I0760353

This novel contains content that might be triggering. Please check my list of possible triggers here:
https://www.abbeyfox.com/the-wicked-kingdom-trigger-warnings

Cover illustration and design by: CD. Lohr (abbeyfoxauthor)
Front of the book Couple Illustration by: CD. Lohr (abbeyfoxauthor)
The Crow's fountain illustration by: heathersouliere
World map, city map design and shields by: aaguirreart
End of the book Couple illustration by: artbybrina

Obsidian City
Sable Forest
Iron Kingdom
Plume City
Leona Sea
Iron City
Rama Sea
Tatum Ocean
Pearl Island
Grey Island
Willowbrook

Alver Mountains
City of Casti
Bold Kingdom
City of Bold
Ender Desert
Ochre City
Eros Ocean
City of Milania
Ilian Town
Sin Forest
Copper
Sky City
Silver Kingdom
City of Silver
Rust Island
Briar City

THE SILVER KINGDOM

THE IRON KINGDOM

THE GOLD KINGDOM

THE CURSE OF THE CROW

BOOK 1

THE COPPER KINGDOM

NORTH
WEST
WILLOWBR

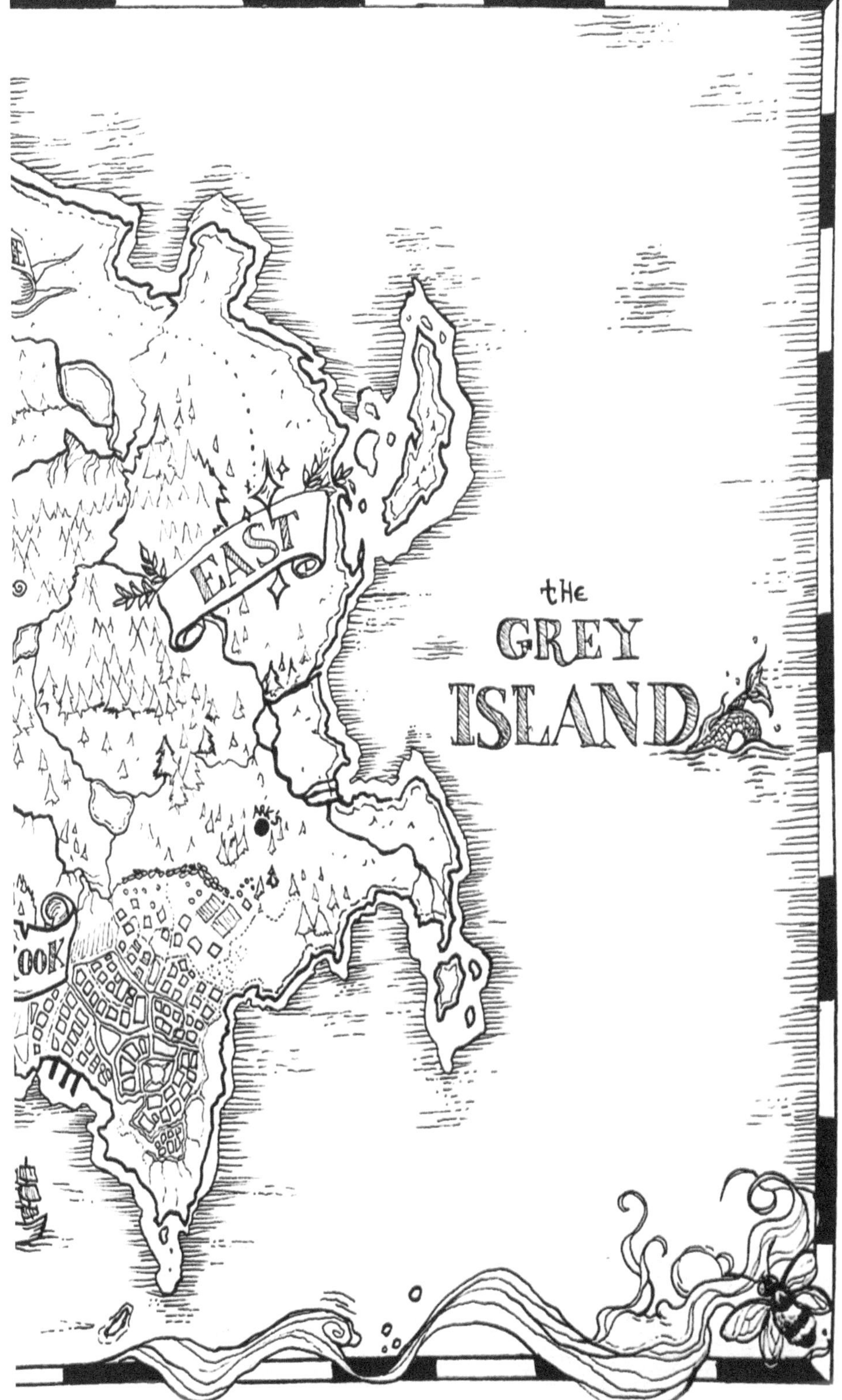
EAST
the
GREY
ISLAND

CHAPTER ONE

They came like a summer storm, bringing bleakness and terror into her life. Two riders wearing darkness galloped down the long pathway to her home. Like beasts on top of their giant steeds, sending thunder roaring over the dull cobblestone road.

Nava regretted disobeying her mother's curfew. As the men dismounted, she stared around, trying to find a suitable place to run or hide in the garden. The stone rails of the terrace offered little cover. Both men took the stone steps two at a time, and when they reached the top, their gazes were heavy on her.

Time seemed to slow as they said nothing, clearly surprised to find her there. They wore ebony outfits with blue accents, the hoods of their cloaks large enough to hide most of their features.

"Excuse me, do you know if anyone is home?" A deep male voice like honey made her body go tense and soft all at once. His voice ignited flames that burned in the pit of her stomach.

What was going on with her? She swallowed, her hair standing on end. "N-no one's home."

He took one step forward to get a better peek at her. "Do you live here?"

Her body blazed when the weight of his eyes settled on her. Something was off with her body. "No, I'm just . . . the gardener." The moment the words left her lips, it was clear they wouldn't believe her. She was fifteen and the spitting image of her mother, with the olive tones of her skin, her unruly brown hair, and her full lips.

Nava tried to mask her nerves by pulling another dead plant from the ground, the painful pricks of the stem distracting her.

She lifted her gaze, something divine calling to her. Her heart fluttered as her gaze came upon him again. The sharp line of a jaw was barely visible outside of the shadows of the hood. The trail of a day-old stubble, and the start of thick lips that got lost outside of her view.

She couldn't see his eyes but knew deep within her that they were staring back at her.

"You have peculiar eyes." The second man's voice, cold like icy fingers, trailed down her skin, breaking the moment. He stayed back, however, his posture straight, observing while the other drifted closer to her.

"I get that a lot," she said, her hands growing colder. Her eyes had always been something people commented on since one was blue and the other one was brown.

"You look too young to be a gardener." The second man stepped closer. Nava felt like they were having a silent conversation as they looked at each other. She had to force herself to stay still. Focusing on their long legs, she was aware she wouldn't make it far if she decided to run.

"Do you know when Miss Celeste will be back?" the cold voice asked, startling her.

She shook her head, her long, wavy hair sticking against her sweaty skin. "She's out in the market with my mother because we are the closest neighbors she has." Nava tried to sound casual, but her voice shook. "I can tell them—I mean, tell her you came around."

She could see jet-black hair peeking out from the blue accents of the hood of the man with the cold voice. "Where did you say you lived?"

"I didn't." Nava placed her gardening tool inside the basket. "You aren't supposed to tell strangers where you live. I can tell Celeste you came by or you can try to catch her at the market." Her breaths faltered. Her mother always said Nava was a terrible liar. Would the men take her away? Like all the stories her mother had told her about children being seized.

The other man hovered for a moment that was like an eternity. They eyed each other in silence, in a daze. The first man shook his head, somewhat distracted, turning away from her. "Please tell her the Society of Crows came to see her."

She stood, focusing on his retreating shape as he followed his companion down the steps to their horses. He mounted a large gray horse, and as he settled into the saddle, so did the movements of the horse.

Nava. Something shook her, a tug of her shoulder, a voice far in the distance.

The prickling of her nerves settled in the pit of her stomach. She watched him go, trembling as heat coursed through her body and landed in her chest. An ache grew into a burning sensation.

Nava, wake up.

She slipped her fingers under the linen fabric of her shirt and moved it aside with a gasp of pain, revealing lines that marked her skin with the shape of three intertwining ovals that formed a flower.

Nava's body shook. It was like her parents' mark, though not the same symbol.

The mark of a soulmate.

Nava, please.

She wished she didn't have to wake up.

"Nava. Nava."

The pull of someone shook her as she tried to hold on to the dream for a little longer.

Nava's eyes opened. Her brother hovered over her face. A messy head of tight red curls, a small button nose covered in light freckles. A shadow of concern tinting his youthful expression.

She grumbled, moving her heavy arms outside of her worn cotton sheets. Her focus changed from the red curls of his hair to the gray tones of the wood beams of the ceiling.

"What a relief. You're finally awake." His hands dropped from her shoulders.

She smiled. "My eyes are open."

"You are a sleepwalker, though."

"I am not. Stop making things up." Her words were thick with sleep.

He laughed, getting up from her bed and straightening his pants. He was wearing his heavy wool school uniform. Indigo pants, a jacket, a stark white shirt with pearl buttons, and a striped vest. All were a bit tight on his body, getting too small for him after his summer growth.

She made a mental note to get an appointment with the local tailor. She'd have to dip into their savings once again to cover the expensive uniform. Not much she could do, as it was the only school on the island.

Nava refused not to send Cameron to get a proper education, even though Laurie, their housekeeper, had insisted she could tutor him from home.

"I'm not making this up!" His eyes met hers again through copper eyelashes. "Were you dreaming about him again?"

She propped her body up with her elbows. Her muscles complained as she scanned the room. Judging by the light that filtered through the large double windows, she could tell it was early morning.

She shrugged, knowing he already knew the answer.

"Your dreams are getting worse, Nava. The bed was shaking this time." His hand grasped hers. "I don't want what happened to Dad to happen to you too."

She forced a smile. "It won't."

He studied her features, searching for a shake of her voice that would give away the lie behind her words. "You suck at lying. At least if you're going to lie, you should make it more convincing."

"It's not my fault I can't cater to your lying needs when I first wake up." She took a deep breath. "You don't have to worry about me, though. What happened to Father—it's different."

"Maybe you can tell Laurie about the dreams getting worse. I'm not great at keeping secrets."

Nava shook her head, knowing she was not about to go to the older lady with concerns she could do little about. "We don't need to add to her worries."

"I know you want to protect me. But I'm not a child anymore—I'm thirteen now. I can handle it." He pulled at the lapels of his jacket with uneasy hands.

"I know."

"He didn't wake up from the last dream about Mom. Lately, it seems like you don't want to wake up, either."

She tightened her lips, not wanting to worry him any more. Because the truth lay somewhere between his words; at times, she didn't want to wake up.

Her body longed to know more about the man she was supposed to be destined with, anything that would feed the incomplete mental image she had of him. She wanted to see his face, to learn if the softness of his voice matched his features. Was his hair dark? Were his eyes mischievous or gentle?

"Why don't you help Laurie with breakfast? I'll be downstairs soon." Her voice was hoarse with sleep.

Cameron tapped the wooden frame of her door before leaving without another word.

Her mind wandered, caught in a fog left behind by memories. It had been ten years since she'd met him on that fateful afternoon when she challenged her mother's restriction of never being outside the house during daylight.

The songs of seagulls flying overhead brought her back. She pulled her legs out of the warmth of her covers, wincing when her feet touched the worn wood floors. Fall had arrived, making the rooms dry and cold. Her room lacked a wood-burning fireplace or a stove that would warm it up.

She would have to get the wool blankets out of her closet that evening if she planned not to catch death this winter.

The narrow stairs creaked under her feet, alerting the bottom floor of their home to her descent. The smell of smoked bacon enveloped her like a hug, and her stomach rumbled. Nava scanned the room as she padded to the kitchen, finding Cameron already seated at the table, happily eating his eggs.

Laurie puttered around the room, her age not slowing the quickness of her steps. She wore her favorite burnt-orange dress that had been pressed with care without a wrinkle in sight, the white apron a stark contrast against the bright color beneath. Her skin sagged with age. Her wise black eyes came to greet her as a smile graced her features. "Awake at last, Nava. If I didn't get Cameron to come get you, you would've missed breakfast again," she reprimanded, pointing a finger to a spot at the table.

It was like she was fifteen again, not the twenty-five-year-old woman who held the well-being of this family on her shoulders.

The table was rustic and well-loved, with ornate chairs painted in white and a vase filled with orange mums from her back garden.

"Thank you for breakfast."

The woman shook her head, her brow wrinkling as she stared deep into her. "You are skin and bones, girl. You've got to put on some weight if you want to carry children."

Her skin heated, her eyes flashing to Cameron, who had started to choke on his food. She was not skin and bones; nature had graced her with curves and an easiness to put on weight, but she didn't need to mention this. "I'm not having children anytime soon."

"You are twenty-five." Laurie's tone carried the burden of the societal pressure she'd been getting more lately, with all the pitiful stares people in town gave her.

Nava lifted her chin. "I won't wed anyone in this town. You know I haven't felt a true connection here. So no need to worry about my childbearing abilities." She had to worry about keeping food on the table for both Cameron and Laurie; she didn't have time to worry about missing breakfast.

Laurie's voice softened. "It'll be hard to make a connection."

Nava took a deep breath. There was no use getting into this conversation again. A full plate appeared in front of her. Before she was able to muse her thanks, Laurie was already walking away, drying her hands on her apron.

"It's not like anyone is coming to see her lately, not after she booted Hale." Cameron shrugged, pushing another large bite into his mouth. Chewing loudly.

"Manners, Cameron," Laurie hissed to the boy as she walked around the kitchen, dropping dirty dishes into the basin. "She doesn't need to be courted by these fellows. She has a soulmate waiting for her."

A pit of dread started to build in her stomach at those words. Nava never asked about him, even though she wanted more. She didn't need any part of a false love where she had no real choice in the matter. She was sick and tired of magic and people making her life choices.

Because that was what a soulmate was, magic dictating who she was to love and be attracted to. Not that she was having much luck in the latter, as she hadn't been attracted to anyone.

"I told you before, I don't need my soulmate. I don't know him, and I don't want anything to do with him. I want to live in peace and be able to provide for the both of you the best I can."

"The gods brought you two together. It's not something you can outrun, Nava," Laurie said with a soft tone that hid a bite behind every word. "You should know this after what happened to your father."

Silence descended upon the table. Nava's eyes flashed to Cameron. She expected him to be saddened by the reminder; it had been a couple of years since they'd lost him. Cameron didn't appear sad. He was alert as he stuffed his mouth with a spoonful of eggs. "My soulmate is not here. I doubt I'll ever see him again."

Cameron coughed loudly then, his face red as he shifted in his seat. He sprang up from the table, pushing his empty plate away from him. "Well, this was great and all." He cleared his throat as his freckled hand brushed over his hair. "I guess it's time to go to school."

"Wait up. I'll walk with you," Nava said, pushing a couple of spoonfuls of eggs into her mouth and grabbing one slice of bread on the go, the loud complaint of the woman behind the only sound as she rushed up the steps to her room.

CHAPTER TWO

Their home sat at the top of the town that was built on the side of a cliff with long serpent roads of warm-colored stones of all shapes that were worn smooth by centuries of use. Their house was quaint, a two-story home built of stucco that had cracked with age, showing gray stone underneath. Sun-bleached large wood beams held a roof of terracotta tiles, much like all of the buildings in town.

She loved the little cottage and the small garden in the front that bloomed in spring, with hydrangeas that lasted all the way to late summer.

They walked down the street as Nava shrugged on her long coat. She wore her simple grass-green skirt she'd tied a brown belt over. A dagger was shielded within it, something she had carried around with her for the last decade, always prepared to defend herself from an impending attack.

"I wish I didn't have to go to school today. I could come help you at the shop like old times," Cameron said. His hair shone under the sun, freckles dancing on his cheeks. A feature they both shared, freckled skin, though Cameron's was fair while Nava's was a few shades darker like her mother's had been.

"I would have done anything to go to school when I was your age, back when we lived in the Iron City and not on this island. To be able to make friends, to be *free* to leave the house," she said, lost in the moment.

"That's what you keep saying," he grumbled, shaking his head, half annoyed and half amused. "You can't keep moping about your stolen childhood. You are supposed to be the grown-up here."

Her mouth dropped, just before he started laughing. "Here I thought you had matured overnight." She pushed him by his shoulder with her own.

He was no longer that gangly, short, skinny boy. She hugged him close to her as they walked, the sound of their heels clicking over the hard stone to the rhythm of the birds flying around them.

He was tall, just a couple of inches shorter than her five-six, caught in that time where the proportions were too awkward. His voice was that of the boy she loved.

"My point was that you should enjoy your childhood with peers your age. It got lonely for me."

"You're still a hermit. What excuse do you have?" he challenged her.

Nava paused for a moment, taken aback by his observation. She guessed it had been naïve to think Cameron wouldn't have noticed how difficult it was for her to make connections. "I'm not a hermit—I see Simone often," she defended.

"One girlfriend. It's hardly a lot of friends. I'm saying I haven't seen you go out with anyone else. Hale courted you, then there was the excuse of me—which is a terrible excuse because I quite liked him." He shrugged.

"Cameron, the matchmaker," Nava joked. He narrowed his eyes. "Fine, he was boring, okay? There were zero sparks. Also, he kept implying I needed him."

Nava didn't need anyone, not even the man the gods had sent her.

Worry flashed through her brother's eyes, but in a blink, it was gone. He was much better at masking his feelings than she was. "Maybe . . . we need to leave this town, go back to the Iron City to try to find *him*. I know you hate for me to bring him up, but I'm afraid to lose you too, Nava."

"We aren't going to find him. There was a reason we ran away from the Iron City. I'm not about to put you in danger for my gain." After all, it was thanks to her they were in this mess. Had she not disobeyed her mother, the Society of Crows wouldn't have found her, and they wouldn't have had to run away from the city like the Devil himself had been chasing after them.

She was just thankful they'd never learned about Cameron's existence.

"Mom and Dad are gone. I want us to do more. It feels like we're here just because they said so." He crossed his arms, his brow dipped.

"Morning, witch boy." The voice startled Nava. She stared into the face of a fair boy who was smirking at them.

Cameron saluted the caller.

"Did he just call you witch boy?" Nava narrowed her eyes as she crossed her arms over her chest, puffing a breath out.

"Yes, he did."

She gazed at her brother before settling on his freckled face. Her anger wavered at his soft, relaxed grin. "It doesn't bother you?"

Cameron shook his head, shrugging. "Why should it?"

"Well, for starters, you aren't one," she stated. Those words had been used to mock her behind hushed tones, through tight lips and frowned faces—witch *girl.* The memories made her heart heavy.

Her whole time in this town, she had heard this. It was no secret her mother had been a spell wielder, and her father's gift with potion-making had shaped them into the outcasts of a town that had no magic.

Them calling her a witch was the worst insult, as witches were known for their cruel ways and working with dark magic. The reminder of side-eyes and mocking faces came to her, making her stomach heavy as if lead had filled it to the brim.

"Maybe not a witch. But maybe a warlock—or a powerful sorcerer." Cameron's excitement was a complete departure from the churning in her stomach as the words escaped his lips. "Stop shaking your head, Nava. You're going to rattle your brain." He smirked.

"You are most definitely *not* going to become one."

"You are free to be afraid of who we are or what we might be. I'm not. I want to figure it out myself."

A rush of energy ran through her body, and the sensation in her stomach grew more significant, making it hard to breathe. The chilly autumn wind moved her wild hair across her face. "Y—you never said you wanted to leave this town." Nava scanned around them, making sure eavesdroppers were nowhere to be found.

"I just did."

"Well, yes, I know. You were talking about my soulmate. Not about you and what you want." It was too early for her brain to fully take on Cameron's intent. At least she was glad no one was watching her panic. The town was still half asleep, the roads empty except for the odd student walking to school that morning.

"This town was picked by our parents, not by us." He shrugged.

"To protect us from the crown." Her voice came a bit louder than she intended.

"You don't have to come with me when I go, but I want to see what my nature is."

"Maybe we have no magic," she pressed, panic closing her throat.

"Then what are you so afraid for, right?" His smile grew lopsided as he gave her a side hug before walking away.

She raised her hand, waiting until he crossed the black iron gate that housed the school. A wooden sign with shiny brass letters spelled "The Walrod Academy." The school that taught no magic, a place that represented safety to her.

THE COOLING AIR OF an early fall morning. The old cobblestone roads were uneven under her steps, winding over a city built onto the steep side of a mountain.

Buildings of stucco, stone, and brick surrounded Nava. The doors of the shops and apartment buildings were bright, intense colors. The constructions weren't as tall as the ones she remembered from the Iron City the few times she'd been allowed to visit.

She stopped by her favorite bakery to buy a few loaves of bread and say hello to Simone, her best friend. The soft ringing of the doorbells welcomed her, along with a waft of delicious-smelling baked goods. Simone was behind the worn wood counter, her platinum hair pulled back into a tight bun that usually didn't let any flyaways escape their confinement. This morning, it was different, however, as wisps of hair were a halo around her head.

She was wearing a sky-blue dress and an apron that had been white earlier in the morning. Now it was stained by a baker's job. Her pink lips turned into a smile as soon as she noticed the new customer was Nava.

"Nava, honey." Her melodic voice broke the silence. She scurried to the baskets where she kept that morning's fresh bread. Her nimble fingers selected the ones Nava wanted before putting them inside a linen bag. "I was going to come to see you later today. I have completely run out of my migraine medicine and was hoping to bribe you with some of your favorite bread for a couple of bottles." She handed the bread over with a smile.

"Already?" Nava tilted her head. "I gave you some last week."

"Yes, you did—but Mother came by yesterday for dinner. We both ended up with horrible headaches after it. She took half of it, and I took the rest." Her flour-covered fingers came to the back of her neck.

"Is she still pushing you to marry Kyle?"

Simone winced. Nava turned, checking her surroundings. It wouldn't be the first time she'd spoken a bit too loud where strangers could hear a private conversation. Destiny had been kind to her this morning. The bakery was empty.

"Don't remind me." Her friend groaned. "I don't even know where she got that I would agree to this. Kyle and I are practically siblings."

Nava nodded. It would be amazing to have her mother here, pressuring her to find someone to marry and give her grandchildren, much like Laurie had this morning. It had been so long since her mother had been gone, she had already forgotten the sound of her voice, the softness of her embrace, or the spicy scent of magic when she'd come home from the garden when they lived away from here.

She remembered her father telling her he missed the tone of her voice as well, that he was afraid of forgetting it. Then the dreams had started. What once had been the healthy, round face of her father had chiseled down into a tired, gray complexion. He'd always wanted to sleep, had always wanted to be in whatever other world of dreams she'd awaited him.

"You went dark, didn't you?"

Her friend's voice took her out of her thoughts. "Yes, I totally did. I'm sorry. I'm feeling a bit—"

"Tired?" Simone worried her lip with her teeth. "Is it the dreams again?"

"Yes."

"Do you want to talk about it?"

Nava shook her head. "I will. I promise it's not something crazy. I know you get a bit anxious when I talk about M-A-G-I-C, even though I'm not one hundred percent sure this is in any way related to that . . ." Nava let her words fade because she didn't like lies. Magic was what was making her tired.

Even in this town that repressed magic, the soulmate bond was still there, beating inside her, haunting her night after night in dreams, reminding her that she had left something, *someone*, behind. The sorcerers and warlocks who'd set the wards in this town were all-powerful, though not more powerful than the gods.

Simone paled; she and her family were the only people in this town who accepted the Forrests openly, even though they were magical in a town that wanted no magic inside it. Simone's mother had been a good childhood friend of Nava's dad once upon a time.

"Honey, I don't want you to stop telling me things because I might get nervous. You know, I have never seen magic before, but from the stories I hear, it's scary but also exciting?" Simone's voice wavered.

"Don't I know it."

"My point is, I want you to talk to me if something is happening to you, even if I don't understand it." Simone reached across the counter to Nava.

"Thanks, and I promise I will tell you more. Preferably over wine and chocolate," Nava murmured with a smile, trying to lift the sudden mood that had fallen over them. The impending doom of what she often referred to as her curse was present in her mind.

"I will come by tonight with both things, and you can spill whatever is bothering you then." Simone's voice carried around the room as Nava pushed the door of the shop open with her wide hips, turning to smile at her friend.

"Don't forget the chocolate or I won't let you in," she said before exiting the bakery, a bag of fresh bread in hand.

CHAPTER THREE

The shop was slow that day. People had been buzzing around about a new ship that had docked earlier in the morning. Nava hadn't gotten around to checking it out, as it was always unnerving when a new boat landed in Willowbrook.

Nava had been a ball of nerves ever since she'd learned there were soldiers and a sorcerer onboard the ship. To most people, it was an exciting novelty. To Nava, it was her absolute worst nightmare.

Few ships landed on the island. Usually, kingdoms avoided sending crews here. The island wasn't wealthy, and magic got canceled inside the invisible shield guarding the town. Treaties made eons ago protected trades. City people rarely came to vacation or moved to the Grey Island.

Nava tapped her pen against the worn wood of her shop's counter, having abandoned the illusion of making any potions much earlier. She couldn't focus with a kingdom's army looming so close to Cameron. Much less if they had a sorcerer or warlock in tow.

Her gaze darted around people passing by her shop. Everyone seemed to be in a cheerful mood, the novelty of the newcomers making the town buzz with excitement.

She took a deep breath and told herself for the tenth time that her paranoid nature got the best of her. The likelihood of one of two sorcerers who knew her face coming to this island was improbable.

The sun kissed the paving stones of the streets with orange and yellow hues at a quarter to five. The bell on her door rang. She lifted her head toward the newcomer, and her heart dropped.

The towering shape of a man, dressed in an ebony coat with indigo and cobalt-blue accents, came in, crowding her small potion store. Shapes embroidered intricate organic patterns across a broad chest. She had seen the exact outfit once before. Her heart pounded and everything went still for a breath as she considered her swift escape.

Once again, she cursed that the only exit of the building was through the narrow front door. Poor architectural planning had been a constant thought when the afternoons were slow. If she survived today, she would not be renewing her lease.

Her gaze reached his face. She expected to see *him*, her soulmate. She knew deep within that he wasn't it. He met her stare with eyes so dark they could have been pools of spilled ink.

Nava was at a loss for words. The knot in her throat grew with every step he took toward her. Like a wild cat hunting for prey. He reached the counter in a heartbeat, one pale, scarred hand resting on top of the glass, tapping a finger to a soft rhythm that sent her nerves into a frenzy.

His focus never left her as he smirked. Nava had never beheld anyone with such a fair complexion before. His skin was so pale he could have been a sheet of bleached parchment.

"Good afternoon," he purred. The scent of blackberries and mint wafted around him.

Nava blinked her daze away, swallowing loudly. The voice sounded familiar. Nava might have heard it that morning in a hazy dream brought by memories she could never forget. She had lost her voice. He lifted a brow, awaiting a response. Perspiration dampened the skin of her hands, and a prickle crawled down the back of her neck.

She managed to find her voice. "G-good afternoon. How can I help you?"

His hair was brushed back neatly, black as a moonless night. He leaned forward, resting the weight of his body on the old countertop. Nava pulled back and heard the clinking sound of glass bottles as she collided with the rack of potions she kept behind her.

He smiled crookedly. "We landed today, after many months locked away in a ship with hundreds of men."

A panther in front of a scared rabbit. Why did he try at small talk with her when he could be anywhere else in town?

Her nerves were driving her closer to a panic attack. She had not seen a Crow for ten years. A secret part of her, one she never gave a voice, had hoped the next time she encountered one, it would be *hers*.

Her Crow. Her soulmate.

“Is there something you want?" Words spilled out of her mouth before she could stop them, something that happened when her nerves took over. "Or are you looking for a potion?"

His eyes sparkled like polished onyx before his voice filtered out of his lips in an unnervingly calm tone. "Imagine my surprise when I see a potion store in a town that is supposed to suppress magic." He straightened to his full height. A whole head taller than her. By his intense scrutiny on her face, he had memorized every single one of her freckles.

"Oh, we don't use magic here—it's alchemy. The name potions is for novelty. No one is expecting a love potion or good luck in a bottle."

"How disappointing. I hoped someone had found a way around the spell that cancels magic inside this town," he said, peering across the shelves of potion-covered walls.

"Sorry to disappoint." She hoped with every bone in her body that he would take his leave.

“Forrest. I knew a potion maker with the same name back in the Iron City."

She stilled, considering jumping over the counter and bolting toward the door. If he was as skilled of a warrior as she assumed, he wouldn’t have a problem catching her.

Still, she didn’t spot a weapon on him, and he had no magic here.

"Forrest is a common last name.”

"Is it?” A charged silence followed. He remembered her.

"Of course. There are a lot of Forrests in town," she lied through her teeth.

One of his brows lifted. He was toying with her, realizing her predicament.

She told herself he didn't have any magic here. No way to detect her aura or whatever other parlor tricks warlocks could do. He had a last name, along with a memory of a young girl picking plants from her garden. She wrapped her shaky arms across her stomach, grasping the hilt of her dagger.

Nava hoped it looked casual. Crows were skilled in weaponry, but so was she—sort of.

She had trained for many years to wield this weapon, to defend herself without the need for magic. No longer a defenseless teenager. Her mother had made sure of that.

"You have such peculiar eyes.” He leaned in. His long fingers reached across the glass. The wood frame creaked with his weight.

"Everyone says so," she said. Her knuckles went white as her grip tightened around the leather handle of her weapon.

Perfect, straight white teeth flashed behind a truly mischievous grin. "I once met a girl with similar eyes. A gardener, a very young one."

Nava swallowed, not saying a word at first. "What can I say? I have a common face."

"No, I don't think you do." His gaze narrowed on her. "A friend and I were together that day. I haven't seen him since. He is dear to me, you see. I have been looking for him for quite some time."

Missing. Her soulmate was missing. Her mind reeled back to his words. Her body went cold and clammy. Why was he not in the Iron City? Was he searching for her? "I'm not sure what you are trying to find here, sir."

"Sir sounds old. Call me Devon or Mr. Black." He took a step back, focusing on the hand holding her dagger.

Her throat bobbed. Her stomach revolted with nerves. She might be sick at any moment.

"The crown became interested in my trip here. It's said Gray sorcerers tend to escape to this island—"

"I assure you, I was born and raised here." Another lie. "I have never seen you before—or your friend."

"Of course." He walked around the shop, his arms coming around his back as he studied the sage-colored walls, the dark worn wood shelves. "Perhaps you have seen sorcerers passing through town?"

She shook her head so hard a sharp pain extended down her neck.

"Another dead end, I suppose," he declared. The intensity behind his expression hid nothing.

"I'm sorry I'm not the girl you were looking for, Mr. Black. I don't mean to be rude, but we close at five, and check the time." She waved her hand, signaling the clock hanging on her wall. Steam poured out of the top, marking five fifteen with its brass arms. "I'm afraid I have to go. I have previous commitments."

He nodded, and the same side smile appeared on his face as he tilted his head, studying the clock on the wall. "Of course."

She walked to the front door of her shop, one shaking hand holding the linen bag with her bread and the other firmly placed on the hilt of her weapon.

"I was not aware this type of advancement had made it to this island," he said, pointing his chin to the clock. Her father had brought it over from the Iron City.

She stilled. "We don't. A tradesman brought it over five years ago. It's handy."

He dipped into a polite bow and sauntered to her. "Apologies for having kept you, Miss Forrest. I'm afraid I could not pick any of your potions to try for seasickness. I must come back at a later date."

"Please do." She clenched her teeth with the lie alongside false politeness.

He *knew* her. The safety of the town provided her a shield from his magic. He would be back and armed with soldiers later on.

She pushed the door open with too much strength. The old hinges screeched before it slammed against the exterior wall. She walked out of her shop, almost tripping over her steps.

He prowled to her, his hands behind him. Nava held her breath, trying not to catch his scent. The heat of his body almost burned her. She stepped back and hit the frame of the door, cursing she hadn't gotten out of the way fast enough.

His eyes fixed on hers, a promise of something wicked and bad shining behind them.

She pressed her lips together tightly, waiting with a forced smile as he turned to her. Devon lingered on her before he sauntered down the cobbled road. People all around ignored their exchange, talking lively about the day, unaware of the danger she was in.

She had never run faster than she did that evening toward her home.

CHAPTER FOUR

Nava had learned from her mother to be paranoid. The run home exhausted her, as she'd decided to take the long road at the last minute. Just in case someone followed her there.

If she lived through this mess, she would have to move out of town since she'd decided it would be a great idea to run through lady Mallory's yard as a shortcut. They would call her not only a witch but also a trespassing lunatic.

She heaved for air when she crossed the edge of her property, past the ornate black iron fence and the browning leaves of her hydrangea bushes in the front of her house.

Nava pushed the heavy wood door open, meeting the eyes of both Laurie and Cameron by the kitchen, the latter holding two plates while he padded to the table. Her blood boiling, she removed her coat, the fabric of her shirt stuck to her back.

She stared toward the street before she closed the door behind her and rushed to the side window, peeking through white curtains while gasping for air.

"Nava, is everything all right?" Laurie asked.

"He found us—me. He found *me*, Laurie." Her shaky hand came to her face, brushing away the hair sticking all over her sweaty skin.

"It can't be." Laurie shook her head as her skin turned a pale gray.

"Who? What's going on?" Cameron's voice wavered.

"The Crow. One of them is here. He came to the shop this afternoon. We aren't safe here. We have to go." Her words rushed out, and silence descended between the three of them.

"Your soulmate?" Cameron asked, his features appearing so much younger as he approached her.

Her hand came to his face. Tears prickled her eyes. It was her fault, after all, that they were in this mess. Had she not disobeyed her mother that afternoon, he would be safe. "No, it wasn't my soulmate," Nava whispered.

Laurie walked to them, and her heavy hand landed on Nava's shoulder. "If it wasn't your soulmate, you're in danger." She tugged her away from Cameron. "Do you think he would find us here in this house?"

It had been the one thing that had occupied her mind during her run home. Devon just needed to ask around town for Forrest, the potion maker residence, and someone would offer the information for the right price.

"We have to leave." Laurie's voice shook with emotion.

Nava nodded as her mind reeled back. "Why do you think I would've been safe if it had been *him*?"

"A soulmate would never hurt you. I never agreed with Celeste on keeping so much from you. You are her child. I respected her choice not to tell you anything until you asked." She moved her hand down Nava's arm, holding her with an underlying urgency. "You never asked."

"Laurie?"

"I did research on the subject of soulmates when you found yours . . . Celeste and I had extensive conversations about what was coming for you."

They walked past the kitchen and down a narrow corridor that led to Laurie's bedroom. It had the house's best view, with large windows facing the town's steep views and Nava's back garden.

Laurie let go of Nava's hand and stepped in, moving around her space, heading toward the heavy black-and-gold trunk by the end of her bed.

"I don't think we have time for this. Devon Black is here and might be coming to the house as we speak. We've got to leave."

"Yes, we do." Laurie pushed the heavy lid open and rummaged through the contents inside.

"I don't understand what's happening."

"Me, neither," Cameron piped up from Laurie's bedroom door.

"The Crows might think they have a claim over you—they might even know one of their own is your soulmate," Laurie said. She rummaged around her trunk, large hands pulling out an old leather-bound notebook. She got up from the floor, her face morphing into a pained expression.

Nava's brows dipped. "Yes, so?"

"We need to go to the Grey Forest."

Laurie's words hit her all at once. Dread crawled like an icy caress down her spine. A shot of adrenaline ran through her body. "The forest is full of magic. It's cursed. We wouldn't make it a day."

Silence descended over them, the weight of her words settling as the truth. Nava had trained with her mother in weaponry. She was barely able to defend herself, let alone Laurie at her old age and Cameron.

"They don't know Cameron exists. They aren't aware you are here with us. It'll be safer for the both of you to stay in this town," Nava said, the air escaping her lungs in a whoosh. She rested her body weight against the cold wall.

It hit her at once, the relief that she hadn't put Cameron in danger. The dread of having to leave him behind . . .

"Not in this house," Laurie said with a stiff nod.

"No. Maybe the inn?"

Laurie nodded. Nava's fingers were thick and uncoordinated as she undid the leather string tying the notebook closed. Stumbling, she caught a piece of parchment that had dropped from it as soon as the bind had loosened.

She opened it and studied the ink lines that made a clear map of the Grey Island's forest. It was easy to see the town by the illustrations, the edge of Willowbrook where the spell ended and the magical lands began.

The forest took most of the island, with the shapes of trees, mountains, and lakes. Dotted lines marked directions she didn't understand. Nava blinked in confusion, her gaze zeroing in on the contrast of red ink circling one area in particular. The familiar scribbles of her mother's letters wrote a name.

"*Arkimedes*." The weight of two intense gazes fell upon her. She lifted her face to Laurie, a question about to spill out. Who was Arkimedes?

"Your mother didn't say much, just that he was someone we should go to if the crown ever found us." Laurie's face fell. "I wish I had asked more questions. I had so little time left with your mother before sickness took her."

"She wasn't one who liked to share truths." Nava's words burned her throat.

"No, I guess not." Cameron's voice shook with anger, his fists clenched at his sides. "We should stay together. That's what family does."

Nava came to him, closing the map inside the notebook to inspect later. Her free hand reached to one of his, grasping it tightly. "Family also protects each other," she said. "You are the most important thing in my life, Cam. Believe I'll be fine and will come back."

His skin lost a bit of the color it had gained when his anger spiked. "I never doubted you would be fine. You're the strongest person I know, even when you are a butthead," he admitted.

A soft knock on the front door had them all jumping in their spot. Nava's skin crawled. Her finger pressed to her lips, signaling them to be quiet. Laurie rushed to the side table by her bed and blew out the candle that illuminated the room, bathing them in darkness.

"Stay here," Nava whispered, coming outside to the living area. The gentle light of candles illuminated the place, and the floorboards creaked under her quiet feet. She walked to the front door to see the shadow of someone peeking through the window.

Nava took a calming breath and took the dagger out of the sheath as she approached the door. She might have the element of surprise. If she did enough damage, it might give her family enough time to run away from the back of the house.

She yanked the door open, raising her dagger. Simone yelped, stumbling back. It was a miracle the bottle of wine hadn't fallen to the ground.

"Nava, what the hell is going on?"

"Come in." Nava pulled her inside the house.

Simone focused on Nava as if she had at last lost it. Her attention followed a spot behind, where Cameron and Laurie were coming out from the back room, somber expressions on their features. "Nava, honey, what's wrong?"

"I don't have much time to explain anything, Simone. I'm in trouble," Nava said.

"Pack lightly, child. We must not appear to be running," the older woman said in an assured voice and pushed Cameron toward the stairs. Nava could tell by the crease of her brows that she didn't know what to do.

Simone paled. "The ship." Understanding shone in her blue eyes. "It's from the crown. They're chasing deserters. They don't know you are—"

"A warlock came on the ship, and he does."

Nava watched Simone's skin turn a sickly green. Her best friend took a couple of steps back, holding herself against the nearby chair. "Oh."

"They never knew of Cameron and Laurie. They'll be going to the inn. We don't know if the warlock and whatever army he has with him will come to look for me here."

Simone shook her head. "They'll go to the inn to search." Her gaze shone with conviction. "They can stay with me."

Nava swallowed, blinking to prevent from crying. "Are you sure?"

"Of course I'm sure, silly," Simone said, enveloping her into a bone-crushing hug. The steps of Cameron coming down the stairs distracted them.

"I'm ready," he whispered, tugging the canvas bag closer to his body.

Nava walked to her brother and wrapped him in a tight hug. The Society of Crows made children ruthless soldiers. She wouldn't let them take him.

"You will be staying with Simone," she said in a shaky tone. "I'll be back before you miss me."

"We should go." Laurie came close to Nava. "You should leave tonight. Don't wait long."

"I won't."

"If you can't find Arkimedes, there is one village in the forest. You can go there, ask for help, and warn them they are coming."

Nava nodded, unsure if she'd make it to any village. At this point, she'd be glad if she survived one day in the forest.

"I will care for him, Nava. Don't worry. Go. Stay away. Don't let him take you, or I fear we might not see you again." Laurie enveloped her in a tight hug; the soft scent of cinnamon and cardamom reminded her of her childhood.

"I guess it's time," Nava whispered, dropping the fabric of the curtain. "Thank you, Simone."

"Of course, honey."

"We'll come back to our home when it's safe," Laurie said.

"Yes." Nava turned to Cameron. "See you soon, caterpillar."

"I want stories when you are back," he answered with a smile.

Nava held back as they said their goodbyes and the people she loved the most in her whole world left her behind. Once again running away from a Crow, from her own mistake. Her cheeks grew wet as she watched them walk down the pathway of their home and past the front iron gates.

CHAPTER FIVE

Nava frantically shoved supplies into a backpack that had once belonged to her father. It was old and tattered, made of thick canvas the color of green olives, with soft leather tabs and worn brass buckles that barely held it closed.

She could hear her neighbors chatting on their back patio, enjoying the cooling temperatures after a hot summer.

She swallowed, trying to rack her brain for tips her father had once given in their many camping trips. What medicine to pack if she were ever to cross the edge of town to venture into the forest. She shoved in the bread Simone had given her, a heavy breath escaping her lips.

Silhouettes came down the walkway to the front door of her home.

They had come for her after all. It had taken less than a couple of hours for Devon Black to find her. She picked up the heavy cloak that hung from the back of one of the dining chairs.

Avoiding making any noise, Nava moved to grab the two daggers she'd lain on the table earlier. She took her backpack and headed to Laurie's room.

The window was heavy to open but large enough for her to sneak out. For once, she was grateful for the neighbor's overgrown, unkempt garden she often complained about. Relieved that none of the men checked the back of the house.

Nava tossed her heavy backpack out, snapping her mother's rose bushes in half as it fell down, and her heart ached at the sight.

She jumped out, and it wasn't a graceful fall. The hardness of the cold ground scraped her hands. Steam left her lips in a surge from the chilled air that burned her exposed skin.

Nava ran across the short, manicured grass. Their yard was a small rectangular space filled with dry plants. She jumped over the hedge that divided her home from the neighbor's, landing on a much more unkempt property.

Overgrown bushes hid her shape as she ran behind the home to the street. Her neighbors had decided to go in, chased by the cold air. She was grateful for the chilly night. The less they saw, the better.

Her feet pounded on the hard stone road. Her backpack buckles shrieked with the movements. The loud crash of a door getting kicked in echoed in the empty streets, followed by the breaking of glass.

Nava glanced and saw two of the guards around the front door, wearing black outfits with furs that adorned their necks.

"Hey, you!" one shouted.

Terrin, who owned the local flower shop, unloaded his empty buckets onto his home's front steps. His attention was behind her, his brow deepening.

Understanding lit his features as she ran past him. Whatever he did next was unclear. Instead, the commotion of water splashing over stone came.

"I'm sorry. I did not see you coming." Terrin's loud voice gave her the fuel she needed to provide her steps with an extra boost of energy.

It was common knowledge to the townspeople that the crown chased deserters. She would forever be grateful for his help.

She cut through alleyways, making sharp turns that only residents knew. She went up the old, uneven steps, so many she lost count. Her lungs burned.

Nava kept going. She had at least two miles to run before she was out of the town, all uphill while carrying a heavy backpack and two steel daggers in her belt.

She struggled to catch her breath, her legs cramping. She didn't stop even as the buildings became sparser. Homes were smaller with larger front yards. Smoke billowed out of weathered, stained chimneys.

The Grey Forest stood tall, trees rising over a bed of mist. The fence dividing the non-magical grounds from the magical ones was near, made of the variance of stacked gray stones, bathed in the moon's blue light.

Nava stopped right before climbing. The shapes of the trees loomed in front of her. She wasn't sure what she was more fearful of, the people chasing her or whatever magical creatures awaited her inside the darkness of the forest.

Swallowing, she steadied her resolve and found the will to keep her freedom.

Sharp stones cut her palms and scraped her legs as she climbed over the wall, her green skirt making it harder. Nava couldn't stop until she was safe in the cover of the thick woods.

Safe—a word she would never take for granted again. At the top, she took another second to think of her family.

She jumped down the five feet of rock, across the invisible line that, for the past ten years, had separated her from magic.

NAVA WAS NOT SURE how long she wandered. Her eyelids were heavy, and she was drunk with exhaustion. She held the old brass compass that belonged to her father—and had given up checking on it.

The new morning sun peeked through the trees' tall branches, allowing her to better take in the magic around her. Trunks, thin and thick, extended high up, with limbs of moss-covered branches. The ground was softened with dried foliage.

She rested against a tree. Her breaths of air were loud. Dread pooled inside her stomach. She expected to see a three-headed something appear out of nowhere. The forest *was* full of life. Not in the frightening way she was expecting, normal somehow. The songs of birds singing with the morning sun calmed her. It smelled like cedar, pine, and morning dew.

To get to the red circle her mother had made on the map, she was supposed to head east. She searched for any shape that could represent danger but found nothing. The magnitude of her situation made her pause. Her house had been raided by Devon Black's goons. Her thoughts went to her neighbor Terrin. She hoped he was fine.

Nava dropped her backpack and lifted the top flap to remove the small notebook. Taking the map out, she studied the ink lines, hoping to find more information that would lead her *somewhere*.

She let her head fall back, the bark digging into her scalp. The truth was, she didn't know where she was or what to do. She dreaded trusting a stranger because her mother had left his name scribbled on a piece of paper.

He was likely an old haggard man who smelled funny and talked in riddles.

Her body heated as her hands tightened around the map, the crinkling paper somehow alien in her surroundings.

She startled at the feeling of a heartbeat that was not hers, a whisper of a tap-tap against the skin of her chest. Her fingertips touched her soulmate mark. It was warm under her touch, alive after ten years of slumber.

NAVA HAD BEEN WALKING for hours. She had occasionally stopped to eat and give rest to her tired feet. She needed to set camp soon. By following random notes her mother had scribbled on the map, it would be near impossible to get to Arkimedes's cabin in the woods until the next day.

The day had warmed up, and the forest was bright with golden colors seeping through the canopy's holes. A lingering scent of burning wood hung in the air. It had to be her imagination, as there was no fire or smoke in sight.

She jumped, startled by the sound of leaves rustling, her eyes fixing on the ground, watching them caress the forest floor. A bee struggled with an injury. It trembled on top of a dried leaf, its yellow body contrasting against the dried foliage.

Her heart pitter-pattered at the heartbreaking sight. Another one nearby, then hundreds of thousands peppered the forest floor surrounding her.

Following the path of the dying insects, she stopped, her mind screaming at her to get out of there, but her heart insisted she inspect further.

She always followed her heart.

The side of the tree moved, and long limbs took shape; spindly arms shifted, pointy shoulders decorated by protruding branches. Moss covered its torso and long legs, each the size of one of her. She swallowed, taking a step back. A scream held on her tongue.

He was a tall creature, his chest made of bark adorned by lichen. His long neck made him appear more fragile. His lips parted to reveal jagged teeth. He was staring at her, his movements frozen. What she'd previously read as a snarl was a pained cry. Her heart contorted at the horrible despair that filled the air.

The bees on the ground weren't dead. They flapped their wings in a futile attempt to fly.

The creature was afraid of her. She wasn't sure if whatever or whoever had hurt him was still lurking around.

She steeled her shaking body, forcing her eyes to find the reason for its pain. She gasped when she spotted another creature a few feet from the tree, the floor of the forest already hiding the decomposing body. Deep gashes ran through, and a thick, gooey substance that resembled honey spouted out of the wounds.

Her focus turned to the smaller shape crying by the tree, and a hand covered her lips on a shaky sob. It was the heart-wrenching pain of the creature in front of her. Whatever had attacked them had killed one of them.

There was a deep gash in the beehive that made the top part of the creature's head. At first glance, she considered it an enormous hat. It gushed honey down its face to its sharp mouth.

Nava was moving before she could think twice, running to the spot behind the fallen tree, where she had left her backpack. She rummaged in the pouch where she had stashed her potions. She'd figured a healing potion would be handy at some point. It was unclear if the medicine would help the creature. However, she was determined to try.

She came to it, her arms out in a sign of peaceful approach. Its pitch-black eyes fixed on her, and it made no move to attack or retreat. Maybe it could read her intentions.

The bees on the ground flapped, their energy dwindling. Panic rose in her chest, but she didn't understand why. He was so high up in the trees she wouldn't be able to reach his head.

"If you can understand me, I have something that might help you. But I can't reach you," she said. Her fingertips couldn't even touch the bottom of the creature's feet.

He cried once again.

It had been many years since she'd climbed a tree, but the broken branches around this one made it a perfect option for her to try. She hoisted herself up the first branch, her leg coming up to secure her stance.

She steadied her hold, grasping the tree's trunk with shaky hands, and stepped onto the next branch, which cracked under her weight. She hiked up onto the next one, a thicker one this time, and continued one, two, three.

Nava was closer. The face of the creature made her pause. The pain in his expression stirred her to put aside any of her biases.

"I promise I won't hurt you," she said and reached into her pocket, fishing out one of the two vials of her healing potions. She brought it to her lips and bit off the cork that held the heavy liquid inside.

Nava reached, but the creature pulled away. She allowed it to come near, her heart hammering when its wooden nose touched her skin, sniffing. It would take a bite for her to lose her hand, her mind supplied, a spike of panic running through her. Her body slumped down as her adrenaline subsided.

"Please let me help you," she whispered. It dipped its head, allowing her to inspect the dripping gash.

Nava poured the potion down, digging in her pocket for the second vial, and repeated the process. She took a small gauze she'd also stuffed in her pocket and pressed it onto the wound with delicate fingers. Her hand became wet and sticky with warm honey, to her chagrin. She could never eat honey again.

She closed her eyes, the warmness in her hand extending through her body like a rush of energy. Nava hoped this could at least help this creature heal. Her skin glowed with power.

Panicked, she pulled her arm back, studying her skin as her heart fought to leap out of her throat. The wound in the creature's head closed a little—the goop had stopped oozing out of it.

Had she done magic? No, of course not.

She brought her hand back and stared—she could go fetch her last two potions to try again—but was interrupted by the creature. Its pained expression lifted somehow from the corners of its sharp mouth. The creature stilled, and his gaze moved to one side of the forest. And then it met her eyes again.

"They are coming. Run," a buzzing voice thundered through her thoughts.

Nava's eyes went in the direction the creature stared. She didn't have to be told twice. Her legs trembled as she tried not to focus on what would happen to her if she were to drop.

The buzzing became louder, the bees waking up from near death. Nava jumped off the third branch, yelping in pain as she landed poorly.

She ran to the fallen tree and picked up her bag, hoisting it up on her shoulders, and she was off.

CHAPTER SIX

Nava couldn't keep running. She was afraid her body would collapse from exhaustion at any moment. Darkness was approaching, the days shorter as summer ended. She was tired, thirsty, and afraid.

The voices from her huntsmen came from afar. She tried to zigzag among the trees, to be hidden by their enormous trunks. She was running out of time. Despair moved her forward. Her hair caught the air with the quick movements.

They covered a vast amount of ground. She counted five, maybe six men in black coats. The buckles of her backpack screeched.

Nava didn't see the shape looming until it was too late. A firm grip locked on her arm as a gloved hand covered her mouth and pulled her behind a tree.

A warm body held her tightly. She writhed against his hold, pushing and pulling. She was against a wall of muscle. Her heartbeat drummed. They'd caught her. Nava bit hard, tasting salt and dirt on the leather glove. A deep gasp of pain was the only sound near her, and the hand pressed tighter against her.

"Stop that or they'll find us both," a throaty voice whispered against her ear. Warm air hit the side of her cheek, raising the ends of her hair. She stopped moving.

He turned her around, and her back hit the texture of the tree. His hand lifted off her for a second before covering them again. He stood over six feet. A brown hood hid his features, much like the one she was wearing. His hold on her loosened, a finger pressed against her lips in a signal to be quiet. She nodded curtly. His hand lowered from her face. He lifted his head and looked around.

"I swear I saw her run this way," one man grunted.

Nava moved closer to the tree, praying it sheltered her from view. She peered out of the hood of her cloak. The soldiers stared right where they were, with no recognition behind their features.

"He said she couldn't do magic," another one snarled. "Promised it would be easy, that she wouldn't expect us to come."

"Since when do Crows speak the truth?" another one asked as if bored, and the stranger next to her tensed at the words. "We are here for the money. All that matters is capturing as many deserters as we can. Twenty silver coins per head."

The other three grunted in agreement and walked on, their heads turning.

The stranger hid behind the tree, listening to the retreating steps. Her legs were cramped from the uncomfortable position she stood in. She moved, trying to bring circulation back to her extremities.

"Are they gone?" she whispered.

"Shh."

A spike of annoyance flooded through her. There was no sound other than his breathing. The stranger's posture relaxed, so she took a deep breath.

He stepped away from her, crunching the leaves under his considerable weight. His hand came to lower his hood. The warm afternoon sun hit the sharp angle of a jaw. Fair skin came into view, gold under the sunlight. Bright green eyes stared back at her. Shades of chartreuse stormed inside his irises with otherworld magic. His umber hair matched his thick brows. His chiseled jaw showed the shadow of a beard.

Nava had never beheld such magical eyes before, the movements of colors. She studied his skin, his broad shoulders. He couldn't be older than thirty.

Her stomach twisted as she took in his features, a warm wave running through her body, spreading down her limbs, and pooling in her stomach. He was the most handsome creature she had beheld in her short twenty-five years alive.

"Why are those men hunting you down?"

She pushed down her hood.

His lips parted, softening his stern expression. He stepped back farther away from her.

Nava shifted the weight of her body as she searched the trees, trying to find her wannabe captors looming in the distance. "My name is Nava. I have been running from them all day. I'm looking for a man who lives near here. At least, I hope it's this part of the woods."

He paled. "You're Celeste's daughter."

Nava knew she had found him, and he was *not* what she'd expected.

She hadn't thought much about her mother's friend as she ran for her life. She had imagined him being old and wise, with a large potbelly and a long white beard. He was a fae of sorts, so maybe he was older than he appeared. "Are you . . . Arkimedes? My— I was told you could help me. My mother knew you?"

He nodded. "We can't stay here. They will come back once they realize you aren't the way they headed." He focused on the direction where Devon's men had disappeared, and he took one long step back. "Come, my cabin is not far."

HOW HAD NAVA'S MOTHER met this man? Why had she trusted he'd help them if the crown were to appear on the island? It wasn't normal for someone as paranoid as her mother to send her off to a stranger.

She didn't know her mother at all.

Nava studied the sharp angles of his wide shoulders. His face turned from side to side, his steps lighter than hers even with his large stature. He was taller than average, and he gave away something that wasn't human. She realized she had never seen any of the magical species before, had read about them in books.

"Not so hard to be quiet, is it?" Arkimedes tilted his face back, his gaze flashing toward her.

"No one to keep up the conversation." Her stomach rumbled with hunger, loud enough it broke the silence. Her cheeks heated. "I haven't stopped to eat or rest in hours."

"We are close," he whispered. "We can't use any light to guide us after the sun is down. It will attract attention from things we don't want to follow us. Worse than the hunters."

She nodded, and her legs shook in protest. It didn't matter if a spirit of the forest or an ogre came out of nowhere to get them. Nava couldn't stand straight for much longer. If they kept going, Arkimedes would end up having to carry her the rest of the way or leave her behind. She tightened her lips, the fear of being left behind to fend off the men on her own too strong to ignore.

The cabin became visible as they walked down a narrow pathway. Nava could hear a stream nearby, the rushing of water. They had traveled in silence for hours; he hadn't spoken much, other than the odd grunt, and she'd been too tired to do even that.

The cabin was quaint, with a thatched rooftop and stucco walls. Rough wood beams held it together in each corner, with moss growing from all horizontal faces. A stone fireplace jutted out from one side, covered by tree branches.

She had a decent warm place to rest tonight, after all. Unless he was expecting her to sleep outside in her tent, which she guessed wouldn't be so bad. Nava was tired enough she would pass out as soon as her head hit the— Wait, she had not packed any blankets.

She paused outside the home, studying her surroundings. It was cold in this forest, and she had her coat to keep her warm.

He was already halfway up the stone steps to the cabin when he turned around to her. His brows lowered.

"I followed you with no idea what I was to do once we got here." She crossed her arms over her chest.

"Other than being safe," he quipped in an amused tone.

She needed to get her plan together or she would mess this whole thing up. "It's presumptuous of me—" she started, and his lips twitched. Maybe it would have been the start of a smile, but he had schooled his features.

"Do you think I would leave you to be taken by the bounty hunters?" he asked in a soft voice, shaking his head. "You can stay here for a couple of days. It will give you enough time for them to lose your trail."

"I know it's moronic. I have no plan other than finding you."

"Most people who end up in this forest have no plan other than surviving." His voice was soft, almost lost in the noises of the forest.

The reality of his words hit her. She was fighting for her freedom. If the Crow took her to the city, she would be forced to a life of servitude for the crown. They would force her to marry, to make magical children who would be slaves all the same.

"I'll set my tent right over there." She pointed to an empty area at the front of his cabin. Dried foliage covered the ground, flat enough for her to set up camp.

He frowned. "What?"

She walked a couple of steps, lowering her backpack to the ground. The tabs screeched with the movement. "I brought one to sleep in."

With an amused expression, he shook his head. "There are wards around the house. The river nymphs tend to come out in the evening."

Nava nodded, opening the flap of her bag, searching for the heavy canvas of her tent. The heavy steps on stone called her attention to him.

He had come down a step. His brow was raised, a shadow of a smile on his face. "They have long, *sharp* teeth."

"Oh? *Oh.*" Her gaze traveled around the grounds. The tall grasses moved with the wind. She did not want to have to deal with those.

"Get in the house, Nava."

She nodded, fumbling to pick up her bag from the ground, and followed him up the stone steps, wondering about river nymphs and the fact that her stomach was doing somersaults.

The wooden door of the cabin was large, heavy, and rustic. She walked in and was greeted by a warmth that embraced her like a hug. It smelled like iris, sandalwood, and leather. Planked walls extended from floor to ceiling in brown tones.

It was cozy inside, the fire rolling in the small fireplace. There was a woodstove at the other end of the cabin, cabinets and a little rustic sink to one side. A small dining table with three mixed chairs.

There was no art, no bookcase in sight. Like he was ready to leave at any moment. Nothing personal in here, except for the weapons. Her gaze traveled to two large swords hung on the wall, their steel reflecting the fire nearby.

There were black lines etched on the blade, intricate designs she couldn't quite study from this far. Her attention shifted across the fireplace to the chair in the corner, covered in blankets and furs. Nava swallowed as she took in this one large room with *one* bed.

She was going to have to sleep in the tent, sans blankets and surrounded by river nymphs.

He moved around his home, taking off his coat and hanging it on a hook by the front door. She stood at the entrance, chasing his every move.

He was wearing a white button-down shirt that stretched over his muscular back, tapering down to his narrow hips. Brown trousers hugged his muscular legs. She bit her nails. He would take the whole bed.

Not that she was considering sharing it with him.

"Make yourself at home, and leave your bag at the door." He pointed at the place to her right, where he had hung his coat before.

He doesn't expect us to share the bed, right?

He huffed a laugh. To her horror, she had spoken the words out loud.

"You can have the bed," he said, his smile widening. Her heart stumbled at the beauty of it.

What was wrong with her? She hadn't meant to act so rudely to him when he was helping her out. "No, I can't take your bed. I can sleep in that." She pointed at a chair by the corner.

"It's fine, Nava. I won't sleep tonight. I'll do some rounds to make sure they didn't follow us."

She swallowed when his intense eyes met hers. She didn't like magic, but for his eyes, she could make an exception. "They will come here?"

How had her mother met this man? Had they been friends, acquaintances?

She could tell he was a sorcerer, not because he was skilled at veiling spells. The scent of magic in the air was a clear giveaway. The extension of his powers was unknown. She was confused why she was at ease with his company; she wasn't afraid of him—wary, perhaps.

"The house is warded by strong disorienting spells. The men who were chasing you wouldn't even know where to start. It will point them in a different direction if they get close." His veiling spell in the forest should have told her Arkimedes was remarkable.

Still, her mother had also been remarkable, and even she had not been confident to hide from a murder of Crows.

That was an exaggeration. There had been two Crows who knew Nava's face—three if she counted her mother.

"Aren't you afraid?" She voiced her fear. It occurred to her as she inspected the peaceful home.

He shrugged a shoulder, handing her a glass of water. She drank it all in one go, remembering how thirsty she was. "No. They are manageable and appear to be looking for deserters in general. They will be annoyed you disappeared. However, they will move to the villages next. My biggest worry is who hired them." He brought his hand to his chin, rubbing across the short stubble.

Nava's mind came to the word. Villages—as in plural. Laurie had mentioned something about one as well. He was in the kitchen, rummaging through the cabinets. She approached the table, unsure how comfortable she should be. Her rational brain told her it was strange she was at such ease. She pulled out a chair and let the weight of her body drop onto it. It screeched with her movement. He took the empty glass of water from the table.

"I know who hired those men."

Arkimedes straightened, his brow lowering.

"A man docked on the island yesterday morning. He made his way to my potion shop in the afternoon. I guess it was silly of my father to use our surname to name the shop. It led him straight to me." Her chest tightened. She wouldn't cry again today.

"Who?"

"Devon Black. I have a strong suspicion he will not stop until he finds me." Reading his stiff posture, she asked, "Do you know him?"

His expression shuttered; she had seen the same reaction on her mother before—always hiding information. The reality of it made her warm with anger.

He nodded, but he didn't elaborate as he walked farther into the kitchen and placed a kettle on the woodstove. "This complicates things," he whispered, deep in thought. "He is powerful. If he's after you, Nava, we can't stay in this house for long."

"Us, as in *you* will come with me?"

"Is it true you don't use your magic?"

The warmness of her cheeks increased. "I don't care about magic." She paused. "And . . . even if I did, I never got the opportunity since I've lived all my adult life in Willowbrook. As you're aware, there is *no* magic there."

He let out a resigned breath. "I have to come with you. It's not safe for you in this forest by yourself. Not to mention you are being tracked by the bounty hunters."

"Your veiling wards could keep us hidden?" A slight tone of hope shone behind her words.

"My wards won't deter him. Devon is highly trained. He would perceive there's something off when he comes close."

The screeching of the kettle boiling broke the silence around them. His attention was outside the window. The sun was setting.

"Oh."

"Your mother was part of the Crows. Gaining you will give him high praise in the Society," Arkimedes proceeded.

"Where would we go? I'm—" Nava's brows lowered. "I'm not going to travel the forest to await capture. The ship was large. He told me there were *hundreds* of soldiers in there."

"Gray sorcerers, sent by the crown," he breathed out and poured boiling water into a mug. She focused on the liquid, the shining metal of a tea strainer. The water inside the cup turned a caramel color. The soft notes of chamomile reached her as the tea brewed.

"We need higher numbers. The both of us won't stand a chance against an army, but if we were to travel north to the larger village in the forest, we might."

She cleared her throat. "I know nothing about this village . . . ?"

"It's safer than here." He nodded. "We need to warn them since they won't be expecting this. They have families. Children." Something dark descended in his expression. He turned away from her scrutiny. "I have to go. Stay inside. You'll be safe here." His expression matched the grave tone of his voice. "There is a bath if you need it."

He left before the sun had fully set behind the tall tops of the trees.

She made her way to her bag and took out her bread to the cabinets by the woodstove. She drank her tea before heading to the washroom. A large wooden tub was in the middle of a decent-sized bathroom. A metal pipe jutted from its side. A chimney twisted up to the ceiling. Her fingers grazed the wood.

Nava opened the faucet, and frigid water started spouting out. Upon further inspection, she found the coals in the small chimney were attached to it. Nava searched for matches all over the house and found none. Arkimedes never had to use them in his life. She left the bathroom to rummage inside her bag. Finding the small wooden sticks would mean a warm bath for her tonight.

Her muscles relaxed after the bath. Her skin smelled like sage and rosemary, some of the oils that were by the tub.

Nava padded barefoot across the room. The cabin was quiet except for the rolling fire burning from the fireplace. She searched for a sign of Arkimedes, but he was nowhere to be found.

The fluffy mattress was so appealing to her overtired body. Arkimedes truly meant for her to sleep in his bed. Otherwise, he wouldn't have offered. Right?

So much unknown was ahead of her. Now she was thrown into this world she had avoided for so long.

Nava crawled over the furs on top of the bed, the wool blanket woven in earth tones. She let her body fall. The surrounding scent lulled her to sleep.

CHAPTER SEVEN

Nava had been awake before the sun came up. Her body buzzed with pent-up energy, even though she'd been exhausted both physically and mentally the day before.

Arkimedes was not back yet. Worry nagged at the edges of her mind. She figured he'd have returned in the middle of the night, and the thought of him being in the same quarters as she had woken at random moments throughout the night. Too self-conscious of sleeping mouth agape, kicking, or—worse—sleepwalking with a man like him around her.

When she was sure sleep wouldn't come back to her again, she rolled out of bed and made her way to the washroom. She tried to tame her wild waves to no avail.

Let it be, for now.

Nava washed her face and changed into fresh clothes. Today she put on her woolen trousers. They had belonged to her mother back when she'd served the Society of Crows. They were black, with a blue sheen, like bird feathers, in proper lighting.

She padded out of the washroom, appreciating the soft texture of the worn wood floor and the cabin's cozy atmosphere. Her gaze landed again on the swords she'd spotted the night before. She approached. There were ornate letters down the blades, spelling his name. *Arkimedes B. Valeron.*

She touched the cool metal, entranced as her pads explored the design's texture. A vague recognition hit her. She had seen this sword before, she thought. Or one like it. She was sure she had never met Arkimedes or his weapon. Nava looked at the second sword that hung above. Instead of his name, there was the etching of a dead tree.

Nava turned her head to the side, examining it in confusion. Curiosity got the best of her as she came closer to the sword, her nose almost touching it.

The door of the house swung open, startling her back. A scream escaped her lips. She leaped a couple of feet and hit the side of a table by the bed, pushing off all the contents as she fell right over it and tumbled down to the ground along with paper, glass, and more.

Arkimedes was by the door, looking tired from a night out. His eyes widened as she rushed to get up, her face warming with embarrassment.

"I'm *so* sorry," she blurted. "I was not snooping. I mean, I *was*. Only because it's such an interesting sword."

His attention traveled toward the sword, then to the ground peppered with his things.

Nava kneeled down and picked it all. She hoped he wouldn't kick her out of his house now that she'd made such a mess of his things.

She pulled her hand back when glass pierced her skin, examining it with a frown. A red drop was coming out of a slight cut. He was by her in a blink, his enormous hands bringing hers closer to inspect the cut.

Nava trembled under his touch. A sensation ran through her skin and warmed her body. Her teeth captured her bottom lip.

Arkimedes's brows furrowed. His touch was leaving her speechless, which on its own was something to behold. She put her foot in her mouth when nervous, never one to lose speech.

"I left for just a few hours. You have already broken multiple of my things," he said.

Her skin grew warmer as she pulled her hand away. "You scared me."

Arkimedes huffed a laugh before starting to pick up the broken glass pieces. He walked to the kitchen while she finished settling the small table back into place. When she was getting up, he was by her, holding a wooden box. There were vials of potions and gauze inside.

"It's just a scratch. Also, what are those?" She studied his potions suspiciously.

His brow lifted. "I see. You destroy my property and snub my potions."

A bite of shame burdened her thoughts. "A good potion maker always questions other people's potions, *particularly* if they are magical."

Arkimedes laughed, shaking his head. He placed his first aid box on top of the table. "You've gotta clean it. Who knows what potion residual was in the glass that cut you?"

Her steps were quick to get to him, and she reached to pick the tiny glass vials from the box.

His hand stopped her before she got a chance to pick any. "I don't want you messing with them, potion maker."

He picked two out of the bunch and cut a small piece of gauze. He handed her the saturated cloth. She brought it down to her cut. From the smell and the sting of it, she could tell it was just a disinfecting potion.

Not unlike the ones she made daily in town.

"So. Nava Forrest. The potion maker of Willowbrook. Doesn't want anything to do magic but enjoys making potions," he said.

"Potions don't ruin people's lives. They improve it," she mumbled.

His playful expression faltered. "I see." He handed her a rag saturated with a different kind of potion, and he followed her movements.

She could tell by the soft lavender notes that it was a healing potion, much like the ones she had used on the creature the day before. She put it against her finger and met his eyes. "There, all clean. You don't have to worry about me losing my hand because you didn't clean your potion bottles."

A smile pulled the corners of her lip, and rolling laughter came out of him in disbelief—the sound making her insides swirl and heat pool in her stomach. "I saved you, let you sleep in my bed, and what I get in return is judgment."

"This will teach you next time you want to save a random person in the woods," she piped in, and his expression danced with mirth before he walked away toward the kitchen, shaking his head.

He reached for the bread Nava had placed on top of the counter last night, her favorite from Simone's bakery. "Yours?"

"Ours?"

"It has been a while since I've had sourdough bread." A wistful tone was behind his words.

"This one is the best one I have ever had." She made her way to the small kitchen, intending to lend a hand with whatever breakfast they might come up with.

It was delicious, the warm bread with melted butter and eggs. Nava had to forgo the honey. After what happened yesterday, she was not about to consume the gooey liquid anytime soon.

"How do you get this food? Are all these things from Willowbrook?"

"I can't enter Willowbrook," he stated.

His swirling green eyes were a stark contrast to anyone's she'd ever seen before. Not even her one brown and one blue eye could compare. "Your eyes

—I mean, your blood. You must be mixed, right? Magical beings can't enter, either?"

"Something like that. I go to the villages in the forest. They hold markets twice a week. There is also the occasional traveling marketer," he explained and took a sip of his herbal tea, looking already less tired than he had been when he arrived.

Her lips parted at the mention of villages and markets. She never expected this forest to be so alive with people. She remembered Laurie's words. Cameron would've been delighted to hear this. To just be in the presence of a sorcerer like Arkimedes would've been enough to send her brother into a frenzy. Her heart lurched.

"I guess I never knew this forest was so alive with people." Her voice was weak.

Arkimedes's gaze met hers, and she stirred under his scrutiny. "Yes, there are a lot of people in this forest."

"Are they all deserters from the cities?"

"All are escaping *something*." He nodded, taking a sharp breath. "We don't get bounty hunters often in this part of the world, much less the crown's army."

"And a Crow," she added.

Arkimedes nodded. "It's not normal for Crows to work with other people. They work alone or with other members of the Society." He paused. "This is unusual."

Nava wanted to ask questions about how long he'd been here, what he had been running from. She guessed he knew about her situation, as he had known her mother.

The playful atmosphere had all but died. Nava popped a couple of tomatoes into her mouth. What would the next few days hold?

"When should we go?" she ventured, bringing the steaming cup of tea to her lips.

"Soon. Maybe tomorrow."

She studied his features. How could she be so attracted to this man she had never met before? Her soulmate bond should prevent it, as it had with all her suitors at home.

Nava paused. What if Arkimedes *was* her soulmate? It would explain why she was at such ease around him. A mixture of curiosity and dread spread through her at the prospect. She had to remind herself that even if he was, she didn't want her soulmate because the attraction would be a lie—something created by magic, not by her own choice.

Still, the attraction was strong. The play of Arkimedes's forearm muscles as he moved his arm across the table caught her attention.

No, he couldn't be him. Her mother would have *never* sent her this way, straight into her soulmate's hands, not after going through so much to keep her away in the first place.

Maybe, just maybe, this travel around magical lands would allow her to find a solution to her *curse*. Maybe these villages would be able to break the bond that attached her to a man she didn't want, therefore allowing her to make a real connection that wasn't forced upon her by divine intervention.

"I saw yesterday that you carry daggers with you." His voice shook her out of her musings. She nodded. "Do you know how to use them well?"

Her cheeks grew warm. "I trained for years before my mother passed away. It's been a while, and I have never used them in actual combat before." Her truthful words just made her that much more self-aware of the fact that she was unprepared for a Crow and an army.

"What about—"

"Don't say magic," she whispered, and his lips clamped shut. "I don't want magic, Arkimedes. I don't feel it is running within me. Maybe I didn't get the gene, after all."

"In that case, we should go outside, see how well your fighting skills are. I need to know what we're working with when out in the forest." Arkimedes pushed away from the table and made his way to the kitchen sink, where he dropped his dirty dishes.

She nodded, letting a mask of calm cover her features. Her hand shook as her insecurity with her fighting skills took over her brain; the rattle of the fork over the ceramic plate was the only sound in the cabin.

The sun was shining through the clearing of the forest. Soft warm light bathed her, a clear contrast to the cold temperature. Morning dew trailed down the black iron railing of the front steps. Now that it was bright out, she could focus on the details of the place.

The smell of grass hung around them, and the soft trickle of a stream nearby accompanied the sound of birds singing in the background. The land where the cabin sat had short grass, getting taller as it got closer to the woods' edge. The trees were different here. White trunks and moss-covered branches contrasted with the background of the dense forest.

Leaves covered the ground with red and yellow tones. She studied the property and met Arkimedes's expectant gaze. Her nerves came back alive, and her sweaty palms told her how ready she was to train with the man.

"We can go over there." He pointed to a spot far enough from the house.

She followed, taking both daggers out of the sheath and turning to him expectantly. He assumed a fighting stance.

"Where are your weapons?" She focused on his broad figure. His hands were empty, and he was wearing his regular clothes. Concern creased her brows.

"I don't need one."

"Wow, confident much?" She narrowed her eyes.

He circled around her like a giant cat sizing his next meal. She extended her arms, trying to keep the distance. Nava moved so she was facing him at all times. He was underestimating her, and it made her blood boil.

She attacked. For his large size, he dodged her with grace. He was well trained. Nava struck again. She was smaller and could get closer without him expecting it.

He grinned as he deflected her attack with ease. She didn't let him get too comfortable and moved quickly, changing directions as she attacked again and again. She was panting for air by the seventh attack.

It unnerved her more that he was quiet. Her mother had always talked to her when they'd been training, giving her pointers and praises when they were due. This silence was driving her insane.

She came at him more aggressively, letting her frustration take hold of her movements. He was close enough when she brought the blunt side of her dagger down. He blocked it with one arm. She brought the other one in, but before it could get anywhere near him, something grabbed her and swept her off her feet.

She screamed when she hit the ground ungracefully, staring at the mist that emanated from him, retreating from her body.

"That's not fair, Arkimedes!" she complained, rushing to get up.

"Why not?" His voice was a mask of clear danger. The dark tendrils rose again, shooting to her.

She gasped, dodging out of the way as she screamed in fright. "We aren't using magic!"

"You are not. I am." He was pleased with himself.

She stared him down in disbelief, right before she had to dodge another smoky tendril. She gasped in horror.

He appeared so calm, standing in the middle of the meadow, surrounded by shadows that could come out of anyone's worst nightmares. The spicy scent of magic enveloped her. She dove out of another one's grasp, swinging her dagger at it. The blade went across it like it was smoke.

She had a moment of confusion when something grabbed her other leg.

She was falling again. This time, she didn't even get to scream, too angry to speak as she got up, threw her knives to the ground, and stormed at him.

The mist and shadow retreated from his body. The only thing left behind was his blackened hands.

"You cheating bastard!" she snarled, ramming into his body. Unable to move him an inch. This just angered her further. "Why did you use magic?"

"You chose your weapon, I chose mine. This forest is not for perfect techniques. We'll face magical creatures, warlocks, *an army*. There is no foul play when your life is at stake."

"I would've known this out there. Here, I thought you wanted to see my technique!"

"I wanted to see how you would defend yourself against someone—anyone out there," he countered, "but you are so afraid of magic, you lost track of who your opponent was. Magic is not your opponent. It's me."

She pressed her lips together, huffing in annoyance. Arkimedes arched a brow, and she choked out a cry when his power came out of his body. She stumbled back and rushed to get her daggers from the ground, heart hammering. A swooping sense of dread filled her.

Nava couldn't battle against magic. She could barely hold her own against a trained fighter with her weapons. Darkness surrounded him, swirling around his looming figure, and it paralyzed her. Her sweaty palms shook as she tried to keep a hold of her two long daggers.

She couldn't fight him. She wouldn't be able to win.

Maybe she didn't have to win. She had to fight just long enough to get away. She gripped the hilt of her daggers, walking with a determined pace toward Arkimedes. The surrounding shadows dispersed. Black tendrils pointed like the sun rays from his body, reaching out to her in thin, wispy fingers.

She found Arkimedes's gaze behind his dark cloud. Nava understood what he'd said. She had forgotten who her actual opponent was.

Nava couldn't hurt the shadows made of mist, power, and magic. She could attack their master. She leaped in the air, evading one shadow that dived for her, and landed with a wince. Her sore legs strained. She jumped again to one side, dodging another shadowy hand.

Arkimedes followed her every move. He was close enough for her to be on him soon; she wished her next jump would be higher.

She bounced, ready for an attack, when a shadow wrapped around her waist. The powerful movement jerked her around. The shadow dropped her, and she landed prepared. She had seconds. She jumped once again, but this time, the shadows came from everywhere and pinned her down.

She writhed on the floor, the heaviness of the spell constricting her. Or was it her panic? She blinked. Steps sounded near her. Arkimedes hovered over, studying her features. She stopped fighting the shadows, letting her body relax.

"That was better. Your focus was always on me," he commended, and the wisps of darkness retreated from her body. The ghost of magical fingers crawled over her skin.

She tightened her hand, and she rammed the pommel of her dagger against his foot with all her strength.

Arkimedes yelled and stepped back, and she bolted upright. Both blades ready, she attacked as he stumbled, not with the same grace he once had. The smugness disappeared from his handsome features.

He was slowed down by his hurt foot, distracted enough by the sudden attack that she had a moment of headway. She pushed forward and attacked, but both blades were stopped by the strength of the black shield.

For a being made of mist, it was hard like metal.

Arkimedes's expression shifted to something like appreciation, if not for her skills, then for her actions. "That was good, Nava."

She stepped back, panting. His shield was up when she dropped the blades to the ground, breaths coming out of her in a big whoosh.

She dropped to the ground with shaky legs and drew in a couple of deep breaths. "Don't mock me," she grumbled, aware of every ache in her body.

He settled next to her. His attention was fixed on his home. "I'm not. I mean it. You knew I would be confident. You could've taken the lead in the fight if this had not been a friendly match."

"It didn't feel so friendly, being hoisted around by your magic."

"I will keep that in mind for next time." His voice was tired. Magic was taking a toll on his energy or maybe it was the fact that he hadn't slept all night.

"Next time?"

"Yes. We'll need to train every day. Next time, if you catch anyone off-guard, wipe them off their feet." He moved to get up and offered his hand to her.

They were quiet, just listening to the song of the birds. Their calls were different to the seagulls back at home.

"Thank you," she said.

He turned to her. "For what?"

"Saving my life yesterday. I realized I hadn't thanked you for it." She met his gaze.

"You are welcome."

NAVA GREW AT EASE as soon as they crossed the threshold to his home, chills traveling down her arms when he hovered nearby. She found him staring past her toward the end of the room. Dark circles appeared under his eyes, making his bright, magical irises pop.

She followed the direction of his stare and found the bed, his bed. After being out all night, he needed to rest. "You are tired." She turned around to face him, miscalculating how close she would be. She met his gaze.

"I'm fine."

"Go. I promise I won't jam any daggers on your feet." She pointed at his bed.

He laughed. "If you promise to behave, I guess I could." They got lost in each other's eyes. His hand landed on her shoulder, just a touch that came and went too soon, setting her nerve endings aflame.

Nava sat on the table, spreading the contents of her backpack on top. She had packed in such a frenzy during the evening. She now had more time to go over her things. The cabin was quiet besides the soft crackling of the fire.

Her attention traveled to the sleeping form of the man she hadn't been able to stop thinking about for the past hour and a half.

Her hand stilled on top of her clothes, finding the leather-bound journal of her mother. She held it open. It was dated, narrating her findings in the forest. Her speculation of who lived here. Nava's heart grew heavy reading the words. She missed her mother, but her anger toward her grew larger the longer she read.

Nava's reckless nature brought us to this point. She was not ready for the world then, not for magic or the soulmate bond that came out of her disobedience.

She focused on the words, her vision blurred.

Nava closed the journal with a snap. She looked at Arkimedes sleeping on his back. Let destiny be cruel and tease her with this, a crush on a man she'd never expected, plus the sharp words of her mother hurting after all these years.

This soulmate bond was so much more like a curse this time. Even if he turned out to be the man, it would mean this was all a lie.

Nava sighed, focusing back on her potions. One of the things she had always been good at making. Her father had always praised her innate skills.

She packed them back with care. Nava hadn't brought much but the essentials and had used a couple of them already. She focused on Arkimedes again. Why was he helping her? Devon didn't know he was here. His hiding spell was so good, they would skip him in their quest of catching as many deserters as possible.

She guessed maybe he wanted to help, not only her but the rest of the villages as well. Perhaps he and her mother had been closer than she'd thought. Nava pressed her lips together, making a mental note to ask him when she got a chance.

CHAPTER EIGHT

Departing from the cabin in the woods had been difficult for her. Nava had started to feel comfortable there. She was also aware that whatever came next was going to be much more challenging.

Nava rested and was well-fed. Laurie would be proud. She studied the wooden walls with minor details that had felt like home for the past few days. The long swords on the wall, the gray-and-silver stones in the fireplace marked by soot. The small kitchen with the wood-burning stove, where iron pots and skillets hung on the wall. The box of potions hidden in a wooden box underneath the small ceramic sink.

Nava's heart squeezed at the realization that she'd never see this place again. What would Cameron think about it if he ever were to set foot here? He would try to pry the swords from the wall. Her gaze traveled to her companion, and she swelled with wonder and desire—the latter something she was too scared to look into.

He wasn't one for many words. Other than the light flirting she'd sensed from him the day she cut her finger, he had kept his distance for the most part. He was a mystery, one she was aching to solve.

"Arkimedes," she blurted, breaking the comfortable silence.

He stood by the front door, shrugging on his large coat, grasping a wool blanket he wrapped around his neck as a scarf. He smelled like pine and leather. He focused on her, his gaze swirling with an emotion she had a hard time deciphering.

She guessed he was not going to talk, but she had his attention, that was obvious. “I meant to say I was sorry to have dropped in on you and somehow dragged you into this mess."

"The crown sending troops to this island to gather people would have affected me whether you had come or not." He took in a breath.

"Oh, okay."

"I also escaped from the city—a long time ago. The likelihood of them knowing I’m here is small but possible. There are many innocent people in the village. Those who were born here have the right to stay. I can't just sit here knowing they will be hunted down and do nothing about it."

"I see." She understood a bit more. "So, it's not that you had a blood debt with my mother then?"

He laughed. "No, I did promise I would help her family if something like this would happen."

"Why . . . ?"

"Something like a blood debt, just not that bloody." He turned away, focusing on getting ready. He wouldn’t say anything else on the subject judging by the tense lines of his jaw and shoulders.

Nava was used to not asking many questions. Her mother had always admonished her and her curiosity in a much less subtle manner than Arkimedes had done.

"Are you ready?" His voice broke the silence.

"As ready as I'll ever be." She bent over to pick up her heavy bag. Her shoulders were sore from the day she had left Cameron behind.

Cameron’s red hair and freckles made her heart ache. She was happy she had at least taken the danger away with her. Was he already at school? She hoped Laurie wasn't driving Simone crazy.

She took a deep breath, her heart heavy with sorrow. Cameron had wanted to see this world. He would’ve loved to see Arkimedes’s magic, however scary it was.

"You wouldn't have to carry that backpack with you if you used your magic." He searched her face.

She tensed her jaw, lifting her gaze to him. Arkimedes put his hands up in a sign of surrender, a smirk pulling the side of his lips before he exited the door.

The cool air of the morning welcomed her outside, the sun kissing the roof of the cabin, highlighting moss and gold hay. The dewdrops shimmered like diamonds sprinkled over the blades of grass. Nava wrapped her woolen scarf closer to her neck, trying to find warmth in the cool morning. Arkimedes walked in front of her, tugging on his black leather gloves as mist billowed out of his mouth.

The forest seemed less daunting now that she wasn't alone. Arkimedes had her back somehow, allowing her to see her surroundings with fresh eyes. It was beautiful, imposing, large, and magical. Enormous trunks jutted out to the sky, branches covered in moss, greenery everywhere. Even though fall was in full swing, it didn't hit these giant coniferous trees.

"You mentioned there are different villages in this forest." Her words came out winded. They had been walking for a while with no rest.

Arkimedes nodded, checking his surroundings before his face flashed to her.

It was no wonder he was in such good shape if he always walked around these woods at this speed with no rest in between. She was aware of her lack of endurance. Her cheeks heated when her mind went a bit south. Maybe he had endurance in other aspects as well. Simone always said that was an essential key with intimate partners.

Maybe if he wasn't her soulmate and they survived, she might get to see for herself. She fumbled in her steps, unused to this kind of curiosity before.

"What are the other villages like?" She pushed back her heated thoughts, giving way to another curiosity.

"There are a couple that are dangerous. Run by criminals." His voice was grave. "A mixture of cruelty and power. Those two are small and on the west side of the island. Most people don't head that route often."

Nava took a mental note of this. These villages were probably the ones the townspeople spoke of when they talked about the dangers of the forest.

"There is one in the north, which is the main village. It's not too different in size than the town you live in. A seasoned sorcerer who used to be a commander in the Copper Kingdom runs it. He transferred to the Iron Kingdom before he too ran away."

Nava struggled to catch on, her breaths coming out quickly. She brought her hand to her neck, using her icy touch to cool down her overheated skin. The terrain had become rocky, and they were trotting uphill. The path seemed to be well-traveled with a defined hiking pathway. "Those in the . . . north village . . . are . . . they good people?" she wheezed out. One would think all her gardening would help her some with endurance, but no.

"Like in any city." He shrugged. "There is one village to the east. Mixed races occupy it. Mostly fae. It's small, and the spells that protect it are powerful."

"Right, and you are sure Devon will be heading north first?" she asked in between breaths. Silence descended upon them.

"I'm hoping he goes there *last*. It will give us enough time to prepare, minimize any casualties," he admitted. He studied her flushed cheeks, his expression softening. "We are almost to the camp area."

"I don't believe you." She grabbed the straps of her backpack, trying to ease the weight on her sore shoulders.

"You have already said no multiple times . . . do you want me to carry your backpack?"

"I told you twenty times I don't want your magic's help." Her voice was sharp.

"I don't mean with magic. I mean *I* can carry it for you until you want it back."

Nava knew she should. The backpack was heavy. She swallowed, considering it. Arkimedes noticed she wasn't refusing him like she had done already multiple times and walked a couple of steps back to her. They were silent as they exchanged the heavy load.

She sighed, massaging her protesting muscles as they resumed their walk. They hadn't eaten since breakfast, and by the coolness in the air and darkness all around, she guessed it was nearing five o'clock.

Arkimedes, much like her, hadn't eaten after their breakfast, but unlike her, he knew the perils of the forest. Who was she to derail these plans?

They slowed down in an area where the trees were sparser. The sound of running water nearby was one of the first things she noticed, followed by how thirsty she was.

As if reading her mind, Arkimedes brought the canteen of water to her before dropping the bag to the ground. "I will gather some wood." His voice broke the tired silence.

Nava wanted to be useful, deciding she'd find the best spot to put the tent up. She cleared the ground from large debris.

Opening her bag, she reached for the thick canvas of her tent and pulled out rope and metal pegs. She had camped a lot while young. Her father used to make tents in the backyard to count the stars. She had continued doing so with Cameron, camping in the plains before the forest.

Her task took her full concentration, her fingers tying rope and finding the correct size branches to keep the tent up. She laid the floor down, a thick canvas coated with wax to prevent the humidity in the ground from seeping up. She didn't hear Arkimedes's approaching steps until he was next to her. He studied her hands as she worked the rope.

"What are you doing?" Arkimedes raised his brows, his deep voice a contrast to the quiet surroundings.

She yelped, jumping, and said, "I'm putting up my—our—sleeping tent," then frowned at his growing smirk. She unfolded the large, heavy canvas for the roof of her tent. "You don't have to do magic for everything. It's rewarding using your own hands to accomplish things. Plus, using magic will drain you, and you already look exhausted."

"You don't hold back, do you?" he said, amusement behind each word. The deep circles around his eyes made it apparent he hadn't slept enough again. He had been out all night and had come back home with sunrise.

Nava had been quiet this morning, trying to allow him rest. She had gone outside at some point while he'd slept and attempted to train. He had barely gotten four hours of sleep. The drawn appearance on his handsome face showed how tired he was.

He was busy making the fire while Nava finished putting the tent up and examined her excellent work. She brought her bag in, taking out the food she had packed earlier.

Dried meat, fruit, bread, and cheese. By the time she was out, the fire was rolling hot. Arkimedes was sitting by it. She extended him his food, and as he took it, their fingers grazed. The charged tension flowed in between them like waves of electricity.

"Thank you." His voice was quiet.

She plopped down next to him, focusing on the dancing flames of the fire, long tendrils of yellow and orange. "If there are all these magical villages, why live alone in your cabin?"

His eyes lifted, framed by his thick brows. "The people in these forests range from criminals to people searching for new beginnings. Because of who I am and who I *was*, I'm not welcomed into the ones I would feel comfortable being a part of."

Nava swallowed down questions that popped into her head. She shouldn't pry as much as she wanted. She had just met him and didn't want to be too nosy in his affairs. Still, they were to travel together, and a part of her craved to learn more, whatever he would give her. "I know about not fitting in. I guess that's not what you are saying—but what I'm saying is I understand about feeling alone, even when surrounded by people," she whispered. Memories of a lost childhood, awkward conversations, being an outsider.

Nava brought her hand to the spot on her chest where her mark lay, and her fingertips rubbed the area in a soothing motion. She often did this when she needed reassurance. Arkimedes zeroed in the movement, and she dropped her hand down.

"How did you and my mother meet?" There it was, the question that had been going around her mind ever since she'd met him.

"We met in the Iron City."

Silence.

"Just that—you aren't going to elaborate?" She frowned.

His cheeks turned red, and his features changed with embarrassment. "We met when I was very young. Celeste used to be a weaponry instructor for the Crows. She also oversaw the army camps' training. When we met here years later, the fact that one of the high-ranking commanders had ended up here was a red flag for her."

"Why would it raise a red flag if he was also running?"

"Because high-ranking officers of the army are not dismissed. They are a lot more likely to pursue him, to make an example out of his betrayal. Still, I guess it was safer for her to keep you and your brother here than in one of the cities." His voice was even, and it was clear he was studying her reaction.

She gasped. Her mother had spoken to him about Cameron. This tidbit of information shook her to her core. Her mother must have trusted Arkimedes much more than she'd thought. "You know about Cameron?" The words escaped her lips without permission, her heart stumbling over heartbeats.

"Not his name, but I knew of him," he answered.

"No offense, Arkimedes, but why would my mother think you would drop everything to help us if we needed it, if not because of a blood debt?" She gasped, filling the blanks. "A life debt?"

His lips parted to say something, but the crunching of leaves made their heads snap to the upcoming noise. A gray-hooded shape appeared between the trees, holding a giant wooden cane in one gloved hand.

The newcomer stopped at the edge of the woods, his face barely visible under the shadows of his cloak. Nava could tell by his build and frame that it was someone tall but likely human.

"Arkimedes Valeron, fancy seeing you in this part of the woods." The man's booming voice echoed around them. He was walking toward them with quick steps and without an invitation. His cloak swallowed his thin, tall frame. He pushed back the hood covering his face, revealing dark skin and a long face—sporting a crooked nose and a pearly white smile. Nava had never beheld teeth so large in a human before.

"Andreas, it's been a while." Arkimedes stood and walked to the newcomer, his eyes crinkling as his smile widened.

They embraced in a brotherly hug. "I was going to come to you after I went to Elise's," the man said, and when his attention came to meet Nava, the expression on his face faltered.

Arkimedes turned, following his gaze to her. By his expression, he hadn't forgotten the conversation they were having. It surprised her that she could tell it relieved him to have been interrupted. She crossed her arms over her chest as a wave of frustration built in her stomach.

"Nava, this is Andreas Mortimer, a friend," he said as if answering a question written all over her face.

She guessed it was evident by how comfortable they were. She stood, realizing she had been frozen in her spot, approached them with tentative steps, and offered her hand to the man. "It's a pleasure to meet you, Mr. Mortimer." Her voice was quieter than usual.

As his smile grew, the tension in her stomach lifted. "Please, call me Mort," he said, shaking her hand vigorously. "The only person who calls me Andreas is this bastard here. I'd rather not have anyone else use that name. My mother used to call me that. It makes me feel like I'm in trouble."

"Andreas is one of the traveling merchants I mentioned," Arkimedes explained, sitting down on a tree stump near the flames of the campfire.

"So what brings you two to this part of the woods?"

"We learned a Crow might be on the hunt on the island," Arkimedes said.

The man dropped onto the ground unceremoniously, his skin paling. "Are you certain?"

"I'm afraid so. Nava and I are looking to warn Roman's village. Also, staying in larger groups might be our safest bet. He has bounty hunters and an army."

"A Crow working with bounty hunters?" Mort repeated in disbelief, his brow bone lowering into a deep frown. "That is most strange."

"He can't be up to anything good," Arkimedes agreed.

"I'm on my way to Elise's village. I can tell her to up her wards for the time being."

Nava's eyes traveled to Arkimedes in question. His lips silently moved to form a word, "East," which answered her question.

The fae village.

"So you two are a thing . . . ?" Mort started.

Arkimedes lifted a hand, pointing at this friend. "Now, Andreas, I thought you knew better."

Mort laughed out loud, staring at Nava. "You can't blame me for being curious. I have never seen you in the company of someone as lovely as her."

Nava's cheeks warmed at the praise.

"What is a beautiful lady like yourself roaming around this part of the woods with this scoundrel?" the man asked gallantly.

Arkimedes's brows lowered, his hand up. "Stop."

"Always in such a foul mood." Mort pulled a bottle out of his coat pocket. She stared wide-eyed at the large size of the bottle. "Rum, to celebrate the occasion."

Nava had one cup before she retired to her tent, a bit drunk and afraid her lips would be too loose to reveal something embarrassing.

Who had traveled with Arkimedes before? Her stomach sank. She had no reason at all to be jealous, so she blamed her curious brain for it.

She wrapped the wool blankets Arkimedes had brought in earlier around herself, grumbly admitting that even though magic had provided storage for them, she was grateful for them on that crisp fall night.

They smelled like the cabin, and the scent calmed her nerves. Soft voices of the men outside gave her a sense of safety. Would he come to her tent tonight? Her body prickled with excitement at the possibility.

It had been interesting to learn about how Arkimedes had met her mother. She had been an instructor of his, perhaps in the army. He could be a Crow. Nava had the distinct idea that if he had been, her mother wouldn't have trusted him to help her and Cameron in this situation.

She stared at the blank ceiling canvas on top of her. He could be her soulmate, even if it made no sense why her mother would send her on a gold platter back to him.

It was a possibility. She shouldn't let her heart get too carried away. Whatever this was, it was doomed before it even started.

Magic would always win. Her soulmate would always be first. She guessed it was better Arkimedes had not shown interest in her thus far.

The sounds of the night enveloped her, and soon she was asleep.

CHAPTER NINE

When Nava came out of her tent the next morning, it felt like winter had arrived. The ground had frozen over, as it had dipped to below zero during the evening. The ice cracked under her boots as she made her way to the campfire. Rubbing her hands together, Nava tried to bring warmth back to her fingers. The sun was coming up, the rays sneaking in between branches and lighting the forest ground.

Mort sat by the fire, his hands clasped together in knitted gloves that didn't cover his fingertips. Brown eyes trailed the sound of her steps and settled on her approaching form.

"Mornin', sweetheart." His voice was throatier than it had been the night before.

A pot was boiling on the fire, and the fragrant scent of coffee came to her. She groaned as she took a seat. She hadn't had coffee for days. Arkimedes always made tea. A potent brew of herbs and spices that would wake up *anyone* but tasted like death.

"I take it you missed coffee." A big smile stretched across his thin face.

"Not sure what Arkimedes has against coffee. I have missed it dearly." She nodded.

Mortimer handed her a steaming cup. "Oh, he swears by that disgusting concoction he makes."

Nava's nose wrinkled at the memory of the mentioned drink, and she inhaled the aroma of the fresh-brewed coffee in her hands. The bitter, earthy scent of roasted beans came as a warm hug, and a smile tugged at her lips; she basked in the warmth the drink provided her cold hands.

She studied her surroundings, not finding Arkimedes anywhere. Mort's tent was still up. It was a monstrosity made of magic, two times larger than her modest setup. Her lips pursed as she stared at what appeared to be a house, thick gray-and-brown canvas, sewn together with gold stitches that matched the garish gold trim around the door. Tassels hung in places as decoration. It reminded her of a circus tent. She had never been to a circus before, but she had seen many illustrations.

"Where is Arkimedes, by the way?" she asked.

Mort took a loud sip of his drink, shrugging. "The man is a night owl, always gone when the sun goes down. Almost like a vampire—except reverse, I guess." His voice was amused.

Nava got the impression he found himself hilarious. He handed her a shiny apple. "Thanks." She took the fruit but didn't move to eat it. Her stomach swirled as she took in the reflective skin. Arkimedes trusted Mort, but to her, he was a stranger.

Her mother's warning voice telling her not to eat food from a stranger boomed inside her head.

She guessed Arkimedes was also a stranger she had met four days ago. But getting to trust him had been as easy as breathing. She couldn't say the same for Andreas Mortimer.

"It's cold for being the start of fall." She spoke to break the silence.

"It's this part of the forest. It's charmed to be always cold, you see."

It must have been why Arkimedes had brought her so many wool blankets the night before. At first, she assumed it was one for him and one for her. He had never come to sleep, so in the end, she had hogged all the available blankets.

The soft ruffling of steps and leaves moving across the ground made both of their heads snap in that direction. Arkimedes ducked under a particularly low-hanging branch. He had to be at least six foot three. He strode as he approached them. He had not slept much at night. His short, wavy hair was awry, as if the wind had brushed it. His sharp gaze came to her first, a flash of relief passing across his features.

"Mornin', fae," Mort said and lifted a cup of steaming coffee up to Arkimedes.

He took a seat by his friend, a grumble of disapproval escaping his lips. "Good morning." He studied his newly acquired drink before his focus shifted to her. "Did you sleep well?"

"Wonderful, actually. Thought you would never ask." Mort's false excitement tickled Nava.

Arkimedes sent him an exasperated glance.

Nava huffed a short laugh. "I did sleep well. Thank you for the blankets. I didn't know it would get this cold so early in the season." She put the shiny, possibly poisoned apple in her lap and held her warm drink with both hands.

"You're welcome."

She missed being the two of them. She craved more of Arkimedes, her natural curiosity fueled by the fact that he always disappeared at night.

Mort extended him an apple, shiny and red like the one in her lap. Nava looked at it with the intensity of a hawk. Arkimedes lifted it to his lips, one of his brows raising as he read her expression before taking a large bite.

The movement made her body heat. Her focus zeroed in on the tip of his tongue as it caught some of the juice on the corner of his mouth. A grin tugged his expression, and his gaze flashed to her, a wicked realization in his features.

Nava cleared her throat, a wave of anxious excitement flowing through her.

"So what had you running away to this forest, Miss Nava?" Mortimer asked.

She brought the cup of her untouched coffee to her lips and took a tentative sip to prevent words from spilling out in a fit of nerves. She wasn't sure when she'd get to have coffee again and might as well enjoy it. "Why do I need to be running from something?" she asked, aloof.

Arkimedes sat still, to her surprise.

"My dear, everyone here is running from *something*." Mortimer bellowed a laugh.

Nava half shrugged. "I guess that must be true. I'm running from the Crow who came to town earlier this week—and the Iron Crown."

"Let me guess, a forced marriage? Maybe seventy percent of the people in this forest have run away from those. You would think the crowns would abandon their ridiculous law."

The law forbade magical people to marry regular humans and make families of their choosing. The one that had forced her family into hiding since her father had possessed no magic. Their whole relationship had been in defiance to the crown. They had been soulmates, which meant the gods had approved their relationship.

Once, Nava had read the soulmate bond ruled over any other law, but with the greed of more power, the Crows had chosen to turn a blind eye to this.

"I guess you could say that." Nava swallowed.

Arkimedes's back straightened as he looked at her intently. She had not told him about her soulmate and why they had run away from the kingdom. But she had to assume her mother had, given that she had been so forward to share the existence of Cameron with him.

"What had you running away, Mr. Mortimer?" she ventured to ask.

"Call me Mort," he said.

"He was running away from debt collectors," Arkimedes pitched in, and Mortimer opened his lips in false offense.

"Excuse you, *fae*, I was running from bounty hunters. Get it right."

Arkimedes's rolling laughter made her smile.

"How so?" Nava asked.

"Well, for starters, I could have easily taken care of the debt collectors. They have no magic and deal with measly Grays. I, Andreas Mortimer, am *way* more powerful than that." Confidence oozed from him. Arkimedes's laughter grew stronger.

"And you, Arkimedes, what made you run from the Iron City?" she asked, and his laughter stopped. She blinked. Both pairs of eyes came to her.

Had it been an arranged marriage or debt, like it'd been for Mort? A crime of passion? Defiance in the army?

"Miss Nava, you will learn this one shares very little about his past," Mort said.

Nava pouted, meeting Arkimedes's gaze, her own heart hammering inside her chest.

"Self-preservation." His voice broke the silence. He took another bite of the fruit in his hand. "I had to leave to survive, or stay and die."

"It's extra scary *you* were running from someone, maybe *something*." Mort's voice was filled with wonder. Arkimedes didn't elaborate. He didn't smile any longer.

The heavy sinking settled in her chest. Arkimedes excused himself from their company and made his way to her tent, presumably to rest. She stayed by the fire, lost in thoughts. Movement in her peripheral called her attention.

Mortimer's tent was groaning and shrinking in front of her. She dove onto the ground, magic taking over her senses. There came the sounds of fabric ripping and folding. The spicy scent of magic overtook her, and just like that, the tent was out of sight.

"Woo, the look on your face, Miss Nava. It seems like you've never seen somethin' like it before." A smile tugged at Mortimer's lips. His hand was holding the cane he had the night before, the heavy fabric of his traveling coat swallowing his shape whole.

She found her voice. "I—I hadn't."

"Fancy that." The man's curious expression settled on her before he shook his head. "Well, here is where I say my goodbyes. It was a pleasure. I hope I get to see your lovely face again."

"But . . . Arkimedes, he is still sleeping."

"Oh, don't worry. We never say goodbye, him and I. I will see him when I see him," he said, lifting the hood of his cloak. With a small bow, he was off—a limp in his right leg.

She chased his retreating shape until the gray of his cloak camouflaged him, leaving her alone in the cold enchanted forest.

CHAPTER TEN

Nava was bored stiff. B-o-r-e-d. *Bored.* She was also tired. The crunching of forest debris under their feet broke the lack of sound around them.

Where were the birds? Weren't forests filled with them? Even when they'd been at the cold camp with Andreas Mortimer, she'd absently recalled listening to their songs.

It was hard to keep her mind from going to places it wasn't supposed to when the landscape was the same. All she wanted to do, other than wonder if Cameron was all right, was ponder how handsome Arkimedes was and over read any attention he paid her.

She had become that pitiful.

"So, Arkimedes is a long name," she started. "Maybe I should come up with a nickname."

"Please don't." His voice was stern, but she couldn't care less. It wasn't like he kept up the conversation.

"How about Archie?" His whole muscular back became rigid. She chuckled. "Okay, fine—not Archie, though. I think it's cute."

"I don't need to be cute."

"Oh-kay, how about . . . Arch? No, too weird? Maybe Ark? I like Ark—"

"No."

"Val. That one is good."

He took a sharp breath. She was sure he tried not to show the full extent of his annoyance, or maybe the contrary. Maybe he acted this way to show her how annoyed he was. "Fine, I will bite. Why Val?"

"From your last name. I read it on your sword."

Silence. "I'd rather not have that one."

So he *was* considering a nickname after all! She would take the small wins where they came, happy she was wearing him down. A smile tugged at her lips, then faltered when something else came to her. Something a lot juicier than a nickname.

He didn't like his last name, Valeron. Why?

"Why do you ask so many questions?" he growled.

She had asked that last bit out loud. What in the actual hell was wrong with him? "Have you been cooped up in your cabin for so long, you forgot how to treat people?" she fired back.

His steps slowed down, and he faced her. "Perhaps most polite people are not this nosy."

Nava's mouth opened in shock. Why would her mother send her here with this hot, stubborn, insufferable man? "You are *so* nice." Her words dripped with sarcasm, her body heated. "I ask questions because I know little about you and we are traveling together. Seems normal to me."

Arkimedes was quiet for so long, she had given up on any hope of getting any answer at all. Her pride told her she didn't want him to give her any information. "The name Valeron means little to me. I barely knew that family. And I'm sorry," he added.

Some truth, but definitely, he kept most of it guarded. She was happy he'd shared *something*. It gave her an insight into him not being close to his family. Nava also had the keen impression he didn't say sorry often.

"I'm curious by nature," she said.

"I'm finding that out." His face softened, and he resumed his walk.

"I will keep asking questions—*and* using nicknames." She would set a mental clock to know how long it took him to snap at her in annoyance again.

"You ran away from an arranged marriage?" he asked.

Her face went warm. "Oh, it wasn't that precisely. What did my mother tell you?"

"I— She told me enough." His face angled toward her, his bright green eyes turbulent. "But I want to hear it from you."

"Fine." Nava took a deep breath. If she wanted him to open up to her, she also had to do the same. "I found my soulmate back in the Iron City, ten years ago."

"How old were you?"

"It's rude to ask women their age," she pointed out with mock offense. His lips twitched. "I was fifteen."

"It's not quite an arranged marriage," he said, and she wished she could read his expression.

"I guess it's not." She shrugged. "But I don't want the soulmate bond either way, so in the end, it ends up the same."

He nodded, turning toward her. The light of the afternoon burned a highlight across his profile, marking his straight nose. "If you don't want the bond, I guess it would be even more suffocating since the gods, not humans, dictate it."

"Exactly." She paused. "Have you ever been curious if you would find your soulmate?"

"No," he said. "I don't want a soulmate, either. Someone like me is not cut out for that kind of relationship."

Her whole body sank at his words.

I HAD TO LEAVE TO SURVIVE, or stay and die. Arkimedes's words had been going around her head throughout the night as Nava tossed and turned under the wool blankets he had given her days prior. She hadn't gotten much sleep with her busy mind.

The wind howled across the tall trees. The canvas moved like a sail in the wind. The thick wooden sticks she had found during the afternoon rattled along with her tent, and she half expected it to fall on her at any moment.

She had liked this campsite after they arrived, with ample flatter ground and massive trees.

When Arkimedes said he would do rounds around the campsite, Nava had offered to come with him, not wanting to stay alone to face her feelings, the way she missed Cameron and Laurie, or the comfort of her bed.

He had declined her offer, saying he'd be back and she should set her tent up, as a storm approached. Somehow Nava knew he wouldn't be back until the morning *again*.

Her heart shrank like a raisin, making it difficult to breathe. She wasn't sure if her mood was soured by exhaustion or the frustration of not understanding enough. Not about her nature, her soulmate, what to do, or how to do it. She didn't know about Arkimedes or his past, but she was hungry for more.

On the one side, if he was her soulmate, like it kept popping in her head, it meant he didn't want her. She was ridiculous for being disappointed, especially since she didn't want her soulmate, either.

He'd said he wasn't cut out for that kind of relationship. Whatever that meant. A profound, intense, dedicated love? It annoyed her further that he wasn't asking her questions. He gave her less of an excuse to pry into his life.

She blinked with heavy lids. The blue of the moon bathed one of the sides of the tent, showing the shadows of leaves moving.

Another blink. Why, even though she was tired, did her mind refuse to let her sleep? She focused on the heavy sound of steps, a deep voice in the distance.

Her vision was hazy, and it was bright, a clear contrast to the bite of the cold morning. Another slow blink. This time, her vision sharpened over the approaching shape of a large male body. Broad shoulders and a long, thick neck. Arkimedes.

"Nava! Are you okay? Are you hurt?" His voice carried a panicked undertone. His hand traveled down her arm, his touch warm over her icy skin. A current traveled through her body, awakening every nerve ending where he touched her.

"I—I'm fine." Her tent was a mess—tilted to one side, the weight held by a couple of her wooden posts. The other two had tipped over in the windy storm the night before.

Arkimedes's breath left him in a whoosh, his skin pale. He studied her face as if making sure she was *indeed* all right, then traveled down her body to continue his assessment before they settled on her chest. He didn't move, didn't blink as he stared, his pupils becoming wider. With a sharp intake of breath, he turned away.

"I will give you some privacy." His skin flushed, which was uncharacteristic.

She followed his shape as he awkwardly stood under the half-fallen tent and exited. The heavy cloth of his coat billowed behind each of his steps.

Her gaze came down, and her skin heated when she realized she was wearing her nightgown—made of sheer cotton fabric that hid little of her breasts. Her nipples peeked behind the white fabric.

Her arms came across her chest, her hands grasping her cold shoulders as her stomach churned with embarrassment. A nervous laugh escaped her lips.

She was happy the worst of it was hurt pride over her fallen tent because even though it wasn't pretty, it had kept her safe and warm during the night. She shivered, her skin covered in goose bumps.

Okay, perhaps not warm, but it had kept her *safe*.

Nava got dressed in her traveling clothes and left her tent, finding

Arkimedes by the fire. She was shy from the memory of what he had seen of her body but was determined to make nothing of it.

She had gotten a reaction from him—unknowingly, of course. Her stomach swirled upon remembering the heat of his gaze on her flesh. She found him not meeting her gaze.

No longer panicked and concerned, his expression not soft or worried as it had been a few minutes prior. His chiseled jaw was becoming more apparent by the rigid set of a strained expression.

"Is everything all right?" she asked as she approached.

Arkimedes stared at the pot resting on the fire. The strong scent of the godforsaken tea surrounded her. "No."

Nava's brows lifted up, nearly touching the edge of her hair. "Wha—?"

"You could have been hurt last night in the storm," he growled.

Nava's back straightened at once, heat prickling her skin. Her stomach dropped, making her uneasiness grow. Long gone was his heated gaze on her. "And why is it making you angry with me?" she asked, unsure why his reaction was so harsh. She crossed her arms in front of her chest.

"This could have been prevented if you had reinforced your tent with *magic*."

The contrast of her warm skin against the iciness of the blood pumping through her veins was stark. Anger pooled in her stomach. "I don't need magic."

"But you do." He pointed to the spot where her lopsided tent stood. "Clearly."

"I have camped many times with my non-magical tent, using my own two hands, without a problem."

"Avoiding learning about your magic is not protecting you. It has given you a great disadvantage in this forest. In life."

Her chin lifted in the air. His imposing stature made her feel short, even though she wasn't. "How so? From where I stand, magic has been the one constant in my life that has brought me pain, has torn apart everything I held dear to me. It's magic that brought me to this forest in the first place."

"If you had used magic last night with your tent, you would have been protected from the elements and from the cold," he insisted.

"I'm *fine*. This has to do with more than my tent failing your standards. But the way I see it, I've been doing fine just the way I am."

"You had to leave your brother with someone else while you came out here to this dangerous *magical* place in searching of protection."

His words cut through her, the way he had intended them. The unpleasant churning in her gut wasn't anger any longer. She had a hard time putting her finger on what it was, but it was ugly and scary.

"You are running away from a world you don't understand."

"I know *something* about it."

"And what is that you know?" he challenged.

"People with magic have to serve, no questions asked, whether or not they believe in what they have to do. They're forced into arranged marriages, the sole purpose being procreation, even though you might not want children at all!" She took a deep breath. "Children are taken away to be forged into weapons. Do I know something or did I make all of it up in my naïve head?"

"It's true." His face softened. "That's the negative side of magic."

"It tore my mother apart to have to hide us from this. My brother and I were allowed to stay with our parents, to grow with their love, unlike most—if not all—magical children." Her throat thickened.

"But at what cost, though?" His gaze was hard on hers, unblinking. "Were you able to discover your true self? Are you happy with your mother about it?"

His words stung, reminding her of Cameron and the conversation they'd had before. Her brother wanted to find his true nature. If it weren't for a sorcerer and the crown, she would be with him.

"I don't need magic." She was supposed to be caring for her brother. It was her job to protect and care, but to do that, she needed love and strength. "So instead of judging so hard because of what I believe, maybe you can try to understand I'm not so ignorant."

"No, you aren't. But you are afraid—that often leads people to make decisions that hurt them in the end."

"Did I do that?" Her voice raised. "You must know all about me. Tell me, Arkimedes, were you a believer of whatever they asked of you when you served their army? Or did you hate all of it like my mother did?" she asked, and his lips clamped shut in an instant.

"I— It wasn't so black and white." His throat bobbed. "We are not one extreme or the other, not usually either way." He paused. His large hand rubbed his face, out of frustration or plain exhaustion. The deep color underneath his eyes was more pronounced. "What I mean is if you push this other part of you away—"

"It's not another part of me," she interrupted him. "I have lived in the City of Iron. I have lived with magic. I'm happy with myself the way I *am*." She didn't believe her words, but Arkimedes didn't need to know that.

They stared at each other for a long, uncomfortable moment, neither of them saying anything else or making a move to leave. This first argument hung heavy between them.

Nava was the first to turn around, making haste toward her tent, not wanting to leave it up for a second longer than necessary. Her skin prickled with the weight of his stare following her. She touched one of the ropes before the poles fell with a loud thump.

Her annoyance with her tent spiked. She knelt, proceeded to untie her rope from the poles, and pulled the canvas away. The cold bit at her bare fingers, making her joints numb as the morning dew burned her skin.

Nava didn't put her gloves on. They were buried under the mess, and she was too self-conscious to try to find them under the thick canvas.

She turned around, and Arkimedes was still staring at her. He hadn't moved to get tea or even sit down. His jaw was tense, a clear warning to stay the fuck away. She proceeded with her task.

Eventually, he stopped following her. The intensity was driving her crazy, but it eased slowly. He had fallen asleep by the fire, his large body slumped against a tree. Her own heart leaped as she allowed herself to linger on him.

He was unlike any man she had met before, an otherworldly beauty that was more than human. The straight profile of his nose. The long, black lashes and the bow of his lips.

Her heart squeezed because he was so close but so distant. She had never experienced such an attraction to anyone before. Her hand touched the spot where her mark painted her skin.

You don't want a soulmate, Nava's mind repeated for the tenth time.

She wasn't available to fall for anyone and waste time in things like attraction. No, she had a task at hand, which was to stay alive and survive long enough to make it back to Cameron and Laurie. But it was more than that. Her quest for survival had grown when she learned other innocent people lived in this forest, and much like herself, they shared her fate.

Her anger subsided somewhat as she took in the way he slept. He couldn't be comfortable in the position he lay.

She had finished folding her tent and made a neat pile of the woolen blankets Arkimedes sent away with magic every morning. She took a deep breath and grabbed both of those. Her heart came alive in quick pitter-patters as the decision formed in her mind. She padded toward him, making sure her steps were quiet so as not to awaken him.

Nava unfolded one of the large blankets and laid it over his body. Maybe if he were warmer, he would get better sleep. She startled when his eyes opened and focused on her. Though no words left his lips, his brows furrowed. She continued, however, steeling her resolve, and put the second blanket on top of him, hoping he took the olive branch for what it was.

His lips twitched up into a whisper of a smile.

BY THE TIME ARKIMEDES WOKE, the sun shone in the middle of the sky, and Nava had packed her things away. She always admired how he was able to be fully alert as soon as he woke. He stretched like a cat, the movement making the muscles underneath his clothes more apparent. Her gaze followed from a distance.

He lifted the fallen blankets from the ground and eyed them before his curious gaze landed upon her. The blankets disappeared from his hand in a blink. Her heart sputtered at the vision.

"Are we leaving?" she asked, making scribbles over the mud by the fire with a stick.

"Yes." His voice was still deep with sleep. He cleared his throat. "Er, thank you for the blankets."

"I hope they helped. I like to sleep toasty," she said, avoiding his gaze.

"They did."

Her eyes lifted to meet his. They both stared at one another, and it wasn't uncomfortable but charged with something else entirely. She swallowed. "So . . . how far away from the village are we?"

They had been traveling for a week already. For an island she'd assumed only held her town and a vast amount of wasteland with magical creatures, it was huge and busting with human life.

"We're a few weeks from it. It will depend on the weather and what we might encounter in between here and there."

"What might we encounter?" she echoed.

He grabbed his kettle and poured himself some of his energizing tea. The smell alone made her nose crinkle. "The Neems, the spirits of the forest."

"The spirits?" Her voice was high-pitched. A pit of dread grew in the middle of her stomach. "What spirits? Like ghosts or like fluffy, leaf-covered forest spirits?"

"Fluffy? Where are you getting your information?" He eyed her with rakish amusement.

"Well . . . I have studied. Some forest spirits vary. I read some are protecting the forest and are not harmful to people who are passing by." She didn't mean for her voice to sound so defensive. She was trying to get along, after all.

He ignored her tone. "These spirits are angry. Those who were murdered here stayed behind. There is little known why these forests make it easy for them to stay. As we move north, we will cross some of their haunted grounds."

"Just great news all around."

He nodded, taking a long drink from his mug. "We could try to go around. If we do, we might get a bit too close to the West Village—which might be worse and would add an extra two weeks to our trip." He paused, frowning. "I'm not sure we have the time to do that. The village might be attacked before."

The reminder of her task was clear—innocent lives rested in their hands with the knowledge of the looming threat.

"Right." She nodded.

Following Arkimedes's cue as he killed the fire, she bent down and lifted her backpack and the remainder of their things.

CHAPTER ELEVEN

Haunted didn't begin to cover the feeling around this part of the woods. As Nava and Arkimedes progressed through steep climbs, their trips became shorter.

It had become of the utmost importance not to travel when the sun was setting. The trees had also changed, growing thinner and longer, the bark painted in silver tones. Nava had picked a couple of plants she hadn't encountered before, remembering from her studies that they were rare and full of heavy medicinal properties that would help with more potent healing potions.

The forest became muted, the chirping of birds and the croaking of toads ceasing altogether. Arkimedes seemed to be more on edge as the day progressed.

"Do not leave your tent in the night, at any cost." He studied the darkening sky, and he would be gone soon to do whatever he disappeared in the evenings for.

"I won't leave my tent at night. I got it," Nava said, taking a bite of her meal. The bland flavor of stale crackers and hard cheese wasn't exciting, even with her hunger. It was the third time he'd said the same thing with different words.

"Even if you hear cries."

She met his hard stare. "Cries?"

He nodded. "We are in the spirits' grounds now. It's *not* safe, much less at night."

"Are you leaving tonight as well?"

His face turned into a mixture of guilt and worry, his brows lowering over his eyes as his skin lost all color. "I have to. The wards . . ." His whisper died on his lips.

She guessed he was done lying to her about this. "Are you a werewolf?" She had not meant for the words to leave her mouth, but this was her life, and her mouth had no filter.

"What?" His face snapped back, his eyes wide in shock at her question.

"You disappear at night. I know there is supposed to be a full moon with werewolves—but maybe there's something I don't know," she continued.

Silence descended upon them before Arkimedes laughed, first a low sound that became rolling laughter.

She furrowed her brow. "Well, I'm glad *someone* finds me funny."

He shook his head. "No, I'm not a werewolf, Nava."

"A vampire, then?"

His lips twitched. "Not a vampire. Wouldn't you be concerned about being so close to me if I were one?"

She shrugged. "I guess that made no sense. I have seen you eat. Maybe that disgusting tea of yours curbs your appetite."

His smirk turned into a full-blown smile. Her stomach churned with the sight of those straight white teeth, such a blinding sight that she lamented she could count with one hand the times she had seen it. "It's not that bad," he said, half shrugging. "Maybe I shouldn't have let Andreas stay with us that night. Ever since, you haven't been drinking it. It's good for energy."

"Have you heard of coffee?"

"Not the same."

She scoffed. "Either way, don't think I didn't notice you changing the subject." She crossed her arms around her chest and leveled him with a stern gaze. "Why are you always gone at night?"

His face fell, his attention moving up. The blue tone of the sky peeked around sparse foliage, the smoke of the firepit billowing up. The expanse of his thick throat bobbed as he swallowed before he met her stare. "I'm cursed."

"I'm sorry. What do you mean?"

In a second, he was up from where he sat. He unbuckled the belt that held his sword and dropped it to the soft ground, taking a couple of steps around the area before facing her. "I was cursed many years ago. I can't speak about it much, but . . . the reason you haven't seen me at night is because when the sun goes down, I take the shape of a crow."

Nava's lips slacked. "Why?"

"I guess she thought it amusing," he said in between tight lips.

"How can you break it?"

He observed her, shaking his head. Was he unable to speak much about the curse or was he putting his walls back up?

"So, do you sleep in the trees?"

"Not usually. Sleeping is dangerous."

"Do you keep your consciousness?"

"Yes."

"What do they call you, the man with one-word answers?"

"I haven't spoken about it with anyone. I'm not used to divulging a lot of the information." His hands went over his head, the waves of silky hair falling over his face.

"No kidding."

The silence that surrounded them was long. What was going on inside his head? His shoulders were growing tense.

She took a few steps to him and reached for his shoulder. He stopped all movement when she touched him. A zap of energy ran through her hand, and she gasped, pulling her hand back. His gaze met hers. "Did you use magic on me . . . ?"

"Must have been static energy," he said, staring at the sky again and letting out a soft breath. "I have to go, please—"

"Stay inside my tent. *I know*."

He nodded, and without another word, he turned around and disappeared behind the shapes of the twisty trees.

NOT WAITING FOR ARKIMEDES to come back didn't help with her nerves. Nava wasn't worried he would leave her, as she had been in the past, though it did morph into being concerned he would get eaten by a larger animal instead.

That night, however, she was worried about something else; much like Arkimedes had said, moans and cries happened through the night. Whispers sounded a lot like the howling wind, except she could listen to words mixed in between laments. Latin, the language of the fae, and others she didn't know. She couldn't tell them apart.

They whispered threats, cried for loved ones. They begged for mercy and asked for help.

The end of her hair stood up as the temperature dropped, so cold that mist billowed out of her mouth. Nava knew deep within her that she would not be able to sleep tonight, expecting a ghost to barge into her tent at any moment. The spirits, however, seemed to stay outside, as if her tent were warded.

She had the sneaky suspicion Arkimedes had worked up a spell while she had excused herself to take care of bodily businesses. She was so freaked out she wasn't mad about it. Of the two evils, the ghosts outside were the worst.

Something brown crawled over the roof of her tent, slow but steady, the size of a small coin. Nava blinked. It was a bee. The stripes of its furry body were gone in the darkness of the night. She fell back onto her bed.

Nava remembered the creature she had helped. It felt like a lifetime ago, but the memory was still fresh as if it had happened yesterday. She took another breath. The scent of mud and decay surrounded her, like flowers left in the same water for a while.

She buried her nose inside the fabric of the wool blanket, the soft scent of campfire holding on to the threads of the material. Nava could also pick up Arkimedes's scent, and she didn't want to dwell on the fact that her body relaxed a fraction.

When the sun lit up her surroundings, Nava rushed out of bed, making sure she was ready to run if she needed to. She folded the wool blankets and stuffed her bag. Her hair was wilder than usual, sticking out in all directions in soft curls. The last thing on her mind was to try to tame it. She put it up in a bun, eyeing the door of her tent warily.

Would it be safe for her to leave? To start the fire and wait for Arkimedes outside?

He said to stay in while it was nighttime, but the sun was already up, and he had to be on his way back to their camp.

The daggers would do nothing against a spirit, her mind supplied. She frowned as her stomach sank and the awareness of being ill-prepared hit her full force.

Steps over crunchy leaves made her head snap toward it.

"Nava."

She let out a sigh of relief before exiting the tent. He took her in from where he stood. A wave of intense need washed over her, startling her. "I'm okay. I stayed inside the tent."

"I know—I was nearby," he offered, his cheeks turning a bright shade.

Nava smiled. "Thanks." Even though he would've been unable to help her, he had stayed to make sure everything went okay.

"We shouldn't stay here for long." A crease formed in between his brows. "Did you get any sleep?"

Great, not only did she feel like dog shit, but she looked like it as well. "I guess my face gave it away."

"You look bea—" He stopped. "I *recognize* the appearance of being tired."

She was moving to pack the tent. She turned to Arkimedes in time to see a surge of mist and power form around his body. Black in color. His hand turned a blue shade, and gray smoke lifted from his fingertips. Soon after, a soft fire came to life in the logs.

His head tilted to meet her gaze. She always avoided seeing him make the fire or do magic at all costs, but today, curiosity had won over her stubbornness.

THE TEA TASTED LIKE DIRT water and rotten fruit, but it did give Nava the energy she lacked that morning. Their meal had been light.

This dreary part of the forest made her blood cold. Maybe that was why this place was called the Grey Forest. The trees lacked the normal splendor. Mist covered the ground, and even though she couldn't see them, ghosts surrounded them in between infinite tree trunks that extended beyond what she could see.

Arkimedes walked a few meters in front of her, not resting. Their path was less traveled than all the previous places they had been before.

Nava caught something to her right, a gasp for air. She looked to the side. A shape of a woman stood in between the trees. Her head was down, with her long black hair covering her features. She choked. A rattle that reminded Nava of the last dying breaths her parents had taken.

Nava's steps slowed down for a second as her mind tried to catch up on what she was seeing. Her body already knew, though. The crawling in her scalp and the cold that extended through her body shook her.

The woman's gaunt white face lifted, and she stared at Nava, sockets where eyes once had been. Skin so thin it was translucent, the forest visible behind it. Teeth through a hole in her cheek, and her lips—or lack of them—open menacingly.

Coldness dropped through Nava's body as panic hit her hard. All she could hear was the drums, a hard beat taking over everything. It was her heartbeat.

"*Arkimedes.*" Her voice trembled.

"Don't look at her!" He sounded far away.

Nava's focus fixed on the dead woman's face. Her torn mouth opened again in a snarl. The pits of her eyes shone with light.

Arkimedes jerked her out of her frozen state, and before she knew it, they were running past large tree trunks. Her aching legs struggled to keep the pace, and her mind was behind her with that dead woman.

"Avoid their eyes at all costs!" he panted as they ran.

Nava could see white shapes pop around them, behind trees and closing in. "They're everywhere!"

"You've got to run faster."

It happened quickly; they hadn't been running long before a ghost figure appeared in front of them. Arkimedes changed directions, pulling Nava along with him. The ebony tendrils of his magic crawled over his body. A spell shot from him over one spirit, and the ghost evaporated in front of her.

A white shape reached out in between the trees. A gnarled arm with bone peeking through paper-thin skin. Fingers purple and blue from being rotten for days. They were spirits, but also corpses. Not entirely gone, but not here, either.

A scream escaped her lips as she jolted out of Arkimedes's grasp and the Neem's reach. Nava turned to it, and she stared right into a dead man's rotten face.

Fresher than the one before. Skin still clung to his swollen face. A scream left Nava's lips. Light shone behind his milky stare. A ray escaped out of his mouth, shooting straight at her.

Arkimedes came in front of her, and the ray hit him instead. He collapsed on the ground without a sound. Her gaze was on him as he lay by her feet. She had lost him.

Bile rose in her throat, nausea hitting her hard with the overwhelming sense of defeat. Her knees hit the floor as she dropped next to him. The backpack weighed on her shoulders.

Nava took off the heavy load and pushed it aside, her mind homing in on him. The spirits neared her, their laments coming closer.

A small bumblebee landed on top of Arkimedes's brown tunic. Its body was wide and fuzzy. Another one landed, and in the middle of her panicked state, she had the wherewithal to notice something was off. Her hands reached to the lapels of his coat and shook him. She called his name twice. Her voice was breaking with despair.

She tried to lift him, struggling with his weight. Nava was not weak. She often boasted that she was stronger than the average woman. Arkimedes was bigger than a regular man, however, pure muscle and utter dead weight.

Buzzing surrounded her, bees coming down from the tops of the trees. Wisps of Nava's hair escaped her bun and moved with the wind. She grasped Arkimedes's tunic harder.

"Arkimedes, please," she urged. She wouldn't run without him.

The bees surrounded her, forming a shield, and the gaunt faces of the spirits disappeared behind them. Confusion overtook her as she studied the wall of small insects. The buzzing became a clear whisper.

"They are coming."

She had heard this before. The day she'd saved the bee creature when it warned her about the bounty hunters. Her back straightened, realization hitting her all at once.

Why did she know the bees weren't referring to the spirits, but to another more significant threat? Devon Black.

Without Arkimedes's magic, she was useless with her lack of powers. Tears pricked as anger ran through her. She hugged his warm body close.

She got up from her seating position, grabbed his arms, and pulled. The bees surrounded her.

"Tell me where to go," she gasped in between labored breaths. He was so heavy. She wished she were stronger. With the shield of bees, the spirits seemed to have less of a hold on Arkimedes. His tense posture was relaxing.

The bees opened a hole in their shield, and she could see the forest beyond her. She dragged Arkimedes over forest debris. The bees changed direction, and she followed, sweat breaking out on her skin and rolling down her face.

If she had mastered some spells, she could have been able to protect him better. She would have been able to help somehow.

Nava had been trying to get him away from the spirits and Devon's path for a while. Frustration with her mother and herself bloomed inside her. She spotted a large tree with a hole in the bottom. Large enough for them to hide.

The bees swarmed as she focused on Arkimedes's sleeping form. Ark had saved her, and it was her turn to do the same for him.

The tree was more prominent than she'd expected, smelling of mud. She gained strength once they were inside, hauling him until the walls of bark hid him.

"He is coming." The buzz was distant.

Fear spiked through her blood. She rushed to cover Arkimedes's legs with leaves.

Nava pushed her back next to him, making them as small as possible. She studied her surroundings, and to her horror, she noticed her backpack was not there. She had dropped it when Arkimedes had been hit.

Dread trailed like a cold finger down her spine. Once, her mother had told her that magic was about visualizing what was needed. To home in on all the energy of her body and call for that to happen.

Magic always had a price, usually on your body's energy.

The bees settled in the hole and covered it. They weren't moving their wings. She guessed to an untrained eye it would soon appear to be tree bark from far away. Why were the bees here, helping her?

She pictured her backpack and wished for it to come to her. Cinnamon and cayenne, the spicy scent of magic, wafted to her. Warmth ignited in the pit of her stomach. Her hands tightened around Arkimedes's arm.

Exhaustion came. She pictured her backpack in that part of the forest. She imagined it disappearing, coming to her, and appearing inside the hole in the tree where she was.

Her body became numb, and even if she wanted to, she wouldn't have been able to open her eyes. Her head dropped and laid on something soft. A heartbeat lulled her down to sleep, then there was darkness.

NAVA'S SHOULDERS AND BACK ACHED, it was humid wherever she was, and she was lying on a hard, warm pillow that drifted. Her eyes opened, and she found Arkimedes staring back at her.

"Oh, good, you are awake," she whispered. She wrapped her arms around him in a tight hug.

"You saved me."

Her heart sped up when the weight of his hand landed on her back. She shook her head and enjoyed the warmth of his body. "It wasn't me. The bees saved us."

He stared at the wall of insects. Their wings fluttered, but they didn't fly away. "I must know how you did this," he whispered, exhaustion marking every word that left his mouth.

Nava wished she could answer the question, but the reality was, she didn't get why the bees had helped them.

Her lips parted when she noticed the shape of her backpack a few feet away from her. She gasped with the realization of what she had done.

Magic.

He was sitting up, his large body crowding the space, like too much and not enough for her brain.

"They are still covering the entrance." She pointed to the bees. "I'm guessing it's not safe for us to leave."

He nodded. "The bees have an alliance with you. Can you control them?" His voice was low enough that she could hear him only because he was sitting next to her.

"No, I helped a . . . creature that afternoon, just before you found me. I put a potion on its head, and it warned me the bounty hunters were coming." She shrugged. "I don't know why they helped us today."

Understanding passed through his features. "A life debt binds you to your savior to repay in kind. You probably saved an essential creature. I have an idea of whom."

"Anyone would have done it," she said.

"No, Nava. Only a selfless act would form a life debt." A smile turned up the corners of his lips.

"How are you feeling?" She was glad there was no light in here or else he would see her blushing.

"I'm well."

Her mouth opened to respond when the buzzing interrupted her words. The bees were moving, flying away. Rays of gray light filtered through the hole. Nava brought her hand up to shield her eyes from the brightness.

"We need to go. It's almost nighttime, and it's not safe for us to camp here."

She followed him out of the tree, keeping her focus low to the ground. How long had she slept after her stunt with magic? Dread filled the pit of her stomach. She didn't want to dwell on what she had done as she grasped the straps of her backpack, a reminder that magic had saved them.

Arkimedes turned around and darted in one direction, and like she had done many times before, she followed him.

CHAPTER TWELVE

Magic had drained her. Nava struggled to catch up to Arkimedes, who, like her, seemed a bit off-kilter. She was too caught up in her fears to say anything. The silence was broken for brief moments when Arkimedes mentioned how much longer they would need to walk to make it out of danger.

The trembling started when the adrenaline dwindled. It went from Nava's fingertips, down her arms, and through her body. Her steps died down, and she grew numb as images of dead faces came flashing through her mind, but the worst was Arkimedes collapsing to the ground.

Again and again.

Ghosts were something she would see in a horrifying nightmare. Now it had become a reality.

A loud tapping distracted her, almost as if a woodpecker were nearby. She was shocked it was her chattering teeth. Her arms came around her to bring warmth back to her body. She couldn't find her voice to call for Arkimedes to stop.

Her vision was blurry as a panic attack closed in on her. Why had Arkimedes jumped in front of the hex? It made more sense for her to be hurt. He was stronger and able to carry her around or make it out of there alive. She was angry he had sacrificed himself—angry and touched.

The magic she had so vehemently denied just a day ago, the primary source of their fight, had been the thing that had saved her.

Arkimedes turned around, realizing Nava had stayed behind. His steps were quick to reach her, his face a gradient of emotions. "Nava?" Her name escaped his lips.

"Why did you jump in front of the Neem's attack?"

His brows furrowed, as if her question were the biggest puzzle. "Because."

"Just because? It could have killed you."

"I didn't think about it." His hand came to her shoulder.

"I—I thought they had killed you. Then I realized you were alive, but there was no way I could save you because I'm not strong enough. I have denied this part of me for so long. You were right, Arkimedes." Tears pricked her eyes.

His face softened. "We are fine, and you *are* strong. This is a new world for you. It would have shocked me if you weren't shaken by what just happened."

"They hurt you. I would have been able to do something if I hadn't allowed my prejudice with magic to take over."

"You *saved* me," he corrected.

"No, I didn't—the bees did."

"They were bound to you."

Shivers covered her body when his fingers traveled down her arm before dropping to his side. "That is true." She smiled, and Arkimedes mirrored the expression.

"Yesterday, I shouldn't have said all that I did." His voice turned softer. "You were right. I don't know everything about you, but I want to know more."

His words took hold inside her because they meant something. He wanted to know her, and that was scary and exhilarating all in one. The fight had stirred something within her. She had been angry about him judging her decision to cut magic from her life. "You were right about something, though. I have never given Cameron a choice, much like Mother never gave it to me." Cameron had asked to see the magic books, to go to the forest and encounter creatures.

She had always feared this part of herself.

"However misguided your fear is, there is a difference between acting out of fear and acting out of spite."

"I have done a little of both," she said, lowering her gaze to the ground.

"Calling upon your magic can drain you. I meant to stop as soon as we were out of danger. It's still close to the edge of their haunted grounds. This could do for tonight if you need rest."

She nodded, her body screaming for her to lie down. However long she had passed out inside the tree had not been enough.

She inspected the area where they stood. Now that her nerves had calmed, she could take in her surroundings. Her boots weren't in two inches of mud any longer. The forest was humid, and moss hung from every surface sunlight touched, but it wasn't overwhelming anymore.

Nava laid her backpack on the ground, shaking from the remnants of her jittery nerves that lingered in her body. The tent was easier to set up this time; she let her hands go through the steps by memory, allowing her mind to wander.

THE WIND HISSED THROUGH the trees surrounding her. Nava opened her eyes with a gasp, the ghosts' images from the day before coming to her. She scrambled out of her bed. The furs, blankets, and jacket she'd hugged to her body fell to the ground.

It took a moment to adjust to the darkness. The off-white of the canvas flapped around with the wind, and there was no sign of Arkimedes.

He is a bird now, her mind supplied.

She needed to stop listening to the howling of the wind that sounded an awful lot like the cries of the ghosts and try not to remember the haunted grounds she'd slept on the night before.

She tried to focus her mind on pleasant things, like the smell of Laurie's blueberry pies or the Iron City's summer days. When that didn't work, she tried to focus on the reason she was here. Cameron came to her.

Her mind supplied the image of Arkimedes and Cameron, training outside his cabin, and her heart almost couldn't bear it. Why would it keep bringing this image back? He hadn't shown any interest, and she wasn't convinced this wasn't some magical trick of destiny.

Nava didn't know when sleep took her, but the wind was gone, and the soft light of the morning's first rays of sunshine brightened the canvas ceiling of her tent.

The ruffling of leaves had her jolting up, rushing to the flap that served as the door. Arkimedes was sitting by the fire. His coat lay next to him. The white sleeves of his shirt were rolled a couple of times, showing the play of his muscular forearms. His handsome face was focused on the rabbit he was cleaning.

His gaze came to meet her face and raked down her body. It was a subtle movement she would have missed if she hadn't been staring so intently. As it was, she *had* noticed. A sense of smug pride washed over her. Nava walked toward Arkimedes, putting a bit of extra pep to the movement of her hips. Simone had told her to do this plenty of times before.

"I would like to train and learn magic," she said with a voice she hoped sounded strong, unlike how she felt. Arkimedes's eyes widened at her words. "Don't look so surprised."

"Okay." He nodded. "We can start later today after we make it to the new camp."

"After you get some sleep, of course. I don't want to hurt you with the undeniable power I have running through my veins." She reached for an apple from the dwindling bag of food they had gotten from Mortimer days prior and bit a big chunk of it. She enjoyed the sweet, tart flavor that took over her palate.

He huffed a laugh, amused. "Who knew you would hide such an ego under that big hair of yours?"

She choked, coughing loudly. "I don't have big hair!" Her hand came to her messy waves, puffier than usual from the lack of her everyday hair products from back home. Her cheeks heated.

So much for the wave of her hips. He didn't see her that way.

"You're beautiful," he breathed, and for a moment, she thought she'd imagined his words. Her gaze met his, and she could tell by the color in his cheeks that he was surprised he had said this out loud.

"Thank you." She grinned at him.

The silence that followed was charged with understanding. She buzzed with emotion at the idea that maybe her growing feelings weren't so one-sided. Then it came to her again. "Are you my soulmate?"

Oh, no, had she said that out loud?

"What?" He straightened, his skin turning pale. Now she had shocked him well. His brown, bushy brows dipped. His previously relaxed pose was long gone.

It was her gift to society to ruin something with her big unfiltered mouth. "Well, I just—I . . ." Her face was so warm she could have fried an egg on top of her cheeks. Her stomach twisted, and she swallowed, trying to get down the heavy constriction in her throat.

"What gave you that impression?" His voice was cold.

He had called her hair beautiful. Oh, god, she was so stupid. A compliment didn't equal being a soulmate! "I— Nothing. I just wondered because I never felt . . . attracted to anyone before . . ." Her voice became almost a whisper by the end.

She couldn't dig herself out of this one. Not only had she asked Arkimedes if he was the most important person in her life, but she'd also admitted she was attracted to him. She swallowed and understood her mistake.

There was no warmth of recognition. He *had* told her he wasn't ready for a relationship, then she'd gone ahead and asked him—just because she had a crush? Ordinary people had crushes all the time. She wasn't normal, though, but her pride prevented her from telling him so.

It wasn't like she wanted to dwell on the fact, not after he appeared so put off by her question.

"Just because someone gets along with you doesn't mean they are your soulmate." The almost imperceptible shake of his head made her stomach drop lower.

Fine, he wasn't her soulmate.

"I get it." Nava stepped back. Maybe she would get some of the rabbit later. "I'm going to go and see if I can find a place to . . . die of embarrassment."

"Nava." His voice was a bit softer, but she didn't stick around to see pity. Oh, no, she was out of there.

A good walk would clear her mind, and maybe by the time she was back, he would already be resting inside the tent.

CHAPTER THIRTEEN

The new camp was bright. The trees had changed once again to white bark, and bronze leaves peppered the ground. Unlike the day before, this area felt calmer. Birds chirped. Squirrels ran around the trees.

Or maybe they weren't squirrels. Upon further inspection, they had long fluffy tails, but their ears were large and fox-like, and they had lizard-like hands.

"The Northern Village, can they help you with your curse?" Nava asked, hitting the pegs into the ground that would be her tent. Neither of them had brought her floundering words back up. She pushed back her hurt pride and acted as if nothing had happened.

Arkimedes got up from his spot by the fire, dusting his pants from forest debris. "Unfortunately, they can't break the curse. Only I can unravel it," he said, meeting her eyes.

"What do you have to do?"

His face hardened. "I can't say. The curse prevents me to."

"How long have you been cursed?" she proceeded, walking toward him.

"Nine years."

"Was that what brought you here? I know you said you had to leave the city to survive."

"I was cursed here, not far away from where we are," he said in a reflective tone, his eyes lost somewhere on the horizon.

Nava opened her mouth to ask more. She remembered he had said it had been a she—had it been a companion he often traveled with? Mort had made it appear as if Arkimedes did travel with others.

She would ignore her turning insides and the unpleasant heat that settled in her stomach.

"So, how about we start with your training?" His focus shifted.

A wave of excitement ran through her. "Here?"

He pointed to a clearing a few feet away from where the tent stood. Their steps were a mixture of crunching leaves and rocks. His body turned to face her. She was unsure what was coming next.

Conjuring magic from thin air sounded ridiculous to her. If anyone had told her a few weeks ago that she would try to do this, she would've laughed in their faces.

"Magic comes from within. To call to it, your mind must be free of noise."

"Noise?"

"Distractions—you must quiet your thoughts and focus on calling the energy within you," he explained.

"Fine, no distractions," she repeated, but just thinking about doing magic sent her mind reeling.

She tried, however, not to think about Cameron or Simone, who had offered to help her and had asked nothing in return. About Laurie, who had been by her side since she could remember.

She stared at a blurred spot in the autumnal colors of the trees, and she tried again. Her mother popped into her mind. Anger took over her, suffocating her. Why had she never spoken about magic, taught them to fight back? Why had she never mentioned Arkimedes before?

Why had her father stopped caring about living and left his children behind? Chose to die bedridden like a skeleton over being with them. *Alive.*

"I can see you are spiraling." His voice brought her back.

"Sorry, it's hard not to get attacked by thoughts when there's so much happening here." She waved a hand over and around her head.

"Close your eyes and focus on the noises around you. It's like meditating."

"Do you meditate?" she teased, trying to lift her mood after the sour memories.

"Every time I do magic. Now, focus. Magic comes from the energy within our body, our surroundings. Those of us who have the gift can harness the energy and transform it into what we all perceive as power."

She took a steadying breath and did as he asked. The breeze of the cooling afternoon air hit her face. Her skin prickled in goose bumps.

"It's different for everyone. It differs in intensity and in what it can or can't do." His voice was low.

She didn't have a hard time pinpointing where he was as he circled her. The rustling of dried leaves on the ground, crunching under his feet. She took another slow breath and focused on his steps.

"We know you can heal and enhance your potions. This is true."

Not true. She wanted to protest this. The words were on the tip of her tongue.

"Focus."

The leaves were soft as paper, swaying in the wind. Could she lift them in the air? She remembered how the bees had circled the two of them a couple of days before, protecting them from the spirits that haunted the forest and forming a barrier of winged insects. Nava hoped she could create such a thing to protect Cameron, herself, and Arkimedes.

The silence was suffocating. The nothingness that happened made her skin prickle.

She opened one eye to find Arkimedes looming a few steps away from her. He lifted a brow in a challenge, and she closed them again.

"This isn't working," she said, splaying her hands out before letting them drop to her sides.

"You're overthinking it."

She met his gaze, full of disbelief. "Maybe it was a fluke—the backpack coming to me."

"Did you also accidentally alter your potion with magic to cure the Beekeeper?" he challenged.

Her lips parted in shock. "That wasn't— I didn't."

"You most definitely did. An alchemist potion wouldn't have cured a wound that would have bound the Beekeeper to you," he said with conviction. "Your potion likely had magic, and it runs deeper than just a small dose of power."

"Fine." She remembered how her hand had heated when she touched the creature's wound. "I still don't know how to harness it. When the attack happened, I needed to protect us. I was between a corner and a hard place."

"That is not how the saying goes." He smirked.

"Whatever. You get what I mean."

"Maybe I should make it harder on you."

Her eyes widened. "Like how?"

Arkimedes shrugged, walking around her. She smelled it, the scent of pepper in the air as the dark tendrils of his magic appeared around his body. Nava steadied herself for whatever attack he had prepared for her.

She trailed the long tendrils that surrounded her. But unlike that day training outside his house or the days after, this time she was at peace somehow. The magic didn't scare her as much anymore. It had her in awe.

It rushed to her and wrapped her in a hug of cool mist and spice. She gasped before it pressed her to the hard, warm body of Arkimedes.

"Get out of my hold," he commanded. His voice came out in gasps. He was as affected by the nearness to her body. He focused on her lips.

The warmth of his body molded against her. The rising and falling of his chest was slow as his breaths hit her cheeks. Warmth pooled in her stomach, extending lower, reaching a pinnacle between her legs.

This would not work out. Nava couldn't ever tell him she didn't want to be out of his grasp. She wanted to be even closer, and judging by her body's awareness, Nava wanted much more than his hands touching her.

"I don't want to," she blurted. "What I'm trying to say is *I don't know if I can.*"

Arkimedes held his breath, and she struggled in the magic's grasp. She wanted to disappear. Why, oh why, did her mouth keep running away from her? She had to get these nervous outbursts under control. She didn't want to appear a fumbling mess in front of him, not after what had happened earlier.

Her face was hot with embarrassment. She wished the earth would swallow her whole.

The ground beneath her feet shook. She reached for him, trying to gain balance. The surrounding shadows of his power had dimmed somewhat. Arkimedes's shocked expression told her it had not been him.

A wave of energy pulsed through her body, and shock ran through her. She searched Ark's face, and he nodded before a smile took over his features.

"Unexpected could be very effective," he said.

Nava was aware of how close they were. In her panic, she had jumped to him. Nava needed to put distance in between them. He'd told her he was not available, but neither was she. She dragged her feet while taking a couple of steps back.

A wave of exhaustion hit her almost immediately. Similar to the first time, when her body had drained and she'd fallen asleep. "Is it normal—for this to feel so exhausting?"

"At first. Eventually, you will learn to take energy from your surroundings as well, not only your body." His voice was distant.

Two muscular arms lifted her from where she was standing with a swift movement. One arm under both her legs and one holding her back. She laid her head against his chest and enjoyed the soft drumming of his heart.

"Maybe try not to conjure an earthquake to start with," he teased, and an edge of pride lingered behind each word.

Nava grinned against the soft material of his linen shirt. He laid her over the furs of her bed, which smelled like him.

She was out before his steps left the tent.

CHAPTER FOURTEEN

Caw, caw, caw.

The constant loud sound woke Nava from her dreamless slumber. It shook her awake as if an invisible hand had landed on her shoulder. The bird's cries carried a haunted sound, along with the crunching leaves from footsteps around her.

"Get the bird!" A loud, deep voice.

She stumbled out of her bed, sleep clouding her senses. Her heart was hammering as the shadows came closer to the fabric of the tent, silhouetted by the dim light of the moon.

She reached for her coat, the bone-chilling cold air surrounding her as she abandoned the warmth of her furs. The ominous shadows approached, shooting spells from their hands as they pointed to the sky, trying to get to Arkimedes, as he was stuck in his animal curse. Bile rose in her throat as a wave of panic navigated through her.

She picked her blades from the ground, the cold of the metal seeping into her skin and chilling her bones. She was in trouble. Arkimedes's caws still echoed around the emptiness of the night, along with a few screams of pain.

"What the hell is wrong with this bird?" another voice called. They weren't even trying to be quiet. That was how fucked she was.

Nava took a deep breath, steeling her resolve. She guessed she'd rather go down fighting than cowering inside the tent when there was nowhere else to go. Her knuckles turned white as they tightened around the tan worn leather of her weapon's handle.

She lifted to her feet and bolted out of the tent, ducking through the heavy fabric. She held in a scream when she met three large men in black leathers. Time froze as panic overtook her.

Her fight-or-flight mode kicked in, and then she was dodging out of the thick arms of one and running around the tent. There was no use trying to fight them when she was so outnumbered.

Feet pounded against the wet dirt, and icy wind burned her throat and lungs. The screeches of the bird were distant. For a second, she thought she could do it. She would escape.

A black-gloved hand appeared out of the shadows of the night, holding a shiny blade. It hit the side of her head with its cold hilt. Blinding pain shot through her body, making her lose her footing seconds before it all went dark.

IT WAS BONE-CHILLING COLD.

"Miss—are you all right? She's waking up," a low, raspy voice said to someone, his tone concerned and a million miles away from her.

Nava winced when her head rattled in pain. Her eyesight was blurry, and her body ached all over. Her consciousness became sharper as memories of the night came to her in quick flashes. She squirmed under tight ropes. They'd bound her arms and legs. Nava's shoulders hurt almost as much as her head. There was a large cut oozing cold, sticky liquid on the side of her right cheek.

"Miss," the voice repeated.

Nava blinked up in confusion, trying to find the owner of the spoken words. There were two shapes near the trees by her. The drumming in her ears muffled his voice.

It was still nighttime. The morning peeked soft yellows through the canopy's sparser leaves. She traced back to the last thing she remembered as her blurry vision focused on the shapes. She didn't recognize the voice.

"Arkimedes!" She let her head fall back on the bark behind her.

"Shh, you're gonna call them back in here," another voice said in a higher pitch.

A man and a woman were three meters away from her, both bound to a cedar tree that, judging by its sheer size, had to be hundreds of years old.

Was it the night before? How long had she been out? Was Arkimedes all right?

"Who are you?" Nava asked, keeping her voice low. "Where are we?"

"Move little. You hit your head pretty hard—or I guess maybe they did that," said the guy.

"She asks so many questions. This situation could not get any worse, Gavin." The woman rolled her eyes.

Nava stared at her surroundings in silence, trying to find Arkimedes somewhere. Her body tensed, and anxiety built in her chest, making it harder for her to breathe.

She didn't recognize where she was. Nava's attention came to the woman who had spoken. She had smooth bronze skin, a face that would have been pretty—gorgeous, even—had she not been scowling so profoundly. Her hair was a nest of tight curls that spiraled out of her head at a hand's length.

"What are you looking at?" The woman sneered.

Gavin, who was working the binds around his wrists, lifted his head toward the other woman. "Why do you have to be so hostile?" he said in between his teeth. "Don't mind her. We've been tied to these trees for way too long and are tired and hungry."

Nava didn't answer, her mouth dry like sandpaper. Her headache was too intense for her to focus on anything for too long. How long had they been here before her?

She would never see her family again. Never see Cameron grow older, graduate, and become a man she would be proud of.

There was the noise of chattering around them, the soft crunch of twigs. Nava guessed the camp of their abductors wasn't too far from them. Tears dampened her cheeks. Her throat grew swollen as she swallowed her cries.

"Where are we, and who are you?" she asked again, adjusting to the darkness around them.

"My name is Gavin Luna, and this is Violet Ash. As you can see, we have been taken." He focused on her face before he resumed his task of moving his arms, letting out a groan. "I can't even seem to loosen them up a smidge." His head dropped back, hitting the tree with a thump. His Adam's apple bobbed.

"I told you, it's futile," Violet said.

"I'm not trying to escape them—they're too tight, and it's cutting the circulation from my fingers." His black hair was wet with sweat. He had a nasty gash on the side of his head. He moved his arms again with more fervor, grunting as his face turned red with exertion.

"You aren't going to be able to," Violet said, shaking her head in disapproval. "We won't gain anything by having you out for good from exhaustion as the damn ropes drain you."

"It will be worse if we let them take us back to the Iron City." Gavin sneered.

Nava's stomach dropped. They would take them back to the ship and away from this island.

"Bounty hunters—who would have thought? Probably trying to gather as many deserters as they can before heading back." He stopped what he was doing, studying her. "You don't look familiar. Are you new to this part of the island?"

Nava was aware of both of their gazes studying her. "I was on my way to the magical village of the north."

Violet grunted. "Oh, great. What we needed—a Willowbrook girl wanting to see a magic trick."

"I do not want to see any magic tricks." Her voice matched the woman's tone. "I'm trying to warn them about—well, the bounty hunters." She didn't feel like sharing all the details with these strangers. The bonding of their mutual kidnapping only went so far.

"And this Arkimedes you were asking about . . . did they kill him?"

Nava's stomach dropped, her skin growing cold at the words.

"Violet!" Gavin chastised her.

"What? They probably killed him if they didn't bring his ass back here." She shrugged.

"You are such a bitch." Nava's voice shook with anger as she stared at Violet's passive face.

The woman acted like she didn't care that her words had hurt anyone. Gavin shook his head before pushing it back against the tree trunk.

The sky was turning ominously gray. Nava could have sworn the tones of the morning had been present in the sky minutes ago.

"What is all this fuss about?" That voice was silk and cold.

Dread pooled in her stomach as she met the upcoming shape of Devon Black. He radiated elegance even in these humid woods. He wore a black cloak that was iron-pressed with no wrinkle in sight and a purple silk button-down shirt, which made a stark contrast against his milky pale skin. He fixed the cuffs of the shirt.

"They told me they found you last night, Nava Forrest. I had to come to see for myself." He knelt next to her, his ebony eyes shining with contained excitement. His leather-clad hand touched the side of her forehead.

She winced as pain came thundering in her head. "Don't touch me," she said, moving her head out of the way.

"Feisty little kitten." He laughed. His hand dropped from Nava's face. The scent of blackberries and mint lingered on her skin.

"Let me out of these at once, Devon," she demanded, struggling against the ropes that bound her. The movement weakened all the energy from her body.

"Tsk, tsk. It's no use for you to struggle, kitten. The rope will cancel your power. The more you fight them, the more it takes your energy." He pushed up to his full length. Imposing. Not in the same way that Arkimedes was. Devon looked out of place in these woods with his fine silk clothing and the stiff set of his shoulders. The man was slim, with a sinewy, muscular body.

"I see you have met your people." Devon's voice was elegant, as if they were talking over tea. His hand signaled the other prisoners.

"Why do you have us tied to this tree like we are animals? I've done nothing wrong," Nava said again, her pounding headache making her vision blurry. She didn't miss a smug smile spreading across his features.

"Kitten, your rights are nonexistent, worse than any animal. All of you are a shame to our kingdoms and a disgrace to magic," he said, fixing the collar of his new outfit.

She was aware of the stark contrast between them.

Clear societal differences between Devon's expensive, tailored outfit and their clothes. The Society of Crows was the elite force, detached from the crowns' interests. They were meant to protect the citizens, to guard the balance between magic and non-magical people, but they had been seduced by power and money.

It had been one of the reasons Nava's mother had left the Society years before they had to run away. Nava remembered their manor's size back in the city, a palace if she compared it to her home in town.

She focused on Gavin and Violet, who observed their interaction with murderous intent painted on their features. They were both stained with dirt and blood. Their skin was shiny with sweat, their lips dry from not getting enough water to drink while being tied up.

"You can go to hell, prick. No Crow ever needed a bunch of goons to carry his duties. You, however, might be weaker than most if you have to get help from a lot of them," Nava spat, her attention flashing to the noise in the campground.

Devon's face turned from false agreeableness to one of pure fury. Surprised to be called out and insulted. She guessed no one ever challenged him. He laughed and knelt over her, his gloved hand holding on to her chin. She hissed when a spark burned her skin as he came closer. The peppermint smell of his breath hit her face. Nauseated by his closeness, she turned her head away.

"I'm going to enjoy breaking you," he said, and it was the first time the true fire of anger burned behind his expression.

He got up and dusted his hands before throwing a glance at the other two, as if Violet and Gavin were cockroaches in his way, not worth more than a dismissive gesture.

"Enjoy the rain," he mused.

Thunder roared in the sky, followed by the pitter-patter of freezing rain. Their place among the trees had fewer branches and leaves to shield them from the weather.

Coldness seeped into her body. She followed the retreating form of the Crow. His coat flowed in the air. Gavin cursed in another language, staring at Nava, a spark of curiosity and annoyance tinting his features.

"I didn't know one of the Crows was working with the bounty hunters." Gavin's voice was more concerned than before, his skin pale. Mist came out of his lips, caused by the drop in temperature.

"We are even more screwed than I thought." Violet's gaze fixed on Nava. "You taunt him recklessly, not thinking of what your actions would cause. Not to you but for us by approximation."

"Let me remind you. It's not because of me they tied you to this tree. So focus your anger on the person who did it and not someone who's also sharing the fate," Nava said.

Violet bared her teeth. "No, but it's because of you we will get hypothermia by the end of the morning."

Nava pressed her lips together, forcing down the bitter words that tasted like bile in her throat. There was no point in arguing with someone like Violet. She needed to focus on warmth and how to get out of this mess.

Devon Black had not come to this island in search of the Forrests, but for deserters. She had been found by accident because Devon knew what she looked like. Bad luck, yes, but at least she was happy her brother was not in danger. Not unless he ever decided to find her.

Her stomach sank because, without a shadow of a doubt, her spirited, brave little brother would do that as soon as he came of age.

She studied the cloudy sky as it poured icy rain over them. Sunrise had come; it was only a matter of time before Arkimedes would come. Nava wished he would leave, save himself, and warn the village people like they'd intended.

There was no victory against a Crow. They were the most skilled soldiers —the most powerful sorcerers and warlocks in the kingdoms. Even though Nava had taunted Devon, his strength terrified her.

If she were to judge by her companions' faces, her fears were based on reality. She tried to tune out their voices as they talked about escapes. Her attention traveled up the trees. She blinked at the heavy drops of rain that hung in her eyelashes, her body numb from the cold.

At least the headache was duller, driven down by the temperature and the exhaustion of her body.

A tree moved, and Nava blinked in confusion, her focus sharpening as she followed its movements. Bark sticking off places, a waxy chest, and a deep hollow gaze trailed her. Gnarly teeth shaped from tree bark turned into an expression of despair. This creature intended to come to aid her.

Nava was unsure why she could tell his intentions as if she were staring at her own. She tried to find the sign of bees. The frozen rain would prevent them from coming.

She shook her head at the creature, hoping whatever connection they shared, it would read her mind. Nava didn't want it to get hurt. The risk wasn't worth it.

Stand back.

CHAPTER FIFTEEN

The magical rainstorm didn't waver, not after the temperature had risen with the apparent passing of time.

The agonizing screech of a man by the campground jolted her awake. Arkimedes had arrived.

Clear commotion boomed around them. The three of them stared through the forest where the tents stood, where men in heavy cloaks and furs were running, carrying heavy weaponry. They couldn't see well what was happening behind the screams.

Thunder boomed.

A tree fell with a ferocious bang. Arkimedes rose in the distance, as if suspended in the air. Nava blinked at the sight of sable wings that jutted out of his white shirt. With long feathers that spread out, he perched onto a tree branch. Tendrils of magic radiated from his body like hands, arms—like he was carrying people's souls within his power. His face contorted in rage.

Nava's heart skipped a beat when she took him in, and the palms of her hands tingled as her nerves flared. Her worry shot up for him. He could be harmed, captured, or, worse, killed. She struggled against the binds around her body, ignoring how exhausting it was.

The sight of Arkimedes and the fight against a whole group of bounty hunters rendered her companions speechless. Nava followed Devon Black, who was crouched down on the floor, an arm to his side with the power of ice swirling around his hand. His face was not so polished and cocky anymore.

Thunder roared in the sky again, and a bolt of lightning struck down. Her hair stood on end with static, her ears ringing as one tree went up in flames. Arkimedes dodged the weather attack, jumping out of the tree branch with barely enough time. Shadow figures made a shield and chased after him.

The tree went up in flames. Devon screamed something in a clear commanding voice. Arkimedes didn't answer. His wings expanded, like the most magnificent vision she ever saw. Gavin stilled at the sight of him.

He was muscle and strength. A plume of smoky ink followed his movements as he leaped down on Devon. Ice and snow exploded around them. Smoke billowed out, hiding them from view.

A man's cry of pain echoed in the camp once again, and her blood chilled with the thought that it could be Arkimedes. She resumed her fight against her binds, having stopped to stare wide-eyed and open-jawed at the man she had been traveling with. Her friend. Nava's body ached, her extremities numb.

Nava could see little from her vantage point but could hear the hits of pounding flesh. The smoke cleared, and Arkimedes came into view. His hand raised as an upcoming bounty hunter ran to him, weapon lifted. A wave of shadows left his hand, and the man collapsed to the ground.

He didn't hover, but he met her gaze from across the clearing. His usual stormy green eyes were shaded by anger as he took her in. Nava's stomach dropped. The realization of his power hit her hard, then he was gone.

Her lips parted in shock when the swirls of charcoal smoke were left in the spot he'd been mere moments ago. The screams and the clanking of metal echoed around them.

Gavin became frantic, studying his surroundings.

"It's one of them," Violet hissed. "Gavin, I don't want to go back."

One of whom?

"Don't worry, Love. It seems he is fighting against the ones who took us," Gavin said, his voice winded.

Nava turned to Violet, who also was trying to get off her binds, and the realization hit her: they were afraid of *Arkimedes*, more so than Devon.

Something heavy landing on the ground next to her had her gasping. Gavin and Violet let out a scream. Her attention was on the shape of the Beekeeper in front of her. The stature of it was imposing. Its long, wooden fingers came to the rope and winced on contact.

Its sorrow-filled face came to her, and she realized it couldn't help her even though it wanted to. The magic in the ropes would cancel the Beekeeper's magic.

"Go. I will be fine," she said with a conviction she didn't have before, but it was rooted deep within her stomach.

The creature nodded, its movement jerky, and with a speed hard to register, he vanished up the trees.

Nava met the shocked gazes of her captured companions. She didn't like saying or explaining anything to these strangers. Especially since her own brain was trying to figure it out. When silence descended upon the campground, the eeriness of it became real.

Nothing besides the cold remained. Thunder came, and rain fell heavier upon them, making it hard to see anything.

The silence lasted longer than she cared for. Her sanity hung by a thread as she waited on a string of hope for something that told her Arkimedes was all right. A tall shape appeared from the darkness of the trees.

She recognized the way of walking—no, running as the person came closer to them. He was wearing his coat, also drenched by the rain. Wings no longer grew out of his back.

"Are you okay?" Arkimedes's voice was soft as puffs of breath left his body.

His blade cut through the rope that bound her. Nava shook free of it, and as soon as the textile dropped, the exhaustion lifted from her body. The tentative, soft caress of his fingertips against the side of her cheek ignited the nerve endings of her skin.

"They hurt you." His jaw tensed as he trailed his fingers down, gently touching near where her open wound was. He was examining it with a frown.

"I'm fine. It's just a scratch," she assured him. Her hand came to rest on top of his, giving it a tentative squeeze.

She *was* fine, now that he was here and could scoop her off the ground, where she had turned into a gigantic pile of mush.

"It's more than a scratch." Gavin's voice shook them out of their exchange, making both of their stares travel to him. "You might have a minor concussion. You were a little dazed, and the bright light seemed to bother your eyes."

"Are you a healer?" Arkimedes stood and meandered toward Gavin, who nodded.

Nava got to her feet and took a tentative step, her surroundings spinning as she winced and reached toward the nearest tree, trying to steady the dizziness that engulfed her.

"Easy," Arkimedes urged her and was next to her in an instant. He studied her features with worry etched on his handsome face.

"Might be best if you sit for a moment," Gavin said from his spot on the ground.

"Nava. My name is Nava."

"Nava. If your friend here can let me out of these, I would love to look at your wound," he said, staring at Arkimedes, whose jaw tensed.

"He won't let us out," Violet mumbled, speaking for the first time in a while. Nava had forgotten she was there. For someone who had chastised Nava about baiting a powerful warlock, she didn't seem to take her own advice.

"Of course we will." Nava met Arkimedes's gaze. However, he did little to move from his spot. Nava took a step toward Gavin, intending to get him out of the binds. Her steps faltered, and nausea hit her hard again. The ground spun. Her cold, wet clothes made her movements stiff.

"Don't move. The healer said you might have a concussion."

"Please help him out of those," she said in between her teeth.

"Of course," he said.

Her headache was too intense so she sat down, struggling with her garments that were stiff and half-frozen, taking a calming breath. The rain was ceasing, becoming a drizzle. She wasn't sure if the numbness around her body was due to disorientation or the fact that the cold wind made it more apparent she'd been rained on for a long time.

It was clear by the tense lines in Arkimedes's shoulders that he trusted the strangers as much as they trusted him. They eyed him when he took a knife out of his belt and knelt in front of Gavin. A silent exchange happened before the sharp blade cut through the binds.

Gavin's chestnut eyes focused on Nava. The softness behind them spoke volumes of how thankful he was. He was up on his feet before Arkimedes was done cutting through Violet's binds and walking toward Nava with assured steps.

"Let me see this." Gavin possessed a calming smile. His touch was cooler than Arkimedes's had been, his fingers damp and stiff from the cold or lack of circulation. He studied the unbroken expanse of skin on the side of her face. "Are you feeling dizzy?"

She nodded at his question and winced as the pain in her head intensified.

"We don't have time to play healer, Gavin. We need to warn Roman." Violet's sharp tone drove all eyes to her. She was rubbing her wrists as she stared down at Arkimedes.

"Nava might have a minor head injury. Her speech pattern appears normal. She lost consciousness for a bit when she was brought over and looked dazed. She needs to rest—we're to set camp somewhere safe. The village is three days away. She won't be able to make the trip there so quickly," Gavin said, choosing to ignore his companion.

Arkimedes's face turned to one of more concern. "Devon escaped. I don't think anywhere in this forest is safe." Something heavy was in his expression.

"You cannot seriously be considering sticking around them." Violet's body shook with tension.

"I am, dearest." Even though Gavin used a loving name with her, his voice was anything but.

"We would just be sitting targets for more of the Crow's goons to come and get us." Her purple eyes went to Arkimedes. "Or worse. She's useless and is going to slow us down!"

The tick in Arkimedes's jaw told Nava his patience was running thin. If she were honest with herself, so was hers.

"I would like to remind you this useless person just saved your sorry ass's life," Nava snapped. And it hadn't technically been her who'd saved them, but those were semantics.

The air of Gavin's laughter hit her face as he shook his head, amused. "You don't have to stay with me, dear. For one, I'm grateful to them for saving us and would like to help Nava."

"You gotta be kidding me," she huffed, not moving a muscle to leave.

"Am I wrong to assume our kidnappers won't be waking up soon?" Gavin's attention came to Arkimedes.

"Not in this lifetime," he said with a shrug. His brow dipped into a deep frown. Her stomach knotted. He'd killed them.

But, her mind supplied, if he hadn't, they would have hurt or killed all of them.

He had killed all but one, Devon Black. How was he feeling about this? Had he killed before? It was a silly question. If he had been a part of any of the crown's armies, he'd *had to*.

"We can't stay here. They aren't the only ones in their group. The others will come searching for them. From what I gathered from their conversation, they're expected to be back at their main camp within the fourth night," Gavin said. "That was before the Crow showed up, of course."

Arkimedes nodded. She wished they could talk more freely, as they usually did. Even though she liked Gavin, she wasn't sure she trusted either of them yet.

"I can carry Nava so we can move faster," Arkimedes said.

"With the magic you just used, you'll be drained of energy for a while. We can take turns."

"I'm here, and I'm sure I have a say on whether I get carried around like a fra-fragile doll or not." Nava's words came a bit harsher.

"Kitten does have a bite." Violet's voice was amused.

Nava shot her a glare. "D-don't call me that." The reminder of Devon's nickname rattled around in her brain. By Violet's smile, the intent had been to get a rise out of her.

"I'm sorry, Nava," Arkimedes said, kneeling in front of her. "We have to move quicker than you can manage since you're injured. We need to gain distance from this camp," he said as a matter of explanation.

"B-but is it necessary for you to ca-carry me . . . ? I might be too heavy." Her voice became a whisper at the end.

His expression softened. "You'll be just fine." His smile eradicated whatever resolve she'd had before to be less codependent of him after he'd saved her. *Again*.

"Okay. Fine." She wasn't unreasonable. "Is-is the village that's three days away the-the Northern Village?" she asked Arkimedes, who nodded.

"Roman, who Violet mentioned, is their leader—you might remember him from our conversation with Andreas." Arkimedes's voice lowered enough that she wasn't sure the others could hear him. So close to her ear, the air of his breath hit her skin, raising goose bumps everywhere.

So they had a common goal, the Northern Village, the path they'd been traveling for weeks to warn them about their common enemy. To stay in more significant numbers and avoid being taken back to a life of servitude.

"You should be better within a day. We can reassess then," Gavin conceded with a nod.

Nava met Arkimedes's gaze as his hand went under her knees and behind her back and he lifted her from the ground as if she weighed nothing.

CHAPTER SIXTEEN

It turned out they were right. Nava couldn't walk even if she wanted to. The forest was disorienting on its own. With her injury, she had a hard time focusing on where they were going. As soon as Nava pressed her feet to the ground, everything spun around. They walked and walked.

The camp they found was terrific in the darkening light of the day. Arkimedes sat her on the ground, while Gavin stood in a wide stance and conjured two large tents out of thin air. Those were perfection in a tent. She squinted when she found Arkimedes's amused expression fixed on her.

His lips pressed down into a thin smile as he averted his gaze to the handiwork of the healer. Violet had left to check on the perimeter of their camp and make sure Devon hadn't followed them.

"Ark—medes," she whispered, nausea hitting her hard.

He was kneeling by her in a blink of an eye. The sun was setting, and Gavin focused on them. Curiosity tinted his features.

What did he think when he looked at Arkimedes and her? Was he wondering why Devon Black seemed to pay more attention to her? Or how Arkimedes and her knew each other?

"M . . . not."

"Shh, bee, the tent it's ready. I'm sure it's not to your standards." The playful smirk was back on his face.

Nava narrowed her gaze as a soft laugh escaped him. At least his mood had brightened somewhat.

She didn't want to go in alone; she dreaded going to sleep to find people lurking over her tent once again and taking her against her will. She shook her head, finding words weren't coming to her.

His hand came to her shoulder, squeezing it softly. "I understand you probably don't want to be alone, and you won't be. I'll stay with you tonight. The only way I can, but I will still be there," he promised.

A knot formed in her throat. She lunged at him, hugging him. He held her just as firmly. Perhaps he had been as afraid of losing her as she'd been of losing him. Her energy was dwindling once again, and she was out before she had much more to worry about.

THE SOFT MELODY OF BIRDS chirping around her woke Nava from slumber. The warmth of the morning filtered through the fabric of the tent. This was the most comfortable she had slept since her nights in Arkimedes's cabin. She groaned at the throbbing pain in her head, like her skull was splitting open.

"Are you presentable?" Gavin said.

Warily, she studied her state with horror. She was still wearing her dirty clothes from the day before, caked in mud and blood. Covered in a familiar woolen blanket.

She pulled the fabric up more and brought her hand to her head, patting down her matted curls. "As presentable as I would be in my current situation," she answered.

His head peered in through the flaps of the tent. "How are you feeling this morning?"

"Like my head is being hammered by river-dwelling sprites."

He walked in with a tray of potions and gauze in his hands. He knelt by her and, with nimble hands, checked the previous bandage. One she didn't remember having on.

She sniffed, trying to catch the scents of the potions to get a sense of what he was using to aid her healing. But she couldn't pick a scent. Her injury must be the most annoying thing she'd ever had.

He answered her questioning gaze. "It's looking better already, but you need to lay low and rest for at least another day—maybe two."

"Isn't it dangerous? With Devon Black at our heels, I'm concerned that staying here and waiting for me to feel better will make us be sitting ducks for him to come and snatch. "

Gavin nodded, but his gaze didn't shift from hers, his fingers patting a potion against her wound. Gentle enough not to be too painful, but a simple reminder that she was unwell. The room spun, and she leveled him with a glare.

"We worked some spells last night and a few more this morning. They aren't the strongest, but they should hold for a couple of days." He smiled. "I'm not sure how much you know—but your boy, he is one of the most powerful sorcerers I have ever met, and I've met my fair share. He seems intent on protecting you. I wouldn't worry about it. Concern yourself with recovering."

Nava understood his words. Arkimedes's power was something that had left them all speechless the day before. Still, Nava preferred him to be far away from the Crow. Also, Gavin wasn't aware that Arkimedes wouldn't be able to help them if they were to be attacked in the middle of the night, like it had happened to her.

It wasn't her secret to tell, so she guarded it and nodded.

"We aren't too shabby, either," he said, reading her concern. "Violet and I—and you, if I were to judge a sorceress by the fact that a *Beekeeper* tried to save you."

Her bee creature. Wait, why did she call him *hers*? The thought was so natural, it came to her as easy as breathing. She blinked in confusion.

"I meant to ask you how something so rare and pure came to be bound to you."

Nava shrugged, wanting to protect it at all costs. She didn't want to divulge that she had found it dying, mourning the loss of someone he loved. Another Beekeeper had been murdered. She guessed the culprits were the bounty hunters, though at this point, she wasn't so sure. "I don't know, either," she said; it wasn't a lie, but she kept it simple. Even though she liked Gavin so far, Nava was not so naïve to trust blindly. It didn't mean that because they had a mutual enemy, they would become automatic friends.

Her brain supplied Arkimedes's image almost immediately. Deep down, she knew that whatever was happening with *him* was anything but ordinary. She had to be cautious about letting her feelings drive her actions.

She had never been attracted to another person this way before, both physical and emotional, and at such a fast rate. She was mated to a stranger she had never seen before, and it made her cautious of any man. He had so much power, it could mean he had been a Crow in his past.

But he wasn't her mate. He had told her so.

"There, you are ready. I was going to bring you some food, but I think a bit of sunshine and fresh air might be nice for you." He got up to his feet and left her alone.

Nava got up. Her equilibrium was off but not like the day before. The backpack sat against the wall of the tent. She walked to it, taking slow breaths to calm her sudden dizziness.

She picked her last set of clean clothes and found her canteen of water. She dampened her towel and cleaned her skin the best she could with what she had available. It took time, but by the end of it, she was a lot cleaner. The grime and memories of the day before were fading into another nightmare.

Nava battled with her tangled hair for an eternity before she tied it into a quick braid. She remembered how her mother had braided her hair before going on missions as a Crow.

Her mother always told her that their wavy hair was a blessing and a curse, but it was still better to keep it out of the line of vision when in battle. Nava liked to have hers wild and long, flowing against the salty ocean wind in town. Free, unlike her.

She picked a pocket mirror from one of her backpack pockets. When she shoved it there, she'd thought it was silly. She stared at the reflection of her face, the freckles that speckled her nose, her wide lips that were paler than usual. One blue eye and one brown eye, framed by thick brows.

Her fingers combed her eyebrows. Coming down to her cheeks, where she pinched some color back.

She had lost weight since she'd last seen her reflection back at Arkimedes's house. She guessed it was expected with all the exercise, the energy spent using magic, and the lack of substantial meals. She pushed the mirror back into the pocket and took a steadying breath.

Nava pulled the flap open. Black things hovered on the ground by her backpack, calling her attention. She stared at the fluff floating in the air. Black down feathers, the color of the night.

She picked one up between her fingers. The tiny strands shimmered indigo when the light hit them—the same color as the enormous wings that had grown out of Arkimedes's back the day before.

He had kept his word and stayed with her last night the way he could—in his cursed body.

CHAPTER SEVENTEEN

Her healing came quicker in the forest than a wound this bad would have healed in Willowbrook. Magic had a big part in it. At first, the tingle of worry was present every time Gavin applied the salves and potions to the gap on her head. By the second day in this camp, Nava was less worried and more curious.

Arkimedes slept most of the day and spent the night as a prisoner inside an animal body, perched on top of her backpack while she spoke about Cameron. He was observant, and she didn't know if he understood a word she said but was comforted by the swirling magic in his irises, so much like his human form.

By the third day, the nausea and dizziness had all but gone away. Gavin's wounds were just a small scratch. His face had been swollen, presumably by someone hitting it repeatedly. With the bulges gone, he had to be around the same age as Arkimedes, maybe in his late twenties or early thirties. He was handsome in a rugged way.

She sat by the fire, watching Violet and Gavin spar a few feet away from her, following their movements when fists connected and grunts were voiced. Violet cursed when he connected a mean-looking punch to the side of her arm.

"You dirty slob of a bastard." She jumped back into a crouch, like a feline ready to pounce.

"Tsk, tsk. You've gotta protect your weak spots, dearest wife," he said but didn't sound apologetic. His face twisted into a wicked smile.

"Don't call me that." Her voice went up an octave. Nava's lips parted when her brain caught up to his words. *Wife?*

Violet leaped toward Gavin, who was ready to meet her attack. They weren't holding back. Nava winced at the pounding flesh, watching their every move.

"Intense." A voice behind her made her jump, and a scream escaped her lips. She met the looming shape of Arkimedes. He was holding a steaming cup of his tea in one hand, an eyebrow raised at her reaction.

"You scared me to death, Ark!" She brought her hand to her chest.

"I wasn't quiet." He smirked, sitting down next to her as his attention followed the pair's sparring.

"They aren't holding back at all—aren't they afraid of hurting each other?" she asked, meeting his gaze.

Arkimedes shrugged, taking a long gulp of his disgusting drink. His complexion was golden, rested. "By the looks of it, they want to." He pointed.

Violet screamed, round-kicking Gavin, who stumbled back with a gasp of pain.

"I can't watch this," she said, her focus trailing them with intent. "I can't . . . look away, either."

Arkimedes laughed, and a comfortable silence came over them. It had become second nature to enjoy the other one's company.

"How are you feeling this morning?" His deep honey-like voice broke the insults from the other sorcerers.

She nodded. "Much better today. No dizziness, headache seems more manageable. Gavin said the wound is almost all healed."

"Perfect." He studied the sky. Blue peeked through the tall forests, and it was warm for a fall afternoon. "The wards are fading. It should be our last night here."

She followed his gaze, squinting at the sky, trying to see whatever he saw, but all she could discern was nature. Wind stirred the leaves on the trees, the slow movement of white billowy clouds that painted the sky. Branches shifted when squirrels ran by them. "I can't see anything," she grumbled, staring at her half-eaten bread, annoyed at her lack of impressive magic.

Surrounded by Gavin and Violet, who could fight, or Arkimedes, who had displayed magic unlike she'd ever beheld before. She was not knowledgeable on the subject of magic, but she *knew* she was unimpressive.

"We should resume your training now that you are feeling better," he said.

Her cheeks burned. Memories of their last training session came to her in flashes, how close they had been, how much she had wanted him to kiss her.

She never knew she could be this romantic before. Never again would she poke fun at Simone and her romantic tendencies.

"Like now?" she asked. A rush of excitement went through her body, surprising her. She turned to Gavin and Violet. They were both resting against separate trees.

Violet fixed her shoe, quiet while observing Gavin, who massaged his shoulder and returned her gaze. Their expressions confused Nava, a mixture of longing and anger.

Arkimedes dropped another log onto the fire. "No. Tomorrow if you are fully recovered."

She bit the bread, enjoying the softness of the texture, its delicious buttery flavor melting against her palate. She had woken up to a fresh loaf of bread earlier this morning. When asked how it had appeared, Arkimedes had been intentionally cryptic.

His expression danced with delight. He'd been teasing her previously strong dislike for magic and her change of heart. Still, magical bread tasted better than no bread at all. Even though her skin still prickled with fright when the spicy scent of magic wafted through the air, she was finding comfort in it.

Love was such a big word, one she'd only used with her family. She never imagined she would feel this way for another human, having decided at an early age she wouldn't pursue searching for her soulmate.

Could she grow to love him? It was so easy to care for him. To get lost in this attraction that burned in her veins and extended through her body.

"Yesterday, you said Cameron wanted to travel the world, to get to know his nature." His comment made her head snap back to him.

She had a brief mention as she'd stared at the ceiling of the tent. There had been a black bird perched on top of her backpack. "Yes, I was so afraid that day. Then Devon walked into my shop, and my life changed forever."

"Do you think he would like magic?"

"Oh, yes. Unlike myself, he is so brave and smart." Nava beamed with pride. "If it had been him, he would've mastered a spell by now."

Arkimedes's brows deepened. "You are brave and smart."

Her face warmed at his words. A smile pulled at her lips. "Thank you for noticing."

"Of course." His gaze moved to the other pair.

"Do you have siblings? Family?" Her voice was tentative. "I know the crown takes children away from their families once the magic comes. I always wondered if you had one to go back to."

Arkimedes was quiet for a long time, his gaze back to her. Her breath caught in her throat at the raw pain behind his irises. His expression wasn't guarded, however. "I never knew my family." He added, "I was dropped at the doorstep of an orphanage when I was one. Or so I was told."

She tried to mask anything he could see as pity, even though her soul ached for him.

"I presented magic at a young age. I was five when they came for me. The orphanage had written them, claiming they had a half-fae in their care." Arkimedes breathed and took a long pensive sip of his drink.

"Couldn't they tell before, by your eyes, that you were mixed?"

"The eyes came when I was five. It was the first sign a different kind of magic ran through me."

She had known Arkimedes for weeks, and this was the first time he'd shared something like this. The truth behind his words horrified her. He had been part of the army of the crown since he was five years old? Raised by soldiers. "It's horrible that they gave you away so young."

"The crown pays a pretty penny for a magical child. I'm guessing my bounty alone covered their expenses for a year." He shrugged. "I was treated well, better than the orphanage. It's more than I could have hoped for."

Arkimedes's guarded nature became so clear to her. Abandoned at such a young age, moved around, and raised to be a weapon. "Do you know anything about your family?"

Silence.

"Not a lot." He was quiet after that. They both followed the other pair sparring once again. This time, magic was part of their training.

"I guess they don't deserve you," she said, and the intensity of his gaze burned her. Nava's hand came to his, the warmness of his skin a welcome change to her chilled fingers.

"Your hands are freezing," he said.

Her chest tightened. "That's because there is nothing I can use to warm my hands. I'm talking about a hot cup of something to hold while we talk. All of you heathens like that disgusting tea."

Arkimedes's soft roll of a chuckle made her smile. He had changed the subject, and she was not eager to bring that pain back to his face. She was glad he had shared a part of himself with her.

"I guess I have to start drinking it if I want to be part of the sorcerer team," she said.

"It's a drink they give us in the army," he said with a shrug. "After a while, you grow used to the taste and the energy it gives you."

"Coffee is great with cream or milk. Two cubes of sugar." She sighed. "Oh, how I miss it."

"I'll make sure next time I see Andreas to get you some."

She beamed. "Is that where you got the bread?"

"You would never know." His lips tilted into a rakish smile.

Nava had been staring at him while she chewed her bread in silence. She forced her focus on the other sorcerers.

Gavin walked in their direction, more at ease than they had been before. "Good morning," he greeted.

Arkimedes nodded, taking another sip of his drink. Gavin sat on the other end of the fire. The impacts had reddened his skin, already bruising in places. Nava gaped wide-eyed at the angry hits on his glistening skin.

"They don't hurt anymore," Gavin explained.

"Why train so hard when it's just the two of you?"

"Because our adversaries won't hold back. It's of no use to hold back on punches and not do our best. We don't want to get hurt, so when we are training, we must get out of the way."

Nava focused on Violet, who walked the camp's perimeter, checking the wards that undoubtedly they all saw but Nava.

"Violet holds back," Arkimedes said.

"I know." Gavin shook his head. "I taunt her to see if anger gets her to give it her all, but she is strong-willed."

"Arkimedes can train with her," Nava offered, and the relaxed ambiance darkened around them.

"No." Both of their words came at the same time, with the same intensity.

"All right," Nava said.

Men.

They ate in silence, and by the time Violet joined them by the fire, the tension had lifted somewhat.

"The wards are weaker. We have to move." Her voice was sharp and unwavering. Her smooth skin was tainted red, her knuckles bloodied.

"We can't. Nava needs at least another night." Arkimedes's flat tone matched hers.

"I wasn't asking you." Venom dripped off every word, and distaste painted her features.

Arkimedes's face was unmoving as he shrugged. Nava's turned from one to the other; she stirred in her spot.

"You are more than welcome to leave," Arkimedes said and pointed away from the camp. "No one is holding you back."

"Maybe I will because if the Crow doesn't get us, the Neems will. Tomorrow is a full moon. They will be here come midday." Her words and expression lacked the sharpness of distrust, unlike the day they'd met.

"Violet, please, Arkimedes and Nava saved us. You know better."

"I don't want us to be here and get kidnapped again," she said.

Gavin lifted a piece of bread to her. "Eat something. You're angry because of the lack of sugar."

Nava's lips twitched.

Violet snatched the bread out of his hand and stormed off to her tent without another word.

CHAPTER EIGHTEEN

The next morning, they left their camp when the sun was rising. Nava opened her eyes to a mild headache and Arkimedes's head poking through the door of her magic tent. He'd recently trimmed the beard he had been growing the past few days down to a stubble. He looked absolutely delicious.

When had she become like this?

"We should get going in the next fifteen minutes," he said, and before she could say anything, he was gone.

She jumped out of bed and stuffed her clothes into her backpack, making a mental note to wash them in the next day or so. She braided her hair and resumed the washing routine she had done for the entire trip. As her second foot met the cold dirt ground outside, the heavy scent of magic came around, and wind enveloped her. She blinked and turned to find an empty spot where her tent had been.

She stepped back from the spot, magic still lingering in the air. Violet's hand came down in front of the campfire, and the flames suffocated. Gavin was finishing with his tent, his steps bringing him over to her. His hands reached for her bandage.

"Hey—" she complained.

He peeled the bandage back and leveled her with a glance. "We don't have time for you to complain and proceed to tell me how you have rights, blah blah. The spirits will descend upon us any moment now, from whatever dimension they come from, and we *don't* want to deal with them."

Nava shut up. She didn't need to be reminded of the horrifying truth of the ghosts that haunted these forests, angry spirits taken by magic and brutality, never able to rest, always coming back for vengeance.

"Where is Arkimedes?" she asked after Gavin had finished setting her straight. She helped pick up a couple of leftover bowls, which soon disappeared out of her hand.

Violet gave her a pointed look. "The kitten is always worried about the fae." Violet's mocking ground on Nava's nerves.

"He went to do a perimeter check before we leave." Gavin ignored Violet. "I didn't paint you for someone who cared about whether people were fae or not, my dearest."

"I don't, for regular people *I like*, which is not him," she said with a shrug.

"Do you even like anyone?" Nava's chin lifted in the air.

Violet smiled like a cat. "Not usually, no." Her eyes flashed to Gavin.

Nava was curious once again, then she found she shouldn't care. Violet was rude and mean, and she had better things to do than worry about their love life, even though it *was* interesting.

Arkimedes came back down from a tree. The daylight was dim enough that it gave the illusion of him floating, his wings like shadows. They disappeared behind his back in a blink. Her heart sped up at the jarring image, the beauty, and the strangeness of it all.

In the middle of her recovery from her head injury, she had forgotten to ask him about it. Why did he have wings? Was it something he had inherited from his fae genes? Or was he bending his curse to his will somehow?

She walked to him, curiosity blooming in her chest, and grabbed the straps of her backpack, trying to alleviate the heaviness of the load she carried. The weight of it dug into her shoulders.

"Morning." His gaze avoided hers, swirling with raw emotion, guarded.

"Good morning." She brought her hand to his arm. Maybe her questions about the wings could wait longer.

"How are you feeling today?" His voice dipped lower in concern.

"Just a *very* mild headache left. It's the heaviness of the backpack. It's killing my shoulders."

Nava regretted it when it left her lips. She had forgotten who was around her. All three of them lacked a backpack but were always wearing fresh clothes. It had her face burning.

She pulled at the sleeve of her tunic, trying to hide the stain that peeked from her long-sleeve shirt.

"You can—"

"No."

"Hear me out," he said, and she pressed her lips into a thin line. "It can be part of your training, so you don't drain your body when you do magic."

"Fine, so what is it I'm supposed to do with this training of yours?"

"You can make your backpack weigh nothing," he said with a shrug. "That way, you can stubbornly carry the thing but won't throw your back in the process."

"Ha-ha, it's not that I'm stubborn." She crossed her arms over her chest at his pointed expression. "It's not. I don't know how to do what you do, and I don't want you or anyone else fixing everything for me. The situation is frustrating enough as it is."

"Fine. In this case, it wouldn't be the Grays taking care of your problem for you or me. It will be you alone."

She focused her mind on her backpack, reeling back to what Arkimedes had said. "The Grays?"

He pressed his lips together, lowering his head to the ground. "It's a way to refer to deserters."

Her face was slacked. "Arkimedes!"

"Okay, fine, I'm sorry."

"What are you sorry about? Does that mean I'm a Gray too? Is it a negative word? It sounds like it," she sputtered.

His face lost color with every single one of her words. Regret shaded his expression. "Yes—no." He took a breath. "It makes us *all* Grays. In the eyes of the kingdom, Grays are sorcerers, warlocks, and sorcerers who have mid-level magic and run away from oppression to forests where magical creatures live." He brought his hand over his face. "These lands, where we all ran to—the ones that are habitats for fae, spirits—are usually called the Greyland. The unwanted places."

"Like Willowbrook?" Which was located on the *Grey Island*. It made sense.

"Yes."

"So is it used as a bad word?" she asked again.

"Yes."

"What are we? Why aren't you considering yourself a Gray?" Her voice carried some heat.

Panic took over his features. His lips parted to speak when a bee landed on Nava's hand.

The soft fluttering of wings hit her skin, sending shivers down her body. The bee's fur tickled her. The contrast of its colored body against Nava's olive skin was jarring. Nava focused on the insect with curiosity when another one landed next to it, then another one.

What concerned her wasn't the bees. It was the sense of dread growing in her stomach. Nava faced Arkimedes, whose eyes were wide, staring at them with equal shock.

"Wha—?"

"Run." The voice came into her mind, jolting her. She didn't have to wait to figure it out. She had to be out of there immediately. She grabbed Arkimedes's hand.

"*Run*!" She sprinted. The bees flew, and she followed them without a doubt crossing her mind.

It nudged the back of her mind, telling her it was strange that she trusted these insects, that she sensed their intent and where to go when she followed them. Her human brain thought this wasn't normal, but her magical side *knew* it was right.

Arkimedes ran next to her, checking his surroundings where ghosts materialized. She didn't stare at the dead faces this time. The bees surrounded her, leading her way. Gavin's voice boomed in the clearing, yelling at Violet to run, and their steps tailed not far behind.

She wanted to run faster, make her body weightless. Her backpack hurt her shoulders, so she called it to be light as a feather. The bees pivoted, and so did she, jumping over a fallen tree.

She let go of Arkimedes's hand, using her motion to propel her forward. She needed to be faster. White bodies appeared in the hole between the thick trees in front of her. Her mind supplied the gnarled image of a pale man, dead, having been taken long ago if the state of decomposition was anything to go by.

"Dammit, they are everywhere," Gavin gasped, his voice sounding far.

Arkimedes's presence next to her provided a sense of relief in the chaos. He had no issue keeping up with her, with his fit body and long legs, following her direction even though she wasn't voicing them out loud. This other connection was strange to her.

Five more bees appeared, their round bodies making it clear where she needed to go.

A face appeared in front of her, and her heart jolted in fright.

"*No*!" Nava gasped, memories flowing through her mind of the first time she had seen the Neems.

The ghost, which wasn't so much a ghost but a lifeless body made of pale rotten flesh, opened its mouth, a ray of magic inside the pit of death. She wished for a thousand bees to shield them from their attack.

Thousands of bodies came flying down, some real and some made of light, shielding Arkimedes and her from the upcoming attack. Arkimedes grabbed her hand and pulled her in another direction, running faster.

Nava turned around to make sure Gavin and Violet were following. They weren't far behind, their magic emanating from their bodies in shades of gray. The bees resumed their spot around them, buzzing. The spirits disappeared behind their small bodies.

They ran. Nava's ragged breath burned her lungs, her body hot from exertion, even though the chilled air burned her cheeks. When they left the area where the spirits of this Greyland were haunting, her body relaxed. The forest was alive with nature.

Birds chirped. The air was less muggy. The smell of rot lifted from the air.

She slowed down as the bees disappeared from view, flying off to somewhere else in the trees and around the forest. The ones that remained were made of yellow light, landing on her and Arkimedes protectively.

The bees' brightness contrasted with the gloom of power that emanated from his body.

Arkimedes's green eyes focused on them in awe. The heavy steps of both Gavin and Violet came around them. The four of them were gasping for air, their faces shiny with sweat.

The bees faded away, and the heaviness of exhaustion swathed her before everything went dark.

CHAPTER NINETEEN

When Nava opened her eyes, she was staring at the same ceiling she had woken up to the past few days. Not her beloved handmade tent that had belonged to her father, the one she put up with sticks and flimsy materials. This one was built with magic, making its construction stronger.

She groaned as pain extended down her arms and legs, sore muscles complaining about being overused. Her head spun, but not from her head injury. It was pure unadulterated exhaustion. She racked her mind, trying to come up with memories. All of them came rushing back. Ghosts, them running, and bees—real bees and ones made of *her* magic.

Nava's brain conjured the image of the Beekeeper. It kept helping her. It came for her even though she wasn't calling it. She was not afraid of it, like she had been the day she met him. Her need to protect him was intense. Something had happened that afternoon. An invisible connection had formed in between them, helping her hear it, feel his pain.

She studied her hands. Freckles peppered her skin, but nothing appeared different. She was the same woman who had left Willowbrook, except magic had awoken inside her body. This time, it was she who had saved them.

The idea made her heart soar. Warmth traveled through her body, and she smiled. Her breaths came out easier. She was where she was supposed to be, however scary. Now she needed to survive long enough to bring Cameron to it.

Her spirits deflated. Why would she bring him to danger? To ghosts, murderers, and kidnappers? She bit her bottom lip. She had time to figure things out.

Nava walked out of the tent, bringing her hand to shield her face against the brightness of the fire and the morning light. She met Violet, who was sitting by the fire, picking food out of a brown linen bag on the ground.

Nava hesitated, sitting in front of the woman who studied her movements with interest.

"Kitten." A greeting.

Nava narrowed her gaze at her. "Please stop with the name."

"Why? The guy is a complete dick, but the nickname fits," Violet said lazily.

Nava shook her head and decided ignoring her would be best. She picked up the kettle by the fire and filled a cup with steaming, disgusting army tea. Nava dreamed of the days she could drink something other than this.

"Yesterday's stunt, I must admit . . . it was pretty impressive, kitten." The irony in her voice had toned down a bit.

Nava stared at her over her mug. "Thanks?"

"So, what's up with the bees? Are you and the Beekeeper connected somehow?"

Nava didn't want to talk about this with her. "Are you and Gavin married?"

Violet paled, not having expected this change of subject. Her face changed to a guarded expression. "That is none of your business."

"Oh, well, I guess my issues aren't any of yours, either," she snapped.

Violet's lips curved up into a small smile. "Cute."

"What?"

"You getting flustered. It's cute. I guess I understand what he sees in you," she said and stretched her legs in front of her.

"Who sees what in me?" Nava asked but was sidetracked by the sound of steps.

Arkimedes was coming out of Gavin's tent, scrubbing his face with his hand. He stopped when his eyes met Nava's questioning gaze.

Something was wrong.

She stood and walked to him with long strides. "What happened?"

"Good morning to you too, Nava."

"Are you hurt?"

His brows lifted. "How did you . . . ?"

"It's easy to figure it out. The sun just came out, and you went to find Gavin *the healer* first thing after you transformed back into yourself." She listed the points with her fingers and stared.

He let out an amused laugh and nodded. "I might have gotten hit last night with an arrow."

Nava gasped. She studied his body, trying to find any sign that pointed to a wound.

"It is not visible," he said.

"Where? Are you okay?"

"I'll be fine. It was a clean shot. It happened close to sunrise. I could transform and walk instead of flying back to our camp."

"Did it hit one of your wings?" She shifted her body weight around, her hand dragging down his arms before reaching for his hand.

He nodded, his hand squeezing hers. He was reassuring her when he was the one who had gotten hurt. "Gavin said I should be fully healed within a week. You don't have to worry."

She got lost in him, enjoying the closeness, her worries dissipating. "Who did it? Do you think it was Devon?"

"I know it was him. It wasn't close to our camp. I flew in a different direction—I couldn't tell how many people he had with him."

"Do we need to leave today?" Her body tensed with dread.

"Yes, we need to get closer to the Northern Village. They'll need time to prepare for an attack."

"You should get some rest before we head out."

"I will," he promised. "I'll go around the perimeter to check that our wards are still strong. Gavin and I set them wider this time to hold back any spirits *and* Devon."

Arkimedes walked past Violet with a polite nod she barely responded to before disappearing in between the trees. Would his wound be visible if he were shirtless? She would work on her healing potion while he rested.

She picked her now-cold cup of tea and brought it back to her lips. It tasted worse when chilled by the weather. Maybe this watered-down, mud-tasting drink had started as a way of torture.

"That's never gonna happen." Violet's voice jarred her attention back to reality, to the campfire and purple irises staring right through her.

"What will never happen?" Nava asked, blinking in confusion.

Violet threw another piece of wood onto the campfire and settled back in her spot. "You and him." She stuffed a large piece of potato bread into her mouth and chewed loudly while her finger traveled through the air, pointing to where Arkimedes had disappeared earlier. The exact place she had been staring at.

"I don't know what you are talking about," Nava blurted. Mortified that anyone else, meaning Arkimedes, might hear Violet's words. The woman wasn't quiet.

"Oh, please. You do a terrible job at hiding it." She scoffed. "With all the heart eyes and nausea-inducing smiles."

"I *don't* do that."

Violet stared at her with no words as she moved to cut a slice of apple with her knife. "Look, I get it. Most people would fall for the chemistry, his body, and the pretty-boy looks," she said. "A ray of sunshine will come out of my ass before he breaks his precious rules and does anything with you."

"What rules?" Nava furrowed her brows. "Have I missed something here? Now you and Arkimedes are good friends and he's shared all his secrets with you?"

"Pfft, we would never be friends," Violet said. "He is one of those who followed the crown's rules. He would never get serious with you unless the crown dictated he had to marry you."

"How do you know?" Nava squinted. "In case you haven't realized, we aren't in the city anymore. No one is forcing anyone into marriage here."

Violet half shrugged, as if Nava's comebacks meant nothing. "I guess I owe you an apology from my outsider's point of view. After all, I must have missed all the ways he's been courting you."

Nava tried not to let the disappointment show on her features. She tried but was unsuccessful, clearly, by Violet's softening expression.

"Please don't cry or something."

"I will not because there is nothing to cry about." The knot forming in her throat told her quite the opposite.

Arkimedes had told her he was not available, that someone like him wasn't ready for a relationship—not in those words, but she got the gist of it. She couldn't be with anyone. Either way, she was mated to someone who wasn't him.

Violet's voice broke the silence. "I mean, it wouldn't hurt you to bathe. Perhaps a fresh smell could do wonders."

She brought her nose down to her shoulder and sniffed. "I don't stink!"

"Kitten, you reek." Violet shrugged. "Men in the village wouldn't mind, but pretty fae there . . . he does."

Nava's mouth fell slack. "You don't hold back, do you?"

"Look, I can see a virgin from a mile away. I'm just trying to help you."

"Oh, god, please stop!" Nava rushed to get up, done with the conversation. She took five steps toward her tent before turning back to face the dark-skinned woman sitting by the fire, whose lazy stare came up to meet Nava's fiery one. "I'm *not* a virgin," she declared.

Violet's lips pulled up into a smile.

Nava tried to get along with the other woman. She did. Violet was the only other female in the group, and it would be nice to connect with someone who didn't have massive amounts of testosterone running through them. She tried to fill the void from missing Simone, but she was done.

Nava turned to find Gavin a few steps away. She winced when she noticed his amused expression. His mouth was opening to say something, but she stopped him by lifting her hand and shaking her head.

"Not a word, Gavin," she said through clenched teeth and rushed past him.

NAVA HURRIED TO HER TENT, going for her backpack. She picked fresh undergarments, her thin worn-in towel, and a set of clean clothes she had washed by the stream five days ago. She also rummaged around, picking the handmade soap she had packed once upon a time. It smelled of roses and cardamon, a present from Cameron for her birthday.

He had worked in Simone's bakery during a busy summer day to save enough money to buy it for her. She pursed her lips and told herself she would use it a little today.

Nava hid the clothes under her tunic, pausing, considering taking the whole backpack with her. She shook her head, groaning at the thought of having to carry the heavy thing with her when her neck and shoulders were healing. She could try to make the backpack lighter, but the idea of draining her energy was less appealing than being dirty.

The lake wasn't far away. With the sun out, she hoped the water wouldn't be so cold.

Out of all their camp spots, this one was her favorite. The ground was less muddy and covered in fallen leaves of various red, orange, and brown shades. The colors reminded her of the tones in Cameron's hair.

Nava had always liked camping, her love of nature still a part of her. She'd always had a connection to plants, to the trees around her. Her mother had been good at gardening and had encouraged Nava's love for it.

That was, until Nava disobeyed her, went out of their manor, and got caught by the two Crows. One had happened to be Devon, and the other her soulmate. How a simple rebellious decision and a hobby could change your life forever.

Her mother had hated camping; she used to say she loathed sleeping in uncomfortable beds or dealing with bugs and mediocre food. Nava's ties to nature grew when she was out and away from the town—looking at the stars in the sky.

That was something she'd shared with her dad.

She missed him, missed the way he'd been when he was healthy and robust with so much energy and a jolly mood. Cameron always reminded her of him.

The trees were changing as she got closer to the water. The view was magnificent. The jewel-blue tones of the water reflected the blue sky above her.

Her chest squeezed at memories. She swallowed the thick knot in her throat, urging her mind to move elsewhere. *Anywhere* but her dad. It wasn't hard. Violet's words came back to her brain as she made her way to the shore. She was thinking of Arkimedes, her undeniable attraction to him, and what Violet called his pretty-boy looks.

The vision of his stormy green gaze flashed to her, and she let out a sigh. At first, her feelings had been a gradual thing, the pitter-patter of her heart when he glanced her way with a particularly intense stare. When he saved her from the spirits, somehow it had changed something else, something more significant.

She wished he'd opened up more, share his past like he had done a few days ago. It made sense that he was reserved. After what he had gone through as a child, she understood and wanted better for him.

Her gaze was lost on a spot at the end of the lake, where mist hid the connection between the water and the land, her boots hitting the smooth rocks in the shore with a crunching sound.

Pff, a virgin.

Nava might not be experienced in the lovemaking department, but she was not ignorant. She grew aware of the growing needs in her body. After that disappointing first time with Hale when she was twenty, drinking had never been the same since. She stayed away from hard spirits.

She made it to the lake, distracted as she admired the splendor of her surroundings. She stopped at the sight of the naked chest of Arkimedes. A large expanse of golden skin and overbuilt muscle. Thick strong core marked with cut abs that looked a whole lot like the chocolate bar Simone used to bring to her.

Her eyes followed a drop of water that glistened as it dripped toward the taper of his navel to the beginning of hair and more. Her eyes zeroed down on the promise of something great.

She flailed her arms, dropping her clothes, undergarments and soap to the rocky ground.

Arkimedes gazed up. "Shit!" He submerged himself back in the water.

Her throat was dry as she stood frozen, fingernails digging into the palms of her hands. Of course, she'd never expected him to be bathing.

Stop staring! But her eyes refused to move, too afraid to lose a second to marvel at his toned physique. Heat traveled down her body and pooled in her core, throbbing with want.

Nava had imagined him, fantasized about what it would be like to touch him. To kiss him all over. She had fantasized more heated exchanges; the reminder of those made her blush intensify.

Her imagination had not done him justice.

"Nava," he called. His cheeks were also a deep shade of crimson that was crawling down his neck.

"I'm *so* sorry!" she exclaimed, urging her body to move, to turn around and give him the privacy he deserved.

Her legs refused. Her gaze was fixed on the way his skin wrapped around the muscle—he was the prime example of health, and Nava ached to touch and savor it. Her breaths were coming out in puffs. She wanted the earth to open up and swallow her whole immediately.

She stopped, remembering the near earthquake she'd almost caused before. Maybe she didn't need the earth to swallow her up.

Turn around! her mind bellowed.

Arkimedes's embarrassment eased when he noticed her immobile. He raised a brow and rose from the water. Steam was coming out of his body. He was so goddamn *hot,* the water evaporated from him.

"I'm so sorry. I didn't know you were going to come here when you said you were going to check on the wards!" she babbled, and finally, her body moved. She crouched to pick up her items, her hands shaking.

Moving water had her turning in another direction. She exercised extreme self-control not to turn around to get another look at his . . . manhood.

"I promise I saw nothing. I mean, I did see *something*. A lot of muscle and . . . things." Her voice lost its power in the last word, and she cursed her awkwardness.

She picked at the last remnants of her things. Nava lifted her head at the sound of approaching steps, and Arkimedes walked toward her. He was wrapping a towel around his waist, his eyes shining with much more than amusement.

Nava bolted up, her back straight, her legs shaking. She tried to ignore the tingling sensation between her thighs and swallowed the thickness in her throat.

"I'm done here if you need to . . ." His voice was deeper than usual. Arkimedes's arm moved across his chest, holding onto his shoulder. She guessed he was trying to hide his wound from her.

But the wound was the least of her worries.

He was going to kill her. She shook her head, and long locks of waves hit her cheeks. "No, no, it's okay. I will come back later." She was dying for a bath, if just to cool down her heated skin.

"Are you sure?" he asked. Why had he decided to walk to her? There was no way he wouldn't be able to notice the red in her cheeks now.

"Yes, *very*. Sorry again, Ark." She took a step back, her attention drawn back down, raking the planes of his chest, so close she could lift her hand and touch.

Bad idea. Nava couldn't remember why she had to keep her extreme lust for him under control. It had something to do with an army coming for them and the fact that she had a soulmate.

When she reached the top of his towel, his skin shook from the cold. She snapped her focus back up. His pupils were blown wide, and he was not bothered by her admiration. Her mortification grew as she kept ogling him.

"I'll see you in the camp." She had never walked so fast before, running past the trees she had been admiring the splendor of a few minutes ago. The soft gray color of the smoke of their campfire billowed in the air. It reminded her of the way magic swirled around Arkimedes when he was in battle.

Both Gavin and Violet turned to meet her approaching body. Her unmentionables were held against her chest. She hoped her undergarments weren't visible but couldn't care less to check. Things could not get any more mortifying.

"How was the water?" Violet asked in a sing-song way.

Nava halted, focusing on the other woman. Her full lips pulled up into a smile.

Nava gasped in horror. "You knew? You conniving, evil—"

"Mastermind," Violet supplied.

"You would like to think so." Nava scoffed, shaking her head.

"I feel I'm missing a critical piece of information right now." Gavin's voice was soft and entertained.

"I figured you needed a bit of a push. Trying to help another girl out." Her smile grew, her eyes dancing with laughter. It was all a fun game for her, embarrassing Nava further.

It wasn't like Nava needed to be fueled into it. She did and spoke her fair share of embarrassing things already; she didn't need for her self-awareness to grow.

Gavin turned to Violet, a brow raised.

"Don't"—Nava pointed her hand to the other sorcerer; she might have been holding the soap in said hand—"help me again."

With those words, she left the campfire, intending to stay in her tent for the rest of the day before they had to go.

CHAPTER TWENTY

The sun had set over the horizon. The sky was painted with oranges, reds, and purples. The soft scent of the fire Gavin had been working on for the past ten minutes surrounded them. He was at last successful.

It was a bet he and Nava had struck earlier in the day. She'd challenged him to make a fire without the use of magic. His laugh of victory echoed around their campsite, and even though Nava had lost, a grin tugged at her lips.

The air was crisp as fall carried on, getting colder by the day and dropping lower in temperature at night. The color of the changing leaves of fir and maple trees was a welcome change to the constant pine and cedar they had been in for weeks. It had been almost a month since she'd left home. Much had changed in her since, like the nature that surrounded her.

Nava tugged at the tent Gavin had put up for her. She was deciding how she could improve her regular human tent when someone came behind her.

She turned and yelped, her hand coming to rest on top of her chest as she met Arkimedes's looming form. Gavin laughed, staring at the pair with increased curiosity.

"Archie, you are going to kill me sneaking up on me like that!" Nava said, and she had no moral ground to be complaining about him sneaking up on her. Not when images of his naked body flashed through her mind as she stared at him. She turned away to hide the blush that crept onto her face.

He chuckled. "I guess you're not the only one sneaking up on people when they least expect it."

Her lips parted with complete shock and mortification.

His grin widened. "Also, we said no to the whole 'Archie' thing?"

"*You* said. I happen to be still deciding which nickname I like best." She would tease him with all her ideas except for Val.

"Archie sounds like a child's name, and I don't look like a child, do I?" His gaze shone with a rakish light.

Her face boiled with heat. They both knew the answer to that question. She looked at him before dropping her gaze down, her stomach churning. "I'm *so* sorry for earlier. I didn't mean to see anything. I saw *nothing,*" she babbled. "Not a thing, just a large . . . tattoo?"

His lips twitched. At least he didn't appear to be furious with her. Though blurted in a panic, her words made her rewind back to what had happened earlier. The expanse of his skin. She *had* seen a large tattoo. Black ink wrapped around his shoulders and arms like feathers.

"It's fine."

"I swear, I didn't intend to . . . intrude. In my defense, I thought you were checking on the wards, and it never occurred to me that you would be there bathing."

"Nava, it's okay," he repeated.

"Violet knew. I don't understand how." Arkimedes lifted a brow. "She told me I needed a bath—so." Nava's lips clamped shut.

Arkimedes's eyes lit in recognition. "When you were asleep, I mentioned to them that I would do a recognizance of the area and strengthen the wards. Gavin offered to come with me, but I said I intended to take a dip in the lake by myself."

"Ha! That conniving . . ." *Genius.* "Still, I'm sorry."

"I meant it when I said it was fine," he said. "So—training tomorrow morning?"

"Yes, training. I want to hone my skills and do more." An awkward silence followed her words.

His hand rose to her shoulder in a soft touch that ignited the nerve endings of her skin. He read her like an open book, every single one of her insecurities spelled out in a language he understood well. She turned away, not wanting to be so bare with all her shortcomings to him.

"Hey, there is nothing wrong with the way you are. I keep telling you this." His voice was low and intended for her ears only. "It's not ideal in such a volatile situation that you haven't gotten proper training with your magic.

Being kidnapped by trained fighters, or attacked by the Neems, isn't something even a trained sorceress can handle with ease."

"You're saying that to make me feel better."

"Gavin and Violet, they have both endured more than we know. Battles and hardships have shaped them. They were trained since they were children, and they also got kidnapped."

"Yeah, and what about you?"

"I was a Crow. They didn't even know they should have paid attention to me when I was stuck in my animal shape. Maybe the one good thing that has come out of this whole curse situation." Arkimedes's slow grin spread across his features.

She tugged the magical canvas of the tent, not moving it but an inch. How could it be this strong?

"You seem extra annoyed at your tent. Put up a complaint with Gavin. His tent-making skills must be abysmal if they do not measure up to your standards." Arkimedes could barely hold back the smirk.

Nava turned around, hitting the side of his arm. "Stop it, you tent snob. My tent is normal and would pass any test. It failed me in the wind storm."

"Be careful with your use of strength. I'm injured."

Nava brought her hand back, searching his face, expecting him to be in pain, and instead found a knowing smirk. "You are incorrigible." She shook her head, focusing on his shoulder that was covered by his thick tunic. Would the arrow wound be on his back, or perhaps his arm? She didn't remember it from earlier when he'd been with no shirt on.

Though, to be honest with herself, and she often tried to be, she was looking elsewhere.

"Getting easily distracted today, bee."

Nava smiled at the use of such a fitting nickname. She shook away her memories of naked bodies and the desire pooling within her. "It's hard not to get distracted with all that I did manage to see." She was surprised she admitted this and didn't fret about it.

Arkimedes's expression intensified over hers. What had been a light ambiance became charged with much more.

They stared at each other. His gaze dropped to Nava's lips. He was so close that if she lifted on her toes and kissed him, he might not pull away.

She had to be careful about her fast-developing feelings when it came to him.

"You have a tattoo?" she asked instead.

He lost some of the heated darkness that had taken over. "Yes."

"Your wings?" He was so close, the scent of leather and cedarwood still surrounded her.

"They represent my wings, yes," he whispered.

She understood this was information meant for her alone. "I meant to ask you, are those wings part of your curse? Have you found a way to make it work for you?" She hoped he had. It would be a great way of giving the middle finger to the woman who had cursed him.

"No, it's not the curse. I have been able to call upon my wings since I was five." Arkimedes's eyes evaded her, as if he were battling a harrowing memory.

Nava's lips opened, and her heart squeezed at the sorrow that shaped his handsome features. She didn't want him to be in pain, not by a memory from her questions. Her hand came to his chest. He met her gaze. "Was that how the orphanage found you possessed magic?"

He nodded. At first, the giveaway had to be his eyes, so beautiful with raw power. "It wasn't the only thing that I developed at that age," he said. "They are pretty large, and I was unable to call them off. So they were always there, a constant reminder that I was different."

"Are you a shapeshifter?"

"Yes and no." He turned to the steps of someone near them. Violet was walking toward Gavin by the fire, not paying any attention to them, not even acknowledging that they were standing so close. "I can change my shape as I call upon my wings and withdraw them at will, but I don't shift into an animal." He paused, his brows furrowing. "Except now, because of this curse."

"Is it because of your fae origins?" Nava hesitated, her hand still on top of his chest. She was aware of the touch. However, she didn't drop her hand. She liked it there.

If Nava were to judge his emotional state by the thundering in his chest, she would venture to guess he was nervous.

"Yes, or at least that is what I believe. They didn't leave a note that explained what to expect from my powers when they abandoned me." His expression darkened.

"Food is ready," Gavin called them from the fire, and both of their gazes traveled to the other pair. Nava dropped her hand, the cold air prickling her skin at losing his warmth.

She was happy he had decided to open up to her. It helped her understand, to fill in one of her many questions. Nava opened her mouth to say something, but her stomach decided to speak instead, making them both aware the scent of bread and meat by the fire was of the utmost importance.

Her cheeks grew warm. "I'm sorry." She should stop being sorry for everything.

"I guess we'd better get you some food then." He smiled, the heaviness of the last subject lifting from his features. He pointed to the fire where Violet was sitting, filling her plate with food.

She and Gavin were immersed in a lively chat that mentioned sweet liquor and wine. For the first time, they all ate in a companionable conversation, not with a lack of ironic remarks from Violet or grunts from Arkimedes to her.

Nava enjoyed the casual conversation right until Arkimedes had to leave, before the sun dropped behind the treetops.

WHEN SHE WOKE UP the next morning bright and early, Nava went to the lake before having her first drop of what she called war tea. By the time she was clean and back to their camp, she was crankier than usual. The water had been freezing. She couldn't understand how Arkimedes was at peace, like a statue carved by a skilled artist.

She had managed to make her body warmer. Magic had flown to her easier than the last few times. Her walk back to the camp had been slow and tiring. At least this time, she'd managed not to deplete her body's energy to zero. She plopped down on the ground, taking the mug Gavin extended her and wrinkling her nose at the bitter dirt taste. At least the warmth was pleasant.

Positive thoughts.

"Good morning." Gavin's voice took her out of her sulking.

Nava grunted. It had been good and bad. Bathing in a lake that held magical beings made the freezing dip in the turquoise waters more unpleasant. The coolness of the bath had cleared her groggy brain, however, so even though her exhausted body needed food and rest, her brain was sharp.

She imagined Cameron screaming at the cold water but braving it either way.

"Arkimedes . . . is cursed, right?" Gavin's words took her out of whatever trance her mind had gone to.

"Uh . . ." She blinked as her brain caught up to his words.

"It's easy for us to know. He is *always* gone at night and sleeps during the day. I'm guessing he gets trapped inside something. I'm thinking an animal. By his injury and his clear experience with wings, I'll guess a bird?"

Nava shifted, uncomfortable by the line of questioning. "I don't think it's my place to say anything," she decided, and the man in front of her nodded. Nava didn't like lying, but she wasn't doing that now—she was deflecting.

"It's fine. It was more a comment than a question. He came back and has gone in your tent to rest."

"Is his injury better?" She glanced at her tent.

Gavin agreed with a hum, taking a substantial bite of the half-eaten apple he was holding. "I thought you would have seen it by now, with all the questions about the healing potion I applied."

Arkimedes's naked skin still played in her mind. She deviated her attention somewhere else because she had no shame and was apparently a pervert.

"He was lucky. Wherever the arrow hit, it was a clean shot. It didn't harm any tendons or ligaments."

"That's very good." She took a plate and filled it with food.

By the time Arkimedes joined them by the fire, the sun was nearing the sky's highest point. He was wearing all dark clothes, a navy shirt, and black pants. His brown jacket had been replaced by a thicker gray one.

He quietly took a seat by Gavin and poured a cup of warm tea, accepting Nava's offer of a food plate.

"We aren't too far from the village. I'm concerned we are leading Devon straight to it," Violet said.

"It's not like we have any other choice. Devon will get there. We can keep running around, but it's best to warn Roman. There needs to be enough time for us to gather the children and elderly. To take them to safety." Gavin's hand tightened on top of his knee, his knuckles whitening.

They had been talking about this for a while. Nava was listening. She didn't know about the village other than by mention, but she wanted to help and prevent families from being torn apart, everyone rounded up and taken to the city to be slaves.

It had stopped being about saving Cameron and herself alone. It had ceased being about running away from magic and all that entailed.

"Maybe the bird here can bring the warning to the Commander on his own. He can fly, after all."

Arkimedes's groggy gaze sharpened. "I won't be leaving Nava. Also, I don't believe Roman would listen to me on my own, even if I were to do so."

"You got the point—why would he trust one of your kind?" Violet's words dragged, and for the first time in a few days, her eyes narrowed into slits.

"Hey!" Nava complained. They were past this. Anger flourished in her chest as Gavin rested his hand on Violet's leg, giving her a warning.

Nava didn't understand why Violet held such a strong dislike for Arkimedes's kind. She remembered the other woman mentioning he was a hybrid and Gavin reminding her she didn't have those biases. Somehow, whatever Arkimedes was, it made a difference.

She wanted to save the innocent people of the Northern Village, and she would not stand back and let Violet bully Arkimedes because of his breeding, even though he seemed to be unaffected by the woman's opinions.

"Please, let's eat—we will leave this campsite tomorrow morning as planned."

The rest of the meal was quiet and uncomfortable, and by the time they were done eating, Arkimedes was up as if sprung by something else. "It's time."

Why did he often speak in such short sentences? She turned around in confusion. "For training?"

He nodded, walking away without another word.

"Well, *someone* is in a foul mood this morning—multiple someones." Nava side-eyed Violet.

"Not all of us need to be a ray of sunshine at all times, kitten."

Nava shook her head and stormed off, shadowing Arkimedes. The area he picked was in between significant trees. He stared at her as she prepared for training, dropped her coat to the ground, and searched around for a couple of sticks she could use instead of a weapon.

His face darkened as his black aura of magic enveloped his body, tendrils coming out. The sight was no longer scary. It filled her with awe and wonder, nonetheless. Why was his aura black when Gavin's and Violet's were gray?

She widened her stance. Nava gripped the stick she had just foraged, the same size as her actual blades. She was no longer in the mood to train against him with something so sharp. No matter how great of a warrior he was.

She took a measured step, and a bee landed on her hand, the buzzing of its wings sending a shock of power through her skin. However, it didn't jolt her. She followed Arkimedes's body. He walked around like he had done that day in the clearing of his house.

Nava had changed ever since. She was like a different person. She was no longer scared of everything that surrounded her. No longer would she be able to see the shadows in the forest and not remember the gnarled faces of dead people with vicious intent to kill.

No longer would she be able to eat honey.

Magic was not only evil but also beneficial. She was not a regular human; she had never fit in because she wasn't around her people. She focused on Arkimedes, knowing without a doubt she was where she belonged. Cameron had been right.

That alone was scarier than the magic had been the afternoon they'd trained for the first time.

Nava exhaled, her breath billowing up to the sky. She attacked him, her movements as fluid as her mother had taught her. Black tendrils pushed her stick away and wrapped around her body, lifting her off the ground as if she weighed no more than a leaf. She winced as air escaped her lips. Her weapon sliced through mist and fog. They were not harming it.

Bees kept landing on her skin, more than she could count. This time, though, the pinch of impending doom was not there.

They weren't here for a warning; they were coming because she had been calling on them. Nava was not aware she had been doing so.

When had bees begun to signify her power? At some point in the past three weeks, she had accepted them as if they were part of her. It was still confusing, yet here they were, responding.

Nava imagined what would happen if they wrapped around Arkimedes, blocking his view of her, enveloping him in a small bubble. As if she had whispered the command out loud, the bees flew at incredible speed toward him. Arkimedes gasped, and the magic that held her wavered. Her body weight fell a fraction before his magic held her up again.

Her own body was warming up, and the mist evaporated from where it touched her. She dropped to the ground and landed on her feet, wavering but recuperating her balance before toppling over.

The bees enveloped him, and she took the advantage to run toward him at the maximum speed her legs could carry her. The bees opened up a hole when she was close enough to him, and she hit Arkimedes on his side with her stick before jumping back when an arm of black mist came out for her. The bees covered the hole, and a gasp of pain came.

Were they stinging him?

She could do this, though her strength wavered as magic sucked the energy out of her body. Nava's arm shook as she gripped the stick harder.

She ran to the other side, her steps slower, and the bees opened a new hole. Arkimedes's surprised face was now covered in crawling insects before she swung the stick once again and hit him on the side of his arm. He winced, and before the bees could close in, his giant wings expanded, sending bees flying everywhere. Darkness enveloped him, and she gaped, wide-eyed and in complete awe of the magnificent sight of him.

His wings were at least seven feet long, with black feathers that shone an iridescent blue and gray. She took a few steps back when his magic's spicy scent burned her nose. He attacked her this time, and she winced at the unexpected move.

His body was surrounded by shadows popping out and around him. The precise shapes made her skin crawl.

His magic was made out of nightmares. Nava had time to cover before he struck, but the wood of her training sticks shattered with his power. Black tendrils sent her back flailing to the ground.

Arkimedes' wide hands wrapped around her arms, bringing her toward his body The force of his pull brought her floundering into his chest. The soft raising and falling of his rapid breaths told her he was as flustered as she. His warm breath touched her face… and he was so close.

Gooseflesh raised over her skin when his fingertips traced her skin, down her forearms before he gripped her hips. "You hit me hard."

"Twice. So, the winner is the one that strikes first, right?" She said in a breathy tone, feeling half proud of how much better she had gotten with her magic. It was an accomplishment.

"You can't make up the rules as you go," Arkimedes brought her closer to him. All the solid planes of his body touched her. His eyes trailed down her face and stopped on her lips.

"Pff. Why not? That's what you do, you are a *terrible* loser." She teased with a grin, and his own lips tilted up, he captured her chin in between to roughened fingers, and her heart jolted in her chest. Was he going to kiss her? Were they still talking about training, or something else?

"I've a strong argument that I didn't lose."

She raised her chin to him, exposing her neck in hopes his breathing would caress her sensitive skin. His pupils were blown wide, but it was much more primal than she had noticed before.

Her limbs shook under her, and heat rushed through her body, pooling in her stomach. She licked her lips when he pressed his forehead to hers. She could discover what it felt to kiss him, if she lifted her head…

The sound of clapping had them breaking apart from whatever spell they had been under. Arkimedes stepped back as if she had burned him. Nava let out a breath. Gavin and Violet were standing nearby, their faces shaped with different emotions.

"That was something else!" Gavin's smile took over his face, with dimples and all. Unaware of the tension in the air.

How *not* to be annoyed at their presence? Nava shot a glare at Violet, who dropped her hand and grabbed Gavin by the arm, hauling him away. He complained but let himself be dragged back to their campground.

Nava met Arkimedes's gaze, her body cooler than it had been seconds before. She was shaking with want. Would it be too off-putting if she kissed him now? He pulled back another step, adding to the distance, and shook his head as if trying to get rid of fog.

"That was impressive." He cleared his throat.

"T-thanks." Her teeth caught her bottom lip as she tried to distract herself from her desire.

His eyes zeroed in on the movement. "The bees—they are still coming to aid you." His voice was quiet. She didn't get protective when *he* spoke about them, like it had happened when Gavin or Violet inquired.

She nodded. "I don't know why they seem to keep coming. I think about it all the time." It made the worries clearer. "I—I want to protect it. The Beekeeper, I mean. It's almost like we are linked."

His face grew concerned, but he kept his distance.

"Maybe the creature has taken the place of my actual soulmate," she joked, and a soft laugh escaped his lips.

"It seems that when you healed it, the connection went both ways. It came to you in Devon's campground. If it had been a life debt, it would've been repaid when it saved you from the Neems the first time."

"Yes."

"The bees are with you, not only real ones but ones you create with magic." Arkimedes's brows met in the middle. "When the Beekeeper is around, does it speak to you?"

"It does—and doesn't. I sort of sense his intent, his and the bees."

Arkimedes nodded, shoving his hands in his pockets.

"It's not a bad connection." She walked to him. His whole body tensed at her proximity. She realized belatedly that he was trying to put space between them. Her stomach churned, and her warm body turned cold.

He was regretting almost kissing her. She dropped her gaze. Her pride took over. If he wanted not to talk about it, she would oblige. "It's natural, like breathing. Like it feels being with you," Nava whispered. To hell with her pride.

"Nava," he pleaded.

She lifted her gaze to him, searching for something that told her he might feel the same way. His expression was guarded, his body rigid while his fingers rubbed together in a nervous tick.

She took a step back, her heart contracting. "I'd better go. I'm just making this more awkward than it needs to be, like usual."

"It's not that."

"I felt . . . We had a moment, right? That wasn't me making it all up in my head." The words were spilling out. Magic had weakened not only her body but also her sense of self-preservation.

"We did. It was something," Arkimedes said, keeping his feet grounded in his spot. The pit inside her stomach grew. "It's not the right time, Nava."

She nodded. Violet's words came back to her mind. She had warned her

Arkimedes would not be with her, even with their undeniable chemistry. She hadn't paid attention at the time, focusing more on the flirting and the intensity of what they'd shared after their training session.

Anger was coming at a fast pace. Why would he flirt with her if he wasn't ready for anything else? Why lead her on—almost kiss her—then push her away?

Nava didn't want to risk falling for anyone, but she was willing to do so with him.

She opened her mouth to say that before snapping her lips closed. There was her pride coming to her again, maybe a bit too late. She turned on her heels and walked away before she could pass out from her drained energy and embarrass herself any further.

CHAPTER TWENTY-ONE

Nava's surroundings had not changed for hours. Tall trees covered in green moss extended high in the sky, making their walk dark and cold. The air was more humid the more north they went, and she was happy this was their last day traveling.

Everyone walked in relative silence, alert for possible attacks. Arkimedes was in front of her. The tension was palpable in between them, and it almost suffocated her.

As desperation hit her, she considered telling him to forget their almost-kiss ever happened. She didn't know if it would make things even worse. Nava didn't understand what he wanted but wished they could go back to being normal.

She studied the surrounding trees. If she were to be here on her own, she wouldn't be able to find her way. Not to this village but back to Cameron and the town she avoided thinking of much.

Nava's heart contracted with dread as she imagined being immersed in Willowbrook's boring simplicity once more.

"I haven't been forthcoming with you." Arkimedes's whisper had her head snapping up toward him. His face was beautiful and lethal, with the sharp angles of his high cheekbones.

"What do you mean?" Her steps were longer and quicker to keep up with him.

He was quiet for a moment that extended too long. Nava didn't reach to grab him, however. She had been trying to keep her distance since the day before. "When Devon's army shot me, I did notice he might have come with a larger army like you mentioned when we met."

Her lips parted in shock. "How large are we talking about?"

"Hundreds."

"Why didn't you tell me before?"

He pressed his lips into a thin line, evading her pointed gaze. "I wanted to give you a few days of normalcy and allow you to focus on training. I'm sorry." Honesty tinted his last word.

The heat of annoyance still swirled inside her stomach. "Are we going to stay at the village or leave and keep on the move?"

"Our best option is staying with bigger numbers still. He didn't come looking for you or me. I believe he had been tracking Roman since he used to be a high Commander in the army of the Iron City, but after finding you and, in return, me, he is after us more so than them at this point."

Nava opened her mouth to say how little sense it made that Devon Black had his attention set on them when he had a whole village of sorcerers to raid and capture. Still, her mind supplied memories of the day in the clearing when his magic had rained down on her. Devon had made it a point to come and talk to her. He had ignored Gavin and Violet.

She swallowed. Devon knew her from before. Her mother had been a Crow once upon a time. Arkimedes had defeated a small camp full of bounty hunters. That alone would drive the warlock insane. She was sure of it.

She said flatly, "No more secrets, this includes withholding information."

His eyes held hers for a long time. "No more secrets."

"Are you two lovebirds coming?" Gavin's words shook her. Heat traveled to her face.

Arkimedes turned and walked toward the other pair without another word.

THE VILLAGE APPEARED as they crossed the wards that protected it. Nava took in the magical ambiance. Homes and buildings made of stucco, wood, and stone were built against tall trees with massive tree trunks as large as her house back in town.

Lanterns shone with magical flames, lighting up the dark streets shaded by the giant trees that hosted it.

Three-meter-wide roads were paved with smooth stone aged by lichen and moss. Life burst through the seams of this little section of the world.

Carts were being pulled by large stallions or donkeys, but upon further inspection . . . said donkeys bore large horns in the middle of their heads.

Her head moved to the sides as she studied the people who walked by. They wore earth-colored tunics similar to Violet's and Gavin's. Children played in the streets, chasing each other. Their laughter echoed around, mixing with birds chirping and the casual conversations around them.

Kids ran around her. They couldn't be older than five, maybe six. Two women wearing dresses and heavy coats chatted among themselves as their offspring played. Not a worry in sight, ignorant a monster was coming to take them away.

Nava had come to this village first for protection. Now she wanted to help them. Devon Black arriving here without warning would lead to failure for these people. Seeing this place, the life here made her aware of how similar her situation had been when she was a child and her mother had protected her from slavery.

Her anger toward her mother, the one always burning beneath her skin, subdued a bit.

The air smelled of a mixture of spices—saffron, cayenne, cumin. Incense burned in the air, and beneath all these scents was the particular smell of magic. It was different from what she remembered from the Iron City. This was breathtaking and booming with life.

Dread bloomed in the pit of her stomach as she took on all these people who could lose if Devon Black got to them.

She followed her group of people as Gavin and Violet greeted a few who were walking by. Arkimedes walked next to her, his own gaze fixed on a point ahead. A tall man wearing a black tunic with a dark fur collar stood by, talking with someone, unaware of them approaching. Both men in front appeared militant, even though their hair was long and wild. Their statures were imposing, much like Arkimedes.

"Roman." The man's gaze searched for Violet's voice, relief and surprise flashing across his worn features.

He had to be in his mid-forties. His expression was of a much older man, worn by battle and hardship. His face was a mixture of strength and wariness, high cheekbones, and a straight nose. A large scar marked the right side of his face, sparing his dark eye. His hair was peppered and tied into a low ponytail.

"Violet, Gavin." His face twisted into a smile that morphed his face. "I'm so happy to see you. We have been hearing rumors of a crown ship landing in Willowbrook and expected the worse."

"I'm afraid the rumors were correct." Gavin shook the man's hand, turning toward both Arkimedes and Nava, who waited behind. "We met these two in our captive time."

Roman's focus shifted to them. He scanned her before moving on to Arkimedes. He paused. "Arkimedes."

"Roman."

"I hope you had nothing to do with this." His voice held an aggressive undertone, and Nava's skin prickled.

Violet's face showed no signs of embarrassment by the words of the Commander.

"He did not, Roman. He was the one who released us." Gavin's hands came up.

"Or that's what he wants you to think," Roman said.

Arkimedes's jaw tensed. "Why would I do that?"

"Who's to tell with you?" Roman's eyes narrowed.

Nava pushed forward, much more petite than Arkimedes, but still, she walked in front, wanting the man's attention to be elsewhere.

Curiosity caressed her mind at this, settling on Arkimedes and his tense jaw. It was ridiculous that this man would blame him for this. Yes, Arkimedes had been part of the army, but so had this Roman guy. Arkimedes had also run away and was living in exile in this forest.

Nava's breaths came out quicker as heat traveled through her body. It was clear Arkimedes was an outsider, much like she had been in Willowbrook. He had not shared many things about his past and was an enigma, but she also knew he had wanted to help them.

"He did not plan this." She took a sharp breath and squared off her shoulders. "The bounty hunters who took them also took me—and Arkimedes was there to get me out."

When she finished, a weight lifted off her shoulders. She wanted to speak up for him. Even if they had met not that long ago, he was her friend.

"And you would be . . . ?"

"Nava. I met the Crow in Willowbrook. We have been running away from him for a few weeks."

Roman shifted his focus to Arkimedes, ignoring her words.

"Roman, he took care of the bounty hunters. *I* saw him fight the Crow—please, there is no need for this," Gavin said, his brow furrowing.

Violet let go of a sharp breath, her face soured. Nava guessed she had been enjoying the way Roman was making Arkimedes a villain, right until the point Gavin decided to side with her and Arkimedes.

"What brings you here?"

Arkimedes stiffened, but other than that, his expression remained neutral.

"We were on our way to warn you of Devon being on the island and targeting *you*. He comes with a large army."

"Targeting me?" Roman snarled. "What makes you think he is here for me and not *you*?"

Nava turned to Arkimedes, her heart pounding.

"He didn't know I was here until I attacked his camp to get Nava out."

"Rather convenient no Crow or crown has an idea where you are."

Arkimedes shrugged. "I have been on this island longer than you. They had stopped looking for me. However, you left with a big splash, didn't you? The crown probably put a pretty penny over your head."

"Crows don't work for money," Roman said.

"No, but bounty hunters do, and he comes with those as well." Arkimedes seethed.

Silence descended upon the group. Nava swallowed.

"He is also after us. We figured if we stayed in larger numbers, everyone would fare better luck," Arkimedes said.

"I see."

Conversation followed, and Violet explained what had happened and how they had been ambushed in the middle of the night the day before they had taken Nava.

Nava glanced at the trees around her, curiosity taking a firm grip on her thoughts. This was the first time she had been inside a magical village, and it was unlike anything she had ever seen. Something moved, long limbs made of tree bark. She blinked, and the vision was gone.

She walked away from the group, searching for her Beekeeper up in the foliage. Nava pursed her lips and considered the possibility that she was going crazy. A small fuzzy body flew down in a zigzag and hovered close to her face.

She turned her hand and offered it her palm. As it landed, Nava waited, holding her breath for words to echo in her head. The bee walked and turned up its little head as if waiting for a command.

Nava's eyes changed focus, from the insect standing on her hand to the shape of someone in front of her.

She met irises the color of vibrant cobalt blue. The woman's skin was blue and leathery, its shine reminding her of the pearls sold in the town's market by the ports. Her dark blue hair was in an elaborate bun on top of her head, and she had long, pointy ears. A fae.

The closest she had ever been to a magical creature like this before was Arkimedes, who talked little of his past but had shared a small fraction of what he knew. Her lips parted as both of them stared at one another with increasing curiosity.

"I haven't seen you in town before," she sing-songed, walking around Nava, studying every inch of her body. The movement made her want to cover herself somehow.

"We got here with Gavin and Violet," Nava said, pointing behind her, where the four of them still stood.

"Your name, girl?" the woman whispered.

Nava blinked, a daze forming around her mind. "Nava."

"Nava," the fae repeated, long white teeth revealed in a smile sharper than she cared to dwell on. "I'm Thea. The Commander called, so I came," she said as if this would answer the question going through Nava's head.

Steps came behind her, but she couldn't move much. She was entranced by the cobalt eyes and an increasing prickly sensation inside her head.

"Is everything all right?" Arkimedes's voice shook her out of her trance. "Roman said there is a cabin for guests. You can have it." He fixed his gaze on the fae, who stared from Nava to Arkimedes, buzzing with excitement.

"What about you?" Nava lowered her voice.

"I don't need it. You know why."

"That's not true—"

"Oh, how exciting! Anima-mate. I haven't seen the likes of you for so long, I almost forgot what it looks like." Thea smiled, buzzing with delight.

Nava focused her attention on the fairy before lifting a brow. Arkimedes's expression differed from what she was expecting. His face was suddenly pale. He shook his head, his lips pursed together.

"The likes of who?" Nava said.

The fae's leathery hands landed on each side of her cheeks. Thea chuckled with excitement, turning Nava's head as she examined all of her exposed skin. *So, I guess me?*

"Um," she said.

Arkimedes's hand landed on her hip, pulling her back a few steps and away from the eager fae. "I'm sure we should get going," he whispered into Nava's ear.

From the air of his breath hitting her neck, goose bumps awakened and traveled down her body, making her aware of how close he was.

He held her against his warm body, but his attention was fixed on the woman in front, wariness tinting his features. It hit her with the realization that whatever the fairy had said had him in a frenzy.

"She doesn't know. How is it possible, girl?" Thea asked, her brows dipping down into a frown.

Confusion was creeping in as she took a sharp breath. She was tired of always being the one out of the secret. Never understanding what was happening around her. Was the fairy referring to her connection with the Beekeeper?

"*What?* About . . . the curse?" She turned to Arkimedes in a warning she hoped he heard. She was not buying his need to get her away from the fairy.

"You must have missed the sign or something is blocking you from finding it."

"Get out of our heads, Almathea," Arkimedes warned.

The fae took a step back and crooked her head, studying him. "The Commander demands if you are to be trusted," she said, her sing-song words dying down.

Nava understood the prickliness inside her head and the fogginess that had occupied her mind. Thea was a seer.

"I don't care what he says," Arkimedes hissed.

Nava crossed her arms in front of her chest. The woman had been inside her head, and she had found something that was different in there—had alluded to something Nava ought to know. Her mind reeled as she took Arkimedes's features. Something he didn't want her to.

"Roman, what is the meaning of this?" Arkimedes's voice boomed.

The Commander, who had been talking with Gavin and Violet, came hurrying. His expression shuttered, his hand resting all too casually on top of the hilt of his sword. "What is the problem?"

Arkimedes turned and pulled her along with him, still holding her hips. It wasn't as if they didn't touch. As a matter of fact, the longer they spent together, the more touch became part of their routine. A shoulder graze here, a caress to one's arm. He had never held her like he was doing now, however, and she couldn't help what blossomed in her chest.

"You had the fae get inside our heads," Arkimedes snarled.

Roman's lips twitched. "We do it with *all* newcomers. It's a way to ensure we have no moles."

"Let me remind you. You need us as much as we need you—you do not get to get inside our heads without us agreeing to it." Arkimedes's expression didn't waver.

Roman's tense shoulders relaxed a bit. "I apologize." His eyes flashed behind them, where Nava assumed Thea still stood. "It seems it's all okay. With that, we will escort you to the guest cabin. You can rest tonight, and tomorrow we will prepare for whatever might come our way."

Silence passed with a beat as Roman walked away, followed by Violet.

Gavin walked to them, both hands inside his pockets, his face apologetic. "I'm sorry for his behavior—but I hope you have grown to trust me. You will be safe in here. We need you to help us fight against the Crow." Gavin's face morphed to one of concern, his attention fixed on the children playing in the street, the laughter, the normalcy. His pronounced Adam's apple bobbed. "I will take you to your cabin. There will be a small celebration this afternoon. I hope you two will join us for drinks and dancing."

Nava smiled, eager. It had been a while since she had been able to do something she loved. She and Arkimedes fell behind Gavin's steps, walking down the wavy stone roads of the village. The smell of burning wood, dirt, and moss was a pleasant combination.

Gavin stopped in front of an old tree. A small cabin jutted out with ceramic tiles on top of the roof and small windows. The door was much too small for someone the size of Arkimedes.

"Your home." Gavin's hand moved in a grand gesture, making Nava smile. It was pleasing that someone's mood was not being shifted after arriving at this village.

The door was heavy, and as she walked inside her home for the night, she studied the warm, rustic wood tones and the wool rugs over terracotta-tiled floors. A small living room surrounded a stone fireplace and worn leather chairs with thick colorful blankets layered on top.

To the side, under a small window covered in forest-green curtains, there was a small shelf filled with curiosities: a half-burned candle, three hastily stacked books, and a glass vase filled with dried flowers.

Someone had once lived here. Nava turned to ask Gavin whose cabin this was but stopped when her attention landed on both Arkimedes and him. They were whispering outside. She took slow steps toward them, trying to make out anything of what they were saying.

Curiosity was her worst trait, her mother had said. She happened to think it was one of her best.

"He understands we also need you, but you need us too," Gavin said.

"I won't leave Nava, if that's what you are thinking. I'm not going anywhere while she's still here."

"Good, I will see you later."

"I'm not one for parties."

"Don't do it for you but her. It's clear Nava has never been to war." Gavin added quickly, "A large army, you said, is coming this way to take every deserter—but we both know what they do to the elderly, the disabled. You and I have fought on the other side."

Nava walked closer to the door and peeked through the small opening, focusing on the hard planes of Arkimedes's back. The afternoon light graced the sharp angles of his features.

"Yes." His face turned dark.

"The ones who are worthless to them will get killed. We'll put up a fight, and this will become a bloodbath. War is coming, and you are aware of what that entails. Drink some wine, make love to your woman, and prepare for hell."

"Gavin—"

Nava stepped back. The war was coming, whether or not she was ready for it.

CHAPTER TWENTY-TWO

Arkimedes entered the house shortly after, bending under the worn doorframe. He straightened while he studied the small space, and then his eyes settled on Nava.

His cheeks blushed, and she knew he was remembering Gavin's last words. To make love to her and prepare for battle. The tension increased as her own blood boiled in her veins.

"Do you think we need to get dressed up for the celebration? Because I have nothing other than trousers and shirts—in various states of filth." Her voice was less convincing by the end.

Her mind supplied the image of her green skirt. She had worn it little on the trip because the excess fabric made it hard for her to walk in the forest, but maybe she could use it for today's festivities.

"I won't get dressed up, either," he offered with a shrug.

She studied his dark clothes and wind-brushed hair, which had gotten longer in the past few weeks. It swooped over his forehead. He was the most handsome man she had ever seen with his stubble.

She grimaced. "Of course, it's not like you need to, with the way you look." Realizing all the words had left her lips, she winced but decided it was too late to salvage it. "It's something silly to be concerned about, not with what's coming." She walked around the home, her cheeks flaming. "This reminds me of your house." She took in the play of his muscles as he removed his coat and dropped it over the back of one of the kitchen chairs. "I like yours better." She met his gaze as he turned back to her.

Curiosity piqued his attention. "You do?"

She nodded, walking around while her fingers brushed over the stucco walls. "Yours felt like home."

His lips twitched into a smile she might have missed had she not been staring so intently at his face. He took a step forward, and she held her breath, unsure what he would do. They had been dancing this strange game of giving in, then pulling back.

"Have you thought about what you want to do when all this is over?"

Silence. "Are you going to return to your town?" The muscles of his jaw tensed.

Nava's throat went dry, her palms sweating with uneasiness. "I have to go back to Cameron and Laurie," she admitted. "I don't want to be in that town, far away from . . ." *You.* This time she held back, afraid to say too much and have him pull away again.

Music drifted through the air, reaching them. They both turned their heads at the sounds of the cheerful tunes.

"I'm going to freshen up before we head out." She carried her backpack with her. For once, she wished all her clothes weren't inside a town where no magic reached or else she might attempt to bring something new for the celebrations using her magic.

That alone made her pause as she dropped the heavy backpack on the floor. Her lips parted as she stood still and enjoyed the quiet to reflect on the changes that happened within.

The washroom was narrow, illuminated by a tall stained glass window with intricate designs, arranged in a mosaic that formed trees and leaves. There was a wooden tub with a coal-burning stove attached to it, similar to what Nava had seen in Arkimedes's home.

There was a small vanity with a copper bowl and a pump faucet to the side. This whole village would have been connected to a septic system, unless it all worked with magic—which, based on where she was, she guessed was plausible.

Nava splashed cold water on her face, taking a deep breath to calm her nerves. She was not only nervous about her lack of proper attire for the celebration.

Water filled the tub with steam. The air was thick as she took another breath, closing her eyes as her mind rushed through memories of what she knew before and knew now.

This village proved she had been misguided her whole life to fear, hating what she was, a magical person with power running through her veins. She was not a damsel in distress. She should have been able to protect Cameron and herself.

Her mother had been an instructor, a powerful sorceress, and part of the Society of Crows. A respected weapons master. She had been Arkimedes's teacher, for god's sake, yet she had chosen to leave Nava in the dark. To let her believe the best option was to be wary and afraid of magic.

Nava guessed she could understand why she had been so sheltered. Her mother had gone through a lot to protect them. She wished she had thought of their future more.

Arkimedes's question came to her mind—would she return home to Willowbrook? The answer was an easy *no.* Nava craved knowledge, wanted to work on her confidence and self-worth. For the first time in her life, she was not feeling inadequate, but powerful instead.

Cameron had wanted to learn this side of their nature, and she would work on that. They could move to this village, or she'd search for somewhere they could go, because it was clear the crown would not stop seeking deserters even in this remote place.

She got in the tub and let herself soak in the warm water as it soothed her sore muscles, and for the first time in weeks, she was truly clean.

She settled on her green skirt and a shirt she had washed in the lake. She braided her hair in one of the styles Laurie had taught her. By the time she was out, Arkimedes had settled into one armchair and was paging through a book.

His gaze raked over her body before settling on her face. "You look beautiful, Bee," he breathed.

Her stomach woke up in a flutter. "Thank you." She didn't need to dwell on his appearance. "I like the nickname, by the way."

"Yes?"

"It suits me, I think."

He smiled, and the expression reached his eyes. "I like it too. Ready to go?"

THE VILLAGE WAS ALIVE with people on the streets, loud voices, and laughter. The smell of tobacco, beer, and rum filled the air, along with something spicy. Magic was everywhere.

Nava and Arkimedes followed the crowd to the village's center, a small plaza shaped like a circle with smooth stones that matched the roads and walkways. Large planters housed four weeping willows that clashed among all the other trees. A band played music on a wooden stage, all wearing matching outfits of moss-green tunics and brown hats. People of all ages were dancing.

Lightning bugs flew around in the air. It wasn't night yet, because Arkimedes was still here. Under the trees' dense canopy, it was dark and magical.

She followed the men, women, and children wearing dressier attires, unlike herself. Women wore long dresses in saturated colors that popped against the trees' brown bark and the yellowish tones of the stucco buildings in the background. Her insides sank with self-awareness.

Even though she wore her best attire, her skirt was torn after climbing that wall when leaving town. Still, green suited her.

Nava's gaze followed the direction Arkimedes was staring and found Roman and Gavin, both men wearing dressy attires. Gavin's face was shaven neatly, making him look so much younger. His nose had a shadow of a scar from their captive days.

They made their way to them, around the dance floor and between a sea of people. She spotted Violet by one of the willow trees, wearing indigo pants and a clean black tunic. One of the few women she had seen *not* wearing a dress. The weight of self-doubt lifted from her shoulders.

"You made it." Gavin's voice was cheerful as he patted Arkimedes's arm twice, then took a drink out of a pint of beer. "Nava, may I get you a drink?" Gavin searched Arkimedes's face, as if checking he was not overstepping on some alpha male thing.

She squirmed in her spot at the heaviness in her chest. What had she been expecting? That Arkimedes would offer to get her a drink instead? It was precisely what she'd wanted, him jumping at the chance of courting her. Instead, he was keen on keeping the distance he had set since their *almost*-kiss.

"I don't want to trouble you. Where may I find one?" She was also not ready to deal with a possible hostile Violet if the woman was a jealous type. She spotted a lady with a tray filled with cups of overflowing drinks. "Never mind. I think I found her. I will be right back."

Nava made her way across the crowd in search of something to calm her nerves. The three men fell into a hushed conversation, reviewing what had happened in the last few days while they'd traveled.

She didn't need to stay behind to hear what she already knew, reliving moments where she had been paralyzed with fright or swiped away by another array of feelings she cared not to dwell on. The woman holding the tray couldn't be older than forty. Her ash-blond hair was pulled back into a bun with ringlets framing her thin angular face.

She was beautiful in an otherworldly way. Nava knew she wasn't just human. She paused and stared for longer than necessary before those magical orbs came onto her, a thin brow lifting in question.

"Is there something wrong?" Her voice held a bit of a bite.

"Oh, nothing wrong. May I have one?"

The fae hybrid sized her up from the bottom of her worn, dirty boots to the top of her head and shrugged. "You look old enough." She extended Nava a pint of beer.

The foam spilled over her fingers as she tried to steady it so it wouldn't make a mess. "T-thanks."

The fae with the drinks was already walking off. Nava shook her head and brought the glass to her lips. The fermented taste of homemade beer came to her palate. She had never been a particular fan of the drink, preferring wine any day, but this celebration called for it.

Nava walked closer to the dance floor as if hypnotized by the dancing. She stared at the shapes, sipping on her beer. Her legs ached for her to let go, to loosen up a bit and forget the things that haunted her dreams or her concerns about whether she wanted to return home or stay in this new world.

Or the fact that she was falling for an unavailable guy when she should be uninterested.

A female voice called her attention. "Have you seen the new guy?"

She was near enough that Nava could tell she was young and eager. Nava studied the crowd as curiosity piqued her interest.

"The one next to Gavin? How could anyone *not*?" another voice replied.

Nava blinked as she found two girls huddled together, a couple of meters away from where she stood, their eyes fixed on a spot in the crowd.

"He is scrumptious," said the blonde, whose hair fell down her back, contrasting with her shiny silky blue dress. The shade reminded her of one Simone wore often, and her heart contracted with the memory of her friend.

"He *is*, Mina. Mother told me he was dangerous," the other said. This girl had warm copper skin and jet-black hair. Her dress, much like her friend's, was a silky gown but light green.

Nava took another sip and followed their gazes, peeping across the crowd. Her gaze landed straight on Arkimedes, and her cheeks flamed at the vision of him. His arms were crossed over his chest, the pose displaying the bulge of his muscles. His attention traveled across the sea of people as he studied his surroundings with a bored stance. Gavin was near him, still chatting with a man of medium stature, muscular build, and long, wavy caramel hair. She didn't recognize him, which wasn't surprising as she was new here.

Nava breathed her disappointment. She had hoped he would come and look for her, but instead, he was biding his time before he had to depart, forced by his impending curse.

"I'll let him do whatever he wants to me. You know how I like a bad boy," said the girl with the pale hair.

Nava's chest burned with flames that flowed through her body as she huffed at the girl's words. She couldn't be older than twenty, and her rosy round cheeks and clean face made Nava ruffle like a wet hen.

Arkimedes was indeed too old for her. She grumbled, tilted the pint to her lips, and finished her drink. When the last drop was gone, she stared in awe as the ceramic cup disappeared from her grasp. Her lips parted in shock, but she held it together long enough not to make a scene.

As Nava followed the dancing bodies, a man, not much older than the girls she had been obsessing over, came to her. He was tall and slim with blond hair and bright blue eyes. He reached a hand out with a broad smile, and she tried to find who he was inviting to the dance floor, only to realize he had come for her.

People moved in circles in a lively rhythm, a dance pattern she knew from back in town.

"Could I interest you in a dance?" His voice carried a heavy accent, and his cheeks were flushed.

Giggles came from nearby, and the girls, Mina and black hair, were staring at them. His smile faltered at her hesitation. She took a sharp breath to steel her nerves and took his hand, letting herself get carried away to the dance floor.

Her smile grew as they jumped around and forgot about everything. He smelled like pine, and his hands were much softer than the large hands she longed to hold. She stared over her partner's shoulder to the spot where Arkimedes stood, and she was shocked when her gaze met his across the dance floor.

His shoulders were tight with tension, his expression filled with emotion. Nava swallowed and looked away, back to the present.

She clapped to the sound of the music, following everyone else. Their complexions were shiny with sweat, all happy and *free*.

Devon Black was still out there, getting closer to them with every second that passed by. These people, like her family, had run from the crown and made their lives away from servitude.

She sobered a bit, and her attention stopped on her dance partner as she took in his features. Much like what had happened to her in town, there was no connection or attraction, though her brain supplied he was handsome. His face was sharp and smooth.

The song was ending. She jumped around the dance floor along with the guy with blue eyes. The last notes of the song were hanging in the air, and everyone stopped dancing and clapped at the band.

"Thank you for the dance." Nava managed to curtsy. Laurie would be proud she had not forgotten her manners.

The man who had invited her smiled and bowed to her. "It's my pleasure." He paled as he looked behind her shoulder and then he disappeared from her view before she could say anything else.

She turned around and found Arkimedes looming. His jaw was tense, his stance wide. He stared at the retreating form of her dance partner. A part of her wanted to be annoyed at whatever this display was. Another, more significant side wanted to rejoice.

"You have scared away my dance partner." She eyed him sharply.

He extended her a hand. "Then I'd better rectify it. Would you join me for the next dance?" he asked in a refined, high-society tone she hadn't heard before. It was like he had grown up going to such events, maybe even much fancier than this one.

Nava took his hand, and butterflies flew inside her stomach. She hoped he didn't notice the tremble as he brought his body closer to her and his other hand came to rest on her lower back. They moved to the slow rhythm of the ballad playing.

She broke the silence. "So what was that about?"

His dark lashes lowered. "What?"

"The display with . . .him."

His lips lifted into a side smile. "So you didn't even get a name?"

Her cheeks went warm. "We were dancing." She smiled. "Maybe I was too lost in the moment to speak."

"Or too busy looking elsewhere," he countered.

"Do tell. Since you were paying attention."

"*I was* paying attention." His hand squeezed hers, his eyes dipping down to her lips.

A breath caught in her throat, but she didn't want to fall into the abysm of her desire. Not this time. They had gone down this route before, and it had burned her. "So, what was I looking at, Arkimedes?" she pressed.

He spun her, making her stomach swirl. He pulled her back and held her close. The warmth of his body seeped through the layers of clothes, burning her. His breath caressed the side of her neck, his lips against her ear. "You were looking at me," he whispered.

"I was reading the room." She could tell by his amused expression she was not fooling anyone. "You can't keep doing this to me, Arkimedes, playing with my feelings."

"I'm not playing. I told you it wasn't the right time a couple of days ago—and maybe not now, either."

"It makes no sense." She huffed. "Why not? Last time I checked, neither you nor I are with anyone. We are free to be with who we want, and I want . . . you." Were they moving to the sound of the music or standing still?

Silence.

"Is it because of my soulmate thing?" she asked.

His brows met in the middle. The song ended, and he pulled away from her as if she had burned him. Her mind went haywire. Was he retreating because he thought she was trying to pin him about being the one again?

She was *not*—right? A prickle crawled across her scalp.

"I'm going to head back. I only have minutes before nightfall, and I don't want to transform in front of all these people." He took a couple of steps back, facing her, before spinning around and stepping past the crowd.

For such a large man, he was a quick one. She followed behind, steps faltering as people came in front of her, covering his retreating form.

"Excuse me." She pushed between bodies but was unable to make any headway. Instead of moving away, they came closer together. She pushed and pulled and soon was out of a wall made of people.

Everyone was laughing behind her. She studied the darkened streets. Nava's stomach sank. The tall trees crowded her in the noisy background. A spark of recognition. Somehow she knew where to go, which made little sense to her human non-magical brain but worked with her awakened senses.

The whisper of magic caressed her mind, giving her flashes of images that told her where to go, showing her a way back to him. She would not stop their conversation there.

She would take any minute he still had this evening. Nava wanted to use it to clear the air. Questions swirled in her mind, Amalthea's words coming to the forefront.

Nava hated secrets having grown up in a family that said too little and left her living adrift.

Arkimedes was swift on his feet. Even though she was practically jogging behind him, she could not catch up.

By the time she made it to the cabin, the light of the fireplace illuminated the windows, and as soon as she opened the door, the largest raven flew out of the house, cawing as it disappeared between the shadows of the night.

CHAPTER TWENTY-THREE

Nava woke up in the morning to a cold cabin. The fire had gone off in the middle of the night, and with the dropping late-fall temperatures, the stone floors were frigid when her feet touched it.

She made her way to the fireplace, searching for kindling to light it up again. When she found none, she moved to her backpack, but her matches had gotten soggy.

Nava dropped back onto the floor. The smooth stones' coldness seeped into her body, and she wallowed for a couple of minutes—before she would pull herself together again.

She had never relied on anyone so heavily that despair took over her, not being able to do something so simple as making a fire. Lighting a fireplace was something she'd done over and over with non-magical human tools.

Life had forced her to grow up when her father had fallen into the daze that had taken him. He had chosen to die with his soulmate instead of living with his children. Her body warmed as anger flowed through her veins at that.

If anything, these weeks had made her aware of her resentment toward her parents. Sure, her father had taught her to make a fire using matches. He could have demanded her mother teach her how to make such things with magic, instead.

Her world closed in, suffocating her. It was not because of her soggy matches or because she was cold, hungry, and alone. It was because of the constant feeling of being the weak one—something she was unused to.

She was used to being the aloof person who didn't need help. Taking care of her home, her brother, and the family business when she'd been twenty.

She didn't need a man. Nava had dismissed her suitors when they'd implied she *needed* their support. Like hell she did. Sure, her funds were dwindling because people in town were unwilling to give a woman of her age a shot, even though her potions were just as good as her father's. She didn't need a man or her soulmate.

Being rejected for something she had no control over made her blood boil.

Her lips shook as she swallowed down a heavy knot in her throat. *You don't want a soulmate. And if it's not your soulmate, then it shouldn't be anyone.* Her brain repeated the words Nava had been telling herself since she was fifteen.

While she had been attracted to Arkimedes from the get-go, it had developed slowly, from attraction to friendship to more. Or maybe it had come all at once, and she was better at lying to herself than she thought.

Nava stared at the fireplace. The ashen wood stared back at her defiantly. She had magic. It was about time she used hers for things other than a panicked attempt to save herself.

Focusing on the energy that coursed through her body, on what she wanted to do, she buried away all negativity. Her mind narrowed to the cold that surrounded her and called on fire.

A tingling traveled down her spine, over her skin, through her veins, and to her fingertips. She smelled spice, smoke, and burning wood. Nava gasped when orange-and-yellow flames danced in front of her. She fist-pumped the air, right before a wave of tiredness ran through her body.

She got up and headed back to bed, plopping down while her eyelids drooped. A smile tugged at her lips, and exhilaration mixed with exhaustion.

The knocking brought her back to the present time. She must've dozed off at some point, and she blinked at the haze inside the cabin before she moved to the door.

The door was heavy, and when it cracked, a wave of frigid air hit her like a hurricane. She squinted against the bright light outside, coming to the familiar shape of a woman. Flawless copper skin, wearing a burgundy coat and dark pants, hair pulled back in careful braids that made her already fierce expression even more intimidating.

"You are alive," Violet said, walking into the cabin and examining the area.

"Good morning to you too," Nava said, closing the door behind the other woman.

"You mean good afternoon."

Nava swallowed. "Afternoon," she corrected, emphasizing her annoyed tone. "Can I help you with anything?"

"We're preparing for an attack. Roman thinks it's prudent to have you train with me since the Crow seems especially keen on you."

"Oh?"

"Gavin and I noticed how even though he didn't bother to come to us after we were captured, he made it a point to see *you*." Violet studied her nails, but by the vein throbbing on her forehead, Nava deduced this didn't please her, her pride not too happy with the revelation that Nava was somehow more prized in the Crow's eyes.

"Why you?" Nava challenged. She would prefer to train with Roman himself rather than with the woman in front of her, remembering how she had hit Gavin in their training sessions.

"Why not? Are you afraid of me?"

Nava frowned. "Maybe I am," she admitted. "Look, I'm not here to measure our pride. I'm not an experienced warrior. I never used magic before a month ago."

Violet scoffed. "You expect me to believe this, that you have discovered power. Yet you have a significant amount of it. You control the bees. The Beekeeper comes for you. One of the scariest men I have ever seen protects you, and the Crow hunts you."

Nava lifted her hands in a sign of peace, and Violet's frown deepened. Why did people keep saying Arkimedes was scary? Powerful, yes. But scary . . . ? Her mind supplied the image of him raising his hand and one of the bounty hunters collapsing to the ground. The man had been alive one second, and next, he was dead.

Yep, she guessed he was scary.

"The Beekeeper is something I'm trying to figure out myself, but I don't control him. Arkimedes is not that scary, and my mother pissed off the Society of Crows when she married a non-magical man, lied to them, then escaped with me in tow." *And* Cameron, but Violet didn't need to know that.

"I'm not sure if you are just naïve or stupid. Maybe both."

"You are so nice. I wonder why I even try with you."

Violet's lips pursed as she walked around the house, abandoning Nava. "Let's give you the benefit of the doubt, kitten. You are new to this life, that much is clear. Why would I risk everything I love to protect you?"

"What—?"

"Arkimedes bringing you here put us all in danger. Devon will come for you *and* him. To him, we are insects. You two are his prize. Why should I not take you there myself?"

"Oh, you think Devon is here for us alone?" Nava challenged. "He came searching for *deserters*. He didn't even know I was on this island until he found my shop. Taking me to him won't stop him. Once he has us, he will keep coming for more. His ship is large. It will fit this whole village in it, and the ones who don't fit will likely get executed."

Violet's nostrils flared, her face and throat flushed.

"You are counting on Arkimedes to help." Nava's voice was unwavering. Violet had come of her own will to train her so she was ready for what was coming. She was not a burden but an asset in the eyes of this trained warrior. Her soul soared. "You need me."

"We don't need you." Violet's gaze narrowed. She walked toward her bag, trying to find a set of clean clothes.

"No, you do." Nava's throat became a knot, the knowledge making her dizzy.

Violet's lips pressed down, and she didn't argue any further. "We have been sending sentinels to see if they can find the army, if they are coming north or heading east. Arkimedes and Gavin went with them earlier today. They haven't returned."

He had left without saying goodbye, even though he'd said he would never leave her behind. Her heart squeezed at this, and she sobered her features. This situation was more significant than whatever was going on between her and Arkimedes. This meant freedom for everyone on this island, including Cameron and Laurie.

"They left before I woke this morning. He should have come to get me as he promised." Violet shifted, her face tinted with concern, and Nava understood. While her concern had been for Arkimedes, Violet's was for Gavin.

"I want to train," Nava said.

"I won't go easy on you, kitten. Not like he does."

Nava opened her mouth to counter that Arkimedes didn't go easy on her, but Violet's knowing expression made her shut her mouth. "Fine, but please don't kill me."

"I'll try my best since, according to you, we need you." Violet's voice held mockery.

"I'll get dressed and will be right out." Nava headed to the small bathroom in the back of the house.

"Hurry up. We need to get you fed before you pass out on me, as you like doing."

NAVA HIT THE GROUND WITH A GROAN, her hands scraping over rock and dirt, her muscles sore by their training intensity. Violet was standing over her, still in a fighting stance. This time they were training sans magic, per Nava's request after she had hit the ground more times than she cared to admit.

Violet had street fighting skills, and she moved with precision over grace. Her hits were hard, and by the third punch, she had left Nava winded right before the woman had swept her off her feet.

Nava had, however, gotten several hits, and Violet's pointers were helpful.

"C'mon, kitten, I'm not getting any younger," Violet said, her voice never abandoning that bored tone that ground on Nava's nerves.

She pushed up, her arms trembling from exhaustion. They had trained with magic before, and that duel had gone better for her. Now, her body was too tired even to get up.

"Draining your body of energy while using magic might as well be a death sentence," Violet said.

Heat flooded Nava's cheeks. "Everyone has failed to teach me how to avoid it." The heaviness of her limbs refused to move, dragging over muddy soil.

"It's not something we can teach you. It's something you learn by practicing every day. Things like energy from your surroundings become more apparent." Violet lazily poked at her side with her foot.

The movement made Nava's blood boil.

No.

Heat rushed over her body, and her muscles trembled as power ran through her, her limbs not so sore anymore. No, she would not get kicked while defeated on the floor. She had fought her entire life to keep afloat, head over water, preventing her from drowning, and her body would not give in yet.

She swept her legs under Violet's and pushed her body from the ground with unnatural power. No, it wasn't artificial. It was *her* power. Her skin buzzed with energy, shining white and yellow.

Violet gasped as she fell to the ground and stared back at Nava's glowing skin. "You are cheating."

"There is no cheating in war, especially against someone who kicks the person who's down." Nava's power was shining brighter.

Violet was up from the ground in a blink. Both attacked, hitting a target as they grunted, and pain extended through her extremities.

Nava knew she had little energy left. She had to get the other woman down one more time. She shifted her attention from the energy that ran through her body to the earth beneath her feet. Her power hummed with recognition of the natural magic around her, pulling energy from her surroundings instead, as Arkimedes had once told her.

Nava stepped back away from Violet. The brisk air burned her lungs. Her eyes snapped to the large tree roots by Violet's feet, thicker than her legs, and she imagined them moving, grabbing the woman, and holding her down.

The trees moved, and Violet gasped as thick roots lifted from the ground and shook the two women on their feet, making them lose their balance. Faster than she could imagine something so significant moving, the roots grabbed the slim figure of the warrior and pinned her down.

Everything went quiet except for the intense buzzing inside Nava's head. She stumbled forward to check if Violet was all right. Her face slacked in shock, facing the open sky that peeked over the tall branches of trees. Nava held her weight against the wood of a nearby tree. The noise around them became louder. Voices exclaimed, and the loud steps of people approached.

"A-are y-you all right?" Nava's words were slurred.

A genuine smile appeared on Violet's face. "Not so much a kitten," she groaned.

Nava leaned against the tree, closing her eyes

"I'm impressed, tiger."

Nava's lips twitched before her legs gave in. She was falling before it all went dark.

CHAPTER TWENTY-FOUR

Nava . . . Nava . . .

Her eyes fluttered open, burning from the brightness around her. She closed them again before letting them adjust as strong hands held her head, and her blurry vision focused on a familiar shape of a man.

"Welcome back," a soft voice said.

She focused on Gavin's face as it became clearer in front of her, his crooked smile more apparent.

"Thanks." Her voice was hoarse. "Water?"

Quick feet behind her and a canteen of water appeared. She drank as if water hadn't touched her lips in years. And she didn't stop until there wasn't a drop left.

"That was quite something you did, pinning Violet down with a tree—I had never seen that before," Gavin said.

"Is that judgment I hear?"

Gavin laughed, shaking his head. "On the contrary." His gaze came up, and she followed it toward Violet, who was standing nearby with her arms crossed, eyeing him with anger.

"Well, she's up now, so I'm going to make myself useful. Not all of us have the luxury of sleeping in the middle of the day," Violet snapped.

Nava didn't get to ask her if she was okay. The other woman had already stormed off.

"She is fine," Gavin reassured her. "The anger isn't directed at you."

Nava blinked. Understanding rang inside her head. Gavin and Arkimedes had left them to go on a mission and hadn't bothered to let them know. Her brow furrowed at the memory. "Arkimedes?" The word left her lips before she could stop it.

She turned her head, trying to find him among the people nearby. Gavin's hands left the back of her neck, and she pushed herself up with her elbows, muscles screaming in protest. She spotted him talking with Roman in the distance, not here checking on her.

"He is fine," Gavin said.

"I get it." Her bitter tone said more than her words.

"It makes me happy I'm not the only one in trouble." Gavin's voice was amused.

Nava eyed him, shaking her head. "It's not funny, Gavin."

"It's a little funny," he disagreed, and his hand came to her head again. She winced when his fingers grazed a susceptible spot. "You've got to stop injuring your head. It's not smart to pass out and fall straight on it. Every. Single. Time."

"I'll remember it the next time I lose consciousness—to make sure I don't hurt my head in the process."

"Your healer appreciates it."

Nava sat down. "Why did you leave without saying a word?"

Gavin put a vial of potion back into a leather pouch that hung from his side. "Not all of us have to go all the time," he said with a shrug. "I have my reasons not to tell Violet. The last time I asked her to come with me, we were kidnapped, held, and tortured for days. I'm sure Arkimedes has his reasons."

Nava frowned, and her mouth parted to refute, but she caught Arkimedes's approaching form. His tentative steps brought him over. Her eyes narrowed.

His hands dug inside his coat pockets. "How are you feeling?"

Had he come to check her when they arrived or had he been too busy to care before? How much of the whole thing had he seen?

"Never been better," she said, moving to get up. Ready to go back to her cabin and take a long warm bath to soothe her muscles. Maybe if he was so eager to distance himself from her, she should do the same. She was never one to pine and beg for attention. It was annoying her heart had decided to start now.

"Take it easy for the rest of the day. No more training." Gavin's voice broke the uncomfortable silence that had fallen in between them before he lifted to his feet. The man's hand landed on Arkimedes's shoulder, and they both shared a look of mutual understanding before the healer walked off, leaving her alone with him.

She winced, her muscles and sides protesting from the hits her body had taken during her sparring with Violet. Her head throbbed, still weakened by her display of magic from before.

"Do you need me to—"

"Don't say it," she snapped. "I can't believe you left this morning to find Devon's army with these people who hate you and conveniently forgot about me."

He shut up. More hurt than she cared, she pushed the knot that had formed in her throat down.

Her legs moved, anger driving her forward. She wanted to be out of there and away from Arkimedes. His steps followed. The temperature was colder today. The sun was hidden behind heavy rain clouds.

"It was early, and I thought it would be best for you to rest."

She turned around, and he almost ran her over. Nava poked the hard planes of his chest, raising her face to meet him with a challenge. "No, you felt I couldn't handle it."

His brows lowered into a deep furrow. "*Not* true. I wanted to protect you."

"Please. I'm not a child." She turned around. Nava spotted the cabin as raindrops started to fall, rustling the trees' leaves with the wind, first a slow pitter-patter and then thick, heavier drops.

She pushed the door and went inside but didn't bother to close it, aware he wasn't far away. She turned after the door locked. Arkimedes stood ruffled, his hair pointing in different directions.

It was clear they had left before he'd gotten much rest, if his tired face was anything to go by.

"It's dangerous. You have never been in something like what awaits us," Arkimedes rushed to say, taking wide strides straight to her.

"And you—"

"Yes, I have."

"Well, since you like to keep secrets from me, I barely know anything about you. What did you do before coming to this island? Why are you alone? Why do these people dislike you?"

Hurt flashed through his features, and he crossed his arms over his chest. "What do you want from me?"

"For you to tell me things!" she snapped. Groaning, she stepped around the living area.

"It's not a good story to tell. It's not nice to remember my family abandoned me and that I have spent my entire life being feared for something I don't understand! I don't know much of where I come from. The little I know, I don't like."

"I also did things I'm not proud of when I was trying to fit in. It's hard to find a moment to explain all of this when we are trying to survive."

Her ire softened a fraction, the fire burning in her veins dimming somehow. Arkimedes had told her he had been abandoned before, and when his magic presented, the orphanage had been eager to get rid of him. "I guess I understand," she said, but something kept nagging at her, scratching in the fog of her memories. "Why does everyone here say you are dangerous?"

Silence descended upon them. She shifted her weight around. He would not say anything of the matter. Disappointment took over.

"The magic that runs through me is dark and old. It comes from an fae bloodline in the Copper Kingdom." He shrugged. Judging by the tense set of his jaw, this was anything but trivial to him. "I stopped trying to find my origins a long time ago. I accept people will not trust me and that I'll never understand why."

Silence took over. The only noise around them was the heavy rain falling.

"How can they sense you are different?" She didn't understand.

Arkimedes's expression softened on her. "It's my aura. Unlike most people with magic, mine is always present."

Nava blinked, confused as she studied his body. Flesh and blood. "I don't understand. I don't see anything but you."

"Have you ever seen my aura before?"

She nodded. "Your magic aura is black. It's present when we are training. It's like mist."

His lips flattened, and his hand came over his head, brushing his hair out of his face. "Most people here can see it, even if I'm not using any magic. It's a curse on its own. It stirs fright in people, mistrust." He paced around for a while and stopped, his back straighter. "My magic works in sinister ways. It takes energy from people. Suppose I hurt someone. I kill, even if it's in self-defense. I absorb part of their power—of their souls."

Nava gasped, and her mind supplied a memory of the day he'd rescued her from Devon's army. The mist that had followed him around showed shadow arms and hands. Her skin went cold.

"You have seen it." He deflated.

"I—I think I have, the day the bounty hunters took me from our camp."

"Well, that's what they see of me all the time."

"Ark, I just see you," she admitted, swallowing. No wonder everyone feared him.

"I have been alone in this world since I was born, bee. You are one of the only people I have let get this close." And by his morphing expression, she couldn't tell if this pleased him or made him even more hesitant.

The sizzling of affection and trust surrounded them. They had been through so much already and had fought to protect each other. Had confided in one another—more so her than him, but still.

He walked past her toward the fireplace and leaned against the cold stone while he got lost in the dim embers, the fire coming to life.

The scent of magic surrounded her, and it didn't make her panic as it once had. Much had changed in such a short time, a life of prejudices shaken so. After so many weeks together, him using magic was as normal as breathing.

She remained quiet, allowing him time to come up with another slice of truth he would share with her. He would shut down if she pushed him too hard. He was afraid, but she didn't understand why.

His nature reminded her a little of her mother, and it made her pause. Her mother had always had a problem opening up. She'd liked to keep secrets, not saying anything when it could help.

Why did life keep making her care for people who were afraid to let others love them?

"Do they have reasons to fear you?" she asked, trying to focus on the present, to take advantage of the fact that even though she could sense he was close to closing himself off, he was still sharing.

Maybe leaving her behind today had made him feel guiltier than expected.

"Yes," he said. "Whatever is in my nature, it's not light. My thoughts sometimes are harsher than normal. I have an easier time making hard choices, but it doesn't mean I lack empathy, though."

Nava came one more step closer to him, giving in to the pull between them. She was close enough that her body touched his. Arkimedes's head dropped, his forehead pressing into hers. She had never been so close to him. The scent of cedar, leather, and the intoxicating smoke from a campfire enveloped her. She enjoyed the intimacy of it all as the air of his breath hit her face.

She forgot her insecurities.

You should pull away, her mind supplied, worrying Arkimedes would pull back once again, as he had done before.

Maybe this was magic-induced love, after all. No, not love—she couldn't go there with him.

"You don't have to be so afraid of letting people in, of letting *me* in. You won't lose me," she said and met his gaze. Her hand came to his face, and a spark of electricity ran from her fingertips.

Her body shook with anticipation, and she was drunk with desire, needing to explore his body with more than her thoughts.

She trailed her fingers across his face, over skin that was golden after traveling for so many weeks. He went still under her touch. She wasn't sure when she'd become this bold. Maybe she had always been.

Nava took a calming breath, waiting for him to pull back again. He stayed, his black lashes fluttering. His eyes opened, and without preamble, he kissed her.

It was unlike anything she'd ever experienced before, and it took her by surprise. Her body buzzed with awareness. Her skin raised in goose bumps when his lips demanded more of her.

A wave of desire crashed into her, pooling in the pit of her stomach and extending to her core. She wrapped her arms behind his neck as his skilled tongue caressed the bottom of her lip and his arms dropped to her hips, lower, resting on the curve of her ass.

She opened her mouth, meeting his tongue in a delicate dance as her hands held strands of his hair. He grunted in response and dove deeper into the kiss as he pulled her closer. She was burning up. Nava's fingers teased his hair, and she gasped when his hands grasped both her legs and lifted her off the ground.

Nava wrapped them around his hips. He was so close to where she wanted him. She let out a soft moan when the hard shape of his cock pressed against her. She straddled him as he walked blindly. Wherever was he taking her, she hoped it was somewhere horizontal and soft.

She rocked her hips, and they broke apart for a few seconds after he hit the side of a table. He was great at this. While Nava was not experienced, she had been kissed a few times before. None had caused her toes to curl and her desire to spike.

She gasped when her back touched the hard cold wall, and her stomach tightened. He pushed against her center. There were too many layers of clothes in between them. She traced her lips down the thick expanse of his throat, rejoicing in his taste and the soft sounds he made. His hands weren't idle as he pushed her coat off, and this time she was the one pushing against him, trying to calm her burning desire.

Her head thumped against the wall. Arkimedes took that as an invitation, and his teeth nipped her neck, sending shivers through her body. The way he pressed against her told her how he would move when he was inside her, and her blood burned hotter.

It wasn't lost on her that he could hold her body weight up while moving and not have to put her down. His strength made her hunger for him grow, and she moaned.

She pulled his shirt out of his trousers, an edge of desperation in her movements. The fabric was off his body, and her hands lost no time exploring his newly exposed skin.

Mine.

It made her pause. Arkimedes's lips trailed down her chest, his fingers unbuttoning her shirt.

She blinked. Desire pushed aside the random possessive thought that had crossed her mind. Her shirt pulled open, revealing the freckled skin of her chest, her breasts covered by a sheer layer of lace and thin cotton.

His lips traced feather-like kisses down her clavicle, down and down. She writhed against his hips, trying to no avail to bring him closer.

He stopped.

Nava stared down to find him paralyzed, his face a few inches away from where her soulmate mark was. Three circles that could have been confused for a birthmark to an untrained eye.

"Ark?" Her voice was small. She traced a few strands of hair out of his face, and he tensed.

He pulled away, and his hands came to her waist, making it easier for her to unwrap her legs' firm grip from around his hips.

She stood, shaking under her weight, and he was off her body as if she were on fire and it had burned him. "What's happening?" His reaction was making her self-conscious about her state of undress. She pulled her shirt closed, her brows furrowing.

"I can't." He shook his head.

She pressed her lips together. Her soulmate mark was visible, and suddenly, he wanted nothing to do with her. She guessed knowing it and seeing it made a difference.

She couldn't believe she had allowed herself to get pushed away *again*. She swallowed her anger, as it had formed a thick knot in her throat. *I guess you don't want me, after all.*

"It's not that."

Of course, her brain filter had failed to do its job once again, and she had spoken all those insecurities out loud because the situation wasn't mortifying enough as it was.

She didn't want his pity, and the way he was staring at her grated on her nerves. She clumsily closed the buttons of her shirt, aware of how much easier it had been for him to work them open than for her to close them. "Well, it feels that way." Hurt seeped into every word. "I would like to be alone." She stepped away from the wall with shaky legs, her vagina demanding something to happen. She had clearly not gotten the memo.

Not tonight, and not ever again.

"Bee," he pleaded as she walked past him toward the bathroom.

She appreciated that he didn't follow her or try to hold her back for a heart-to-heart. His self-preservation was not *that* lacking.

She slammed the door behind her and leaned against it. The kisses, hard and passionate, flashed through her mind, and she let herself slide to the floor. Her heart felt tight, as if it had been shrunken down after being so full.

Tears spilled down her cheeks. She hugged her legs and let herself think. Nava shouldn't be this upset. She had made it possible for him to hurt her this way. Arkimedes had told her from the beginning that he wasn't ready for this. She understood he had the right to change his mind. Maybe he didn't love her the way she did him.

Love—did she love him? She had never been in love before. It was the first time it had come so clearly that she allowed herself to admit her feelings.

He might be the one, her soulmate, hidden in plain sight. He had told her that he wasn't, and yet, she had still fallen.

Something in between a laugh and a cry escaped her lips. Leave it to her mother to play with her truth this way.

She didn't hear him leave.

So Nava allowed herself to cry over her broken heart on the cold stone floor of the washroom. The light of the fading afternoon seeped through the stained glass window in colorful speckles that slowly fell away as her heavy lids closed, giving way to the darkness of sleep.

Powerful arms carried her, and she nuzzled her nose against a chest that smelled like home. Nava was caught between reality and a dream, but she was being moved, the coolness of the surrounding room a clear contrast to the warmth of the body against her.

"Arkimedes?"

"Shh. Sleep." His voice was whisper-quiet enough that if she hadn't been so close to him, she would have missed it.

A soft feather-like kiss to her forehead and the heaviness of sleep pulled her under. She hadn't dreamed of him for so long. She'd almost forgotten what it felt like to be in his arms.

The arms of her soulmate.

CHAPTER TWENTY-FIVE

Knock. Knock.

Soft knocking woke her up. Nava blinked her sleep away, focusing on the pale gold-and-beige tones of the dry bamboo ceiling. Its imposing rustic wood beams held it up.

She had cried all her tears away the night before. The heaviness of her breathing reminded her that her heart had been shattered. Nava didn't understand why it had happened. Her raw and well-kissed lips, and the memory of how his body had responded to her, told her he had felt the connection like she did.

Knock. Knock.

She pulled the soft wool cover higher, trying to wrap herself in the comfort of the bed, so different from the cold hard floor in a sleeping bag. She sighed and enjoyed the feather mattress beneath her.

His scent lingered on her skin.

Nava sat up. How was she in bed? She racked her brain for memories and an explanation of how she had gotten here. The last thing she remembered was being on the washroom floor.

Had she sleepwalked? She guessed it wouldn't be the first time, according to Cameron. She had been known to walk to the kitchen in search of evening snacks.

Knock. Knock. Knock. Whoever was outside was getting impatient.

"Nava." Gavin's voice took her out of her sleepy musings, and she pushed the covers aside, swinging her legs out of the soft comforts of the bed to the floor.

She winced as the cold traveled through her body, and she rushed to the door on her tiptoes, combing a hand through her wild hair, surveying the state of her undress. She was wearing her indigo trousers and a lopsided shirt, none of the holes matching.

"Coming!" Nava brought her hands to the buttons and fixed them. She took a calming breath and put on her best forced smile.

The chill of the morning enveloped her, but the warmth that radiated from Gavin's smile was as contagious as ever. She found her smile grew when she met his gaze.

"You are hard to wake up." He inspected her ruffled state.

Her hand patted down her hair again. "Don't you have someone else to torment? Violet perhaps?" she said in a false snarky tone.

He shook his head, laughing. "Oh, no, I value my life too much to mess with Violet this early in the morning. Plus, she is pissed at me."

Maybe Nava was too soft. Had she been more rigid and taken longer to forgive Arkimedes for leaving her behind, she would have avoided the big mistake that was last night. "What brings you here?" she asked and opened the door to allow him to enter as she made her way to the washroom.

"Roman wants to speak with you," Gavin said, walking in with both hands shoved in his pockets. He was wearing a forest-green shirt and gray trousers, his face bright and rested.

"Please, make yourself comfortable. I need to freshen up." She pointed awkwardly to the door at the end of the narrow hall.

Gavin nodded, walking to the fireplace, a spot where Arkimedes had kissed her senseless the night before. She wished she didn't have to be reminded of it.

Nava found Gavin sitting in one of the leather armchairs, his legs crossed casually as he flipped through the same book Arkimedes had the day they arrived here.

"Ready?" He closed the book with a snap.

"He doesn't waste any time. Roman, I mean."

"We don't get town dwellers here, much less a magical one who brings us news of impending doom. One who comes accompanied not only by a powerful sorcerer, but one that seems to have a history with the Commander."

To her, Arkimedes being powerful was no secret. They had all seen him fight that morning when Devon held them captive. It made sense now that she was aware of his history, of what the others saw. "I would never lie about Devon coming. Arkimedes is powerful, but he wouldn't hurt you or the people in this village," Nava said, even though there was a piece of the puzzle she didn't have.

"I'm aware of that . . . now." He paused, sauntering out of the house.

The splendor of this village took her breath away once more. Buzzing with life in earth tones, the setting was beautiful. People of all shapes and sizes walked by her in colorful robes and tunics. Pointy ears. People with horns. Small children who seemed to have shadows following them around. The view would have been creepy, but the child was laughing.

Here in this village in the middle of the forest, magic didn't look like a curse, but something that brought life and joy. Her heart squeezed.

Why had her mother decided to live in a non-magical town when this was a possibility?

Well, had it not been for the name of her shop and her peculiar eyes, Devon Black wouldn't have found her. She begrudgingly gave her mom a point.

If it had not happened, she wouldn't have made it here to warn them about the threat. She wouldn't have learned about magic and her Beekeeper and . . . love.

"Roman doesn't trust your boy yet," Gavin said.

He was unaware of Nava's train of thoughts or the way she cringed at him calling Arkimedes hers. His words were a bucket of cold water to her senses. "He is not *my* anything, I told you."

"Does he know that?"

"Gavin, he's the one making it so." Nava shook her head. "His hot and cold is giving me— He doesn't want me."

Her brain supplied plenty of memories of Arkimedes pushing against her the night before, his groans and kisses. Nava pressed her lips into a thin line. Maybe he wanted her body, but there was something else preventing him from letting go, and the other side was stronger than whatever attraction he had for her.

Gavin stared at Nava with a raised brow. "I don't get it, and I'm a pretty good judge with these things."

They walked through roads of dirt, rocks, and pine needles. There were homes against and up trees as if suspended in the air. A street market, where people gathered and chatted vibrantly, bustled with activity. The smell of saffron, rosemary, and other spices wafted into the air. Wooden crates were filled with fruit and vegetables.

Dried meat and cheeses hung from tent roofs. The place was popping with life, and if Nava didn't focus on the different creatures surrounding them and the magic scent sparkling in the air, she could almost forget she was in a magic forest away from home.

She focused on a small creature inside a cage. It was scaled and small, painted in bright colors. Pink, teals, and blues. A Dragon?

"Yes, a young one," Gavin answered with a laugh. "I assume you have never been in a magical market before?"

She shook her head, pressing her lips together. Her mother had gone alone to the magical markets when they lived in the city, always leaving her behind with Laurie, and when Cameron had been born, he had also stayed. "My mother said it was dangerous for me to come, back when we were in the City of Iron."

Gavin nodded. "She was right."

"I have feared magic for so long, for it to cause despair and death. It shocks me to see it so alive."

"Magic can be both death and life. It's up to us to find the balance and to defend our freedom, to have the choice to do so."

Nava understood Gavin's words more than he knew.

"I was taken by the army, never to see my family again, until I was old enough to get a break. I was one of the luckier ones who got to stay with them longer. Most, like Violet, are taken when they are twelve years old, and then the training starts." His words matched his sad expression.

Nava stared horrified at Gavin. The Society of Crows took their members as children, but she had never heard of the army recruiting theirs so young.

"I found another family here amongst all these people after I escaped the kingdom with Violet."

"Did they make you do things you didn't want to?" she asked.

Gavin's face turned more severe, and his Adam's apple bobbed. "We were prisoners. We had to follow or face the consequences."

"Did they try to force you to wed? Violet and you, I mean," Nava asked.

"Aye, they did. The crown doesn't care about who you love, whether you are already with someone or have a soulmate. They will match you with another equal sorcerer or sorceress, and you have to procreate. They want to keep their army going."

A crawling sensation traveled down her spine. "You had a soulmate?"

Gavin raised a brow. "No, no. Soulmates are hard to come by, Nava—one in a million, they say. I was young, and I was lucky I had not found anyone at the time."

He kept talking, unaware of how she had stumbled on her feet, her throat going dry all at once. She was grateful she could avoid this prison and ungrateful because she didn't want her soulmate. Right?

"What happens if you are barren and can't have children?" she asked.

"Oh—they will cancel your marriage and arrange another union."

"Wow."

"Either way, it was better to join Violet on her crazy escapade than be murdered on our wedding night," he joked, and a breath of a laugh escaped his lips.

Nava shook her head, smiling. From both of their interactions, they had grown to care about, if not love, one another, so at least, even though they were forced, the crown had not ruined them. "I guess I felt like I was in prison as well," she admitted, remembering the long days inside their manor when she was fifteen, wanting to feel the sun, to make friends. "Except mine wasn't imposed by the king and queen's greed, but by my mother." It was the first time she had voiced it, and it shook her how bitter she sounded.

"Sometimes we do stupid shit for the people we love most," he said.

Both of them fell silent as they walked past the market to a quieter part of the village.

There was a large campfire and a long table with mixed food laid over it—cheese, crackers, dried meats, fruit, and bread. People walked around with bowls and plates, filling them with food and heading on their way to unknown places.

She spotted three large men speaking on the side of the campfire, their expressions solemn. Roman, Arkimedes, and the same guy Gavin had been speaking with the day of the celebration.

Her heart dropped when her gaze settled on Arkimedes. He was wearing new clothes, a black shirt, gray pants, and brown leather belts that held his enormous sword.

Nava's steps slowed when his eyes met hers across the way. She swallowed as the images from the night before came crashing down, and she cursed her vibrant memory and hurried to catch up to Gavin, who didn't seem to notice her falling behind.

Her heart hammered in her chest as they made their way to the three men. Arkimedes's arms dropped when she was but three meters from him.

"Good morning, Nava," Roman said, taking her out of her inner turmoil. His voice was a lot less tense than the day she'd arrived. Nava wished the passing days had brought her the same peace.

The night before, she had imagined sleeping deeply after a few hours of intense lovemaking, but that had been replaced by intense crying instead.

She slept well, and today at least, she was rested. It was more than she could say for Arkimedes. His expression was shuttered and tired. He had come here right after changing back to his human form.

"Morning," she responded to the Commander because the good part was debatable.

"Nava." Arkimedes's voice was a plea.

She wished he wasn't so ruggedly handsome with his fresh clothes and trimmed stubble. Her attention deviated to Roman.

"You called for me bright and early, so here I am." A forced smile tugged at her lips.

"Let's talk about Devon and his ship," Roman said.

Her cheeks warmed. She was afraid the information she had was lacking. "Uh, okay."

"We are trying to figure out the number of Devon's army. It's hard to tell what to prepare for by something so ambiguous," Roman started.

"I'm not sure I will be much help. I didn't see his ship—had intended to go and take a peek at a later date, but he came to my store, and I had to run." She shrugged. "He told me there were hundreds—but I didn't see it myself, so I'm not sure."

"You are right, that's not helpful at all," Roman said.

"Better than what you had a week ago." Arkimedes's voice was low and cold. "We could go and investigate again today, make it closer to their camp."

"We are not in the kingdom anymore. You do not call the shots." Roman's body had gone rigid with tension, his golden skin turning red.

These beasts of men couldn't wait to jump at each other's throats, and by the looks of it, they would get there before Devon even made it here.

Her money was on Arkimedes, if she were a gambler.

Her mind reeled back to Roman's words. Arkimedes had called the shots over the Commander, a high-ranking soldier in the army?

"Let's calm down. We aren't enemies here," the third man said, and Nava turned to him. His expression was gentle, his face was all sharp angles, and his caramel-colored hair was wavy and long. He was in his late thirties. Unlike the other men, this third guy didn't appear to be a trained fighter.

"I agree," Gavin said next to her.

Roman's gaze fell on the third man, and his own expression relaxed. He cleared his throat. "You are right, Mars."

Mars approached the Commander, and his hand came to his back, rubbing calming circles up and down, a smile on both their faces. She understood by their body language they weren't friends but lovers.

"If you want to do another round, I will send some men with you," Roman agreed, and Arkimedes nodded.

"Breakfast?" Gavin's voice startled her.

She nodded and was happy to be pulled away from that uncomfortable conversation. "Are the Commander and Mars together?" she asked when they were far enough from ears to reach.

Gavin chuckled. "Curious, aren't we? But yes, they are. The reason why Roman left the kingdom was because of their relationship, if I'm not mistaken. You could ask Mars. He is an open book."

"He doesn't look like you all. He looks . . . normal."

"Ouch, normal? Who wants to be normal?"

"I used to," she mumbled. "What I mean is he doesn't give me the soldier vibes."

"He is not. He was an actor in the city—a quite popular one at that. The girls used to flaunt themselves at him, or so he says." Gavin chuckled. "The kingdom forces us to marry but never listens to what you desire. Who you love. A man and a woman are forced to marry because they are after our children. We were all screwed."

When would this crazy world rebel against them and claim their freedom back? Nava hoped it was in their lifetime. Maybe Cameron would be free to visit the kingdoms and chose who to marry outside of the Greylands.

CHAPTER TWENTY-SIX

Nava filled her plate. Her stomach rumbled at the sight of the food. Bread, butter, and cheese. She gazed at Gavin as he put a healthy serving of honey on top of his bread. She took a deep breath to calm her uneasy stomach and filled her plate with it all, except for the honey.

"Comfort food today, eh?" Gavin commented, glancing at her plate.

"Oh, shush." She appreciated him. He wanted to cheer her up, and it was working. Distraction over food made her not be consumed by rejections or heart-melting kisses. Her eyes traveled to Arkimedes, who was sitting by the fire with Roman and Mars.

Violet had joined them, and the four of them seemed to be caught in a vibrant conversation. Judging by Arkimedes's frown, whatever the subject, it wasn't a pleasant one. A warm wave of protectiveness washed over her.

It didn't matter what had happened in between them. She didn't want him outnumbered by people who clearly mistrusted him. "We should go back there."

Gavin stared at the heated conversation with a curious expression.

They weren't sitting too far from the table of food. She walked around the fire and plunked down across from Arkimedes. She wanted to be there for him but not too close. She took an absent bite of her bread, and the salty flavor of butter dominated her palate.

It took her a minute to note the conversation had paused. She studied the group. Gavin was sipping on his steaming drink with a wondering expression. Roman was giving Violet a warning.

She focused on Arkimedes. He was sitting tenser than usual, his face troubled.

"So what? We're supposed to stop talking because Nava is here?" Violet snapped, and it was Nava's turn to straighten up. It was a miracle she had not choked on her food.

"Violet!" Roman's voice was a warning.

Arkimedes didn't flinch, his stormy green gaze coming up to meet Violet's with a cold, unmovable expression.

"What's happening?" Nava's gaze moved across the fire to Violet, who was scowling at Roman. It had been a while since she had seen that severe expression on her face.

"You two are here talking about how she doesn't know yet. She deserves to!"

"About what?" For once, she agreed with Violet, albeit blindly. She had the inclination it had to do with the secrets between her, Arkimedes, and whatever hostility these rebel sorcerers harvested toward him.

"It's not ours to tell. We don't have all the history," Roman warned.

"I want to know," Nava whispered.

Arkimedes's face turned into one of pure panic. Long gone was the calm, collected expression. His mouth opened as if to speak, and the knot in her throat became thicker.

Violet's voice interrupted the thick silence surrounding them. "He was sent to hunt us, over and over. Keep us under their shackles. Am I supposed to forget this?" she challenged Roman.

"Before two weeks ago, I had never met you in my life." Arkimedes answered this time, his voice matching the coolness of Violet's voice. "Last I checked, I saved your life from the ones who were keeping you prisoner."

Violet's lips pursed. If her stormy gaze could kill, Arkimedes would be dead. "You are all alike." Venom dripped from her words. "Breaking families apart, not caring that besides our magic, we are people."

"We are not servants of the crown," Arkimedes snapped. "The Society is meant to keep balance. We take on the task and teach magic. We defend innocent people. The crown and civilians are all subject to the law of life."

"Is that so? You are more focused on maintaining their armies, following their nonethical coupling rules—taking children away from their families," Violet hissed.

Arkimedes took a sharp breath, eyeing Nava, concern back on his features. Nava's brain was fighting to catch on. Society . . . ?

"We—they don't take children away. The Society only takes the ones who offered to join because it's an honor to serve our gods. But not everyone's intentions are good," Arkimedes agreed. "There is good, bad . . . and in-between. There are people in our—the Society who are fighting for people's rights."

"Yet here you are, cursed by a sorceress you chased down, and the Society of Crows is not tailing your whereabouts," Violet said. "This is because you are one of them. You leaving doesn't bring the same repercussions as *us* leaving does. We are hunted down like animals."

Nava tensed, her mouth as dry as sandpaper as she met his eyes across the fire. Nothing and no one was around them. The silence that descended was absolute. Her breathing was loud to her own ears.

She'd known it from the beginning. A fog lifted from her mind, taking her own stubborn denial. She focused on his lie, clear as day. At first, she had been doubtful her mother would ever send her straight to him, but Nava hadn't wanted to accept it as the days turned into weeks.

He was part of the Society of Crows, and in a flash, she could see him, behind the blueish tunics, his voice asking her if her mother was at home in a distant memory.

The earth shook beneath her, and she bunched the fabric of her coat in a fierce grip. She shook as adrenaline ran through her veins. Trying to discern the truth behind his tumultuous expression, to find something that would ground her, to tell her what she was conjuring in her mind was not true.

Even if he was a Crow, that didn't mean he had lied to her about being her soulmate, right?

No, she was doing it again, making excuses and trying to find other truths when reality was staring her straight in the face. It had ever since the beginning.

Regret, worry, and pain were etched on his face as his lips parted, his expression changing to one of pure panic as he realized she had put all the pieces together at last.

"Nava." He rushed to his feet, and absolute silence descended upon the group.

She stopped him with a raised hand, going over memories, things her mother had told her when they'd been escaping the kingdom. How afraid she had been because *he* had been chasing after them.

Him . . . the one Crow with the most power her mother had known. From that fateful afternoon, he'd turned her life upside down. Her mother had been afraid of him, of the darkness in his power. Arkimedes had revealed as much the night before, how people feared him for what he represented.

The magic of her *soulmate.* It made sense why she was not afraid of him. Why, even though everyone could focus on his aura, she could only see him.

"You are *him*," she murmured. Adrenaline pumped through her veins as she stumbled off the log she had been sitting on.

She tried to gain distance in between them. He was around the fire and over the log she had been sitting on. As he took slow steps toward her, his voice turned pleading. "No. *Yes*. Nava, please let me explain."

She could barely register the shapes of the rest of the group in the background. When had Roman stood up? Her mind was spinning, her hands shaking more as tears ran down her cheeks. "You *lied* to me."

"No. I . . . diverted," he said, and there was a ruffling sound around them.

She turned to Roman, who clung to the grip of his sword. The weapon meant nothing. All Arkimedes had to do was raise his hand and point it at the leader of this town for him to crumple down.

However, Arkimedes wouldn't hurt the man.

"Arkimedes." Roman's voice was filled with a warning.

"Stay out of this, Roman," Arkimedes seethed.

"You are my soulmate—all this time." Her voice shook with pent-up emotion. He was quiet, and his silence was all the confirmation she needed.

She had asked him before, and he had denied it. The answer had been there all along. In her mind, he was always the one, but each time she'd come close to admitting it, she had pushed that away, overlooking something so obvious. Like his voice, how easily she'd fallen in love with him when her entire life she'd had no connection or attraction to anyone.

Why would her mother send her straight to him? Her mother, the most aggravating person she'd ever known.

There was a gasp from around them, and both Nava and Arkimedes turned to face the others. The audience made her already clammy skin prickly with their stares. They were too close. Her clothes were too tight, suffocating her.

Roman dropped his sword back to its sheath and, with a quick nod, walked off without another word. His large hand grabbed Mars and pulled him along. Gavin followed behind, a bowl of food in his hand as he pushed a spoonful of eggs into his mouth, chewing like nothing else was awry.

Violet stood frozen, her features twisted in so much confusion.

"Violet!" Roman's stern voice shook her, and without another look back, she walked off.

Nava wrapped her arms across her stomach as a wave of dizziness ran through her body.

"Can we speak in private?"

She shook her head. Walking might not be an option for her with her trembling legs. "We are alone now."

"We are never alone in this forest." He came one step closer, and she took a step back, desperately putting distance in between them. "Please."

Her mind rushed through memories. All the rightness of his kiss. Was that even real? Was it all a magic trick? She wasn't sure anymore.

She turned on her heels and forced her body to move, numb as she walked the stone road toward the cabin that had been theirs for the past few days. He opened the door for her. She stepped into the home, flustered, unsure, and confused.

"Let me see it," she said in a biting tone, turning to face him.

"Bee . . ."

"Let me see it," she begged, her voice shaking with emotion.

He stared. "I don't think—"

"You owe it to me," she snapped, a wave of pure rage rushing through her.

He didn't move, his breathing hard, matching hers.

"Show me your mark, Arkimedes. "

His hand came to his chest, dabbing the center between his two pecs. She knew where it was located, a place she had so eagerly touched and kissed the night before. "Why? Would that change anything in between us?" he challenged, his expression shuttering.

"What is that? I don't know anything."

"How does this change anything of what you feel—what I feel?"

"And what is that?" she snapped. "You haven't said anything. I have been throwing myself at you since we met, unable to control this crazy attraction, while you knew all along why and you—"

"What? I didn't take advantage of you. At first, I didn't want this either, Nava. You might remember our conversation."

How could she forget? He had all but told her he didn't want her. Granted, at the time, she had said the same thing . . .

"Much like you, it was also a surprise to find a teenager who was meant to be mine. Before I even figured out what I felt, your mother was already taking you away."

"She was protecting us." Cameron and her.

"From whom?" Arkimedes lifted both hands in frustration. "From her selfish decisions? You are aware we cannot outrun fate. The mate bond will claim us whether we accept it or not. She doomed us both."

"You chased us down across towns, villages, and a whole freaking ocean!" she exclaimed.

"What would you have done? Little is known about soulmates and how it works, other than we are rare and that if we are apart from one another, the dreams will become our reality. If I were not at least close to you by approximation, I wouldn't have survived—neither would you."

"Well, maybe she was scared of you!"

"We already established everyone is scared of me, whether they have to be or not," he said. "She was not letting you decide anything. You were a prisoner in that house."

Nava wanted to refute this, but it was true. She had grown inside the four walls of her home without meeting anyone or anything else. Tears spilled down her cheeks. "I was just a kid. Not ready for a forever match," Nava whispered.

His face morphed into a pained expression. The words hurt him, she could tell. "I was twenty when I found you. Wouldn't say I was experienced and mature. Or ready for a forever match, either."

"She was afraid for me—of you, like all these people, Arkimedes."

"I was young and craving acceptance when she left the Society. She was not perfect, either. She was just as quick at hunting down people who broke the law." Arkimedes shook his head. "They told us lies, and I realize it now, after being away for this long, after meeting all the people who run from who I was."

"Why did she curse you?" She pressed her lips together after the words left her mouth.

"The spell the town has, it doesn't allow magical beasts to enter. As part fae, I was already pushing the limit. She threw in the curse to make sure I could not make it to you."

The conniving, brilliant mind of her mother would never cease to amaze and paralyze her with anger. "Did she tell you how to break your curse?" She knew by his conflicted expression that she would not like the answer.

"Yes."

"Arkimedes, out with it."

He hesitated. "Nava—"

"How do you break your curse?" she pressed.

"I'm supposed to do a selfless act for you," he said.

Silence descended upon them. Pieces came together in her head. Her mother had been mindful that she couldn't stay away from Arkimedes forever. It would eventually kill her.

"You accepting to help me, it was always to break the curse, not to save all these people?" Disappointment flooded her system. She stormed to him and pushed against his chest.

"No, I wanted to help these people. It's not only about us."

"It was always a lie! You never wanted to be with me, to help me. You have been lying to me all this time."

His face was tight and flushed. "At first, I didn't know you. I had been cursed for ten years. I wanted to be free of it. Don't mistake that for being the sole reason. I also wanted to keep you safe. Protecting you was always my primary goal."

"Somehow, I doubt it." The ground beneath her shook, and she wasn't aware if her emotions had been kicking magic around and she was causing another earthquake. "Why did you lie to me when I asked you if you were him?"

"I—I wasn't ready. I wanted to tell you. I was afraid you would pull away."

"If you are here in this village to be *selfless* and break your curse, congratulations, you brought me here. You can go."

"You don't have to do this."

"I don't want you here, and they don't want you here, either," she said, hoping the words would hurt him at least half as much as she hurt.

The memories of the first time she'd met him, *truly,* inundated her brain.

He winced and frowned. "I can't leave you. Devon is almost here. I can't go."

"Whatever. You can stay if you choose, but don't expect me to speak with you—and when this is all over, I will be going back to my town."

He paled. "It will be a death sentence to us both."

"What do you want from me? You lied. You have done all in your power to reject me when you could have been truthful. Yesterday you left me here, and you didn't consider telling me anything."

"It's not true. I held back yesterday because I did not want our first time to be like that. With a secret so large." He paused. "I've never desired anyone or anything as much as I do you."

She had wanted him. Ever since she met him, her dreams had always been of him. She'd held on to his voice, imagined how he would be. She'd never expected Arkimedes. He was too powerful, too handsome, and apparently too wicked, at least in his past.

She took a breath. Tears spilled down as her throat thickened with emotion. "You should have told me," she repeated.

"To have you run away when I had just found you?" he pleaded.

"Please go."

He hesitated, but Nava stayed where she was, her face unmoving as she pointed in the direction of the door. She was done with the conversation and with the lies. Her heart sank when he turned around and walked away from her.

CHAPTER TWENTY-SEVEN

Arkimedes did leave, but not permanently. When Nava went out during the evening for food, she learned from Gavin that he had gone with other sorcerers from the village to investigate how far away Devon's army was and gauge its size.

She took her food and excused herself home, or the home she had for the time being. She didn't eat much, hunger escaping her. The light in the room changed, and she didn't know how long she had been sitting in the leather chair, staring at the red embers of the rolling fire inside the fireplace, lost on the spot in between the gray tones of soot and the dancing flames in front of her.

It could have been an hour, maybe a day—perhaps two. Time was going slower than normal. By the ever-changing shadows across the room, its passage registered in her mind.

She woke up to dreams on and off, of dark gray trees and bloody feathers. Her chest burned with an intensity that made her eyes tear. She guessed the dreams were back, though these were different from what she was used to, full of despair and pain.

Nava wished she were not worried for him as the anger settled in her chest, but she would be lying, and she was going to try to be truthful with herself from now on. After all, nothing came from denying truths to oneself.

She had lost him before she'd ever had him, and who was to blame? Him, her mother, herself, their destiny? Even though her logical mind had let her do it, her heart rebelled against this development.

Nava never got a good glimpse of him in the dreams, and that was even worse. Seeing him again, though briefly during sleeping hours, allured her.

She had been so distracted by her developing love that she had never reflected on why she'd stopped dreaming of her soulmate. She had somehow convinced herself to not acknowledge him for what he was. It was so much clearer now that her actions were there for her to obsess over.

Getting to know him, fighting alongside him, fighting *for* him. A sob escaped her lips. The sound of the fire was too loud in her ears, the weight of her body too heavy. Her chest contracted.

"Well, this is even more depressing than I believed it would be, and believe me when I say I could conjure a pretty depressing image when it comes to you." Violet's voice made her jump in her spot. She was standing right beside her, her purple gaze studying her, and even though her words were snarky, her expression was soft.

Nava didn't care. Violet was the last person in the world she wanted. She narrowed her eyes. "Is there a reason you are here? If you're looking to feel better about your sorry existence, congratulations, mission accomplished. Now, leave me alone."

There was a pause, and Violet put down the tray filled with bread and soup that she had been holding onto the table next to Nava, but she didn't move to leave. "You are doing this to yourself, self-punishing. It's weird, coming from you."

"What does that even mean?" Nava's tone had a bite to it.

"It means he is your *soulmate*. What did you expect by rejecting him? That you were going to be fine after sending him away? You have given the both of you a death sentence."

"Why are you here?" Nava exclaimed, getting up from her seat, not wanting to hear this. Concern took over her. "And what do you mean, I rejected him?"

"Did you deny the bond?" she asked. "You have been pining after him for weeks. I don't understand what the big deal is about. So you have this gift, that it's real, and you send him on a mission when his head isn't right, to get captured or worse. Do you think what you're feeling is happening to you alone?"

"No." *Yes.* Her mouth went dry.

"Refusing your mate when you are already half bonded would mean certain death for the both of you," Violet said matter-of-factly.

"Half bonded . . . what are you even talking about? We haven't half bonded anything."

"Do you love him? Did you say it to him?"

Nava closed her lips before the next words came out of her mouth. Violet seemed to know something more, and she was at least sharing the information.

"From what I have studied, admitting the connection already sets the process in motion."

"I didn't say that I loved him, not out loud. He doesn't love me. He never said it."

Violet's brows furrowed. "Oh, god, you are even more stupid than I thought."

What the hell? "If you are trying to help me, which I'm not even sure that's your goal here, can you please stop insulting me?"

"Look, kitten, it's not a secret I don't like him. I have been running away from the Crows my entire life. I found out he was one recently. I obviously knew he was a Dark One. But having a soulmate, it's a gift from our gods."

"A gift?" Nava's voice echoed with anger or with sadness—she didn't know. "You have been claiming you want freedom, you want to choose your destiny, no? How is this different? I have no choice *but* to love him. I have no say in the matter."

"You have a say. How is it working for you?" Violet asked. "You were all about him before you knew who he was, so did a title change it for you? You have stopped caring for him?"

"No, of course not."

"So what then? You found out who your destined love is. God split one soul into two bodies for them to find each other. Someone most of us never get to have—is that so bad?"

Silence. Did knowing it was him change her mind? She loved him desperately. She always told herself she wouldn't trust this affection being true once she'd found him, but did it make a difference for her?

Her heart ached the same. Her desire for him was still there, untouched. She was angry, sure, but she had been angry with him before.

"When a child is born, a mother loves the baby. Most do, anyway. Nature dictates that for the preservation of *any* species. No one questions it because it's meant to be. Do you question a mother's undying love?"

"No." And for all the wrongs her mother had done, Nava had never questioned the woman's love for her and Cameron. Not ever.

All her decisions were making more sense to her.

"So, nature—the gods, it gave *you* that out of everyone."

"It's not the same. It's magic. Magic gave me this."

"And what is magic, if not our own nature? You have denied it to yourself for whatever stupid reason your brain has come up with. Don't get it wrong, Nava, you are blinded by ignorance."

Even though the words hurt and she wanted to ask Violet to leave once again, deep inside her brain, she got it. She had angrily sent him away, had abandoned him like she had promised she would never do.

Just like his family and the orphanage had done.

Her heart hammered as she lifted her gaze to the other woman.

"And there it is. She gets it."

"You seem to know a lot about soulmates," Nava commented.

Violet nodded and came to sit next to her by the fire. "When I was young, I was one of those who secretly hoped I would find mine." Her delicate brows came down. "Of course, that was silly. One in a million people might find theirs, and many times, they aren't matched."

"What do you mean?"

"I mean, even if they find each other, if one happens to be the wrong gender, non-magical, or the wrong species, the crown would void a soulmate bond over having a sorcerer for their army."

Like her parents, Nava thought, and the pain on Violet's face made her keenly aware of what her mother and father could have gone through had they chosen to follow orders.

"That world is not one for love, kitten," Violet said.

"Unless you end up falling for your assigned partner," Nava piped up.

Violet's attention fixed on her, a smile pulling at her thick lips. "Unless you fall for your assigned partner, eventually," she echoed, nodding, and they both shared a look of understanding. They didn't need to say more. Nava knew that, while it hadn't started as a love match, Violet loved Gavin.

VIOLET STAYED, AND THEY both ate in companionable silence. It was a first for the both of them to converse and not bicker.

When the sun came down, a blinding pain bloomed in Nava's chest. Her mark. She hissed, and her hand came to it. Her skin was hot to the touch.

"What's happening?" Violet's brow rose in questioning.

"I don't know." Nava rubbed the sensitive spot, and her heart stumbled. Something was wrong with Arkimedes. She got to her feet, a cold wave spreading through her. Nausea hit her hard.

"You are pale." Violet rose to her feet.

"Arkimedes is in trouble." Her gaze turned to the other woman. Her voice sounded panicked even to her own ears.

Violet's face sobered. "We can ask Roman where they went. I will go with you."

Nava probably said thank you or something of the sort, but she didn't remember anything as they exited her provisional home and walked the streets. Cold dread crawled inside her, clogging her throat.

Roman was giving orders to a couple of men by the plaza where she had danced what felt like ages ago. When his eyes locked on them, he dropped his hands and came to them.

"Where is Arkimedes?" Nava's words escaped her lips without preamble. Violet grabbed her elbow, and she wasn't aware she needed the support until it was there. Why was she so panicked? Her throat closed in. Her mind provided images of gray trees and bloody feathers.

Something was very wrong. She could sense it.

"He hasn't returned." Roman focused on Violet. "None of my men have. What's going on?"

"Something is wrong, Roman. I can sense it. My—" She hesitated but pushed forward. "My mark aches, and I have had dreams. Something happened." No one in their right mind would believe her.

Roman's jaw clenched. "They were going southeast, retaking the path we traveled before."

So she was wrong. They did believe her. They believed and cherished soulmates, she realized, remembering how all four of them had walked off when she'd revealed Arkimedes was hers. She guessed they'd understood why he was here trying to protect everyone. He had something larger to lose.

As panicked as she was about something hurting him, she had time to figure out how furious she was with him once he was safe and sound. Her mind was supplying another set of questions of how she could get to him when a bee landed on her hand.

Her stomach dropped, and she got the message: it was a warning sent not by the insect but by a powerful old creature that was somehow linked to her.

Something bad was going to happen here.

Nava turned to Violet, grasping the thin shoulders of the woman. "He is here, " Nava said, and Violet followed another couple of bees.

"What's going on?" Roman demanded.

"I have to go to Arkimedes," Nava said with urgency. She had not walked even two steps when thunder boomed in the air, and heavy rain fell out of nowhere.

Her heart contracted, and panic came upon her. It wasn't the rain scaring her, but the fact that seven bees landed on her arms. She remembered how Devon had called in a storm when they'd been his prisoners. She studied her surroundings, paralyzed, with her feet glued to the wet, muddy soil.

"He *is* here," Violet said in an icy voice. She also remembered.

"What? Who?" Roman looked around the place, on high alert.

"Devon Black. He can control the rain." Violet's words were louder, and Roman took a step back. Urgency took over his battle-worn features before he took off running. "Go now," Violet said, pushing her by her shoulder. Gray tendrils of magic emanated from her body, and a couple of bees landed on Nava's chest. Violet's face was void of any color. "I can't come with you. You have to find him—we *need* him."

"But . . ." She needed Violet. How was she to travel in the forest on her own?

"Find your soulmate and come back! He is stronger than any of us and knows how to fight Devon. The small army Devon has with him might be held back for a bit. We are families here. Not many warriors."

Nava nodded, and her hand came to the top of her mark. The dread in the pit of her stomach grew.

With the third boom of thunder, the start of screams filled the humid air, along with the loud hissing sound of magic and fire. Both Violet and Nava ran as sorcerers and fae rushed in for cover, pulling children along with them. Nava chased after Violet.

A couple of soldiers loomed in the distance, wearing black and gray tunics. Smoke raised over a house next to a tree. Their hands were covered in blue flames that rolled near their skin, their faces covered by their hoods.

These were not the Society of Crows. These were the army of the Kingdom of Iron, formed mostly by sorcerers. Violet was right. They needed Arkimedes to help whatever chance they had of defeating them.

"Go!" Violet said to her before she ran in another direction.

Nava pulled out one of her blades and ran as fast as she could, her steps faltering as soldiers appeared behind a cloud of mist in front of her. Their attention fixed on her, and her blade wouldn't be enough.

She was no longer shocked by the prickling of her magic awakening. After training day after day, the sensation was familiar.

The energy of her nature. She focused on the large trees that surrounded this town. The long, knotty branches twirled, thick with age and memories, the earth beneath their feet, and the energy coursed through her body as anger pushed her forward. The trees groaned, and the branches lifted from the earth, pulling chunks of dirt with them.

Nava didn't overthink that she was able to sense nature this way. It was not the first time she had moved the earth or commanded the trees. If she thought about it, she had always had a connection with plants. Her hands always focused in the garden.

The soldiers ran toward her, unaware of the movement beneath their feet. Still, blue flames raised from their hands. The men lost their balance as the ground shook. Her energy soared as she took some from her environment.

She had to persevere to get to Arkimedes. They yelled as branches shot to them, pinning them to the ground with a heavy thump.

Nava didn't stick around to see how hurt they were. She jumped over the large branches and the hidden boots beneath them, the buzzing of bees around her becoming stronger, and her soulmate mark seared her skin.

Was it true she was somehow connected to him already and the mark was telling her this?

Panic flooded her veins, and another fire of motivation lit within her as she pushed forward. Her boots made a wet sound in the mud. The whizzing sound of magic and the screams grew stronger.

People's cries pierced her ears, and she almost stopped. The heavy knot in her stomach intensified. The rain was falling harder, but it didn't stop the blue fire from burning the Northern Village's treehouses.

She dodged a blinding light coming for her, her own heart hammering with adrenaline. Her lungs burned with the heavy intake of cold air.

The secondary white light hit her straight on the back, sending her tumbling down onto a pile of mushy leaves. Blistering pain extended through her back where she had been hit. Her vision blurred as a cry escaped her lips.

She dug her hands into the soft mud, and bees landed all around her as she rolled on the ground, putting out the fire that scorched her tunic. She did not let the panic or the intense burning pain slow her down as she tried to get up, but she slipped on the wet ground. Steps came close as she struggled to gain speed before falling again.

Heavy hands pulled her hair up as she yelped in pain and met the gaze of a man in dark gray clothes.

"This is the one, the one with the blue and brown eyes." He pulled her up to her feet by her hair. Her scalp burned.

Her hands grasped his arms and she thrashed, trying to kick. One of his fists met the side of her face, making her vision blur. She tasted the tangy flavor of blood on her tongue and knew her teeth had cut her mouth by the intense blow.

"This one?" The other man came closer, his eyes raking down her body. "I can see the appeal. Maybe the Crow wants to have some fun before the trials."

Nava tried to push against them, panic rising in her body. The grip on her hair tightened before another hand wrapped around her throat.

"We can have our fun before he gets her." The man leered, and bile rose in Nava's throat.

Her body went limp as she waited for the moment he believed she was losing her grit and loosened his grip on her, so she could make her move.

It came sooner than she expected. His hand loosened just a touch, and she smacked her head back with all her strength and heard the loud crack of his nose breaking. Warm liquid fell over the skin of her neck.

"You bitch!" he screamed.

Pain radiated through her scalp and neck. A breath escaped her lips.

"Maybe he doesn't want her alive. I would enjoy killing her."

She was going to die today. Panic rushed through her body. The surrounding screams matched the ones inside her. Tears ran down her cheeks, and the freckled face of Cameron came to mind.

"No, Tiberius, we have our orders. He would have our heads on a pike if we killed her. He is keen on bringing her, along with the one we captured yesterday."

Her blood chilled, her movements freezing. There was one person Devon Black would obsess over who wasn't her—Arkimedes.

She stared at the one talking. His dark skin peeked through his gray hood.

His rotten breath made her want to retch the contents of her stomach. He stepped closer. A mocking smile appeared on his features. "Have you met a fae with brown hair and darkness that follows him? The Crow insisted we set a trap for him."

"She knows the bastard," Tiberius hissed, and he squeezed Nava's throat tighter. "Did he make you feel good, sweetheart?"

They had Arkimedes. They had hurt him. The bloody feathers, the gray trees. Her fear was pushed down by anger.

She focused on the man in front of her, and she imagined him being swarmed by bees. The sky darkened as bees made of light appeared everywhere, furiously swarming the thinner man with the gray hood and rotten breath.

His screams were loud and pained, and the hand holding her neck lost a bit of its grip as Tiberius shrieked his friend's name. She didn't care to listen to it. The screams died down in front of them as he fell onto the ground, a pile of swollen meat.

She used the distraction to move and grabbed the hilt of her dagger. She pushed with all her strength out of Tiberius's grasp, took her blade out swiftly, and stabbed him.

Her eyes bore into his until the light behind them vacated and his heavy body fell to the ground.

Warm blood had splattered her shaky hands. One second, she was standing surrounded by swarming bees, and the next, she was emptying the contents of her stomach onto the ground next to the bodies of the men she had *killed*.

CHAPTER TWENTY-EIGHT

Nava moved through the forest at a quick pace. The sound of the attack fell behind, her ears drumming in the quietness that surrounded her.

Her breaths came out of her lips in pants. She didn't slow down, however. She was exhausted but not as she usually was after a display of magic like she had just performed. She was learning to take some energy from her surroundings—the skill was yet to be mastered in so little time.

When they'd traveled this forest, she never imagined her way home would be racing to her soulmate. She guessed it made sense.

Arkimedes had become one of the most important people in her life when he stepped in her manor that fateful summer day. Her mark throbbed, and Nava knew somehow deep within her stomach that she was going the right way.

The bees still swarmed around her, following or leading, she didn't know. It was unclear when they had become one entity with her.

It had been wet and humid in the Northern Village when the storm had hit them. Her steps were loud with the crunching of dry leaves and sticks. Between trees, the poking shapes of tents appeared in the background. Smoke billowed out of a campfire, and her steps slowed down until she was walking. She made sure the trees covered her.

The bees followed suit, landing on top of the bark and crawling over her hands and face, on top of her coat. Branches moved over her, and her gaze lifted to find the shape of the Beekeeper.

It was staring at the campsite, ten feet up in the air, its twig fingers gripping the tree. The Beekeeper had been with her the entire time.

Nava swallowed. Her shaking hands pulled the hood of her tunic up, covering her wild, wavy hair. She took a couple of deep breaths to calm her breathing and heart rate.

Crouching down closer to the ground, she strolled behind the trees. No one had spotted her yet. The campground wasn't empty, as a few soldiers seemed to have stayed behind. A couple by the fire, talking calmly, not expecting anyone to come here.

Nava peered over the brush she was hiding behind and counted two by the fire. She stared at a couple who walked and talked in low voices. She focused on a particular tent. One guard stood by the door, arms crossed over his chest.

It had to be where Arkimedes was. She hid behind the bush, and her attention came back up to the Beekeeper. His brows morphed into a concerned expression, but it didn't move or tell her to stop this suicidal quest.

"I don't have a choice." She swallowed the thick knot that had formed inside her throat.

Her body was yelling at her to get in there and save Arkimedes, stat. Every cell in her blood was angry that she had sent him away to come here on his own.

Tears pricked as guilt invaded her.

She was not strong enough to battle five men on her own, especially ones who were sorcerers—better trained in both magic and combat. Devon had left them all behind to guard one powerful prisoner.

She studied her surroundings, making sure they did not see her. She had the element of surprise. She was not alone, and she was angry.

Nava let it wash over her and tasted her magic as it coursed through her veins. She studied the areas where she could hide.

If Nava were to get to the tent without being noticed, she had to make sure the walking soldiers were on the other end of the camp. Then she could take care of the one guarding Arkimedes's tent.

Her mind supplied that she would die today, but she would do so trying to save her soulmate, and that was a good way to go.

Nava willed her steps to be light as a feather. Power rushed through her body, and her feet were weightless on the ground.

Her palms were clammy as she came closer. She unsheathed one of her daggers and took a calming breath. The two soldiers on foot were almost out of sight as she walked between tents, making her body as small as she could. She moved quickly behind the next one.

Nava's power hummed through her veins. Her hand gripped her weapon tighter. She had to catch the guard by surprise. She focused on his back.

It smelled like mud, body odor, and tobacco in here. The soldier was unaware of her proximity. She was about to pounce on him when bees landed on the yellow-stained canvas of the tent by her, making her pause.

A muffled voice came from inside the tent. The tent flaps moved and revealed a man she knew. He was thin and tall, his cloak swallowing his body. Andreas Mortimer, Arkimedes's friend.

His face still sported the same smile she had seen that morning when they shared stories. Once, she had thought that smile to be friendly, curious, but in this new light, it was a wicked pull of loose skin.

He was massaging his red-stained fist as he came close to the guard. Her stomach rolled. "The prisoner is incapacitated. As promised, he won't be giving you grief at the moment. Can I go?" His voice was easygoing, like it had been that night she'd first met him.

Nava's eyes narrowed, heat rushing through her body as her hands went clammy.

The soldier nodded, grunting something Nava couldn't understand.

"The gold?" Mort inquired.

"Martin has it."

Her mind built a puzzle that told her with blaring awareness that Mortimer had betrayed Arkimedes.

"I will go to him then and be on my merry way." Mort dug his hands inside his pockets before walking with his limp and a cheerful whistle.

"Did you say goodbye to your friend?" The guard's voice dripped with sarcasm.

Mortimer smiled as he turned to face the guard. Wicked large teeth appeared behind thin lips. In the light of the day, tiredness drew his face, and he was not as lively or healthy as he had been. "I try not to befriend faes, much less a Dark One, my man. They are evil creatures, you see. They will snuff your magic away from you." Mort snapped his fingers. "Like that."

The guard shook his head, muttering something under his breath, and the absurdity of the situation hit her. The sense of betrayal was bitter on her tongue. Arkimedes deserved better.

She took advantage of the guard who followed the retreating form of Mortimer as she ran to him, her steps no heavier than the wind, and she brought her blade up, hitting him in the back of the skull with all of her strength.

The crack of bones shattering rumbled, and her hand shook with the impact of the hit. Blood stained the bottom of her dagger's pommel, and the man crumpled to the ground as a heavy, unconscious mass.

Blood splattered the skin of her fingers, still warm against the cold air of the afternoon. Acid churned in her empty stomach again. Nausea hit her fast, and her body grew cold and shaky.

She cleaned her hand against the cloth of her tunic before reaching the door of the tent. It was made of rough canvas, dirty with age and wear. Inside was dark and musty, but she could see the shape of a man tied to a pole in the center.

Arkimedes's head lifted, and when his eyes met hers, they widened in shock.

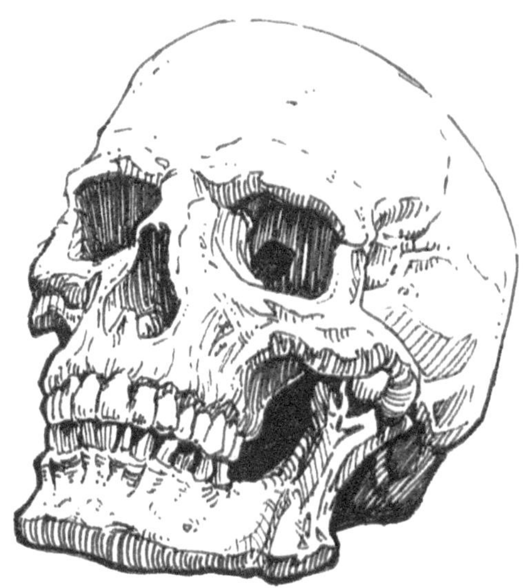

CHAPTER TWENTY-NINE

They had tied a dirty rag in between Arkimedes's lips. Gashes and blood marked his face. One of his eyebrows was swollen and discolored, and a heavy cut on his brow was still dripping blood from a recent hit.

Nava grabbed the guard by the shoulders and dragged him inside, making sure he was fully covered, and ran to Arkimedes, kneeling in front of him. She dropped her dagger as her trembling hand pulled down the cloth in his mouth.

"I'm going to get you out of here," she whispered, guilt tinting her every word. Her fingertips lingered close to his eye. The blood underneath was sticky and cold. His skin no longer held the healthy glow she was used to.

Nava didn't linger. She got up and walked behind him, pulling out her second dagger and slicing through the ropes wrapped around his arms. His body slumped forward, a pained sound escaping his lips. She caught him before he toppled over. His skin burned like hot coals, and he was too heavy.

Her arms shook from the strain, but she willed her body to be strong, holding him with one arm as she pushed the ropes away from his body. Touching them made her energy drain. She had felt these before, the same ropes they had used on her.

"Go." His voice was a weak, muffled sound.

"What?"

"You—have got to go," he pleaded, his parched lips pressing into a thin line.

"No." *Never.*

"Nava, I can't . . ."

She paused as something wet seeped through the fabric of his shirt. She gasped in horror as she stared at her blood-stained hand. Their gazes met, and her resolution grew. Long gone was her weak stomach. No longer was she afraid.

"Who did this?"

His face lowered. "Andreas."

Of course, it had been that sleazy snake. Nava wished she had brought her potions with her, but she had left them all inside her backpack. Her world closed in on her, but the desperation extending through her body came to a halt.

Nava didn't need to have her backpack here. She could call on the potions with her magic like she had done before. She closed her eyes and pictured the exact spot in the cabin she had left it. She could almost smell the fire around the village.

She focused her attention on the olive-colored canvas of her bag and the pocket where she kept her potions, the same ones she had used to cure the Beekeeper. She pictured them and willed them to come to her. Her skin heated as energy coursed through her veins again.

"Please," she murmured, and the cold glass vials appeared in her open palms. A wave of exhaustion reached into her, but she refused to let it take her.

She opened both bottles, holding them as she lifted the fabric of Arkimedes's shirt. A deep gash was right below his rib cage. Deep crimson blood dripped down from it. "Can you lean over?" Her voice shook at the end, and she pressed her hand to his shoulder.

He did as she asked, his arm braced against the ground. His body shook as she poured the liquid over the wound and placed her hand firmly over it.

How did she do it with the Beekeeper? She needed Arkimedes to be healthy. She needed this wound to heal faster. Her fingertips tingled as her skin warmed, and white light shone in between their skins.

His gaze met hers before tilting down to examine what she was doing, his features illuminated by the brightness of her magic.

"Bee—" His voice held a tone of reverence.

She pushed the second vial to his chest. "Drink this, please."

Arkimedes eyed the potion before emptying it in his mouth. His brows knitted together. "Let the record show I drank one of your potions." His lips pulled up into a grin that disappeared as steps came closer. Both of their eyes snapped to the entrance of the tent.

"Igor, where did you go?" said a male voice with a heavy accent, the shadow of his shape coming closer to the tent.

Nava stood, holding her dagger with white knuckles. Before the person finished pushing the flap open, Nava pounced. Anger fueled her movements. She sliced through the chest of the soldier, who screamed and fell backward. She stumbled out of the tent, her face snapping up to the sound of men running to her.

She grabbed her second dagger from the floor and straightened. No, she wasn't as trained as these men, but she was much angrier.

Arkimedes's wounds flashed through her mind, and she jumped, the memory giving her an edge of strength. The earth shook, and the men lost their footing, gasping as the tree roots lifted from the ground with a clamor, and some of the large lower branches swung.

They dove out of the way, screaming, and Nava got closer, unafraid of the branches, as they were avoiding her.

The tree branch hit one of them hard and caught him by the stomach, and the man's eyes went blank before losing consciousness. The tree swung him through the air and across the field.

The other soldier lowered his long sword on her, and she met his with one of her blades. Her muscles shook with the power of the strike. His blade was blazing, making her wince as her weapon lit up.

She pulled back. Her skin sizzled while she focused on the soldier. His own power rose around him as a light gray aura. She brought her other blade across and sliced his arm. He gasped, and she barely dodged his long sword.

Nava's shoulders slumped, her body aching in places they hadn't since the beginning of her journey. Her energy was nearly depleted. The rest of the guards were coming closer and closer.

"There is no way you can win, bitch," the man snarled.

Her lips curled, and waves of energy came to her, out of every pine needle, leaf, and bark. The strength in her body soared. She wished the forest would help her again, and the trees cracked. The man's attention darted around, trying to find the direction of the attack. She took advantage of this, ignoring the upcoming steps, and attacked him.

She jumped high and brought down both of her daggers in succession across his chest. Blood stained his cloak, and his hand dropped his weapon, coming to hold his chest before he too fell.

Nava turned to the upcoming men. She had used too much power in too little time and with no rest. Her vision blurred, but she willed herself to keep going.

A spell hit her and sent her flying back. The pain scalded her skin, and her bones shook inside of her, aching through her body. She cried, her palms sore from the burn and the rough landing.

The sorcerer's steps were slow as he approached. A sneer painted his weathered face, and his hands lit up as energy swirled around his fingers, then a tree fell on him with a bone-crushing crack.

Nava gasped, pushing away from the fallen tree and the dead man under it. Branches and leaves stuck everywhere. Her heart stuttered at the vision. The second guard screamed as the Beekeeper landed on the ground. It was tall and slim, its sharp teeth twisting in a ferocious snarl.

A swarm of bees came around him and straight to the retreating body of the last sorcerer. His screams of pain echoed in the clearing as the bees caught up to him.

Nava lifted to her feet and ran to the creature, studying his face, making sure he was all right. His gaze fixed behind her shoulder.

Arkimedes was coming out of the tent. His body slumped, his skin green and pale, almost getting lost against the fabric behind him. His hand pressed to his side, and he was turning around, trying to find her in the chaos. She was walking to him before her head caught up to the fact that she had not died.

She wrapped her arms around him, careful not to do it too tightly. Arkimedes's chin rested on top of her head. His hand landed on her lower back, bringing her closer. The heat of his touch seeped through the cloth of her coat. His hands and body were feverish.

"Are you hurt?" he asked.

She shook her head, ignoring the pain around her body. "Mortimer is still out there." She glanced from side to side, trying to find the dark cloak between the sea of yellowed stained tents.

Arkimedes left out a forceful breath. "He doesn't stick around."

Her hand trailed up his arm soothingly. "Devon attacked the village. Violet said you might be their only chance—"

"They put too much faith in my power." Arkimedes groaned, clenching his jaw. "We have to go and help them."

"Shouldn't you rest? You are hurt."

He straightened, his brows meeting in the middle. "I will rest when we are there. We can't stay here, not knowing if sentinels will come back. I don't want you alone when I turn into a bird at night."

It was irrational to expect that he could rest when heading into war. Nava guessed at least this way it was somehow on their terms. "I'm sorry this happened to you, Ark. I shouldn't have told you to leave. It was selfish and . . . Had I not pushed you away—which I had every reason to do, by the way—you might have been less distracted, and maybe Mortimer wouldn't have double-crossed you—"

His lips came crashing onto hers in a short, hard kiss. "I am the one who has to apologize," he said, his face hovering near hers. "I shouldn't have kept that from you. I hope you can forgive me."

Nava's fingers came to his cheek. "We can take it one step at a time once this whole mess is over. "

"Thank you."

"You are still in trouble," she said, but the heat had escaped her body when she realized Devon had taken him. She was happy he was alive and free.

"I know." His expression softened. His lips came down on hers again in a slower kiss that made her skin tingle.

The sound of steps broke the moment. They focused on the Beekeeper. He poked one of the dead men on the ground with his long fingers.

"We have to go."

"Are you fine to head back into battle? You don't look too good."

"I have been better," he admitted with a grimace, his eyes flashing to her, and a smirk brightened his features. "Your potion is surprisingly effective. Who knew?"

"He did," Nava quipped, pointing to the Beekeeper, who had straightened and was staring at them with curious intent. "What about Mortimer?"

"Andreas is halfway to your town by now." Arkimedes studied the surroundings, but the only sound around them was that of the crackling campfire.

"What happened to him?"

Arkimedes shrugged. "Andreas came to us yesterday when we were setting camp. He said he was coming to meet us in the village. He was happy to find me alone and was curious as to what had happened to you." He shook his head, pinching his lips. "I didn't think of anything because he had met you. It seemed natural for him to be curious. I mentioned you had stayed back at the village."

Nava ached for him. "There is nothing wrong with trusting someone you thought was a friend."

"It doesn't feel like that, Nava," he said, and his voice shook. "It's like I led Devon straight to you."

"How would you have anticipated Mortimer working with Devon? How did that even happen?"

"Andreas told me Devon had made him an offer he could not refuse. Right as he stabbed me."

"What a piece of ogre shite."

Arkimedes's chest rumbled, and his lips parted with a laugh.

Her lips pulled up into a half-smile. "Should we be worried about him?"

"He is not a fighter. The reason he got to me was I trusted him enough to drink some of the wine he offered."

Nava had not been incorrect not to want to eat Mortimer's apple that one morning.

"He killed Roman's guys. They were good people, out here trying to protect their families." Arkimedes lowered his gaze as he walked up the hill stiffly. "Devon counted on me trusting Andreas enough and was waiting for me. He always knew I had a weakness for my friends."

Nava's chest ached as anger took over her. "Well, Devon's weakness was being a cocky bastard. He misjudged that I would come and save you."

"Thank you."

"Not too shabby of a soulmate you got yourself. Who knew?" She smiled as he turned his head and studied her features.

"I did."

Her cheeks warmed as Nava and Arkimedes edged over a well-traveled path toward the village. She slowed when Arkimedes paused, his face morphing with pain as he took a deep breath and leaned on the side of a tree. They needed to rest, for Arkimedes to find time to regain some energy and allow her potion to heal him.

"I have meant to ask you about your past. Now that I know who you are, you might share more?"

"There is one way to find out."

She nodded and took a deep breath, steadying herself. "If the orphanage sold you to the Crows when you were five, where does the name Valeron come from? Do they have anything to do with you?"

Arkimedes dropped his gaze, his jaw tightening. "The Valerons crave power. They want to be feared. Brody, my adopted father, wanted to be able to brag about my skills being in his family."

"So . . . they weren't a family to you?"

"I was no more than a showpiece. They expected me to attend celebrations, dress to impress, and speak little."

"Well, you being quiet wouldn't have been difficult for you. It's hard to get you talking."

He huffed a shadow of a laugh. "Do you want to know or not? You curious creature."

"I do."

"They made it clear behind closed doors that I was no more than an abandoned hybrid. They mean *nothing* to me."

"I'm sorry, Ark." She stepped closer to him, wishing she could somehow make up for that sense of abandonment that loomed over him.

His fingers caressed the side of her cheek. "You have nothing to be sorry for. It brought me here to you."

She smiled. "I guess that's true. What about the B?"

"The B?"

"Yes, on the sword, it said Arkimedes B. Valeron."

"Oh. It stands for Black."

Nava gasped. "Black, as in Devon *Black*?"

Arkimedes's cheeks flushed. "We were like brothers. In the Society, they assign you a partner. He was mine since we were twelve."

That would explain why both of them had shown up at her house that afternoon.

"So you decided to make a last name and share it?"

"I couldn't tell you before that we had been close. We had no surnames in the Society. At some point, we decided we would be each other's family." Arkimedes shrugged. "When the Valerons forced their way into my life, I kept Black as a defiance."

"It makes sense why Devon said you were very dear to him." Nava leveled Arkimedes with a glare. "You have got to stop with these secrets. Your *brother* had you stabbed."

"Sometimes it is hard to open up," he admitted. "Especially when everyone I trust—"

"Stabs you in the back?" she offered.

"Yes." He took a deep breath and held her hand. "I get that's not you, but give me time, Nava. I promise I will give you everything."

"Okay. Like I said, we can go slow. I think we both need it."

His eyes lowered to her neck and his brow dipped. "What's this?" he growled, and the touch of his rough fingertips lingered on the sore spot of her neck, where Tiberius had choked her.

"Oh, on my way here, two soldiers got a hold of me." Her hand came up to his. Her stomach dropped as she remembered their dead bodies on the muddy ground of the village.

She was not going to be sick again today.

"Did you kill them?" He knew the answer already by studying whatever was painted on her face. "War is not easy. The first person you take will haunt you for a while, but the fact that you did this in self-defense will help you keep up with the guilt," he said in a gentle tone, and his finger caressed her bruised skin.

It did make it better somehow. Her hands were still soiled by blood, and she had changed so drastically today she might never be the same.

"I'm here if you need to talk."

"Thank you," she said back, and they stayed there resting for a while before they continued up the hill and toward the village.

SOCIETY OF CROWS

CHAPTER THIRTY

By the time Nava and Arkimedes made it to the village, the whole place was a mess of smoke and fire. The laments of people were a whisper in the air, not loud enough to discern if it was the howling of the wind or the cries of war.

Nava and Arkimedes held back behind the trees, trying to get a hold on what was happening. Her eyes burned from the smoky fog that lifted from the earth. The sun was fading behind the trees. Her attention deviated to Arkimedes, and they had little time left before he turned back into a crow.

"They don't know I'm cursed," he said. "I might be able to use this to our advantage and get closer to their camp that way."

"They shot you when you were one."

His brow deepened. "Yes, I guess that's true. I'll still get close."

She nodded and swallowed. "How were you able to avoid it last night while you were a prisoner?"

"The ropes. It cancels magic—even the curse." He shrugged. "The first time I haven't been a bird at night in nine years."

"Not the most rewarding way," she murmured.

"I could think of better ways," he agreed.

Even though it was clear he didn't mean anything sexual, Nava's mind went there. The wave of warmth that ran through her took over her senses.

She also could think of a couple of things she would rather do with him during the night. Nava should be too angry with him for that to be a possibility. She was embarrassed about her evident lack of control with her hormones.

As he read her expression, Arkimedes's pupils took over his irises, and she could tell that his hunger for her was present.

"I can't tell what to do," Nava admitted after clearing her throat. She hoped Gavin and Violet were safe. The village wasn't as small as she had once thought. Housing hundreds of sorcerers and fae. She guessed even with Violet's urging, they would have held them back for a day.

They waited as the sun dipped down lower, and the time for them to be apart grew near. She had never witnessed him turn before.

Arkimedes's voice filled the quiet space. "I'm going to fly over to get a sense of what's happening."

She nodded, for once not finding words—the idea of separating not appeasing the nerves that had surged through her. "You are injured. I'm extra concerned about how that will affect your transformation."

He swallowed, and his head tipped back. He studied the night sky behind smoky clouds. Time extended, and they both waited and waited, and nothing happened.

Nothing happened.

She blinked and studied him as the darkness enveloped them. He was here, in his human form.

Arkimedes's expression lit with understanding. He lifted both of his arms, inspecting his body with a frown. "What's happening?"

Her hand came eagerly and grasped his coat. Walking around his body, she focused on the large planes of his muscular shoulders and his handsome face.

"Is the curse broken?" she questioned in a voice that was almost too small.

He swallowed and dropped his arms, grabbing each side of his coat, opening it and inspecting his stomach and legs. "I don't understand." A smile pulled his lips. "I don't know."

"But why? How?" Nava's mind went back to what had happened, trying to find an answer that would explain what had lifted the curse. Had it been because Arkimedes had urged her to leave him behind and save herself? Or maybe it was another layer her sneaky mother had set to the curse, her forgiving him?

She doubted her mom had thought that through, but maybe it had something to do with them being in mortal danger and choosing each other?

They stayed in silence for a while longer, waiting for the curse to settle, but it never happened.

Arkimedes let go of a breath. "I still have to go. Devon won't expect me—

since they think I'm a prisoner. The smoke and the night will be a good cover." He studied the trees and the quiet buildings by their hiding spot.

Nava pressed her lips together, holding back her comment. She had no better ideas, and walking into the village without knowing what to expect was reckless. Arkimedes's expression softened when he noticed the worry that etched her features.

He brought his hand to her face and caressed the side of her cheek, smoothing the crinkle that appeared over her nose. She jumped at the touch.

"You don't have to worry."

"Promise me you will be back."

His expression faltered, and she understood it was not something he could guarantee. He came closer, and his lips landed on her forehead. She enjoyed the softness of his touch, her breathing shaking.

"*This* is something I have done before," he said instead as he pulled away, his face changing to one of stern determination.

The wind that came from the reappearance of his wings whipped her hair around, and she took in the magnificent shapes of them.

She would never get used to them because they were fantastic and something she had only seen in books. She reached to them, caressing the edge of one particular feather and the soft hairs that formed its shape, smooth like velvet under her touch.

She swallowed when his darkened eyes met hers. He had cleaned the blood from his forehead earlier in the afternoon, but his right eye was swollen and bruised.

"Don't move from here."

She studied the wings as they flapped with ease, sending leaves and stones back. His face morphed as his brows knitted. Before Nava could say a word, he flew away, a flurry of dark mist following closely behind.

Nava heard a whimper and turned around to find the face of the Beekeeper. He was holding on to a tree, his gaze following the retreating shape of Arkimedes. She could sense his distress toward her soulmate, and her hand came to the spot on her chest where her mark lay.

Come back to me.

The soft pant of the creature was the only response in the quiet evening. He landed next to her with a thump.

"I'm worried too," she mumbled.

The creature didn't say a word but stayed right next to her. Bees buzzed around both of them as if it were the most natural thing in the world.

Once upon a time, the vision of a swarm of bees would have petrified her.

Even one little winged bug would have made her cautious of its sting. But her feelings had morphed to one of strange care and admiration.

Nava took a moment to stare at the bee creature. "I'm confused about us, about our link," she said, and his eyes bore into her. "Are we somehow connected?"

Even though it could talk inside her head, the creature said no words. It seemed to reserve speech for life-and-death situations. She was disappointed about being in the dark once again. The creature nodded.

"Because I saved you?"

He looked at her, and Nava knew deep within her that wasn't it.

"Was it my magic that bound us?"

He shook his head.

Nava's lips parted in shock. "No?"

"Destiny binds us." His voice came inside her mind, and the bees around them stopped flying. Some landed on trees nearby. Some went into the beehive on top of the Beekeeper's head.

Nava's fingers came to her lips as she held a breath. "What do you mean, destiny?"

"My name is Aristaeus, but you might call me Ari, dear one. Alongside you, I am the keeper of the bees. We keep the forests alive." His voice was louder in her mind. Their eyes connected.

What could this mean?

"There are always two Beekeepers in the forests. Never has a human been one of us. But the gods decided we needed you to defeat our enemies."

Their enemies? Which enemies? Devon?

Ari shook his head, reading her mind.

"The ones who killed the other Beekeeper?"

Ari nodded, and his brows, or what could be his brows, dropped. *"We are bound together to protect the world from the Zorren, demons that come to our dimension, seeking destruction."*

Her lips parted as his words caught up in her brain. The gods wouldn't tie her to two people.

Aristaeus tilted his head as if it had read her thoughts, and it amused him. She could *almost* sense his laughter. She didn't find the situation funny at all.

"I already have a soulmate, Ari!" she said sternly, shaking her head.

"We are not soulmates, dear one. We are companions. Arkimedes, your soulmate, is our protector."

"What?" she breathed.

Ari's branch-like fingers came to her and touched the mark on her chest.

Her eyes dropped down to it. Her skin sizzled under his touch—magic awakening.

"Three circles. Three of us."

CHAPTER THIRTY-ONE

Her eyes came to Aristaeus's chest, and Nava gasped when noticing that in the texture of his torso, three circles made a flower.

Her soulmate mark.

Out of all the strange shit that had happened to her since she'd left home that fateful morning, this had to be the strangest one. "I don't understand."

"The day we met was set in motion, not by chance. It put me in your path, and it called Arkimedes to us."

Her lips parted, and her mind filled in the gaps. Yes, of course. Arkimedes had been near her and Ari, something calling to him. Their marks. She hadn't known how to travel the forest, but she had found her way to them.

Something landed next to them, and both of their heads snapped to the newcomer. The wind tossed her hair back as she focused on the shape of her soulmate.

Arkimedes lifted his handsome face to meet her gaze, his full height imposing. His wings disappeared behind his back. His turbulent green gaze traveled from Nava to Ari next to her.

If he thought it was weird that the Beekeeper was around, he didn't say a word about it. Maybe he could feel the connection between the three of them.

"Is everything all right?" he asked. He was reading her tense pose.

She nodded, curious how he would react when she told him their insane destiny. It would have to be a conversation for another time, however, so she kept the secret burned in her mind.

"What did you find?"

Arkimedes's head snapped around the place, as if he expected something awry. His brow dipped. "You are acting odd."

Nava shook her head and forced a smile. "I'll tell you later. The war situation is more pressing."

Arkimedes's gaze cut to Ari. "Devon and his army have taken prisoners. Some of the fae didn't make it. It seems the Iron Crown isn't interested in them."

Almathea and the fae who had served her the beer at the party flashed in her mind as well, and a heavy knot settled in her chest.

"The rest have barricaded themselves in the west side. Their wards are strong. I did see some of Devon's sorcerers attacking them. They might have until nightfall tomorrow."

Nava's brows creased. "Gavin and Violet?"

"I was too far," he admitted. "We can go around and reach Roman's people from behind. None of Devon's soldiers had made it there, and we will be safer inside their warded shield than here."

She nodded. Exhaustion peeked around the corner of her brain. Her stomach grumbled with hunger, and she was aware she was pushing her body too hard. Nava wasn't sure how she had managed to endure all she had with an empty stomach, then Aristaeus's presence scratched the back of her mind, and she had borrowed someone's energy, after all.

They were the same. Keepers of the bees and the forests helped each other, as their safety was imperative.

She would protect Ari and the bees the best she could and would learn whatever knowledge he needed to teach her to do so.

"How is your injury?" Nava said, reaching to her soulmate. She pulled the side of his coat open and studied his shirt, searching for any possible traces of blood from his wound. It was clear.

"Sore," he admitted. "I need to rest. I won't be able to get too far like this."

"Would it be safe to stay in one of these vacant houses?" she asked.

"Safe is not the word I would use." He focused across the trees and on the homes in front. "It might be better than walking around the dark forest without energy and with the spirits on the hunt."

Right, the spirits and the constant haunting.

Ari made a rough sound that came from the back of his throat. It seemed he was not happy with either option. It wasn't like Nava or Arkimedes could climb a tree and blend in, though.

"We will have to stay in one of these homes tonight. Get some rest and depart west before sunrise. Devon and his people don't know what

"It was always a lie! You never wanted to be with me, to help me. You have been lying to me all this time."

His face was tight and flushed. "At first, I didn't know you. I had been cursed for ten years. I wanted to be free of it. Don't mistake that for being the sole reason. I also wanted to keep you safe. Protecting you was always my primary goal."

"Somehow, I doubt it." The ground beneath her shook, and she wasn't aware if her emotions had been kicking magic around and she was causing another earthquake. "Why did you lie to me when I asked you if you were him?"

"I—I wasn't ready. I wanted to tell you. I was afraid you would pull away."

"If you are here in this village to be *selfless* and break your curse, congratulations, you brought me here. You can go."

"You don't have to do this."

"I don't want you here, and they don't want you here, either," she said, hoping the words would hurt him at least half as much as she hurt.

The memories of the first time she'd met him, *truly,* inundated her brain.

He winced and frowned. "I can't leave you. Devon is almost here. I can't go."

"Whatever. You can stay if you choose, but don't expect me to speak with you—and when this is all over, I will be going back to my town."

He paled. "It will be a death sentence to us both."

"What do you want from me? You lied. You have done all in your power to reject me when you could have been truthful. Yesterday you left me here, and you didn't consider telling me anything."

"It's not true. I held back yesterday because I did not want our first time to be like that. With a secret so large." He paused. "I've never desired anyone or anything as much as I do you."

She had wanted him. Ever since she met him, her dreams had always been of him. She'd held on to his voice, imagined how he would be. She'd never expected Arkimedes. He was too powerful, too handsome, and apparently too wicked, at least in his past.

She took a breath. Tears spilled down as her throat thickened with emotion. "You should have told me," she repeated.

"To have you run away when I had just found you?" he pleaded.

"Please go."

He hesitated, but Nava stayed where she was, her face unmoving as she pointed in the direction of the door. She was done with the conversation and with the lies. Her heart sank when he turned around and walked away from her.

CHAPTER TWENTY-SEVEN

Arkimedes did leave, but not permanently. When Nava went out during the evening for food, she learned from Gavin that he had gone with other sorcerers from the village to investigate how far away Devon's army was and gauge its size.

She took her food and excused herself home, or the home she had for the time being. She didn't eat much, hunger escaping her. The light in the room changed, and she didn't know how long she had been sitting in the leather chair, staring at the red embers of the rolling fire inside the fireplace, lost on the spot in between the gray tones of soot and the dancing flames in front of her.

It could have been an hour, maybe a day—perhaps two. Time was going slower than normal. By the ever-changing shadows across the room, its passage registered in her mind.

She woke up to dreams on and off, of dark gray trees and bloody feathers. Her chest burned with an intensity that made her eyes tear. She guessed the dreams were back, though these were different from what she was used to, full of despair and pain.

Nava wished she were not worried for him as the anger settled in her chest, but she would be lying, and she was going to try to be truthful with herself from now on. After all, nothing came from denying truths to oneself.

She had lost him before she'd ever had him, and who was to blame? Him, her mother, herself, their destiny? Even though her logical mind had let her do it, her heart rebelled against this development.

Nava never got a good glimpse of him in the dreams, and that was even worse. Seeing him again, though briefly during sleeping hours, allured her.

She had been so distracted by her developing love that she had never reflected on why she'd stopped dreaming of her soulmate. She had somehow convinced herself to not acknowledge him for what he was. It was so much clearer now that her actions were there for her to obsess over.

Getting to know him, fighting alongside him, fighting *for* him. A sob escaped her lips. The sound of the fire was too loud in her ears, the weight of her body too heavy. Her chest contracted.

"Well, this is even more depressing than I believed it would be, and believe me when I say I could conjure a pretty depressing image when it comes to you." Violet's voice made her jump in her spot. She was standing right beside her, her purple gaze studying her, and even though her words were snarky, her expression was soft.

Nava didn't care. Violet was the last person in the world she wanted. She narrowed her eyes. "Is there a reason you are here? If you're looking to feel better about your sorry existence, congratulations, mission accomplished. Now, leave me alone."

There was a pause, and Violet put down the tray filled with bread and soup that she had been holding onto the table next to Nava, but she didn't move to leave. "You are doing this to yourself, self-punishing. It's weird, coming from you."

"What does that even mean?" Nava's tone had a bite to it.

"It means he is your *soulmate*. What did you expect by rejecting him? That you were going to be fine after sending him away? You have given the both of you a death sentence."

"Why are you here?" Nava exclaimed, getting up from her seat, not wanting to hear this. Concern took over her. "And what do you mean, I rejected him?"

"Did you deny the bond?" she asked. "You have been pining after him for weeks. I don't understand what the big deal is about. So you have this gift, that it's real, and you send him on a mission when his head isn't right, to get captured or worse. Do you think what you're feeling is happening to you alone?"

"No." *Yes.* Her mouth went dry.

"Refusing your mate when you are already half bonded would mean certain death for the both of you," Violet said matter-of-factly.

"Half bonded . . . what are you even talking about? We haven't half bonded anything."

"Do you love him? Did you say it to him?"

happened in his other campsite, and from the looks of it, this side of town was hit earlier and is empty," he said, walking to her and reaching for her hand.

Nava wanted to protest about invading someone's home, but her body was too tired to be able to do much else today. She found herself nodding, and they both walked across a ghost town.

What once had been roads filled with laughter and children were empty, with rubble and debris polluting the streets. Most buildings were charred and smelled like soot and death.

Scorch marks went up half of the length of the trees. Nava walked behind Arkimedes, scanning the place and avoiding anything that appeared like it had once been a human.

This peaceful village in the middle of the forest had been destroyed by greed. Why wouldn't they let these people go? Why kill faes? Why kidnap children and take their parents for trials that surely would end in executions?

Her heart slowed down to a painful beat that cried for this destruction, the dark side of human greed. Her mother had warned her about the horrible sight. She had been so angry with her mother before. For once, she understood why she'd gone to such depths to keep them safe.

"Wait here." Arkimedes went inside a particular home, one that was less affected by the destruction of Devon's army.

Ari was walking next to Nava, his eyes shaped in horror as he also took in the forest's destruction. The cold, dreary air chilled her to her bones.

Arkimedes scanned the area and, with a silent signal, told her this was where they would stay for the night.

The home was dark and messy. Someone had left in a hurry, leaving everything behind in their wake. The dining table, a small rustic-looking thing, was still set for breakfast. The food had long gone cold. Even with her previous hunger, her stomach revolted at the sight.

"We will be safe here," he told her in a soft voice. "I will walk the perimeter to make sure there are no soldiers around and will set wards so we can rest."

"Arkimedes, I fear you forget you were stabbed and are *injured*. Maybe it's smart for you to take it easy," she said. "Maybe I can do something?"

"Do you know how to set wards?" he asked, raising a brow.

"No need to be a smart-ass about it," she grumbled, crossing her arms over her chest.

He took a deep breath and walked a couple of steps to her. "I *need* to do this. It will guarantee your safety."

"Maybe I want your safety, as well."

He mimicked her stance as a frown darkened his features. "I won't go far,

but it needs to happen. I'm aware this is hard for you, bee. But I am feeling better."

She understood Arkimedes's reasoning, even though it crushed her spirit not to be able to help. Her attention went around the room, and she noticed their Beekeeper wasn't around.

"Where did Ari go?" she whispered.

Arkimedes lifted one brow. "Ari?"

"Yes, Aristaeus. The Beekeeper," she explained.

His face changed from a brief amusement to confusion. "You know his name? Did it talk to you?"

She nodded, gripping her hands together to keep them from fidgeting. She avoided his curious gaze. "He did—" She took a deep breath and knew the truth was about to spill from her lips. "He also told me we three are bound together."

Arkimedes held his breath, his eyes widening. "What?"

"Maybe you should sit down."

"Out with it, Nava."

"How to say this . . ." And not ramble? "Ari has our mark."

Arkimedes's back straightened, and his whole body stilled.

She swallowed. "He said I'm one of the Beekeepers and that you are our protector."

He shook his head. "No."

"Ari also said his—*our* enemies, the Zorren, whatever they are, have been coming to our dimension more and more."

His complexion paled. "The demons of destruction?" Well, at least he knew what they were. He reached for her. "Nava, little is known of the Zorren or the Beekeepers. I don't like this."

"Same with soulmates, yet here we are."

His lips pinched. "He has our mark?"

She nodded. "Ari said the three circles represented the three of us."

"Why don't I have the connection, then? Why can't I call the bees like you? It makes no sense. Does this mean we aren't soulmates?" His voice came a bit louder, his skin turning red.

"Oh, no, we are soulmates all right. He said we aren't his soulmate. However, our destinies bound us. Me being a Beekeeper, you being our protector."

He growled. "No."

"I don't understand, either. The day I left town, he said we called one another. I met him—he was in my path, and so were you. Did something call you that day?"

His brows lifted. "Yes."

Her lips pursed together. "Maybe we'll focus on this when this whole Devon war blows over?"

Arkimedes's jaw was tense. His breath shook. "I will be right back." He stepped out into ash-covered streets. Nava could listen to the laments of people around in the distance.

She forced her eyes away from the door. Tears pricked as the intensity of the horror hit her. It shook her to her core, and her hands muffled a cry. She hoped no children had been captured with all her might, however unlikely.

Mother was right. Right for protecting her at all costs to save her from this destiny—but instead of being a victim, maybe she would've been the one inflicting the punishment.

CHAPTER THIRTY-TWO

There was a large brown sofa surrounded by a stone fireplace and a wooden table with books neatly piled together on top. Nava's gaze traveled up to a loft area above. A mattress lay on the floor with piled linen sheets and wool covers. She dragged her feet, trying not to disturb the things that made this someone's home.

Her focus came to the kitchen, and hunger became too strong to ignore any longer, so she begrudgingly walked there and opened the cabinets in search of something they could eat.

She was finding bread, dry meat, and cheese. She made a platter with these and chopped an apple into quarters. Every creak and whisper of the wind made her heart jump.

Her muscles shook with tired spasms that screamed exhaustion. Her eyelids were heavy. These past few weeks, she had pushed her body to the limit again and again. Nava had grown stronger. Her previous soft curves had trimmed and now showed the apparent shadow of muscle under her skin.

She was used to being hungry by now. However, she hadn't eaten anything since this morning with Violet, and she had thrown up most, if not all, of her food right after.

Magic, constant running, and panic had led her to complete and utter exhaustion. Her back was still sore from the times the spells had hit her and burned her skin. She didn't even want to check that.

Moans filled the air, carrying haunted undertones that could have been the

Neems in the forest but weren't. Her vision blurred as tears accumulated, and she took another shaky breath.

Arkimedes came in the door, a large shape of muscle and strength. His gaze raised from the floor to meet hers, and the normal healthy glow in his skin was gone. His complexion was pale, and his frame slumped unlike how he usually held himself. He closed the door shut behind him, and Nava kept busy as she watched his familiar body move around the home, closing blinds and curtains.

His breath billowed out in front of his lips. It was cold inside the home. He approached her, his attention going straight to the food as she removed her daggers from her belt and placed them on top of the table.

She studied her fingers that were marked with dirt and dried blood, and her stomach churned.

Nava went into the bathroom, and the whole day's events caught up to her. She held her body against the bathroom sink, trying to keep the food she had just consumed inside.

She met her reflection in the mirror in front of her. Brown dried blood and dirt marked her skin, and her hair was a mess of tangled brown waves. She turned on the faucet and splashed icy water on her face, scrubbing it clean. Her breath shook as the images of the men she'd killed flashed through her memories. A sob escaped her lips, and a deep cry overtook her body.

Nava hadn't locked the door and didn't see Arkimedes come in until his hand touched her back. She straightened and met his eyes before crashing her face into his chest and breathing him in. Never again would she take a moment like this for granted.

He wrapped his arms around her body and buried his face in the crook of her neck. Neither of them said a word.

"I killed them, all of them," she mumbled.

"Shh, Nava. If you hadn't, they would have done worse." He held her back, grasped her chin, and lifted her head. "War is not easy. I wished you hadn't had to experience it."

"I thought I had lost you."

"I'm here now." A side smile appeared. "We should get some rest. Tomorrow will be a long day."

He pulled her out of the bathroom in silence. Both of them were aware they had to be extra quiet not to call any unwanted attention if someone was walking outside. Nava focused on the loft and the only bed available. Her cheeks burned hot, and she swallowed, avoiding his eyes.

It was silly to be getting nervous about sharing a bed with her soulmate after it had been a fantasy of hers ever since she'd met him. Especially considering how exhausted she was. Yet her mind was not tired enough not to go there. She studied his profile in the darkness.

His jaw was tense as he also took in the bed. "I can sleep on the couch."

She shook her head. "Aren't we past that?"

His lips tilted up in a whisper of a smile. "Are we?"

Memories of their kiss in the last cabin flooded her mind, and her blood lit within. "Yes, we are," she said, resolution settling in her stomach. Nava climbed the steps that took her up to the loft, managing to calm her breathing and shaking hands.

If they were to be taken as prisoners or die tomorrow, she was at least going to enjoy this last night of peace with him.

It took Arkimedes some time to come upstairs. She couldn't see much in the blackness of the room, but she noticed he was fidgeting. Arkimedes was not the nervous type who held back. He was the one who stormed in. For as long as they had been traveling together, this was the first night they had to share one another.

She kicked her shoes off, removed her dirty coat, and got in between the sheets. She followed his movements as he imitated her and then his gaze raked down her body. The mattress dipped as he got settled next to her, his large frame occupying most of the bed.

He stayed over the covers, and she found herself annoyed at his gentlemanly behavior and endeared by it at the same time. She cuddled the pillow, closing her eyes, and her body sank into the soft mattress beneath as sleep reached in.

"Good night, bee," he said.

"G'night." And she was out.

CHAPTER THIRTY-THREE

"Nava, wake up. It's a nightmare." A heavy hand shook her shoulder as Nava teetered on the edge in between consciousness and the nightmare that held her.

Her eyes opened quickly, blinking away the daze, barely needing any time to adjust to the darkness of the room.

"You are fine." The voice appeased her nerves, allowing the weight of her body to sink back into the soft mattress beneath.

Arkimedes was leaning over her, the hard planes of his chest touching her shoulder. The warm air of his breath caressed her face. Her breathing calmed, her mind becoming more lucid. The clutches of the nightmare had lost their hold.

Her gaze traveled to her soulmate's, meeting eyes that shone with green shades and illuminated the room, like something magical she had never seen before. The beauty of them was hypnotizing.

Nava's hand came to his face, the pads of her fingers going over the rough texture of his scruff. His beard had grown in these past few days. She allowed herself to enjoy the feeling of him near her, of being alive and free. The distance between them was too large.

Her teeth caught her lip, and a wave of warmth ran through her body, her hands tingling.

Arkimedes's fingers pulled her lip from the rough ministrations of her teeth. "Nava . . ."

The room didn't feel as cold anymore, his heated gaze warming her.

"What?" Her hands traveled down, caressing the skin of his neck and down his chest, stopping where his mark lay.

His expression shuttered. "We need rest. This is making it harder for me to keep my hands off you."

"I don't want to sleep. I want *you.*" She was shocked she'd said those words out loud.

A breath caught in her throat before his lips crashed down onto hers with barely contained desire. Energy crackled in the kiss, and an awareness ran through them with the knowledge that this was more than either of them had experienced before.

Nava understood that coming together would forever change them, even if the extent of how much was uncharted territory. Arkimedes's tongue swiped across her lips, and she pushed off the blankets that covered her body in an attempt to be rid of an extra layer that separated them.

He deepened the kiss as her hands fumbled over his shirt's buttons. She groaned in frustration, her fingers stiff and uncoordinated.

Arkimedes's hand skimmed over her clothes tentatively. His fingers were reaching down to where her shirt gapped. His soft caress of the sensitive skin on her chest made her warm and wet.

His lips abandoned hers, traveling across her face, down her jaw, and to her neck. Her wanting hands pulled his shirt out of his pants and settled against the exposed skin of his lower back.

They rolled in bed, and he was over her. She sank into the mattress as he finished opening her shirt, and his lips followed a trail to the newly exposed skin. Her body quivered as soon as his kisses met the raised skin of her soulmate mark.

The intensity of what ran through her took the air out of her lungs . . . Heat traveled through her body in waves and settled in her core. She spread her legs open to allow him to come closer, finding him hard and wanting.

His fingers came around to her back, working the strings of silk ribbon that tied her bustier to her chest. Her breasts came out as the loosened piece of clothing sagged. His fiery gaze raked over her body, making her squirm.

He was kissing her again, making her forget the wave of insecurity that had taken over her thoughts. It wasn't enough. The feel of his hand over her breasts, his fingers raking over her hardened nipples . . . She needed *more*. To find relief somehow for the ache that lit her with desire.

He groaned and rolled against her, relieving some of the pressure in their aching bodies. His tongue stroked a path over her chest and drew a nipple into his mouth, sucking.

With a held breath, she grasped the edge of his pants, her finger dipping behind the fabric and reaching down as she ached for more of him but was a bit too nervous about committing a whole handful.

He pushed his hips up, craving more of her attention. A soft moan shaped his lips as her hand reached in after such encouragement. The space between his clothing and the heated skin of his hard member barely gave her enough room to move.

He rocked into her hand before his lips captured hers with urgency, his own hands coming to the clasp of her trousers, having a much easier time getting through them than she had with his. She lifted her hips as he pushed her pants down her legs. The cold air of the room collided with her feverish skin, raising goose bumps along the way. He pulled away from her to his knees.

A complaint formed on her lips, but before the words entirely left her, the hungry look in his expression intensified as his eyes raked down upon her newly exposed skin. His hands came to his pants, and she focused on the way he unbuttoned and pushed them down along with his underpants.

His whole length sprang out, and *oh, wow.*

"Big boy," she breathed out, and her cheeks heated. Had she said that *out loud?*

Mortification hit her hard, and her stomach turned with embarrassment. Why did her brain-to-mouth filter fail her so? She covered her face, and Arkimedes's hand pulled it aside. He seemed to find it funny or possibly endearing, if the sappy smile that stretched across his lips was anything to go by.

He finished taking off his shirt and was gloriously naked on top of her. She ached all over, wanting to touch and taste all of him. His lips traveled the side of her ribs and down her body.

Nava squirmed, and a laugh escaped her lips. He grinned against her skin, sending a wave of gooseflesh along the expanse of her body. His expression lit up with amusement as he proceeded south.

"That tickles," she huffed, and he rewarded her with the most beautiful smile she had ever beheld.

"It will be worth it." His voice was deep.

Her insides fluttered as he proceeded with his ministrations. She grew more nervous, and as his lips reached the top of her underwear, she swallowed the thick knot that had formed in her throat. What followed next shocked her system. His lips crashed over her sensitive center, over the thin cotton fabric of her clothing. A moan escaped as pleasure exploded through her.

Her hips bucked under him, and soon his hand landed on top of her navel, pinning her to the mattress. As he continued down her thighs with open-mouthed kisses and a trail of his tongue, his stubble burned the sensitive skin of her thighs, and they would be red in the morning.

It was as if he wanted to taste every inch of her skin, and the feeling was new and scary.

She had been intimate with one person in her life before this, a stupid mistake when trying to prove to herself that she didn't need to wait for her soulmate to have fun, to enjoy the company of a man. She had liked Hale. At least she'd been more attracted to him than any other male in her life.

But the experience had been *so* lackluster, and she hadn't been able to see his face ever since. This, with Arkimedes, was different. Her heart nearly bursting out of her chest was enough of a sign to tell her. They hadn't even gotten to the best part yet.

Her gaze was unfocused somewhere on the top of his head. He pulled down her underwear, and she grasped the mattress, trying not to squirm and fighting the feeling of wanting to cover herself.

The only light in the room filtered in from the closed curtains and the supernatural light from his eyes. When his attention came to her sex, his expression grew more feral.

A stroke of his tongue made her tremble, and she brought her arm up to her lips to quiet the sounds that started to escape her. Pleasure extended through her body. The softness of his tongue moved up and down and over her clit. His lips closed over the sensitive nub and sucked softly, making her toes curl. She blinked at the sensation as she held her breath and tried not to moan as loudly as she wanted.

It built through her body. Something was going to explode inside her. Not sure of what to expect but wanting to ask him to stop *or* keep going—she didn't know what her mind wanted. She grabbed the strands of his hair and pulled. It was like trying to move an unmovable force. His merciless tongue was going up and down and around.

"Ark—" She gasped.

She went rigid for one second before ecstasy exploded behind her closed lids. She gasped and moaned loudly, and with the last strokes of his tongue, he carried her down from the previous waves of her orgasm.

This was what Simone had been talking about all along.

Nava grabbed his shoulders eagerly, and he came up to her. His lips crashed down on hers as she brought her hips up to rub against him. His lips tasted like her and desire. His body fit hers perfectly, like a puzzle made by the gods for her.

Arkimedes's cock was trapped in between her navel and his abdomen, throbbing as her lips came down his jaw and her tongue licked his throat. His skin was soft, a contrast to the prickly sensation of his beard against her well-kissed lips.

He moved then, and his length fell into the place she craved him most. The kiss deepened, and a moan escaped her lips as she tried to get him to move. He stilled.

"What?" Her voice didn't sound like her own.

"I— Have you been with anyone?"

Her skin grew warm as an intense flush took over her face. Her complete mortification over his question dampened some of the burning desire that had been raging through her veins. "Er . . ."

"You can tell me. I'm not going to judge you if you have." His finger traveled down her face. "But I need to know because—"

"I was with someone else!" she blurted.

He leaned away, his brows coming down into a deep frown. Well, she guessed he *did* mind, after all. It wasn't like she wanted to learn if he had been with anyone before her, but judging by his clear experience before going down on her, she would take a wild guess that he *had*.

Nava's stomach churned, and a possessive part of her she hadn't even put thought to burst to life, and her fingers dug into his skin. *This* had to be a part of the soulmate thing because Nava had never been one for being jealous or anything of the sort.

But he made her break that gentle side of who she was, and her nature took over.

She pushed up with her elbows and captured his lips, trying to make a point that he was now *hers*, and by the way he answered said kiss, he was making the same claim.

It wasn't like the kisses before; this one was teeth and tongue and everything raw in nature. He pressed into her slowly before his face buried deep within her neck.

He pushed, his girth filling her, and she was captured between that fine line where intense pleasure met a bit of pain. She had been with one person, and he had not been this well-endowed.

"Please." She needed more.

"What?" he breathed against her ear.

"I need more, Arkimedes. I need you."

His eyes found hers. "To do what? What do you need?"

The tingling sensation of embarrassment rushed through her mind.

"Don't go shy on me, Nava." His voice was like honey and sex.

Who knew Arkimedes would be one to like dirty talk? "I want you to fuck me."

"That's my girl," he purred.

Before she could even quip something funny about that, he pulled out, leaving just the tip in before he slammed inside her. She enjoyed the feeling before his teeth nipped at her skin, making her moan with need.

His tongue soothed the area he'd bitten before, and he fully sank into her. Their gazes met, and something else lingered in between them, the intensity of hearts beating together in the same rhythm.

A connection, her mind supplied behind the daze of lust.

Arkimedes's rhythm picked up as he moved in and out of her, their flesh coming together with a mixture of wet slaps and heavy breathing. He groaned, setting a torturous pace that drove her senseless. Her lips were unable to keep her pleasure in any longer, and her moans filled the room.

"This is unlike anything I have—" He roared before she lifted her body in a way that brought him in even deeper. His hand traveled down her leg and pulled it up over his hip, and he pounded into her, in and out, over and over again. "You feel so good."

Pleasure fully took over and expanded through her body as it grew hot like coal.

His rhythm didn't stop, and his groans filled the air. Nava's body was coiled with tension as he hit the spot within her again and again, bringing her higher.

"Let go," he whispered.

Her breaths stuttered, and she tensed beneath him once again, feeling the waves of pleasure through her body. This orgasm hit her out of nowhere. He pushed past it, extending it as his movements became more erratic. His face morphed into one of pure rapture as he climaxed within her inner walls.

They tangled together in a pile of limbs and heaving bodies. Arkimedes pulled out, bringing her into an embrace. With the heat of the moment, the room's frigid temperature hadn't registered; she shivered. He got the cover over both of them, and she smiled against his skin.

He looked down, raising a brow in question. "What?"

"I think it's funny. In the thrust of passion, *you* are the chatty one," she said, and her grin grew more prominent.

He chuckled, shaking his head. "Thrust of passion? Who says that?" he teased her back.

"I do." She snuggled closer to him, enjoying the warm masculine scent of his skin, feeling fulfilled and happy. Her fingers patted the taut skin over the muscles of his chest. His face morphed into an unfocused smile. "I'm not broken, after all," she murmured.

Arkimedes's hand stopped caressing her back as he looked at her with curious intent. "Broken?"

"I— Um, I thought maybe I couldn't, you know . . . come." Her cheeks warmed.

He lifted a brow. "Why would you think that?"

"Well, I was unable to do so the one time I was with Hale—" She paused, a bit unsure.

Arkimedes took a sharp breath, and his brows furrowed. "He didn't make sure you came?"

She shrugged, and his hand brought her closer to him, his lips crashing on top of her head, but then he shook his head.

"Selfish bastard—you'd better hope I never cross paths with him."

Nava's lips pulled up. She had never considered it, but once upon a time, when she had talked about it with Simone, her friend had seemed to believe Hale lacked in that sense as well. Nava had had such a difficult time connecting with anyone romantically before. She figured that had been part of the problem.

"You are *not* broken. To me, you are perfect," he said.

"You are not so shabby yourself." Her lips came to his cheek before she let out a sigh. Now that they had gotten this out of the way, exhaustion caught up to her. Nava closed her eyes slowly, enjoying this warmth. "When we were . . . When you were inside me, did you feel a connection?" she asked tentatively.

"Yes." His hand resumed the soft calming circles on her back. "The bond might have grown stronger tonight—I guess we will find out together."

She nodded and yawned. Nava didn't want to spoil this with concerns about secrets and lies, about how her heart ached from what had happened before. There would be other times to speak, and she wanted to enjoy this intimacy, even if for tonight.

Tomorrow war awaited them.

CHAPTER THIRTY-FOUR

A distant buzzing pulled Nava out of her dreamless slumber. An insect flew across her face, making her grumble. She swatted around. The warm body lying next to her beckoned her to keep still and go back to sleep, but the nagging insect wouldn't go away.

Nava snuggled back, enjoying how the muscles of his arm flexed, receiving her, as his nose buried behind her neck. Lips traveled across her skin toward her shoulder, and the tingling sensation spread.

"Mmm." The sigh escaped her lips, encouraging him to keep going.

She pushed against him, and the hard shape of his cock pressed into her lower back. Her stomach swirled, and her inner thighs moistened as she let her mind wander to how much she would enjoy that hard part of his somewhere else.

The body of a bug landed on her forehead, cold and hard contrasting against her heated skin.

She opened her eyes, the hair of her arms rising as the bee crept across her skin. Her whole body filled with tension, and something else came into her mind.

Arkimedes realized the change in her and lifted his torso with one of his arms, his brows dipping as he took in the bee.

There was not a sound inside the house except for the howling of the wind. Her stomach sank as another bee landed on top of the bed's covers.

She turned to Arkimedes, and his skin was pale. A finger came to his lips, signaling her to be silent, and he moved out of bed with the grace of a feline, barely making a sound. He picked up his pants and shoved his legs through the holes, and Nava followed suit. By the time she was dressed and ready, bees filled the home.

Thunder rolled through, making her stomach drop. Devon Black was close and unleashing another storm.

"He knows you escaped," she whispered.

Arkimedes nodded. His arms extended, and he patted the roof over them. "I'm not sure how close they are. I would fly us down, but there isn't enough space for my wings."

Nava knew her nerves would enhance her clumsiness, but she followed him down the narrow steps of the loft, trying to keep her arms from shaking as adrenaline coursed through her body.

The rain fell hard as Nava tied the belt holding her two daggers across her hips. Arkimedes was by the door, she assumed checking on the wards he had set the night before. His face tilted to her, and she understood without words that they had to get out of the house or it would soon become their prison.

Arkimedes waited by the front door, resting a hand on the handle for a second while he took a sharp breath in preparation. He cracked it open, studying the street from his vantage point.

Ebony tendrils of magic lifted from his skin. The blue light of the early morning highlighted the side of his face. It was colder today than it had been the past few weeks, with the wind howling outside, moving the remnants of ash and dust that had covered the stone roads the night before.

The heavy raindrops were unforgiving as thunder roared high within the sky. The air smelled like wet ash, smoke, and charred meat that made her insides churn, a smell she would never forget.

His eyes cut to her, and they were as ready as they could get in their current circumstances. Bees circled her body. The heavy drumming of her heartbeat was high in her throat, muffling any sound around her.

Even if they were nearby, the army, however big, still didn't know they were in this particular house.

It was now or never.

Arkimedes opened the door and exited first, the waves of his magic covering the whole doorframe. The dreary light from outside peeked through. Nava rushed behind him, her dagger out as she studied her surroundings. Everything was dark, wet, and cold.

She shivered when the icy caress of water hit her exposed skin. A blinding light came rushing to them. Bees flew everywhere in front of them. Arkimedes's magic wove in between their bodies, and the attack bounced off.

Nava hissed. Her heart pounded as the charred bodies of her insects fell to the ground, a sob dying inside her throat.

No.

Arkimedes's wings were out in the blink of an eye, and before the gasp had escaped her lips, his arms banded around her waist, and his wings flapped, lifting them in the air.

Her arms wrapped around his neck. Nava's stomach dropped with the motion. Arrows whizzed by, and spells followed them with different shades and brightness.

Arkimedes barely dodged them, his arms straining around her tightly. Nava buried her face in the crook of his neck. She was heavy, and flying already strained his injured body.

The cold wind burned her exposed skin, and Nava focused on the energy around her, calling for something to shield them. When she opened her eyes, a swarm of bees made of light flew around them.

"Hold on." He flew them quickly over gray skies and out of the heavy rain cloud. The momentary brightness was soon extinguished when he dove under the thick canopy of the forest.

Nava's stomach churned, and she nervously looked at the approaching shapes of trees and branches. She held on tighter and tensed all of her muscles, awaiting a crash.

They were going to *die*.

"No, we are not."

Arkimedes's arms jolted, taking the brunt of the fall. His legs buckled under the heavy weight of their bodies. She was cocooned inside long soft feathers and thick muscle. The wings fell to the earth, and Arkimedes's breathing settled. She pushed up over her arms, examining his body and face.

He was scraped all over, blood peeking through his shirt from his old stab wound.

Nava's shaky hands came to him. "Why did you do that?"

"I'm not used to flying with someone else."

She rushed to her feet, her gaze snapping to each side, examining the area as bees flew around them. The feeling of impending doom had settled somewhat, but they still needed to hurry.

He took a sharp breath while getting to his feet. His wings disappeared behind his back. Something fast and heavy landed right next to Nava. She winced, and Arkimedes's magic flared to life around them. She focused on the long, looming shape of Ari as his head tilted to the side.

"Tell him not to do that again!" Arkimedes's brows furrowed as he stared at the creature.

"He can hear you."

"That was close," Ari said. His tone of voice was reproachful. He gazed at Arkimedes and then back at Nava. Something seemed to click behind his expression. *"We are finally mated to the Dark One."* His voice was soft, and her face flushed in embarrassment.

"Oh, no, we are not talking about that." She shook her head, walking past the creature and toward Arkimedes, whose brows raised in question.

"What?"

"You don't want to know." She shook her head. She would have a conversation with Ari about the use of terms because *she* alone was mated to Arkimedes.

Arkimedes looked like he wanted to argue. However, he chose to let it go for the time being. "We need to get to the camp. One thing I did notice was Devon didn't have as many soldiers with him this morning. I'm guessing yesterday's attack weakened him greatly."

NAVA AND ARKIMEDES TREKKED FOR HALF a day over rough terrain, on muddy paths that had not been walked on by humans in a long, *long* time. The earth was soggy, and the scent of moss and wet dirt surrounded them.

They had been quiet, keeping alert for any possible noise that would tell them they were in danger from either Devon, the Neems, or anything else lurking in the forest. Real bees and ones made of light flew sparsely and protectively around the three of them; their message wasn't one of pure panic like it had been that morning in the cabin, but one of constant alert.

"Does it take a lot of magic to put your wings away?" Nava asked in between breaths. She was determined not to complain, especially since Arkimedes was injured and still managed to walk faster than her.

"Yes." His face turned to her as he dipped under a large tree. "Blending in is not easy for me."

Ari made a noise that was hard to decipher, just as interested in the conversation.

"Well, I like them." She gasped for air. "You can leave them out always."

"They do get in the way."

"You are large everywhere," she said and stumbled on her feet. "Not like that! I mean as in tall and strong. But I guess . . ."

Arkimedes cleared his throat, and her words stopped. "It was a close call earlier today. We need to keep alert now."

She narrowed her gaze on him. "Is that code for shut up and be quiet?"

He flashed her a look that shone with amusement. "Yes."

"Fine."

It wasn't like she couldn't keep her mind busy with all that had happened during the early morning. Not the attack, but them mating. The bond was strong and present, like an invisible string that tied them together. If Nava let her mind grow quiet, she could feel the murmur of his emotions.

Pain was present in his tired body, his wound aching deep in his rib cage. Her brows creased in concern, but there was no point in bringing it up. After all, he needed rest and a healing potion. And they wouldn't get any of those until they got to Roman's camp.

She remembered Arkimedes's words from earlier and held onto the silver lining that maybe Devon was debilitated and they might have a chance to get out of this alive and with their freedom intact.

CHAPTER THIRTY-FIVE

It was past midday by the time Nava and Arkimedes made it to the west side of the village. The wards meant to detract the enemy held them back as an invisible shield for hours before they were able to break through.

The vision of the town in front of them was chaotic. The trees that had been full of life were now columns of blackened wood. The town smelled like burnt pine and cedar and other scents that made her pause.

In the background, behind trees and buildings, the billowy smoke lifted through the air from homes still burning with blue flames.

People rushed in between buildings. Everyone was dirty, bloody, or both. The people of the town stared at them but dismissed them as they approached the center of town. At first, Nava didn't recognize the place. Tents were lifted around the area where she had danced with a blond man and listened to two girls gush over Arkimedes's hotness.

It seemed like such a long time ago. So much had passed since. The willow trees still stood tall around the small plaza. Tents were housing people lying on cots and crying in pain. Nava's hand flew to her lips as they approached the wounded, coming across bodies, searching for a familiar face.

A mixture of anger and complete despair ran through her as nausea racked her body. Unlike anything she had ever experienced, the smell was overpowering—a combination of burnt flesh, blood, body odor, and magic.

There was a table with food around. No longer could she hear children in the street. Her heart churned as she took in the despair around her. She reached for Arkimedes's hand and held it as he led her forward.

"Do you know where we can find Roman?" he asked a woman walking in front of them. She was carrying clean bandages, wearing pants and a blood-stained green tunic.

Her lips went slack as she studied Arkimedes's face, then her gaze flashed to Nava's, then fell on the tall body of Aristaeus behind her. The Beekeeper's face was devoid of any natural expression, and his pitch-black eyes stared back at the woman expectantly. Bees raced around his beehive.

Her face turned pale, and Nava expected her to run. However, her shaky hand pointed them to a spot deep within the tents. Arkimedes walked past her without another word.

"Thank you," Nava said.

They marched on until they found the Commander's familiar shape. He leaned against one of the posts that held up the main tent. His face was scraped and darkened with soot and dirt. Worry etched his features as his attention went to a bed where a body lay.

Nava followed his gaze, and a scream escaped her as she dropped Arkimedes's hand and ran to the cot where the unconscious body of her friend lay. "Gavin!" she exclaimed.

His face was pale, and his head was wrapped with a tight gauze tinted in angry red. One of his eyes was visible and closed. His breathing was slow but steady.

Nava almost missed Violet kneeling by the cot with her hand grasping his. Violet's eyes narrowed when they landed on both Arkimedes and her.

"Oh, now you come," she grunted and pushed to her feet. Nava huffed as Violet shoved her shoulder back with one of her hands, making her lose balance and nearly fall.

Arkimedes was by her in the blink of an eye, holding her by her elbows, giving Violet a stern warning. "Watch it," he growled, pinning the other woman down.

Violet was seething in anger. A spike in her own emotions got the best of her, but she took a deep breath and tried to get herself to calm down. Violet was in an emotional state Nava couldn't even begin to grasp.

"How bad is his injury?" Nava asked, turning to Roman, who looked at both of them. His face, however, unlike Violet's, was relieved.

"We don't know. Gavin was our senior healer. Marianne, our second healer, has had her hands full, and her experience in combat healing is less." Roman studied the tent toward where the red-haired woman they had seen before was. She was wrapping gauze around a man's chest.

"What happened?" Arkimedes asked.

"What do you care? You left us here to handle your poison on our own." Violet's eyes raked up his body. Fire burned behind her pupils. Her aura was coming up in gray wisps. She wanted to release steam, but picking on Arkimedes was not the best idea.

"Violet, stop it," Nava snapped, coming a step closer to the woman who had helped her a day ago. "Stop trying to make Arkimedes into a villain when he had nothing to do with this attack, much less with what happened to Gavin."

"You are right. Maybe it's you I should be blaming," Violet said.

Nava breathed, and her weary gaze stayed with the other woman.

Roman stepped in, and his large hand landed on the woman's shoulder, squeezing it. "Calm your fire. Nava is right. We could use all the help we can get. Devon's army has already done enough damage, and the wards won't hold much longer. We don't know how much manpower he has."

It was clear he had not slept through the night, and a pang of guilt crept into Nava's head. She had slept and more. Nava should have been here. Even with their exhaustion the night before, they should have tried to make it.

The knot forming in her throat became larger, and her vision glazed with unshed tears.

"I flew over his campsite last night. His army has dwindled. One hundred, one fifty max," Arkimedes said.

Nava silently pleaded, stepping closer. Violet knelt down, giving her a reproachful nod.

Nava had healed both Ari and Arkimedes. Maybe due to a healing gift she was not trained to use. However reliable, it was worth a shot. Her eyes landed on the young healer who was tending to another injured man. Nava walked there, drawing everyone's attention as Ari, her Beekeeper, trailed after her. "Excuse me, Marianne?"

The young woman's face snapped to her. Recognition painted her tired features, but a fire lit behind her expression. "Who told you my name?" She squinted suspiciously.

"Roman. I was hoping I could bother you for a couple of healing potions?"

Marianne stared at Ari before letting out a resigned breath. "I don't have much left. What do you need it for?"

Nava's jaw clenched, and her eyes flew to the cot where Gavin lay.

"If it's for Gavin, I already applied a dose of it this morning, which I told Violet *three* times. Not that she ever listens to me."

Nava nodded. "It is for him, and also for my mat—man, I mean, boyfriend." The word was too insignificant, as Arkimedes was so much more than that.

They would have to talk about titles at some point. "I'm a potion maker and could help you make larger quantities of it as soon as we are out of danger. I need a little bit of it . . . to try something."

Marianne started shaking her head when Ari's lips opened in a snarl that would have scared the bravest out of their pants. The redheaded woman jumped back, her features turning pale once again.

"Please." Nava forced a smile to her lips.

The woman gaped at Nava but searched the apron's pockets underneath her green coat and handed over two vials with a purple liquid. "It's Gavin's. It seems appropriate that if I'm going to be *bullied* to give a couple away to you, it would be his."

"I assure you my boyfriend does need one. He was stabbed a day ago." Nava didn't feel an ounce of guilt. She turned around and walked toward Gavin, knowing Ari was behind her. Whatever she had done before, she hoped she could replicate it.

Nava pulled the lid of the vial with her free hand and brought the potion to her nose. She could make out most of the ingredients by the freshness of the brew. It was probably three weeks old, not new enough to be at its full potency, but not fully expired, either.

When this was done, she would have a talk with Gavin about keeping his potion stash fresh.

The burn of Marianne's gaze followed her as she knelt in front of the cot, next to Violet, who gave Nava her best mean stare.

"What do you think you are doing?" she asked with menace.

Nava steeled her temper. "I'm going to apply a healing potion on his head. Is there anywhere else he is injured?"

Both Roman and Arkimedes had approached the bed, following the interaction.

Violet's face softened. She cleared her throat, and her hand came up to his shoulder. "One of the explosions broke part of a building from the trees. Gavin pushed me aside—it fell on top of him. We don't know how bad his inner bleeding is," she admitted, her face colored with guilt.

"It's not your fault," Nava said, but Violet's hand came up, pausing her.

"I don't need your sweet words."

"He would also be saying to you to stop being so unpleasant," Nava said without missing a beat.

Violet's lips twitched. "Yes, I guess he would." She let her body sink onto her knees.

Nava held the potion in her hand and perused her friend's body, swallowing as she took in his bruised skin.

Ari stood beside Arkimedes—his inky eyes bored into her, and she had to try. Nava had to trust in herself that she was good enough to help him. She had done it before, not once but two times.

She took a sharp breath, her body vibrating with pent-up energy. The scent of spice surrounded her, her skin glowing yellow and white.

She brought the liquid to Gavin's slacked lips. Her free hand came to his neck, lifting it as she pushed the vial closer and dumped the whole potion inside his mouth. His Adam's apple bobbed. Nava brought him down gently to the soft wool blanket beneath him. They waited for a charged moment in silence, but nothing happened.

The disappointment grew within her like a festering wound. Her lips pursed together as she studied the pale complexion of her friend.

One warm hand landed on her shoulder and squeezed. She lifted her face and found Arkimedes staring down at her. The side of his mouth pulled up as he nodded in encouragement, understanding shining behind his sable lashes.

She pushed to her feet and fell into his arms, letting the soft caress of his embrace soothe her. Her cheeks were wet with tears.

"I know what you did," he said against her ear. "Give it time. Have faith in yourself and him."

She blinked. His hand brushed the side of her face, and she nodded, bringing her hand up to wipe the tears that streaked down.

"We need to prepare for the wards to collapse. Any able body available to protect the village needs to be rested and ready." Arkimedes's voice was stern as he took a look at Roman. "Including you."

Nava expected Roman to tell Arkimedes where to shove his opinions.

"Yes, I need to rest—and so does everyone else," the man said tiredly. "Devon took a lot of our strongest people as prisoners yesterday. We might have a chance now with you two here." His words made her head snap to him.

Something warm shook her stomach. The Commander's attention came to Nava, and something that wasn't there the day she'd met him bloomed. Respect and *hope*.

The hope of something being better because of her magic startled her. She was not a simple woman making ends meet to keep her brother alive while empty and unfulfilled. This rang truer to her character, someone who in the past month had grown to be much more than Nava Forrest, the potion maker of Willowbrook.

Her whole life, she had been afraid of this, of being around magic, sorcerers, and creatures. She had been afraid of falling for her soulmate, something legend said was sacred and special. She had been afraid of it all, and now she had given in to every single one of her previous biases.

Her gaze cut across people around her, all the things she had once feared that were now her people. She would fight for them, for their freedom and hers and Cameron's.

She wouldn't run anymore.

"You guys should get some rest. There is food outside." Roman's voice broke the silence. "You can take the house with the blue door. It's hard to miss it from here. Please make sure you take the Beekeeper with you."

He scares the shit out of everyone. Roman didn't need to say the words. He eyed Ari, and the Beekeeper's mouth opened. Sharp teeth made of wood made an appearance, a gaping black mouth dripping with honey.

It was hard to tell if that was a smile or something a lot more menacing. Nava opened her lips to complain, to say she was not hungry or tired, but Arkimedes grabbed her hand and pulled her away.

They walked to get food in quiet companionship and then retired to the offered home, where she proceeded to apply the second vial of potion she took from Marianne on Arkimedes's wound. And then they laid down to rest.

CHAPTER THIRTY-SIX

Nava had barely closed her eyes for what she told herself would be a quick nap when pops and cracks jolted her awake. She was alone in the soft bed of their home for the day. Her eyes traveled around the room, and she swung out of bed, touching the floor's worn grayish wood.

The room was sparse and impersonal. White painted walls, no art, the bedding a mix and match set of sheets and blankets. She didn't linger and instead padded outside of the room barefoot.

"Ark?" She pulled up her pants from the belt loops as they lowered down her hips with each step she took. The clean clothes Roman had provided were made for a much larger person. Earlier in the day, Nava had thrown her daggers on top of the table before she had gone to sleep.

She studied the room with neutral worn furnishings made of leather and wood. Nava's hand came to rest on top of her soulmate mark. The pit in her stomach settled at the emptiness around her. The soft humming of the magic that ran inside her body calmed her nerves. She wondered if somehow she was feeling Arkimedes beneath the layers of her magic.

Arkimedes was not only away from the cabin, but farther than she would like, judging by the pit in her stomach. He was gone.

Screams started outside as she dropped her hand in a rush and finished tightening the belt around her hips. She hustled around, picking a pair of socks that were on the clean pile of clothes Roman had dropped earlier. They were made of scratchy wool but were warm for the late-fall day ahead. She put her boots on as she jumped across the room, scanning for the rest of her things. Her chest vibrated with energy and nerves.

Nava picked up her tunic on her way out of the door. She stared at the sky, her lips slacking. Beyond the trees' foliage, a red fiery crack opened in the invisible shield. It burned with flames as arrows plowed toward it, though most of them bounced off.

Her attention followed the frenzy of the crowd. Most people were dressed in battle gear and ran through the cobbled streets, carrying weapons, their faces twisted in determination. Their auras formed a glow around their bodies in various shades of gray. She tried to find someone familiar, the face of her soulmate, to no avail.

"Where did he go?" she mumbled.

Something landed right next to her. This time she didn't jump. Ari's gaze fixed on the fading wards over them, bees flying impassively around his head. His face pointed to the direction where most of these people were heading. Likely where Devon's army was about to plow through once the wards fell.

Arkimedes had left her behind *again* with some noble cause of protecting her. Nonetheless, her stomach burned with anger. He would hear about it.

Ari grunted and nodded, and they both made their way toward the commotion, following the river of soldiers.

Another pop echoed around, louder this time. With horror, she followed the cracks in the shield, and the pieces fell. She brought her arms up and around her head, expecting large amounts of debris to fall on them, but nothing came, just the heavy scent of burning spices.

"Arrows!" someone yelled as dots flew in from the sky toward the river of people. Most buried in trees and foliage that provided natural shelter from the attack. Few made it through and bounced off people's magic shields.

Nava gaped, her heart beating as adrenaline rushed through her body, and she waved between the multitudes. Ari jumped to a tree, his jerky moves more fluid as he made his way from branch to branch, a swarm of bees trailing him, calling the bystanders' attention.

Arrows rained in again, and Nava took immediate cover behind a tree when the shout came. This time, their shields were less strong, as some had exhausted their energy. Screams bellowed around her. She ran around and behind trees, following the pitter-patter on her soulmate mark.

It was coming alive and acknowledging his presence. He was close.

Ash drifted in the air as the never-ending blue flames still burned buildings in the distance. The path was littered with debris from the day before and some from today. Mushed leaves and mud stuck to people's feet. The buildings made of stucco were cracked and broken.

As an inexperienced fighter, she kept behind buildings, her skin crawling with the appearance of enemy soldiers wearing the same tunics as the day before.

Magic wafted through the air, and the tingling of her own came to life inside her blood as she pulled both daggers out of the sheaths. Bees made of light swirled around her.

The scream of a woman nearby forced her out of her hiding hole. A soldier was upon her, not killing her. She realized ropes swirled around the woman's body like snakes, wielded by an enchantment.

Nava didn't hesitate and sliced the soldier across his back. His high scream burned in her memory, and he turned to her. Nava stumbled back in shock when the face of a child came into view.

Not a child, a teenager, not much older than she'd been when she met Arkimedes.

She gasped, and hot air burned her throat as the man—no, the boy—fell to the ground, a scream on his lips. The ropes that had been wrapping around the woman fell. She recognized the face of the blonde who had been gushing about Arkimedes that one night. Their eyes met and then she was off.

She kept going, knowing she was closer to Arkimedes by the increased fluttering in her stomach. The battle raged, people of both sides fighting for life and freedom or power and dominance.

Magic and weapons were swinging around the narrow roads of a fallen town. Nava's anxiety debilitated her. Her legs froze as she relived the memories of the day before, of killing and fighting for her life.

She couldn't move, barely able to breathe as her blunt nails dug into the hilt of her weapon, and everything grew slow and fast at the same time. The prickle of fear crawled across her scalp and backbone.

She found Arkimedes in the distance. His majestic magic billowed as he moved with lethal grace. Dark mist plumed around him and followed his moves as the arms of his power pulled people high up in the air. His wings flapped with power and grace, allowing him a higher vantage point.

Arrows bounced off the surge of his magic, and the shadows of soldiers around him became alive, attacking their masters.

Arkimedes's eyes shone with green light like they had the night before when he made love to her. However, the anger in them was nothing like the heated expression she had seen before.

She froze when his eyes fell upon her; even in the distance, his growing panic pushed through their bond. He threw a soldier across the street and into a large tree. The man's body cracked, bent into angles a body shouldn't, and fell to the ground with a loud bang.

She couldn't move. Nava had never had an anxious breakdown like this. It blindsided her.

Snap out of it, she told herself, and her hand shook the metal of her dagger. She stared at a couple of soldiers who approached her in a run, their faces twisted.

Ari landed on one. His long twisted arm reached to the other with sharp fingers, clawing at his chest where a red stain bloomed on his gray tunic. The man screamed and stepped back, taking in the appearance of the Beekeeper in front of him.

A wave of calm reached her as Ari faced her, his face contorted in worry.

"You were under a spell," he said.

She blinked the daze of her panic away. "By whom?"

Ari shook his head. The upcoming attack shortened their conversation. Two, *no,* three soldiers rushed to them. Their screams were lost among all others. Nava's magic flared as she met their attack, a long sword against her blades, while Ari battled the other two. Their magic fed one another, and bees attacked their enemies.

She separated from the Beekeeper and chased down a soldier. The roads that once had been green and alive with moss were covered in red and gray.

The town was chaos. She could tell Devon's army was failing as they claimed back part of the town they had lost the day before. Nava ran down the streets. The trees shook with the beat of her steps. Branches swung like arms, hitting thatched roofs that sent large pieces of a building flying toward the fleeing soldier. His body was buried under rubble with a precision she wouldn't have had under normal circumstances.

Nava stopped heaving as she studied her surroundings and followed the shape of Arkimedes. He landed a block away from her. Fire burned from the buildings, making ash rain over them. Her view was hazy, his magic contrasting against the white billowy shape of smoke.

Arkimedes's body was taut as he took a few steps toward her. The shadows of soldiers retreated behind the smoke while being pursued by the village warriors. They were *winning*. She scanned the bodies around her.

Black stains of soot marked Arkimedes's face. His eyes raked down her body, checking for injuries. She smiled at him, but her stomach sank when her soulmate's expression shifted to one of pure unadulterated fear.

A chill ran down her spine when a body pressed against hers, so fast she barely had a chance to gasp for air. Nava was as frozen as she had been moments ago when Ari helped her. Someone had cast a spell upon her once again. A hand wrapped around her neck and another one around her arm. The air became heavy as the tightening grip burned her skin.

"Well, well, well. Look who we have here." His voice was silk and poison. His warm breath hit her. Goose bumps rose in its wake, prickling her skin as her stomach rolled.

She made no moves. The grip on her arms tightened. She gasped as pain ran through her arm and neck. It wasn't regular strength but the magic that chilled her bones.

Arkimedes had made it to them fast. "Devon, let her go." His magic flared around him.

Devon's grip tightened again, and the smell of magic wafted around them. "And why would I do that?" Menace dripped off each word. "Keeping her will ensure you don't kill me, *brother*."

"If you don't let her go, I *will* kill you," Arkimedes promised, but he didn't move a muscle. His arms opened in a sign of yielding. His throat bobbed.

"Tsk, tsk. You aren't in a place to make threats," Devon said in a mock tone.

Nava tried to move, to writhe in his grasp, but couldn't. She cried when a bone-melting wave of pain coursed through her body once again. He had paralyzed her, but not her ability to scream or cry. A way to torment Arkimedes. Tears streamed down her face, blurring her vision.

"Imagine my surprise when I found you had escaped yesterday, even after I commanded them to make sure you couldn't so much as *think* about leaving. I guess I underestimated this kitten." Devon's lips touched her neck.

A cry escaped her, and Arkimedes came toward them a step closer.

"Don't!" Arkimedes warned.

"I knew the day we found her something had changed with you. I always guessed your friendship with Celeste was the reason why you left." Devon's voice became sharper. "The golden boy of our Society had found his soulmate in the fugitive daughter of Celeste Forrest. And to think they all mourn your death. I knew better. Something was off in the way Forrest vanished. But also you, and this cat."

Nava screamed as the pain that coursed through her intensified. She tried to bend over, to curl up and wallow in her misery, but he gripped her in his magical clutch.

"Devon, you don't have to hurt her, please—"

"Where is the fun in that?" he snarled. "I came here looking for deserters, following a blind lead of maybe finding my brother. To find what might have happened to my best friend. And here you are, happily alive, waiting for some pussy to show up."

Arkimedes's face sobered. "If you were searching for me, what makes you believe I would be okay with this crazy behavior? Hiring bounty hunters—

working with the crown like we're theirs to command? This is madness, Devon."

"I had to bring as many deserters as possible. You know they can't just leave—we hang in a fine balance before extinction," Devon snapped. "We swore to our gods to maintain it."

"How much did the crown pay you to bring them back?" Arkimedes challenged.

Devon cursed behind her, and a sob escaped her lips. She tried to keep her eyes open, but the pain was too much. Bees swirled around them. She doubted Devon could even see them, as he focused solely on Arkimedes. He knew nothing about her and her connection to nature or bees.

He wasn't aware she was a Beekeeper.

"We don't work for the crown. We swore to protect, to keep balance," Arkimedes said again.

Devon's laughter shook her. "So naïve, brother," he said, amused and also sad. "I'm tired of living under your shadow. I'm going to prove to them how weak you are, how much of a two-faced liar. Even with all your powers, your wings, and your boring bravado, you have been hiding for all these years. While I was there in the kingdom, trying to save magic from disappearing."

Nava grew tired of his voice, of his hands touching her. It was Arkimedes's shifting expression that sobered her mood.

"What is it you want? You lost. Why are you doing this?" She forced her words out and tried to distract him.

"I will take you back home. He will follow, I'm sure. The Society can see what they want to do with the two of you then." If the context had been different, she would have assumed by his calm pleasant voice that he wasn't torturing her.

"I'm not going with you anywhere." Anger burned in Nava's body, and the buzzing around them became louder. She focused on the pain, and magic wrapped down her arms like ghostly fingers on the fabric of her tunic.

She had to unwrap them or, better yet, burn them away.

Once, her mother had told her magic was part of her essence, that she controlled her energy and, with enough practice, could bend it to become what she needed.

Nava was earth and fire, and the pain was no longer coming from him but the growing pit of anger in her body. Anger with Devon. With the crown and Crows. With her mother and her secrets.

The memory of the young sorcerer soldier she had cut not long ago flashed through her mind, as if her subconscious brain was giving her a fraction of a reason why her mother had done what she had.

Nava always hid behind a mask of pleasant smiles and fumbling words, but she was angry. With herself. For turning a blind eye to her nature and allowing fear to dominate her.

Her disgust toward the man behind her burned hotter than her pain. Her body was warming up to scalding-hot. The earth shook beneath her feet. Devon gasped in pain, yelling as he backed away, and Nava stumbled forward out of his hands, onto the cobbled street. Her hands broke her fall, and it shocked her to see the blue fire burning over her skin like a halo.

She turned to Devon. His face was red and burnt, his inky gaze wide with surprise.

"You are a slow learner, Devon. You have underestimated me again." Her voice came out rushed, and she bolted toward Arkimedes, whose own magic swirled around him.

The bees descended on Devon, a cloud made of swirling brown and light. The screams that followed were terrifying. Their bodies landed on him, but where he burned them away, more appeared. Thousands of bees came upon him.

Arkimedes welcomed Nava into his arms. She buried into his large chest, and they both stared in horror as Devon fell to his knees, screaming, trying to save his life with magic.

Arkimedes flinched and stepped toward Devon. "We can't let them . . ." His face paled, and his gaze moved around his old friend's body, brows lifting as panic settled.

She tried to find Ari, but she couldn't see him in the smoke of the burning town.

"Nava, stop them."

Her stomach shook as understanding hit her hard. This wasn't Ari's doing. It was her anger fueling the bees to protect her and Arkimedes from the crown and the Crows.

Her face snapped back to Devon's body as he barely held himself against the ground. "*Stop*." The word was loud even to her ears.

The bees all lifted from the warlock at the same time, hovering close to his body. His shaky arms held him upright before he collapsed to the ground.

Arkimedes rushed to the man, and Nava followed behind. Devon's skin was red and swollen, covered in black stingers, and she couldn't bring herself to care enough about what had happened to him. No, this man had killed *many* innocents and had tortured others, including herself, Gavin, Violet, *and* Arkimedes. He had terrorized her, forced her to leave her brother behind.

She crossed her arms over her chest and stilled when Arkimedes's hand came to Devon's pulse and he breathed in relief.

"He is alive." He met her gaze with an expression that was hard to read.

"I don't understand *why* we care." Her voice was clipped.

Arkimedes lifted to his feet and cut the distance in between them. His hand landed on her shoulder pleadingly. "He is my brother, Nava," he whispered, lowering his gaze.

"He is a monster."

"I'm not saying he doesn't deserve a punishment for this." His sigh made her tense posture relax a fraction. "He doesn't deserve much mercy, but it shouldn't be our decision alone to make. He hurt the people of this town. They should be the ones deciding his punishment."

She shook her head, and her eyes landed on where his wound was. "He tortured you, commanded Mort to hurt you."

"Killing for self-defense, it's different from killing out of anger. I'm damaged because of what I have done in my past. I don't want you to go through that."

Nava knew he was right. She had not been in danger when the bees had kept going. Devon was fully incapacitated, a pile of swollen flesh barely hanging on after such an attack. Still, she'd almost kept going. A bit too far, probably to the point of no return.

"He is a crappy-ass brother."

"He's not a great one," he agreed.

"Also, I haven't forgotten the fact that you left me asleep today and came to this battle on your own."

He shrugged. "I would do it again."

Her lips slacked. "What?"

"I promised I wouldn't lie to you again. I'm never going to stop feeling protective. If I can keep you away from danger, I will."

"Well," she huffed, and she could tell him who was not getting laid tonight, but she took a sharp breath and turned her head to face Devon once more. "So what do you suppose we do with him?"

"Roman can decide," Arkimedes said.

Nava assessed the body of her enemy. It was over—at least for now.

The echoing steps in the distance called their attention from the body on the floor. The silhouetted shape of a tall man approached at a slow pace, his sword drawn out as he investigated the area with careful measures.

She recognized him even among the gray mist and smoke around them. Roman's feet moved with caution, his head snapping from empty homes around them, coming to fallen bodies that peppered the ground. His face contoured in a mixture of anguish and anger.

The blue-and-black shades of Devon's outfit let him know who that was.

Roman brought down his sword and put it back in its sheath with a quick movement. His steps were faster to reach them. His black hair stuck to the sides of his sweaty face, his skin marked with blood and soot. "Is that . . . ?"

Arkimedes nodded, stepping away from his brother's body. He didn't say a word, but she could tell by the tense line of his shoulders that he was teetering on the edge of something dark.

"Is he dead?" Roman asked, the large tip of his boot pushing on Devon's leg.

"No," Nava ventured to say before taking a deeper breath. "We figured it would be fair for you and your people who suffered the most from his attack to determine the level of his punishment."

Roman's warm brown gaze snapped to Nava, his thick lips pursing before he nodded. "We are not savages," he mused with understanding. "Here, we adhere to and follow the rules of our village. We will lock him up to wait for trial. I understand you two were close once upon a time. I remember."

No wonder Roman had been so hostile when learning about Devon's impending attack.

"He deserves his punishment. He attacked a village of innocents and was not following our—the Society's law I grew up believing and the reasons why we upheld certain things." Arkimedes shook his head, pursing his lips. "With the dwindling number of magical humans being born, we were supposed to be doing this for the benefit of people. It was never about the crown and doing their bidding."

He took a deep breath and rested his hand on her lower back as if needing contact to steady his nerves. Her own body trembled as the adrenaline dwindled from her system.

Her heart filled with hope, and it relieved some of her momentary anger. They had to work hard on their communication. She had a broken man, someone who had suffered disappointment and pain. The kind of abandonment she'd never had to deal with, other than when her father had decided to let himself die.

"We are not executioners," Nava said with a nod, and she focused on the body she'd almost, albeit unknowingly, killed. Her stomach churned with the realization.

"Good," Roman said, and more people approached. The three of them relaxed as they took in the approaching shapes of the villagers.

"Would you stay here with us?" Roman asked.

"If it's not much trouble, we would appreciate somewhere to rest before we have to go back." Arkimedes's eyes came to her, a question painted on his features.

She nodded.

"We didn't start on the best terms, but you're welcome back here anytime." Roman extended his hand to Nava, who shook it, and to Arkimedes, and the previous tension that had flowed around them melted as soon as Arkimedes's hand grasped Roman's.

"Thank you."

The older man nodded and bent down, lifting Devon's limp body with ease and dropping it over his broad shoulder.

Nava eyed their retreating shapes, focused on Devon's previously pale features, which were now covered in angry welts.

"We should go help with the injured. Hopefully, we will get some rest tonight," Arkimedes said, and she nodded, letting her mind go blank as she got to work.

CHAPTER THIRTY-SEVEN

It had been a tiring three weeks since Devon Black's army had attacked the northern town in the forest. The days grew shorter and colder, and the sky was no longer gray with smoke and magic-induced storms. The sun shone, but everyone was aware bright winter days were the coldest.

They had moved patients back to their respective homes with the dropping temperatures. The few army sorcerers who had not escaped that day had been taken as prisoners and were held in the town's jail.

Nava had been surprised this existed in a lost village in the middle of a forest, but the longer she stayed, the more she realized the place wasn't as small as she had once imagined.

She found herself among the healing team, including Marianne, who disliked her but tolerated her based on her potion-making skills. Nava had been hard at work, brewing healing potions and pain management medicines every hour of the day she wasn't sleeping.

She had not performed any other healing spells, like the one she had done with Arkimedes, Ari, and Gavin.

Her steps were loud in the quiet morning, her boots clicking over stone roads that serpented the village. The sun shone through the tall trees. The homes protruding out of the giant trees no longer appeared jarring to her; she knew this area well.

She turned left and headed to a home she had been in and out of each day for the past week. The façade was thin and tall, the walls made of clay and sticks painted a warm cream that made the red door contrast against it. Pine needles were scattered all over the entrance steps.

She knocked on the wooden door a couple of times before she buried her hands inside her pockets, trying to shelter her skin from the biting weather. Nava heard quick steps before the door cracked open, and Violet's face appeared in front of her with a scowl that morphed into a somewhat pleasant expression.

"Oh, you are here," she said, opening the door wide to allow her in.

Nava cleaned her boots furiously on the doormat, not wanting to be scolded by Violet like she had the first day she'd shown up. She studied the warm home with a comfortable red couch in the center and a wood table that held multiple volumes of books, like the bookcase behind it.

The kitchen was quaint. There was a woodstove in the corner surrounded by sage-green cabinets, and copper pots and pans hung from the wall.

Nava's icy fingers came to the back of her neck, cooling her heated skin from her brisk walk here. Violet kept her home warmer than she was used to, and she was too afraid to take off her coat and drape it anywhere, as the woman was particular about how neat she kept her home.

"Is he in the bedroom?" Nava asked, shrugging off her coat after some deliberation.

Violet pointed to the coatrack by the front door. "Yes, where you last left him, kitten."

Nava grumbled, deciding not to say anything about the forsaken nickname this time.

She picked the potions out of her coat pockets and followed Violet past the narrow hallway of her home to the master bedroom, where Gavin awaited. "Good morning, sunshine," Nava said cheerfully when she found Gavin's bright face tilted at her from the bed.

It was a decent size and was covered in multiple blankets of different bright colors. The room was neat and homey. Nava came close and put the three vials of potions on top of the side table, her fingers coming to the bandage that covered half of his forehead.

"Nava," he greeted, his voice a bit more like himself and less groggy and tired. His face was less pale, though the gashes were still present and likely to leave a scar. "You have taken well to being a healer."

"What can I say? I can't let Marianne have all the fun." She was happy the wound on his head was healed. She applied the potion on top and wrapped the gauze around him again.

"She can be difficult sometimes," he agreed with a nod. "I seem to find myself surrounded by strongheaded women."

Nava's grin grew as a huff came from where Violet stood. "Please, the girl is barely a woman."

"Who, Marianne or me?" Nava handed Gavin one of the vials.

He scrunched his nose, and his coffee-colored eyes came to her, his expression imploring. Healers were the worst patients.

"Marianne," Violet answered with a growing smile. "You were a virgin, not a girl."

Nava turned to Violet, lifting a brow. "I was not a virgin. I told you."

"Oh, you were, in a way. Glad that's not the case anymore." Violet laughed louder.

"We can stop talking about it now."

"Please. As much as I like Arkimedes and you, I'd rather not imagine you two going at it like hungry beasts." Gavin's face scrunched.

"I wouldn't mind hearing more about it, soulmate sex—it's gotta be special."

Nava gaped before shaking her head and getting up from the bed. "This is weird, and I'm going to go home."

"Soulmates are so rare, and when they find each other, they keep it to themselves. The connections that undoubtedly happen in between you are a mystery." Violet's gaze shone with curiosity, and she followed Nava.

Nava grabbed her coat and shrugged it on. "Make sure he takes the second vial this afternoon. Marianne told me to tell you she will be coming here tomorrow morning."

Violet paused a few meters away from Nava, searching her face. "And where will you be, kitten?"

"Arkimedes and I are traveling back to Willowbrook tomorrow morning. My brother is waiting for me," she said, and they both stared at each other in silence.

"Will you be back?"

"I'm sure we will be, someday." Nava nodded. "Never thought you would be so sad to see me go."

The woman in front of her scoffed and crossed her arms over her chest, shaking her head. "Don't get it wrong. I'm curious because I want to learn more about the . . . soulmate bond."

Nava laughed. "If you say so." She opened the door, and a wall of freezing air hit her body, a clear contrast to the warmth inside. "I'm really terrible saying goodbye, so please tell Gavin I will see him soon."

Violet didn't say another word. Clearly, goodbyes weren't her forte either, and with this bittersweet moment, Nava walked back to the home that had been theirs for the past weeks, a place where they had been able to spend time together and not worry about the impending capture.

No more running. No more hiding.

For the first time, she had been able to breathe and enjoy him and their connection. It wasn't always pleasant, and there was that wedge he drew with secrets.

With the danger of war removed, it was easier to open up and live. Arkimedes worked hard to help Roman capture the soldiers who had tried to escape, a chase that had lasted at least a week. It was fitting that they had been the ones being hunted down.

The rebuilding had started a week after the battle. The broken bits of the town's east side were piles of rubble, ash, and buried bones. The blue fire that hadn't ceased to burn for days had taken down buildings and century-old trees. Gray ashy rain had fallen upon the town for days, and the smell of burning cedar and pine lingered almost a month later.

She had not wanted to know how they'd disposed of the battle's dead bodies, but some rituals had to happen for the spirits to rest in peace and not haunt the grounds where this village stood, to not become part of the haunted souls that still plagued her nightmares.

Leaving this place gave her a mixture of feelings she had a hard time reconciling within herself. A yin and yang battle over what she wanted.

She had always struggled to find her place, to connect with people. Here, it had been easier to let go and embrace all facets of what made her.

And to think her little thirteen-year-old brother had been right all along.

She spent the whole day making potions for Marianne and the rest of the healing team to use when she was gone. Her heart was full of excitement to see Cameron, Laurie, and Simone again when the sun was setting over the trees and the door opened to Arkimedes, who was coming home.

CHAPTER THIRTY-EIGHT

Nava opened her eyes with a flutter and focused on the sharp features of Arkimedes in front of her. The morning sun burned warm against the skin of his cheeks, outlining his sharp jaw and chin.

He eyed her intently, and he beamed at her. Her stomach flipped as her heart stumbled in its beats.

"Morning." Her voice was tinted with layers of sleep as she cuddled closer to him, enjoying the heat of his body.

"Good morning."

She sighed against him, goosebumps rising along her skin. The sheets smelled like him and like home, even though she had been here for such a short time.

He pulled away, and his expression turned amused. "We should get some breakfast."

Nava groaned a complaint because she wanted a different kind of breakfast. It surprised her, the sex fiend she had become. She'd had to up the doses for contraceptives three weeks ago to make sure a surprise didn't pop up when she least expected it.

The potion was an easy one to make, and it had been one of her best-selling brews back in town. Here in magic land, the recipe was different, and it carried ninety-nine percent success in pregnancy prevention, according to the local gossip.

"I'd rather eat something else entirely." Both of their faces turned bright red. "I didn't mean to say that out loud!"

A rolling laugh escaped him. "I imagined that was the case." He stole a kiss. "We should talk, though—about what happens next."

Nava's stomach fluttered, and she cuddled her pillow. His hand traveled from her shoulder to her back, the caress of his fingers igniting her nerve endings. "What do you mean?"

"I mean past today, about Cameron. Are we going to go back to the town and stay there?" He was nervous, and it was endearing.

They had been taking things slow, or as much as they could for being two bonded soulmates who could feel each other's moods and had to be close to survive.

She was concerned about him being in that non-magical town, what it would do to his half-fae side. She was also uneasy if Cameron would love him, or vice versa, though even, in her biased position, her brother was pretty hard to dislike.

"I—I guess I thought we would take it one step at a time?" she conceded, meeting his gaze and finding it nonjudgmental.

"I don't want to force you to be here because of me."

"What do you mean?" She searched his face for better understanding. He didn't mean them apart, right? Her previous insecurity reared its ugly head. She reached into the depths of their connection and learned he wanted the opposite.

"I would stay in that town if it's what you want."

She released a deep sigh, her mind going around everything that had happened in the past months, all the horrors she had seen in the forest, all the wonders she had encountered. Her life had changed irrevocably.

No longer did she feel magic was her crutch. She brought her hand to his face and smiled. She also couldn't be away from Ari—he was a part of her, and it was her duty to be there for him.

"This journey didn't only bring me to you, but it made me accept this part of me that was always missing," she whispered, and the flutter in her chest became more pronounced. Was it her heart or his? "While in Willowbrook, I always felt *numb*, like a hole I always assumed was my missing soulmate, but it was much more than that. I was missing a part of what makes me, me. That made a lot more sense in my head."

"It makes sense."

"What I mean is . . . I want to go and get Cam and Laurie and bring them with us, maybe back to your cabin?" She scanned the room of their provisional home in the Northern Village, and a crinkle formed in between her eyebrows.

"What?"

"Actually, your home might be too small for the four of us. I don't really want to share a room with Cameron, much less Laurie."

Arkimedes blinked before snickering, letting his head fall onto the pillow. "No, that wouldn't be good, especially with how you have been lately." He paused, waiting.

Her lips parted in offense. "Arkimedes Valeron, how dare you? You won't be getting in my pants again, since apparently, I'm this sex monster perverting your sensible elven ways."

He breathed a laugh that grew and made her stomach flutter, and she found herself laughing as well.

"I'm serious," she insisted, but with her clear sexual awakening, she wasn't sure she was fooling anyone in this room.

His eyes fixed somewhere on the ceiling. The thick wood beams were sturdy and rustic like everything here. Somehow, when they'd arrived at this house, it felt like it didn't have any personality. Bland, even. But now it gave her space to focus on all she had around her. "I built that cabin filled with so much anger and loneliness. I had left my whole life behind, the family I knew, to follow the unknown and also something that at the time I disagreed with wholeheartedly," he explained.

"You mean being a deserter? Or having me as your soulmate?" she offered with a raised brow.

"No, not you. I didn't want to be a deserter. At the time, I believed blindly in what they preached in the Society. I still do believe in some things. It's not black and white for me—there is a problem with magic fading in our world."

"Maybe it's what the gods want." She shrugged. "There is the gift of magic being given. Look at me. Born from a non-magical father and a magical mother. They came together as they should have, and I was born *with* magic. Forcing a hand breaks people apart. It doesn't make for a healthy nation."

"No, it doesn't. I don't agree with them forcing people together or apart. And the cabin, it reminds me of that past belief. I think maybe it would be good if we make our home somewhere else," he suggested and awaited a reaction.

"Where do you suppose?"

"Roman did offer for us to come back. He said his village would always welcome us in." His voice was unsure.

Nava lifted a brow. "A month has changed a lot of your dislike for Roman and how badly they treated you."

"Roman and I have a rocky history. I don't blame him for not liking me," he said. "And it doesn't help that the Crows tried to force Mars into marrying some high-society sorceress."

"No way." Her lips slacked.

He nodded. "Yes. She fancied him and worked her influence with the crown."

"Ark, you are a gossip master." Nava gasped.

His cheeks turned a deep shade of crimson. "Mars talks a lot," he defended. "I have never met anyone who gives so much information in a minute."

She chuckled. Never in her life would she have guessed she would be sharing gossip with the stoic, hunky man of hers.

"*Either way.* Here, Cameron will grow close to kids his age and learn magic the way he is supposed to."

"What I'm hearing is you don't want him to always be around us. Which means I'm not the only one around here burning for . . . intimacy."

Arkimedes pinned her to the mattress. His movements were so quick, it made the air leave her lungs. His lips met her jaw in a wet kiss. "We are recently mated, bee. I definitely don't want your baby brother around us all the time."

Her cheeks warmed. "Well, technically, we found each other ten years ago, when I was working on the garden and you so rudely interrupted me."

Arkimedes's eyes danced with mirth. "Is that so?"

"Yep, get it right."

"Hard to forget. My mate was a gangly, pimply teenager."

Nava hit the side of his shoulder, her lips parting. "I didn't even have pimples."

"Are you sure?"

She pursed her lips. "I might have had a couple because it was summertime, and it was hot." She fumbled over her words. She had looked an absolute mess that day. "Who's to tell? Maybe you weren't this perfect, handsome, strong man. Maybe you were also a skinny, pimply twenty-year-old."

Arkimedes raised a brow, and her annoyance grew, because who was she kidding? There was *no way* Arkimedes had been that. Her memory supplied the image of his strong, tall body filling his Society of Crows outfit.

She somehow knew his face had been as striking as it was now. Maybe with rounder cheeks.

"Your ego has no end. Not all of us have perfectly perfect elven genetics and are gorgeous always."

"You were cute then, but now you are gorgeous," he said, and his expression softened.

A warm wave ran through her body, making her light and happy. "Thank you."

"It's the truth."

"The Northern Village, then? It would be nice to see Gavin more often," she whispered, lost in her own thoughts.

Arkimedes's growl made her giggle as his fingers tapped the side of her ribs where she was the most ticklish, something he'd found soon after the war was over.

Laughter exploded from her lips, and she squirmed to get out of his hold. He held her against the mattress, his fingers relentless as she gasped for air, trying to escape.

She bucked under him as he held her close, leaving her breathless. She moved against him again, the hard planes of his chest pressed over hers.

She stopped when his growing desire became more apparent. His naked body was against hers with a thin sheet separating them. The movements of both their bodies had brought them closer. His hands stilled as their gazes met, his pupils hiding most of the turbulent green shades in his irises.

"We are going to need some boundaries about you bringing other men up when we are in bed together." His voice was husky.

His words shook her all the way to her core. "So sensitive," she breathed and pushed her hips to him, rubbing herself where she needed him.

He zeroed in on her mouth as her heart stumbled. His touch traveled to her hips and dipped past her navel in a soft caress that made her tremble with building desire. His hand pulled aside the sheets that had tangled around her in a slow, calculated move.

A breath shook her as his fingers dipped into her, and pleasure exploded through her body when his touch met her throbbing center. She held his shoulders, her nails digging into his golden skin where his wings were tattooed. She held the moan, bringing her lips instead to his chest.

"Let me hear you," he commanded.

She panted as he added a digit. In and out of her in a torturous pace that built her up and tied her into an endless knot. Her breathing was loud. The soft roaring of the fire in the fireplace provided warmth to their bodies in the chilly morning.

His lips traveled the base of her throat, his tongue marking her skin.

"I need you," she urged him on, gasping when his touch abandoned her.

The tip of his length pressed against her entrance. The hard length of him pushed in, stretching her in a way that was too much and not enough.

His lips captured hers in an open-mouthed kiss that moved fast and asked for all of her. His arms landed on each side of her head, muscles contracting as he held himself up and rocked into her, pushing her closer to where she needed to be.

The coil in her core grew tighter with each thrust of his hips, and both of their moans filled the room.

"Let go, Nava."

"I love you," she gasped as ecstasy exploded inside and around her.

His movements faltered, and she found his fierce gaze on her. Her heart was drumming from the last waves of her orgasm, but in the haze of her pleasure, she had said the words out loud. Before she could say anything else, his lips crashed onto hers, and he resumed his punishing pace.

"I love *you*, too," he said against her lips, and she held on to him tighter as his own movements became erratic, and soon he was also pushed past the edge and collapsed onto her.

CHAPTER THIRTY-NINE

Nava's things lay scattered on top of the table. The half-used cardamom soap Cameron had gifted her. Her tent was folded into a pile. Her vials of potions had been refilled, with a new, fresher batch containing improved brews with magic inside.

She moved her gaze over her things until it fell onto the leather-bound journal her mother had left her. Nava swallowed and reached for the item, unwrapping the rough leather bind. The parchment map tumbled to the wood table. She focused on the familiar scribbles of her mother's writing.

Nava took a deep breath and opened the page, passing notes of travels around the forest. Plants she'd picked for her father to use in potions.

She paged through to the end where the pages became sparser with content and paused.

Nava,

If you are reading this, I fear I never got around finding the strength to speak with you. I know you will be angry and confused.

I'm ashamed of what I did to protect you, and this has been a secret eating at me for the past few years.

In this journal, you will find a map that will take you to Arkimedes, your soulmate. Please don't go to him until you are ready, because the soulmate bond is wonderful but all-consuming.

We don't talk about him. In truth, it's hard to see you so young and already destined to something dangerous.

Arkimedes is too powerful, and with it comes the dangers of what might corrupt his soul. We have never known of his kin, but few can inherit such power and not have to answer for it.

He is mostly good, and I always thought he would pull away from his own darkness. Eventually. I cursed him to prevent him from coming to get you too soon. He is not ready. Neither are you, but I wasn't ready to let you go.

The curse I used was black magic. To use such hexes, you have to give a part of your soul away. His magic is so different. The curse has backfired on me. With the passing of days, I've become weaker. It's the price I pay for acting out of selfishness, for defying the gods.

I told him he had to do a selfless act for you. The real way of breaking the curse is for you to accept him fully as yours. I hope this will give you the choice you deserve.

I love you.

Nava gasped. Tears streamed down her cheeks as the journal shook in her grasp. Answers. She'd had all of them here with her the whole time.

Laurie had told her she had been holding back until Nava asked. They had always wanted to give her a choice. She could have broken Arkimedes's curse before. She would have known who he was had she read on.

Had she not been so angry, so stubborn.

Nava closed the journal with shaking hands. Her mother had died for cursing Nava's soulmate. For trying in vain to slow down time.

TRAVELING TO HER OLD town was bittersweet, the short days and long nights making it harder to journey along the forest's winding trails. The trip back had been quicker than their whole journey to the Northern Village, backtracking to areas she remembered well, some with longing, some with dread.

It had been three months since Nava left the town. She and Arkimedes approached the edge of the forest, where the trees became more sparse and less imposing, where tall grass of golden tones stood dancing in the wind. She could see the houses nearby, starting with ranches with terracotta tiles on their roofs and the warm stucco walls.

She took one step after another, her stomach churning with the anticipation of seeing Cameron once again, and as she walked, something shifted inside her.

A hollowness that grew somehow.

Arkimedes paused, studying his surroundings, and he was no longer walking by her side. She turned around and adjusted the weight of her backpack, the one thing she had refused to leave behind, much to Arkimedes's amusement.

It was no longer heavy, as her own endurance had grown exponentially from the start of her journey, and she had been working on practicing her magic by making it light as a feather and not exhausting her energy. The straps had marked her skin with angry red marks that told her they hadn't taken a rest in a few hours.

Arkimedes hesitated, his hands buried inside his pockets.

"Is there something wrong?" She took a few steps back to him as he frowned at the nothingness. Nava's lips parted, and she understood the predicament ahead.

It was the invisible shield that held magic outside of town. Her gaze traveled up the trees in the distance; maybe she had imagined it. Ari lurked in the background, unable to follow them past this point. A tortured gaze from afar morphed his features.

It had been something she had discussed with her Beekeeper. She couldn't stay in town without visiting the forest at least a couple of times a week. It was unclear how her being in the forest would set things in motion, but whatever magic she had in her helped maintain a balance.

The buzzing of her magic had gone dormant once again. The hollowness inside her made her breathless. Her hand came to her chest. This had been the way she'd felt all these years, as if missing something.

The village's spell had taken this away from her. She couldn't stay here long.

"I feel a pushback." He hesitated before his hand rested against the invisible shield. It resisted allowing him in, and they both held their breaths before it popped and allowed his arm in. His throat bobbed, right before he forced his body through.

They stayed frozen in silence, and she stared at his tall, strong figure. It was the same breathtaking sight of a handsome man, but her lips parted when she stared into his eyes. Gone was the magical storm raging inside his irises. Staring back at her were pale green irises, and he appeared more human than before.

She walked to him, grabbing his face as she examined every single inch of him. "Your eyes—they changed," she blurted.

His hands came to his face, patting over his black eyelashes. "They feel the same," he started, squinting around him. "Maybe the colors are a bit duller."

"Really?" she gasped.

"No, not really." He smirked, and a soft laugh escaped his lips as she whacked his shoulder.

"You wicked man. Do you feel all right, though?"

He nodded, and his hand came to her shoulder, squeezing it softly. "I'm fine."

They started down the hills that led them to Willowbrook. Cattle roamed around fenced fields, the landmarks peppered with trees of changing sizes, naked except for the occasional evergreen.

When she crossed this path months prior, she had been running for her life, not taking a second to breathe in the clear air on the edge of town or appreciate its beauty. The sun was midway through the sky, not quite as hot as in the summertime, bringing a pleasant warmth to their bodies as they hiked the winding dirt roads.

They walked in silence. The day of nonstop trekking caught up to them as they approached. Her heart was already beating as the vision of the packed cliffside town and its cobblestone roads came into view. The homes closed in on them.

She hadn't written or heard about her family for months. She suspected they would be in Simone's house since Devon's ship was still likely docked in town, waiting for him to come back, something that wouldn't happen.

Large arches of caramel-colored stones marked the town's entrance, with buildings of similar tones surrounding them. Wooden flower boxes were outside each window, painted in greens and reds. All vegetation had died and wilted from the cold weather.

The pleasant scent of burning wood and the crisp feeling of winter welcomed them in as people wearing various attires walked past them, barely sparing them a glance.

Arkimedes's gaze hovered over shop windows and studied a town lacking magic. His hand was firmly placed over the small of her back as she paused to allow a cart carrying large metal cans of fresh milk from the local farm to pass by them.

"We aren't far away from Simone's," Nava said, tilting her head to Arkimedes, who nodded, his face morphing with a curiosity she found endearing.

She smiled as they pushed past shops and mundane life by making their way down alleyways she knew well to the home of her best friend.

She half expected the vision of her house to be nothing but rubble. She had even entertained the idea that it had been burned to ashes in a fit of anger by Devon's goons after her escape, having found Simone was hiding the fugitives.

Her stomach churned as her attention fell upon the familiar shape of it, her friend's modest home. Narrow and close to her neighbors, it was made of strong stucco walls and white paint. Smoke was puffing out of the chimney as she pushed open the gate of the small front yard. Simone, unlike Nava, had never had an excellent green thumb, so Nava usually made her way here in spring to work in her garden.

It was all dead and brown.

Her hands were shaking when she reached for the door handle and stopped a few centimeters away from grabbing it. Nava's stomach awoke in a flutter, and her hands moistened with sweat. A warm touch grounded her as Arkimedes came close to her, giving her strength without the need for words.

"I bet you want to see him," he encouraged. A handsome smile illuminated his features.

She took a deep breath, steadying herself before she knocked on the door a couple of times. Where before there had been soft noises coming from inside, silence descended.

He nodded, his chin pointing to the door.

"Simone, Cam?" Her voice quivered even to her own ears.

Steps came rushing to the door. Clumsy long strides pounded over creaking wooden floors. It had been a few months since she'd held the freckled boy who stood in front of her with a gaping mouth as he took her in.

"Nava?" His voice was the one of a kid. If she closed her eyes, she could almost forget he was so tall.

"Of course, caterpillar," she said with a smile as tears blurred her vision.

Her brother jumped into her arms with a bone-crushing hug. "I thought I would never see you again. I— Simone said you would be back, that you were strong, and of course, I *know* you are strong. I never doubted that for a second. The house was such a mess. Like they had taken you. We were so afraid." The words tumbled out of his thick lips, but she enjoyed the smell of his skin and the feeling that she was home.

"The quickness of talking is something you *can* inherit." Arkimedes's voice broke the moment as both siblings pulled out of their embrace and turned to him. He had a smile on his lips, but he twisted his fingers as he stilled under Cameron's gaze.

"Cam, this is Arkimedes, and he is— Well, he is my soulmate." There was no use beating around the bush. Her brother's lips parted in shock as his bushy red eyebrows lifted to the edge of his forehead.

"Nice meeting you, Cameron."

"Whoa, wooow, wait—*wait,* you found your soulmate? The Crow?" Cameron shook his head as if trying to get his thoughts in order before pushing himself from the door and walking inside.

Nava followed behind. She knew Simone's house well, and while she studied the clean, neat place, she was unable to find a sign of her friend. The woman was likely in her bakery and wouldn't be back here until later that day.

"Yes," Nava answered her brother's questions and turned around to make sure Arkimedes was following. He had, but he stayed by the door with both hands in his pockets as his gaze followed the boy walking around the room in a wind of energy and emotions. Clumsy steps of someone who had grown too fast in the past few months.

"But . . . they are our enemies, no? Wasn't it a Crow who came and forced you to leave?" Cameron's gaze landed warily over Arkimedes, who looked at Nava for help.

"Cam, you might want to sit. It would be good for us to explain."

Cameron stopped and nodded, walking to the large sofa in the living room and letting his body fall unceremoniously onto one of them. "Are you having dreams? The ones of him, the ones that can take you away?" His voice was small. His attention focused on both her and Arkimedes as they settled as well.

"I stopped having them when I met Arkimedes. I know you are going to ask, but no, I wasn't aware he was my soulmate when I met him," Nava said, and she told him all that had happened, skipping a few bits of information he didn't need. She didn't want to scare him, after all.

"Where is Laurie—and Simone?" Nava got to her feet and made her way to the kitchen. She was starving and wanted to get something in her before making a trip to her house to see what state the bounty hunters had left it in.

"Laurie went to the market, and Simone is working."

Nava nodded, her palms damp from anticipating the two women reacting to her being back, with her soulmate in tow.

"So, you are a Crow? And we are fine with that?" Cameron's attention snapped to both adults in the room with a held breath as Nava nodded.

"We are okay with *Arkimedes,*" she agreed.

"I don't want to lose you like we did Dad. I was afraid you would never want or consider us going back to Iron City to find him. So I wanna say . . . I'm happy that for whatever reason, he was here, instead." Cameron's brow raised. "*Why* were you on the island? You aren't some stalker, are you?"

"Cam!"

"No, it's fine. It's a fair question. I wasn't stalking your sister. I wasn't able to even get into this town. I had to be on the island to be near her and not be taken like your father by the dreams. Soulmates need to be close."

"The dreams . . . happen because the soulmate is away? Well, that makes sense."

"Yes."

"But Mom, didn't she know it would happen? Why would she take Nava away from you and risk it?"

Her stomach dropped as she cleared her throat. "She did, and she expected he would follow."

"Which I did."

"It doesn't seem fair. Nava suffered through dreams for years," Cameron said.

"Mom left me a note," she admitted, lowering her gaze but feeling both of their eyes boring into her. "She explained it all, who Arkimedes was—" She met the man's confused gaze. "I found it in her journal when I was packing."

His lips parted.

"So you are accepting the bond? You didn't want it, right?" Cameron asked, unaware of the intensity hanging in between them.

A silence extended, and Arkimedes's brow lifted as a smirk appeared on his face.

"I wish I hadn't been so eager to voice such things to everyone," she mumbled. "It doesn't feel forced. It feels natural and real. I didn't understand the magic of it because I hadn't been able to experience it. We got to spend time with each other before we both chose one another."

"So—you love him?"

Nava's skin warmed as she held her breath.

Cameron turned to Arkimedes. "Welcome to the family."

"Thank you."

Nava was truly and unabashedly happy. They were not to stay here. The loss of her magic, being away from Ari, and her concern about whatever this was doing to Arkimedes's fae side were too much for her to grasp.

Sure, it would take them time to figure out what to do, to sell all their belongings and move across an island, but she was ready for this new life to begin.

She caught the brown body of a bee flying around the house. It landed on the arm of the sofa she had settled on. She turned her hand and opened her palm, and the bee crawled to it. Its soft humming energy coursed through her body.

Her eyes lifted to meet Arkimedes, and her mark soared.

It was *magic*.

The Silver Kingdom

The Iron Kingdom

The Gold Kingdom

THE CURSE OF A KINGDOM

BOOK 2

THE COPPER KINGDOM

THE COPPER CITY
Society of Crows
Marni's Woven M
Society safe's House
Society safe's House exit
Leela's house
The Lost Chariot Inn

Flying Boar

CHAPTER ONE

NAVA

Nava had been waiting for a while for Arkimedes to join her in the bath. She stared at her pruney fingers, moving her arms over the milky water. What was taking him so long? Surely getting wine from their kitchen wouldn't have meant leaving her alone for the evening. Not when he'd been kissing her senseless recently.

"Ark?" she called, frowning at the water around her that now cooled her heated skin.

Her heart skipped a beat at the silence. She lifted out of the water, and there was a heaviness in her stomach that hadn't been there before, something that made her pause.

She got out of the tub, reached for her nightgown, and draped it over her body, not caring that it would get wet.

Thunder rolled, and the pitter-patter of the rain fell harder against the glass window. She walked to the door, unsure why she tried to keep her steps weightless, but the uneasiness grew more assertive.

The prick of panic settled in the back of her mind like a whisper. Nava's steps slowed down as she tried to understand what was happening. She stilled her hand, then extended it to the doorknob. The only sound other than the rain was her loud heartbeat.

Out of nowhere, a stab of pain rattled through her. Her soulmate mark was aching like someone had branded her with burning iron. A loud bang roared from downstairs, followed by the cracking of wood.

She couldn't move and her vision blurred with tears as the scent of cayenne wafted around the room. Magic always carried a spicy note.

Devon, the member of the Society of Crows who attacked the village a year ago, had frozen her under a spell similar to this one in the middle of a battlefield.

Her body glowed as her magic awakened. Bees made of light formed over her skin, giving her the power to snap out of whatever had her frozen. She and Arkimedes were under attack. Her fingers twitched, and Nava focused her attention on them and closed her hand into a fist, grasping at the door and stabilizing her body weight on the frame.

Arkimedes had taught her earlier in the year how to battle a paralyzing spell by focusing on each part of her body and funneling her magic to it. Her muscles spasmed before she regained control.

She rushed down the stairs, her power around her like a shield. Candle-light illuminated the first floor. The sound of soft crackling came from the fireplace. The door that led to their garden swung with the loud wind from the storm outside.

Nava studied the space. The green glass of the bottle of wine on top of the wooden table mocked her. Her stomach churned.

Arkimedes. She tugged on their mating bond like a string, but panic tasted bitter in the back of her throat at the lack of response.

She ran past the threshold of the door and out into the rain. Her bare feet pounded the ground as she followed the pull toward him. Arkimedes held his head in his hands, kneeling and hunched over. A gasp of pain escaped his full lips. Her heart wrenched as she felt his pain vibrate through her body.

Their bond was aching, unable to contain this anguish any longer.

The darkness of the night veiled them, but she knew this area well and could roam it almost blindly. The scent of wet grass and summer rain enveloped her in a humid embrace, the tall trees of the Grey Forest their constant companions.

Nava was closer to him. His white knuckles tightened around his brown hair, pulling harder. "Ark—" She reached to him.

Arkimedes's head snapped up, and his wild green gaze came upon her. "Stay back, bee." He forced the words through tight lips. His handsome face was usually bright and healthy, but it had lost all its color.

Shadows of mist and smoke billowed around Arkimedes. It had to be the aura of his power. But these were wrong, like an evil presence of torture—ghosts made of dark magic and ancient, raw power.

Her heart lurched as an icy caress went down her spine, and she stopped panting for breath. Her body broke out in a thin layer of sweat. The aura around him resembled Arkimedes's power when he was in a fight.

The smell of magic and a mix of smoke enveloped her. The weight of the shadows' stony gazes made the hairs on her arms stand. Nava watched with horror as Arkimedes's face contorted, his lips opening in a silent cry. She took a step closer, but he shook his head in a plea.

"No!" he shouted in her mind. *"Stay. Back. Nava."*

The bodies became sharper, almost taking the appearance of a human. Tall, with slim waists and broad shoulders, something wicked blooming behind their bodies. Wings. She couldn't tell their shapes in the darkness of their yard, but the clear silhouette of feathers became apparent, so similar to Arkimedes's.

She counted seven, maybe eight winged creatures who flickered in and out of focus. Her chest burned, and she tried to swallow the thickness that had formed in her throat and made it hard to breathe.

The tendrils of a dark spell approached her. They grew like a weed over the ground, fingers extending at a rapid pace. Nava took a few steps back as a distance buzzing tickled the edge of her mind.

She was quick on her feet, backing away, focusing upon her soulmate. The ache emanating through their bond distracted her.

The bees surrounded her, but for the first time since Nava had learned she was a Beekeeper, they did not offer relief.

Nava was losing sight of Arkimedes behind the shapes of her insects.

No, *no*. She pushed her hand through the shield that enveloped her. Bees covered every inch of her body, constricting her movements. Her power blinded her, even as it tried to protect her from harm. But she didn't want this —she wanted to see Arkimedes, to help him.

Nava waved her arms around, the scorching sensation in her soulmate mark intensifying. The bees lifted her body in the air. The buzzing grew louder as a desperate cry left her lips. Was Ari controlling the bees? Was the second Beekeeper nearby? "Arkimedes!"

The bees uncovered her face, and the humid air of the summer night hit her skin. From the ground below, his face lifted, staring at her with pained eyes.

And then he was gone, disappearing in a billow of mist.

"No!" she gasped, and heat spread through her veins and her skin. The bees flew away from her body, and she dropped a few feet down. She landed poorly, but even as she stumbled, a deep hollow pain in her chest grew like a festering wound, making it hard to breathe.

Nava made it to where Arkimedes had been but a few moments ago. The weight of his body depressed the grass. She dropped to her knees and ran her fingers over the blades of grass. They were warmer than the cool ground. He had been here, and they had taken him away from her.

She heard something land behind her, but she didn't need to turn around to see it was the creature who was bound to her and Arkimedes. Aristaeus's presence had become second nature. Her friend, companion, and the first Beekeeper.

"He is gone," he said.

She lifted her head, and the raindrops were warm in contrast to her icy skin. Her chest seized as tears ran down her face. "Where?"

"The Dark Ones' kingdom, I presume." But she couldn't form a cohesive idea as she gasped for air like she was drowning. Aristaeus tilted his head, wood groaning at the movement. *"Sleep, dearest one."*

The hard sticks that were his fingers wrapped around her shoulder, the touch numbing. Her vision became spotted and the stale taste in her mouth was replaced by the sweetness of honey, and then there was darkness.

Nava squinted in the warm morning light. The storm had passed, giving way to a sunny morning.

The shapes of trees and twisty branches hung above her. Her body ached from sleeping on a bed of leaves. Nava sat up and took in her appearance. Her white cotton nightgown was stained with greens and browns. Mud crusted her bare legs and feet.

It wasn't her appearance or the fact that she'd slept outside that gave her pause, but the sinking inside her chest. The slow ache reminded her of all that had happened the night before.

Nava brought her shaky hand over her soulmate mark. Her chest caved in, and the wrecked sound that escaped her lips was empty. Not a dream. The shadows had taken Arkimedes.

She stared at a lost point between the trees as her body shook with the intensity of her sobs. The sparse grass made the puddles more visible.

Her body was numb and heavy like lead. She had not an ounce of energy to move, and her thoughts were muddled. From her vantage point, the movement between the trees called to her.

Ari's wooden frame appeared in front of her, thick trunks and branches covered in lichen and moss. He took her in with a gentle, ebony gaze. It was hard to read his expressions since he was a creature made of wood. But the underlying pain through their strange bond was present.

He'd used his magic to put her to sleep the night before. Had settled her on this pile of garden brush that Cameron had refused to throw away before he left for his travels with Gavin and Violet.

Her younger brother had taken an immediate liking to both sorcerers as soon as they'd moved to the village earlier in the spring. It had surprised Nava that Violet liked children. For someone who'd been so standoffish the entire time they'd traveled together, she had warmed up to her younger sibling rather fast.

"You put me to sleep." Her voice sounded broken to her ears, wobbling at the end.

"You were about to faint, and my magic has numbing qualities that would allow you to rest."

Nava rushed to sit down, and the hard edges of wooden sticks buried into her back and sides. "We should've followed the Dark Ones. Find Arkimedes and help him. I didn't need to sleep, Ari."

The Beekeeper tilted his head, slowly blinking. *"And how were we supposed to? Did you master your transporting skills overnight?"*

Her Beekeeper had been spending too much time with her little brother. His sarcasm levels had shot to the sky during the past few months.

Nava took a deep, calming breath. "I don't need the attitude right now," she huffed. "You know I haven't mastered it yet." It was imperative she learn to harness her Beekeeper's magic and transport, the way Ari could move around the forests. Magic connected them to nature, and thus they could become part of it. She rubbed her chest, going over the memories of the night before. Something came up. "Yesterday, you said you presumed he was in the Dark Ones' kingdom?"

The Dark Ones—the name people liked to call Arkimedes, the reason the entire town had was so afraid of him months ago when she and Ark had been in the village for the first time, battling Devon's army.

Arkimedes had once told her that everyone else but her always saw him surrounded by his power. Something wicked and dark. She hadn't understood what that would look like. Why would people be so afraid? Today, she knew better.

Ari nodded, and the tremor of dread in her stomach grew. The shapes from the night before were part of whatever he was from. When he shared about his past, he'd mentioned where he'd tracked his origins before he had stopped searching further.

She got up from the ground and dusted off her nightgown. "He found his kin in the Copper Kingdom. I have to go there. What does that mean for us?"

The Beekeeper nodded. *"Magic bound the three of us long ago. I shall go with you and stay in the forests near the city. We should be able to maintain the balance in nature from there."*

Balance in nature, words Ari liked to throw at her, even though she had a hard time grasping whatever he meant. It had been almost a year since she'd discovered she had a larger fate than being a potion maker in Willowbrook.

Not long ago, she'd thought she would always stay in that non-magical town. But once they'd returned after the Crown's attack, she couldn't take it for longer than a couple of months. They'd stayed there long enough to pack a few things and make their way back to this village. She wanted to raise Cameron in a life that embraced their newly accepted nature, and she also needed to be closer to Ari.

Nava wished she hadn't been coddled her whole life, so maybe leaving this island toward the unknown wouldn't add to the dread already piled over her. There was no other way, however. She had to get to Arkimedes as fast as possible; their soulmate bond demanded them to be close.

How long would it take her body to deteriorate now that he was continents away? How long did they truly have?

Weeks, months? She didn't even want to consider being away from him for longer than a few days. Nava wished she could ask someone about how her bond might affect her by being away from her soulmate, even though they were both still alive—at least she hoped that was still that case. Her heart constricted at the way her thoughts twisted, and after a forced intake of breath, she took her mind away from that line of thinking.

There was one person who knew more about soulmates than she did—Violet. However, the sorceress was away for a month to do research in the enormous libraries of the Pearl Islands.

Cameron had begged Nava to let him go with Violet and Gavin, fascinated to learn more, and the largest magical library in the world had made her little brother tremble with excitement. She could use his hug to bring back her strength.

"We don't have long," Ari said, and Nava met his eyes, her stomach dropping. *"Your bond is fully formed now. We will deteriorate fast."*

"You are full of good news, Aristaeus."

The bark that made his brows dipped. *"The Zorren will come for us in our weakened state and make sure they finish what they started months ago when we first met."*

Great. The pit of dread in her stomach grew. She'd found Ari nearly dead almost a year ago. The Zorren, creatures of a shadow dimension that sought destruction in the world, had attacked him. The only information Aristaeus had given her was that they fed on life.

They were the mortal enemies of the Beekeepers. *Her* mortal enemies, even though she'd never seen one before. "So what then? We transfer there? How long would it take me to master this?"

"We have been working for a couple of months. You tell me."

She tightened her lips. "Cut the sass."

As if to prove his point or to annoy her further, Ari disintegrated in front of her. His looming body faded to shapes of bees, dust, and pollen. He flew away from her and headed to the forest, leaving her standing on her land.

Whatever peace of mind Ari had given her was gone, throwing her back into despair. She walked to her home, ready to get on with her tasks at hand. First, get dressed. Second, get her weapons. And third, find Roman.

The Commander knew about the Copper Kingdom. She remembered that detail being mentioned before and was hopeful he would aid her. Nava couldn't march there and bring Ari along with no actual knowledge of what to expect.

Had she honed her power and transfer, maybe they would already be there. She took a breath to lighten her heavy heart, to not be annoyed at herself and her failings. She'd been doing magic for less than a year. Arkimedes always told her she was her own worst critic.

Nava lifted her hand, chasing the cool brass handle of the back door. The aroma of leather, lavender, and cedar hit her in a wall that reminded her of home, but also of the clear hole staring at her with a sense of growing doom. She'd be of no use to Arkimedes if she crumpled now.

Like the dining chair that lay on the floor, turned on its side, the leg twisted and broken. The sound of it falling had been the only alert she'd gotten that something had been wrong the night before.

Nava walked to it, grasping the cotton fabric of her nightgown as she went over the splintered wood. She kneeled down and studied it longer than time itself. A few drops of dried blood stained the floor, and a breath caught in her throat as anger exploded inside her stomach, spreading like wildfire through her veins.

Nava wasn't the scared woman who'd run from her town a year ago. She was powerful and determined, all in one.

She would find him, whatever it took. And they would pay.

CHAPTER TWO

NAVA

Midmorning sun passed through the tall foliage of the forest, hitting the cobbled roads of the center of town. The buildings that jutted out of the trees were spaced closer; their shapes loomed over her and increased the sensation of claustrophobia that squeezed her lungs.

She ran down past her favorite restaurant, and curious looks from passersby trailed her steps. The streets hummed with life, the warm humid air of summer embracing them all.

With every step she took, her heartbeats became louder, the pounding of her headache increasing. The distance between Arkimedes and her was already affecting her.

The Commander held meetings during the day. She spotted him from afar, his long salt-and-pepper hair pulled up into a bun, his skin golden from being under the sun. He wore a forest-green linen shirt and sat at a table in front of the largest building in town, the Commissary. As he listened to the first person in line, he crossed his leg over, nodding every so often.

Roman wasn't alone. Next to him was one of the law enforcement recruits who protected the village. Nava jogged to him, and her quick steps alerted them to her approach. Everyone was still on edge, even though it had been a year since Devon's attack.

Roman's rum-colored eyes met hers; his brow deepened as he took her in. "Nava, is there something wrong?" he asked, rising to his feet. He studied her face and then his eyes traveled down her body.

"The Dark Ones took Arkimedes last night."

His face lost its color as he rounded the table to meet her. "What do you mean?"

The heaviness in her throat settled and her limbs grew numb. "They came to our home, and they kidnapped him. I need to find him. Arkimedes once told me he traced his kin to the Copper Kingdom. I know you are from there. I—"

"Nava, I can't just go back there." Roman's brows pinched in the middle.

Her body broke into a sweat. "Why? I— We have to find him."

"To do what?" He pressed his lips together tightly, his hand going over his face. "It was always going to happen. I told her they'd come for him."

"You told who what?" A spike of nausea hit her in a wave that built up and weakened her stance. Light-headed with the information she could not follow, Nava swallowed thickly and took a step closer to the man. "It doesn't matter. We need to go."

Roman's lips tightened. "I can't leave the town, and even if I could, we wouldn't make it there in time. It will take us months to travel there by boat. My small force here won't stand a chance against the Copper Kingdom's army. The king hates me, Nava. If I step foot in that kingdom, not only will Arkimedes die, but so will anyone who comes with me."

Drops of sweat scoured her skin, and her world closed in. She steeled her back. Bees were coming to her in her panicked state, swarming with a loud buzz.

Roman looked to the darkening sky and swallowed. "Nava, please calm down. I can't go with you," he repeated. "We need the defense against any potential residual attacks. You know that."

They did. The village had been getting attacked in the subsequent months since Devon's arrival. The soldiers who'd escaped had traveled to the West Village—finding allies among the wicked. No one was impervious to the kingdom's gold.

She swallowed but pressed on. "There is much more than our lives at stake."

Not that she didn't understand his point. To him, it was just two people in an entire town. She didn't want to divulge that their destiny was greater than politics and wars. It was even more significant than her love for her soulmate.

"If it was on this island, we would lift every rock to find him. But this is across oceans. To a force stronger than what I offer."

She drew a step back. "I will find another way."

It wasn't a grand plan. There was one other person in the world she knew who had knowledge about Arkimedes's past and power beyond what was expected from a sorcerer, however scary he was. Devon Black had been a brother to Arkimedes once upon a time, and he was her only choice.

She walked toward the building that held the prisoners. It was an asymmetrical construction built inside an ancient tree. The trunk was hollow but reinforced with many layers of magic.

Nava peeked from behind a home as the guards chatted in front of the rusted iron gate. Lunch hour crept in, and it always took them a few minutes for their replacements to come back. Arkimedes complained about this lacking system often, mentioning there would be a time someone would break in. Roman's answer was always to say no prisoner could escape on their own.

She swallowed, trying to keep herself from fading as her legs and arms turned heavy with the passing time. The soul bond affected every inch of her body with each breath she took, demanding to be near her mate. The Copper Kingdom had to be much farther than she'd originally thought.

Nava had to make it inside the building somehow and then find Devon's cell. Arkimedes had visited him often, ever since they moved to town. Her soulmate seldom spoke on the matter with her; she supposed it was normal since she wasn't Devon's biggest fan.

The bees hadn't stopped circling her body ever since she'd left Roman's company. Nava could sense Ari nearby, waiting for her to do the most stupid thing she'd ever done in her life. Judging by her failing health, there was little time to come up with a third idea.

The guards, one man and one woman, walked away, their long gray tunics billowing with each step they took. The male's laughter trailed behind, masking the sounds of their heels over the stone ground of their path. Nava took a steadying breath and followed their retreat. After what she was about to do, she would forever be the enemy.

Her home for the last few months, the only place she'd ever fit in. She pressed her lips together tightly and allowed herself to wallow and then ran toward the building.

The heavy gates were unlocked, and they screeched as she lifted the lever and pulled it wide enough to squeeze through the hole. This would be a perfect opportunity to use her transferring Beekeeper spell if she wasn't feeling so weak.

Nava had transferred once before, only a few feet.

Her shoulders eased as she settled in the entryway. No one was here; she rushed to the front desk and rummaged through a rustic wooden box that was stained with age and held brass skeleton keys. The bees crawled everywhere, and the sensation of doom grew in the pit of her stomach, warning her.

Nava cursed under her breath and headed to the steps. She would have to release a man, who was hated by everyone, out of the prison she put him in, without the keys.

She ran up steps carved from live wood into the massive tree. The energy of it vibrated through every inch of her skin and blood, healing her body as she pushed forward. She was getting used to this part of being a Beekeeper, being the same with nature.

She and Ari protected it, whatever that meant. Nature, in return, responded to their calls, lending them energy when needed.

The sorcerer's magic bound the tree to repel people trying to release prisoners or prevent them from escaping. Nature, however, was aiding her, even though her intentions were clear.

Once, Ari had mentioned that they were one with the forest and its creatures, that it would help them and then would come around when it was their turn to replenish it. Nava had seen Aristaeus bring spring flowers out of thawing grounds before.

She climbed hundreds of uneven steps. The farther up she went, the stronger the surrounding magic became, almost suffocating her.

Nava took two steps at a time. Devon's ship still awaited his return to the ports in Willowbrook. They could take it to the Copper Kingdom, and maybe she wouldn't die before they got there.

Torches on the walls illuminated the top floor, casting long shadows that moved over the ground. The energy emanating from the tree's core enveloped her like a shield. Bees flew around her, crawling over the ground and the walls. The stairs stopped in the middle of the room; now that she was here, she counted nine cells.

Only one of them had the lights on.

Nava cleared her throat and made her way with tentative steps. She hesitated when she came upon a man sitting on a white cot. He wore simple black pants and a black striped shirt. His hair was longer than when she'd seen him in Willowbrook a year prior. It was similar to the way it'd been the day they'd met in the front garden of her manor eleven years ago.

Dread pooled in her stomach, and she stopped. Nava couldn't do this; she couldn't release this monster after all he'd done. Even if it meant she would die.

She took a step back. He was her chance of survival for both Arkimedes and her, and she had made it all the way here. Devon knew where the Copper Kingdom was and had the ship to take her there.

The world demanded two Beekeepers—Ari had revealed as much. Even if she died, another would be born, right? It didn't have to be her. Arkimedes didn't need to be their protector.

She took another step back and froze, her soulmate mark throbbing as if in response to her thoughts. Tears dropped from her eyes, and a booming voice came into her head. It spoke in tongues, a language she didn't recognize. However, she understood.

"You will find your soulmate and defeat the demons."

It wasn't a voice she had heard before, and the sound of it made her hair stand on edge. Warmth rushed through her as she remained in her spot. Her insects crawled up her glowing skin. She understood with clarity; the Zorren's threat was much more significant than her, and a higher power refused to let her give up.

Nava steeled her fading resolve and walked a step closer to Devon. His head snapped up, and his lips parted as he took her in. She must be something to behold, with golden bees crawling over her body, her face visible and covered in sweat.

"Devon," she said in a commanding tone, or at least she hoped it was.

He came to his feet lazily, his head arching to the side, exposing his long, pale neck. "Now, this is something I didn't expect to see today." He walked closer to the cell bars.

"I need your help."

He barked a laugh that lacked warmth to it, shaking his head. "That might be the most ridiculous thing I've ever heard."

She took a couple of steps forward, closing the gap between them. "The Dark Ones took Arkimedes last night."

Her body almost touched the iron bars of the cell. It was so small in there, just a bed with thin blankets. The walls were plain dark wood, covered in a thick layer of moss that extended to the floor. A basin to the side of the room, nowhere left for privacy.

"Help me find the Copper Kingdom." Her voice wavered. She knew so little of the other kingdoms of this world. Geography and politics were not her favorite subjects. "We could take . . . your ship?"

Devon's eyes raked down her body, and one corner of his lips tilted. "Have you looked at yourself in a mirror? You don't have that long."

Nava didn't understand why her health deteriorated so quickly. It had taken her father much longer than a few hours to die after her mother had expired—a dreadful year of him suffering and sleeping.

The reality of his words hit her like stones dropping into her stomach. "Do you know any other way? To get there, to save him?"

He studied her quietly. "Perhaps I do."

"How?"

"You are thinking of sauntering to the Dark Ones' kingdom, and what? Politely ask them to return their prisoner back to you? You're naïve, and it will get you killed." He shook his head and added, "Not that I care if you do."

The Crow said it was the Dark Ones' kingdom. That information alone had her mind reeling. She'd always assumed it was just a village inside a kingdom, a continent, but if Devon's words were correct, fae ruled that land. Did they share it with humans?

The Iron Kingdom didn't welcome fae species openly. The name alone was a deterrent to most, if not all, as fae were allergic to iron.

"I will not ask them to return him to me. I will just—free him." Once she was in the same area as him, she'd have more time to come up with a better plan.

He scoffed. "Are you going there alone? Or have you somehow convinced that crew of greys who hung around you two last year?"

The greys Devon referred to, Gavin and Violet, weren't here. She wished they were the ones she had to rely on. This would be a lot easier with her friends around. Clearing her throat and taking a step closer, she realized that even in his cell, Devon stood with an air of grandness Nava almost admired. Further scrutiny showed he had ropes around his wrists that were tight enough to leave bruises on his skin.

She clutched the metal bars. Her energy dwindled immediately. They had spelled it to cancel magic, something she assumed would prevent a prisoner from escaping. She dropped her hand as if it had burned her. "You were so close, like brothers. Don't you care even a little?"

"It was always going to happen." His sharp jaw clenched as he avoided her gaze.

"It bothers you."

He bristled. "He locked me in this cell."

Nava ignored his words. "You probably were with him when he was doing his research on his past—before he found them. You know how to get to the Copper Kingdom and where he's being held."

Devon's inky gaze cut to her. "What if I was there? It's not like I can help you, even if I wanted to . . . And let's make something clear, *I don't*."

"I can let you out if you help me," she whispered. The bees lifted from her body all at once, circling around her with an intense buzz.

Devon's back straightened. He took in the surrounding spectacle, his gaze tinting with a bit of panic. He remembered the bees that had almost killed him a year ago. "You would release me?" He took a step back, his long legs almost bringing him to the edge of his bed.

"I would, but only to go to the Copper Kingdom and save Arkimedes."

A bitter laugh escaped his lips. "Even if you could, why would you be so naïve as to think I would help you and not kill you myself as soon as I'm free?"

"You won't." Her voice came out strong, and she lifted her chin in the air.

His lips pulled back, revealing straight white teeth. "Please release me. I would love to prove you different."

"He saved your life, didn't he? He didn't do it for his own gain. He did it because he didn't want you to suffer." Devon's eyes came to meet her and his lips tightened as she continued. "You owe him a life debt."

His pale complexion turned green. "No."

"Yes, and I'm calling on it."

"You can't call upon this. You aren't him."

"But I'm his soulmate." Nava had been piecing this together, but as her confidence grew within, she knew this was the right path to follow. "Which makes him and me one soul. If I don't get to him soon, he will die, and you will fail to repay the debt I'm here to collect."

Devon shook his head. His skin glowed yellow, matching the color of her aura. The binding of the life debt settled between them like a strong rope tying them together in an unbreakable spell. "You conniving bitch." His wide ebony eyes looked at his glowing skin. Magic lit the cell. "How are you doing magic inside this building?"

He would never know that the tree was allowing her to do so. "It doesn't matter how. What matters is to get you out of there so we can—"

"Die in that kingdom," he interrupted her, dropping his arms to his sides. "You seem like a fit mate for him, stubborn like no one else."

That, she couldn't refute.

CHAPTER THREE

NAVA

Her brain always worked in funny ways when put between a rock and a hard place. Nava was always good at making up plans to survive.

It wasn't like she was proud she'd ended up in this prison, making a deal with someone she hated. She wasn't sure if her shaking knees had anything to do with the tightness in her chest due to her betrayal of this town or the growing weakness in her body. It was likely both. She hoped Arkimedes would forgive her for calling a life debt in his name.

"So, how are you breaking me out of here?" Devon's voice was gruff and dangerously deep, his face disjointed with rage.

Nava took a step back, keeping a healthy distance from him. "I'm not, not until you say how you're bringing us to save Arkimedes."

He surged forward, taking a few steps to the cell bars but not reaching for them. It was then that Nava realized the palms of his hands were blistered, likely from holding onto the spelled iron bars. She almost pitied him. "It's of no use to me to reveal anything to you if I don't believe your skills will get me out of this fortified prison."

Her mouth became sandpaper, and the word "imposter" flashed through her mind. Even after learning she had a bigger destiny than just being a potion maker, she was unsure of her strength, in whether she was indeed worthy of all this.

Ari often told her this crutch stopped her from achieving her full potential, but what if the universe had been wrong all along? What if she couldn't do it?

She swallowed down the knot that had formed in her throat and took a step back before turning around to leave. Two could play this game. It wasn't like he had anyone else lining up to release him.

"Wait!" His eyes nearly bulged out of his head. "Where are you going?"

She shrugged, keeping her expression neutral as she fixed her gaze back on him. "I don't have time for your games. I will leave you here to rot and find another way."

He straightened to his full height, towering in the small room as he took her in a different light. Like he'd never truly seen her before. "I can create a portal that will get us both there."

Dark magic. A warning bell rang inside her head, and she blinked in silence. "You can make one that strong? What do you have to sacrifice in order to gain such power? Kill a baby?"

"Perhaps a kitten." His lips tilted up, but the gesture didn't reach his eyes. "You asked what I could do, no? I find it rich for you to judge me when you're so desperately trying to break a prisoner out of jail."

She hadn't been able to shake the damn nickname he'd given her a year ago after his bounty hunters took her as a prisoner. Violet had thought the nickname fit, and it had stuck. "What's the price?"

"One I won't be paying, that's for sure." He turned, walked to the bed with lazy steps, and let his body drop on the mattress, crossing his legs and putting both hands behind his head.

She scowled. "What's that supposed to mean?"

"You know there's a price to open a portal, and I'm telling you I won't be paying it. It means you will be the one sacrificing something dear to you." He lifted his head and his eyes danced with mirth. "A hand? Perhaps your teeth? Your sight? The possibilities are endless."

Her stomach dropped; her skin prickled like a thousand ants were crawling over her.

"Does Arkimedes mean that much to you?" he asked.

"Yes, he does."

Devon sat up, his eyes wide like circles before he caught himself. "Fine. Now get me out of here. Because you, kitten, are on borrowed time."

Nava studied the cell in front of her. They'd secured the iron frame that held the bars to the wood with thick metal hinges and bolts.

"How are we going to make it out of this building? Have you even thought about that?" Devon's voice broke her concentration.

She was making her plan on the spot because no one had prepared her for the fae coming to her home and stealing the love of her life away in the middle of the night. She was also growing sicker by the minute and had gotten no help from the Commander or this town.

Gavin, Violet, Cameron, and Laurie were elsewhere, unable to support her. Her only companion, Ari, couldn't leave her behind and save Arkimedes on his own. She was alone.

"I have thought about it," she snapped back. "You will open the portal here."

He barked a laugh. "Here?"

"Shh, yes, here. You speak Casztinian, no?"

Devon crossed his arms and stared at her with an indifferent expression. "This shall be interesting."

Nava ignored his words and studied the tree. Her bees crawled on the roof and the energy of her surroundings became thicker as she called for more. She needed the wood to expand and contract, to weaken the iron gate, to crush it enough for them to kick it aside.

A tremor ran beneath her feet, and Devon stood from his bed. "I'll be damn—"

"It won't take much time for the guards to be up here when I break the gate. How long do you need to make the portal?"

His lips parted as his dark eyes studied the ceiling. "A minute or two."

"Good." She drew her dagger out of the sheath. Bees lifted in flight and surrounded her protectively. "You so much as move to attack me, and I'll finish what I started last year. Don't let my magic fool you. I intend on saving Arkimedes, whatever it takes."

"The life debt won't let me harm you, you know that," he said in a low tone.

"Get ready." She let her eyes drift to the tree and the moss. To the energy that came out of them and fed the power of her magic. The tremor became a full-on earthquake. Screams erupted from underneath, the prisoners' and guards' fear echoing around them.

Devon steadied himself against the wall, and the iron gate shrieked. The sound grew louder, and the wood above them contracted, the metal bending at weird angles. Heavy bolts loosened and fell to the ground; her knuckles whitened around the hilt of her blade as her stomach churned with fear, anger, and anticipation.

She felt a trace of an emotion that wasn't hers—pride. From Ari, not far away.

The screams came louder from the floors beneath, and she took a few steps back as the gate in front of her shook and then fell with a loud bang over the wooden floor.

Devon gasped. "No shit."

Nava's legs shook as the tremors of the tree died down. "The portal, Devon."

He lifted his arms, showing her the straps that prevented him from doing anything.

She swallowed and fixed her gaze on his. "Do not think about leaving without me."

He smiled. "Don't give me ideas, cat."

She ran the sharp edge of her dagger through the binds, and they fell to the ground with a heavy thump. Without the rumble of the tree, she could hear the clear voices of people beneath. She studied Devon as he rolled his wrists. For a breath, they stood in absolute silence, and she waited for him to pounce on her.

He stood a whole head taller. Nava squared her shoulders and brought her dagger closer to her body, assuming a defensive stance. Her magic soared around her as bees and a yellow glow.

"Open. The. Portal," she said.

Devon's own aura shifted, a color of indigo so dark it almost appeared black. Then his fingers shone with power. A crackling noise and the heavy scent of spice enveloped her. Peppercorn and cayenne.

A surge of wind whipped her wild hair over her face. Devon's brows dipped in concentration as he looked at his fingers, where inky trails came together and twisted into a circle that rose between both of them. The sizzle of static raised her hair, and she struggled to see behind the traces of debris and flailing insects.

A bead of sweat trailed down his temple. "When we cross, the portal demands a payment. The first thing that comes to your mind will be what it claims," he said. The black hole of dark magic was now the size of her whole torso.

She thought of Cameron and urged her mind to put that away, to not think of Ari or Arkimedes. "You mean the portal will claim my memory?"

"Yes, it will become his."

"His?" Nava repeated, blinking rapidly, trying to understand the information. "Who is he? Would he hurt me?"

Devon's black eyes flashed to her, and his lips twitched. "He is the guard and ruler of the shadow world. The portal will hurt you, but it won't kill you."

Nava swallowed, and her skin became clammy and cold. She hoped her mind wouldn't give something she couldn't live without or this would all be worthless in the end. "Why are you telling me this?" she asked, trying to distract herself.

"It will be of no use to my life debt if you wind up not remembering why we're there in the first place, would it?"

She guessed he had a point. The portal zapped, and behind the whirlwind of inky magic, she saw the mirage of tall buildings with patina-green rooftops and warm stones. A city made of copper. Behind the carriages, stone roads, and people, a giant castle loomed in the back.

"Now?" she asked. His hand shook as he dropped it to his side. She vaguely heard steps dashing up the staircase and met his gaze as he pointed to the raging circle in front.

"Ladies first."

"Oh, gee, thanks." Nava's voice dripped with sarcasm, but she stepped forward, lowering her dagger, and hesitated for a second. Then something—no, someone—shoved her in.

She staggered toward the portal. Her arms flailed for a moment, and then she couldn't see the prison she'd been standing in before as she fell down into the nothingness. Floating in a place without gravity or scent. Not cold or warm.

She wasn't even sure if she was breathing. Then her thoughts became sharper as she focused on her surroundings; the aching hole in her heart was present, and she still was sore and tired, but not dead.

Nava had to be careful what to think of next, as the portal—or the gods—demanded payment for magic such as this. They always wanted something. Then she smelled it, the soft scent of burning, like smoke over a fire.

Something moved through the darkness. It had to be a play of her imagination. Everything was as black as night. Her pulse quickened, and somehow she knew she was being watched. Her eyes strained as she followed the shape, sure it was a trick of her brain.

"Look, Father, a Beekeeper has come to us in our land," a whisper echoed in the cave, a sinister hiss that somehow hurt her ears and was familiar at the same time. Gooseflesh raised over her skin. The movement in her peripheral was choppy, like a nightmare coming to claim her.

Her throat clenched and her skin became cold with sweat. "Who is there?"

A laugh reflected in the empty shadows. Her skin glowed as her magic came to her calling, warm, bright yellow light. A pale-skinned man stepped back into the void with a hiss, black feathers moving to shield him from the light. His red eyes were forever burned in her mind.

A demon? Had she gotten stuck in the shadow world?

"This is not a normal Beekeeper. A human crossing *has* to pay," another voice said, this one deeper and detached, ignoring the pale man with red eyes who'd disappeared. "Give me a memory."

Nava held back a scream that threatened to spill as the same demon moved closer. He had wings, she realized, and was shielded by the shadows, however she sensed him coming near.

"A memory, girl," the deeper voice that came from everywhere reminded her, spiked with annoyance.

This didn't sound good. She tried to focus on anything but the winged man who approached her, wishing she could go back to the simpler days of training in the forest, camping on higher grounds, and the constellations above her. Like she'd done with her father.

No, no, no.

"Yes," the deeper voice gloated.

Memories flashed through her mind: starry nights, her father struggling to put the tent up when camping. The familiar burn of the rope fibers against her grip as she laughed at something he said. But his words faded.

Gasping, she screamed, "Not him, *please*!"

She tried to force her mind to focus on something else. The gods could take her hand, instead. But the rolling laughter of her dad disappeared, and so did the mornings eating brunch or him explaining how to make the perfect healing potion, which midnight flower would give her the strongest brew for migraine medicine.

Tears wetted her cheeks as the knowledge escaped her. One by one, they all flew away, even the bright blue color of his eyes. She brought her hands to her face as she tried to hold on to something, anything, a name.

Oliver Forrest—the potion maker of the Iron Kingdom. Her mother's soulmate.

But soon, that too disappeared.

CHAPTER FOUR

NAVA

Nava fell onto something soft but prickly and was blinded momentarily by the bright light around her. The scent of lavender and other florals enveloped her. She opened her eyes, blinking rapidly, and took in her new surroundings. The sweet, warm air of summer caressed her skin.

Sitting on top of manicured grass, she wiped her cheeks as her body racked with sobs that weren't as silent as she hoped. Tall hedges stood a few feet from her, crafted into the shape of a spire.

Devon landed next to her, his hands barely catching him before he fully ate the dirt. She might have laughed at his wild expression had she not felt so wrecked. She'd surrendered something so important. Her mind was struggling to provide her with what, but the hole left behind was too large to be anything but catastrophic.

Devon was up from the ground just as fast as he'd fallen, his face snapping to each side as he took in their surroundings. She followed suit, albeit slower, feeling her legs and arms shake under her weight. Her soulmate mark ache had lessened, and some of her energy was coming back.

Arkimedes was close.

She let go of a heavy sigh, relieved as the realization hit her that he wasn't the one who'd been taken from her. She scoured through her mind. Cameron's freckles came quickly, her mother's warm voice, Laurie— The soft trickle of a fountain nearby distracted her.

It mixed alongside her heaving breaths, a song of birds with melodies she hadn't heard before. A castle stood out in the background, hazed over by its size and distance, behind the layers of shaped bushes and vegetation that separated them. Yellow marble blocks layered neatly, and massive windows with lancet arches decorated the tall edifice. The towers' pinnacles were topped with aged copper-green roofs. Nava had seen nothing like this before.

"Snap out of it. They will be on us soon." Devon's sharp voice took her out of her reverie. With wide strides, he made his way past the hedge.

"Do you know where we are?" she asked, rushing behind him, glancing at beautiful white flowers that bloomed with geometric patterns. So similar to camellias, however . . . not. This enchanted vegetation followed their movements closely, angling their petals with their passing.

A chill ran down her spine as she hugged her arms closer to her body, eyeing the walls of flowers. The pit in her stomach grew.

"Do you even know where we are going?" she asked between clenched teeth.

He tilted his face, leveling her with a glare. "I have never been here in person. Since you talk to nature, apparently, why don't you tell us where to go before the guards are upon us?"

She reeled back, aghast. "What do you mean, you don't know where we are?" She pointed to the wall of creepy flowers in front of them. "This is not normal. This is magic— Someone's tracking us."

Being in tune with nature had its perks.

His lips tightened. "We need to get out of this garden."

"You said you've been here before."

"No, *you* did. I just didn't correct you." Listening to his unaffected tone, she would've thought nothing was worrying him. What gave him away were his tense shoulders and traveling gaze. He continued down the path they were walking. The sun of the afternoon highlighted his profile. A straight nose, with proud, pale lips and large black eyes.

"Wait, wait. You didn't come to this kingdom with Arkimedes?"

"We have no time to get into semantics."

"Oh, no. We do." She quickened her steps, trailing him. "That changes things."

"Does it? You told me once here, you'll figure out a way to save him. I brought you here. So far, I'm holding my end of the bargain." He paused, and his gaze tracked down her face. "Now, you aren't dying. You're welcome."

She huffed her annoyance but chose not to dwell on his words. "Where are we, either way?"

He eyed the castle looming in the background with apprehension. "Looks like the castle's garden."

Her mouth dropped. "T—The castle, what?" She groaned as she looked at the marble statues between the bushes. It was carved into the likeness of someone beautiful. Were their eyes chasing them as well or was she going crazy?

This kept getting creepier by the minute.

"Why did you bring us to a castle? We just needed to land near Arkimedes, in a safe place to come up with the next move."

"It's not like I had a lot of time to set up coordinates," he snapped, not pausing in his strides. "You were the one showing up to my cell, making demands and forging life debts."

"Believe me, you were the last person I wanted to ask for any help at all."

Devon stopped, turning to face her, and she almost ran into him. Reeling back, Nava tried to keep her distance. "Let's call it what it is, shall we? You forced me here, and now that your pathetic plan is backfiring, you need to put the blame on someone else."

Nava's mouth hung open. And she wanted to tell him to go to hell, except maybe his words had hit some deep guilt brewing inside her.

"Probably have never had to work with a team before, have you, kitten?" He continued walking after her lack of a response.

She cursed that this man's sharp tongue could get under her skin so fast. "I thought all of you Crows are supposed to be all-powerful," she breathed as she caught up with him. "To a truly remarkable, trained sorcerer, a portal would've been a nuance. Especially since I was the one paying the price."

"I hope they took something that pains you." His tone dripped with venom, and her heart contracted at the emptiness within herself.

"At least I had something to lose. You probably only have yourself—since you even lost your brother."

Devon reeled back, his expression shifting rapidly with fast blinking and paling skin. He pressed his lips together before his hand brushed away strands of greasy hair that had fallen over his face.

She could've felt the ugly grasp of guilt clutching at her, but she wouldn't allow it. Not when Devon had done all he had the year before. Nava cleared her throat. "You said the guards are coming?"

"You know what I said, you just like to hear yourself talk."

They took a sharp corner to what felt like a maze. It was hard to see where to go when the hedges were so dense, and the sweet scent of the blooms nauseated her. She might be in the only garden in the world she didn't like.

Something was very wrong with these flowers.

"In the name of His Majesty, stop at once or face the consequences!"

The sky darkened above them. Nava stood paralyzed at the sight of angels coming down from the sky, their large wings flapping in the air, contrasting against the copper shades of their shiny armor.

She turned at the sound of retreating steps. Devon had clearly decided he was not sticking around and was already eight feet away from her. A spike of panic ran through her as her instincts took over, and soon her legs were moving, chasing after the Crow.

Both Devon and she ran down the aisle of the maze, the hedges closing in. The sound of flapping wings wasn't far away. Bees came down around her body, circling her as her steps became lighter over grass; even though this bush wasn't helping her, her bees were.

"This way," she panted, and Devon turned and followed her blindly. His face morphed into a determined scowl.

She wasn't sure if he was annoyed at the soldiers chasing after them or at her. It was probably both. Air burned her lungs as the ground beneath transitioned from short grass to loose gravel, and the hedges were no longer covered in white flowers but were spires of cedar.

The sky darkened, and the air crackled with spices and magic, becoming humid out of nowhere. Thunder rolled, and mist appeared around them. It became difficult to see. Devon's magic was making an appearance, hiding them in plain sight.

They wouldn't make it; there were too many following them, even with both their powers combined.

"Shit!" Devon's voice echoed in the empty garden when a fae landed in front of him. The angel-like man assumed an attack pose, holding a two-bladed sword in one hand. His face was covered by a helmet of orange-and-pink copper, aged in greens and whites.

Wisps of ink bloomed around the fae's body, similar to what Arkimedes's magic did when he was amid battle—except not as impressive of a sight. Floating leaves and the shape of a dead tree embossed the center of his chest plate.

"Stop at once! This is your last warning." The fae's voice boomed in the clearing, and her steps faltered as she lost her footing over the loose ground.

"Fuck!" the Crow cursed louder, but he lifted his hands in a sign of surrender. His onyx gaze flashed to her.

Nava wasn't so ready to give up. She turned and faced the approaching shapes of the Copper Kingdom's army, their wings large and mostly black. The reminder of her soulmate made this moment that much more painful to bear.

She had gotten so close.

"We aren't looking for trouble," Devon said, though his eyes shone with murderous intent.

She dropped her arms to her sides, and the swarming of bees became larger, almost fully covering her body as the steps of the soldiers slowed around her.

"Stop that, witch," one barked, and indignation flared inside her stomach. Her skin glow intensified.

"Nava," Devon started.

"I'm not a witch," she said in a clipped voice, unsure why she was choosing to pick this battle. It certainly didn't help that winged shadows had kidnapped Arkimedes the night before. The portal bringing them to a place where winged fae lived was not a coincidence.

These were her enemies, and she would make them pay.

The soldier who'd spoken took a step closer to her, his shoulders wide and tense with anger. "I will kill you right now. You are trespassing, and the use of portal magic inside the palace is a grave offense."

Well, splendid news all around.

"Boys, boys—a simple miscalculation. We didn't intend to transport to the castle, clearly. Just show us the way out, and we'll be on our merry way," Devon said.

They all fixed their eyes on her, their weapons tilted toward her body. She felt the ground tremble beneath her feet as fear settled in with her anger. She wouldn't get captured, not without a fight.

"You will get to claim your innocence to the king. However, His Majesty does not easily dismiss the use of dark magic in his kingdom," said the one with the tarnished helmet. His wings were brighter than the rest, a light gray speckled with black spots.

The one by her took another step closer, and the bees started flying faster. The soldier swatted and hissed as some landed on his armor and quickly crawled to any open skin. "Stop that or we will kill you!"

"Don't come near me or I will—"

"Nava!" Devon snapped from his spot, his eyes wide. She stared at him as he shook his head almost imperceptibly.

"Kill them both now," one gravelly voice said from the background.

"I wouldn't if I were you." Devon's polite mask melted, his features twisting into the scary, confident face she'd seen the year before. "Unless you want this place to be swarming with the Society by midnight."

"A Crow." The fae swatting at her bees spat near their feet. "We don't fear you."

"I'm sure the king wants to prevent bloodshed, according to the accords he signed last year."

The one with the gravelly voice grunted a curse, and the one with the spotted wings took a step closer. "Then call off your magic if you care about the accords."

Devon's pointed look was not lost on her. She dropped her hands to her sides, calling her bees off. The bees flew away up into the clearing sky, leaving Nava naked among the enemy.

A hand clasped her arm, and she winced when he drew her closer to him, her body crashing against the metal of his armor. He brought both her arms behind her back and soon she had shackles around her wrists, the coolness of the metal a contrast to her skin.

They spoke in a language she didn't understand, but it sounded like a mix of elegant romantic-sounding words and beautiful unique tones. She walked with her head held high, her eyes prickling as her anger burned hotter. They were all men, taller than average and about the same height as Devon.

Muscular and built for battle, with wings as large and majestic as any painting of fae ever depicted. The rumors of faeries being fallen angels could be true—or demons that had escaped from the shadow lands.

They didn't hide their wings, unlike Arkimedes. Their armor was made to accommodate their shapes. A wispy dark mist radiated from their bodies in different shades of black, present at all times. The fae and the mist that constantly surrounded them gave her the creeps.

The castle wasn't far, and soon they were walking down well-kept stone pathways that led them to its back door. The entrance stood hundreds of steps away from them. Doors made of heavy metal and vaulted frames rose alongside majestic walls.

Now that she was this close, the variation between each brick of marble told a different story. Age had softened the sharp angles of the building as a whole. It was beautiful.

The fae who held her pushed her forward, and her foot caught on one of the uneven steps. Nava stumbled to the ground; every jagged edge of stone dug into her legs and stomach. A pained sound came out of her lips, and then she was hoisted up by her arms, sharp fingers digging into her skin.

She turned her face to the soldier and leveled him with a glare, trying to move out of his grasp. "Let go of me. I'm walking where you're taking me."

The Dark One pushed her forward with more strength than needed, and she almost tripped to the ground again. "Let's gag the witch," he said instead.

The one with the greenish armor and lighter spotted wings turned his head and studied her. "Calm down, Herous. She is restrained, and the cuffs have taken the magic away. The king will tell us what to do."

A year ago, she'd had her first encounter with magic-canceling ropes and the horrible sensation that came from them draining her magic. These shackles had a similar burning feeling against her skin; however, this time it was different.

While her body wanted them off, her magic was alive and still running through her veins, even though she wore the cuffs. She wasn't sure why the shackles weren't working properly, not that she was complaining. Maybe it had to do with the fact that her magic as a Beekeeper didn't work the same as a warlock or sorceress.

She wasn't powerless here, not like they wanted her to be. Perhaps the fae had a reason to be dubious of her, after all.

The inside of the castle was bright. Tall, ribbed vaulted ceilings loomed over them, all a mixture of warm marble and copper. The tapestries hanging from the walls depicted moments in history she had no time to study, but what called her attention were the large stained glass windows that framed the aisles. Showing battles of beautiful winged figures, the bright colors kissed the floors in mosaic patterns that made her heart skip a beat.

Herous pushed her shoulder forward. She had fallen behind while staring at the surrounding beauty.

They walked for ages, down corridors and through rooms she supposed no one of importance frequented, if the subdued furnishings were anything to go by. She didn't encounter any other Dark Ones, beyond the ones escorting them. Was the king of the Copper Kingdom fae or human?

She had never heard of the kingdoms' royals being fae, but it was possible, considering all the Dark Ones around. Arkimedes had told her very little of his time here in searching for his kin. He'd said he found them in a village here, so she'd assumed the faes weren't everywhere.

She hoped their luck would improve after seeing the king and that maybe they would make it out of the castle alive.

CHAPTER FIVE

NAVA

The doors in front of Nava were majestic, made of wood stained in ebony shades. Settings and images were carved into four panels. One was of a winged man standing over hills with both arms raised in the air; under his feet, roots grew deep into the ground. The second one was a beautiful blooming tree. The third was a queen who wore an intricately carved dress, and in her arms, she carried a child. The fourth was flowers, much like the creepy geometric ones that had spied on them in the garden.

Nava's eyes lingered on that fourth panel. Out of the four, this last one was odd, newer than the rest, lacking the details of aged gold leaf, and shinier in finish.

Nava forced her gaze away from the image, taking a deep, calming breath. She had never met a royal before. How was she supposed to address a king? She didn't even know his name. The king who apparently hated Roman. Maybe she needed to bow? Curtsy? If that was the case, how low?

Was she meant to go onto her knees and beg forgiveness so she and Devon could make their way into a forest village and find her soulmate?

Out of all she'd learned from Laurie, who had been Cameron and her caregiver since she could remember, how to address a king had never been a part of her studies. Much less if this king was a fae. One would think a book would have said as much.

The fae with the green armor, whom she assumed was the leader, took a step forward to the large doors, holding his double-sided sword all too casually in his hand. It was as if he expected someone to jump out of a dark crevice in the never-ending halls.

Perhaps he was expecting Devon to attack.

She swallowed and followed each one of his movements. They kept Devon and her in the middle, caged between the six of them.

"You will address the king as His Royal Highness. Do not look him in the eye unless he addresses you. Hold your tongue or you will lose it." He turned and faced her, and she could almost see his bright magical eyes behind the shadow of his mask. Her lips parted when she realized he was speaking to her.

The day kept getting better by the minute. She didn't need to be treated like she had no self-restraint when Devon Black was standing next to her, being a perfect little captive.

Nava's gaze traveled to the aforementioned man. He stood with his back straight, a calm but bored expression on his face. What the hell? What made him so relaxed when they were captives to these maniacs?

The doors groaned with their weight as they opened. Her stomach tightened as she tried to peek between the large wings of her captors, but the men were too large for her to get a clear view of what surrounded her.

The room was circular, with vaulted ceilings so tall she couldn't see the end in the haze. Light streamed in from the large stained glass around the room. Colorful shades of blue tinted the polished floors beneath.

Candelabras hung from the pillars that surrounded the room, and wax dripped down them, permanently suspended in mid-drip. The light of the flames burned hot, illuminating the space with orange light.

A shiver ran down her spine and dread grew inside her stomach as they walked in, their steps echoing in the mostly empty room.

She looked at the three thrones in the center of the room. The one to the right was empty. Large men occupied the other two. No, not men. Fae, judging by the large wings behind each of their backs.

The king of the Copper Kingdom was definitely a faerie.

Between the two, Nava wasn't sure who was the king. If she took a wild guess, she would think it was the one who was swallowed by black swirling power; she could barely tell what he looked like with the shadows that wrapped around his body.

This wasn't like the small ink emanating from the guards. This was genuine raw magic, the scary kind.

They were closer now, and she squinted, trying to see their faces, but still the shapes were blurry with the distance.

"Bow to the king, witch." Herous's voice took her out of her reverie, and her stomach churned when the warm air of his breath hit the side of her neck. He pushed her forward, and she stumbled to the ground unceremoniously.

Nava hated the man and struggled to get up as the other guards stood watching. She cursed, trying and failing to get to her feet, unable to use her arms and hands, which impeded her. She met Devon's gaze as it dropped to the ground, following her with a tensed jaw.

His chin twitched, and she understood. He was hurrying her to get on with it. The shackles that held her arms shrieked with her movements, and her joints protested from all the times she'd fallen today.

"Your Majesty, King Oberon Yearwood, and His Royal Highness, Prince Orion Yearwood. We found these trespassers in the west garden this afternoon."

Finally, taking pity on her, one guard came down and lifted her from her shoulders, settling her near Devon before he took a stance back.

"Keep your eyes low to the ground," Devon whispered between tight lips.

A voice deep and cold broke the silence. "How could these humans make it past our walls and gates?"

"They used a portal, sir. The man claims it was an accident—"

"An accident, you say. How would a sorcerer manage to portal into our heavily warded palace?" The king's voice was less than impressed if she had to guess. "That's a better question, Fael of Heira. Aren't my people's magic more powerful than that of a human?"

Nava frowned and chanced a look at Devon; his lips tilted up almost imperceptibly. He didn't need the ego boost, that was for sure. The silence that descended was charged. They weren't the only ones in trouble with the king.

"Of course, sir." Fael, head of the soldiers, dipped into a deep bow that showed her just how low she needed to go.

"Bring them forward. I'm curious to see the two humans who've challenged me." Oh, no. That didn't sound like a good start.

Alarm bells rang inside her head. She needed to get out of here, quickly. A hand wrapped around her arm, so tight that pain extended through her limb and all the way to her shoulder.

Herous brought her forward, and even though she wanted to squirm and fight, she kept her eyes low to the ground. Her heart was beating so fast, it stumbled with double beats. Nava might have a panic attack if her sudden surge of fear was anything to go by. "I will enjoy seeing your head on a spike, witch." He whispered the words against her ear, and she winced.

Did the kingdoms around the world still do such macabre, ancient practices like put heads on spikes?

He halted, but his hand jerked her around, as if trying to get her to look up.

Fael's words echoed in her mind, not to look the king in his eyes unless he addressed her. Keeping her gaze low was imperative. If the king was the man covered in shadows, it would be hard to tell where his eyes were to avoid them.

"Why would magical humans be so bold as to come to my home without an invitation?" His crisp voice commanded answers, and she felt a spike of magic trailing down her skin, an icy caress that made her want to speak truths.

"The king asked a question." Fael's voice shook her out of her trance, and she lifted her head to the fae, and then her gaze trailed up, as if called by something larger. A prickle of recognition lit behind her panic state, a familiar warmth that extended through her body.

Her eyes came to the throne chairs. The polished wood was stained black. Then she studied a set of booted feet, pants black like a starless night. Her gaze went up and up; her heart stumbled in her chest when she met the eyes of forest and moss.

Arkimedes sat on the throne like it was made for him, wearing a black silk tunic that hugged his broad shoulders and skimmed down his chest and narrow waist. They'd adorned the fabric with gold embroidery of a design she couldn't place from this far.

A copper crown, made of thorns and twisted branches, lay on top of his thick brown hair. He looked different from the night before, but it was the same man who'd been kissing her lips.

He stared back at her and his forehead twisted into a frown. Anger, she realized, burned in the pit of her stomach, but it wasn't hers anymore.

Had it been his anger driving her short mood this whole time? No, if she looked deep within herself, she could feel her own braiding itself with his. The fire driving her was his and hers.

His intense green gaze stayed with her for a while longer as the silence stretched. Her skin went cold and clammy all at once, confusion and horror settling in the pit of her stomach.

Why was Arkimedes sitting on the throne, wearing a goddamn crown that looked made for him? Why were his eyes so distant? What was going on?

"Arkimedes." The words left her lips with a gasp.

"No shit." Devon's voice was a whisper or maybe it was drowned by the loud drumming inside her ears.

Arkimedes looked down at her without any recognition in sight. She knew he was a master at masking his emotions, but he had never done so with her, not even when they hadn't known each other well. Much less now that they'd bonded and she could feel his powerful emotions, as if he were shouting them down their connection.

"Release them at once," Arkimedes growled. His features remained impassive. The only sign that he was as affected as she was the whitening in his knuckles against the arm of his chair.

The king's shadow twitched, and his voice bloomed with curiosity. "Do as he says." He waved a hand in dismissal, but she could feel the hot coals of his eyes burning her skin.

Herous's fingers dug deeper into her arm, and she gasped from the pain. The sudden movement was a shock to her system. "But, sir, this witch—" the man next to her started, but no other words came out, just a gurgling sound low in his throat.

She turned to him, and even though she couldn't see his face behind his helmet, the skin of his neck turned purple and blue.

The hand that held her twitched and dropped, and she skittered away. Her soulmate was now standing from his throne. His hand reached out toward them. Shadows enveloped him like a storm; wispy arms flared from him as his aura deepened to the color of slate.

Plumes of smoke emanated like waves, and the air around the throne room became musty with the scent of magic. Another gurgling sound and the guard fell to his knees. Other than his choking noises, silence descended upon the room.

No one moved a muscle to help or said anything.

"I said, release them." Arkimedes's voice was icy, unlike she'd ever heard it before. A shiver ran down her spine as the man next to her fell to the ground into an unmoving pile.

The king's hand grasped Arkimedes. The love of her life stepped back and sat on the throne once again, as if nothing had happened. His eyes avoided hers entirely. "Pick him up and take him to the infirmary," the king said to his soldiers.

Two men from the back rushed to pick Herous from the ground and dragged him out of the way.

The king stood from his throne, the shadows that enveloped him dissipating momentarily. His lips were full and youthful, as though he couldn't be older than thirty. Straight nose, thick black brows that framed cerulean eyes. His hair fell past his shoulders, silver, the color of starlight. He looked too much like Arkimedes.

She swallowed and looked away, hoping her curiosity didn't mean he would kill her now.

His frown deepened. "I must admit I'm curious as to why my heir has spared you two."

Heir, as in . . . Arkimedes was a goddamn prince?

CHAPTER SIX

NAVA

Nava understood why at first glance she hadn't seen that the prince had shadows around him. She had never seen what others did with Arkimedes's aura. He'd always looked normal to her.

Not like the scary fae hungering for blood—or like a prince.

What had they done to him? Her eyes raked down his face as he avoided her, his own fixed on Devon.

He'd almost killed a man. However, his face wasn't twisted with remorse like she'd expect him to feel. It was in his nature as her mate to want to protect her at all costs, but she knew Arkimedes often refrained from using his shadow powers, as she liked to call them since it absorbed parts of other people's souls.

"You called my son by his human name," the king said, and she squirmed under the weight of his gaze, quickly facing the ground. "Have you met this woman before, Orion?"

Nava brought her eyes up, meeting Arkimedes's heavy gaze. He narrowed his eyes at her, and her breath caught in her throat. Her skin was tight with pressure. Nava reached for the bond to find what was in store, but it told her nothing. There was recognition, yes, but none of the burning love he'd had the night before.

Her stomach tightened as her mind ran rampant with thoughts that were too wild and scary. Something was off.

"I have not met her before," Arkimedes spoke, standing from his throne, and took the steps down the polished marble stairs with a trot, his tunic billowing in the air.

What did he mean, he didn't know her? Her lips parted, and her body temperature dropped when she felt his confusion and wariness—toward her.

He didn't remember her? Then why was there a spike of something churning between them? She guessed it could be the bond making him feel something. Was this all a charade? Was he buying her time or was there something she was missing from his blank expression?

"I see." The king's intense blue eyes shone behind the dark smoke of his aura. Nava averted her gaze when she realized she'd been staring at him once again.

"Devon is my brother from the Society," Arkimedes continued, calling the king's attention back to him, and her entire world went still.

He is—as in, present tense?

"So, Devon . . ." The king's gaze reluctantly traveled to the man next to her, his hand moving in graceful circles as if trying to fill in the void of his name.

"Black, Your Majesty," Devon chimed in with a polite dip of his head.

"A Crow in my kingdom. That would explain how you could open such a portal." A frown morphed his gentle features into a wicked expression. His youthful expression fell apart as wrinkles tainted his face. "The Society isn't welcome in my castle. They stole my heir away."

No. Freaking. Way.

Nava had gone to sleep and had woken up inside a nightmare. Was Arkimedes the stolen heir? It was obvious by the crown resting on his pretty head.

She took a deep breath to calm her racing heart. The king's words didn't match the tale Arkimedes had fed her a year ago about him being dropped at the doorsteps of an orphanage.

"It took us too long to bring him back, where he belongs."

Her mouth opened in indignation. Arkimedes didn't belong here. He was supposed to be back home with her. Making hot chocolate and practicing magic in their backyard. Building their life together.

Preparing for an attack from the Zorren.

"The Society also took Devon to serve them, Father," Arkimedes chimed in, and he stood next to Devon.

There was a silent conversation happening between the royals. Arkimedes's emotions were all but shouting down their bond. Confused but determined, her mate didn't waver or look at her.

How could she get him out of here if he didn't even remember her? Nava's whole plan, albeit not a great one, had been to get to him so they could work together in the escape. She'd expected to have time to come up with the next steps, but now, how was she supposed to do that from a cell with an unwilling partner?

Her powers were still there; she could transfer—even if it was a few feet at a time. There was also the possibility of doing the same thing she'd done at the prison on the island, to get to Arkimedes and somehow get him out of here.

"Well, if Orion considers you family, then you're welcome in our kingdom, of course." The king's tone was definitely not the friendly, welcoming kind. His gaze came upon her again, and she steeled her spine, ready to be accused of something. "What about the . . . sorceress?"

Would Devon let her burn now that he was safe and Arkimedes didn't remember her?

"She is my fiancée," Devon said without missing a beat.

Her mouth fell open as she took a step back, looking at Devon. *What?*

"Your fiancée?" Arkimedes echoed, and warmth pooled in her stomach with an unwelcome churn that didn't belong to her.

"Recently matched, I'm afraid. She is a spirited little thing. I can't leave her out of my sight." Devon nodded, and his onyx eyes came to her, a brow lifting at what was surely her dumbstruck expression. An unpleasant shudder ran through her.

"You shouldn't take your eyes off her. Humans with magic so earthy are hard to find." The king took a step toward his throne. His hand moved dismissively at them. "The Society must be rejoicing at the possibility of an offspring of you two."

She was going to throw up all over this polished ground, whether it was from anger or disgust, she didn't know. They spoke about her like she was a decorative piece and not a person. Was it common in the cities? Her scowl deepened, and she gave Devon her best murderous look.

"They're most eager." Devon's lips twitched with contained amusement. Arkimedes's complexion became sickly pale, and his scowl deepened.

The soft buzzing of a bee landing on top of her finger was a wake-up call. She swallowed down the rage burning through her. It wouldn't be helpful if she called on a swarm of insects and revealed that her magic was very much awake.

"You will join us for a banquet tonight. Orion can show you to the guest quarters. Take a couple of guards with you, son." It was an order, and a clear sign he didn't trust them.

Which made it mutual. Nava now knew who the kidnappers were. The reasoning was obvious, though murky. Arkimedes nodded and stepped away from the king, beckoning them to follow.

"Oh, and, Orion, make sure your guests get their jewels."

Arkimedes turned to face the king and his expression sobered. His eyes came to Devon, avoiding her entirely.

Guilt.

Whatever the jewels were, they weren't good.

This whole thing was bizarre, as if she had stepped into a different dimension. She blinked and wished to soothe her aching soulmate mark. It burned under the linen fabric of her shirt, like the first time it appeared a decade ago.

Nava dragged her feet past the heavy doors of the grand throne room, trailed by a couple of guards. She had found Arkimedes in less than a day, and that alone should be a cry of triumph. Had she stayed in the Northern Village, she would likely not have made it past tonight.

Arkimedes talked with Devon in a hushed tone that left their conversation in the shadows. The sounds around her were magnified, the clicking of their boots over stone, the guards' armor screeching with each step, the buzzing inside her ears.

Nava rolled her shoulders, trying to ease the pressure forming in her neck. Maybe if she focused on that woe, she might not obsess over the glaring issue walking in front of her.

She studied her soulmate's clothes; they were finer than anything she'd ever owned, the crown polished. Her brows furrowed as she focused on his hair. It was longer than she remembered.

How could that be?

The wind howled between the cracks of aged stone. They walked to an area of the castle with warmer, more inviting furnishings. Different from what she'd seen earlier that day. Clearly, these were areas of the palace meant for visitors, not prisoners.

The halls consisted of long, unbroken walls. Hanging tapestries of midnight shades decorated the place, and fancy arrangements of violets, white camellias, and other greenery stood on each side of the corridor.

Fae walked around, wearing silk clothes in similar shades of burnt orange, with delicate embroidery details of gold tones. Based on the tasks they were handling, these were palace staff. Some were carrying buckets and sweeping the floors. She even saw one lady cleaning cobwebs that had accumulated in a corner.

Didn't they use magic for these things? Nava had always assumed in these cities they would use magic for everything. She guessed that was the main issue the crowns were facing. Magic was disappearing. Nava had never considered it would affect the fae, as well.

She rolled her shoulders again. The dull ache in her joints wouldn't go away.

"Release them from their binds," Arkimedes commanded and turned to the guards, crossing his arms over his chest.

The guard nearest to her fumbled over his feet. He reached her in a matter of seconds, and the smooth texture of his gloved fingers touched her wrists. After Arkimedes's earlier demonstration of magic with Herous, this poor soul was terrified.

"The woman is a witch, sir. Should we fetch the jewels first?" the second guard asked.

Arkimedes's aura exploded around him. Dark tendrils of magic emanated from his body, showing his temper. Both the guards shrank back. "Get the jewels, bring Callisto, and do not question my orders again, Rilu."

It was a part of him she had never seen before, Arkimedes Valeron the Crow. Someone she'd assumed he had left behind after a decade away from the kingdom.

"Yes, sir." Rilu's voice shook before he rushed past them and down the corridor.

Arkimedes, however, still refused to look at her. Could he feel her emotions right now? Or had the bond somehow been affected by the loss of his memories? Why didn't he remember her?

He and his captors had left that island so quickly, they had to have taken a portal, like what Devon created. Had Arkimedes been the one to pay the price? Had he been thinking of her at that specific moment and lost her?

Her chest squeezed and the knot in her throat became giant, making it hard to swallow, let alone breathe. Her eyes prickled as tears blurred her vision, and she forced her gaze away. Unsure if her emotions were only acting this way because of the possibility of him never remembering what had happened, but also because of the possibility of her never regaining whatever she'd lost.

"Stop frowning, kitten. You're going to wrinkle," Devon said.

She narrowed her eyes at him; however, she didn't trust her voice not to crack if she spoke a word.

The metal around her wrist loosened, and the discomfort in her skin eased slowly. The guard stepped away but stayed behind. She suspected he was buying himself time before his friend returned with whatever the jewels were.

"It has been a while since I have seen you, brother. Ever since you've been away from . . ." Devon let his words die down.

"The Iron City?" Arkimedes's voice deepened, and she could barely see his expression from his sharp profile. "We can speak about it at another time—when we are alone." His eyes flashed to Nava, and her stomach sank.

Devon nodded but said nothing. She could feel her soulmate's shoulders grow tense. Perhaps he was sensing some of her despair. If he really didn't remember her, then that alone would be disconcerting.

"Is she always this quiet?" Arkimedes asked flatly, finally fixing his gaze upon her.

Devon laughed as the second guard approached him with careful steps, reaching for the cuffs on his back. "Not at all, but I'm enjoying it while it lasts."

"Well, you can start by asking me the question instead of asking Devon, Your Highness." Those last words tasted bitter. This was all too much.

Arkimedes's frown deepened. She heard the distinct noise of someone gasping in shock; she guessed the poor guard behind Devon was expecting Arkimedes to flail her for her response.

He opened his mouth, but the upcoming steps of Rilu and a fae woman had them all turning their way. She held a polished metal box in her hands and approached Arkimedes with wide, shiny eyes.

She was slim and tall. Her deep burnt-orange dress skimmed her narrow hips and hugged her chest. Her hair was pale and long, cascading behind her back with each step she took toward them. No wings showed behind her back, unlike the guards. Had she put them away with magic?

Nava didn't need a soothsayer to figure the fae was swooning over her soulmate. Not that she blamed her. He was handsome, dark, and powerful. The wide coquettish smile, and the wave of the woman's hips, made her blood boil.

"Your Highness called?" Her voice was tones of melody, and she extended the box to Arkimedes with a flutter of her eyelashes.

What a stupid question, because . . . duh. If Nava could vomit somewhere, she hoped it would be on the woman's dress—or maybe Arkimedes's shoes.

"Thank you, Callisto." Arkimedes opened the box, and inside were two gold bracelets encrusted with sapphires and emeralds. Rune letters in a language she didn't understand marked the sides.

"Is it necessary for me to wear this? I came here looking for you. Surely you know I won't leave," Devon asked. For the first time since they'd left the throne room, his calm mask shifted.

He would totally leave if it weren't for the life debt, right? Devon's expression showed a rare vulnerability she hadn't seen before. The way his Adam's apple bobbed when he swallowed, his crestfallen face.

It hit her then that Devon Black had never left Arkimedes. He had been searching for his brother for a decade. He wasn't going to leave him behind on the island. Nor was he going to leave him here. Life debt or not.

"I'm afraid so." At least that had not changed. Arkimedes was still a man of brief words. He handed the cuff to Devon, and the Crow hesitated for a moment, his eyes fixed on her.

This was it. Maybe now that the Crow had his magic, he could open a portal again and they could leave this horrid place behind. She still had her magic; they could stun Arkimedes for a moment and take him away. He would not expect it. This could be their only shot.

Devon's black eyes fixed on her as if he were reading her thoughts. Shockingly, he closed the bracelet over his wrist, and just like that, their chance of escape was gone.

Arkimedes took a step toward her but hesitated to approach. Maybe it was the way she looked at him, the churning in her gut, or a spark of memory? He lifted the delicate bracelet to her, and her jaw grew tenser. No, not a memory.

"I don't want your family jewels on me."

Devon snorted before his head tilted back with a deep, rolling laugh.

Arkimedes's lips twitched. "What's your name?"

"Nava."

"Nava," he repeated, and gooseflesh awakened over her skin. The way her name sounded out of his lips was like a prayer. "Is that your given name or your family name?"

"Given name."

His eyes danced with curiosity; however, his expression was null of further emotion. "The king demands you wear this bracelet while you're in his kingdom." He held her gaze, and Nava knew she had no choice.

As he fiddled with the jewelry, she could tell he wasn't happy to give her this; it had not been his decision. "Fine," she said in between her teeth, lifting her arm toward Arkimedes to allow him to put the bracelet on.

He appeared to debate whether or not he wanted to do so. However, she felt the burning of something else through their bond, maybe desire. It was hard to tell when their connection was somehow fractured. It took but a second for the cool metal to touch her. The skin beneath the bracelet sizzled, but the soft caress of his fingertips warmed the ache left behind by the sting of magic.

Arkimedes didn't blink, look away, or move a muscle. His only reaction was the tightening of his jaw and the longing pushing through the bond.

"Sir, would you be requesting adjacent rooms for your guests?"

Adjacent—a room that shared a door between Devon's and her accommodations. Because they were supposed to be engaged. Something crawled in her spine at her horror, like fire-bending ants.

But then, upon further inspection, it might be the only way they could plan how to get out of here because she was running out of ideas. Even bad ones weren't coming to her.

Arkimedes's jaw was set at a sharp angle when he turned to Callisto. His aura darkened around him, and the air sizzled with energy and the scent of cayenne. "No. She will stay on the west side of the wing."

Devon eyed Arkimedes with an entertained expression, clearly enjoying their torment too much for his own good. "Oh, worry not, my brother. You don't have to protect her virtue. That ship has long sailed."

"Hey!" Her voice echoed in the hallway. "It's not like he's making it sound at all," she huffed but let her words die down, knowing Callisto still was around and eyeing Nava like she was below dirt level. Judgy wench.

Devon's eyes danced. "Sorry, that was uncouth of me. I merely wanted my brother to allow us privacy, my dear."

Arkimedes cleared his throat loudly, the vein on his forehead becoming more apparent. "We don't have rooms next to one another."

Callisto opened her mouth, her delicate eyebrows wrinkling in confusion, but closed her lips as soon as Arkimedes's eyes landed on her. Nava didn't even need to feel his emotions to know he was lying.

"Please set the rooms, Callie. I will take Devon to the gold room and Nava to the green."

"Your Highness." She dipped down before she walked ahead of them, shaking her head.

Devon's eyes chased down the retreating shape of the woman whom Nava assumed was a maid. Her narrow frame was almost swallowed by the large hallways. "It's a shame I can't be closer to you, cat, really." He turned to her, and his straight teeth showed in a wicked smile. "No way to protect you if an assassin were to try to kill you."

Nava would have retorted that she didn't need his protection. But in this castle surrounded by enemies, she wasn't sure that was true.

CHAPTER SEVEN

NAVA

Callisto stood poised in front of what Nava assumed was the gold room, studying their approach with wide blue eyes. The imposing door reminded her of the one she'd seen before in the throne room, except this one was all bright yellow metal.

Devon whistled as he peeked inside, and his eyes cut to Nava with a smile. "This is an improvement to my previous arrangements from earlier in the day."

"Your apartment?" Arkimedes paused his movements, studying Devon as if looking at him for the first time. From the top of his greasy matted hair, the dark circles under his eyes, and the black-and-white prisoner outfit he wore.

If he found it odd, and the confusion pushing through the bond told her he did, Arkimedes didn't mention one single thing about it.

Devon blinked a few times before regaining his usual stance. "I haven't been in the city for quite some time."

Arkimedes didn't remember the island; he thought Devon had come straight from the Iron City. Eleven years of memories were gone.

"Where have you been?"

"Searching for you." Devon paused and sauntered into the room, peering in with tense shoulders. "You left and said little."

The Crow turned and met her gaze, and they both stared at each other in silence, understanding passing between them. This was not a lie. He had been searching for Arkimedes a year ago when he entered her shop that fateful afternoon.

Nava pondered if things would have been different had he not scared her off that day. Had he not sent the bounty hunters to chase her down, would their relationship be more akin to family now?

No. He would have still chased down deserters, destroyed families, and killed innocents he deemed useless. Devon Black was not a good man. She needed to keep remembering that, even if they were allies of sorts.

The bigger issue was Arkimedes's lack of most, if not all, of his memory from the last decade. It was odd that he knew everyone in this castle and also had a fair amount of comfort talking to the king, which would indicate he'd been here for a while.

It made no sense—he'd been taken from their home the night before. Maybe time in this kingdom worked differently or somehow magic was involved.

"True." Arkimedes's fingers went through his hair, making the thick strands stand on end. "I had not intended to stay for long. Callie, take Nava to her room. Make sure she has what she needs, as they will join us for dinner." Nava fought her urge to squirm under his gaze. "Rilu will come with you."

Oh, so he thought Callisto—or Callie—needed protection from her? Nava focused on the other woman, who was practically glowing, her face flushed and eyes glossy with desire. Maybe he had a point. After the day she'd had, her crankiness had gotten the best of her.

Though the one getting stung might be Arkimedes and not this girl.

"Your Highness." Callisto beamed with a bow and headed down the corridor. "This way, miss."

"Do you need me to call on a maid to help you wash?" Callisto opened the curtains that led to a sizable terrace. A pleasant view of the garden opened ahead and, beyond that, a vast forest. "Miss?"

"What? Oh. No, I don't need help bathing." Nava focused on the trees, wondering if Ari was waiting for her.

"The rooms in this castle are alive with magic," Callisto said. "When you want a bath, it will run on its own. The fire will turn on the moment you enter the room if the air is chilly. Clothes for you to wear are already in the armoire." She eyed Nava's clothes, and her brows met in the middle. "It's a great privilege to stay in this wing. Especially in this room."

Nava huffed and walked toward the terrace. She didn't need fancy accommodations. Something simple would be perfectly fine. Arkimedes was all she needed. "What do you mean?"

Callisto walked to the door, her pale hair shimmering with the sun. "This is the prince's wing. Where he hosts his guests." Her sneer swelled. "The guard will escort you to dinner tonight—don't be late. The king likes to eat before the sun sets." She opened the door and left before Nava could ask anything else.

Nava basked in the splendor around her, the warm tones of the stone wall, the imposing vaulted ceilings. The room alone was larger than the whole second floor in her house. Now that she was alone, she studied every detail. The linens on the bed were rich forest green. Multiple wool rugs were layered under the bed, in complementary shades of lighter greens that reminded her of Arkimedes's eyes.

The mantlepiece was green marble; carvings showed swirling rosettes and leaves, an imposing oil painting of a forest hanging on top of it. Her heart ached from what she'd left behind and what the men in the shadows had stolen from her.

The same flower arrangements she'd seen in the halls decorated each side of the fireplace in the room's corner. Nava paused as her gaze stopped on the weird geometrical flowers she had foolishly thought were camellias when walking down the corridors.

Spies.

Nava walked to the arrangements, plucked every single one out of the vase, and threw them out of the balcony. She breathed in, relieved that even if it was paranoid to throw away the beautiful arrangement, she would not let them spy on her.

The hole in her heart grew like a festering wound, unlike anything she'd felt before. Something was off with the encounter she'd had when crossing the portal. That shadowy shape was all too eager to have seen her.

She was unable to come up with what she had lost but knew it was something irreplaceable. Her cheeks dampened with tears, and she held the weight of her body against the cool banisters, feeling as if everything was closing in on her. This elegant room was a prison in disguise, oceans away from home, where she didn't know how to save her soulmate.

Nava had only her magic against an entire kingdom, against powerful ones everyone feared. How was she supposed to start when she'd just learned about her magic a year ago?

She had never been this far away from Cameron and Ari—but there was one familiarity with her current situation: being forced to face everything she didn't know.

Her clothes constricted her breathing, and she stripped off the layers, taking a deep breath to calm the pressure forming in her heart. The shadows of the room traveled across the floor, and the warm, humid air of summer kissed her skin.

Her legs groaned with pain from standing for too long. She made her way to the washroom, ready to get the grime off and face whatever was coming for her next.

Just as impressive as the bedroom, green slate extended through the floor and up the walls. There was a tub—or a pool—in the center of the room. The water inside was steaming and a milky shade of blue, and the scent of honeysuckle drifted in the air.

Nava lowered herself into the hot water, hissing as it burned her skin but calmed her aching muscles. She picked a sea sponge from the side and dampened it in the water; she used to use these to make potions, her mind supplied, though she couldn't pinpoint what potion that had been.

By the time she got out of the tub, her fingers resembled prunes, and the sun grazed the treetops with orange hues. Nava wrapped her body with the most luxurious and fluffiest towel she had ever encountered and made her way to the bedroom.

The closet smelled like a mixture of sandalwood, mildew, and a side of peppercorn. She wrinkled her nose as she took in the wall of gowns in front of her, all in different shades of blue. Some shimmered under the afternoon sunlight.

She brought her hands to a specific gown. The color of sky blue reminded her of something she had a hard time placing. Her fingertips skimmed over it, and the knot in her throat grew thicker.

Why was she getting so emotional because of a dress, or the color of it? Nava picked it out of the closet and slipped it on, as if doing so would bring her closer to whatever was amiss. It fit like they'd made it for her, a modest high neck that covered the skin of her chest, hiding her soulmate mark under layers of sheer fabric and carefully stitched beads that formed a beautiful motif.

A knock on the door had her jumping in her spot, and she realized to her chagrin that she'd gotten little time to do anything with her hair, which still hung slightly damp against her bare back.

"One moment, please." Taking in her reflection in the nearest mirror, she ran her fingers down her locks. It was silly for her stomach to dance with the spike of adrenaline. Arkimedes had seen her at her absolute worst, covered in grime, mud, and blood, and had still fallen in love with her.

He'd always liked her hair—even if he teased her about it.

She reached the door quickly and took a steadying breath to give herself some gumption as she opened it, but it all escaped her when she met Arkimedes's gaze. "Oh, I didn't expect you to come and get me," she blurted.

His eyes quickly darted down her body. "I wanted to make sure you didn't get into trouble on your way there."

"What trouble was I supposed to get into?" She made her way out of the room, discreetly taking him in. He looked so handsome, wearing a black tunic and pants. His crown still rested over his head. He had brushed his hair back, making his cheekbones more prominent.

"Hard to know, but the guards were keen on monitoring you—and so was Devon."

"I'm not complaining. I enjoy spending time with you," she said boldly.

He turned to her sharply, his eyes narrowing as he took in her expression. "What does that mean?"

If destiny was going to hand her this crappy situation, she was going to make the most of it. There were some benefits in knowing you were irresistible to the person you loved. "That I'd like to get to know you better."

He grabbed her wrist, stopping her mid-walk. "Do you make it a habit to bewitch people you don't know?"

"I'm not sure I'm following."

He stepped closer, towering over her. "You need to stop this nonsense. I'm not interested."

Her skin heated at his words. "Still not following."

"I've been dreaming of you for months." The familiar scent of cedar and leather washed over her.

Months?

The soulmate dreams wouldn't spare him if he'd been here for a while without her. Without all their memories from a year together, he was likely remembering part of their past while he slept. That gave her hope.

It also fed into the idea that the way time passed in this kingdom was different. This was the only explanation of why he'd been dreaming of her for months.

For her it had been a day, but their souls had been apart for much longer. No wonder she had deteriorated so quickly yesterday.

She grinned. "You lied to your king."

"What?" He shook his head, taken aback.

"You told him you had never met me before, but you just said you met me in your dreams."

He scowled. "Dreams don't count. I have never met you in my life."

"What dreams have you so worked up?" She refused to back away from whatever intimidation tactic he was trying to enforce.

He swallowed, and she rejoiced in the way his cheeks turned a bright shade of red. "Nothing important."

"Well, then I guess I don't see the problem." She shrugged and stepped away.

He pulled her back, his body colliding with hers. "It is a problem. You are engaged to my brother—"

"I haven't put a spell on you. I just arrived in your kingdom, and the entire time I've been here, I've been wearing this." She lifted her hand and waved the bracelet in front of his face.

He dropped her hand. "I don't believe you, and I won't let you out of my sight."

"Good, I already said I like that." She continued down the aisle with a smile. Even though she didn't know where to go, she assumed he'd follow.

He reached her in a few strides. "How old are you? Usually the crown doesn't match members of the Society so quickly."

"Twenty-six."

He turned to her, raising a brow. "Devon is too young to be matched, especially with someone older than him."

"Well, aren't you pleasant?" she said between her teeth. "He hasn't complained to anyone. He actually seemed quite pleased by the match."

She would own up to the fact that her words were a cheap attempt to hurt him like he'd hurt her. In reality, she doubted Devon would have been pleased to be matched with her at all; their disdain for one another was quite mutual.

Arkimedes's brows dipped as he studied her features. It was hard not to get caught up by the intensity of his emotions. Mistrust and jealousy.

Nava wondered if this would've been how their interaction would've gone if her mother hadn't taken her away when they met eleven years ago. She found herself rubbing at the spot where their mark lay. "When you look at yourself in the mirror, do you see anything new? Maybe a scar that wasn't there before?" She remembered the old stab wound he had received last year. "Maybe something more . . . ?" Like their soulmate mark.

She could just reveal right now what they were to one another. Show him her mark and explain it all. But then, what if he didn't want her? He had told her a year ago that at first, he hadn't wanted the soulmate bond, either. And this version of Arkimedes was from a decade prior to that.

He wouldn't want her. Her breath burst out in a whoosh, and she struggled to keep her steps steady.

She couldn't tell him they were soulmates—yet.

A loud crash broke the surrounding silence, followed by the sound of splashes over stone. Arkimedes's arms wrapped around her and brought her behind him before she could blink. Her nose itched with the scent of pepper as his aura expanded around him.

"I'm *so* sorry, sir. I didn't mean to startle you. It slipped my hand." A youthful voice came from the open room to their side. A young maid exited, holding both her hands in front of her. She wore a dress the color of tangerines, the fabric darker in areas where it had gotten wet. Her shaky hands pushed back strands of bright red hair behind her pointy ears.

"Leela." Arkimedes nodded and stepped away from Nava. His face grew darker. "Listening to other people's conversations won't be tolerated. You won't speak a word of what you just heard to anyone."

Her face lost all color and her wide eyes came to Nava as she nodded. "Yes, Your Highness."

Arkimedes strode off, and Nava followed, shaking with pent-up adrenaline. He didn't trust her yet, but she got the idea that he trusted this kingdom much less.

CHAPTER EIGHT

NAVA

They walked in silence past Devon's gold room and down long corridors that led them to the dining area. The castle was breathtaking, with decorated arches that faced the expanse of royal gardens, where her eyes lingered.

Her steps were heavy over stone, and the closer she got to where he was taking her, the larger the pit in her stomach grew.

"Is there any way I can skip this dinner?" She turned to Arkimedes the moment she realized the words had actually left her lips.

"Aren't you hungry?"

She shrugged. "I've been hungrier before."

Arkimedes's lips tightened. "The king requested for you to join us tonight, as my guests."

"He wants to monitor us because he doesn't trust us." She wrung her hands together, the bangle on her wrist pulsing against her skin. Even though the damn thing didn't cancel her magic, it zapped her like a current that didn't fully die off.

Arkimedes's eyes flashed to her and then toward the room in front of them. "Yes, and neither do I," he said after a moment, the words slowing her steps down to a stop.

"Fine. Though not sure I have done anything to deserve your mistrust."

"If you can put a spell on me from a continent away, who's to say Devon is not under one as well? He looks . . . different." He was saying he didn't trust her, but Nava got the impression he was battling with himself on this.

She could feel his interest grow as his gaze met hers; this was so different from the first time they'd gotten to know each other. A year ago, he had held back his emotions because he'd known she meant more.

Now this "younger" version of him threw her off. He was a bit more direct and guarded. He had no clue who or what she was to him but was clearly feeling something. Much like what she had dealt with a year prior, except they hadn't fully formed the connection then.

"That is the most absurd thing I have ever heard," she said. "If that was the case, why don't you lock me away somewhere else, far away from you?"

He clenched his jaw. "Maybe I will."

She took a step closer and challenged him. "Do it—but just so it's out in the open, I believe you are under a spell. But I sure as hell didn't put it on you."

"What do you mean?"

Nava turned around and started off toward the dining area, following the scent of food and baked goods. "I have no reason to say anything since you won't believe me either way."

She was ready to put distance between the two of them after letting part of the truth out. Nava clutched her stomach, trying to bring warmth back into her body.

The dining room was grand and meant to hold large gatherings. The scent of roasted pork, potatoes, and something buttery draped over her, making her stomach rumble as she took in the variety of dishes in front of her. Maybe she was hungrier than she'd thought.

Dark stained wood wainscoting encased the bottom half of the room's walls, and vibrant painted murals decorated the top, depicting scenes of hunting, woodland animals, and fae surrounded by shadows. A long wooden table occupied the center of the room, carved with intricate patterns and motifs. The room was mostly empty except for a group of Dark Ones who were sitting together while they talked in hushed tones.

All of them stood at once as soon as they noticed Arkimedes had entered the room. Their wings were of various shapes and colors. Soft gray mist emanated from their bodies, almost like they were starting to catch on fire.

"Your Highness." They bowed as one, keeping their shifting expressions low.

Nava studied the mood in the room, unsure if it was reverence or marked with a tinge of fear. The prickle in her skin intensified as soon as their gazes landed on her. She swallowed and slowed to a stop as she tried to avoid fidgeting.

"Please take a seat," Arkimedes said to the fae, and even though all of them sat at once, the room stayed quiet. The tension was palpable, and she startled when Arkimedes's breath hit the side of her neck, awakening goose bumps down her body. "You may sit next to me." His voice was like honey and sex all in one.

Her lips parted at the same time her body grew warm, longing pooling in her stomach. Still, she had to keep her head on her shoulders if she was going to survive the night. "Would that be near the king?"

"Are you afraid of sitting close to the king? He won't hurt you, you are my guest."

"Right . . . I'd rather not."

"Are you afraid of me?"

She met his gaze, trying to decipher his turbulent expression. "No. I'm not. Does that disappoint you?"

"Yes, and no." His lips twitched into a shadow of a smile. Nava got the impression he was more surprised she didn't fear him when everyone else around him always did.

Even if Arkimedes believed that his father wouldn't get rid of her, she wasn't so naïve as to count on it. How was she supposed to get him away from this kingdom before the king got rid of her?

A portal could be their only way out of here. She had to get the bracelet off Devon, so he could open another one. They might be able to leave and explain to her soulmate the truth at a later date.

Would that make her any different from the king? Kidnapping Arkimedes when he didn't remember her? Her shoulders sagged as she lost some of her gumption.

Nava couldn't do it. Neither could she tell him they were soulmates. He would just send her away, and that wasn't an option.

She might have to camp in the forest nearby, biding her time, like he'd done for a decade when her mother took her away. She didn't have Arkimedes's patience.

Maybe the only option would be to convince him to leave with them, to help him remember.

His hand hovered near her lower back. However, he held himself back from that intimate touch. A day ago, that touch would've been as easy as breathing for either of them. The sudden loss of it had her heartache growing.

It was then that she caught sight of Devon, standing by one of the large windows, staring at them from afar. He wore a dark blue tunic with silver embroidery down the lapels of it.

"Finally, you two. I started getting worried," he said with an indifference that didn't match his words. "I see who gets the preferential treatment here."

"It's not you he mistrusts," Nava whispered.

Devon's face brightened with delight. "Smart man."

Arkimedes ignored their words. "You two can sit next to me."

"Next to your father? I'd rather stab my hand with a fork, repeatedly."

For the first time, Nava agreed fully with the Crow.

The king entered the room then, followed by a group of women and a couple of guards. His aura billowed out of his body like smoke in a campfire, and his gaze landed on the three of them. However, his steps took him all the way to the head of the table.

All the fae at the table stood and bowed. "Your Majesty."

"Sit," he commanded, but his attention never left them. "Orion, would you join me?"

"Father." Arkimedes dipped his head, and at that same time, his hand actually touched the skin on Nava's back, jolting her as a wave of warmth traveled through her body. She swallowed and met his gaze, finding she had lost all the air from her lungs. "Stay out of trouble."

She very much intended to do so, but Devon spoke instead. "And where is the fun in that?"

Arkimedes's lips tilted up into a shadow of a smile before he walked away

They sat away from the royals, in wooden chairs with thin but tall backrests that were meant to accommodate wings. The king's attention never came to her directly, but she knew he had been the one who'd sent his guards to kidnap Arkimedes and was likely plotting a way to get rid of them.

She picked at the flaky butter bun that had appeared on her plate soon after. Nava peeked behind her hair to where they sat and wished that she sat next to Arkimedes, even though he didn't remember her. She missed the warmth his presence gave her.

Roasted pork, salted fish, and a casserole of peas and golden roasted potatoes appeared next. Her mouth watered as she took it all in before she followed the rest of the party and served herself a heap of food.

The idle chatter stopped when the king stood. The black fabric of his tunic billowed with an unnatural movement that mixed with his shadows. "We gather today among my court to celebrate the fortune of our kingdom. This year we welcomed my heir back home." His eyes shone across the table, and he raised his glass in the air. "To our prosperity. Our forces will take out those who try to break us apart, again."

Nava swallowed as the king's aura grew and the candlelight flickered under the constriction of his power. Even though his words were light, the ambiance of the room was anything but. As everything grew darker by the moment, the wood of the table shrieked and trembled under the pressure building around it.

"Father."

The king's hard gaze fell upon Arkimedes. "Orion's good friend from his past life, and his *fiancée*, join us today," the king continued, and Arkimedes stilled in his seat. His magic billowed around him, so similar to the king's. No one would be able to deny they were related.

Nava's back crawled with an icy touch, and her stomach contracted as it grew more suffocating. Her knuckles whitened around her silverware, but just as it had started, it stopped. The room's darkness retracted to the man sitting at the head of the table, and the candlelight stopped flickering as it settled into a gentle dance.

"Please enjoy your meal. We will do a full celebration in a week's time during the summer solstice."

The room's ambiance shifted as the king took his seat. Nava let out a breath and focused on the plate in front of her. She had been so hungry a moment ago, but now her stomach churned with nausea.

The message was loud and clear: stay away from the heir or die a horrible, suffocating death. She guessed she knew where her life was taking her.

They ate in silence, and slowly everyone forgot what had transpired a moment ago. The idle chatter resumed once again.

Nava took a sip of her wine, her gaze fixed on a nonspecific point by the wall. Her hand came over her heart, massaging an ache that didn't go away. It had been easy to forget, if just for a breath, what had happened in her travels here. Tossed inside a palace to find out her soulmate was a prince and had completely forgotten her.

But now that she had filled her stomach and the looming pressure of what she needed to do weighed on her, it was obvious she had not only lost Arkimedes, but something else as well. Someone important she couldn't place.

She faced Devon, lowering her voice below a whisper. "Is there any way to regain what was taken from me when we crossed the portal?"

He shrugged, his cool, calculating gaze crossing the room, following the shapes of a couple of court people who were excusing themselves from dinner. "Not that I'm aware of. It wouldn't be much of a price to pay if you could take it back."

The weight inside her chest grew heavier, her breaths coming shorter as the world suddenly became too small. She had lost it forever—him, her? What? "Well, who took it . . .?" She hesitated. The shadowy shapes in the portal felt different from the voice that had spoken with her when she'd released Devon from his cell. "There was someone there with me—multiple people. Did they speak to you as well?" There was one in particular who'd been more interested in her.

Devon's attention snapped back to her as he dipped his head closer. "You saw someone when we crossed?"

She nodded, moving her mashed peas across her plate with her brass fork. "It was a shadow." But was it? No, it was a male, pale and familiar. "It— He *knew* me."

More importantly, he knew she was a Beekeeper.

The silence extended for longer than she'd expected; Devon was a bit too close for comfort, and his scent of mint and blackberries hit her straight in the face. She pulled her head back, eyeing him warily.

His skin had lost whatever little color he had to begin with. "What did he take?"

"It's not like I could know, would I?" she said between clenched teeth. "I can't remember what I lost, only that it feels important."

Devon tsked before bringing the brass goblet to his lips and taking a healthy swig of fruity wine. "I warned you it will take your first thought. Not a smart move to think of something important."

"It wasn't like I consciously picked." Nava tried to keep her voice down. "It felt like he took my first simple thought, and it pushed me to spiral. He took more and more, until it left me with emptiness."

"It might've been the Lord of the Shadows. The ruler of the place in-between. We don't know if these legends are true or not, but he is supposed to be a demigod. It's said he likes to lurk between worlds." Devon put his glass down and warily looked at the king at the end of the table.

"Have you met him before?"

He let out what sounded like a forced laugh, shaking his head. "No, he doesn't just show up to people. Even if he is claiming his portal fee." Devon's eyes narrowed on her. "Which makes me think, what is it you have to capture his interest?"

Well, so much for getting unfiltered information. She had gotten too close to the lion, and it had scented fresh blood. "You know well who I am," she blurted. "I was living my very peaceful life, in my boring-ass town, until you showed up."

"Kitten, I showed up way before that."

"Right, but you weren't alone then." She looked across the table toward

Arkimedes and found his green eyes staring right back at her. He stiffened as his attention moved from her to Devon.

When had this all gotten so messed up? How would she be able to get him out of here when he was so keen to play the prince?

"I enjoyed finding a flustered miniature version of your mother eleven years ago in the manor," Devon said with a side smile, his focus lost somewhere in the room. "I didn't expect what followed, but that afternoon was entertaining."

"How are we going to get hi—"

"Shh." He dipped his head and gave her a hard look. "Long, pointy ears are bound to hear you."

She growled. "You thought to remind me of this now that we've been talking for a while?" Her tone was so low, she was surprised he even heard her at all.

"Talking about a payment for crossing is something our host knows."

"Right," she said, and silence descended over them, while they just listened to the muted conversations around. No one else paid them any attention, but Nava knew better.

"You have my interest now. When we can talk at ease, I can't wait to hear more about you speaking to a shadow figure while crossing a portal," he whispered.

Dropping her fork, Nava gave him a hard look. The sound of metal against porcelain echoed across the room. "I'm not one hundred percent confident I want to confide in you with anything."

"You must." Devon's poised stance grated further on her nerves. His grin extended through his features. "After all, we are in this together, fiancée."

The lie hung heavy over her; she allowed herself to look upon her mate one more time. He had been away from both Devon and her the whole evening, chatting with the king and all the women who'd come with him.

Devon was her ally in this. She had been the one to release him after the king kidnapped her mate. What she hadn't expected was eleven years of his memories gone, taking away not only her and their bond but all the emotional growth he had done while away from politics and power.

CHAPTER NINE

NAVA

The air was heavy, like the storm raging above. Wet ash and smoke burned her eyes. She stood perched on the tree. Embers of red-and-yellow fire lit beneath blackened wood. A soft cry escaped her lips, encouraging the critters around the forest to scurry and survive.

The scent of death hung thickly in the air. Sulfur and burnt flesh.

The roar of the flames competed with the thunder in the sky. A dark shape of a demon surfaced from the smoke. Two horns shaped like antennas grew from each side of its head. Charcoal skin wrapped tightly against a plated thorax, a narrow waist, and long, segmented legs that bent in weird directions.

It looked like a wasp, except its face was demonic, with a flat, wide nose and a mouth that opened with jagged teeth.

It wore no clothes, nothing to shield it from the elements, much less from the fire it was causing. Hell had arrived in this land, burning it to ashes with fire from below, leaving no life behind.

She moved on her perch, feeling the rough texture of bark beneath her wooden claws. Anger flared in her chest as she took in the destruction. Embers blew in the wind with fallen trees, and the cry of animals surged within the chaos beneath.

Her body faded, becoming pollen, dirt, and leaves as it traveled to the ground. Pain scorched through her skin at the heat. She bared her teeth at the demon; its black, beaded eyes came to her and the rumble of a growl started in its chest as it lunged for her.

Nava moved out of the way, and her sharp wooden claws slipped over the demon's chest. Her hands burned from the contact, but its chest split open, showing embers of magma behind the wound.

It screamed, and the fire behind her claw marks subsided as nature reclaimed the demon's body. Branches grew from its heart, and its pained scream filled the air.

At some point, Nava would've been sorry to see a life sucked away like this, but not with a Zorren, their mortal enemy. Not when she was so angry.

It was the nature flowing through her that called on the dying trees, and its branches swung low, catching the demon and sending it flying up in the air. It became a pile of ash and fire when it landed.

The demon materialized back in front of her, and she attacked it again, slicing over its head and neck. It cried out, its eyes staring right at her before they grew slack, and slowly it dissipated in the air, following the ash of the burning forest.

Nava gasped for air as she woke, drenched in sweat beneath layers of silky blankets. She studied the room but found no ash and no forest, and definitely no demon.

In the green room, she was still a prisoner in the Copper Kingdom.

However, she knew deep within this had not been a dream but a reality for Ari. It wasn't the first time she'd dreamed of him this way. He usually was awake in the forest while she slept. It had been the first time she'd seen a Zorren, however, and she hadn't been there to help him.

A ray of lightning illuminated the dark sky, and a few moments later, thunder rolled in the distance, and wind swept into the room like a storm. Nava rushed to her feet and ran across the room to close the terrace's doors as the rain fell sideways, drenching everything in its path.

The gods were angry, and the Zorren had arrived in this kingdom. A coincidence? Unlikely. The three of them in this land just meant the demons would gravitate here, right?

Unlike the rain in the Grey Island, this was unnaturally warm, as if the sky was telling her hell was coming. Releasing Arkimedes from this new curse of amnesia was her first job.

After quickly closing the wood doors, Nava wrapped her arms around her body and stared out past the terrace to the forest that surrounded the palace. It had been raining a storm where Ari was, much like this one, which meant he was there, waiting for her.

Nava needed to get to that forest, away from these four walls that constricted her. It was true the bracelet didn't work on canceling her magic. However, it numbed her skin with whatever power it had, like mild poison.

The likelihood of her leaving the palace was low, and making a plan with

Devon had become another hurdle. In hindsight, she wished she had gotten an adjacent room to the Crow. Maybe both of them would have better luck finding a way out of this mess.

Where was her soulmate? He had to still be in the palace and close by since she hadn't been dreaming of him. She'd half expected to see him at some point.

They had locked the doors of this bedroom, and even though she had been speaking to the door every day, no one answered. It was almost embarrassing that the first couple of days in the room, she hadn't wanted to get out of bed, the heaviness in her heart too strong. She had cried until she'd had no tears left and her head hurt.

Nava wasn't sure what she was mourning. Her stolen memory or the fact that Arkimedes also didn't remember her and their love story had been sabotaged in such a horrible way. She missed Cameron, Aristaeus, and Laurie.

Then after sadness had come anger. He had been the one locking her in this room, even though he didn't intend to visit. Devon had likely gotten more attention since he was remembered fondly, maybe had even been outside of his gold room.

Leela, the redheaded maid, had brought her food every day but hadn't stayed or said much. The message was loud and clear. Arkimedes didn't give a flying rat's ass about her. After getting a sneak peek of the nightmare Ari was going through, Nava understood she had been wallowing in her self-pity long enough.

The sun had come up to the highest point in the sky, casting sharp shadows. Nava couldn't stay inside this room for a moment longer. She grasped the brass door handle, shaking it with pent-up frustration. The thing didn't budge.

She pounded on the heavy wood so hard the skin at the heel of her hand discolored purple and blue. "You can't keep me a prisoner here forever!"

No answer.

A sensation crawled over the back of her skull, and the oppression in her chest grew stronger. The energy in her body had dwindled since this morning, and she didn't know if it was because Ari needed her. Not being able to touch the rough texture of wood or the leaves and dirt and bask in the scent of the forests had to be affecting her.

There was no guard by the door. She hadn't heard or seen anyone during the time she'd been locked inside the hellhole. Hitting the door again, she put more strength into it this time. "If you are there, let me out at once."

Silence.

The weight of her skull touched the cool surface. She took in air deeply, trying to calm her ragged breathing. Not knowing how long she stood there, she opened her eyes with new resolve.

It was time to stop avoiding using her Beekeeper magic. Nava had transferred before—granted, with the direct guidance of Aristaeus, but she knew how to do it. She was not as helpless as the king intended her to be, and the thought comforted her.

Resolve settled in her with each step she took toward the balcony in the room, the only connection she had with nature. Soon her eyes drank in the wonderful visuals of the trees beyond the garden. The sky was hazy. With smoke, perhaps? Knowing her dreams weren't dreams, and the Zorren were causing havoc, only made her more eager to get out there.

She had no plan on how to get Arkimedes out of here yet, but at least she wasn't standing still.

The light summer breeze hit her skin as she focused on a place behind the palace's palisades. Closing her eyes, she allowed her magic to come alive, feeling weightless as the air carried her away.

She could taste freedom, so close as she floated over the banisters; however, her body just hung there, suspended in the air. She was stuck in between wanting to leave and being too afraid of not being able to get back.

Her energy dwindled at a fast rate, unable to borrow from nature. Her body materialized and then evaporated again.

In her panic, instead of going over the balcony, she backtracked inside her cell. She was unable to feel her limbs, and panic took over her senses.

Her body transformed into wind, pollen, dirt, and other organic things. It allowed her under the crevices of her door, and she rushed down the hall before her magic gave up on her.

She materialized with a pop and crashed onto the floor, pulling the runner with her. The skin of her knees burned from the friction.

A vase shattered as it hit the ground, and her blurry vision sharpened with the noises down the hall. Quick steps and deep voices approached. Nava was on her feet, looking around for a place to hide, but she found only long sections of unbroken walls and closed windows.

Other than the columns on each side of the hall, which provided little cover, there was nowhere to hide. Her heart pounded near her throat as she ran back toward the forest-green door of her room.

Nava closed her eyes and tried to transfer again, but her body remained solid and her anxiety wrecked her mind. *Please, please, please transfer.*

She reached for the forsaken handle but met resistance. The steps grew nearer as she pulled and pushed. Trying to get inside was proving impossible, but her body was too weak and her mind too panicked.

Her grasp became heated, but the handle didn't budge. "Please, please."

She could force her way in, but if she ruined this door, how could she explain such a thing? They would know the bracelet wasn't working, and then surely she would get killed.

A couple of guards turned the corner and froze when their eyes met her. Nava's stomach sank, and the ants that had been crawling over her scalp descended over her body.

They took off running toward her, and her adrenaline spiked. Not tired anymore. Before she could think twice, she bolted in the other direction.

"Stop there, witch!" one shouted, and she had a looming sensation of déjà vu.

Nava couldn't hear their steps over the sound of her heavy breathing. She ran and ran until freezing air sent her flying forward.

The scent of magic surrounded her as she collided with the ground. This time, her arms buckled under her weight and her jaw hit the cool marble floor. Her teeth went through her lip, and all at once, pain erupted everywhere.

The hiss of burning crawled over her back, and she turned around, screaming, trying to put out the fire—or calm the freezing crawling over her skin. The metallic taste of blood mixed in her mouth.

Their steps brought them to her too fast. She opened her watery eyes and gasped when a gloved hand grasped her by the neck. The same icy touch of magic from her back extended down her throat.

Why did they always go for the neck? She wished she could scream at them that they weren't that original.

Nava grasped his wrist and tried to pull him off as he lifted her from the ground, still choking her.

"You can't kill her," the other man said from the back, keeping his distance.

"For Herous, I should." The man slammed her against the wall, and her head hit the rock with such strength, sharp pain rattled through her brain and black dots danced over her vision.

"The prince will kill you."

"He can't. We found her outside her room. The king will protect me."

Their voices became muted, and the hand around her throat tightened. It wasn't large enough to hold her entire neck, but magic aided him.

Nava's hold on his wrists tightened as she clawed his leather glove, struggling against his hold like a fish out of water. There wasn't any more air left and her vision closed in.

The man behind her assailant tsked loudly, taking a step back or forward, she didn't know. "I don't want to be a part of this."

Panicked, Nava kicked and pulled, and the man slammed her into the wall again. She picked up her leg and kicked his metal-clad crotch.

Even though protected, the metal screeched under her strength. The man hissed and briefly let go. She gasped for air, but before a scream could leave her lips, he was back on her, his magic overtaking her senses.

She flailed under his grasp. Her strength was so low, she didn't have it in her to fight. It was as if her life was being sucked away. A fresh sense of panic took over before the weight of the man flew off her.

Nava fell to the ground like a boneless pile of meat. The surrounding commotion was unmistakable. Footsteps running toward her, wind blowing over her face with the scent of magic.

Nava was too cold to feel much. However, she opened her eyes and focused on the looming shape of a man with ebony wings. Warmth spread through her body as relief took over, but it wasn't her relief.

"You shouldn't have done that." Arkimedes's voice was colder than the magic that had been used to attack her. For a moment, Nava thought he was speaking to her as the gentle caress of his glove touched the side of her jaw. His features sharpened when their eyes met. Arkimedes frowned before rising to his feet and turning away from her. "What made you think you could touch her?"

"Your Highness." The man's voice shook with fear. Nava guessed he wasn't so cocky now that he was face to face with her soulmate. Arkimedes grabbed the fae's neck, so fast Nava had a hard time following from her spot on the ground.

He slammed the guard against the wall, much like the man had done with her a moment ago, and his armor bent under such force. "Answer me. I'm not a patient man."

"We found her outside her room!" the fae said, trying to inhale behind Arkimedes's hold. "It's the law. We . . . execute . . . if we find a prisoner outside their cells!"

"She is not one for you to punish!" Arkimedes slammed the fae again, and the helmet caved before it fell to the ground with a loud crash.

That's when Nava took in the man's features. He was gorgeous, with a pointy nose and wide, round eyes partly covered by red wavy hair. His lips twisted in a grimace as his skin turned from golden to gray at an alarming rate.

The mane on his head reminded her of Cameron so much. She tried to speak but gasped at the sharp pain that awoke at her attempt to prevent Arkimedes from killing this man. Bringing a shaky hand toward her throat, she tried again, but the sound was croaky at best.

"I thought . . . she . . . was . . ."

"You thought wrong!"

She wasn't sure why she cared if this man died or not. He had been trying to kill her, no questions asked. But his bright blue eyes were so close to the ones of her brother—she couldn't allow it. "Ark—"

The second guard approached her with reluctant steps and reached out a gloved hand. She recoiled against the wall, trying to avoid his touch. Her heart drummed as adrenaline bounced in her body.

Arkimedes's gaze snapped back to her, and the swarm of anger that took over her body wasn't hers. "Stand away from her," he growled, and the other guard put both hands up and took a few steps back.

Her soulmate dropped the redheaded guard and was kneeling by her in a matter of seconds. His warm touch was gentle on her shoulder, and his eyes studied her closely. "Get Fael and Leela," he said to the standing guard, who bolted out of there so fast, all she could hear were his retreating steps.

Her gaze met one of green moss, and he reached over, picking her up like she weighed nothing at all. It didn't take him long to get her to her room. Nava had been so eager to leave, never imagining being relieved to be back.

He laid her on the bed, and a gasp of pain escaped her lips when the fabric of her covers touched her raw back. "I will get a healer."

"No," she said, not wanting any fae to touch or tend to her. However, her voice was a whisper; it hurt too much to speak. Nava rolled over, and the burning ache in her back subsided. Arkimedes gasped a moment before she felt tentative fingers over the uninjured expanse of her back. She had come so close to dying, and now, as she lay in bed, her adrenaline was fading, leaving behind her shaking body.

"You are cold."

"I'm fine," she whispered, closing her eyes, letting her body drift away into a more peaceful time.

"What were you doing outside? How?"

"Magic," she answered. Her limbs were too heavy, and she was too tired to care whether or not this got her into trouble.

He was quiet for a while, probably assimilating the fact that she all but admitted to doing magic. "Why leave when you must have known there were guards outside?"

"I got lonely." She didn't hear this reply as sleep pulled her under.

CHAPTER TEN

NAVA

The night before had been a blur of people coming in and out of her room. Besides a couple of the royal healers and a few female maids, Arkimedes had been hovering around most of the morning.

Her back and neck were healed for the most part, not just with salves and potions. Healers in this city possessed magic unlike what she'd seen in the village. Ancient healing powers. They weren't too happy to use them on her, but it was hard to say no to the prince when that answer could get you killed.

By the time the red-haired fae who'd brought her breakfast last week came over, Nava was already dressed. When she opened the door to greet the maid, her eyes met the golden gaze of a guard by her door.

The man nodded in acknowledgment before the red-haired fae closed the door behind her. "I'm Leela. We haven't met properly yet, though I have been bringing you your food."

"I remember you from my first night in this castle."

She smiled prettily, placing the tray of food at the end of her bed. "I would love to fix your hair for you this morning."

Nava combed her fingers over her tresses in response to Leela's offering. She liked her hair the way it was, wild and free. However, she winced as her fingers tangled in fresh knots. "Has the prince put you up to this?"

Leela's face fell before she shook her head. "Oh, no. But I would love to spend some time with you. I know it gets lonely here."

In other words, yes. Arkimedes had commanded this poor girl to keep her company, and that alone had her stomach fluttering with a pleasant wave of gratefulness and hope.

"Thanks, and who's the guard?" Nava rearranged one gold jewelry box neatly placed on the dressing table, allowing the girl to play with her hair.

"Fael," Leela said, and she remembered that name. Arkimedes had mentioned it yesterday.

"So is he going to be guarding me from now on?"

Leela met her gaze from behind, her thin fingers pausing as she held a lock of Nava's hair. "After what happened, yes."

"Is the other guard all right?" Alive, she meant.

Leela dropped her eyes to what she was doing. "He will survive."

"Good."

"Good?"

"I don't want to be responsible for that man's life." Nava shrugged, unsure why she cared. But for some reason, she did.

"He is lucky our prince spared his life after he attacked one of his guests." Leela clicked her tongue, shaking her head. "Nimb should have known better."

Nimb, the faerie who looked like an adult version of her little brother, had almost killed her for no reason other than being outside her room.

"You are precious to our prince. That alone should have sent a warning to the guards to keep their hands off you."

"What?"

Leela swallowed and stepped back, bringing a cup of steaming tea in her shaky hands. Nava grabbed it from her before it spilled all over. "He put you in the green room when he could have assigned you a room closer to Mr. Black." Her words startled Nava. "What happened could have been avoided, had Nimb used his thick head."

Both of them had red hair, and Nava couldn't help but wonder if they were somehow related, or maybe this kingdom housed a bunch of redheaded people.

"He is all muscle and no brain," Leela continued, and Nava got the impression that even if they were related somehow, the girl wasn't a fan of the guard.

"I don't know if that says I'm precious to him. Devon and I are . . . engaged. He didn't want his brother to lose his soon-to-be bride, that's all." That lie tasted more bitter than any other she had ever told.

The fae hummed, dragging the boar brush over Nava's hair. A spike of panic moved through her as she imagined how puffy her hair would be after such attention. This fae had clearly never dealt with curly locks. "Well, he placed you in the room next to his—he must want to ensure your safety. He's put no one in here since he returned."

"Oh, I don't think that's the case," Nava said in what she hoped was a casual tone. However, her lips twitched as she fought to keep a smile under wraps, and warmth settled in waves inside her stomach. "Has he—um, has he brought anyone to his room before?"

The mere thought of it had her in knots. Arkimedes had no memory of her, and even if their bond prevented him from feeling true attraction to anyone other than her, he might have been trying to prove a point to himself. Much like she had done once upon a time in Willowbrook with Hale, the only man other than Arkimedes she had been with.

That whole experience had been a fiasco to both Hale and her since she couldn't have been less interested if she'd tried.

"Oh, he hasn't shown interest in anyone these last months." The girl clearly didn't notice how Nava's whole body relaxed at her words.

"Either way, him putting me here is more to ensure I don't do something reckless," Nava supplied with a smile. It wasn't that she had any reasons not to trust this girl, other than the fact that the king had kidnapped Arkimedes and she was under his allegiance.

"For that, he could have assigned you to any room with multiple guards. Instead, he put you right next to him." Leela worked on her hair with nimble fingers. Her wide blue eyes met Nava's through the reflection, and it was easy to see that this faerie was a hopeless romantic. Leela wasn't that far off, since in this case Arkimedes and she were soulmates, in love, and fully bonded.

"If it makes you happy to think this, then go for it."

"It does, my lady. It has been awfully dull in this castle for many years, ever since the queen—" Leela let her words fade and lowered her gaze back down to Nava's hair.

"Ever since the queen what?"

As she shook her head, her long locks of fiery red hair whipped across her face. "I can't say any more, my lady."

"Please call me Nava. I'm not anyone's lady." Except she was a prince's soulmate, however weird that was to grasp. Cameron would have a major freakout when he learned this. He had always been so curious about the royals and their kingdoms.

"Of course, miss. However, I think you're someone's lady. Aren't you going to be married to Mr. Black?"

Right. "That's what I keep hearing." Lies to appease Arkimedes and buy them time to form a plan she was struggling to come up with.

"How exhilarating! To have these two men fight for you! I mean, we both know who will win. Our prince is one of considerable power, and I haven't sensed the Crow's power yet since he is wearing the jewel, but he is very handsome."

Was Devon Black handsome? She guessed he could be considered a more typical handsome man if you took away the evil veil that covered him. With his height, muscular build, and sharp cheekbones. It was hard to see him as anything other than a bully who'd tortured her and her friends. Someone who'd tried to kidnap a whole village to take them back to the crown and enslave them.

However, the perk . . . or downfall of having a soulmate was the lack of attraction to anyone other than the person the gods bound you to.

"I guess I never thought about it." Nava shrugged, inspecting the intricate braids around her scalp that met into a low bun behind her neck.

"But the prince, now he has the beauty of our royals. The women of this kingdom have been swooning over him ever since he came back." Leela finished pinning the bun back. "Wouldn't you say he is the most handsome?" This girl could give Nava a run for her money for fitting so many words in one conversation. Leela was an utter gossip and a breath of fresh air in this prison.

Nava felt her cheeks warm as her mind supplied images too heated for someone who appeared as young as the fae behind her. "I agree. He is handsome—and seems tense."

She had known Arkimedes from a soul-sharing level for a year. He was different now, like his soul was weighed down by things he didn't have a week ago when they were back home together.

"He is also wicked," Leela added with a delighted expression.

"How so? Has he done something bad since he's been here?"

"Not quite." The fae placed a pin in Nava's hair, a large white pearl with a hanging charm. "But it is known that in the Society of Crows, they called him the Reaper."

"The Reaper?" Nava repeated, a wave of annoyance running through her. Why was it that everyone knew more about Arkimedes's past than she did?

"I have no idea why, but it sounds dark and wicked, doesn't it?" By the large smile on the fae's face, they had a different understanding of those words.

First thing she would inquire about next time she crossed paths with either of the Crows. "Where has he been going during the day? I half expected Devon and I would see more of him as his guests." Nava's casual tone could have fooled anyone. She tucked a strand of wavy hair behind her ear.

"I guess it won't hurt if I say anything. No one has told me to keep quiet." Leela exhaled, lowering her attention to the ground as her delicate eyebrows twisted. "There have been rumors of attacks in the forest. We dispatched guards during the week."

"He has to go?" Maybe seeing Ari would jolt some memories back.

"His Royal Highness likes to go on the hunt with the guards. It's said around the halls that hunting helps him gain power—when he takes others, it happens with His Majesty the king as well. They are so alike. It's like the king was reborn in his son, and of course, none of the mixed blood is hindering his powers. The queen couldn't take our heir away, after all."

Mental note, say nothing to this girl that could paint the queen in a positive light. "So it's only the royals who have that power? I notice only them and the guards have wings as well. Are most of the fae asked to put their wings away?"

"Put the wings away, how could someone do such a thing? Fae that have been gifted by the gods with wings should proudly walk amongst us with them on display." Leela's brows almost hit the edge of her hair.

Why indeed? Arkimedes had always chosen to do so. Maybe it was an insult? Nava had a lot of learning to do.

"I—I don't know. I haven't met many of your kind. I grew up in the Iron City, and there aren't many fae there."

Leela relaxed a fraction and nodded. "Iron is toxic to us." She took a deep breath and continued in a lighter tone. "Not all fae have wings, Dark Ones do. So the royals and the guards possess them, but not me, for example."

"Oh." That would explain why so many of the people working in the castle were wingless. "I thought this was the kingdom of the Dark Ones."

"Eons ago, only Dark Ones walked these lands. But the Copper Kingdom is a habitat for many races, including humans. Fae have been intermixing for generations, and so I guess we all have a bit of Dark Ones' blood in us, just not any of their magic."

"So that's why only the royals have their aura?"

She nodded, distracted by Nava's hair. "Some of our most powerful guards have a fraction—but not quite the same." At those words, Nava swallowed and watched as Leela's face lost all of its color. "I think your hair looks beautiful, milady. I appreciate you letting me braid it today. His Royal Highness will be pleased." Leela could compete with Cameron over who was the best matchmaker.

"Thank you, Leela. I appreciate your time. I wouldn't have been able to get my hair to do this."

Even though the words being exchanged were happy ones, Leela drew herself away. It was as if speaking about the queen was forbidden, even if no one else was present to chastise her. The air in the room practically crackled with tension, and the fae was already walking away, her skin shining with perspiration. Why was the mention of the queen so bad? Was the king able to listen to them somehow?

Nava had gotten rid of the creepy flowers, but the castle was run by magic. "I'm sorry, I'm a bit confused. Did I say anything wrong? Is speaking about the queen bad somehow?"

"We loved our queen. I will never speak ill of her again," Leela rushed to say, though Nava wasn't sure she believed her. However, the weird tension in the room did ease. The feeling alone had her skin crawling with self-awareness. Was she being watched? Or was it the particular subject that made the castle react?

Looking around the room, Nava ventured to say something more. "I'm curious what happened to her."

Leela's gaze turned pleading before she said, "It's forbidden by the king. Even the prince knows little. If His Majesty learned of someone divulging false information or any rumors, he would . . . It would be bad." Had Arkimedes been asking this poor girl about it as well? How else would she know that he knew little about the queen?

"Don't worry, Leela. The king and I are far from pals. I'm practically a prisoner here, so please don't feel the need to panic. I will keep your secrets, and I hope you keep mine." But Nava would never, ever divulge a secret to this girl, however sweet she was.

After a few beats, Leela grinned, relaxing her posture. "You have gained a confidant, milady. I will be on my way then. I will bring your dinner at the same time." She bowed and, without another word, rushed to the door.

Nava stood from her seat by the dressing table, feeling the walls of herself collide as she was left alone inside this room once again. Her chest constricted, and suddenly it was hard to breathe. She rushed to the door as it closed in front of her, reaching for the brass handle, half expecting it not to move as she turned it.

Click.

It opened. *It opened!*

She let out a whoosh of breath as she peeked out into the hall, meeting the expectant gaze of Fael. He held his rusted copper helmet in the crook of his arm, and his golden eyes studied her as if reassuring himself that she was fine before he lifted a brow.

"May I help you?"

"Uh, no. I mean, yes!" She cleared her throat, bouncing on the tips of her toes as she looked down the hall to the retreating shape of Leela. "I'd expected to be locked in here like I was before."

Fael turned to her, letting out a contained breath. She had a hard time deciphering what it meant. "The prince has been busy with his duties and has been unable to tend to his *unexpected* guests. He understands it's unpleasant to stay inside the room all the time, so I've been placed as your guard so you can leave your accommodations at times."

A little more friendliness or hostility would help Nava place this man onto her friend-or-foe list easier. She straightened and crossed her arms over her chest. "So . . . will I be able to visit the castle grounds?"

"With limitations, and always escorted."

"What about seeing Devon?" So they could plan *something.*

"When the prince is around, you may see your fiancé."

In other words, Arkimedes didn't trust them together. Whether because of jealousy or whatever reason, she was on her own.

CHAPTER ELEVEN

ORION

His long mist of shadows followed him as Orion entered the forsaken area of the library. The sound of his steps was muffled as his boots met the bumpy terrain of fallen books over rotten carpet.

The walls of bookcases were as tall as a common house in the Iron City. Even though this had once been as majestic as the rest of this library, it was now black and ashen after a fire long ago. Crusted with age and destruction, like the remnants of an old campfire.

The king had forbidden anyone to rebuild, rummage, or dissect the area after its demise. To the few who could step inside, it was a constant reminder of what had been lost long ago. Their queen, who they believed had betrayed them; their heir, who they thought dead; and all the history that once had been rich inside these shelves.

Four months ago, he'd boarded a flying ship from the Iron Kingdom that had brought him here to search for answers about his lost family, never expecting to find who he'd turned out to be. However, in the beginning, accepting a role in this madness had been more about finding why he'd been abandoned, rather than anything to do with the kingdom or the king's expectations.

That was, until the ghost of the queen had haunted him for the first time. It had begun when he entered this very same library three months ago. She'd been standing by the window. A woman wearing a black dress, with a full skirt and a tight corset. Her hair had billowed in the air, as if submerged in water. The crown had been barely visible between the strands, and he hadn't realized who she really was, until she'd shown up in his nightmares days later.

After that, he'd learned quickly that no one spoke of the queen. The kingdom believed she had died in a fire, in this very same library. Orion had believed the same, but the nightmares had shown him otherwise.

It hadn't been ideal to alternate dreams of Nava—a woman he knew nothing of—with nightmares of his mother dying in a fire. Confusing didn't begin to cover it; he didn't know what was real or a figment of his imagination.

Now that Nava had turned out to be real, he couldn't ignore the nightmares any longer. There was something larger hidden here, and he was being asked in a not-subtle way to find it.

Orion wasn't afraid of spirits; as a matter of fact, they constantly haunted him. It came with being a Dark One. This ghost of bones and ashes, however, had had him freezing in true fear the first time he'd seen her.

That day, many months ago, he had questioned the keeper of the library if he knew a ghost haunted the space. The old man had actually laughed in his face, clearly unable to see the figure of said queen standing a few feet away by the window.

Orion's mixed feelings of whether he should be resentful toward the woman who had birthed and abandoned him pulled him in a different direction. He hadn't wanted to learn anything more about her at first. Still, seeing her suffering, nightmare after nightmare, and the ghostly remnants of silent sorrow that followed him around the castle, had taken down brick by brick the wall he'd put up throughout his life.

The guardian of this place claimed all records of the queen had been burned when she died. The man had expected Orion to blindly believe the tale everyone else did. That she had taken him away, then returned to burn all records and killed herself in the same fire.

No one needed to know that he didn't trust much of what anyone around here told him, not when everything sounded like a lie.

Much less now that Nava and Devon had landed in the castle, claiming something was off—or at least she claimed. He had to find time to talk to his brother about it.

Tucking his wings closer to his body, Orion scanned the shelves for anything that would call to him. Searching for a name, feeling for a pull of magic.

Why had the queen been killed? She'd stolen the heir away. However, according to the king, he would never order such a thing. She had been treasured by him. Orion brought his hand to his temples, trying to massage away the pounding headache that kept building up as the hours passed.

It was a fool's errand to return to this place every night when, for the past three months, he had found nothing other than growing frustration. It didn't help that all he wanted to do in this particular moment was go and see if Nava was, in fact, safe.

She was a magic wielder who had bewitched him from across an ocean and was engaged to his brother. A bitter laugh escaped his lips as he shook his head and walked deeper into the ruins that once had been a guarded part of his family's library.

The worst damage of the fire lay ahead, leading him to areas he hadn't fully explored yet. He wondered if the ghost of his mother would await him in the shadows of this place.

He closed his eyes and let his magic pull him forward, following the instinctive pressure forming in his stomach as the scent of mold and ashes wrapped around him. Destruction often spoke the same language.

The moans and whispers of those he'd taken long ago stirred to life in dark, misty shapes. His power consumed kernels of other people's souls if he ever took their lives. It didn't matter if it was for self-defense or if he had been forced to do so.

An echo of a soul, forever bound to him.

The king had been teaching him to block them out, and he *had* learned. He was able to block them for the most part these days, but every time he stepped foot inside this place, they came back with a vengeance.

"There is nothing here, other than filth," one cackling voice whispered, angry and disgusted.

"A waste of time, really," said another.

The debris crunched under his weight, and the heavy scent of burnt matter had his eyes watering in response. It was even more unsettling that all the voices sounded alike these days; he had forgotten who they came from. His mother, however, never spoke to him. But it wasn't like he was an expert on how spirits worked. Unlike the ones who followed him around, this was the first time he'd been chased by an actual ghost.

He traced a gloved finger over the decaying ledge in front of him and wondered if he would be escorted out of this place once again. If he would leave empty-handed. The deeper he went into the darkness, the more his chest tightened with the wrongness of it all. He knew she was around when the icy whisper of a touch of bone crawled down the back of his neck.

Goose bumps awakened, and he turned his gaze, searching. It was dark like a moonless night, but his fae eyes never disappointed, and even this remote, lonely space still looked bright to him.

The drumming inside his skull intensified as he walked deeper into the shadows, his own power blending into his surroundings as he followed a sinking feeling in his gut.

The scent of pepper lingered in the air, faint enough that most wouldn't notice it. A spell likely to disorient and push people away. Orion was close to finding *something*.

The ghost appeared then, snapping movements of charred skin over bones and empty holes where eyes had once been. He had to fight his innate reaction to flee. She raised her hand, bone pointing toward the case to his right.

Sweat beaded on his brow as he reached for one of the books, his fingertip tracing over the spine of it, and just like that, it disintegrated under his touch. Orion's wary gaze flashed to the spirit, who preserved her pose, floating in the air with teeth showing behind worn lips.

He continued, touching books here and there; his shallow breaths had him on the edge of hyperventilating when one book didn't fall into a pile of mush and ashes, and an embossed gold letter peeked out from behind charcoal.

"*There*." The three voices of his mist perked up, but the ghost of the queen disappeared in an instant.

Swallowing, he reached for the book with gentle hands. Chunks fell off, but for the most part, it stayed solid between his fingers. His wings twitched as his fear morphed into contained excitement that ran through him like a wave.

His fingers trembled as he brought the delicate tome under his tunic in the crook of his armpit. It wasn't like the keeper of this place could stop him from reading it, but taking this without anyone being the wiser would give him a chance to get a leg up in this situation.

Orion took a deep breath and exited the burnt wing of the library, looking around for the curved old man who guarded this place, listening for the shuffling of his feet or the feeling of being watched. But nothing came to him, and he spread his wings before coming downstairs with quick steps.

He hadn't fully made it to the bottom floor when the wavy tones of a shrill voice had him stopping. "Leaving already, sir?" For someone as old as this man, he was lethally quiet when he wanted to be.

Orion half turned to meet his hazy gaze, making sure the burnt tome wasn't visible to the man. His schooled features would be hard to read, as he'd been trained to do by the Society of Crows. "Yes. Is there a problem?"

"No, of course not." The man wrapped an arm over his stomach and came one step down the marble stairs, his other hand grasping at the decorative black metal railing. One more step down and then another. "Did you find what you were looking for?"

He took a deep breath to calm his sudden irritation at his nosy behavior. His aura expanded, turning a deeper shade of black around him.

"Let's show him what happens to the ones that question us," hissed a voice near his ear, and Orion's hand twitched with the vibrations of his magic.

"Are you intent on wasting my time today?" he asked instead, and the man's expression shifted from inquisitive to cautious.

"No, sir. However, if you were to find anything in the forbidden area, I'm bound by my duties to record it."

"Let him try to take it from us." The voices weren't helping with his mood, and Orion had to take a calming breath to quiet them.

He had to give the old geezer something; the man was persistent and not too afraid of him. Orion guessed the keeper had to deal with his father often, whose temper was known to be short, much like his own. "I didn't find anything other than burned books, Ellis. I'm sure you already know that," Orion said and turned to leave but paused. "I will be back tomorrow."

By the time he was out of the library, the shadows of daylight stretched over the castle halls. The air was warm and humid, almost as suffocating as the forbidden area in the library. However, the pleasant smell of summer blooms surrounded him as he walked at a quick pace toward the dining hall.

The book ground into his side, and his throat tightened as he thought it might be falling apart with friction. He took a corner and inspected the empty place; surely everyone was back in their homes, eating or working to serve the king.

He took the book out of its hiding place and looked around once again. He didn't have time to find answers right at this moment, so without preamble, he sent it away to his room, the scent of magic burning his nostrils.

Orion was greeted by the smell of roasted pork and buttered potatoes when he entered the dining hall. His gaze settled on the king, who sat at the head of the table. One of his cohorts was draped over his lap, her thin arms wrapped over his shoulders while his face worked the nape of her neck.

Her half-closed lidded gaze snapped to Orion. Her eyes were a rich brown that contrasted against her very pale skin. Her hair was long and straight, the color of spun gold. He slowed down, hesitating near the table.

"The prince is here, sir," she purred. A smile curved her plump pink lips.

Orion cleared his throat, shifting the weight of his body, not knowing if he should look elsewhere or pretend this was normal. "You called, Father?"

The king lifted his face, and his cobalt eyes darkened as he studied Orion closely. "You are late."

"I got caught up in the library."

The king hummed, straightening in his seat. His hand draped over his mistress's hips, his other holding a half-full glass of wine to his lips. "I don't like waiting. Don't let it happen again."

"You were . . . entertained without me."

The king narrowed his eyes at his heir. "Sharp tongue, like your mother."

Orion swallowed, remembering the shape of the ghost. Burnt and shallow, pointing at a book in the library. Dead.

The female sitting on the lap of the king straightened, her skin turning pale as her aura bloomed a darker shade of black; the scent in the air soured with her displeasure. He guessed she didn't like the reminder of the queen, especially when coming from her lover's lips.

Orion took a seat by the king and proceeded to fill his glass with some of the grape wine in front of him. Then he piled his plate with a healthy serving of meat.

"The forest fires, were they handled?" the king asked. "Have you found a guilty party yet?"

"What you mean to ask is, have I found a human to blame?" Silence hung heavy in between them, so Orion continued. "I haven't found signs of any human that could lead us to what the guards have been claiming."

"You have a sensible head on your shoulders but are also clouded by biases that might lead you to overlook things our people are seeing."

"This whole place is swimming with prejudices against humans. It's worth a reminder that I'm half one."

The king moved forward in his seat, and the mistress hung tighter to his neck as if afraid he would push her off at any moment. It wouldn't be the first time the king had done so in front of Orion. "Don't use that tone on me, boy."

"You asked me to go with them, and I'm reporting back that there is no human sign in that forest. No use of gray magic will cause such destruction in such a short time."

The king settled onto his seat once again, bringing the grape wine to his lips. "I heard that the witch has been tended to by my healers."

It was a miracle Orion didn't choke on his food, the change of subject was so abrupt. He tried to act casual as he washed the rich taste of pork, potatoes, and gravy from his mouth with wine. "Nava was badly injured by one of the guards."

"She was caught escaping her confinement. Our guard was allowed to punish her how he saw fit."

"I didn't like the way he behaved in my wing," Orion countered. It had been the king who'd told him he was free to make his rules on that part of the castle.

"Don't play the fool with me, Orion. It doesn't suit you."

"I told her she was allowed to walk outside her room if she needed a change of scenery. She wasn't disobeying anyone's command." Silence descended upon them, heavy and infinite, broken only by the hissing of the fireplace by the table.

"And why would you do that?"

"I learned she is claustrophobic." His jaw ached with tension, his need to protect almost overwhelming. "I'm keeping an eye on her, Father."

"But how close of an eye?" the king challenged. "Perhaps too much, as I was also informed you placed her in the green room next to yours."

His heartbeat raced and his hands prickled with sweat, but he didn't cower from his father's scrutiny. "So what? I didn't want her near Devon."

It wasn't even a lie and was something that had been bothering him for days since she'd arrived at the castle. The incessant need to protect her, like it was second nature. It didn't die there. He'd rather face the ire of his father than have her sleep next to Devon, and that thought alone was even scarier.

"*Divert. Now*," one of the misty voices whispered against his ear.

Shrugging noncommittally, he said in a flat tone, "I don't trust her with my brother."

"You don't trust her near the Crow, but I'm supposed to be at ease with her sleeping next to *you*?"

He didn't believe for a second the king was truly worried about Nava hurting him. The king's aura vibrated with pent-up tension, his expression sharpening. He was trying to find a hole in his tale.

Orion swallowed, counting on his expression not to give away how he truly felt for her, which might give his father a reason to jail them. The female sitting on the king's lap, Elly or something, shifted uncomfortably, avoiding either of their gazes.

"She is wearing the bracelet that cancels her magic. I'm capable of protecting myself from her, unless you doubt me," Orion countered with a lie that was far too easy to spout, especially since she'd been able to do magic just fine, and he wasn't so sure he was able to protect himself against her at all.

"What about other powers she might have over you?" The king's voice came down an octave. "She is beautiful."

"She is also my brother's fiancée."

"And I'm supposed to believe that makes a true difference? You almost killed two of our guards because they were hurting her."

"I would think after what happened with Herous, the other guards would've learned better than to harm her."

"Why do you care?"

Why, indeed? Orion wasn't sure why he was risking it all for a woman he didn't know, and he shouldn't care as much as he did. He had been telling himself he wasn't wicked, unlike the blood that ran through his body. Even though everyone back in the Iron City liked to remind him his very essence was evil, he wanted to be more. "Because I'm not a monster." Or at the very least, he hoped to avoid being one.

"She entered this palace without an invitation from either of us, which is punishable by death."

"I believe my brother when he says it was a miscalculation. When I left the city, I told him I would be gone for a month at maximum. It's natural he would come looking for me. He was all I had while I was there, and I accepted staying with you if you respected some boundaries, which includes my family."

The king stayed quiet for too long for Orion to feel at ease. This man's wisdom and wickedness were not to be outsmarted. "I see in you the way I used to be, the power, the hunger. You have the level head needed to make decisions in a moment's notice." The king picked a grape from his plate, holding it between relaxed fingers. "But then you speak and sound just like her. Idealism is the murderer of powerful societies, and we have no room for it." His gaze burned like blue fire when it landed back on Orion.

He didn't need to tell his father that idealism had saved his heart when he'd been a lonely child in an unwanted place. It wasn't his craving for power that allowed him to be human and pardon people the Society of Crows wanted dead for no reason other than wanting freedom.

Human or fae, he'd rather just be true to himself.

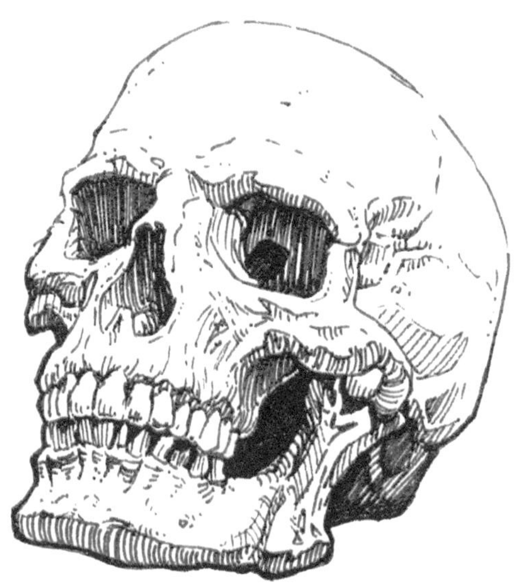

CHAPTER TWELVE

ORION

"I thought the next time I saw you, the cat would be dragging you in." Devon's voice carried through the walls of his room, his ebony eyes studying him. "It surprises me that I'm disappointed she wasn't the one bringing you to me."

"I have no idea what you're talking about," Orion said flatly, making his way into the room without waiting for an invitation. The door clicked behind him, and his brother followed him, crossing his arms over his chest.

He already looked ten times better than he had the day he arrived. His sunken cheeks had filled some. The darkness under his eyes had lifted.

"I have many names for her—cat, kitten . . ." Devon used his fingers to count, his lips twisted into a shadow of a smile. "*My* fiancée."

Orion flinched at that last word. Devon calling Nava his fiancée had his blood boiling. The smirk barely reached his brother's eyes, however, and it was as if he knew deep inside the word alone would grate at him. "I see," Orion growled.

It was odd with the way Devon held himself around him, like a wound that had festered between them. They had been close just four months ago, before he'd come to this place . . . unless something was off.

Devon could be under a spell that was forcing him to be here, acting strange. Manipulated by the same beautiful woman who had *him* under a spell.

Clearing his throat, he took a step closer and changed the subject. "You look thinner than four months ago." He studied Devon's complexion with a frown.

The aforementioned moved with floating steps toward the sitting area by the hearth, unbuttoning his deep blue jacket before taking a seat in the plush gold chair. "Arkimedes, brother, your manners are horrid. I would think they would beat you into shape in this hell, teach you better."

"Just call me Orion."

Devon tilted his head, showing straight teeth behind a tense smile. "Changing names in such a short time seems rather abrupt. Are you determined to stay here, then?"

Orion shrugged, making his way to the chesterfield sofa in front of his brother. The silk cream fabric was soft, with golden botanical patterns that shimmered with the light of the fireplace. His brother chased his every move, like a caged animal waiting to bite. His chest constricted at the realization that behind the false confidence, Devon was terrified of him. The only family he truly had hated him.

Orion laced the fingers of his hands tightly, bouncing both legs as the uncomfortable silence descended over them. "Arkimedes reminds me of someone I wish to leave behind." His throat thickened, and it was hard to swallow. Not knowing what to do with his hands, he raked his fingers in his hair. Arkimedes B. Valeron was a name associated with so much pain. With feeling like he didn't belong, like he wasn't wanted. Always feared. A monster.

"Ah." Devon allowed his body weight to rest on the back of the couch, crossing his ankle over his knee. "The tormented act."

"It's not an act. If someone were to offer you a chance to turn the page, to start fresh and not be who we were, you would also take it in a blink of an eye."

"I'm sure it doesn't hurt that you turned out to be a prince."

"You know me well enough to know I don't care about status or money."

"Yet somehow you always end up with both." Devon sneered, and Orion sat back, mute for a moment. His brother's eyes burned with a fire he hadn't seen before.

"What's happening here?" he wondered after a moment of extended silence. "Did we have an argument I'm not remembering?"

"You have no idea."

"What?"

Devon let out a heavy breath, his jaw tightening. "Never mind."

"Speak your truth. What's happening?"

Devon opened his mouth, and gurgling noise came out. His cheeks turned red, and he tried again. Silence, not one word. His thick black brows met in the middle. "Fuck."

"Are you under a spell?"

"You know well enough I wouldn't be able to tell you. But no, I'm not under a spell, per se. I'm under something much bigger."

"What, then? Is it something Nava did to you?"

Devon's eyes widened when no words left his lips again, and then he was up from his seat, a heavy groan leaving him as he walked around the room in a frenzy. "I guess I won't be able to say what I really want to about it."

She *had* cast a spell on his brother! Orion's body heated as he also stood, his hands turning to fists. "I will have her break it now."

"Calm down." Devon waved him off. "She can't break it. Only I can once I fulfill my end of the . . . bargain."

That damn woman would be the end of him. Orion hesitated but took a seat again. "So the match, when was it ordered? Can you break it?"

Could it be broken? Had it been an order from the Crown itself or was it a mere suggestion that his brother had blindly jumped into because of her breathtaking beauty? His skin prickled with anticipation as he waited for Devon to answer.

When no words came, Orion sat forward. "It's rather odd they matched you so quickly, and I find it suspicious you are suddenly here, under some sort of magic bond. She shouldn't be matched to you."

His brother barked a laugh and let his body unceremoniously fall onto the chair in front. "Oh, tell me how you are feeling, I beg you."

He should leave before this ridiculous jealousy came out in any way that could harm their trust further.

Leaving before asking Devon the questions that had brought him here in the first place was ridiculous. The scent of spice wafted, and the palm of his hand heated before the charred tome he'd taken from the library last night materialized in his open hand.

Devon wrung his hands together before straightening in his seat. Leaning forward, he studied the book and then raised his eyes slowly to meet Orion's.

"I have been searching for information ever since I arrived as to why my mother took me to that orphanage when the kingdom clearly wanted me here. Something is not adding up—"

"And you brought me a barbequed book to solve your mystery because . . . ?"

"The wing in the library that held the history of the kingdom and the royal archives burned around the time I was taken." Orion shrugged and placed the book on the polished wood coffee table in front of him. "I paged through it this morning, and there are some pages that are legible but in an old fae language I can't understand."

"Ah, there it is. I told you the language arts class was important to not fully flunk, didn't I?"

"You also love to dish out the 'I told you so' with no remorse."

"Touché." Devon's grin reached his eyes for the first time, and Orion relaxed a fraction in his seat.

The memories of ditching class to go and master spells while Devon stayed behind were still fresh in his mind. Like they'd happened yesterday, not when they had both been in their teens. His brother could speak many languages; they always came easy to him.

"We all have our strengths and weaknesses." Orion's lips twitched into a smile. "You and I both know I'm abhorrent at languages."

"Indeed." Devon grinned before leaning forward to inspect the book, his fingertips going over the charred cover with a gentle touch. "I'll page through it, but I won't make any promises."

"Thank you."

It had been hours, and the cool air of morning had turned warm and humid. Long ago Orion and Devon had abandoned their coats and moved to more casual positions in the same sitting area. They talked little as Devon scribbled on a clean parchment, his knuckles stained with black ink as the feather plume scratched the paper.

The document being so incomplete by the destruction of the fire made it harder; it didn't help that it disintegrated if held the wrong way.

The whole experience was like déjà vu. Devon hunched over a table, muttering unintelligible words as Orion sipped on whiskey from a gold cup, biting the inside of his cheek not to ask for the tenth time if he had found something of use.

"Don't you have anything better to do?" Devon asked finally, reaching for his own drink. "I can't translate this damn thing with you breathing down my neck. The least you can do is go and get me food."

Feeling his cheeks warm at his brother's words, Orion raised to his feet. "I will get something."

"And you'd better believe I require payment for this."

"What kind of payment are we talking about?"

"For starters, I would like to leave this room once a day, at least." Devon dipped the tip of his quill inside the pot of ink. "And I would like to see the cat."

Orion's back tensed over, his stomach churning suddenly as heat settled in his chest. He hadn't mentioned to Devon that she'd been hurt or the fact that she was able to do magic even while wearing the jewelry. "I will see what I can do." He forced the words through clenched teeth. "You probably can guess that I was barely able to save you two. It's a fine balancing game."

"I have seen you accomplish harder things." Devon tapped the dirty pages on the table. "This is not easy. Call it a favor for another favor."

Orion nodded before he left the room.

CHAPTER THIRTEEN

NAVA

Facing the garden, Nava sat on a cold stone as a gentle summer breeze came through the open doors of her room. The walks in the garden had been short and far between; however, she was happy she got to inspect some of the castle grounds while out. It helped her set a goal of where to go if she were to try transferring again.

Not that she was too eager to do so after her last attempt had nearly gotten her killed. Her back was mostly healed by now, but the mental scars were ever-present.

Her fingers tingled as she focused on the way the air felt against her skin, the wrinkle of magic pushing to come out of the curves of her body. Even though the energy inside her was practically begging to be let out, she'd been hesitant to even try.

What if she transferred into the hall again and Fael realized she was able to do magic? Then he might decide to punish her and call for reinforcements, and Arkimedes might not be close enough to save her from the king himself.

She took a deeper breath and closed her eyes. Her hair moved with the wind. The sounds of people working around the castle were almost as loud as nature itself. The power building in the pit of her stomach swelled as she tried to become one with nature, as Ari had told her dozens of times.

Maybe if she quieted the what-ifs, focused, and believed she could do it . . . she could save Arkimedes. Get back to Ari and fight the demons wreaking havoc in the forest.

The magic was there, buzzing beneath the surface. She just had to learn how to tap into it and let it flow, without letting self-doubt drag her under.

She had tried to run when she hadn't even learned to walk, too preoccupied with what was happening with the Zorren and Arkimedes to focus on her task of learning to transfer, to map the area with her mind and allow her energy to bring her there.

Steadying herself, she emptied her thoughts. Her limbs became lighter, and she focused her attention on the room next door. She wanted to transport herself into the washroom; it was safe and close.

Her stomach became alive with dozens of butterflies lifting, and now it wasn't only her limbs but her hair that billowed like air. Dust and pollen surrounded her before her body disintegrated, cell by cell, becoming one with the air, and she moved quickly toward the washroom, feeling the hot, humid air of the surrounding bath.

Her body became solid again, and she stumbled on shaky legs as adrenaline pumped rapidly through her limbs. *I did it!*

Light-headed, she sat on the bathroom floor to prevent falling due to her weakened limbs; a wide smile spread across her lips as her heart doubled in speed.

"Ha!" She pumped her fist up in the air. For the first time in days, she allowed herself to squash her fear and believe she could do it.

Throughout the day, she transported more times than she could count, taking quick cat naps in between to recuperate her energy, for once happy that no one came to fetch her. The blue sky had warmed to bright orange tones, the highlight burning a trail down the top of the garden hedges and stone paths.

Nava made her way out to the terrace. The sky-blue fabric of her dress billowed in the air, and each small gem that was beaded on the skirt shimmered in the sunlight.

Summer had always been her favorite season, but not this year. She frowned when the hint of burnt wood lingered in the air. She squinted into the forest but couldn't see smoke in the distance. Still, the pit of dread bubbled in her gut.

The dreams of fire and Aristaeus fighting the demons couldn't be a coincidence. If she could smell something burning nearby, there was a possibility Ari was in that forest, losing a battle that she should be helping with.

The sound of metal-heeled boots over stone floors came from the room next door. The terrace mirrored hers, but the whole time she'd been here, the room had been closed. Arkimedes came into view as he stepped outside. His green eyes met hers, and she noticed them softening as he took her in.

He was far, but even in the distance, the sun brightened his features with light gold tones. He wore armor, she realized, similar to the guards'. The insignia of a dead tree on the chest plates called to her. Silver chain-mail mesh wrapped around his arms and neck like a scarf.

She had seen that tree somewhere before, but where? Her mind couldn't reach the memory.

Soot stained his face and armor, and his large wings flicked behind his back, the feathers moving with the wind, catching blue highlights. He hesitated but continued toward her, his gaze dropping to her neck, clearly trying to find remnants of her attack.

The skin of her hands became cold and sweaty, and she was back to being a nervous wreck under his scrutiny.

"It's cold out here," he said as a greeting when he reached the edge of his balcony and held onto the banister.

"It's not too bad." It wasn't a lie. It was cool, yes, but her body was suffocating with a bothersome heat underneath her skin. The coolness of the approaching evening felt good.

"How have you been feeling? Has Leela taken good care of you?" It was hard to hear him, and her brows met in the middle as she came closer.

"I think I heard you right, but yes, she's been wonderful. You didn't need to force her to keep me company, though."

He scowled. "She said that?"

"Oh, no, no. I just—" *know you* "—figured it out."

Arkimedes's wings expanded, so large they barely fit in the area he stood. He flapped them and soon he was landing on her balcony. Her heart threatened to leap out of her chest. She would never be tired of the vision that was him flying.

He tucked his wings behind his back but didn't put them away, like he would have if they were back home. "Have you left your room again?"

She had been dreading the possibility of this conversation ever since she'd woken the morning after the attack, not wanting to explain or lie about how she was able to use magic, especially since she didn't know the answer to that. "Other than the garden walks Fael takes me on, no."

Arkimedes focused on the landscape, his jaw clenching. "I'm not talking about him taking you anywhere."

"I know what you are asking. I'm not sure if you are ready for my answer."

That called his gaze back to her, and she struggled not to squirm under it. "How did you do it?"

Nava shook her head, letting the silence wash over them. "It smells like smoke. Have there been fires in the forest?" Her eyes cut to him.

His frown deepened, and a lick of mistrust reappeared on his handsome features. "You can smell it?"

She shrugged. "I'm sure anyone can smell it. It's pretty strong, no? I mean, I don't see any smoke around, so maybe not . . ." Oh, she had not missed the babbles.

"No, it's not apparent to anyone. But there have been some fires. We don't know what's causing it." He squinted at her, clearly forming his own wild ideas inside that thick head of his.

They didn't know what was causing them. She did. "Before you try to blame it on me, I have nothing to do with those fires," she said sharply. "I have been stuck in this room for days."

"You can also leave this room, apparently." He reached to her wrist, touching her bangle with a finger. "It's active."

"Yes. It works just fine. It just doesn't work one hundred percent with my magic." She fidgeted, trying to prevent anything else from spilling out. It was difficult when it was second nature to want to be open and confide in him.

"So you can bend a magic-canceling jewel and can smell a forest fire that is miles away." Arkimedes was close enough that she had to crane her head back to meet his gaze.

"My magic works with nature." She hesitated when his attention burned through her. "Um, you could bring me along. I'm sure I can help."

"Isn't all of our magic supposed to work with nature?"

Nava scowled. "I'm not exactly like you or—other magic wielders. I guess it's of no use to explain since clearly you are mocking me."

"No. I want to understand what you mean." If he did, why was his voice loaded with irony? "If you aren't the one starting the fires, can you find who is? Are you a soothsayer?" His skepticism dripped off every word, and it grated on her nerves. Sure, this Arkimedes didn't remember her, but that didn't mean he had to be such an ass.

"Stop mocking me."

"I'm asking questions." His voice dropped an octave, becoming dangerously low. His aura billowed out. "How can you do magic with the jewel on?"

"I don't know."

"Liar."

"I don't!" she huffed, crossing her arms over her chest. "My magic is earth-based, not fire, water, air, or dark." Though, that was a lie as well. Nava didn't feel so connected to fire but had been able to call it before.

The kingdoms rarely specified the inclination of one's magic, but magic wielders usually had an inclination or two. It had always been one of Nava's favorite subjects when reading her mother's books.

"You won't leave this palace," he said.

"Why the hell not?"

"Because you trespassed when you arrived here, and the king doesn't trust you."

Well, duh, the king didn't trust her because she was sure he knew she had been there the night they'd kidnapped him.

She wrapped her hands tightly around the terrace's balusters. "Well, for someone who just claimed I wasn't a prisoner when your guard almost killed me, you sure treat me like one."

Arkimedes hovered closer and his body brushed hers, his energy a mist of cool air against her heated skin. "Don't fool yourself. I did that because you are to be Devon's bride."

Nava raised a brow, feeling the wave of dangerous fire churn between them. "In that case, can I at least move next to my fiancé? I sure would love to spend some time with him."

Arkimedes held the railing so tightly his knuckles turned white. Nava was sure it would explode under the pressure of his power at any moment. "You are to stay here, where I can keep my eyes on you."

"One would think you are jealous of your brother, sir."

"Don't flatter yourself." His eyes dropped to her lips.

The swarming heat that took over her body left her breathless, and she pulled away. Being so close strengthened his emotions within her, and she didn't need to feel his jealousy when he was so clearly trying to be an asshole. "Speaking of, when will I see Devon?"

A fake smile appeared on his handsome features. "Are you going to stay out of trouble if you do?"

"Is that what betrothed people do?" Her words came out harsher than she'd intended them.

His nostrils flared. "Good girls do."

"Who says I'm good?"

A wave of burning desire that was all him had her blood boiling. She gulped at his darkening gaze. "No, I supposed you mustn't be." He brought his hand to her face but stopped himself short of touching her. "My name is Orion. Use it."

"I'd rather not, Your Highness." She curtsied, and his expression morphed. Out of annoyance or interest, she didn't know. Maybe it was both.

CHAPTER FOURTEEN

NAVA

The warm air was suffocating, clogging the lungs as she sat on a tree branch, watching the forest burn. Her hand grasped at the blackened wood, still warm to the touch even though it had stopped burning hours ago.

There was no life left in this tree—hundreds of years of memories gone. The knot in her throat became so thick she couldn't swallow. To think of the centuries of magic, life, and love lost to the shadow demons.

This was the end of whatever had been set in motion the day the gods had bound her to her other two parts. Her eyes focused on the branch she sat on, her skin bark and lichen. Long fingers that resembled sticks, and nails of iron that cut through fallen angels, fae, and demons alike. Her power lightened beneath the rough texture of her skin, and soon the burnt tree regained its luster.

What they had burned became alive with her touch. The tree creaked under her, and the ash and soot that covered it fell to the ground. Her body weakened as the tree greedily took all she offered. Soon, leaves sprouted out of the dead branches. Moss regained its emerald-green color.

She took her hand off the wood and her energy dwindled further, too low if she were to be attacked at that moment. There was no way they could revive an entire forest. No, not even their magic could save the tragedy of what was being lost here.

Nava woke up with a gasp. Her dreams about Ari were coming to her every night. It was the only connection she had to what was happening out there. Even though she had been asleep for hours, her body was drained and tired.

She reached for the glass of water on her nightstand, something she'd been leaving there every night to battle her parched mouth.

Nava was exhausted but buzzed with the need to be out there in the forest. Knowing her Beekeeper was hurting, alone, made staying here that much more painful. Her unsuccessful attempt to get Arkimedes to take her with him was maddening. A part of her knew she could have tried harder.

Groaning, Nava let her body flop back onto the feather-filled mattress. A commodity she'd never had before. However, in her current state, it was almost suffocating her. Her breathing was quickened as fragments of the dreams she'd been having flashed through her brain.

He didn't trust her, didn't love her, and that alone was heart-wrenching. Telling him they were mated and that he'd been taken from her could help matters, but he might also just send her away to live in town alone. There was no sentimental attachment, just the damn bond.

One of the options was to give him time to fall back in love with her all over again. To trust that he would with time, like he had done last year. She *had* to believe in them.

On the bright side, she'd been successful at transporting the entire day and was ready to risk it farther.

With the Zorren attacking Ari every night, she feared her time was short. She would try to get to Devon's room tonight and figure out how to remove the bracelet from his wrist. Once he was able to do magic again, they could portal Arkimedes and her back home.

Her heart slowed down, and her body prickled all over. *No.*

Grabbing the silk cover of her bed, Nava pulled it harshly. The fabric tensed under her fingers as a profanity left her lips. She would not kidnap him like *they* had done. Nava had to battle those dark thoughts every day.

Nava just needed a few minutes alone with Devon to figure out how the damn jewelry worked. She had been trying to remove it for days with magic and other small objects in the room, to no avail.

A knock on the door had her jolting in her spot. Leela came in, holding a tray with food. The scent of eggs and bread wafted through the air, along with black tea. The fae put the tray on the bed's foot and rushed to the doors of the terrace to open them wide, the way Nava liked to keep them.

"Good news today. His Royal Highness has requested for you to join him for lunch." Leela was practically shaking with excitement, her face blushing as she walked back, filling the ornate porcelain cup with steaming tea.

"Really? No outing to the forest today?" Nava wrapped her silk robe around her body, hoping her question would get her more answers than she had gotten from Arkimedes yesterday. Her leaving him outside the afternoon before had struck a nerve, she was sure of it, and was likely the main reason he'd set this little lunch date. It might be the perfect time to try to get him to bring her along or maybe slip some information that he could use to help Ari.

"I guess not. Aren't you excited?"

She was and wanted to wear something other than blue to celebrate the occasion. Didn't these people like variety? Judging by the orange dress Leela wore every day, Nava got the impression they had designated colors.

"Would we be alone?" She tried to sound casual, but the shake in her voice gave away her nerves. She picked a light blue day dress with embroidered silver flowers down the bodice. It draped down wider than the ones she'd been wearing lately, in layers of distinct tones of blue.

"That one is gorgeous. He won't be able to take his eyes off you," the young fae gushed, rushing to take it out of Nava's hands. "Neither of them will."

Oh, so Devon was joining them as well. The pleasant warmth that had been running through her body dimmed. She had wanted to see Devon, to plot if he had any ideas on how to get out of this mess.

He couldn't plot against her since Arkimedes's life and hers were so intertwined. The life debt would demand he didn't act in any way that would harm them while the bond was latent. That didn't mean she trusted him one bit near her soulmate.

"Where are we eating?"

"Out in the garden—very romantic."

Leela needed to find another hobby that wasn't gushing about Nava's love life, because whatever she was imagining was happening wasn't the case.

By the time she was ready, Nava's brown wavy hair lay past the middle of her back, not half as frizzy as it usually was.

"Leela, your matchmaking skills are really something to behold." Nava shook her head with a smile.

"I apologize for my enthusiasm, my lady. I know they betrothed you to another, but my romantic heart is just— When you two were bickering in the hall that night . . ." She sighed, and Nava's smile grew. "This is the most exciting thing I have seen in the last ten years. Other than this, I only get to clean cobwebs and dust curtains."

"Oh, yes, that sounds dull. At least it's a beautiful castle. Also, there must be gossip that doesn't involve the royals."

"Yes, my lady, but this is so much more exciting." The fae's fingers retreated from Nava's hair with the soft knock on the door. She beamed down at Nava and scurried toward the door with light feet. "The guard is here to escort you to the garden, my lady."

"I'm not your lady, it's just Nava."

Leela nodded and cracked open the door, revealing the looming shape of her mate. Arkimedes rested against the doorframe, his brow lifting as a rebellious strand of hair fell over his forehead. Nava heard a gasp to her left and could only imagine the young fae's face right now.

With the silence that descended, she battled the need to fidget.

"Your Highness." Leela bowed from inside the room, and Nava remembered where she was and who this was supposed to be. Not her rugged soulmate from the forest or the Crow chasing her across an ocean. This was a prince.

She curtsied. "Your Highness."

"Orion," he offered with a secret smile.

Her cheeks warmed at the sight of it. "I like your other name better."

He shook his head and allowed her space to exit the room. Today it was warmer, and within the humidity in the air, Nava could still scent a trace of smoke.

"I didn't expect you to escort me," she said, bringing her hands down the skirt of her dress, straightening nonexisting wrinkles. "Sir," she added for good measure.

"I was on my way there." His eyes grew darker, and he pushed both hands inside the pockets of his ebony tunic. While the words said something, his inner emotions were a lot more complex. He was excited to see her. Waves of warmth and bubbling nerves pushed through their bond.

Nava had a hard time hiding her trembling smile. He had the gift of an impressive blank expression, but it was hard for him to hide all of his emotions from her. "So, is this lunch to make it up for having locked us away for days? I assume Devon has been treated the same way . . . since I haven't seen or heard of him." She paused, taking a deep breath after she'd pretty much blurted out all of the words.

"I thought Fael was taking you out for walks," Arkimedes shot back, lifting a brow at her.

"Well, who is taking Devon out? You?" And she didn't mean to sound as petty as she did, but the words left her before she'd gotten hold of her feelings.

His lips twitched. "How are your wounds healing?"

"Fine."'

"Are you sure?"

"Yes. Um . . . could you reconsider the option of taking me with you next time you go to the forest?" she whispered, and his face snapped back to her, his eyes narrowing. She wrapped both hands together in front of her.

He let a deep breath out and shook his head. "You don't understand your current situation. Even if I scream that you are my guest, the king doesn't see it that way. There is no walking out, not yet."

Nava *did* understand, but she couldn't just accept it. The forest called to her; Ari needed her there to balance, lend, and borrow each other's magic. There was a lot she had to learn about her own power before she could confront a demon alone.

Transferring was her only choice.

She looked forward and didn't broach the subject again, and they walked mostly in silence, all the way to a part of the garden she hadn't seen before. They crossed under arches and down stone steps. Sage-green grasses lined the stone pathway, and the tips caressed the stone with the light breeze.

Past that, shrubs of camellias were in full bloom with pink-and-white flowers. Her heart soared as the energy of nature embraced her. Here, she could almost forget the scent of burning around them.

They meandered to a large veranda on the side of the castle. Its roof was molded metal that swirled with leaves and branches. A massive wisteria tree climbed it, draping lavender blooms on the sides.

Nava slowed as she took it all in. The large circular table in the center filled to the brim with food. Tiers of buttery pastries, bowls of fruit, and platters of dried meat and nuts.

Devon stood from his spot at the table, straightening his coat. His hair was slicked back behind his ears, making his high cheekbones and porcelain skin practically glow. "I wondered if I would eat by myself." He crossed toward them, patting Arkimedes's arm as his dark eyes met hers. "That perhaps the approaching summer solstice had already gotten to you."

"What does that even mean?" she asked, taking a seat.

"The solstice affects all magical creatures. Warlocks, sorcerers, and witches are affected the least, as we are the most human—but the fae have curious parties."

"What do you mean by curious?"

Arkimedes took a seat across from her.

"Seductive. Stimulating. Sexual," Devon continued, and his eyes shone with malice.

Nava's face heated. "That answers nothing, Devon."

"He means the fae have sex all night long while the party is going," Arkimedes said, filling his dainty cup with steaming tea.

Her face slacked, and her whole body grew warm from something entirely different. She pressed her legs close together, squirming under both their gazes. "Oh."

"Oh, indeed." Devon filled his plate with food. "But not only the fae are affected, of course. It's said soulmates are . . . how do you say this without being crass? Well, they go through a heat spell. Like animals, really."

Nava reached for the collar of her dress, her cool fingertips calming her flaming skin. "Huh."

"Whoever has a soulmate around—well, let's just say, all the crannies in this garden will be occupied. Won't it, brother?"

Arkimedes's gaze all but seared her alive. She swallowed, reached for a glass of water in front of her, and drank it all in one go.

"Are you two soulmates?" Arkimedes's growl had her jumping in her seat.

Devon's rumbling laughter filled the space a second later. "No, no, brother. She is not mine."

Damn right she wasn't.

"How did you two become engaged? It takes years for the Society to consider a match, and I have never heard of her before."

"You have heard of Nava—or the possibility of her," Devon said, his face abandoning the lightness of before.

"What do you mean?"

"Does the name Forrest ring a bell to you?" The porcelain cup shook between his bone-white fingers. His onyx gaze deviated from Nava to his brother.

Arkimedes's face dropped. "Celeste's daughter?"

"The one and only," Devon said, popping a ripe green grape into his mouth.

"But she couldn't be. Nava would have to be—"

"Fifteen?" she asked, and his eyes burned through her.

"You are not fifteen."

"Ouch, kitten, you must up your face moisturizing rituals." Devon smiled wickedly.

"Devon, you aren't making this easy." She seethed. "But he is right, and so are you. I'm Celeste's daughter and I'm not fifteen."

"Right, and she had you when she was, what, eleven?" Arkimedes's voice was drenched in sarcasm. "She wasn't even pregnant when she left the Society."

"Well, there must be something wrong with your timeline. I'm sure you can see the resemblance—I have been told I look just like her."

"Maybe her sister, but not her daughter," Arkimedes insisted.

"She is her daughter, brother," Devon said. "Her and the potion maker made this wonderful creature, and we—I—discovered her."

Arkimedes paled, but Nava's vision of him glazed over, her skin breaking into a cold sweat. The potion maker? Her father. Why couldn't she recall him?

He was missing completely. Was he alive? Dead? Had he been a part of her life growing up? Her chest constricted as the walls of her mind closed in on her, and she became a prisoner of her panic.

The memories of darkness and emptiness from when she'd crossed the portal slammed into her like an iron wall. There had been two entities the day she and Devon had passed through the shadow lands toward this kingdom. The voice that had demanded payment, and the shape that had loomed closer.

One of them had taken her father away.

Her breaths became shallow, and she sank deep within herself, putting her half-eaten scone back to her plate, her appetite lost.

"Her skin is lighter. A mixture from her father. And she has the one blue eye like him." Devon reached to the three-tiered stand that held the pastries. He hummed while deciding which buttery cake to pick. "She is also a potion maker. Like father, like daughter."

"You look a lot like her," Arkimedes acquiesced, then his expression shifted. "Are you all right?"

The air left her lungs, and her grip tightened on the edge of the table. She wanted to swallow, but her tongue was as hard as a rock. She couldn't breathe, or was she breathing too fast?

"Nava?" Arkimedes's tone was far away, and his face became closer as his hand rested on top of hers, his touch scalding her skin. Why were they looking at her? Was she speaking out loud? Was she screaming?

A couple of bees landed on the table, crawling over her fingers. Why couldn't she remember how her father looked? Or his name, the sound of his voice? Had he enjoyed singing? Cameron had red hair, so very different from the dark brown of their mother. Perhaps his hair was the same color as his father's.

Nava gasped for air, stumbling to her feet. The chair crashed against the stone floor. She tipped over it when Arkimedes wrapped his arms around her, bringing her straight to his warm chest. Her knuckles whitened as she grasped the silky fabric of his tunic, feeling his breath hit her face as she closed her eyes.

"You're fine." His arm reached behind her back, drawing circles over the fabric of her dress. The touch grounded her somewhat.

Silence descended. Even the birds had stopped singing—or perhaps she couldn't listen to them.

"Ark, take me back home, *please*," she whispered against his chest. She wanted to be back in her house in the Northern Village, wrapped in her favorite, fluffiest blanket that Laurie had knitted last winter.

He scooped her from under her knees. Soon she was flying off the ground, and the flapping of wings moved her hair with the air.

"Take a deep breath, Nava. Don't pass out on me." His voice was like honey, and her skin raised with goose bumps. However, it was the soft beating of his heart that helped calm her down.

Nava didn't remember what happened next, just that she was inside his warm embrace in one moment, and the next she was lying on a mattress made of feathers, under covers of silk and fine cotton. The scent of leather and him pulled her to sleep.

CHAPTER FIFTEEN

ORION

It was not lost on Orion that he'd been the one who'd jumped to comfort Nava when the panic attack hit her in the middle of breakfast. It was even stranger that his brother hadn't reacted at all to the fact that he'd touched his fiancée.

She'd asked him to take her home, like he knew what she meant. Maybe in that moment, when the wave of desperation hit him out of nowhere, he would have taken her anywhere.

Orion sat on the green velvet couch. Flames rolled in the fireplace; however, no heat reached him. His fingertips grazed his lips as he studied the frame of her body as she slept. The waves of her dark hair lay across the mattress, covering the points of her shoulders. He followed the gentle curve of her back and the soft curves of her hips.

He had never burned like this for anyone. To drop whatever he was doing just to get her out of the situation. To want to fly, to fight, to kill. What was going on here?

A sob escaped her lips, and the sound alone had his back straightening. His fist tightened as he tried to rein in his feelings. He would find and hurt anyone who'd harmed her this way. Flipping the sofa over wouldn't help the situation at all. The fact that that was his first inclination as to what to do had him stopping before he did it.

His fingers stilled over his chapped lips, and he blinked away the fog of protective anger that had settled within him. The deep knot in his throat was hard to swallow, but he knew he needed to get out of the room before he just took her in his arms and left this place for good.

To hell with his mission of finding the reasons for his mother's betrayal, her death, his past. He was up and storming out of the room like a soul traveling to hell. He hesitated for just a second before he flew off the balcony.

Nava only represented danger to him. She was forbidden and would only distract him from something he had been searching for his whole life. He needed distance.

The guards were pushing Devon out of the gazebo by the time Orion entered it. His aura bloomed against the greenery, almost as opaque as the night. Their gloved hands immediately abandoned his brother's shoulders, and his ebony hair lay in disarray over his forehead.

"Your Highness!" The two guards took a healthy step back from his brother before one dared to speak. "We thought you would be occupied, and we were bringing the pri—your guest back to his accommodations."

"Was he even done with his meal before you two decided to push him around?" Orion growled, and silence descended.

These two guards were part of his troop, and he usually had to work with them when they went into the woods or to town to deal with any issue that might have arisen. They respected him and were amicable enough that he didn't sense they feared him. However, the scent of the area was sour with the spike of anxiety emanating from them.

He knew his answer then. They hadn't waited for Devon to be done with his food. They had decided to take him away whether or not he had eaten.

"You are dismissed. I will take Devon back into his room *after* we are done eating."

The two men didn't have to be told twice. They pretty much piled toward the exit of the gazebo, trying to get away from there.

Devon looked back with a scoff and straightened the cuffs of his shirt before his pale hands combed his hair back in place. "I thought you had forgotten about me."

"They shouldn't have pushed you around like that." Orion walked to the table and took the seat he had previously occupied, his gaze traveling toward the metal chair that still lay on the floor.

"I'm guessing the cat is fine?"

Orion's attention snapped back, and his jaw ached with tension. It was hard to battle the need to go back to where he'd come from. "She is asleep."

"Rather an intense reaction to scones, if I do say so myself."

"Do you know why she acted that way?" He had lost his appetite in the middle of the commotion.

Devon piled extra food onto his plate as though nothing was amiss. He didn't care what had happened. "Not a clue."

Orion went over everything they had said, trying to find what had triggered it, and it was the mention of her parents—not her mother, but her father. "Did her father hurt her?"

That had his brother looking up from his food, his brow crinkling as he thought over his answer. "As far as I know, the man is dead. Nava was working at the potion shop by herself. Why?"

"She has a potion shop? Where is Celeste in all of this, and why would Nava panic when reminded of her father?"

Devon dropped his pastry on the dish and dusted his hands. He was buying himself time from speaking. "She is elsewhere. You know how she is—hiding all of her family from us."

"How did the Society find them? Did you . . . ?"

"I found her, which is why I got stuck in this predicament in the first place." His sigh of annoyance was telling, and damn if his brother's reluctance didn't make him confused. "But enough of that. I found something with the . . . item you brought me."

The book. Orion perked up in his seat.

Devon pulled something from his pocket and slid it to Orion over the table, while his other hand took the bone china cup that no longer held steaming tea. "The translation might be off. I'm a bit rusty."

Orion looked around him but found no one was around. This meant little, as his father had spies everywhere, even in the damn vegetation. He opened the folded paper; Devon's neat scrawls were familiar. "It's not much," he commented, looking at his brother over the paper.

"There wasn't much left in what you brought me. Most of what was there was not important—recollections of yearly expenses on improving the garden and some updates to the town. There was a brief mention of the Society visiting, but the juicy bits were burned. I did find a few tidbits that might interest you."

Orion dropped his gaze back to the parchment. The more he read, the slower his heart drummed. The sudden dizziness that hit him had his head spinning.

The child of royal blood came to this world sick, poisoned by evil, and was taken into the world of shadows, away from the land and our people.

Did this writing mean him? The world of shadows was considered the transition place. Where souls went to get winnowed to a better or worse fate. Purgatory.

He swallowed and fought the urge to crumple the paper in his hands; he kept coming back to the words sick, poisoned, evil.

Evil.

Had his mother led him to find this book to show him that she'd had a reason to get him away? She had not killed him . . . but people considered him dead until not long ago.

"Oh, you got the tortured face on. Am I going to have to convince you this might not be about you?"

"No."

"This could be any other royal, Arkimedes."

"It doesn't matter." The thickness in his throat told him otherwise, and he wished it was true. "This is something I can work with, ask questions."

"If you were evil and sick, the king wouldn't have received you with open arms. But by all means, we can just leave and be done with this madness. Go back to our city and—"

"I'm not going back to the Society of Crows, Devon. I don't want to go back to that life, I told you. I feel this is where I'm supposed to be."

Silence took over for a moment before he continued reading, but the left-over paragraphs just spoke of resistance toward accepting the human soldier in the royal guard. No mention of the queen.

"Oh, there was something else. I didn't get to write it down, as I was in the middle of reading when the guards came to get me. The book mentioned a prophecy. It was at the end of the book, and since most of the pages were charred, the dates were a bit difficult to access."

"There is likely another record of it in the library."

Devon nodded with a hum. "It would be strange if they only tracked it in one book."

Orion folded the paper his brother had given him before putting it inside his pocket. Now he had a task—go back to the library and find that prophecy. "Thank you, Devon."

"Sure. But the true payment is not being stuck inside that room. I would like to see the cat again, at some point."

Orion nodded, even though he felt cold and sick at the idea. He had to battle this urgent need to keep them apart. Nothing good was going to come out from trying to prevent her from seeing him, not when they were engaged, and she was a distraction he didn't want or need. "I will see what I can do."

CHAPTER SIXTEEN

NAVA

Nava pressed the sliced cucumbers against her swollen eyes. She'd cried until she had no tears left. This morning, the redheaded fae who'd tended to her for the last week had woken her up by opening the balcony windows.

Leela had gotten one good look at her face and disappeared from the room for almost an hour. She'd returned with sliced cucumbers and a juice she'd claimed would help with heartbreak.

How the young fae knew about her broken heart was a mystery Nava wasn't sure she'd ever find the answer to. She appreciated her immensely.

"He is off riding today," Leela said as she worked on Nava's hair, untangling the mess of curls that had matted over while she'd slept.

"The prince?" Nava's voice cracked.

"There are rumors circulating the castle that he flew you here yesterday. That there was a fight in the garden between him and your fiancé."

Nava's lips slacked when she realized that Leela thought her sorrow today was due to a romantic upheaval. Not the fact that she'd lost her father. She cleared her throat before she went down the same path. "If they fought, they didn't do it over me."

"Why are you so sad then?" Her eyes shone behind thick black lashes. "I'm an excellent listener, my lady. I know I talk a lot, but I promise whatever it is, it won't leave this room."

Nava tightened her lips. If only she trusted her. But her mother had taught her to believe in herself and her family. Her eyes ached from the lack of moisture, and she blinked rapidly, trying to bring some back. "It's—it is heartbreak, but not the romantic sort." Nava took a deep breath and pressed her palms against the dressing table's top, letting the coolness of the wood ground her. "On my way here, I lost something very dear to me. Something I won't ever get back—" Nava swallowed the ache in her throat. "I'm not ready to speak about it."

Leela stared but nodded. "I will bring my lady some grape wine for this evening."

Nava's lips turned. "Now that's what I was hoping to hear you say."

The fae left not long after. Nava looked at her reflection in the quiet morning. She had been a potion maker since she was a teen. Her blood sang when she sat on her stool to ground herbs and play with metals and oils. She loved helping people, but it was more than that. Being able to create had given her purpose.

Now, all the memories of potions were gone—most of them, anyway. And even if she remembered making them, the techniques were murky, as if someone had punched holes in the recipe.

It was all gone, all she'd fought to learn for the last decade of her life. Her career.

She allowed herself to bask in her pity party for a while longer. But eventually, she reminded herself she was not one to wallow for long. Forrest women didn't let problems take over. She wasn't no one. The gods had given her a task: to protect the world from the demon realm. Her magic was wonderful and alive, even though someone had tried to snuff it.

To think she'd always assumed that when Arkimedes would give her a piece of jewelry, it would be an engagement ring—not a magic-sucking bracelet.

Nava stood from her chair, resolution settling in her stomach. Ari always told her something was holding her back, but it wasn't something. It was someone. Herself.

She would leave this castle and get to that forest to see her Beekeeper at whatever cost. He called for her, night after night. The bees crawled the walls of her room, blending against the warm tones of the stones, a reminder that she was still very much a creature meant to protect.

Nava stood and dashed to her armoire, rummaging until she found her old clothes. Brown pants and a white shirt. She pulled on her well-loved boots; they fit her like a glove, the leather worn and caked with mud.

It was time.

After what happened, Nava wasn't ready to attempt transportation all the way to the forest. She had to tackle it differently. First to the garden, and then to the forest from there. Easier said than done, but hunger for the result gave her resolution a well-needed push.

She looked at the expanse of the garden. This would be a long distance to go, and she was going there half-blind. Her connection to Ari, and his need for her, would guide her there. Sort of.

"Stop being a chicken." Her knuckles whitened with her tightening hold against the banisters. "You've got this. You are a badass Beekeeper."

Apparently a crazy one at that.

She closed her eyes and held her breath, focusing on the mental image of the garden and the meadow between the palace's grounds and wilderness. Her insects crawled over her skin, answering her calls.

Nava reached down into the bond, trying to sense where Ari was, feeling the tug across her bond, calling for her, as she wished to be there. Letting out her breath, she transferred away. Down the terrace, hugging the rock walls of the palace. However, she veered back inside again. To the lower floors and inside an open window.

No . . . No . . . No.

Walls of large wooden bookcases that extended to the ceiling caged her in, with volumes upon volumes of aged manuscripts, ancient if the musty scent was anything to go by. She materialized in the darkness of the vast room.

Nava held herself behind the cabinet, the wood smooth under the pads of her fingers. It smelled like leather, beeswax, and old paper. Why the hell had she ended up here? It was the complete opposite of an open garden filled with plants.

She eyed the tones of books warily, remembering all the hours she'd spent hunched over some like this in the manor before she'd met Arkimedes. Forced to read hundreds of pages of boring history lessons and ancient politics that didn't help anyone.

Nava was much more of an outdoorsy sort of learner. She absorbed new information from experience; she craved the feel of nature's air against her skin.

What a waste of time. Just when she closed her eyes to transfer again, she heard them.

"Look for them again," Arkimedes growled, and Nava stumbled back, hoping the shadows of the heavy furnishings would hide her from view.

"I will, Your Highness. I—I'm trying. The king ordered we burn all the books that mentioned the queen—" The man paused, and she heard the shuffling of feet.

Nava held her breath, too afraid to call anyone here to her in the room's silence. It was now clear that she had ended up in that library because of Arkimedes; he had been in despair and calling for her. Nava now knew her soulmate was hunting for answers about his past.

"I'm sure there are more here, and I hate to think you are holding information. I need to know what happened before my mother left the kingdom."

"Before you were born?" the other man asked, and the candlelight flickered as Arkimedes's magic burned through the air.

"Yes. I know when something doesn't add up, and I need more information."

"I will turn every book, every page, in this library."

Silence descended, and for a moment, Nava thought they might have left. She stood still, her back pressed against the cool wall.

"What about the prophecy?" Arkimedes's voice lowered, and for a while, nothing broke the heavy silence.

"The prophecy," the old man repeated, clearly buying himself time. "I don't know what—"

"Save yourself the trouble, Ellis. I know about it. Where is it?"

Nava let her body relax against the heavy bookcase, breathing slowly as she listened.

"Someone stole it from this library around the time you were taken, s-sir."

"Are there any records of it?"

Nava peered behind the wood corner of the shelf. The old fae pointed at a spot, his twisty old finger shaking. She followed the direction of where he pointed, finding a section of the library burned to the ground. The metal gates were still black with burn marks, and soot extended along the walls and ceiling.

"They are all gone," he said.

Arkimedes said nothing, but the churning disappointment in her stomach told her more than he could say with words. "You may now go."

"Sir," the other man said, and Nava heard the distinct dragging of feet.

She took a deep breath and chanced another glance behind the rack she hid behind.

Arkimedes pinched the bridge of his nose, closing his eyes. "Come out of the shadows, Nava."

Her throat ached as she tried to swallow, making her body as small as she could between the heavy bookcases. She could try to transfer now to avoid this terrible situation.

He exhaled, and she could feel his annoyance pulsing down their bond like a wave. She hesitated but stepped out of the shadows. The sun pierced through the massive windows behind him, grazing their skin.

He considered her in silence, and his already sullen expression darkened. "What are you wearing?"

"My old clothes. I'm tired of the dresses," she whispered. He prowled toward her, and she shuffled back, pressing her back against the bookcase. A rim of fire haloed around his wings. He towered over her.

"Why are you wearing traveling clothes, and how did you get in here?" His voice was significantly lower than what he'd used with Ellis.

Her body shook from the top of her head all the way to the tips of her toes. Based on her fast heartbeat, scared didn't cover how she felt. And the heat pooling between her legs confirmed this. Her libido was back with an appetite. That horny bitch never knew when to lie low. "Back away, Arkimedes."

"Don't call me that name. How. Did. You. Get. Here?" His body was less than a foot away from her. Tendrils of darkness rose from his body. Oh, he was pissed. "This area is warded. No one but the royals are allowed in."

"What about—Ellis?"

Both his hands caged her in. So much for having him trust her.

"I said, back away!" She pushed against his chest with all her strength, but he didn't move an inch.

"That was the custodian, the only other person allowed to enter." His gaze narrowed on her. "You shouldn't be able to enter."

The solstice was affecting them both, she realized. Nava had been off-kilter ever since she'd woken up, her blood flowing hot under her skin; her thoughts about her mate weren't just focused on how to escape but more about how to get him trapped somewhere, preferably under her and wearing a lot less clothes.

Still, she would not let him think he could talk to her this way, even if she was secretly loving it. She was technically in a forbidden area of the castle—and had gotten caught eavesdropping. Those were semantics.

"Stop whatever this is, *now*."

"I'm going to ask you one more time, and then . . ."

Nava lifted her chin, narrowing her eyes at him. She called upon her magic, and it came soaring through her veins with the heat of her scorn. She dissolved midair as Arkimedes staggered forward, his hands desperately grabbing a breath of pollen, dander, and dirt.

CHAPTER SEVENTEEN

NAVA

Nava's legs buckled when she materialized between sculpted hedges in the garden. She took in her surroundings with a heated breath. The emotions inside her weren't hers alone but his as well. She bolted forward.

She transferred three times, each occasion bringing her closer to the forest. Her energy flared along with her adrenaline; however, transporting so many times in a row made her dizzy.

The pounding of gravel under her steps and the clear buzzing in her ears muffled all other noise. The large flapping of wings came behind her, and then Arkimedes had landed with a mighty roar. She turned and her eyes widened when he met her gaze.

His frown deepened. "Nava, stop."

She ran as if her life depended on it. Repeated inside her head that Ari needed her. Arkimedes also deserved to see this side of her, of them. Her actions only kept feeding his mistrust. Something had to change.

He groaned when it became clear Nava would not listen to him. "Stop!"

She turned back around but ran faster. Her strides down the path led to an imposing copper gate, rusted in mint-green color with drips of white and dark browns. Walls made of stone caged in the garden. Here, so far from the castle, the heavy scent of smoke lingered heavier than before.

They were playing cat and mouse, and the excitement of it made her blood simmer. Whatever the gods did to magical creatures like them in the solstice was not helping.

The gate's intricate designs let her see beyond the carvings to a misty forest where Ari awaited her. She could almost feel Arkimedes's heat as his steps boomed closer. If he caught her, she knew somehow it would take a lot to convince him to let her leave.

But if she made it out and Ari found them . . . then maybe it would spark his memory. His fingertips brushed the end of her hair, and her body lost matter, floating in the air and through the holes of the closed gate.

"Fuck!" His voice sent a thrill of excitement down her back. She almost smiled as she materialized back on her own two feet outside of the castle grounds. "Dammit, Nava."

He flapped his wings and was over the gate and heading toward her. He had to be using his magic to propel his movements.

The exhilaration that ran through her was a mixture of magic and something more primal. The strong wind stirred her hair before a wall of steel landed on top of her, sending her flying to the ground. An iron arm snaked around her waist and twisted her in his grasp.

The air escaped, and she shut her eyes, awaiting the impact, but all she saw were dark feathers that wrapped her in a protective cocoon.

His muscles reverberated with the impact of the landing. Arkimedes grunted in pain, and the soft, velvety texture of his wings touched her skin.

Nava was draped over him, her arms pulled around his chest. She felt the quickness of his heartbeat under her cheek. This was the closest she had been to him in so long. Her mark soared at the touch. His wings spread open, letting the warm light of the day fold over them. His dark lashes lowered as he blinked multiple times, confusion flashing through his features. One of his hands came to his chest and massaged the spot where his mark lay.

Nava stirred, feeling the long expanse of muscle tense under her movement. He was hard wherever she was soft, their angles and curves perfectly molded to fit one another, just like their souls. His pupils dilated, and the thrill of desire that traveled through her body left her breathless. Whatever this nonsense Devon had been blabbering about, it was not untrue.

Arkimedes rolled over her, and his warm breath hit her cheeks. "Don't run away again," he commanded.

"Or what? You will lock me away in the dungeons?" She'd heard castles had dungeons. Her complete ignorance on the matter was not lost on her.

"I will tie you to my bed if I need to."

Her mouth went dry. Now, *this* was the kind of submission she could get behind. "I would like to see you try."

His gaze dipped to her lips, and her heart leaped. Maybe he would kiss her and his curse would lift. She kept thinking if she made him break this iron grip he had on his feelings, he might remember her.

He clenched his jaw and pushed away from her as if she burned him, leaving her on the ground, lamenting the loss of his body heat. "If you leave again, I will." His voice sounded throatier than usual. However, his eyes burned with the intensity of the promise. He meant every word.

"I need to be in the forest," she whispered. "I can't be locked in that room forever."

"Even if you survived that forest, the king will hunt you down, and this time I won't be able to stop him." His hand went over his face. "They will kill Devon too."

Nava was about to tell him she didn't care whether or not the Crow was killed but hesitated. Not only would that reveal the lie of their supposed engagement, but she wasn't sure that was the case anymore.

Did she hate the man? Yes. Did she want him dead? Maybe not . . . and it had to be due to how important he was to Arkimedes because the Crow couldn't be growing on her.

No way.

She rushed to get up from the ground. "I would not leave"—*you*—"permanently. I will be back before sunset."

"The forest is dangerous right now, and the king doesn't trust you."

"What about you?" Hope bloomed in her stomach as she held his eyes.

His lips tightened. "How did you get into the library? How were you able to disappear like that?" He inspected her, as if she would grow an extra head at any moment. "How can you work your magic while wearing the bracelet?"

She pressed her lips together. "I already told you I don't know."

He reached for her wrist with gentle fingers. "What spell did you put on me?"

"None. I swear." She swallowed and knew she had to take a leap of faith. Lying would only push him away further. Plus, she hated lies. "I haven't lied to you. I don't know why I could enter the library, but I know my magic is different—and I can show you."

He dropped her wrist and brought his hands over his face, taking a deep breath. "How?"

"You can come with me to the forest," she started, and he was already shaking his head.

"It isn't safe in the forest right now."

She knew this! His words only lit the fire within her to be out there. "No, it's not. But it doesn't mean I don't need to go." She took a step toward the trees behind her and called to Ari, hoping he would hear her.

His brows dipped, and he followed her. "If the king finds out you were here, it won't be good. This is not a matter to take lightly. My rational mind tells me I shouldn't trust you, that this is strange." He moved his hand around them, pointing at their surroundings.

"Then why are you trusting me?"

"I don't know." He groaned. A spike of annoyance rushed over her body. Hers or his? Likely both of them. She could feel Ari nearby, could sense her strength growing. A bee landed on her shoulder, and Arkimedes's eyes came to it.

"Nava . . ." His brows raised as a spark of recognition lit his face, his eyes never leaving the insect as another landed over her hand. He paled, staggering back. "I have seen this before."

"Ark—"

"Don't call me that."

"Do you want to be a prince that badly you have to abandon who you were?"

"No, but does it matter? It's who I was meant to be." He stirred under her scrutiny, but his expression hardened. "I don't know why you think you can talk to me like you know me."

"Maybe I *do* know you," she snapped. "You must not fully trust what you are being told around here, either. Because something doesn't fit, does it?"

"And you do?"

"I know where you were four months ago, and it wasn't here or the Iron City," she said but hesitated to continue telling him, too afraid that the truth might spook him.

Arkimedes hadn't wanted or planned to leave the Iron City ten years ago to go to an island in the middle of nowhere to find her. If Nava told him, he might ask what had happened with Devon, and she feared the truth would make this harder.

She needed Arkimedes trusting Devon so they could get him out of here. If he didn't trust either of them, this whole thing would be a mess. "I'm going in that forest, whether you or the king try to stop me. Unless you plan to take me to that castle against my will." For a moment, she really thought he would take her up on it, and she wasn't ready to go down without a fight. "Aren't you at least curious about what I have to show you?"

His tense pose relaxed a fraction, his eyes narrowing on her. "Fine."

Nava turned around and headed into the forest before he could change his mind. She let her intuition guide her. Here the air was thick and dry; moats of dust and ashes floated in the air as if gray snow was falling from the sky. Even though she couldn't see a trace of flames anywhere, it was sweltering hot the farther in she went.

Her eyes watered as she moved forward, knowing Arkimedes followed closely behind. The knot in her throat thickened as bees came to her. The forest differed from the ones in Grey Island. Moss didn't hang from every surface, and the trees were sparser, with a gentle mix of conifer species and others, like pecan and maple trees. Their energy embraced her, welcoming her.

Her body was weightless as she walked forward, the tentative smile she wore had her cheeks aching. But it wasn't only happiness that had her giddy.

This was home, the scents of wood and soil. The rattling of the leaves as the wind passed through them. Her body refilled with energy she hadn't known had been depleted until this very moment.

The treetops waved with unnatural force, and Arkimedes pulled her behind him, his magic exploding into a plume of black ink that embraced them in a protective shield. "Stay behind me."

"It's fine. I know who it is." She pressed her hand against his back, right underneath where his wing protruded from his coat. A creature of wood and bark landed in front of them, crouching on the ground before he stood over seven feet tall, looking down at them with black eyes.

"It's nice to see you, dearest."

"I wasn't allowed to leave. I had to escape today—and barely made it."

Ari stared in silence. *"Blackness hugs the mind of our protector like poison."* The Beekeeper turned his head to the side, studying Arkimedes with an expression that morphed into one of worry. *"That is why he didn't bring you along the last few times he has been in the forest."*

"He doesn't remember us," Nava said and heard the loud intake of breath coming from Arkimedes. She chose not to turn to face him, not to dwell on the lack of recognition on his face. With a few strides toward the Beekeeper, she placed her hand on top of one of his wooden legs. "It's good to see you again, Ari."

The creature nodded. *"You have finally let your body unleash some of your power. You have transferred. I can sense it in your skin."*

Even though Ari didn't speak out loud, the creature's mouth ticked up in a prideful smile, and that alone took some of the burden that weighed her heart. She turned to Arkimedes, who was staring open-mouthed at the both of them.

"I have never seen a Beekeeper this close before," he breathed.

If only he remembered all they'd gone through, their adventures, the knowledge they'd both gained, their life together. "You have," she whispered.

He turned toward her, a brow raising. "How would you know?"

"It's easy." She shrugged, but her eyes stayed on him. Unblinking. "You have seen *me*."

And to prove her point further, she lifted her hand, and bees came flying down, circling her palm. Tens. Hundreds of them. The buzzing grew louder, and Arkimedes staggered back. His eyes widened as he followed the swarm.

Ari grasped her shoulder, and their energy blended together, soaring with their nearness. *"He doesn't quite remember us, but the memories are still there. Trapped under an enchantment."* The Beekeeper's eyes shifted to Nava. *"You, dearest, lost something greater. The shadow man's touch was on you."*

Her body crumpled down, or maybe it wasn't her physical self, but everything inside. An emptiness in her heart grew like a black hole, sucking the energy she had just regained.

She didn't want to be reminded of it, not now. She had cried enough already.

"It can't be. A human can't be a Beekeeper." Arkimedes shook his head, but his eyes traveled from the bees to her.

"Surprise." Her lips turned into a weak smile, but the heaviness that lingered in her heart was anything but happy. "The Zorren have been coming to our dimension more and more. Ari needs me here."

"The Zorren?" Arkimedes repeated, his skin growing pale. "We suspected it was humans using dark magic to burn the forest, but we didn't expect demons."

"I sent one back to their realm a couple of days ago. There is one more I have tracked down. They have opened a gate in this forest, but my power alone doesn't let me find it."

"Does he talk to you?"

"Yes, we are connected." The three of them. However, she hoped Arkimedes didn't see the mark carved in Ari's chest. She didn't want to have to go through the soulmate-bond thing while she had to deal with everything else. Cowardly? Perhaps. But after realizing she'd lost her father and her ability to make potions, she was determined not to lose Arkimedes as well. "He says there is a gate opened in the forest, but he needs our combined forces to find it."

"We have seen the destruction scattered around the west side. They've killed a few hunters, and our farmers claim the land has been poisoned."

"We should go there, right?" She turned to Aristaeus, who quietly observed them.

"There is a legend that claims the god of the night had two children. One with a mortal, and one with the goddess of the moon. Both offspring were so wicked, they

were cast away to roam the earth. One became the first fae to walk on this land. The first Dark One, our protector's ancestors."

The information, though shocking, didn't pertain to their current predicament. "So?"

"What's happening?" Arkimedes's brows crinkled with worry.

"The Zorren power works similarly to the Dark Ones. They feed on life and were created by the other sibling, whom you met. His claws have been on you, dearest."

Nava's lips slacked. The shadow that had taken her memories was the person commanding the Zorren? Which one of the two? "What?" Her body went cold, shaking at the memory of the dark shape with an icy voice that had ripped a part of her soul open. "Didn't you think that information was important to tell us before?"

"The gods work in mysterious ways. Them making our protector the Dark One's princeling was a surprise to me, but it makes sense, as Arkimedes's power works similarly to theirs, and so different to ours." Ari sounded passive, clearly not understanding why she felt so upset about this new information.

"Nava," Arkimedes started, "what's going on?"

She hated lies, and not being able to unload all this information on him right now was difficult for her. "Did you know he was a prince before?" she asked, ignoring Arkimedes's gasp.

"No."

Nava let out a sigh of relief, but the creature continued speaking. At least Aristaeus wasn't a liar, unlike Arkimedes, who had lied about them being soulmates the year before—and her, who was doing the exact same thing now.

"But I suspected his powers were connected to the gods in a more direct way after I saw him fighting against the bounty hunters."

Arkimedes grasped her arm with a gentleness that wasn't reflected in his impatient tone. "Are you talking about me?"

"Yes, we are. But we don't have time to get into this right now." The scent of smoke was too strong around them. She wrinkled her nose. "We have to find the gate and try to close it."

Arkimedes was ready to argue, but he closed his mouth and nodded instead. "Are we heading west?"

"With you two here, I should be able to close it for the time being, but more will come."

"What did he say?" Arkimedes shifted his body weight around, his shoulders tense. He stared watchfully at the Beekeeper as she repeated what Ari said. "With the both of us?"

"Later," she promised, laying her hand over his arm, and they stared at each other in silence. "I will tell you more later, I promise."

"All right."

CHAPTER EIGHTEEN

ORION

They trailed the forest with haste; dew saturated their clothes from the slick leaves of the low-hanging branches, and it was harder to move in the muggy surroundings.

His wings were too large to walk in such a confined space. They slowed him down, and he'd been fighting against the urge to put them away every damn second. If he wanted not to be an outcast for once in his life, all he had to do was to learn and adapt.

His ability to do so had saved him when he'd been picked by the Society of Crows at the age of five.

The sun trickled down the path as they moved farther east. The forest rapidly changed from healthy and living to the sicker nightmare he had been fighting against. Hanging in the air was a disease of evil that burned in his lungs. The foliage withered with brown-and-black tones and crunched under their feet.

"It's gotten much worse." Orion turned toward Nava. Clenching his jaw, he studied the area. "It wasn't like this a couple of days ago."

The Beekeeper creature whimpered, and Nava's expression shifted as the shock of the visuals hit her full force. The mystery of this woman drove him mad—she was reckless and an enigma he craved to unravel.

Seeing the mask of fortitude she slid over her features was endearing. Her face appeared stern, but her hands trembled as she held onto a burnt tree. Those strange eyes flashed to every corner visible. "How much longer until we get to the gate?"

"We are close."

"You two are synchronized!" she said with a smile that reached her eyes, the freckles on her cheeks multiplying. His heartbeat raised, and he wished his body stopped reacting to her this way.

She had given him a half-reasonable answer as to why she could do what she had, but it didn't mean she was trustworthy. No matter what his senseless body was telling him, he had to keep his distance.

He lifted his brow, staring blankly at her.

"What? You both said the same thing at the same time. Find some sense of humor, you two."

His lips twitched, and he struggled to school his features from her curious eyes. It was peculiar that the mythical creature spoke with her.

They reached the area where the open gate quivered in the air. The forest became hazy with smoke, and their travel slowed down as they moved forward, keeping their steps as quiet as possible.

There were no noises here, no animals, no rustling of the leaves with the wind. The air hung stagnant with something malicious. In this destruction, even their breath echoed.

The ends of his hair stood on end when a smoky shape fluttered between the trees. Orion's steps froze alongside the rest of them. He was not wearing his armor or carrying any of his weapons—not that a metal sword could help him against a demon.

Immersed in this destruction, Orion's power rejoiced at the possibility of battle. It always hungered to take energy and life.

Something warm called to him, like a lover's embrace. Orion turned to his side and let out a breath when encountering the beauty of Nava's aura. Yellow and blooming like the sun. Her power embraced her as she prepared for the evil presence that approached them.

The smoke took shape, and a demon formed in front of them. A giant insect-looking thing that could come from anyone's nightmares. Taller than seven feet and looming with a snarl that showed ebony teeth behind a gaping hole.

The Beekeeper's stance widened and his magic billowed around him, yellow like hers—no, his was gold, shimmering like metal. Orion's own aura exploded around him, mist, smoke, and shadows that looked so alike the ones around the demon.

The Zorren's eyes traveled to him, shining red as it also realized how alike the two magics were. Orion's stomach sank deeper. No wonder people always feared him.

The child of royal blood came to this world sick, poisoned by evil, and was taken into the world of shadows, away from the land and our people.

The words written on Devon's parchment flashed through his brain as fire bloomed from the demon's clawed hands. Soon, a ball of fire came their way —toward Nava. It burned a path of charred dirt and everything that once had been alive and green.

Nava gasped when the heat scalded their skin. Panic bloomed inside him, and without thinking, he stepped in between her and the enchantment. His shield of black ink came over them, and the fire bounced off, dissipating in the air. His energy dwindled.

"It shouldn't take it long to fire back." He heaved out of the way as the Zorren ran to them, its segmented insect legs kicking ash and dirt in the air, steam pouring out of its wide mouth.

The roots of the burnt trees moved, and the dirt groaned under their feet. Orion struggled to keep standing, gazing at the two Beekeepers by him. Nava shone like a beam of light, her anger burned into her beautiful face. She strode forward as the branches swung low toward the demon.

The Zorren weaved out of their reach. The wood of the tree withered away in large coal chunks.

Roots lifted from the ground, not just from one tree. All around them lifted, causing a tremor on the forest floor and forcing Orion to take flight. The land stayed still as the demon tried but eventually failed to run from the attack.

The forest soon pinned it under roots, rock, and debris, and the evil thing screeched as fire lit from its skin, charring everything in its path. The trees burned, and the soil melted with stone, but the woodland didn't release its hold. The three of them ran to the demon. From this close, its features were even more horrifying. Its snappy movements were jarring to his eyes.

It smelled like charred flesh and burnt acid. Orion lifted his hand to it, and soon the smoke around the demon started dissipating, rushing to his extended fingers. The creature's eyes widened as its fire dimmed; a high-pitch scream left its mandibles again, lacking some of the energy it previously had.

It was never easy seeing the life of a living creature flicker away under Orion's destructive pull of energy. The demon's eyes became vacant as his magic fed from it.

With the destruction surrounding them, his human compassion dwindled, and instead, the bitter tug of resentment took over, and he wasn't sure he wanted to fight against it this time. Why was it on him to always turn away from his natural urge to steal energy from someone else, even when it was against something as evil as this demon?

His depleted energy soared, but with it came an increase of rage and bloodlust.

A small hand wrapped around his arm, momentarily distracting him from the strange veil of anger that had come down over him. He shook his head, trying to clear his thoughts as he focused on Nava's face.

"Are you all right?" she asked, her brow crinkling. One blue and one brown eye studied him closely.

"Yes." His voice came out hoarse, and he wondered if using his power to suck out that evil energy had affected his thoughts. Had the malicious essence of a demon somehow clouded his thinking, made him angrier and ready to enjoy killing it?

The Beekeeper creature held the demon by its neck, and the gold of his power enveloped them both. Soon the Zorren's body turned from burnt matter to vines twining around it. Nature soon devoured the body of its adversary. The only remnant was a pile of ash on the ground of what now appeared to be a fallen tree.

He cut his gaze from the Beekeeper to Nava. Her face had been tense before, but now it rested at ease with her surroundings. Sensing him, she met him with a raised brow.

"Your magic . . . is incredible," Orion breathed as her hand dropped from his arm. He had all but forgotten about her touch.

"I know." She smirked, and the air of laughter escaped him before he could stop it.

"Who knew your ego was this inflated?" he teased back, a warm feeling spreading from his stomach and through his body. Maybe he didn't need to hide from her, just now when his darkness had been at a high point. Instead of fearing him, she had grounded him.

He paused at his problematic thoughts. It was beyond worrisome, especially since he knew near to nothing about her, other than she was Celeste's daughter, a Beekeeper, and was engaged to his brother.

"Someone has been feeding said ego for a year. I blame him." Her smile faltered after the words left her lips, and her eyes searched for something in his face that made the pit in his stomach grow.

Whatever she was looking for wasn't there. A spark of a memory, perhaps. But his mind only drew blanks, only pieces of dreams that involved her body with much less clothing. His cheeks warmed, and he turned his gaze away.

"Ari says we should close the gate before another demon appears."

He guessed Ari was the creature's name, a much less impressive one than he'd thought. Who would name such a being of life *Ari?* It felt like a dog's name. The Beekeeper responded to her words as if called by them. The situation was bizarre, at the very least.

They didn't have to walk long before the gate came into view. In a land of nothingness, a wide black circle quivered with pent-up power, the wrongness of it palpable in the air.

They slowed down when the pressure of it kept them away. Voices speaking in tongues came from the other side.

"How do we close it?" he asked.

"Ari?"

The Beekeeper stood forward and lifted his arms in the air, sharp fingers spreading, and soon words came out of his mouth. It wasn't something he had heard before, but the words caressed the back of his spine and were beautiful. A language of gods.

He soon realized that not only the Beekeeper's aura surrounded him, but so did hers, blooming as bees descended from the sky. Orion's throat felt clogged as his own aura also billowed, and he was sure Nava's shocked expression mirrored his own.

Strings of yellow, black, and gold flowed between them, like ribbons of woven silk shimmering with magic. Nava's fingers extended, and her power came in waves from the ground beneath her boots.

The creature kept chanting the same words in that language that soothed Orion's darkened soul. He didn't understand the direct meaning—or did he? His mind tickled with a distant understanding. He shouldn't know what the words meant, but somehow he did. It signified the healing of this world, the closing of a gate between realms.

The dark portal closed another inch and then two more, zapping with magnetic power, now barely a sliver. Claws appeared in the black hole, trying to push through the small space, but soon it closed down, and black iron fingers fell to the ground without another sound.

The three of them stopped at once, and the ribbons of magic slowly faded away, back into their depleted bodies.

It had been a while since he'd felt this level of exhaustion. His legs trembled under the weight of his body, the ache of his shoulders apparent as he rolled them. Nava walked like a newborn fawn toward a nearby tree and leaned against it as her head thumped on the blacked texture.

He pinched the bridge of his nose as he took a couple of deep breaths. This fatigue was unlike anything he had ever experienced, something that took his essence from the marrow of his bones. "How did I know what those words meant, and why did I know what to do? I have never heard that language before."

"I didn't know the language either, but I also knew what it meant," she admitted, and her gaze traveled to the Beekeeper.

Silence followed, and Orion tightened his fists; his stomach churned. "What is he saying?"

"He said it's the lost language of the Beekeepers. Only he knows it fully. Since we are a part of him, it passes the knowledge through the bond."

His back straightened, and he became utterly still at her words. "What did you just say?"

Her skin turned a pale shade of gray, and her eyes dipped toward the ground, her teeth capturing her bottom lip with a sharp bite. "Um—so, perhaps you want to sit down? Or stay standing, no worries. It doesn't make me more nervous or anything." She cleared her throat. "Remember when I said I was a Beekeeper?"

He raised a brow expectantly. Of course he did; she had just dropped the bomb not an hour ago. "Yes."

"There are always two Beekeepers in the world, and with the Zorren coming to this land intent on destroying it, the gods also assign a protector." Nava lowered her gaze to the ground, avoiding him. "Our magic works together. They bonded us to protect the world from destruction."

He stepped toward her, shaking his head. None of it made sense. "Does that have anything to do with me?"

She shifted, restless on her feet. He was closer now, and she hesitated to meet his gaze. "You are our protector, Arkimedes."

His jaw slacked. "What?"

No, I am not.

She flinched, and he realized he had said the words out loud, but the churning of his stomach told him he was not fit to protect anything or anyone. He took lives. He certainly didn't deserve to be one protecting these two creatures of light.

"We are connected and have been so for a year—actually, more like a decade."

"My magic is the complete opposite of yours," he growled. "I'm not at all one of you."

"Maybe that's the point!"

His lips tightened into a flat line. "If we are, why can't I hear him?" he challenged, pointing a finger at the Beekeeper.

Silence came over them again, and Nava turned her face toward the tall, treelike creature. "Aristaeus says you don't let him in—not like I do. He says you have a block in your mind, that you've learned to shield against him communicating with you. Willing or unwilling—"

"I don't want to hear any more of this nonsense," he said and paced away. Not ten minutes ago, he had been deep into thoughts so dark, she would shiver over them. He didn't deserve to be even near these two, let alone protect them.

She cleared her throat once again. "You had dreams of us, right? Maybe those weren't dreams . . ."

Here it was again, the damn memory loss that didn't leave him alone.

"Stop." Arkimedes lifted a hand, while the other rubbed a circle on his forehead.

"Shh." She shot the Beekeeper a pointed look. "Arkimedes, there is a reason—"

"I said I don't want to hear it," he snapped. "We should head back. I don't want the king to send guards looking for me and realize we both left the grounds. It will be bad if he gets suspicious."

"He is already suspicious of me." Nava lifted her arms over her head, groaning in frustration. "He knows I was with you when he took you." She let the words die on her lips, and they both stared at each other.

"Nava." His voice sounded broken even to his own ears. He hated that sound.

Unlike anything his father had told him these last four months, *this* felt like the truth. That alone had his body shaking as it mixed with utter exhaustion. The thought of having lost a decade of his memories was an out-of-this-world notion. He *had* seen them before.

Nava and Aristaeus were familiar in a way they shouldn't be. Devon's distance toward him was like there was a wedge between them that hadn't been there before. The extra scars he'd found on his body didn't lie.

With how much his father needed him to be here in this kingdom, it was no surprise that the king would go as low as to erase Orion's memories.

It made sense, but it still deviated him from his original goal, which was to find answers as to why he'd been abandoned. Why his mother had been killed, and all that had led him here. To have ten years of memories gone.

He didn't have time for strange bonds and falling for his brother's fiancée . . . if that's what she was.

"We should go," Nava agreed, turning to the creature. "We will be back, Ari." She flinched at apparent words he couldn't hear.

"What did he say now?"

"If you didn't want to hear about our connection before, believe me—now is not the time for what he said."

CHAPTER NINETEEN

ORION

Orion had hated these woods ever since the ghost of his mother haunted his dreams. It was a daunting task to come every night and hunt for arson when he knew the darker secret that lay behind. As he got closer to the spot he hated the most, his heart pounded alongside the building headache.

He needed a distraction.

"How are you feeling?" he asked, glancing back.

"Tired." Nava's brows twisted as she took in his features. "How about you?"

Apparently, she could read him like an open book. Did this have anything to do with the supposed bond they shared? He sure as hell couldn't read her that well, but now he was wondering if he had been able to. Magical bonds came in all shapes and strengths.

The bond a shifter had with their claimed mate, forged with a bite at the time of selection. The bonds witches had with their covens. The bonds of brotherhoods and sisterhoods, formed with blood spells. Then there was the myth of a soulmate, chosen by the gods themselves. The only chance a soul had to find their other half.

This supposed bond Nava had blabbered about sounded a whole lot like a soulmate bond, except the creature was dropped in there, and Orion believed in soulmate bonds about as much as he believed the king's lies.

"I'm fine," he said sharply. "We are almost there. I'm guessing you won't be able to do your disappearing trick to get to your room."

"Transferring? No, I'm barely able to walk. Be glad I'm not fainting as we speak—I have done that before." Her cheeks turned a bright shade of pink. "Multiple times."

He faced forward, fighting a smile. "There are some areas of the garden that are heavily watched."

"You mean by the creepy flowers?"

"Yes." That was one way to put it. "I'll take you through a secret passage and then fly you up to your room."

"Aren't you also tired?"

He raised a brow, facing her. "Are you worried I'll drop you?"

"Absolutely. I know you think you are invincible because you're the all-powerful Ar—prince, but it's not the first time you have crash-landed with me in tow." Nava pressed her lips tightly together, as if realizing she had given too much of their past, and once again, silence descended upon them. When and why had he dropped her? He hadn't shown his wings to anyone before he came to this kingdom.

The two of them had to be close, and if the dreams were memories . . . intimately so.

"I won't drop you," he promised. "Say I believe this madness you are telling me, that I have known you from before—you claimed the king knows this?"

Nava took a subtle breath but didn't hesitate. "Yes, if you remember the way he greeted us at dinner, then you know there was a threat woven in there."

Orion nodded. "I have learned in my time here that our kingdom's history is messy. The king wants to prevent it from repeating itself. It's hard for the royal kin to produce heirs. Something to do with our blood not mixing well with others, even our own kind—or humans."

This was it, the area of the woods he hated the most. The trees had become thick with age, and even though it had been years since this part of the forest had caught on fire, it was still all dead.

He slowed his steps and turned to meet her gaze. Nava was not looking at him but at her surroundings.

Her eyes were wide and horror shone through her expression. "The Zorren were here too? So close to the castle."

He walked forward, and the tree of his nightmares came into view, so large it commanded reverence. A huge clearing was around it where no other tree could grow due to what he assumed was poisoned grounds.

He was sure this had been a beautiful place, but it wasn't anymore. The tree's charred trunk and branches were all that was left.

"When my mother took me away, the kingdom mourned us for years." He paused, turning away from the horrible imagery that would forever haunt him. "This tree was where the queen was murdered, though it's not the story told to the population."

Nava brought both her hands to her lips, covering her horror.

He wasn't sure why he was feeling so open and vulnerable with her and the Beekeeper, who trailed close behind, but he was. Orion needed to get this burden out somehow. "My dreams of you are not the only ones that have haunted me these past few months." His chest sank lower despite himself.

"You have had nightmares of her dying here?"

"Yes, though very fragmented, and it doesn't really reveal who did it or why she was here in the first place."

"I'm so sorry, Ark," she whispered, her brow wrinkling as she grasped his hand. Her skin was warm, and it lifted some of the heaviness that had settled in his gut. Her touch should have startled him, made him want to shake her hand and put some distance, but that was the opposite of what he craved.

They stood in silence; the looming presence of the tree hung around him like an oppressive force, and he no longer wished to speak a word of it.

"Is this why the kingdom's emblem is a dead tree?" Nava's voice shook him out of his thoughts.

"No." He cleared his throat, debating whether he wanted to keep speaking or just move on. Her gentle gaze brought him back into the conversation, like a moth to a flame. "There is a mirror tree inside the castle, the queen's tree."

"Oh?" Her brows knitted together, but she didn't ask anything else.

"Since there is no recollection of what happened, it's all my own conclusion. But it's possible this was made to look like the one inside to send a message to the king."

"Do you think it's the same species of tree?" she asked, her voice hesitant.

"I think they look too similar for it not to be so. The only difference is this one is burned, and the one inside is asleep and untouched by fire."

"The king hasn't been able to have any more children after you?" Nava asked, as if knowing to change the subject.

It had been so long since he'd felt he could trust someone. The history of his family came with a heavy load. He hadn't known them personally before coming here to search for answers, but for some strange reason, he cared. "No one but me. After my mother was gone, he took on multiple women to get an heir."

Nava's lips slacked. "I have not read in any books that the Copper Kingdom's king has multiple wives. Though clearly, I have not read enough. How does it work? I didn't know there was a queen in the castle."

"There is no queen. He never remarried." Orion rubbed the back of his neck, the uncertainty of his feeling settled somewhat.

"It explains why he went through the trouble to kidnap you in the middle of the night, all the way from the Grey Island," she grumbled, and waves of images crashed into him.

He was chasing her across a vast ocean. Salt waves crashed against the large ship, the wood groaning alongside the sound of seagulls above. He stood at the end, gripping the rails. The captain had assured him there was an island less than an hour away. The Grey Island, where magic wielders came to run away from the crowns.

A town that held a spell that canceled magic. Willowbrook.

. . .

"Willowbrook," he breathed, and Nava's eyes snapped to him. His skin turned cold and clammy as the memory pushed to come through the haze of his thoughts.

"Yes." Her voice was hesitant, and her lips shook as she studied him closely.

"How long has it been? How many years did I lose?" His voice was barely audible from the noise of the forest.

"Eleven."

The anxious bubbling sensation in his gut didn't allow him to stay in this forsaken place a moment longer. He strutted toward the castle. His breathing was hard as he processed all he'd been told, everything that had happened today. "When did we meet?"

"The first or the second time?" she asked, and he turned to her, raising a brow. She looked so incredibly beautiful under the light of the setting sun with soot marking her cheeks. "We met once eleven years ago and then again last year."

"Why the time gap?" He hadn't meant to sound so harsh. Her back tensed and her eyes shifted away, teeth catching her bottom lip. "Are you going to tell me that's too much for me to hear?"

"It will be too much," she admitted, her rigid tone matching her straight back. For the first time since she had dropped back into his life, true fear took over her expression. He found he hated that look and needed to make it go away.

The air was still muggy, and his skin was rough with the ash that stuck to his sweat.

"Why did the king not remarry?"

Orion stared at Nava, wanting to find answers in the softness of her face, but maybe he wasn't ready for all the truth, not after all he had learned today. "The tree didn't bloom."

"What does that even mean, the queen's tree?"

"Haven't you read about it? It's pretty much shoved down everyone's throats in history." He slowed his strut and turned to her.

"I have not. I was homeschooled, and history wasn't my cup of tea. There are a lot of nuances of all four kingdoms—I don't keep track of every detail." Her tone took a defensive quality to it, and the way her nose wrinkled was adorable. She crossed her arms over her chest.

"The tree signals when the rightful queen has arrived. It can be an heir being born if it's a girl. But it also can be a betrothed."

"So, the tree bloomed with your mother and then died down when she passed?"

"That's how my father learned she had died." Orion's jaw tightened, and he resumed his walk. "And then he found her back where we just were, in an exact replica of the beloved tree of our people."

"I'm sorry, Arkimedes," Nava said between breaths as she struggled to catch up to him. At this point, he wasn't sure he would bother to correct her using his old name, not when it clearly held some sort of history with her.

"I'm fine. I never even met her." The hollowness in his voice told him that was a lie even though he didn't believe any longer. He cared very much as to why she had suffered such a horrible death. He cared too much.

The castle's magnificent sight came into view between the leaves of the trees as the sun set behind it. Orange and golden hues painted the tops of the buildings and trees, like a pastel painting.

"So—do you believe me?" she asked.

"That my dreams of you weren't dreams but memories being repressed? That I'm cursed?"

She nodded. "Four months ago, when they took you away."

"I believe that something is not adding up."

The palisades became clear behind the wilderness as they stepped out of the cover of the foliage. Nava turned around, her face changing as she took in the forest; it pained her to go back to the castle, and now that he knew the why, he would try to get her out of that room more. Even if that meant having to face the king's scorn.

"We can't enter the garden the same way we came out. Because of the attacks, we've increased patrolling during the night."

The sky darkened, offering them cover. "Are we going to walk all night, then? Or are you just trying to torture me?" She groaned, rubbing her hands over her thighs.

"Torturing you? May I remind you I'm here because you had to go to that damned forest today—"

"Right . . ."

She was an eager, beautiful woman, with a sunny disposition and a breath of fresh air.

Orion patted the wall that separated the wilderness and the perimeter of the castle ground, the pattern he had memorized months ago. The grout cracked, and a line was drawn over stone, between the rocks, forming a door with an arch frame and intricate designs.

"So tell me, Nava. In my repressed memories, I remember you being a curious creature. Are you also an impatient one?" His eyes shone when she approached the door.

"I guess you will have to find out for yourself." She smirked, passing by him. The scent of her wrapped him like a warm hug. Wild berries, earth, honey, and, of course, smoke. The threshold wasn't wide, and her body was touching his. She faced him.

With her skin flushed as she stared into his eyes, he wanted to pull out her thick bottom lip from the ministration of her teeth and replace it with his own. He was suffocating, dying to know if she felt as soft as he imagined.

But as soon as the heated thought surfaced, it was quickly pushed down by guilt. Devon's face flashing through his mind had his stomach dropping. Was she even engaged to him? Had that all been a lie to prevent the king from making an example of Nava the day they'd arrived?

It would explain why Devon had been so unaffected the day of her panic attack, when to Orion it had been anything but. He would be asking his brother questions tomorrow.

CHAPTER TWENTY

NAVA

The warm evening enveloped them as Arkimedes flew to his tower, the white moon and stars peppering the sky's veil. The smoke didn't linger in the air any longer. However, their skin was stained by the demon's scorn, and the scent clung to their clothes. A reminder this was not over.

It'd been a while since Nava had been this close to him, with his arms wrapped around her body protectively. Their feet touched the cool stone of her balcony, but he didn't let go of her. Maybe he was also enjoying their nearness for a change.

She held the cloth of his tunic, feeling the quick beat of his heart under her fingertips, and lifted her face to meet his. They were so close, she would only have to lift to her tiptoes to kiss him the way she craved. "I guess you didn't drop me after all."

"I'm offended you even considered it," he mocked and mirrored her smile. "Safe and sound and delivered to your room." Arkimedes's gaze flashed behind her and into the aforementioned space.

She was still determined to get them out of this place as soon as humanly possible. After today, she sensed she had taken a significant leap forward.

He believed her; he knew her role as a Beekeeper and was guarding her secret of being able to call to her magic, even though she was wearing the bracelet. Arkimedes didn't trust these people. She still wished he would have taken her straight to his room, and by his heated gaze, she knew he was thinking the same.

"This is not my room," she murmured.

"No? Where, then?" He matched her tone.

Emboldened by his question, she pushed forward. "I rather think my room is wherever you are sleeping."

His eyes widened at her words, and his fingers combed his hair back away from his forehead. "You keep playing this dangerous game, Nava—"

"I'm not playing. I want you to take me there tonight—"

"I want to," he admitted. His finger caught her bottom lip and pulled it out from under her teeth. "Is that something I have done before? Take you to my room? Touched you?" His hand left her lips and traced down the skin of her cheek. He wrapped his hand around her neck, pulling her closer to him. His body was hot, and that place in between her thighs throbbed in anticipation of more. "Have I tasted you?"

The heat that ran through her was nothing to be trifled with. She breathed, "Yes."

"I keep wondering if you would be as sweet now." He dropped his face down, and her breath caught in her throat as she awaited the kiss that didn't come. "It feels like I'm under a spell, burning for you."

"Why don't you let go?" Was that even her voice? She couldn't tell anymore. The drumming of her heart muffled everything else.

His darkened gaze dropped to her lips. "Why are you with him?" His brows dipped.

"What?"

"Why does he get to call you his fiancée? Every. Single. Time. You tempt me here, and I want to believe this whole thing." He hesitated. "I believe you, at least the part that you are a Beekeeper. However, Devon hasn't come out and said you aren't engaged."

Her breath left in a whoosh as he stepped away, his hand dropping from her neck. "It's not true that Devon and I are matched. He said this to protect us from the king."

"I almost kissed you. I want to do so much more. My brother calls you his fiancée, even when we speak in private. I need to hear it from him."

An icy wave ran through her veins, cooling the heat that had been burning there before. She crossed her arms around herself. Devon technically couldn't hurt them with the life debt in play, but that only protected their lives. He could very well plot to have them both survive but not be with each other.

She had wanted to appear unaffected, but it was too much for her to take. The change of their relationship, the trust they'd always held for the other's words. Even before accepting their bond, they'd both known to trust each other.

But this was too different, and just as this was all a shock to Arkimedes, it was also to her. She *loved* him, whereas he might lust over her now but had not fallen in love with her yet. He was also determined to call himself Orion; he wanted to play prince and had just told her he had never wanted to be a Crow, never wanted to be Arkimedes.

The man she loved.

"If you need to talk to him to believe me, do so. I would love to be present because I sure as hell don't trust what he tells you."

"*I* trust him."

"Well, you are more naïve now than you were before!" she snarled and almost felt sorry for the way his face fell.

"You came here with him. If anything, your actions don't match your words."

"I'm here trying to save you after you were kidnapped! I had few options at the time. I don't know how to open a portal or work with dark magic. All I know is I came here and you didn't remember me, and you aren't the only one who lost memories."

Silence descended upon them, the thickness in the air strong enough that she found it hard to breathe. Arkimedes's frown softened as he took in her ragged stance. "You paid the price by crossing, not Devon?"

"I lost all memories of my father." Her voice cracked.

His Adam's apple bobbed as he swallowed. "Your reaction in the garden was when you realized he had been taken from you?"

"Yes."

"I'm sorry."

The churning coming through their bond made it all worse. "Good night, Arkimedes." Her feet dragged over the stone when she turned toward her room.

"Nava . . ."

But she closed the door behind her.

The sound of the curtains being pulled aside woke Nava from sleep; the morning sun stretched shapes over the floor of her bedroom. She grumbled and sank her face into the pillow, chasing the last remnants of sleep.

"Good morning, miss!" Leela's voice was shrill with excitement.

Nava awaited stiffly inside her warm cocoon. Maybe the fae would take the hint and leave. It wasn't like she had much to do other than transfer to Devon's room and hope she would find Arkimedes there.

Get that damn conversation over with.

Her whole body ached, from the top of her head to the tips of her toes. Her hair still smelled like smoke, even though she had spent a good hour in the bath scrubbing every inch of her body clean of the grime from yesterday.

"Too tired." Nava's voice came out muffled by the pillow, but soon enough, Leela's cool fingers dragged the sheets away. "Hey!"

"I'm sorry, miss. But the king has commanded the guests to get fitted for the celebrations tomorrow."

Nava blinked groggily. "Can't I just wear one outfit in the closet? There is plenty I haven't worn." She pointed at the aforementioned wardrobe.

"Oh, no, there is a dress code for the solstice celebrations. Plus, if the king commands it—"

"Fine." Nava took a deep breath and got out of bed. The morning breeze that entered from her terrace's open door was cool over her heated skin. Unlike yesterday, it didn't smell like burning and death, and she grinned at their victory.

It had been an amazing feeling, the three of them working together, like the gods had intended it to be.

"You smell like a campfire, miss," Leela commented, helping her onto her robe, her small button nose wrinkling.

These fae and their sensitive noses. "I spent a long time in front of the fire yesterday," she said with a wry smile. When did it become so easy to lie? She used to be horrible at it.

"Oh, that makes sense," she chirped. "Let's get you in the bath, then. Marni is rough around the edges."

"The seamstress?"

"Yes. She doesn't like . . ." Leela fidgeted, pulling her red long hair behind one pointy ear.

"Outsiders?"

"Humans."

Oh, the joys of classism. This was not something new. In Willowbrook, she had been looked down on her whole life for being a "witch." The townsfolk had always whispered behind her back in hushed tones about the woes of Forrests' luck.

"Is there anywhere else I can go to get fitted?" Nava wasn't even sure why she asked when she knew the answer. Even if there was somewhere else she could go, it wasn't like she had money to pay for such things.

"Unfortunately, all royals—and their guests—go to Marni." Leela hesitated.

"My seamstress, Renna, is amazing. You would like her. She is just as talented as Marni, but kinder, and beautiful." Her eyes shone with such affection, Nava wasn't sure if this was a family member or something more.

"Is Renna your friend?"

Leela's cheeks turned a bright shade of red. "Yes."

"I see. Maybe something more?"

"Miss!"

"Come on, humor me. I have been stuck in this room forever! I need something to hold on to, hope for what's good in life," Nava continued, and the fae's face turned as red as her hair. However, her eyes shone.

"It's difficult for the kingdom to accept us, not with the Society looming nearer this part of the world."

"Fuck the Society straight to hell."

Leela gasped. "But your betrothed is part of the Society."

"I just said what everyone else is thinking. If you think a girl like me would get matched and just accept it, then you haven't heard me complain enough." Nava laughed, and her fight with Arkimedes flashed through her mind. His jealous outburst, and the mess they were both in.

Leela's shaky lips turned into a tentative smile. "I don't know what we could do."

"You could always leave this kingdom—go to the Grey Island."

The fae's red lashes moved like the wings of a butterfly as she blinked before her thin hand grasped hers, pulling her into the washroom, where a steaming pool that smelled of honeysuckles awaited. "Thank you."

"For what?"

"For your words." Leela's lack of words could mean she wasn't used to any sort of support on the matter. Her voice rang small. "I will set your dress on the bed and make sure Fael is ready to go. Our appointment is at ten." The fae smiled and bowed before she left the washroom, allowing Nava the privacy she had asked for earlier.

How did they keep time in this castle? She hadn't seen a steam clock hanging anywhere in sight. She had seen several sun clocks in the garden when she'd gone out with the guard. Still, everyone here followed time like it was a religion.

She moved her freckled hands over the fading bruises on her neck as she inspected her reflection. Her cool touch was a contrast to her feverish skin. What tomorrow's solstice would bring to her and Ark was . . . worrisome, as if she needed anything else added to her already complicated life.

CHAPTER TWENTY-ONE

NAVA

A polished black carriage with gold trim awaited them by the entrance of the castle, down dozens of narrow stone steps that were lined with cement banisters. Two guards wearing polished copper armor and long blue capes stood at the bottom.

The beasts pulling their transportation were not horses, nor bulls. They were as wide as the latter, with shiny hides of charcoal gray and ebony. Their necks had long, thick, wavy hair that reminded her of sheep.

"The orrus." Fael's voice had her heart jumping out of her chest. "The beasts are bred by the fae in the high mountains. Stronger than a bull and faster than any horse. Stubborn and the males can get . . . scary if females are around."

"I have never seen one before. Are they bred as a mix between a bull and a horse?"

Fael shrugged. "I'm sure they took inspiration from that, but the high mountain fae are known to have the gift of creation. Once a century or so, they bring to life something new. A plant with medicinal powers never seen before. A creature like this."

"So magic is no issue for them?" That thought alone had Nava perking up. It was a disease that affected every corner of the world. The dwindling of magic, the main reason the Society of Crows was wreaking havoc on people's lives.

"No, they are also affected. Before, they were able to create every decade—then every fifty years, and so on." Fael moved toward the door, and the footman made haste from his path, clearly not wanting to interact with the guard. "It's rumored their magic is not as strong as it used to be."

"Oh."

"Either way, these creatures are protected by our laws because they are made by our magic, and they don't reproduce easily. It's forbidden to hunt or trade them, and they are to stay in our kingdom. Of course, poachers happen, but it's not common that they go unpunished." Fael held the door open for her.

Another poor living creature having difficulty procreating in this kingdom. Nava wondered if it had something to do with the water or maybe the magic that fed the lands.

The orrus snorted loudly, their two-fingered hooves lifting rock and dirt from where they stood, clearly not pleased to be holding still while the three of them got in the carriage.

Standing straight and looking forward, the guards with their impressive dark wings shaded the gravel path; they were taller than even Fael, their mists billowing around them like a campfire. Their gazes burned the nape of her neck as she turned around to get into the carriage, past the footman in orange regalia who didn't say a word and avoided her eyes.

It had been a long while since she'd ridden a carriage. Last time had been in the Iron City, when she and her family had been running from Arkimedes and Devon. She could still remember her mother tightening the ropes that had held their sparse belongings to the back of their wooden ride. Her mother's dark chestnut hair had billowed in the wind, wild, much like her own.

If Nava closed her eyes tightly, she could almost smell the soft notes of rose from her mother's body oil. But as she sat on these black velvet seats, the only scent that surrounded her was leather and musk.

The Copper City revealed itself as the carriage pulled past a tall archway under the castle's outside walls, layered in tiers that descended in circular patterns. Tall, century-old trees lined the streets here, with black lamp posts and uneven cobbled roads.

Nava held the leather handle by the roof as the carriage rushed past impressive-sized manors on either side of them.

"The high fae live here," Leela said and intertwined her fingers over her legs, her blue gaze flashing from Nava to the outside. "Are you well, miss? You are looking rather pale."

Her stomach churned as nausea hit her in waves, coming and going with the rocking of the wood that encased her, closing in like an unwelcome hug. "I usually walk everywhere."

They crossed past another archway, the stone walls shorter than the ones that surrounded the castle, but here the color of the city exploded around her. Bright yellow and beige homes loomed over them. Every inch of the city was covered by a stucco building or ones made with burnt-orange bricks and framed in wood.

The city was alive with people. Unlike what she had seen in the castle, they all wore different colors. Reds, yellows, whites, and browns. Beautiful patterned silk fabric hung from a particular store, with greens that reminded her of the forest in the Grey Island.

Children played on the sidewalks; some had wings, some did not. The streets were packed full of other carriages being pulled by less-impressive orrus or by horses. Nava swore she even saw a donkey somewhere.

Her nose touched the cool glass of the window, and her breath caught in her throat when the turquoise water of the canal appeared behind the buildings.

"We are close now, miss," Leela said.

Nava met the eyes of a young man with long, camel-blond hair held down by a tall hat. A polished gray suit fit like it had been tailored to him. He smile at her from the sidewalk, tilting his hat up and revealing perfectly rounded ears. Nava blinked and sat back, finally meeting both Fael's and Leela's amused expressions.

"They are not all fae," Nava murmured.

"We have a large population of humans in the city, and in outer towns of our kingdom, there are other fae races and shifters." Fael placed his helmet over his head, covering his salt-and-pepper tresses.

The carriage shook as they went over a large bump on the road, and Nava struggled to keep herself seated and not lose her breakfast all over the place. The damn thing moved even faster than the steam vehicles from the Iron City.

The carriage stopped in front of a row of red brick shops, and the morning sun hit the uneven copper roofs with golden highlights. Nava jumped down faster than any polite lady of society should; Laurie would have been scandalized if she'd seen it. However, her caregiver was far away in the Pearl Island with Cameron, and Nava was too happy to be out of that can to care.

She dusted the skirt of her dress, staring at the orrus through her lashes. The creatures were fast and strong, without an ounce of elegance in their massive bodies. It took her a moment to calm the storm brewing in her stomach before she faced the shops.

These were undoubtedly a place of elegance where people of money would come to get fitted for their clothes. A bit far from the castle, and Nava guessed the royals didn't really come this way, but rather the seamstress Marni would go to them.

"This way, miss." Leela's gentle fingers wrapped around Nava's arm, pulling her toward the shop.

The gentle breeze brought smells of baked goods from the nearby bakery, mixing with the distinct scent of sea breeze from the canal nearby. Light music tones grew from the distance—someone playing a guitar, perhaps a street performer?

She strolled behind Fael's giant frame, his white spotted wings swaying with his every step. His hand rested all too casually on the hilt of his sword as he looked around for anything amiss. Always alert.

Leela walked next to her, chatting vividly about the preparations for the dance. "At the ball, women wear golds or yellow, while the men wear whites." Leela had not stopped talking. Nava admired how she could fit so many words into one breath. "It will be hard to tell who's who with the masks. Except for the royals, of course. Their aura alone gives them away."

Right. Nava still couldn't see Arkimedes's all the time, but she had to assume it looked just as scary as the king's.

Fael tilted his head, staring at both of them with a raised brow. "Most of us in the guards have the aura as well, Leela."

"But it's not the same, obviously." Leela grinned. "Are you jealous I'm not specifically pointing at the royal guard too?"

Fael choked on a laugh. "You wish I was jealous."

Nava had not realized Fael and Leela were close, but it was clear now with the affection that shone behind both of their gazes. If Arkimedes trusted this man with her protection, and Leela liked him, he couldn't be so bad.

Leela answered an unspoken question while snickering. "Fael and I went to school together. Actually, he was a few years ahead of me. He is an old man."

Nava couldn't help but smile. "That makes sense. I was wondering for a moment why you had gray hair if you were as young as Leela."

Fael's laugh rolled in a carefree way. "To a human eye, we probably look around your age. However, we have to be nearing a century now."

Nava almost choked on her own tongue at his words. Fael didn't appear much older than Arkimedes or Devon, with his copper skin, gold eyes, and smooth face. Leela looked much younger than Nava. Twenty at most.

"Not all of us, even though we are fae, inherit the wonderful genetics of the Rosalors," Fael continued.

"That's my family name," Leela replied, perking up. "But Fael is actually graying now because of the stress, not genetics."

"If you keep going this way, Leela, I will not bring you the honey wine you love the next time I come to visit you."

Leela's lips clamped shut at his words. "What a delicate child you are." She turned to face Nava. "I will bring you some of that honey wine. You would enjoy it, maybe you can share it with your fiancé."

Right. "Oh, you don't have to. I actually don't eat honey." The skin of her face turned warm. "But speaking of Devon, would he get fit with an outfit as well?"

"Oh, yes. I believe His Royal Highness took him earlier in the day," Leela said, and Nava's heart sank in her chest.

It was silly to be jealous of Devon, but her mind hadn't been acting rationally today, and her nerves were still fried from her ride here. Nava clasped her hand together in front of her, trying to hide the need to fidget.

Why would the Crown Prince take her to get fitted for a dress? Not even if he had been courting her would he do such a thing, and he was not. That would raise questions, obviously.

Had he talked to Devon by now about if their engagement was true? If so, had the Crow lied just to make things difficult for them? She wouldn't put it past him to do so.

Even though she liked her current escorts, she would have preferred Arkimedes's company, even after their small fight last night. He had almost kissed her. He believed her. She just needed time to convince him to leave all this madness behind.

"Must be nice to be catered to by the prince." Nava said.

Leela's attention came crashing to her, her face practically glowing as she bounced on the balls of her feet. The fae's plump lips opened to say something but shut the moment she remembered they weren't alone. They had arrived.

Incense hung in the air outside the shop. Notes of patchouli and roses tugged at a ghost of a memory that wasn't present any longer, something she had lost, and it ached for unknown reasons.

Even though she didn't remember her father, who had clearly taught her the art of potion-making, she still had fractured memories of working in her shop. Her roughened hands chopping herbs, of her sniffing oils and boiling potions.

Simone had brought fresh-baked bread in exchange for migraine medicine. She had spent a whole summer trying to teach Cameron the proper way to extract carmine from the cochineal insects. And her shop—it had green walls the color of sage behind the counter.

Nava remembered the imagery and the ingredients were familiar, but she couldn't remember why she had used them. The purpose of it all was lost, much like her father's smiles. It was like watching a dream but failing to understand the meaning behind it all.

Potion-making had been such a large part of her identity. However, she had to keep moving forward. It mattered not what she might be unable to recover, and she needed to focus on what mattered most.

How to get Arkimedes back had to be what occupied most of her thoughts. The rest . . . she could figure it out later.

The entrance to the seamstress's store was an impressive twelve-foot-high archway, framed by decorative sand-colored bricks and a heavy wooden door with glass panels that distorted the inside. A wooden sign hung from a swirling metal arm.

Marni's Woven Magic
Tailored to you

"This is it, miss." Leela's nose scrunched as her sky-blue eyes glared at the seamstress's door. "Don't let her get to you."

"Don't worry, Leela. I'm not a damsel in distress. I know how to handle myself."

Nava lifted her hand to knock on the door, but it swung open before she even made contact. A chime of bells sang as she came face to face with the man she had been dreaming of the entire day.

Her body reacted in kind, burning up just at the sight of him. She focused on the muscles that weren't covered by his light tunic. Black silk tugged over his wide shoulders, and charcoal threads that depicted naked branches. His eyes blazed over her, bright and self-illuminating, and a wave of something warm ran through her, making her dizzy.

Heat. Lust. Want . . . Longing.

That emotion wasn't coming from her alone, but it was being enhanced through their bond by him.

Was this all related to what the solstice would bring for the both of them? It was like she had become starved for his touch even more than normal.

"Nava," he breathed, his gaze lingering momentarily on her lips before shifting to Devon, who approached them from his back.

He wore a light blue double-piece tunic, belted with wider fabric, and dark indigo pants. He seemed less pale than the last time she had seen him, his hair cropped shorter and pulled back behind his ears, allowing his sharp cheekbones to catch the morning light.

"*Fiancée*, fancy seeing you here." Devon approached her with wicked bright eyes, the side smirk on his face growing under her glare.

"Stop with that," Nava said in between teeth, and Arkimedes stirred next to Devon. It was hard to discern if he looked guilty or plain uncomfortable.

Had they talked? Had Devon poisoned Arkimedes's mind with more lies that would bring on his rejection of her? What if the Crow told him they were mated?

The crawl of panic began to take over her body and mind, her chest tightening and making it hard to breathe. She was going to murder Devon and this stupid charade he had put them on. He was doing this to torment Arkimedes *and* her.

"I would have loved to come with the both of you." Maybe that way, she would avoid the possibility of being bullied by a hostile seamstress, if what Leela said was true.

Devon shrugged. "We wanted to spend some time with just the two of us, like the good ol' days before we were split up by . . . destiny." His eyes flamed.

Nava crossed her arms over her chest, meeting his gaze with equal intensity. "Catching him up on what you have been up to, by any chance?" she asked in a fake sweet tone. "Were you able to tell him all the wicked activities you engaged in while he was away?" She hadn't forgotten that both Leela and Fael stood near them, undoubtedly listening to every word the three of them exchanged.

"We were too busy talking about the future to focus on the past." His hand landed on her shoulder. "Have fun in there!"

The future? What future was he speaking of? One where she wasn't in the picture and would be forced to move to be near but never close to the man she loved? Would she be able to put Cameron through this?

Anxiety took hold of her windpipe, and if it wasn't for her mother's stern voice echoing in her mind to get herself together, she would have allowed panic to burst free and pull her down in its attack.

Nava glared at Devon as he sauntered out of the shop, enjoying himself too much for her liking. She turned to Arkimedes, who walked past her, one hand burying inside the pocket of his tunic.

"I have told Marni to take care of you. I—will see you later." His other hand went through his hair, the way he always did when he was nervous.

"Yes . . ." She looked behind her to see if her escorts were close, but they were far enough away and chatting by the carriage. She drifted closer. "Did you ask him?"

"I did." His eyes softened on her, and that alone killed some of her self-doubt, her anger toward Devon appeasing. "We can talk about it later, alone."

"Next!" A shrill voice came from inside the shop, startling her out of her stupor.

"Nava." Arkimedes bowed, his eyes never leaving hers, before he too strode off from the entrance of the seamstress shop. "Fael, Leela."

"Your Highness," both of them said in unison, bowing, and Nava realized that once again, she had not adhered to the formality surrounding them.

Arkimedes walked past the carriage and toward the shops where Devon awaited him, and she trailed their retreating shapes that disappeared in the streets of town.

"Oh, you are here." A woman's voice flowed to her as Nava came into the shop, the scents here much stronger. A tall, slim brunette walked to her with light feet and a raised chin. She wore a wine-colored gown that fell like a cascade of gems and shiny threads toward the soft ground. Her scowl was so deep it could give Violet a run for her money.

"Good afternoon," Nava said, waving a hand.

The shop wasn't large, the ceilings not as tall as she had expected, but the windows were open, letting in the warm breeze of the morning. Rolls of fabric of all the colors of the rainbow lined the walls. Golden gowns lined the display in front of the store. Draped over mannequins were all kinds of different outfits Nava had never seen before. Wide skirts and narrow bodices.

Gorgeous dresses, dyed with rich pigments. Patterns, textures—this time her heart was racing, not due to forgotten memories, but because she was excited to be here.

Never had Nava stepped inside such a fancy seamstress shop before. The one in Willowbrook made and mended clothes that were simple and utilitarian for the most part. She couldn't have afforded to be in a place like this, even in passing.

Well-preserved rugs covered the floors, and in the center of the room, there was a fitting stand and a wooden mirror next to it.

The woman's umber eyes scoured down Nava's body, making her squirm. "It will be hard work to get a gown made in such a rush."

"I'm sorry, I just arrived in town not that long ago."

The woman glowered and headed to the center of the room, waving her hand toward the stand. "Come this way now, human."

She followed Marni with long strides while her blood heated inside her veins. "My name is Nava, not 'human.'"

Marni scoffed, dismissing Nava's words. "It doesn't matter. I will never remember."

It was her turn to frown. If the woman wanted to upset her with her words, she had another thing coming since Nava had had an internship of hostility with Violet last year.

She shrugged. "Suit yourself." And she stood on the pedestal as the seamstress looked her over.

"Your kind is always one to have such wide hips, not the most appealing."

Nava cleared her throat, swallowing her spike in annoyance. "Good news, it seems you make your gowns to overcompensate for the lack of curves. Maybe mine doesn't need as much padding."

Why had she decided to say it out loud *before* the fae made her gown? Marni's glare told her she would be paying for it later.

The fae walked off to the wall that held mounted rolls of fabric, coming back with a roll of the most garish canary-yellow fabric Nava had seen. It shimmered under the light, iridescent colors as she unrolled it unceremoniously over the ground.

"Isn't that a bit loud?" Nava asked, and the brown eyes of the seamstress met hers with a wicked light behind her pupils.

"I'm afraid I ran out of all the other yellow or gold fabric. It is pretty late to get anything brought in since the ball is tomorrow." She smiled.

Nava studied the wall with the rolls of fabric, where at least a dozen of other yellow and gold rolls leaned against the wall. "There are a few more over there." She pointed in the direction.

The fae didn't even move a muscle to turn around. "Those are for . . . higher-class individuals, dear, not for you." So much for this woman following Arkimedes's command of taking care of her.

Nava frowned but pressed her lips together, unwilling to let Marni enjoy getting a rise out of her. She needed the dress; the king had demanded that she get it from this cruel woman.

She pictured her mother's image in her mind and closed her eyes, calling for her strength.

"Do not let them see you affected by their words. Ignoring them is the best kind of retaliation," her mother had once told her, though right now it didn't feel that way.

"Ow." She jumped when the prick of a pin dug into her skin.

"Stay still," the seamstress growled. She wrapped a strap of a hideous, shiny yellow fabric around her waist and pinned it down. The needle went through the fabric and straight into Nava's flesh once again.

She pulled away with a hiss, narrowing her eyes at the smiling face of the fae. "If you poke me again, believe me, you won't be smiling by the end of the day."

Her smile faltered; maybe it was the slight shake in Nava's body, the glow under her skin, or the bees that crawled the walls of the shop.

"I said I was sorry," the woman said, though it was the first time Nava had heard those words.

She had never been one to care about dresses, parties, or makeup and such. She shouldn't care that these were cheap materials set aside for just humans when fae got something else. It bothered her that the gown being pinned together looked like a badly formed cake, decorated by toddlers.

Her skin itched, as if ants crawled over her, biting every inch of exposed flesh. And with the sound of the scissors cutting the fabric, Nava's chin rose higher. She shouldn't care, but she was woman enough to admit it bothered her. However, she would make the most of it.

Fuck the king, his curse, and this woman straight to hell.

CHAPTER TWENTY-TWO

NAVA

By the time Marni was done measuring her for what was to be the most hideous dress the whole kingdom would ever see, Nava was ready to leave and never see her again. The air was cool against her skin when the door of the shop slammed behind her.

Her steps faltered when, instead of Fael and Leela waiting for her, Arkimedes met her eyes from across the sidewalk. He leaned against the carriage, one of his hands resting on his hip, while the other bounced off his leg as he spoke with Devon, whose back was facing her. She saw the footman feeding the orrus, ignoring everything around him.

"Well, this is a surprise," she said, trying to sound casual, but the shake in her vocal cords gave her away.

"You two have been complaining a lot, so I thought we could see the city." Arkimedes pushed off the carriage. Was this a trap of sorts? It sounded too good to be true. Had Devon spoken lies to Arkimedes and this was when they dropped her in the woods to fend for herself?

Devon tilted his face toward her. "Lighten up, kitten."

Nava swallowed and took tentative steps toward her soulmate, searching his face for anything that signaled trouble.

Arkimedes opened the door of the carriage and made space for her to jump in. "Have you ever visited the Copper City before?" he asked when she stood by his side, the scent of leather wrapping around her.

"No, I have only been to the suburbs of the Iron City and the Grey Island," she admitted and looked back at Devon, who buried both hands inside his pockets. "Is this a trap?"

Arkimedes's surprised laughter was a welcomed melody, and his eyes crinkled with amusement. "A trap?"

"Well, yes. Yesterday you weren't happy . . ." She looked back at Devon before raising her chin up in the air. "I don't trust you two all buddy-buddy like this."

"For once, I will agree with Devon and say you need to relax." Arkimedes shook his head, and a caress of his amusement crossed the bond, creating butterflies in her stomach. "It's nothing bad, I promise."

Nava pursed her lips, hesitating just a moment before hoisting herself inside the cabin of hell and waiting by the farthest corner. Devon came in next and sat in front of her with a rogue, elegant pose that required a lot of practice. "What did you tell him while alone with him?"

"Me?" His brows lowered over his eyes, clear confusion tinting his pale features. "What could you possibly mean?"

What she meant was she didn't trust him one bit, and the nervous churning in her stomach was driving her insane. Had Arkimedes asked Devon about their fake engagement, and had Devon told him the truth? "I don't trust you—that is what I mean."

Devon stared at Nava with an unreadable expression before shrugging a shoulder. "I have been working on our combined task. What have *you* been doing? Other than panicking in public and letting the whole castle know he would drop anything to take you away."

Nava's stomach churned at the memory of that morning when she'd realized she had no memories left of her father. The hole that festered in her chest ached with her loss. "I didn't mean to lose my mind that morning. The king already knows who I am; I don't believe for a second they are believing our story. They kidnapped him, and they saw me while doing it." Nava's hands turned to fists, and she hated the guilt creeping inside her. It wasn't like she had full control of what had happened to her that morning. The trigger to her panic attack had not been expected.

Devon looked past the open door. Arkimedes talked to the footman, giving directions perhaps? She didn't know. "The king and his close guards kidnapped him. The rest of the population, I'm sure, thinks he showed up to claim what's rightfully his. Now the whole castle whispers that the prince has it for his brother's fiancée. A human. What a scandal."

"You are enjoying this."

"Enjoying this mess?" Devon's false politeness melted as his brows met in the middle. "I'm tied to protect you two without having a say in the matter. I have hated you both for a year. Don't get things twisted, cat."

"You don't hate him. So stop trying to make me think otherwise." Nava checked on Arkimedes once again. He was still chatting away and pointing in the distance, possibly hearing their conversation. "What did you tell him?"

"The truth."

"Your truth?"

"Who else's?" He smiled.

Nava's annoyance turned into concern, the burning fire in her veins cooling down as she studied the Crow's face. "Don't do anything that would hurt him, Devon. Please."

Devon ignored her words, his onyx eyes following the movements of his brother outside. "When we met, him and I, we had no one but each other. Unwanted children who were given a chance at greatness." Nava was sure he meant the magic in the world. The balance the Crows believed to upkeep. "He always thought of it as servitude. I saw it as a new opportunity to have something worth fighting for. Unwanted by the rest of the world, we found a family in each other." Devon let the weight of his body lean into the seat behind him. "In less than fifteen years, he got not one but two families who wanted him."

"You mean the Valerons?" Nava whispered, not wanting Ark to listen. "They weren't a family to him at all. He hates them."

"Yet they still wanted him." His eyes shifted away from her. "He gets to be a royal, have the gods give him a beautiful mate who travels across the world to save him against all odds."

Beautiful . . .

She stilled in her spot, her heart hammering against her chest, and she let the air leave her lungs. Alarm bells rang in her ears, telling her to get out of there, to disappear and avoid the uncomfortable sickening feeling that awakened within her.

It was the first nice thing Devon had ever told her. However, she didn't want him to think she was beautiful. She preferred him thinking of her as anything but.

He straightened in his spot. "Don't let it get in your head. I find women beautiful. It's not you, it's what you represent."

Her muscles relaxed a fraction as air entered her body once again, and she brought her hands over the fabric of her dress, whipping away the cold sweat that coated her skin. "You are jealous of the idea of me . . . ?" She looked around, expecting to find Arkimedes by the door. What the hell was he up to out there?

"Jealousy is such an ugly word."

"You want a soulmate?" she asked in a whisper.

"Don't we all?"

She hadn't, not one bit. Had fought it every minute of a decade. Arkimedes had fought it tooth and nail last year. "You're envious of all he's gotten when he didn't even want it, aren't you?"

Devon opened his mouth but shut it when Arkimedes's head popped into the carriage. "We are ready." His eyes shone with an eagerness she hadn't seen before; her heart skipped a beat at his tentative smile, as it showed a shadow of dimples.

What was going inside that head of his? Before he was taken, she'd been able to listen to some of his thoughts. That was not the case now—their bond was hurting from the lack of memories. Was he taking them around to see his city? Hoping they would love it as much as he did?

The weight of iron dropped in her stomach, the metallic taste lingering on the back of her tongue. She had been with him not only in the Northern Village, where they had their home, but also in Willowbrook, and not once had he looked this way.

Would he want to leave with her if he did regain his memories—and would she even want to take him away? She brought her hand over the aching spot where the three circles of her soulmate mark formed a flower.

His black wings were there one moment, fitting in the cramped area, and then gone the next, the scent of spices flowing in the air. Her eyes lingered on the smooth plane of his back as he took a seat next to her; she contained her urge to drag her finger over it.

He turned to her, called by her thoughts, and dropped his gaze to where her hand massaged the spot on her chest. His brow crinkled. "Are you all right? You seem uncomfortable."

"Yes, I'm fine. It's just this dark box of a carriage reminds me of a coffin."

His lips pulled to the side into an amused smile that showed straight teeth. "A coffin?"

"Uh-huh. With all this shiny, dark fabric . . . and the pattern." Nava swallowed, moving her fingers over the polished wood of the wall next to her, but held his gaze. His expression softened as he studied her. His fingers twitched closer over his lap, and her lips parted as waves of heat bloomed in her stomach at the intensity of his expression.

Longing. Caution. Concern. Want. So many emotions, she had a hard time picking which ones were hers and which ones were his.

"Ugh. Get me out of here."

She jumped when Devon's voice interrupted the silence. Her face warmed as she tried to ignore his words and annoyed expression. Arkimedes's surprised chuckle had her whole body melting into her seat. He didn't smile enough, let alone laugh, and this carefree expression just fed her doubts further.

"The king would be disappointed to hear that his carriage looks like a coffin," he teased and relaxed in the seat, but he didn't stop searching her features, as if trying to uncover what she was hiding.

Intertwining her fingers over her lap to prevent flapping her hands around, she faced the window as they started moving. "Where are we going?"

"The market, and then maybe we can ride through the oldest part of town. It's a bit bumpy. But there is a lot of—"

"History?" Devon asked with a mocking smile, and Arkimedes side-eyed his brother but proceeded to ignore him.

"Street vendors and art. Does that sound good?"

Breathless at the shine behind his irises, she didn't think she'd seen him so eager since she'd met him. He was happy.

She cut her eyes to Devon, making sure she wasn't the only one seeing this, and by his brother's softening expression, it wasn't just her.

Arkimedes loved it here, and it was a disaster.

By the time they made it back to the castle, the evening light had taken over the sky. Watercolor shades of blues and oranges matched the beautiful silk scarf Arkimedes had gotten her in one of the markets earlier in the afternoon.

She hated to admit she'd had fun. Though she'd been apprehensive at first, life in the city had been contagious. Since Arkimedes's wings had been hidden from view and he hadn't been wearing his crown and regalia, they'd gone unnoticed. Just three humans walking around town.

Time had passed, however, and her body had acted a bit off-kilter. Too swollen in areas it shouldn't be. Even though the night was cool against her skin, she was too warm to stay in her dress a second longer. Having left Devon back in his room, she and Ark walked together down the corridors of the castle, trailed by Fael not far behind.

"Did you have fun?" he asked as they approached the green room.

"I did. Very much so."

Memories of eating frog legs for the first time flashed through her mind. Devon had told her they were chicken skewers; it was her own damn fault for trusting the Crow with anything. She'd been halfway through her second skewer when Arkimedes asked her if she had eaten frog before.

In her defense, it sort of tasted like chicken—with a bit of a swampy aftertaste. Their combined laughter still chimed inside her head, making her smile.

Their rooms grew closer, and with that, the tension in her stomach multiplied, a sort of giddiness she hadn't experienced before. It was what she imagined being courted a regular way felt like. Being walked to her door, unsure what to expect from it.

Unable to look away from him, she was drawn like a moth to a flame. His face had relaxed from the weight of mistrust that had darkened his aura after what they'd done yesterday with the Zorren, and the lightness of today's outing.

He was breathtakingly handsome, and the fact that she was not allowed to reach and kiss him had her aching when she shouldn't be. Fael hung back as Arkimedes leaned against the doorframe, his gaze flashing around the corridor before coming down to her. Nava's back hit the cool texture of the door behind her. Her blood drummed in her veins, and her fingers twitched with the need to grab the lapels of his tunic and bring him in. She missed the way his lips felt against hers, soft but demanding. The softness of his tongue, the burn of his stubble against her cheeks.

"You weren't lying last night," he whispered, and Nava's gaze snapped back to Fael. She gathered her soulmate trusted this man more than he did the rest of the guards. Why? Nava didn't know, but she didn't feel comfortable speaking about yesterday here.

She brought her hand to his chest; his skin burned the pads of her fingers through the fabric. They were both running too hot and treading dangerous territory. "I wouldn't lie about that." Withhold truth, yes. But out of necessity.

"I'm sorry for how I reacted. I was— I have been feeling a bit off-kilter."

So was she. Nava grasped the collar of his tunic and pulled him in just a fraction. He was close enough she could see the spots that moved in his irises and the darkness of his lashes as they dipped.

Nava had to get out of this hall immediately. They had company. "I should get in. I need a good shower." Or ten to cool down. She reached for the doorknob with a shaky hand, struggling to grasp at the metal. "Good night, Ar—sir."

His pupils dilated. "Good night, Nava."

The door clicked closed, and she leaned against its surface for too long, grasping her chest, trying to calm her fast-beating heart and talk herself out of doing something ridiculous like inviting him in.

The reason why she shouldn't was not sounding too important. She struggled to remind herself that there were lies in between them. That being intimate for them was more than just a good time and tousled sheets.

Lying with Arkimedes when he was in a solstice-induced spell was not her goal here. Her nerves were on edge after the day she had today.

She focused on something else. The burning fire in the corner, the fresh scent of a summer night, the memories of the afternoon they had. Nava wanted to hate this city as a whole, but it had been nice to get to know something new, something bigger than where she had been in the past.

Nava walked toward the fireplace, dropping the sleeves of her dress and pushing the gown past her wide hips and down her legs. She wiggled out, her body coiled tighter with each step she took, and the gentle breeze of the early evening enveloped her, cooling her skin.

Her only clothes was a light chemise, made of sheer silk. A low neck and beautiful embroidered straps that tied it to her shoulders. It was light as a feather over her, but even that felt suffocating.

She pulled it down her arms when the ends of her hair raised on end and a pleasant sensation in her stomach blossomed.

Arkimedes's gaze burned across the expanse of her balcony and through the fabric of her curtains. She guessed he'd been outside getting some fresh air—or maybe he'd heard her and had been waiting for her.

Raw and on edge, she closed her eyes and took a deep breath. She should get her robe and meet him outside to talk about what had almost happened yesterday. Ask him details of what Devon and he had discussed.

Her body had other ideas. The pleasurable heat of desire that had started in her stomach spread to the apex of her thighs, making her lose her train of thought.

She smiled and took her time to untie her clothes, and with each brush of her finger over her skin, the desire grew wild. It didn't feel like her fingers were the ones grazing her skin but his instead, rough with calluses and holding the promise of more.

She had memorized his touch long ago. Was it wrong to tease her mate when he didn't know he had no choice but to want her? To hell with that. Life wasn't fair. They had a history that had been stolen from him—from them. She needed to get him on board.

Nava pushed the garment off her body, and after a calming breath, she peered behind the waves of her dark hair and the gauzy fabric of the curtains. Across her terrace, the shadow of a large body loomed behind the banisters, two large wings spread wide.

His bright green eyes lit within the night. She couldn't help the coy smile that grew as she pushed her drawers down the curve of her backside, dropping them to the ground with an unceremonious thump.

She gasped when the inferno in her stomach bloomed. His desire pushed through the bond like wildfire, incinerating everything and leaving her breathless. If she focused enough on her memories, she could recall the scent of his skin. Pine, leather, and something that was solely him. Naked and burning for him, she closed her eyes, drunk from the arousal that devoured her. Nava brought her fingers between her breasts, past her stomach. Her moan would have been embarrassing if she'd been in her right mind.

She didn't want to miss a second of his reaction to her, focusing on his shape outside. The silver light of the night rimmed the silhouette of his body, marking the sharp contours of his muscular arms as he held himself stiffly to the banisters.

Her mouth tasted sweet with anticipation, her body drumming as heat pooled between her legs.

His wings beat, and in two powerful movements, he was up over his balcony and landing on the very edge of hers. Her heart skipped a beat, but she didn't cower or pick up her discarded clothes. Meeting his gaze, she moved one of her hands past her breasts and down her navel, her skin forming small goose bumps and reacting to her touch.

His chest heaved, and she could tell—could *feel*—his all-consuming need. He was burning for her and just holding himself back. Arkimedes was outside looking in, but here with her as well. She could almost feel the warmth of his body behind her as the weight of his hands pulled her to him. Her body hummed and the softness of her fingertips became rougher and more desperate over her stomach. She recalled how it felt to be his.

Nava had a very good imagination, and memories of the last time his hands had dipped into her soft warmth were still vivid in her mind. She took a shaky breath and massaged one of her breasts with her hand, bringing the other down to the place where she ached for him.

She gasped with the touch, and Arkimedes flinched outside, taking a step closer to the doors, his face becoming clear. His irises were no longer bright and green. Chills ran through her body; she expected he would barge in at any moment and take her. He might be even surprised that she would let him.

Arkimedes stopped, and his whole body went rigid as he held himself from taking a step farther. Nava's lips moved on their own into a slow, lazy smile, and she dipped her fingers inside herself.

Moaning, she leaned against the door, hoping Fael wasn't able to hear her but not caring enough to stop since she wanted her mate to be affected.

Her body melted with the movement of her fingers over her most sensitive spot. She recalled the memories of his lips trailing down her neck and her back. The weight of his hard body pressed against her backside as his fingers entered her in and out, and she forgot it wasn't really him doing it.

Soon she was crossing the edge, gasping for air as she came under her touch. She opened her eyes and met his gaze. It wasn't hard to see all the places where he was affected by her. His wings flexed in the air, and the wind moved outside. Nava grabbed one of the sheer curtains and pulled it closed, not blinking or looking away.

Standing still and giving him a full look at her naked body, she smiled before turning around and walking off to the washroom, putting an extra wave in her hips and sensing the weight of his eyes on her until she disappeared into the room next door.

CHAPTER TWENTY-THREE

NAVA

Three fae paraded into Nava's room the next morning, wearing light dresses made of billowy fabric that skimmed their lithe frames. Two carried the yellow monstrosity Marni had made for her, and Nava itched just at the sight of it. Their sapphire eyes fixed on her, dancing with mirth.

Nava sat by the fire; even though she was running hot, the fire produced no heat, and the sound of crackling wood somehow soothed her. With a thump, she closed the book Leela had snuck in for her earlier in the week and made her way toward the door, ignoring the fact that bees had been crawling over the walls of her bedroom ever since she'd woken yesterday morning and had doubled during the night.

It was worrisome, and she was trying to ignore it for now since she wasn't feeling threatened at the moment.

Fael peered in from the hall, his brows raising as he took in the gaudy garment. "I don't think I have ever seen anything as terrible as that." His white teeth made an appearance, showing a straight smile and crinkles to the side of his eyes. "Marni hates you even more than I thought possible."

The three fae wearing burnt-orange clothes, who Nava had at first assumed were servants of the castle, might indeed be the seamstress's minions, as their garments were not orange but different tones of red. They huffed a laugh as they crossed in front of Nava, eyeing her mockingly. She waited with a mask of indifference plastered on her face until they had left her room.

"What did you do?' Fael asked.

Nava brought her hand over her chest, her lips parting in offense. "Why do I have to be the one doing something? She is evil!"

Fael laughed, nodding. "True, but still . . . what did you do?"

"I threatened her, but that was after she pricked me multiple times—and she had already chosen the fabric by then."

"She pricked you?" His face fell as he straightened to his full six-feet-plus height. "The prince won't be pleased to learn this."

Oh, great, now she had to protect the evil seamstress's life from her soulmate's scorn. "Don't tell him, please. I don't want to burden him with something so silly. Plus I took care of it myself."

"You know I can't just keep the secret, right? I swore allegiance to the crown, and to him."

That was good to know. "Why him?"

Fael moved closer, his brows dipping as he checked his surroundings. "He is our future. If he is hell-bent on protecting you and your . . . fiancée, then so shall I." He paused, his deep gaze scanning the room before he eyed her as if it was the first time he had ever seen her. "He put a target on you the moment he placed you in this room." He added in a whisper, "I told him as much, but he is stubborn."

"Why are you telling me this?" She matched his tone, and his deep, gold eyes softened. "You were there, weren't you? The night he was taken from me?"

His lips tightened. "I can't speak about it, not now or ever. But it's not only the catty behavior you should be wary about. While the prince knows he must protect you, he is not aware of whom might try to hurt you and Mr. Black."

Except he did now. Fael wasn't aware that Arkimedes had learned what had happened to him.

"I will be careful."

"And I won't leave my post, under any circumstance. I made a vow to him. You can trust me, Nava."

She nodded, though she wasn't sure yet.

He held her eyes and reached to close the door. "I'm sorry about . . . all of it," he finished, and the door clicked behind him as he left the room.

Leela arrived at her room not long after, carrying a tray with food. She stopped dead in her tracks when she saw the gown hanging by her armoire.

"What is that?" She rushed to the end of the bed, putting the tray on the mattress as she stormed over to inspect the dress.

Nava stood by the tray of food, picking at the flaky pastry, lost in thoughts. When she came out of their home the night Arkimedes was taken, she'd seen several Dark Ones, hidden by the shade of the night and the darkness of their power. How many of the royal guards had seen her? How many knew this "Devon's fiancée" lie was just a charade to buy them time?

Had the guard who'd almost killed her also known she'd been with Arkimedes the night he'd been taken? Had Herous been aware she was the same woman who'd come outside in her nightgown and had tried, but failed, to save him?

The king knew. Did that mean he was counting down her days? Was he going to try to kill her tonight when the castle was especially loud and busy? Yesterday she had gotten a taste of freedom, but today she was forced to face her reality once again. She was seeing the light at the end of this drab mess. With Arkimedes believing her, she had gained something big.

The food, rich in butter and salt, was bland in comparison. She moved her jaw, forcing the bite down.

She didn't have time to wait for him to fall back in love with her, and dread tasted bitter because she knew the secret looming over her—their soulmate bond—needed to come out. But after seeing him so happy in this town, after yesterday . . . What if she ruined it all by coming clean?

She stuffed her mouth with a larger bite of bread to quiet some of the blooming anxiety.

"Is that your dress?" Leela asked.

"Yes," Nava said with a full mouth. Eating was one of her default coping mechanisms. Sleepwalking was how her anxiety presented itself. She had nowhere to go in this castle while locked in this room. "The minions also delivered a wooden box, but I haven't opened it yet. I'm afraid she sent me someone's hand or ear as a souvenir."

Leela's face paled. "Do you think she would do such a thing? That would be a war call!"

"It was a poor joke!" Nava rushed to say, shaking her head. "Please ignore me."

"Huh." Leela eyed the aforementioned object warily, and then her gaze met Nava's and softened. "Come, miss. Let's start getting you ready for the celebration tonight."

Nava wrapped her robe around her body and sauntered toward the dressing table, sitting the way she had for the past few days. Her skin was heated and flushed, her body sensitive and swollen, her mind not as sharp as it usually was.

"The party is not until later tonight. It's pretty early to get ready," she commented as Leela started brushing her hair with a musical hum.

"Solstice celebrations are for everyone to attend," she chirped with a grin. "Including us."

"I like that. Maybe that way, I won't be by myself." Nava smiled.

"I'm sure your fiancé will love keeping you company . . ." Leela hesitated. "Even while wearing that dress."

A surprised laugh escaped Nava's lips. "Please don't hold back how you hate my dress, it won't make me more self-conscious or anything."

"Sorry." The fae's hands stopped all movements in Nava's hair, and she looked sheepish. "I noticed the tension between you and your fiancé yesterday. There is history there, though maybe not romantic?"

"Not romantic."

"What about the prince? I know it has been all in good fun, me teasing you about him. But that night when you first arrived, when you two were speaking in the hall . . . it just seemed like there was more." Leela hesitated, sliding her fingers over Nava's hair, her gentle hands resting on her shoulders. "Do you feel more for him than for your fiancé? The way he looked at you yesterday was different. I have never seen him look at anyone that way."

Nava met Leela's eyes through the reflection.

"I knew it! I'm fantastic at reading. If the gods had given magic to my family line, I bet I could have been a soothsayer."

It didn't escape Nava that Leela had always known Arkimedes was important to her. That they were more when nothing had pointed to that, other than him placing her in the room next to his.

A small voice inside her head, one that sounded an awful lot like her mother, told her she was being too trusting of this girl she had just met. It was hard not to let herself be at ease with the fae, not when her eyes were so round like a doe's or her smile so genuine.

Perhaps Nava was starving for female friendships. To meet a girl who, unlike Violet, wasn't trying to insult her at every corner. Someone who didn't think bonding came over the aftermath of war or a very painful training session. A friend like Simone.

"Has he spoken with you about what he might feel?" Leela continued, undeterred by Nava's silence.

"No. Not at all. We are just friends."

Though friends didn't strip naked and proceeded to intimately touch themselves to give the other one something to dream about. But those were semantics.

The faerie pouted but let the subject drop as she worked in silence over the intricate hairstyle.

Had Arkimedes taken care of his needs while thinking of her the night before? Nava couldn't believe she had been that bold, and her cheeks heated at the memory.

"Please say nothing about Devon and me outside these walls, Leela," Nava blurted, wishing she had been better at keeping her feelings under layers of self-preservation.

"Of course not." Her brows knitted together as she took in the monstrosity Marni had made for her. "This won't do. That hateful wench did this on purpose to shame you in front of everyone."

"That much is clear to me." Nava sighed, rubbing the bruised skin on her thigh where the seamstress had pricked her multiple times. "All the other dresses she had hanging in her shop for the occasion were beautiful."

The loud canary-yellow tulle mocked her from where it hung. The voluminous sleeves made of gaudy sheer fabric and that orange sash in the middle of the dress worsened the already appalling silhouette.

"I will take your measurements. I can't bring you to Renna's shop or the king will have my head. But if I rush there, maybe she has something on the rack that you can use for tonight. Our prince won't be able to look away from you."

Nava laughed again, shaking her head. "I'm pretty sure he won't be able to look away if I wore that horrible thing. No one will."

"Oh, yes, but for different reasons." Leela walked toward the dress and pulled at the fabric, scrunching her nose.

"Wouldn't it get you in trouble?" Nava asked. "My pride can handle this dress tonight. Maybe I'll even make it work for me somehow. I'd rather do that than have you catch the scorn of King Oberon." If only she had learned to sew. Laurie had tried to teach her multiple times but to no avail. Nava had refused.

Leela reconsidered, her skin glistening as perspiration cropped up on her powdery skin. "I might get in trouble." The fae's forehead scrunched. "But maybe we don't have to get you a new dress. Perhaps we just have to alter this terrible thing. It will drive me mad to not do something about it. I despise Marni."

"There is nothing that would make it worse," Nava agreed. "Maybe we can take the sleeves and high neck off."

"And the sash has to go as well." Leela peered inside the garment, and her frown deepened. "Honestly, miss, I doubt this will even hold through the night. It's not properly sewn."

The evil seamstress had had less than a day to sew the whole dress. The lack of proper technique did not surprise Nava. However, maybe she had intended for it to fall apart and ridicule Nava mid-dance. The ballgown had been the least of her concerns earlier when Marni's helpers delivered it. Something had entranced her into the horrors of the way her body was awakening. Not even Fael's words were registering.

The heat taking over her senses, her increased libido, and her mind being stuck in passionate memories and their almost-kiss from a couple of nights ago—none of it was helping matters.

Bringing her hand over her fast-beating heart and her soulmate mark, she took a sharp breath. Nava needed to get herself together. It wouldn't matter if she was wearing a potato sack, if she could not keep it on once she got a good look at her mate tonight. "Do you know anything about the solstice and how it might affect . . . people?"

"Do you mean magic-wielding humans?"

"Sure, anyone really."

"Well, it affects all of us fae much like a full moon affects lycans. We gather to celebrate the longer days, for healthier crops, which means a healthier kingdom." Leela rubbed at the yellow dress, not paying attention to Nava's fidgeting.

"I wonder, if I say I'm sick, would that work for me not to have to go to the celebration?"

"They will send the healers, and they will know if you are in fact ill," Leela warned. "Are you feeling unwell?"

"No. Maybe?" Nava pulled the belt on her robe, deviating her gaze elsewhere. "The healers weren't nice when they tended to me last time. What's with the people of this kingdom hating humans?"

"We're split in between the ones who dislike humans, especially after the queen—" Leela cleared her throat and wandered around the room. But Nava could fill in the blanks now.

The queen had stolen their heir away. A precious prince who wasn't easy to replace, not if what Arkimedes had told her about the royals having difficulty making babies was true.

"But these last ten years, the hate has grown like a rotten thing. The king used to trade with your kind. We used to get delicious chocolate from the Gold Kingdom." Her expression turned dreamy. "And traveling musicians from the Pearl Islands used to tour our land."

Nava's heart shrank at hearing about the islands, where Cameron, Gavin, and Violet were, searching for knowledge about how to battle the Iron Crown and the Society of Crows. Trying to find ancient laws set eons ago that would protect magic-wielders over the crown's army drafting and coupling laws.

It was Gavin's and Violet's hope that there had been a law signed by all kingdoms at some point that protected things like soulmate bonds or families' rights. It was a long shot but worth researching.

"I saw a lot of humans in town yesterday."

"Oh, yes, our locals have always been here. However, they've grown more resentful over getting pushed to the edges of the city. Most of the homes near the castle are fae homes," Leela continued.

"That's horrible, the king shouldn't have so much hate toward his own people."

"I don't believe he does. Not truly." Leela's gaze searched the room. Nava remembered the first day Leela had come to keep her company. How the room had reacted when she'd spoken ill of the queen. Nava wondered if she was waiting for a similar reaction. "He made a human his queen, after all," Leela added after a moment of silence, taking Nava out of her musings. "It's said he loved her, making the betrayal even more heartbreaking."

Nava wasn't sure the king could love anyone or anything. Not if he'd kidnapped his son, erased his memories, and forced him to stay here against his will. "Why are they so sure she betrayed him?" Nava asked.

Leela pressed her lips together, shrugging one slim shoulder. "The king says so, and it must be true since he defended her for years."

If her instinct was correct—and it usually was when it came to her mate—she was sure Arkimedes didn't agree with the sentiment. Something was off, and he was determined to find it.

"I will fetch some needle and thread to fix this monstrosity before the ball. I'm not amazing with sewing, but I know a little, miss. I can help you if you allow me to do so."

"Have at it, Leela. You will make it one hundred times better."

If what Devon and now Leela had told her was true, the way magic worked with soulmates during the solstice would make her irrational when it came to being intimate with her mate. She needed to stay away from Arkimedes B. Valeron, and maybe this dress would help her with that.

CHAPTER TWENTY-FOUR

NAVA

Nava caressed the top of the box, her fingers slipping over the red polished wood. The emblem of Marni's boutique was etched on top with gold foil accents. She undid the clasp, and soon her eyes encountered a feathered, canary-yellow mask to go with her dress. "Does the king allow himself to partake in the ball?"

"Yes, the whole court will be present. He always has his hands full with his ladies . . ." Leela lowered her gaze back to the gown. *Riiiip.* She pulled away one sleeve of Nava's dress with a grin. "I have a good feeling about this, miss. She built it so poorly, I'm able to remove these layers with almost no issue."

"That makes me feel better." Nava grabbed the sash, using the small scissors Leela had provided to cut some of the thread that attached it to the dress. Once the sash was off, it revealed a nice, narrow bodice.

Leela walked to the closet, opening the doors and examining the gowns hanging in there.

Nava stared, curious. "If you are looking for a new yellow or gold gown to magically show up there, I hate to break it to you but I already checked, multiple times."

The redhead laughed, shaking her head. "Oh, no, I want to borrow some pieces from some of the gowns you have already worn."

"Are you looking for something specific?"

"A sash . . . some tulle, anything really." Leela's delicate brows met in the middle. Her lips pursed as she moved the gowns around. "I don't remember them being so dark before."

"Dark?"

"Yes, weren't they all light blue?"

That piqued Nava's curiosity. She strolled to the closet, eyeing the colors of her dresses. Leela was right—they were still blue, but much darker. Some indigo, others navy. "I swear I haven't done anything."

"Of course not. The room is charmed to tend to your needs," her friend said, and it sounded like a practiced speech. Something she repeated often, likely to other guests of the castle. "I have never seen it change dress shades before, but it must go with your mood or something." She shrugged and picked a gown from the bunch.

"Callisto mentioned it, and I forgot to ask her . . . Is it a room thing or is the castle somehow magical?"

"The king's magic feeds the castle—and our kingdom in a way I don't claim to understand, but it's what we're told."

Nava looked around the room, to the ceilings and floors, feeling watched as her spine prickled with awareness. "Can he hear us?" she whispered.

"He shouldn't—"

"Shouldn't and couldn't are not the same."

"He has spies everywhere." Leela's words became almost silent, but she smiled after the room had grown too cold. "His power used to have more of a reach decades ago. I'm sure he has better things to do than spy on you."

Think again, Leela. He was her enemy.

They worked through the morning and into the afternoon. By the time Leela made her way out of Nava's room, the dress looked less like an overly decorated cake. They had picked apart one or two of the other gowns, taking a bit of embroidery from an underlay skirt here, some soft white tulle there.

It was not a masterpiece by any stretch of the imagination, but just the fact that Marni would be upset about them altering her gown had Nava smiling.

Her dress didn't look like two women had pulled it apart at the last minute this morning, and even though it wasn't the most beautiful gown she'd seen, it was pretty enough.

"I will try to bring you a mask to the ball to replace the one Marni gave you. But it gets very busy, I might not be able to find you," she vowed before leaving

Fael peeked through the door, his brows lifting as he met their creation and whistled. "Now that's what I call a full transformation."

"Aren't you going to get changed?" Nava asked when it was just the two of them left. His black aura was a soft, billowy mist, barely perceptible and nothing compared to the royals.

"No, I can't leave the post unattended."

Guilt boiled in her stomach. "That won't do. Maybe I can come with you so you can get changed. I mean, I won't come to see you get changed, of course. What I mean is I can be close by."

Fael's laughter rolled over the room. "Miss Nava. Have you seen how the prince can kill by lifting his hand? It takes the royals just half a minute to break one's soul apart." The guard cleared his throat and shook his head with a tentative smile. "I won't change to anything else than my armor. It lends me better opportunities while I'm there either way."

Nava swallowed, standing on shaky legs. She didn't want to give away the fact that to her, Arkimedes wasn't scary. He was home. "I guess people do like a man in armor."

"It's my preferred outfit for any occasion, and unlike the rest of the crew, we aren't forced to wear white."

She grinned. "I bet you get lots of attention."

"Oh, you have no idea."

Rich red runners flowed down wide spiral stairs, leading to a music-filled room. Crisscrossed columns lined the ceilings, reminding her of the waffles Laurie used to make for breakfast. Her stomach churned, and Nava wasn't sure if it was from nerves or hunger.

The room was vast, with decorated columns and polished marble floors where couples wearing gold, yellow, and white swirled around the dance floor. She found a band in the corner, playing unusual instruments.

Fael walked next to her as they came into the crowd. Laughter filled the air, and Nava met the curious gaze of a mask-wearing fae who snickered at the dress. She would have cared in a normal situation, but the heat soaring through her made it hard to give a crap about the disastrous puffy yellow nightmare she wore.

"How are we going to find Leela?" Nava turned to Fael, who stood a good head and a half taller than her, towering over most people.

He dropped his gaze; golden eyes shone behind a black mask. He lifted a bushy brow. "With that dress, it's more likely she will find you."

Nava lifted onto her tiptoes, trying to find her friend among the crowd. However, her eyes deviated away from their original task, hunting for someone else instead. "Is it too naïve of me to expect that Ar—er, I mean, His Royal Highness to join me at any point tonight?" she asked, wringing her hands together, avoiding the man's knowing look. "I mean, I know he is going to be busy, and I don't expect for him to come to talk to me alone, but since Devon and I are his guests, I hoped . . . You know what? I don't care."

And she shouldn't care! Nava had spent a good portion of the day planning how to *avoid* him. She did want to tell him her life might be in danger, just in case the king decided to attack her tonight when there would be so many people he could put the blame on.

So her mind had settled on having a quick chat with her mate. It would be an in-and-out sort of conversation. *"My life is in danger. Keep an eye on me, but stay away from me. I love you."*

Nava wouldn't utter the last three words, but she would say the rest and then quickly disappear. She would not say they were soulmates when they were both in some sort of lust frenzy.

"I'm sure he will extract himself from duty to be with you at some point." Fael's chin pointed to a spot in the room she had somehow missed. A long table rested above the crowd. It was made of carved wood and painted in rich ebony tones that masked the dangerous aura of the two men sitting behind it.

A banquet of delicious-looking fruit lay in front. The royals wore stark white outfits with gold emblems and decorations. Nava focused on Arkimedes, drinking how handsome he looked. The coat he wore hugged his shoulders, and a golden mask covered the top half of his face, made to mimic his features.

"I just hope that when he does, he finds a moment when no one will miss him," Fael said, bringing her out of her thoughts.

"I need to tell him something quick, and then I will be away." Would he recognize her if he saw her?

Nava swallowed, feeling her body buzz with need. He shouldn't be there, chatting with random women, eating and drinking, instead of here, with her. A distinct sensation boiled within her, one she had not felt in a while. Jealousy.

He wouldn't feel attraction to anyone—she knew this from experience. It didn't mean the king wasn't pushing his own agenda.

It took her a moment to notice that all the women sitting at the royal table had black auras in various shades of intensity. Not as opaque as the king's, and without the creepy appearance of random body parts, very similar to Fael's.

The king's women possessed the Dark One's power. Nava felt her lips part as she took all of them in. Varying in different shapes and skin colors, the cohorts were undoubtedly fae, judging by their pointy ears and the wings behind their backs.

"They all have auras," Nava said, wandering closer to take a better look. "I thought all fae who possess the power were part of the guard?"

"They were once part of us," Fael agreed.

"He forced them to be with him? He took advantage . . . ?" Nava's face warmed. The women didn't appear unhappy where they sat, talking and laughing. They looked at complete ease, unlike the rigid set of Arkimedes's shoulders.

"He didn't force them. They volunteered to give the kingdom a chance for an heir, as we thought our prince was dead." Fael's stern gaze traveled down from the table and met Nava's. "I must admit, some of their choices surprised me . . ." His words trailed as his brows met in the middle. Sadness lit behind his dark lashes, morphing his features and dulling his bright skin.

"I see. Why them when there is a kingdom full of people?"

"It's not for me to tell." Fael put the helmet onto his head and placed a hand on her back, but the sensation his touch gave her was all wrong.

The fire in her veins demanded to be touched, but not by him. Nava stepped away from the guard's hand. She focused back on the royals' table, meeting Arkimedes's gaze from across the room.

Her throat bobbed as he leaned forward, holding the weight of his body on his arms over the table. From this far, she couldn't see the play of muscles in his arms, though her vivid, heated mind could provide her plenty of details.

Frozen in her spot, pinned under his gaze, she was too close and not close enough at the same time. His bright green eyes were brighter than all the other fairies next to him.

"Fiancée, you decided to show up." Devon sauntered into her line of sight, his voice like a drop of ice melting over burning skin.

"I preferred when you called me kitten," she said. It was the first time she'd seen Devon in such bright colors, and he looked almost as white as a ghost under such shades. His hair was slicked back, and the dark circles under his eyes made the pupilless orbs pop.

"I much prefer this new one," he said, stopping next to her with a bored stance. His gaze drifted toward Fael. "Guard."

The fae grunted. "I will get something to drink but will be close. Do not step away from here without me."

It was then that she noticed the glass of red liquid in Devon's hand. "Where are your guards?" she asked.

"I lost them a while ago. Fae get rowdy with the wine," he said with a side smirk. "You, however, don't need such a thing to be in trouble, do you?"

She swallowed, and her eyes shifted toward the table where Arkimedes sat, his eyes burning through the crowd, fixed on them with the intensity of the seven suns. "Is—is there anything wrong with the wine, or do they just drink too much?"

"Everyone knows the fae spike their wine during a celebration such as this to liberate themselves. They like the lack of repercussions or censorship." Devon swirled the liquid again, which spilled down his ivory skin and onto the floor. He dumped half of the contents when no one was watching.

Nava lifted a brow. "What are you doing?"

He took a step forward and lowered his face to her ear. "The guards gave me this wine to drink, no doubt with some wicked intent." One of his hands grasped her lower back, and his lips caressed the shell of her ear.

"You are going to get it all over your white clothes," Nava said, taking a healthy step away from him. She didn't need her dress to become more of a horror show.

"Does it look like I care?" Devon paused and shortened their distance again. They were far enough from the dance floor and other people that most wouldn't be able to hear them. "Neither of you can stay here." He grabbed her arm, something he hadn't done before. Things had changed between them in a matter of days.

She tried to pull away, but his hand held her still. "Let go of me," she said between her teeth.

"Calm down," he whispered. "We don't want to call attention now."

Nava blinked and pulled her head back, meeting Devon's calculating gaze. "Do not touch me again."

He smirked but dropped his hand from her body. "Tell me, have you told my brother that you are soulmates? Does he know why he is burning for you right now? Why he wants to tear away every inch of that dress from your body? And to hell with the consequences."

Nava's cheeks burned hotter than before, and she wouldn't have been surprised if she combusted at any moment. She cleared her throat before speaking, but her insides fluttered with need.

She gazed at her mate from across the room, and her throat became drier than a desert. "If it's such a big deal, why didn't you?"

"I have been busy translating a book for him and assuring him we aren't engaged." He looked around before focusing on her again. "I also thought it was none of my business."

The pit in her stomach grew, weighing a ton. She couldn't tell Devon that she was afraid Arkimedes would reject her. That she was giving him time to fall back in love with her, which was a stupid plan, but it was better than kidnapping, which had been her other idea.

Nava had to be cautious about how much she shared with her mate, and how fast, especially since he'd been so distrusting of her. She didn't want to lose him.

Well, maybe she'd tell him today.

"I'm afraid we are in danger tonight at this party," she admitted. "What if the king plans to get rid of us? It's such a busy night . . . Arkimedes might be distracted to notice us gone."

"He won't be distracted from you tonight."

Her cheeks burned. "Well, still, I thought I would stay away after I told him my concerns."

Devon pondered her words. "Yes, it's a possibility. Why do you want to stay away again?"

"Be-because of consent? I don't think it's a good idea for me to be near him. We aren't in our right minds right now, and it seems wrong to take advantage of him—" Why in the hell she was opening up to this man, she didn't know. Nava must be more distressed than she'd thought.

His laughter shook her out of her panicked thoughts. "Take advantage? You won't be able to avoid him."

Nava's mouth opened and closed a few times before the words bubbled out. "How could you possibly know that?"

"I was not locked away in a non-magical island for a decade like you. I have seen things. Read many other things . . ." Devon lowered his voice. "You have your head on your shoulders now, but at some point, you won't care whatever noble reasonings you've told yourself, and neither will he."

In other words, he would look for her—and she would do the same. She had to get him out of here, and they had to go somewhere away from prying eyes.

Devon's eyes traveled over her shoulder, and his brows dipped. "He doesn't like me being this close to you, but he is not moving away from that damn table."

"It's better not to call for the king's attention," Nava reasoned and was proud of her own self-restraint not to look around.

"Let's dance."

"Um, no thanks."

"Look, I want it as much as you do, believe me. You have to get out of here, and I might be able to go back to my room if I'm leaving with the two of you." Devon scratched his chin with a long pale finger.

Nava shifted the weight of her feet, wanting to squirm out of this dress. The uncomfortable throbbing between her legs grew ever so present. She clenched her thighs together to relieve some of the pressure, to no avail.

Maybe she didn't care if everyone here saw Arkimedes devour her. It might make them understand he was hers, and nothing the king could do would separate them.

Oh, no.

"Good, now she gets it. Let's dance." He offered her his hand, and her stomach dropped as she took it. A year ago, she would have scoffed in horror if someone had told her she'd dance with her arch-nemesis. The one who now had become an ally of sorts.

The ground became soft the farther onto the dance floor they went. Nava looked down, finding stained white coats and shimmery golden fabrics. She watched as the fae and humans shed their clothing. The dance floor was packed, winged people moved alongside wingless partners.

Some wore more clothes than others. She had never seen anything like it. Devon led her forward to the center of the room. Nava wasn't sure she wanted to be so close to all these soon-to-be naked people.

She wrinkled her nose when the Crow turned to face her, lifting his brow.

"Don't tell me you are a prude."

"I'm not!" Nava glanced around her as the strangers of this kingdom writhed against one another in a seductive dance that looked too intimate. She took in the crowd and was astonished by how quickly the party was developing into some sort of orgy. What was going on here?

Devon held her too close for her liking, and her skin prickled with the sensation of being followed. "Don't step on my feet."

"Oops." She smiled when the tip of her heel met his soft boot. "Have you come up with a way to get him out of here? Because, other than giving him time . . . I haven't."

"He is not leaving this place, not until he unravels whatever he's trying to find from his past," Devon whispered. "Unless you break the spell he is under and he somehow evolves to the man you met last year. Which is not the Arkimedes of a decade ago."

She wiggled in her spot, feeling like ants crawled over her skin, the sensation making her lose her footing on the dance floor. "How do I break the spell? I thought the one casting it formed a counter-spell. I doubt the king will offer me the solution."

"You've got that right."

"Well, then what? Is there a way to gain back memories that were taken?" Devon nodded, and her heart stumbled on a beat. "Like-like all memories, even the ones that were taken from me?" Her voice sounded too small.

His face softened. "Cat."

"What?"

"Yours are gone."

She shouldn't have asked. Nava didn't have the luxury of falling apart in the middle of the ball. Her eyes blurred, and she deviated her gaze, focusing on anything but Devon, not wanting to see an expression that mocked her—or, even worse, pitied her.

Devon gave her a moment to collect herself, and she allowed the beautiful music to carry her sorrow, wishing she had her brother close, to get lost in one of his famous bear hugs and find solace that at least she still had him.

"So that's it then?" Devon's words had her mind sharpening back to this reality. "You have been gaining his trust, hoping he'd choose to leave with you in just a couple of weeks?"

She scowled. "Do you have a better plan? I'm open to even your suggestions."

"We can poison his mind to have him kill the king and then take over the kingdom. My debt will be paid, I will be free, and this mess will be your problem."

"You know what? I changed my mind. Your plan sucks." She huffed. "And so we are clear, you will not be free after this." She had to take this man back with her to the Northern Village in the Grey Island or Roman would never allow her back.

His smirk grew to one side. "Watch and learn, cat."

"Nava is a bee, brother. Not a cat." Arkimedes's voice came out dangerously low.

She jumped in her spot, and Devon's hands loosened from her body, dropping to his sides as if he knew he shouldn't push his luck. Her skin raised into goose bumps as she turned to face Ark. This close, he towered over her, standing every inch the prince he'd turned out to be.

His aura flickered, letting her know he was not amused. His temper was not controlled, which in return made his magic act out. It was the only time she was able to see it. "I will steal your dance partner now." It wasn't even a question.

"I'm sure I get a say in the matter," she grunted. However, there was a secret part of her that rejoiced at this alpha display.

Arkimedes took a deep breath, his eyes shining with a heavy dose of amusement. "Can I have this dance?" But his hand was already grabbing for hers before he even heard her answer, pulling her toward him as his wings tucked behind his back. The fairy lights bounced on his feathers, bringing out the blue iridescence shades.

She stumbled forward, steadying herself against his chest. His heartbeat drummed under her fingers, erratic beats that told her his adrenaline was pumping hard. From this close, Nava took in the woven patterns of his coat.

Someone had made it, with beautiful embroidered shapes of feathers and tree branches that held no leaves, like the insignia of this house.

"I will leave then." Devon bowed and met her gaze from the side as his lips formed the words *"Get out of here."*

Arkimedes's eyes bore into her, as if reaching for her soul. His other hand grabbed her lower back, bringing her closer to him. Her body quivered when his fingers trailed up, reaching the bare skin of her back.

She breathed as a spark traveled through her with his touch, and for a moment, it was only the two of them. Even though everyone could tell who he was by the shining crown of thorns that lay over his styled head of hair, he was still wearing a mask.

"What would your kingdom say, seeing you dancing with a human? Isn't that scandalous?"

He lifted a brow. "I would like to see them come and tell me to not do it."

Oh, he was long gone. She had a six-foot-three problem on her hands. Literally.

She didn't want anyone to interrupt them, aware of what was going on between them after her talk with Devon. Nava needed to get out of here, fast, if the tremble of her knees and the throbbing in her center was anything to go by. "I'd rather avoid anything that would upset your father if possible. I don't need him getting any ideas to make me disappear."

"No one is making you disappear," he breathed, and his fingers dug into the skin of her back as he lowered his head to her ear. "I'm afraid my head is not in its right place, especially after last night."

"What happened last night?" she asked in a thin voice, remembering the way she had touched herself when she'd known he was watching.

"You tell me." His lips touched her ear, then moved to her neck, breathing her in.

Oh, god. It was too much. Nava was going to ignite into flames on the spot if he continued on.

"It seemed like you were tempting me to come to you and finish what you'd started."

"I was."

"I'm here now." His tongue slipped over her neck, and her toes curled in her shoes at the sensation that spread through her.

She had to battle to keep the moan inside her mouth, but her eyes rolled back when his teeth nipped at her skin and his wide hands brought her closer to his body. Nava's dress was too tight over her skin.

What if his father was watching them now? It would be hard to explain why Arkimedes was kissing her neck at the moment.

Devon's plan to get too close to her to get a rise out of her mate had worked. Now she had to do her job to get them out of here somehow, away from prying eyes. Maybe gather some courage and confess.

She lifted her gaze toward the table. An ebony-skinned concubine sat on the king's lap, caressing his face as her curves and narrow wings hid most of him from view. They were kissing, and the image was too intimate to linger on.

Alertness descended over her fogged mind. "We should try to not call for attention." She pushed away from him, but desire burned hotter within her as she touched him, grasping the lapels of his coat.

Why should I care? Everyone else seems to be doing it.

"No one cares." His lips traced the side of her cheek, so close to her lips that her body shook with anticipation. But she cared; they weren't a cheap one-night stand. If there was something she'd learned last year, it was that destiny didn't mess around. If soulmates became this heated and uncontrolled during the solstice night, it meant something.

She was scared—maybe a bit paranoid. But she didn't want to regret whatever happened here. "Did you drink some of the wine? I heard it clouds your judgment."

He pulled back a few inches, meeting her gaze, and for the first time, his expression cleared. His gloved finger caressed the side of her jaw, where his lips had just been. "Everyone knows not to drink the wine at these parties."

Nava had his attention; it was go time. "It's hot in here . . . I need some air." No one paid any attention to them.

"Right now?" He glanced around, appearing more lucid. "It is getting a bit . . . intense here."

"Let's leave," she whispered. "Maybe you can show me parts of the garden I haven't been allowed to see. I would love to be close to nature, but maybe somewhere where there aren't any creepy flowers?"

Arkimedes's grin slowly spread, and he nodded, stepping away from her. "There is a place I would like to show you." His hand still held hers as he pulled her through the sea of people on the dance floor, toward the large doors that led them to one of the many halls of the castle.

She caught Devon's eyes on their way out. He was leaning against a far wall and nodded as they walked past. Straightening in his place, he walked behind them.

Last Nava saw him, he was going up the wide staircase Fael and she had descended. She assumed he was returning to his room, but one never knew with Devon Black. She was too far gone to care.

CHAPTER TWENTY-FIVE

NAVA

The sky had turned into marbled shades of apricot and purple by the time they made it out of the castle. Fae filled the wide corridors, dressed in elegant attire. So caught up in their conversations, drinking and laughing, they missed even their prince imposing shape.

Arkimedes and Nava soon walked out to the garden, and when his hand grasped hers, she had almost forgotten this man walking next to her was not *her* Arkimedes. His burning touch was disorienting. She would have to focus on ice buckets or festering wounds. Anything to bring herself to a more level head.

"Not many people come to this part of the garden anymore," he said after they had walked in silence for a while.

Twisty trees with thick green foliage lined each side of the path with manicured symmetry. Her feet clicked over brick terracotta stone, still warm from the afternoon sun, and lightning bugs flew low to the ground, adding to the festive ambiance.

Her heart soared at the sight of it; it was magical being here on the castle grounds, surrounded by masked people in beautiful dresses. When she was young and prisoner to her mother's strict rules, she had always daydreamed about attending one of these.

If she closed her eyes and forgot everything, Nava could almost fool herself into believing this was a normal courtship. That they had met at this age, not when she'd been a teenager. That their meeting and bond wouldn't have sent her mother into a frenzy that had taken her entire family to a different continent.

Maybe Arkimedes would come and get her for the ball, and they would spend time kissing and hiding from prying eyes before a deeper engagement was announced. Maybe if she saw the positives of this terrible situation, she could enjoy falling for each other again.

Her eyes prickled as she focused on their intertwined fingers. A puzzle piece made by an expert, they fit just right, like their souls. Where she was weak, he was strong. Where he lacked confidence in himself, she had it for the both of them.

The string instruments played a beautiful ballad even here, and the percussion of the drums hammered along with her heart. She wondered if the king had a poor band hidden somewhere but didn't care to try to find them in the darkness.

The path continued as they went under an arched gazebo that held white wisteria, hanging low enough to graze her shoulders, and soon people became less of a common sight; the few they crossed here were busy doing other things.

Cedar box hedges lined the perimeter, growing alongside flowers that vined over them. The grass grew wild and uneven, and flowers of all colors rose within the grooves of the rickety brick pathway. The beauty of this area in its wild state took her breath away.

They went under a tall arbor that could have been made of metal or wood, but she couldn't tell with the platinum light of the moon. There, in front of them, was one of the most breathtaking images she had seen. A large pond with turquoise water, no doubt illuminated by magic.

Waterlilies floated above, and in the center, an island held a massive tree that stood twenty feet tall with a wide, knotty trunk. Its texture shimmered in silver tones, and its branches mimicked roots, twisting up in the air.

The sight left her speechless. She had seen this before—no, not this, but one that was made to look the same. Except that one had radiated death and suffering. This was beautiful and full of magic.

"My father brought me here a few weeks after I got to the Copper City."

"How did he find you the first time?"

"I was asking questions, which called the guards' attention." He laughed, shaking his head. "They didn't like that a Crow was nosing around town. Fael found me wandering around. Plus my aura gave me away." He turned to face her and looked at ease while speaking with her. Not guarded. He looked like her Arkimedes, not Orion.

Her heart ached at the sight. "Did they bring you to see His Majesty?"

"Oh, yes. I mean, they had no grounds to arrest me but made it clear it wouldn't go well for me if I resisted the invitation."

"Little did they know," she said with a shaky smile. "I mean, you look like a copy of your father. Same nose and eye shape. Even the lips are the same."

"When you aren't looking for it, it's hard to see it. Especially because my father doesn't like people looking straight at him."

Nava did remember Fael's warning the day she'd arrived at the castle. "Right."

"I'm not sure if those memories are from this time around or the previous time I was here when in my twenties." Arkimedes brought his hand over his head, frowning at the tree. "He wanted to show me my mother's tree. He claimed the future queen will bring it back to life . . ."

Nava didn't want to face him with those words. Oh, no, those were too scary for her to dwell on. Before tonight, Nava had never *truly* considered the fact that he might want to stay, if not for Devon telling her Ark wouldn't leave until he accomplished whatever he was looking for.

Even then, she wouldn't have believed it if she hadn't seen the way his face had shone when exploring the city yesterday.

She'd been dreading that he might not want her if he learned who she was. Now she had gained that trust back, and he was within arm's reach. What would she do if he didn't want to leave with her? Would she feel fine bringing Cameron to this place? Away from the safety net of town?

Even if the king accepted that they were mates and wouldn't just make her go away, would Cameron, Laurie, and Nava be safe in a city that hated humans? So close to the Society of Crows.

Arkimedes's crown glistened under the moonlight, his feathers swaying behind him with the light breeze as they got closer to the tree. She needed a new plan, that much was clear. After the solstice, she would tell him about their bond. Then they could decide what to do together. Any other option was too heartbreaking to consider, and her mind wasn't in the right place at the moment.

She reached the stone banister that separated the pond from the land, and her stomach fluttered when he got closer and the warmth of his body seeped through the fabric of her dress. She turned to face the tree once again. It was clear this was the muse for the kingdom's emblem. And for the queen's killer.

A giant dead-looking tree in the middle of a wonderful garden. So tragically similar to the one in the forest.

"So, this is the queen's tree . . . ?"

Arkimedes nodded, and his brows pulled together as he took it in. "When we were together, did I tell you how I grew up?"

"You told me they dropped you into an orphanage when you were a one-year-old boy."

His throat bobbed. "She was killed after she dropped me—though the literature claims she killed herself."

"How could she have? Didn't they find her tied to that tree?"

"Exactly the questions I have been asking," he said in a low voice before turning to face her. "But she was a magic wielder, and that is their response to all of it. They have erased from all records that her body was there."

"Why?"

"The king said it was to prevent the kingdom from appearing weak. If we couldn't protect our queen, who's to say we could protect our people from harm?"

"Well, that's manipulating true events, it's a lie." Nava huffed. "I hate lies."

Guilt bubbled in her gut. Was she doing the same? No, she wasn't lying, per se. She was . . . momentarily holding the truth.

"Someone attacked her multiple times, once while pregnant. The books don't go into details, but most of the records are still there." His lips tightened.

Nava's heart sank with each of his words. A memory of what she'd heard that day in the library flashed through her mind. "Is the prophecy you are looking for related to this somehow?"

"Your guess is as good as mine." He leaned over the rails, looking at the tree with longing. "It's strange to feel this need to find answers when I didn't know her. But it's a question I have asked myself all my life. Why didn't they want me?"

Nava's heart squeezed in her chest, and she reached for his hand, hoping he wouldn't shut off at the touch. Instead, he wrapped his fingers around hers, his skin feverish. "Turns out, they wanted you very much, but your mother taking you doesn't appear to be the move of someone who doesn't want her baby. It's like she was trying to protect you."

"Right." He nodded. "But from whom?"

"Well, the king kidnapped you and took your memories away. My vote is on him."

"My father wouldn't hurt me. Why go through all the trouble of bringing me here if that were the case?" He had a point. "There is also a book I found that mentions a child born sick, being dropped in the world of mist and shadows."

Her skin became cold as dread spread over every inch of her body. "You think that was supposed to be you?"

"What if that's why my mother did it? What if they believe I was sick somehow, and she abandoned me in that orphanage to prevent my father's people from—killing me?"

"Could the book be referring to her dropping you in the orphanage?"

"I guess it could be. The book was burned in a fire. The dates aren't clear, but its scripture is written in an old language, and it appears to be older than me."

She remembered Devon speaking about helping Ark with a translation. This had to be it. "Too many fires in this castle are linked to you and your mother. If you add the Zorren to the equation, it seems like too many to be a coincidence." She dragged her finger over the stone of the banister before meeting his shocked gaze.

"I had not considered the demons."

"You just found out about them. Well, actually, you have known about them for a long time, but you don't remember, thanks to your dear father." Nava wanted to be there for him and help him with whatever he was going through. Just like he had helped her last year, when she had been the one searching for answers about her nature. She'd gone from hating and fearing magic to embracing it.

She changed from being a scared, closed-minded person to— Her thoughts stopped. Was that what she was now? Scared of something different, of a new world she didn't understand? No, surely not.

No one could blame her for her reservations about this place.

"Do you think the prophecy holds the information about why she took you away?"

"I'm certain about it. Like you said, too many coincidences." His body was so rigid, she almost could see his aura become solid around his body, his magic taking over.

Nava dragged her hand over his arm in a soothing motion. "Have you gotten a clue of who might be behind it? Multiple people?" She hesitated. "The king?"

Arkimedes shook his head. "Whatever feelings he has harvested since her death weren't there when she was alive. The root of it all began with heartbreak. He loved her, and he believes she betrayed him."

"By taking you away?"

"I believe she did it to protect me. Maybe that's a part of that idealistic self he likes to tell me I inherited from her."

Nava tightened her hold around his forearm, winded by the wave of sorrow that pushed through the bond. She took a shallow breath. "If she was being targeted while living here, he betrayed her before she took you away.

He didn't protect her from whoever killed her and then hid the truth from the people."

They stared at the tree. Even this far from the party, the music drifted in the air, reminding her why she'd run away from the crowds. Even though she wanted to keep learning what he had been up to when away from her, something else boiled beneath her skin. A primal need to be closer to him.

"The tree has been dead for twenty years," he said.

"You mean thirty-one years?"

He turned to face her and let go of a deep sigh. "Yes, it's still hard to wrap my head around the time change."

Nava wondered if they kept this conversation, they might fool nature from calling upon them. "I know it looks dead, but it's not." She squinted at the tree, and there she saw it, white and yellow waves of magic vibrating out, pulsing with magic.

"What do you mean?"

"I can sense it's alive—vibrating with energy." She smiled and focused on it. The light of the moon bathed the shapes of the branches, and there in the silhouette, Nava spotted hundreds of small black dots peppering the twisty shapes. "It's one of my Beekeeper superpowers," she teased, though it wasn't a lie. It had been one thing that was unique about her. The way she could see nature's waves. "And I can also see it's budding."

Arkimedes's head snapped back to the tree, his eyes widening. "I see nothing."

"I mean, they aren't opening yet, but I see the start of leaves—maybe even late-summer flowers?" She was not sure why she felt such excitement about the prospect, but her heart soared at the idea of bringing this news to him.

"Nava," he gasped, bringing her attention back to him. His voice didn't sound as elated as she'd thought he would be by the news. "In the life I don't remember, were we married?"

"W-what do you mean?" she stuttered, not liking where this conversation was going. Her neck pickled with the quick building of anxiety. This had better not mean what she was starting to think.

His brows dipped. "Did we get married back on the Grey Island?"

They hadn't even talked about it . . . much. Though she had hoped it was the next step. More of a symbol than anything. "No."

"Don't lie to me."

"I'm not!" She took a step back, and the pleasant heat that had been present in her body the entire afternoon came alive in another way. "And do not talk to me that way!"

"This tree has been dead for twe—thirty years because the queen of this kingdom was murdered."

She swallowed and stepped back one more step. This was going the way she didn't want to go.

"I told you, it's linked to the new queen. It hasn't budded for anyone until you arrived here. I was here last week, and it was dead."

"What makes you think that means we are married? Your father has ten women with him. Surely one of them kicked this tree back to life." And she knew she was reaching for excuses when the truth was pulsing in her mind. She, the soulmate of the Crown Prince of this kingdom, had arrived a couple of weeks ago.

"He has five women," he corrected, "and they have been with him for over a decade. So no, what are you hiding, and why?"

She needed to get them out of here before she ended up trapped into being a queen, which was not something she wanted at all. She took another step back, her heart drumming. "I recommend you to track everyone who's entered this palace in the last few weeks since she has the possibility of giving your father another child, and then we can leave this place and be in peace."

Arkimedes strode forward, and she hit the hedge with the side of her body. "I have been thinking of you for months. I can't get you out of my mind for even a moment. If we weren't married, were we in love?"

Nava swallowed the thick knot in her throat, which felt like it lead to her stomach. "Yes."

He placed his hands on each side of her head, and she squirmed at the intensity in his eyes. "You can't keep pretending to be with Devon. We need to tell my father, and you will become my bride here."

"Arkimedes. Can you even hear what you are saying? The king took you from our home and conveniently left me behind. He knew who I was when Devon and I arrived. He was ready to have us killed. I'm just a human, and everyone in this kingdom hates humans."

His lips parted. "Not everyone hates humans, Nava."

"I'm not a queen." She had to steady herself, to not lose her calm. "I'm a potion—I mean, a Beekeeper, and we need to protect the forests from the Zorren. Being king and queen is not a part of that."

"It's a part of who I am," he countered; however, his eyes glazed over. His expression changed as if a fog had come down his mind.

"Ark," she breathed. Her body shook with something primal spreading over her like a tsunami wave.

"We can talk about it later." His eyes dropped to her lips.

"Not later." She half pushed against his chest, not really wanting to get him away from her. "I'm not staying in a place where everyone hates me, where I don't know what will happen to me. Look at the dress that wench made for me just because I'm a human!"

"I like it." *Off you. Now.*

Nava blinked. Were those his thoughts bouncing in her head? It had been a while since she had heard him so clear. Their connection was sharpening as the night grew closer to midnight.

"It itches all over." The words tumbled out of her lips. She lifted her hands, dropping them on his shoulders, and he stood closer, resting his forehead on hers. "She did this even after you told her to 'take care of me.'"

"I will deal with her tomorrow."

"*No,* just let me complain without murdering someone with your shadow power."

Arkimedes's eyes danced, and his hands caressed the side of her dress over her rib cage. "My shadow power?" He hummed, and that side smirk was all she needed to forget about the whole queen ordeal.

"What else do you call it? Either way, don't go kill Marni, please."

He kissed the side of her cheek with an open mouth, and goose bumps awakened in her body. The arousal that had been simmering under her skin, just waiting to be released, bubbled out on a moan.

What had she been blabbering about? She couldn't think about it with his lips trailing down her neck and with one of his hands tightening on her hips, bringing her flush against his body.

He pushed her toward the hedge. Sticks and leaves dug into her back, and she let her head fall, exposing more skin to him. Their breaths became heavier, and a flow of emotion overtook her. This felt right. She was supposed to be here with him—why was she so worried about everything? She brought her hands to the back of his neck, grasping his hair.

His lips trailed up close to her ear. "When you touched yourself last night, were you thinking of me?" His breath caressed the side of her cheek and down the wet path he had created a moment before.

Nava swallowed as heat pooled in her stomach, growing like wildfire. "Yes." She tried to get her leg around his hips and groaned at the layers of fabric that prevented her from feeling him pressed against her.

She needed to get this dress off. It was suffocating her. There had been a reason she didn't want to do this here, but right now she couldn't care.

Another moan escaped her lips when he traced a pattern over her chest, his knuckles gingerly grazing her nipple.

"Ark . . ." Her voice came as a desperate cry, and his lips crashed over hers in a demanding kiss.

It was wet, soft, and hard all in one. His tongue wasted no time diving into her mouth, claiming her like he had been thirsting for years. He tugged at the collar of her dress, and a rip clamored as the yellow fabric floated to the ground, exposing her under the sheer lace chemise. Arkimedes lost no time, cupping her exposed breast and kneading it with his rough hand.

She had missed him like she hadn't had him for years, not just days.

He pulled away just enough to drink her in. "You are beautiful," he said against her lips, and his wings wrapped around them, black like the moonless night, hiding them in plain sight.

"Thanks." Why was she thanking him? Her mind had the worst timing to come up with the most awkward response known to mankind. She felt her cheeks warm. "I mean, thank you for noticing. I'm ruining the moment. Again."

He smiled and pecked her lips, meeting her gaze with an expression that had softened. Her heart stumbled in its beats. This was how he had looked at her that last night in their home, right before he'd been taken. Like she hung the moon and the stars above.

The reprieve from his heated kisses lifted the fog that had been in her mind for a while, telling her this was too dangerous. They shouldn't be exposing themselves like this in the middle of the garden, even if not many came around this place.

His lips captured hers again, and her skin burned under his day's worth of stubble. She wrapped her arms around his neck and pulled him closer. Whatever magic was running through them was too strong to ignore. His lips trailed down her neck again, across her chest, and closed in on her nipple.

And it felt too good. Why was she so nervous about being here either way? There was no one else around them, not even the creepy flowers. His tongue flicked over her with a punishing pace, and she writhed against him, feeling like she might come apart just from that touch.

She heard the ruffling of leaves and tensed with the noise, the daze clearing from her mind once again. The heat on her skin didn't subside; it demanded more.

Sensing her sudden change, Arkimedes pulled away, his brow furrowing, illuminated by the light of his gaze. "Is everything all right?"

She nodded but stayed quiet, listening. The breeze picked up, and she heard the sound again, realizing it had been the wind.

His wings shifted, revealing the bright night above. "Are you sure?"

"Yes."

He shook his head, as if trying to clear it. "I can't think straight. Please tell me to stop if this is not what you want."

"You are all that I want." She caressed the side of his jaw and down the side of his neck. Why was she fighting this? "But I don't want it here where someone can find us. You aren't forgettable, and I'm not dressed to run."

Arkimedes kissed her again, sucking on her bottom lip, and her toes curled and her mind faltered at the last thought. To heck with caution. She was going to have him now, and she didn't care if anyone got a peep show.

His arms snaked around her body, and soon his wings were flapping and his lips abandoned hers. He lifted her in the air and carried her off toward the castle.

CHAPTER TWENTY-SIX

ORION

The flight back to his room's balcony didn't take long. Nava trailed kisses down Orion's neck, and goose bumps raised over his skin.

"Stop that." Orion tightened his hold on her as his wings moved to slow down their descent and stabilize them for landing. She had been right—the wide skirt of this dress was the least convenient garment he had ever encountered. If only for this, he should pay a visit to Marni when he was back in town.

She didn't stop, however, her tongue tasting his skin instead, and the groan that left his mouth was not a noise he remembered ever making before. His booted feet hadn't finished touching the floor before her lips met his, and he lost track of all thoughts as his blood raced.

He wished he could blame magic for making him this painfully hard and in a constant state of hunger for this woman. But even though tonight his self-restraint had withered to nothing, he had been craving her for months.

His teeth captured her thick bottom lip, and she moved her hands from his chest to the back of his neck, her fingers digging through his hair. Her tongue was divine torture; he didn't know where he wanted it most.

They kissed like rogue teenagers escaping the prying eyes of their caregivers. Enjoying the way her body responded under his touch, he brought his hands down the sheer fabric of the dress, over the naked planes of her back, and down her wide hips to the alluring globes of her backside. Tugging her closer to him, he smiled as she gasped against his lips.

It was not lost on him that *this*—them—was not new to her as it was to him. The pressure of not letting her down weighed in his chest more so than he had ever felt before. She was important to him. Whether he remembered why or when it happened, she had been the main source of his thoughts for months.

He knew deep in the marrow of his bones that what he was craving was more than her body, and that alone sobered his heated thoughts.

He broke the kiss and met her dazed gaze. "Did you drink some of the wine?"

"No, it's not the wine." Was that guilt flashing through her eyes? Did she feel this craze as well? A heat that didn't subside and made his focus narrow on just this. Being close, having her in his bed at this moment.

She dropped her hands from his neck before inspecting her surroundings. She hesitated before she strolled into his room. The fireplace came alive in a soft roll as she made it past the billowy curtains that flowed with the night's breeze.

With the tall ceilings and the dark furnishings, she stood out like a beacon of yellow light. Much like her magic had been that day in the forest. She fit in here, like she was meant to stay forever. In the dim light of the fireplace, she studied her surroundings, taking in all the details that made the room his.

The flames marked an orange highlight over the soft edges of her curves, and just like that, an intense need to protect her washed over him. She had come through a dark portal, losing something dear to save him from . . . his father.

There had been little time to get to know her, but he already admired her tenacity, strength, and stubbornness.

Nava walked toward the four-post bed in the middle of the room. Her fingers drifted over the black sheets, then she turned to him and air escaped him all at once.

Gone were the inner thoughts of someone falling in love, and back was the intense burning he was no longer able to hold back.

She walked toward a large mirror that leaned against the wall by the bed, at least eight feet tall and towering over her frame. In the dim light of the room, her dress, or what was left of it, was muted in the cool light of the night, and it reminded him of her bees.

Orion approached her, following each one of her movements through the reflection. He wrapped a hand across her stomach, steadying her after he brought her back to meet him. His lips came down over the supple skin of her neck, trailing toward her shoulder, where he lowered the strap of flimsy fabric that still held the bodice to her body.

It was too much and not enough. His body was ready, straining with desire and tension. She grasped the ends of his hair, trying but failing to keep his face locked in place. Her skin raised in goose bumps as his lips trailed down the skin of her back. He stored the memory aside for later.

If he closed his eyes and blocked their surroundings, just focused on her and the scent of berries and something wild and earthy around her, he sensed the talons of recognition clawing their way back to him, invigorated by the fire burning in his veins. His lips abandoned the ministrations as he pulled back, unwrapping the ribbons that secured the corset to her body. The fabric loosened and pooled over her chest and down her hips, falling to the ground with a thump.

Her breasts were still under the chemise that covered her, but he could see the clear silhouette. Orion stroke one, and she melted against him.

Nava met his gaze through the reflection with heavy lids, and he was struck by the weightlessness of his stomach and the flutter of his heart. His hand covered the entirety of her right breast and he massaged the supple flesh, bringing her against his straining erection. The rest of her clothing was off in an instant, the scent of magic wafting in the air. Naked in front of him, she stared at him, and they shared the same look. Clarity.

Orion needed her now. He dropped his hand from her breasts, down below her navel. She held her breath when his fingers reached her center, and her face morphed as pleasure overtook her. She was wet and ready, and he was going to burst.

She let her head fall against his shoulder. He slid his finger inside her, arching it to find the spot that would make her squirm. In and out, he let her sounds spur him on alongside her moans.

She trembled in his arms, holding her breath for a moment before her orgasm ran through her body, like waves of ecstasy that bloomed and colored her skin. His stomach tightened, and the pleasure of an orgasm built within him. His breathing faltered as he tried to calm his body and not come all over his pants like a teenager.

What the hell was that?

Breathless and confused, he swallowed down and focused on the woman in front. "I have wanted to do that for so long," he said in a tone he almost didn't recognize. Orion wanted to taste her and not be so gentle when making her shout his name as he filled her.

Nava turned around and captured his lips with hers in a demanding kiss. Orion growled against her lips and dropped his hands to her hips, pushing against her in a way that almost calmed both of their needs. But she needed more of him if her clawing at his back was anything to go by.

She fumbled over the hidden buttons of his coat. It didn't take long for his large hands to replace hers, and soon his white coat fell to the ground, joining the pile of clothes already there. She touched his chest like it was something to be revered, not the marked planes of skin he saw day after day. Goose bumps appeared on his chest when her lips crashed down, her tongue peeking out to taste him, over that weird mark in the middle of his pecs.

She continued down and over the bulges of his abs, licking and nipping as she went, and he could barely hold himself together as anticipation built. But it wasn't only his need to have her wrap her lips around him; there was also a growing sense of worry.

That he couldn't hold a candle to the man she was used to. Maybe he wasn't good enough, not in his current broken state. A shadow of the man he was sure she loved.

She untied the leather strings that held his pants up, and he tried to swallow the knot that had formed there. His blood was boiling too hot, and he was too turned on for his sudden nerves to cool him. Her lips continued across the muscles of his pelvic bone.

His pants loosened as she pushed them down with an eagerness that matched his mood. Nava met his gaze as she wrapped her hand around him, giving him a tentative pump.

A breath caught in his throat just before she took him in her mouth and swallowed him whole. He grunted, holding himself against the mirror with one hand, entranced as he looked at her.

His mouth opened in a silent cry as he grasped her hair. Soon her curls were falling loose over her back and face, and she hollowed her cheeks. She *knew* it would drive him crazy.

He gasped, and the memory of her wet thighs had him breathing harder. He wanted her so badly. Nava read him like an open book and picked up her pace.

"This is going to be over before it starts if you keep—" His breath stuttered.

She pushed forward and sucked him all in.

He pulled out of her eager mouth, colorful words escaping his lips before he wrapped his arms around her and lifted her with ease. His lips crashed over hers. "I want more than just your mouth."

She bit his lower lip before her tongue soothed the sharp pain left behind, and his cock bobbed in response. He couldn't let her go, even if he was damaged. "We have the entire night."

In a whirlwind motion, he turned her around, and her eyes met the reflection. Every inch of her body was exposed, illuminated by the warmth of the fireplace.

Orion's wings expanded, dark like the night outside. He hadn't slept with many women. At first it had been difficult with his duties with the Society to find time to court anyone. Then it had become clear it was pointless to fall in love when his destiny would be chosen by someone else. Much like what had happened with everything in his life.

Then there were the dark, misted shapes that followed his every move. Not many were eager to deal with those. But this kind of attraction, the jealousy with Devon—or with himself—was something new. Too scary at times.

He pressed against her and brought his hand to her stomach, and his lips traveled to her neck once again. "Hold on to the mirror and bend over for me."

The goose bumps that ran across her skin spurred him on. His body hummed with anticipation. He pushed down on her lower back as she followed his command, her round backside lining up just where he wanted it.

He settled behind her, digging into each side of her hips. His cock slid up and nuzzled at her entrance. To make a further point, Nava wiggled her hips. He kicked aside one of her legs, widening her stance, and pushed into her.

Orion dropped his head to her shoulder. His arms shaking, he held himself against the wall as a swarm of feelings and pleasure that hadn't been there before took over him. Like his own, but different somehow.

A rush of moisture ran through her as he set a punishing pace. Her hands slid over the mirror with a screech.

The coil wound tighter with each passing second as he entered her, threatening to snap something within him. Nava's legs trembled, but he held her, pushing her against the mirror fully. Her whole chest and torso slid over the slick surface, and his pace grew erratic.

Her breath caught in her throat, and then stars exploded behind his closed lids. A wave that shook him to his core had him emptying himself inside her.

They might have stood in that spot for seconds, minutes. When he opened his eyes, she grinned at him. And the burning heat that had accompanied him all day lowered to a simmer inside his gut.

He took a step back and couldn't help but grin as she wobbled on her feet. Maybe he had fucked her good enough to have her forget the other man who shared his name and body but not his memories.

She turned and wrapped her arms around his neck before he kissed her.

"I hope you aren't tired because I don't think you'll be sleeping much tonight." He swept her off the ground.

Nava wrapped her legs around him like she knew how this would go, and without another word of warning, he dropped her onto the bed.

CHAPTER TWENTY-SEVEN

NAVA

The room was still dark when Nava blinked her eyes open. Soft rays of sunshine extended over the dark stone floors, hinting at an early summer morning.

She couldn't have slept for longer than a couple of hours, judging by the coolness in the air and how late it had been since their last heated exchange. She ached in the best possible way—a delicious burn inside her thighs, her body still tired from a night of a magical-induced frenzy. The warmth of his body was familiar behind her and still sent her heartbeat galloping in a rush.

She snuggled closer to him, her head on his chest. His fingers caressed the planes of her back.

"I didn't know you were up." His rough voice broke the silence of the morning.

"Hard to sleep with you next to me."

"Last I checked, you fell asleep on me before I was done with you."

Her cheeks warmed, because she had, in fact, fallen asleep on him. "I only have so much energy. Some of us are full-blooded humans."

"What happened yesterday . . . I've never felt anything like that before."

"Me neither." Though she didn't know if he was referring to the weird solstice heat or being with her. Intimate contact always meant the deepening of their bond.

The heat that had burned through their bodies while on the dance floor, it was hard to put what she felt into words when so much had happened in a matter of hours. Her normal thoughts had been fogged, but not gone. She'd been present and able to make decisions, though maybe freer to lean on what she'd wanted.

A prickle of concern trailed her thoughts. The outcome of the sex, the longing—those had been something she'd half expected after all the warnings. For Arkimedes, it had been all new. Their craving for one another came with who they were to each other, but . . . he should have known of their connection before it had gotten to this.

She should have pushed harder to tell him the truth, past her own selfishness.

Turning her face toward the balcony, Nava evaded his gaze. "I should get to my room before Leela comes looking for me." Her stomach revolted at her action, or the lack of.

"They are very punctual in their morning rounds, her and Callie."

His words made her pause, and she shifted back to meet his gaze. "Callie—is that Callisto?"

His bright green eyes focused on her, his expression sharpening to focus. Nava hadn't even given a thought to whether a female fae would be the one tending to her mate while no one else knew of their bond, and the new information sat in her stomach like a bag of rocks.

"Has she come into your bedroom before?" She focused on the door, frowning. "Is she the one coming to wake you every morning?" Weren't there societal rules about this? Nava was sure there should be something like that.

Arkimedes's slow grin lifted the corners of his mouth. "What's happening inside that fiery head of yours?"

She narrowed her gaze at him. "Has she?"

"Are you jealous?"

She huffed, bringing the sheet over her chest to make sure her mark was covered from sight. Now that the morning sun made it more visible, she was glad their heated frenzy had hit them in the middle of the night and not during daylight. She moved her body away from his. "I don't get jealous. I don't have a reason to be."

But the what-ifs came rushing back to her. What if the king had been pressuring Arkimedes to find a suitor? That was something they did in court, right? Laurie had never pushed her to learn much about this. It wasn't like Nava was ever supposed to be exposed to a situation that would make the study worth their time. Little had they known . . .

The burning embers of something angry lit in her stomach. Nava had no reason to be annoyed with him, not when he didn't remember her and was a victim here. But whatever possessive nature their bond brought upon them was hard to battle.

"Good." Arkimedes angled toward her as his hands chased after her hips. "Where are you going?"

"I'm going to my room to allow you time to get yourself dressed before she shows up."

His rolling laughter almost thawed the ice in her veins. "I don't want you to go. Stay with me."

"No." But her body was already sinking back into the mattress. Damn the tone of honey and sex in his voice; she had no defense against it.

His warm hand wrapped around her stomach, bringing her flush to his body, his lips tracing the skin of her back. The intense heat from last night was mostly gone, but his lips were getting her there once again. "I haven't looked at a woman the way I see you ever since—" His words got lost somewhere, and she turned to meet his distant gaze.

"Ever since . . . ?"

"I can't remember. The memory evades me." Arkimedes frowned. "But even if I did, I'm not sure if I have ever felt this way before."

She grinned, and hope bloomed in her chest. It had taken him much longer to admit his feelings for her a year ago. However small, this progress was good. Maybe the idea of waiting for him to fall for her wasn't as ridiculous as she'd thought. "You will get your memories back," she said. Devon thought so.

However, there was a possibility that he would never remember the last decade of his life. Much like she would never remember her father again.

They both stared at each other in a heartbreaking silence, and Nava couldn't handle that pain in his features a moment longer. She cleared her throat. "Has she seen you without clothes?"

A shocked roll of laughter came out of him. "No, bee, she has not." His expression softened.

There it was again, her nickname.

With the light of the early morning flooding the room, she allowed herself to relax in his embrace. It had been a little over a week in her time since he was taken, but it had been much longer for him.

She lay down, facing the canopy above her, closing her eyes as her mind reeled. Unable to imagine the confusion he must have felt from being apart from her, not knowing what was happening.

Even knowing he was taken, she had been perplexed as to why her health had faded in a matter of hours. It made sense now with the time difference between the kingdoms. Maybe her soul had always known they'd been apart for longer.

His touch raised goose bumps as he trailed his hand from her shoulder, making a path to her heart.

"What's this?" His whole body tensed as he stared at her chest, his calloused finger tracing the raised edges of her soulmate mark. The warmth in her body drained away, replaced by the icy caress of panic. Her scalp crawled and she put both her hands on top of his. He pulled out of her grasp as if she had burned him and sat straight in the bed, his eyes widening, his face losing all color. "Is this some sort of trick?"

"No, no." She sprang up, reaching for him.

"You'd better start talking, and I hope this is not what I think it is."

Nava sat straight and fought the urge to fidget under his scrutiny. She covered her chest, and the taste of guilt was bitter. "I wasn't sure when to tell you."

He hissed out a breath, and in a blink, he was standing by the side of the bed, his wings spreading as his eyes took her in. "You had plenty of time yesterday when I was asking you if we were married."

"I didn't lie. We aren't married—and I didn't want to divulge our information in the middle of the garden."

He leveled her with a look that made her shut her mouth. "You were diverting about you being the future queen. You know well a soulmate overwrites any marriage in the eyes of our gods."

"I don't want to be the queen."

"Don't change the subject," he growled.

"You changed the subject, not me!"

This was the most ironic thing she'd ever thought could happen to her, the complete mirror image to what had happened almost a year ago when their situations had been reversed. After all, Arkimedes had hidden that he was her soulmate for almost a month before the truth had come out, thanks to Violet outing him as a member of the Society of Crows.

"I wanted to tell you ever since I first stepped foot here! It was hard with you not remembering even meeting me. You thought I had bewitched you, Arkimedes," she rushed to say.

He walked around the bed, picking up his discarded pants from the night before. "That is not an excuse."

"I tried to tell you yesterday . . . for a moment." But Nava knew she hadn't tried, not really. She crossed her arms over her chest, her blood boiling. "You don't get to be mad at me for this."

"What?"

"You did the same thing to me last year and—"

Arkimedes's lips parted before his aura exploded around him, black and sinister like fingers and arms emanating from his body. "I don't know what the hell you are talking about, Nava! I don't remember anything of what you are telling me. I'm trying hard to trust you, but how can I when you are lying to me about no less than being my soulmate!"

The temperature of the room lowered, and Nava pushed back against the headboard, her heart hammering. "I was waiting for you to trust me before I dropped the soul bomb," she blurted. "I was waiting for the right moment."

He pinched the bridge of his nose and took a shaky breath, the black tendrils of his power coming closer to his body as he regained some of his control. "You can't be here. I need to get you out of this castle unharmed."

"What are you talking about?"

"I'm talking about the enemies I have inside these walls! The people who tried to kill my mother when she was pregnant."

Oh, that was rich. "So yesterday you didn't care when you told me we should go to your father and get married, but today you want me gone so you can keep going on your solo mission?"

"I was not in my right mind yesterday!" His voice might have been the coldest she had ever heard. "This place is too dangerous for you because it's not only my father who has his eyes on you."

She brought the sheets up, trying to shield herself from him. "I won't leave without you, and even if I wanted to—which I don't—I couldn't. We would both die."

"You said the king had taken me from our home, that he knew who you were the whole time." Arkimedes's tone dropped, and she met his gaze. "And you didn't think to tell me we are bonded?"

Her lips shook, and desperation clawed at her from within. "That is why we have to leave, *right now*. Back to our home. We can put Devon back in the prison. Roman might not even be mad since it would've been just a few minutes for him. Next time we will be prepared if they come for you—"

"Back to our home? You mean a place I have no recollection of, to a life I don't remember?" He looked away from her to the side of the bed, his jaw coiled with tension.

Nava gripped her hands, and the prickle in her eyes told her she was close to losing it. This was going wrong. She needed to fix it. Rushing up to her feet, she shuffled to him. "You will love it there like you did before."

"And I'm just supposed to blindly believe this?" Arkimedes scoffed, shaking his head. "I have been alone without a family my whole life, wondering why I'm this way."

"You know a portion of what they tell you here is not true," Nava said.

"They are lying to you. They kidnapped you from our home. Took away your memories and our lives together!"

"And you haven't been?"

She flinched, her shoulders tensing. "I have not lied to you until this moment, and even now I was going to tell you as soon as I thought you were ready."

"What gives you the right to choose when I'm ready or not?"

The words got stuck in her throat. She lowered her face, and tears fell down her cheeks. "I was afraid. This has also been a tremendous shock to me, Arkimedes."

"The Arkimedes you knew is not me, and it is about time you understand that." A cold mask descended over his features, and she knew the conversation was over. "In this castle, I'm Prince Orion, and I will not follow you blindly across the world. I'm not leaving."

Tears swelled in her eyes as her heart split open. It was as if she was losing him all over again. This kingdom had stolen him from her. Stolen their memories, their lives, their identity.

Now it was her and him. A sob escaped from her lips, and his already closed expression softened.

His pain and confusion swirled within her, and even though she didn't want to go, she knew they needed space. It hadn't been easy for her when she accepted that Arkimedes was her soulmate. Even then, she'd had an entire month to fall in love with him. He'd had but a handful of days to fall for her. She was asking him too much.

He needed time. The one thing she didn't know how much she had left to give since the king might strike her at any moment. She guessed that now that Arkimedes knew of the danger they were both in, things would change.

Maybe he would tell the king, and the two of them might lock her away, safe from physical harm but away from him. No, Arkimedes wouldn't do that to her, even as angry as he was.

She swiped at the tears that wet her cheeks. "Even if you don't remember, you have had a family for some time now, and you are not alone."

With those parting words, her body became air, pollen, and dust, floating out of the window and toward her room.

Society of Crows

CHAPTER TWENTY-EIGHT

ORION

A soulmate. He'd had a goddamn twin soul all along, and no one had deemed it important for him to learn the truth.

His blood boiled as he stormed into the solarium. His brother sat at the table, drinking tea from a small bone cup. He raised a brow as Orion loosened the button of his coat and shrugged it off. It was too hot to be wearing so many layers outside in this sweltering heat.

"Did you know?" he demanded, tossing the offending piece of clothing over the black painted metal chair.

Devon placed the cup on the table, his face giving away nothing. "So I'm guessing the solstice brought the truth out, *finally*."

Orion pushed one of the chairs, the noise of metal scraping over the brick ground the only noise around them. His magic burst out of his fingertips. "You didn't think of telling me that my—" He stopped himself and took a calming breath. His brother's challenging smirk was anything but apologetic. "You don't care a thing about what could have happened to us if—"

"On the contrary, I'm *forced* to care about your relationship," Devon snarled and pushed off the chair, fixing his white cravat with both hands. "And for the record, I did tell her to tell you. Maybe that way, we would be out of this place by now."

"Well, she didn't, and I'm not leaving."

Devon shrugged, walking around as he looked at the purple flowers that hung from the winding plant above them. "I'm sure she was mistaken to be afraid of your reaction—you are taking it quite well."

A prickling sensation crawled down his spine, and he rubbed his fingers together, trying to calm his speeding heart. "I never wanted a soulmate, but I have wanted her every minute of the last four months, even when I thought she was your . . . bride-to-be."

"Oh, the joy that gave me." His eyes shone, and Orion didn't know if he wanted to punch that smirk off his face or just keep asking questions. "The world gives you what all of us mundane people want, yet you are too good for it, as always." Devon's eyes blazed on him.

"I don't need your passive-aggressive shit right now, Devon." It was confusing to know what his real feelings toward Nava were when he now knew magic forced some into him. His need to cherish and protect her had been there since the first day. Those were magic-induced, right?

The way his heart skipped a beat when she smiled or his stomach dropped with her magic; her stubbornness drove him mad in the best and worst ways. Those were real. Orion wiped his hands over his face, pacing around.

What he felt had grown to more than something physical, more than good chemistry and desire. The way she challenged him, her sense of humor and laughter. He had been in awe of her magic and the beauty of what she truly was.

Too good for him to taint. She intrigued him, and it wasn't just a magic-induced want. This was real.

Devon returned to the table, his dark gaze studying him before he lowered back into his chair. "Last year when we met, you didn't want to be without her. As a matter of fact, you wanted to stay in that place."

He didn't want to be without her now either, but the man he'd been before . . . that was scarier than even the bond he had formed with Nava. Why had he stayed on the Grey Island and forgotten about his own duty?

Orion needed to protect a whole kingdom, yet he had forsaken them all.

The fact that he had gotten kidnapped from his own home said a lot about how relaxed he had become, not only putting himself in danger but Nava as a result. "I don't want to remember who I was four months ago."

Devon paused halfway in reaching for the forgotten cup. Lifting both brows, he faced him. "Are you saying you can remember if you choose to? Or is this more of a—"

"I was able to get a memory back a few days ago. I remember chasing them across the ocean to the Grey Island. I have an idea of what spell was used to fog my memories, and I could use some of the dreams I have had to unravel more."

"But you don't want to?"

"What kind of man would have stayed on an island full of deserters when this whole kingdom fell into despair because of it?" His voice grew heavy, and he remembered the ghost of his mother, burned and blackened. His heart soared with the need to find answers. "It's likely I didn't even set wards to protect Nava. I knew who I was and the fact that my father would come for me at some point, and I didn't do anything to prevent it."

Devon's long, pale fingers wrapped around the handle of the cup. "Those were my exact thoughts last year. You grew soft there, brother."

Orion nodded and sat on the chair with a heavy sigh. He needed to get the keys for the bracelets from the king. He didn't claim to understand the ins and outs of how the magic worked in this kingdom, but with them, the king could track both Devon and, most importantly, Nava. He couldn't get her out of this place and into temporary safety while she wore the bracelet.

The tree burned bright red. Hissing demons surrounded it. Its wide trunk trembled as the rolling flames devoured the previously green leaves with orange and yellow shades. She screamed, her throat raw from her pained cries and the burning smoke. Her skin blistered as the heat crept closer. But she was too weak to move against the ropes around her body.

Her voice soon gave away, breaking with pain so raw and unlike she had ever felt; however, deep within her soul, she was calm. While this was the end of this life, she had succeeded in a way. It had been a fool's errand to come to this forest to make sense of this madness. To see if it was him after all. To have him call these demons away. Maybe her death would be what he needed to finally rest in peace.

Then darkness coiled in from the sides of her eyes. For a moment, she floated over the burnt tree in the forest, anger and sorrow stealing in her breaths, but she couldn't moan out loud. She couldn't reach those she loved anymore.

Her most beloved had killed her.

Orion inhaled, and it took him a panicked second to understand in the haze of sleep that he wasn't really in that forest. Every inch of his body ached as if he had slept on the hard ground instead of his feather-filled mattress. It had been days since the nightmare of his mother's passing had plagued his sleep.

He peeled the sheets from his sweaty skin, which felt like sand rubbing his body raw. The atmosphere of the room changed with a heaviness that lingered. He wished he could say it was the first time the suffocating sensation of being watched had loomed over him, but it happened right before the ghost of his mother appeared to haunt him.

Looking around the room with his heart beating in his throat, he expected the burnt corpse to appear in front of him at any moment now. But his room remained empty. He took another breath and rested his face in his open palms, wishing he knew better what the spirit wanted from him. It was known that spirits remained in this realm because their souls were restless and needed closure.

Orion had been grasping at straws. He'd considered he had been the one killing her, the heir born sick. But how could he have, when he'd been just a toddler when she'd been killed, and on another continent? Her last thought was always that her most beloved one had killed her—could that be his father?

The sun rose behind the banisters of his balcony, tinting the sky in gold tones as the warmth hit his face. It was too early for most in the castle to be up, and the scent of smoke lingered in the room—could be his mother somehow or an impending attack from the demons.

It had always been strange that he was able to smell them before anyone else in the castle could. That was, until he'd gone to the forest with Nava and found out he was somehow linked to the Beekeepers, the natural enemies of the Zorren.

If he were going to be dispatched early to fight them, he needed to make it to the king's room and find the keys to the bracelets before then. He finished tying the straps of his trousers and reached for one of his favorite black tunics. It had dark gray embroidery that depicted leaves and flowers sprouting out of a branch.

He traced the silk thread, his mind going back to the night of the solstice when he'd kissed Nava in front of the queen's tree. She was his future—*his* queen. He shifted his hand over his chest, trying to massage away the sudden ache that bloomed there. Did he want that longing? She was in love with a man who wasn't him—one who had his face but didn't share his beliefs.

What if Nava hated the person he was today once she realized he was determined to stay this way? Pressing his lips together, he finished doing up the clasps of the tunic and walked out of the room.

The first month of him being back—or stolen back—the king had shown him his private library. He had seen the bracelets and the keys displayed in a glass case. That was when he'd learned how the jewelry worked. The ins and outs of their magic-canceling properties, the fact that they didn't affect the royal kin, and that they were trackable by the king himself.

The library was adjacent to the king's bedroom, but Orion also knew the king was likely visiting with one of his ladies. So if he was quiet enough, he might be able to get the keys without him being the wiser.

Both libraries in the castle were closed off to everyone but the king, Orion, and Ellis, the keeper of the records. The doors of this particular one were ebony with gilded nature-inspired patterns and gold handles. He opened them quietly, and his footsteps were muffled over thick, red-and-wine-patterned wool rugs.

The room was vast, with large arched windows at the end, black ornate frames, and painted glass on the top panels. The pink and orange shades of the morning outstretched over the floor. The small sitting area by the fireplace had three large winged chairs in front of it; the scent of leather and old paper hung in the air, mixing with the soft notes of lavender and flowers—maybe camellias—from an arrangement on the coffee table.

On the far left wall, floor-to-ceiling bookcases held thousands of leather-bound books in various shades and stains.

The clear glass display case for the keys was past the bookcases, perched against one of the stone walls. There were many magical artifacts inside. A blade with three large rubies in the handle, an old book that was held together by worn bindings. He searched for the wooden case of the bracelets and the smaller one that held the keys . . . but it was missing.

He gripped the handle, and the glass shook with his pent-up emotion. If the keys weren't here, that meant they were in the king's room, which really complicated things.

Groaning, he pushed away, gazing around the room, hoping to find them misplaced somewhere else. His eyes came upon a wooden panel hung next to the glass case like art. He didn't remember seeing it there before, but it called his attention now.

He approached it, studying the intricate carvings of wood and gold details; the king stood tall with both hands extended in front of him as he dropped a child toward a sea of clouds. Orion's heart started to beat at double speed, and he traced the carvings, so similar in detail to the one on the throne room's door. The one that had the queen holding a child.

"Orion."

He jumped in his spot, dropping his hand off the wood panel like a child caught doing something wrong, which he guessed was accurate.

Orion turned to meet his father's curious gaze. The king strolled into the sitting area of his private library, holding both hands behind his back. The light rolled over his silk robe and matching wide pants.

Behind him, the doors that connected the library to his private chambers were open wide, which hadn't been the case before. Entranced by his search for the keys and the strange art piece, Orion hadn't heard it open.

"Father." He dipped his head into a bow, his skin prickling as a drop of sweat formed at his temple.

"I didn't know I was supposed to expect you this morning or I would have had breakfast served here. It's already difficult enough to get you to join me for dinners." The king sat on one of the large leather chairs by the fireplace, crossing his legs and hands in front of him, his eyes shimmering like the cat that caught the bird.

He was in trouble. So much for his half-baked plan to sneak in here and retrieve the keys. Orion didn't want his father knowing he was hunting for a way to remove the tracking bracelets from Nava and Devon. "I had a dream about the queen again," he said after clearing his throat, going for a partial truth in hopes of distracting his father.

The king stiffened on his seat, his features shadowing with a haunted expression. "She is still visiting you in your dreams? She hasn't visited mine for quite some time now."

The queen more than haunted his dreams. She appeared out of nowhere, especially if Orion was in the library. "I kept searching in the main archives but haven't had much luck finding much about her, or me for that matter. I didn't want to bother you if you were busy with one of your cohorts."

The king's eyes went vacant as his lips twisted into a grim expression. "How did she look in your dream? Do you remember?"

Orion shook his head. The first time he told the king he dreamed of his mother, his father had asked many questions. A man starved for any piece of information that would fill a void. However, Orion had always felt very protective of these particular dreams. There was a reason the queen wasn't haunting his father, so he would work this up on his own.

"You aren't finding anything in the main library? I should have a talk with Ellis about his lack of help."

"You know well most of it's burned to the ground, and the keeper breathes on my neck the whole time. I don't need him hovering any more than he already does." Orion hesitated in his spot before making his way to where the king sat and taking the other seat. "You did say I was allowed to check this library . . . if I ever needed it."

The king pushed forward, assessing him with increasing interest. "*If* I were to be in the room, Orion. However, this will be all yours. There is no need to rush into anything—your mother is gone, and you can find all the answers soon enough."

Of course he hadn't missed that part of the information; the whole point was he had assumed the king was occupied elsewhere. He looked at his father. Old, thin skin over youthful features. A weird combination that had taken him long to get used to.

"What is that?" he asked, gazing back at the mounted wood piece he had been staring at. "It looks so similar to the one in the throne room."

"It's art. I like to collect it." The king's pleasant features shuttered, and the prickling sensation in the back of Orion's head increased. This was more than art, an aged intricate carving that showed the king throwing a child to mist. A complete opposite to the one of the queen holding a small prince in her arms.

Had this been the one next to the queen's panel in the door and had been replaced at some point? If that was true, why? His father had always been fine with letting the kingdom believe she had taken him away, but what if people questioned why that had happened?

It made him wonder if the king had ever tried to get rid of him when he'd been a child, which might be the reason why his mother had run away with him in tow. Had his father killed his mother in retribution?

Orion itched to be out of there, or to stay and check every single one of those books and find answers. His search would have to wait, however; he couldn't rest until Nava was out of this castle and safe.

"The forest fires woke me this morning, Orion. It has been your job to catch the culprits *before* they get out of hand. They are already getting closer to our city."

"The fires are not caused by humans like the guards are telling you."

"Then by what?"

Orion hesitated before releasing a breath. "The Zorren. I saw one the other day—"

"The demons are crossing to these lands?" The king stood from his seat and paced around the area toward the bookcase. "No one else has reported this to me before."

"It's the truth."

"I need proof. The high fae are convinced the humans that call themselves the Fallen Crows are behind this mess and are demanding retribution. If the demons are the ones wreaking havoc in our land, killing our forests and poisoning our soil, I need some of the guards to back your word—or for you to bring me proof."

"They become ash when killed. How am I supposed to bring you anything but ash?" Orion pointed out, shaking his head.

"Their nails are made of iron, deadly for our kind—yet you are half-human, so picking one up shouldn't be a problem. Cut one of their hands, and bring me the nails."

Orion stood from his chair and bowed to the king. Last time he'd seen a Zorren close enough to see said nails had been with Nava and the other Beekeeper, Ari. That day, it had been just one, but lately there were many more, if the fires were anything to go by.

"I will leave to get them for you then." He walked around the living area, scanning the shelves and the display case where the keys were supposed to be.

"Take as many guards as you think you will need," the king said. "I can feel the kingdom becoming stronger ever since you arrived. Our magic feeds the castle, and the spells that connect this structure to the city, to the lands beyond, work out the rest."

It was the same words the king had said to him the first time he'd been in this castle, learning he was the stolen heir. At the time, he'd half believed them. However, when he returned four months ago, the land had been dry. The castle walls cracked under the demands of a hungry kingdom. A high power that demanded things he didn't claim to understand. The citizens, animals—everyone had been struggling.

Not because of the lack of magical-born children, like in the Iron Kingdom, but because of the lack of children in general. The land and the citizens had become barren. A curse placed on this kingdom eons ago, eased by the power of the king. Lifted by the queen's tree.

Orion paused by the door. He had seen the city regain life, though he wasn't sure if it was due to him returning or just the change of the seasons. "I don't feel different."

"Our power eases the way the magic flows. It allows other magical creatures to help us. The queen's tree is the missing puzzle. A kingdom is barren without its queen."

Oh, the tree was already alive—his father was not going to like the how, but the process was in motion. Orion considered telling the king about the tree and that Nava was his soulmate. It would stop whatever plot his father might be brewing to hurt her.

However, he held himself back; even though he believed his father wanted him to stay, he wasn't quite sure what had happened to his mother. And now with that wooden panel, the rock of dread in his stomach just grew heavier.

What if his father sent Nava away, kept her alive but hidden, and then erased his memories of her? Orion wasn't willing to give her up to whatever fate that was. Sure, he had not wanted a soulmate, but he wasn't going to give her up.

"It's our job to find the queen. It might be time for you to start courting women in the kingdom."

His skin went cold. "I'm not interested."

"Orion. Our kingdom depends on our bloodline to be alive to keep our land strong. The spells that make it run are linked to us. I have told you this. We need your children."

There was one woman in Orion's life he would tie himself to, and he had already chosen her, in his past life and in this one. He opened his mouth to say the truth, but his father continued.

"A fae woman, of course."

"Why does it have to be a fae? The queen was human."

"She was my . . . biggest regret." His voice sounded sorrowful. Orion wasn't sure what the mistake was. "It would make our fae blood too diluted for the spells to keep working. You are half-fae and already struggle to keep the voices at bay. A quarter fae . . . They wouldn't be strong enough to hold them back from taking over."

While he had told Nava they should go to the king and get married the night of the solstice, Orion wasn't sure Nava wanted the life of living in this castle as a queen, which was the life he wanted.

There was also the fact that she was in love with a version of himself that didn't exist anymore. She was the only woman he was interested in, but he wasn't interested in marriage, at least not now.

"I'm not marrying anyone in your court," he growled with a finality that shocked the king. "I will bring you the proof of the demons."

The king nodded and waved his hand in dismissal.

CHAPTER TWENTY-NINE

NAVA

It had been a day since Nava had seen Arkimedes, and the hours dragged by. At least this time, she wasn't forced to stay in her room for the duration of it. Smoke hazed over the sky, thicker with each hour. She stood almost immobile in the wide hall, staring in the distance; wingless fae walked behind and in front, minding their own business as they took care of chores around the castle.

The cool stone column grounded her, and she searched for a sign of a forest fire nearby. It would be her excuse to leave at this moment and damn the consequences.

A few dozen bees crawled over the banisters and walls, camouflaged against the warm tones of the surrounding marble. It hadn't taken the Zorren long to return, and the pressing need to be out there in the forest with her Beekeeper was growing like a weed.

She had hoped the next time she escaped this castle, Arkimedes would be with her. It had been ignorant to think this would be anything but difficult.

Deep inside, she knew his reaction was her fault, that she had acted in a similar way a year prior when he'd hidden the truth from her. It was a humbling experience to choose to lie to protect oneself, knowing the truth always came out to hunt you down.

Maybe it was time to admit that, buried within the crevices of her heart, she had half expected the curse would break if they kissed or lay together. That foolishness had driven her to hide the truth from him for longer than she should have. Like her lips would be magic on their own.

It didn't help her morose mood that she was also worried sick about Ari. Knowing he was fighting their battle on his own was another kind of torture. Nava was being pulled in both directions, torn apart by her love and her destiny, which were supposed to be one and the same but weren't fitting properly.

She rubbed her eyes, and her mind took her back to the nightmares that had plagued her dreams the night before. She had slept little, between dreams or memories of being hunted by demons and Arkimedes's hard features telling her she had to leave.

With the scent of ash and burning wood, she knew he had to be thinking of the Zorren, and the Beekeeper as well. At least Cameron was safe, away from this danger. Nava closed her eyes and swallowed the heavy knot that had formed in her throat.

Please be fine. She trusted Gavin, Violet, and Laurie to keep the vibrant teenager at bay. Still, he was a ball of energy and curiosity, and she hoped he was staying out of trouble.

If she didn't make it out of this mess alive, at least she knew he would be all right.

Out of nowhere, her heartbeat sped up, bringing the nervous reaction down her body as her stomach did somersaults. Arkimedes was nearby. She straightened and turned, searching for him in the empty halls.

"Is there something wrong?" Fael was next to her in three strides. He had been waiting while she got some fresh air away from her room.

The thudding of heavy boots on stone came soon after, quick steps and the screeching of metal as Arkimedes turned the corner, followed by five of his guards. Like the rest, he wore his copper armor, layers of chain mail under his breastplate, and cognac leather belts that held its placard in place. His face, much like the rest of his outfit, was marked with soot and dirt. His golden skin gleamed with sweat. Vibrant green eyes sharpened over her, and his expression turned from fierce to haunted when he noticed she was there.

He held his helmet in the crook of his arm as the group strode toward them, and her heart matched their quick steps. They didn't stop when they walked past her and Fael. His gaze barely held hers before he turned around, abruptly facing forward, and continued his journey down the corridor.

Not a word or a sign of a greeting. The Zorren were back, and he was back to fighting them on his own, and it was all her fault.

"Are you ready?" The fae next to her sensed that something was off, his voice gentler than she was used to.

"Yes, I guess so." She hesitated. "Have there been forest fires nearby?"

Fael's face turned solemn as he nodded. "Been fighting them all summer."

"Do you know what might be causing them?"

He paused as they walked down the corridor to her room. "We believe it might be an attack from an organized group of the citizens who are unhappy with the king, though there is no proof of this theory. Yet."

It was vague but also wrong. Still, Nava was glad she'd gotten an answer at all. It might mean that Fael was trusting her more, and she would take that as a win on this bleak day. "Are there many unhappy citizens in the city?" Curiosity had gotten the best of her again. Her worst quality, her mother had said. But if you didn't ask questions, how were you supposed to get answers?

"Isn't there always at least someone unhappy?" Fael raised his brow as he examined her. "Let me guess, you are one of those people who like politics?"

"It's more like I'm here for the foreseeable future, and I'm curious by nature."

His lips tilted into a smile. "Yes, I guess you are going to be here for a while." Nava didn't like that comment one bit. "Our kingdom is vast, and the city's usual lack of presence from the Society of Crows made it an ideal place to migrate years ago."

Now, that piqued her interest. "The Crows don't monitor you as much as in other kingdoms?"

"We are the only kingdom in which the king possesses magic greater than the most powerful Crow."

"The prince was once a Crow," Nava commented.

"And now they have lost him." Fael's brows deepened into a frown. "We didn't know he was there, rumors of one of our kind being spotted in other kingdoms wearing black and blue. It could have been anyone."

They walked in silence, and her mind hoarded all the new information. She wished her room wasn't so close so she had more time to get answers.

"The Crows are less inclined to come searching for people here and avoid confrontation with us, just like we do with them." Fael let go of a tired breath and rubbed his prominent brows. "A while back, the king signed a new arrangement with the Society. To maintain amicable terms, they were to keep their quarters here and still hidden; in return, they would make themselves scarce from the kingdom."

"So this group, are they upset about it enough to burn a forest?"

"Oh, yes, but they are a minority. The rest of our citizens understand that one king and his army can't battle the Society if they rile up the other three kingdoms against us."

Arkimedes's mother had to have known the crown was less likely to search for him if he was part of the Society. So why leave him in an orphanage instead of leaving him with them and staying herself?

From what Arkimedes had told her, the Crows didn't take people who didn't volunteer, and the young they took were homeless magical beings. The queen would have been recognized by them, and they wouldn't have taken the child of a royal. Leaving him in an orphanage, knowing he would develop magical traits like no other, meant direct transference to the Crows, without the Copper Kingdom ever being the wiser. Had Arkimedes thought of that?

Both their mothers had been masterminds of their own plots with their children's lives. Nava's mother had cursed Arkimedes so he couldn't come to Willowbrook and get close to her, time that had turned into a decade. Then had gotten herself killed by his magic in return and had left a notebook behind with answers for whenever Nava felt like asking questions.

Which was why she was determined to ask as many questions as possible. Still, she didn't understand why the queen would want to escape and leave her child to strangers, to suffer as a misfit for life.

Fael's voice took her out of her musings. "Our kingdom is more of a mixed-race population. In the last few decades, humans have been growing angry against the fae."

Not a shocker. "Does this have anything to do with the obvious animosity that exists from the fae toward the humans?"

"The question is, what came first, the chicken or the egg? Tonight the king has demanded that I escort you and your fiancé for dinner."

The change of subject gave her whiplash. She guessed Fael didn't want to talk about the subject any longer. Nava tightened her fists, feeling the sharp sting of her nails biting her skin and the soft buzz of her magic coming alive. She didn't want to be anywhere near the king, especially now that there was this rift between Ark and her.

It was easier to direct her anger toward the man who had kidnapped her soulmate, instead of her own faults.

Fael swatted near his face, and it took her a while to recognize he was trying to get rid of a bee. She let go of a deep breath and called her insect off.

"Is this a casual affair, where the king might murder Devon and me without Ar—Prince Orion being around?"

Fael looked around, alarmed, and then lowered his face to her as he hissed, "Be quiet or you will get yourself killed, for real." He straightened. "But no, the prince will be there. You just have to be ready before sundown."

"Fine."

The beautiful archway of her bedroom door came into view, and she dreaded the loss of information about the queen and whatever was happening with the fires.

Ever since the solstice, it had been eating at her about why the women of the king's concubines were all Dark Ones. Fael had been disappointed about this.

"I have another minor question," she said with a voice she hoped sounded neutral and small. He turned to her, his lips set into a sharp line. "It's about the king's women. I'm just curious because I never knew they were once part of the Royal Guards."

"Ah, yes."

"Were you involved with one of them?" Ugh, why did her brain keep doing this to her?

"I beg your pardon?"

"In a relationship, perhaps . . . with one of the cohorts?"

His face fell. "Wow, you humans do know how to ask inappropriate questions."

Nava took a shaky breath, her cheeks warming with embarrassment. "It's not all humans, it's me. I have a problem with curiosity and lack of a mouth filter."

Fael shook his head. "One of them is my sister, Rhoan."

"Oh, and her choice disappointed you?"

He placed his helmet on his head, hiding the crestfallen expression that had flashed across his features. Nava got the impression no answers would come, which would be fine since she was being extra nosy. "I don't like it because he will never love her the way she does him."

"How do you know that?"

"It's said the queen and the king were soulmates, and we all know once they find each other, they don't fall for another person."

Nava's throat thickened, and she darted her gaze away so the fae couldn't see her anguish, remembering Arkimedes's cold expression toward her a moment ago. "They couldn't be. She has been dead for decades. I know this because—my parents were soulmates, and they died close to one another. He wouldn't have survived this long."

"Our king is the closest one gets to a direct offspring of a god," he murmured with a shrug, clearly thinking this was answer enough. "He has been alive for centuries. Much longer than any fae I know. However, he never took a wife until the tree bloomed." Fael's eyes were bright behind the slits of his helmet, much like Arkimedes, except his were amber and gold.

"So you think the tree blooms when a soulmate crosses paths with the royal heir?" This would mean everyone would know she was Arkimedes's soulmate within weeks at the most when that tree finished blooming.

"Why else hasn't it done it in centuries?"

Nava fidgeted with her clammy hands, and Fael studied her expression.

"Your heart is beating quite fast."

Great time to learn he could hear her heartbeat. Could Arkimedes do so as well? That secret keeping, annoying man wouldn't have told her so if he could. He was also part human, so maybe that didn't give him hearing superpowers.

"I have a lot of reasons to be nervous in this castle, Fael."

He didn't look convinced; however, he proceeded. "Laws of life don't affect our king like they do all of us, much less a human." The fae paused as they arrived at her room. "I don't know, or want to know, what Prince Orion and you have going on. I swore to my prince that I would protect you. But the king won't allow you two together. Our prince is too precious to us. If you care about your life and his, let him go because there won't be a new human queen in this kingdom."

Nava wanted to scream that she didn't want or care to be a queen here. She hated this kingdom, the king, and, so far, almost all the guards. However, her stumbling heart made her hesitant to voice her thoughts. The city had been a breath of fresh air, and Arkimedes had been so happy.

She had never wanted to be a queen, but neither had she wanted to be a Beekeeper or a magic wielder. Both things she now loved. That had also been the case with Arkimedes and their bond. Nava had been so sure she didn't want a thing to do with it.

Last year, she had learned to open her mind when life threw her into uncomfortable situations. Ultimately, it would be Arkimedes's and her choice, not these people's.

Her eyes prickled with fiery tears that rolled down her cheeks without her permission. "I can't stop it, and even if I could, I wouldn't," she said and turned around, slamming the door behind her. It felt like the entire world had gone against them, and it was difficult to breathe as a sob escaped her lips.

She hadn't cried this hard since remembering she had lost all memories of her dad; at the time, she'd mourned not only him but her identity. All the information her father had given her about potion making was all gone. This kingdom wanted to also take away her soulmate. To hell with them.

Nava made her way to the bathroom, wanting to splash cold water on her face to calm herself down. This kingdom had taken almost all she loved. Had stripped her down and had her fumbling for days. It might be time to tell the king she wasn't going anywhere, and that the tree was already blooming.

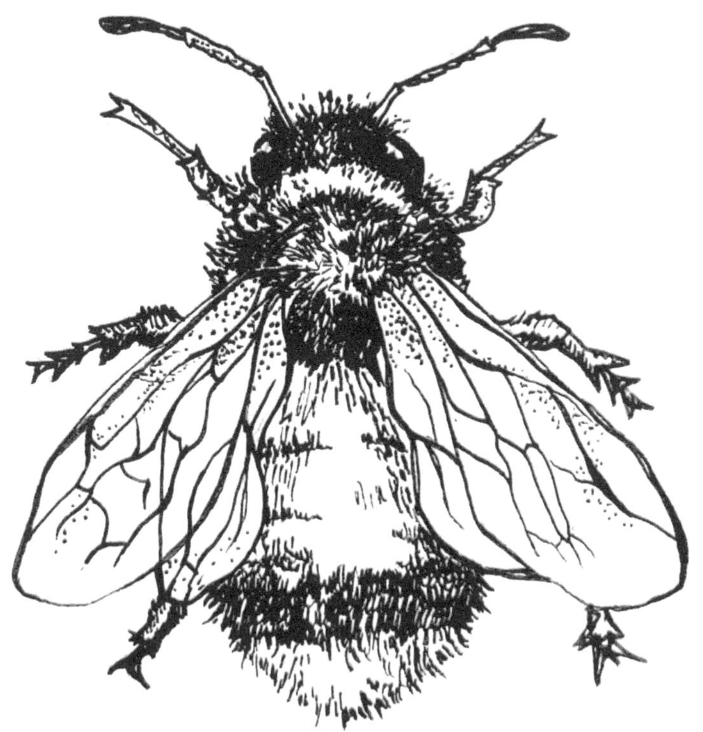

CHAPTER THIRTY

NAVA

The outfit constricted Nava's pacing across the room. It was a tan gown, almost the exact color of her olive skin, with shiny ebony beading that formed beautiful panels. It had surprised her to find this beautiful dress in her closet earlier in the day, especially since it wasn't blue. She and Leela had noticed the day of the ball that her dresses had been getting darker.

Was this something that happened with the change of seasons? The magic feeding things like this, the garden, or the fireplace is still a mystery to her.

The bodice hugged her curves until it reached her hips and then flowed like a mermaid's tail toward the floor. She was grateful the neckline was modest enough that it didn't reveal her soul mark. Nava let her hair fall wild over her shoulders. Today, for the first time since arriving, Leela hadn't come to fix her tresses into something more elaborate.

She didn't have time to worry whether her hair was proper for the king and his court, not when the forest was burning and she had to prepare herself and her magic for a possible confrontation.

Taking a deep breath to calm her nerves did nothing when all she could smell was smoke. Bees crawled over the walls and floor, no doubt answering her subconscious calling. It was hard to transfer to the forest when Fael and a new random maid had been checking on her at every hour.

Suspicion rose within her whether Arkimedes had expected her to leave the castle when the fires restarted and had upped her guard and maid rounds to be random and often.

She huffed at the spike of annoyance within her. Maybe tonight at this dinner she could talk some sense into him. If not, she might have to leave and deal with the consequences later.

Fael's gravel voice boomed over her frazzled senses. "It's time for dinner, Miss Nava."

She stood, debating whether leaving at that very moment was the best chance she would get. No one could stop her if she did.

The knock on the door startled her. "Nava?"

What was she thinking? That she would leave her soulmate here when he had lost his trust in her after her lies? No. She couldn't harm their already fragile bond any more.

Her heart shrank as she pushed down the sudden need to cry. Not wanting to be in this situation for a moment longer, needing to be near Aristaeus, but having to stay here instead, playing with pretty dresses and fearing that someone might kill her if she strayed out of this room for long.

"Be right there." She took a fortifying breath to ready herself for the night.

Devon's indigo suit and cobalt velvet cravat reminded her of the one he'd worn the day he walked into her shop almost a year ago. "You are looking rather ravishing today, cat. I would have loved to match your gown color today, but I'm afraid all my clothes are the same shades of blue." He picked her hand up in a blur, his touch scalding and wrong.

Before his lips could touch her skin, she pulled her hand away. "Do *not* put your lips on me," she hissed.

His lopsided grin became a full-toothed smile. "No fun. So who do I have to bed around here to get a different color outfit?"

The origin of such a dress was still a mystery, and in the middle of her fogged-out thoughts this afternoon, she hadn't stopped to think whether or not it might be a good idea to wear it. Should she have questioned it more? "The clothes just appear in the wardrobe. I found it and thought it would be nice for a change from the regular blue clothes."

Fael's eyes had just caught up on her outfit as well. If his furrowing brow was anything to go by, he was not happy with this news. "I thought the dress was indigo." He stepped closer, his gold eyes raking down her body. "Only the royals wear black."

"What?" She shook her head, her bottom lip trembling as perspiration built up. "Then it must be indigo."

Except it wasn't. Nava lowered her gaze to the gown sleeves, semi-transparent black. She hadn't seen Leela since the day of the ball; earlier in the day, she had gotten dressed on her own, not questioning a thing. What if this wasn't a dress facilitated by magic? Maybe someone had placed it there to get her in trouble.

Or maybe . . . the changing in the tree somehow signaled the magic of the castle to change this as well?

She exchanged a look with Devon. "Do you think someone was trying to sabotage me tonight by putting this gown in my wardrobe?" Leela? The thought alone made her heart shrink. Part of her never had trusted the friendly questions. What if this was one of Leela's partner's creations? She was a seamstress, after all.

Devon shrugged. "Probably."

"We don't have time to do anything about it," Fael said. "We are going to be late, and that will get more attention than the gown itself."

Her skin turned clammy. "I should go back and change."

The fae grunted in front of them, shaking his head. "No time. We have to be there before they close the doors."

Or what? What could be worse than appearing in a crowded dinner wearing the royal colors in front of the king?

The garment itched on her skin. Maybe it wasn't Leela but Marni's doing, as a form of revenge for the way she and Leela had changed the horrid yellow gown the night of the ball. Nava had wanted to blend in with the crowd, not call more attention to herself. This was what happened when one didn't have their head in the right place.

"I have a bad feeling about this," she whispered in the same rhythm as her stumbling heart.

They turned a corner around the hall, which became busier with the sheer number of people gathered by the entrance. This was not a regular quiet dinner with a few people from the court. Fael took them across the crowd toward a room they had never been in before.

It was like a secondary throne room, similar in shape, with an impressive ceiling made of beams that formed an intricate honeycomb shape. Large stained glass windows lined the sides. The late sun's rays made the colors of the art cascade onto the crowd in a shimmering rainbow. Nava spotted the royals at the center of the room. Both sat on their large ebony thrones.

The king's aura swarmed around him like spilled ink in water, and his cerulean eyes snapped upon her as if called by a magnet. Nava's legs shook under her weight just by the sheer fear running through her veins.

She had been so self-assured earlier, thinking she would be able to confront this man, tell him who she was. Nava shouldn't have worn the damn dress. It would have been better to be naked, judging by the prickling sensation of all eyes fixed on her.

Trying to look elsewhere was proving to be impossible. She found herself a captive to the king's deepening scowl, and the warm swarm of panic that raged in her stomach wasn't only her own. Arkimedes's emotions were so strong they sent hot and cold flashes through her body. Her steps slowed down, and she was too dizzy to keep walking.

Arkimedes's hands tightened on the arms of his chair, his body tense. Feeling off-kilter and dizzy, she tried to get air back to her lungs. The light warning of insects crawling over her arms was a clear sign this was moving to a fight-or-flight situation.

Had this always been meant to be a setup, about a stupid dress that would end up getting her killed?

An icy hand grasped hers, bringing her hand across the crook of an arm. The velvet touch of fabric distracted her for a moment. "Look at me, *now*."

Devon's distant voice cooled the raging flames inside her, and she took another step forward, following his pull. If she could break eye contact with whatever magic had her locked with the king, she might be able to blend in the crowd.

"Close the doors." A deep, masculine voice that felt like honey to her senses broke the murmurs in the crowd. Arkimedes's voice had been all but collected, showing some traces of the tension Nava felt through their bond.

The words had the desired response since the king's gaze had broken contact, which freed her from whatever she had been paralyzed under. It had felt too similar to the way she froze when the Dark Ones took Arkimedes from their home. Or the day she'd been frozen in the middle of the Northern Village by Devon a year ago. Mastering these sorts of spells should be at the forefront of her learning at this point.

She took a couple of quick breaths, filling her lungs with precious air as Devon pulled her into the multitude. People followed their retreating steps toward the back of the room, surprise reflected on their beautiful faces. Everyone was a fae in here, except for Devon and Nava. The two of them stood behind the crowd, illuminated by the light of the candelabra. The scent of incense and expensive perfume hung in the air. Nava allowed herself to release the panic that had her nerves tense and frantic.

Since this was not a dinner where she could talk to the king and maybe convince him to not kill her, she would gain nothing by standing like a lamb awaiting slaughter. She needed a plan A and B and C.

Inspecting every inch of the room to find a way out, she clutched Devon's arm like a lifeline. Her enemy had become her savior tonight, and the realization wasn't lost on her. She didn't want the warmth that bloomed in her stomach, thawing the hateful feelings she harbored toward this man.

But she was grateful for Devon's help—even if it was to save his own life due to the life debt.

"Next time, maybe stick to the damn blue colors, yes?" Devon murmured close to her ear.

She glared at him. "You think? I did ask Fael multiple times to let me go back and change."

"It would have helped if you weren't so ignorant about the kingdoms. It's known everywhere that black is the royal color inside this castle."

But she didn't know this, not when she had learned so little of the four kingdoms and their cultures. Her mother had always intended for her and Cameron to be sheltered. To live inside a non-magical island where no king could ever harm her, let alone kill her. "It wasn't my choice to know so little about . . . the world," she whispered. However, the words didn't ring true. Her mother had been gone for years now. What excuse did Nava have to turn a blind eye to everybody outside the Grey Island for so long?

She avoided Devon's gaze. Being vulnerable in front of this man was not her idea of a fun evening, but he had just saved her, and that left her a bit off-kilter.

Devon hummed, studying their surroundings. His sharp jaw caught the highlight of the candlelight like a blade. "The universe is intent on shoving you out into the outside world, despite Celeste's attempts."

Nava allowed her eyes to drift back to the man and her shoulders eased. The universe, the gods of this world, destiny. They all had picked their players in a game she and Arkimedes were forced to play—dragging this man alongside them.

She was a woman tied to a kingdom hell-bent on killing her, and she needed to find a way out.

There were three large doors around the circular room, each one closed with a couple of guards at each side. For a supposed dinner, this was suspicious. Were they expecting trouble?

If the worst came to pass, she could transfer out through one of the door crevices. Maybe if that happened, Arkimedes could save Devon and not have to worry about her. She reminded herself that the only person who knew she wasn't helpless was her soulmate, and she trusted him with her life, even in their rocky circumstances.

Nava focused on Arkimedes, who rose from his seat as if called by her thoughts. His skin was clean of all the soot from earlier in the day, which meant he had been back in his room and had avoided seeing her. She would know, as she'd waited for him on the balcony after she returned from her walk.

His green eyes met hers across the multitude of fae around them, and the room went quiet at his solemn face. "The forest is burning," he said, and murmurs erupted around. Nava could hear the angry inflections in their whispers.

"The humans are doing this."

"It's too close to the city."

"Silence." The king's voice boomed over the room, and every whisper quieted in an instant.

"We have been using our best guards to locate the culprits. Following leads, as some of you suspected a local group from the village was responsible for the attacks. However, this is not the truth. The royal guard and I have been battling demons in our woods for the last week."

Nava's stomach dropped as she clasped her hand over her chest, feeling the bond toward this man, toward nature, ache. Murmurs of panic and alarm spread like an echo in a cave, and Arkimedes found her again. "Today we battled at least fifteen."

Even Devon was quiet, though she felt his eyes burning on the side of her face.

"Be at ease, my people. It's not the first time I have encountered the Zorren in my life." The king stood from his throne, and for the first time since Nava had arrived at this castle, she could see his pale features through the mist of his power.

His almost translucent skin lacked the natural glow Arkimedes had, and for someone so beautiful and young in appearance, his jaded expression didn't hide an ancient air about him. Fael had said he was the oldest fae he had ever met, and according to Leela, both she and Nava's guard were pretty old themselves, to Nava's twenty-six.

"I don't believe it's a coincidence my heir came back, led by his need to help his people. His magic, much like my own, feeds the castle you stand in tonight, the roads you drive and ride on. The grounds this very city is built upon. I have no doubt with our powers combined, we will have no problem finding and fighting this new foe knocking at our doorstep."

He came back . . .

She studied Arkimedes's features, the way the copper crown rested on top of his thick brown hair. He looked at peace with the king's words.

Nava's mind reached deep within herself, and the bitter taste on her tongue grew more pronounced. Her eyes snapped to the kingdom's emblem stitched on the backs of both thrones. A dead tree, with roots and branches that mirrored one another. The queen's tree.

Nava knew this already; she had talked about it with Arkimedes when he showed her both the real one and the one in the forest where his mother had been killed. But the nagging sensation that she was forgetting something told her it wasn't a memory from this kingdom, but from a different one.

Nava's throat closed in, her vision hazing. When she arrived in the kingdom, her first reaction to the emblem was that she had seen it before. Not in a book or in a dream, but etched onto the blades that decorated her soulmate's cabin walls a year ago.

There had been two swords. One said his name, Arkimedes B. Valeron. The other had the image of this kingdom's tree. It had been the sword he'd taken with him to battle, choosing this weapon over the one from when he was a Valeron, a Crow.

"He always wanted to be back," she breathed.

Arkimedes had been here like he had told her and had left, maybe intending to return to what he'd always perceived as his destiny, the one he was so adamant to fulfill now. He had wanted to be back because the kingdom needed him. Had his plans been derailed the day he found her when he'd been forced to run away across the world to survive and not die?

Her mother's choice had made it so. Because they were soulmates and being apart after finding each other meant death. He'd had to run away from this life because of her.

"The royal army will begin preparing for an attack, and until further notice, all civilians, *including humans*, are banned from entering the forest. This is for your protection, and defiance to my command will be your end. By my hands or the demons," the king finished and sat again.

The heat in her body swelled, setting her nerve endings aflame.

A dry cackle escaped Devon's lips. "I guess he didn't tell you he always intended to be back."

Swallowing, Nava turned around, not able to look at Arkimedes any longer with the guilt that sank in her stomach. No wonder he didn't want to leave. He had already sacrificed a decade of his life to wait for her, alone and unwanted in that forest she was trying so hard to force him back into.

Devon was in front of her in a few strides. "So are you this quiet because of the Zorren?"

"Oh, no, I know about the Zorren," she breathed. "I didn't put together that he knew he was a freaking prince."

"Ah." Devon's eyes shone with mischief. Like he had been waiting for this kind of dessert. "So he didn't tell you last year he had a big life responsibility awaiting him elsewhere? He does like to keep his things quiet."

Nava's jaw ached as her vision blurred with unshed tears. "I didn't know."

"You don't know many things, cat. However, I figured he told you, with you both being . . . so close."

Had her mother known? She hadn't mentioned it in her diary. Nava's heart was pulling and pushing her toward angry feelings her mind didn't think it had the right to go to. "He is a man of secrets," she said, lowering her gaze to the floor, trying to calm her erratic breathing. Horror clutched her at the thought that he had given up so much for her.

"He had been back for three days the day we found you. We wanted to check on Celeste, and her involvement with a shady group, before he went to the Society and explained he had to leave." Devon's casual tone in the oddest moments always surprised her.

Shady group—Nava filed that comment for later. Right now she didn't want to ask about her mother.

"Would the Society have let him go?" Was that even her voice? She sounded so beaten down.

"Of course. The Society has no claims over the crown's heirs. The king and Arkimedes alone are dangerous enough to piss off, let alone with an army of Dark Ones."

Nava swallowed. "That's why he wants to stay now. He always wanted to be back here."

Devon's smile faltered into a grimace. "Arkimedes of ten years ago wanted this. The man I met last year was not the same brother I knew, for better or for worse."

Nava loved the man he was; she was hopeless at loving him even now when he was a stranger wearing her lover's skin. "How much longer do we have to stay in this room? I'd rather leave when the king is not looking to murder me."

"The doors are still closed, so unless the prince or that guard who follows you around comes to get us out, we are very well stuck in here."

Nava raised her hand to her temple, trying to massage away her building headache. She would have liked to leave this kingdom, but now things were different. She had more information that made her own selfish needs take pause.

She wished Arkimedes had confided in her, but she also understood him. Circumstances had made her walk the steps of someone who withheld information due to fear, and she wouldn't be so quick to judge him again.

Maybe he didn't want her to feel the way she did now—like she had stolen his life away.

She had to believe he had been trying to protect her from a kingdom that hated humans. From a place that might be dangerous for her, as he didn't know why he'd been abandoned in the first place. She understood now that however misguided either of their reasonings were, the truths they withheld weren't meant to hurt one another.

CHAPTER THIRTY-ONE

NAVA

When the prince of the Dark Ones walked to you in a crowd, it was expected the eyes of every stranger to follow. No longer frozen by the king, Nava could study everyone around them. There had to be at least a hundred people inside.

She spotted the king's cohorts near the two thrones. Unlike the night she'd seen them for the first time, tonight they wore armor. Some made of aged copper, some shiny new metal. Their blackish auras billowed around them as they stood waiting for their king.

All of them held their helmets in their arms, their hair pulled back or braided, awaiting a battle to come soon. Nava wasn't sure if she was feeling jealous of them being able to fight or admiration that they would choose to do so, even when they were no longer part of the guard.

The fae parted ways to allow Arkimedes to cross toward them with long steps. He wore a black suit with gold embroidered details on the jacket. By the time she had to crane her neck to meet him, she could hear the screeching sound of the doors opening in the distance.

"What are you wearing?" he asked between his teeth, his eyes blazing as he studied her.

"It was in my wardrobe," she blurted, battling her need to fidget. "I assumed everything in there was acceptable for me to wear."

"There was nothing black in mine," Devon piped in, studying his fingernails with a quirk of his lips.

Arkimedes glared at his brother. "We've gotta get you two out of here."

They walked out like souls traveling to purgatory. The tight skirt of the dress and her pointy heels made it difficult to keep up with the two giants on either side of her. Neither spoke as they went up the stairs toward the prince's wing.

When the halls were quiet and no one was around, she couldn't hold the silence any longer. "If what makes you so mad is that my dress is black, you have to know I didn't do it. I didn't even know black was the royal color until Fael came to get me. I have no reason to want to get myself killed." Plus, there was the thought she'd had before that maybe his own magic had pushed the change to start.

"I know, Nava." Slowing his walk, he turned to her, his voice below a whisper. "I believe our connection was what made it happen."

Ha! She had been right; the change of her dress was related to Arkimedes's and her connection.

"Like my father said, my magic is linked to this land. The moment you arrived here, it knew who you were because of our bond. The tree is alive, and the clothes have shifted." It was the first time he'd looked at her so intently since their argument.

"Why didn't it happen sooner?"

"I wouldn't say it has been long. We have been here for, what . . . a little over a week?" Devon chimed in. "But the king did say both their magics are connected to this place . . . so it might have something to do with the king's feelings about you."

Nava remembered the day Leela spoke about the queen in her room, how the air had shifted. Had that been related to this as well?

"When Fael brought me to this castle, my clothes changed from the Society of Crows' uniform to a deep black shade in a matter of days," Ark said. "There is no fooling this magic from what runs through our blood."

For once, Devon's face was not one of mocking triumph. "We need to leave, *now*. If the king finds out she is your . . . you know what, he can hold her to get you to do things you might not want to."

He was an expert in evildoing, after all. Was that what he'd intended to do last year when he captured her in battle? He had been so sure Arkimedes would follow. She held her tongue; it wouldn't help their circumstances for her to pick a fight with Devon at this moment.

They had stopped in front of Devon's door, and Arkimedes's hand hovered over the door handle. "I won't leave when my kingdom is being attacked by the Zorren."

"So what then? We stay here and wait for the king to take her . . . and kill me?" Devon challenged, stepping into the room without a look back.

Arkimedes's eyes landed on her. A pained expression that matched the churning in her stomach stared back at her. He had not said the words, but the dread building in him . . . she felt it clear through their bond.

Nava shook her head, wanting to reach to him and hold his hand, but her throat tightened with the realization that she didn't feel like she could. "Whatever you are thinking . . ."

"It will be better if we speak in Devon's room," he said instead.

Her stomach dropped, and cold shot through her body. With the screeching sound of the door opening wider, he shifted his body and waited, silent.

Nava straightened her back. The prickle of her magic came alive under her skin, and white bees hovered over her, a protective shield to guard her breaking heart.

The room was as opulent as she had imagined it. With natural drapes and white-and-gold couches. The floor and fireplace were polished white marble, and the click of her heels echoed in the quiet room, right before the door snapped shut behind her.

Devon cursed out loud, his wide eyes staring at her as the bees circled her body. "Has she been able to do magic all along? Why the hell are we still here, Nava?"

Her chin shook with pent-up emotion as Arkimedes's morose mood pushed through the bond. He didn't even need to speak the words for her to know he wanted them to be separated.

"Devon . . ." Arkimedes warned, but the Crow continued.

"We could have been gone a day after we arrived at this place! Just get this thing off me." He lifted his hand and shook the bangle.

"We can't remove it from you or I would have done it already, Devon. It will poison you." Arkimedes took a step closer to her. She was shaking, the adrenaline of all that had happened in that circular room and the pent-up tension finally catching up to her.

He stood a bit too close to her, but instead of calming her nerves, it made them flare up. She knew he didn't want to be close to her. This was his own nature telling him to be so when he so desperately wanted space.

At this point, Nava wasn't sure her pride could let her enjoy it, not when her gut told her something was wrong.

"So, what then? We stay in this castle?" Devon lifted both hands over his head and dropped them in frustration. "And what's with the demons? How long have they been attacking the kingdom?"

"A week or so before I was brought back. The king thought they were fires from a particularly warm summer. Then it was thought to be arson by the Fallen Crows . . ."

Devon cursed, and recognition tainted his pale features. Nava turned to Arkimedes, her lips parting as her mind went into overdrive. The Zorren had been attacking this kingdom for a while, not because of her and Ari being here. Had they been waiting? Was it a coincidence?

Not once had Aristaeus told her that they needed to go back to the Grey Island so the demons would leave this kingdom. Did this mean the three of them were where they were supposed to be, against all odds?

Had she been the only one trying to be out of here when she should have been focusing on something else?

"You are right, Devon." Arkimedes's eyes burrowed into her instead of looking at the Crow. His forehead crinkled as the color drained from his features. "You two are in danger here. If the king doesn't know you are my soulmate, Nava, he will soon. It would have been easier for me to protect you had you been a regular human. Even though there is a stigma, the king doesn't hate humans."

"He hates soulmates? I heard around here that he and the queen were soulmates."

"Before I knew about us, I didn't believe in the whole concept of it myself, so I brushed it off as hallway rumors."

"What are you saying?" She turned to face him. He was so close, his scent wrapped around her like the hug he wouldn't give her.

"You and I have to go, while he stays here playing prince." Devon's voice was like a bucket of ice over her, and Arkimedes's warning gaze flashed over her head to the man behind.

"You can't seriously consider this," she said, crossing her arms over her chest. "We can't be apart. It will hurt us. It almost *killed* me. Plus, I'm not leaving when the Zorren are wrecking the forest. You . . . you know better."

"I don't intend for you to leave the city. You will be close but removed from the king's reach." He raised his hand toward her but hesitated before his fingers reached her shoulder. "I will be coming often to see you, and it will be easier to plan where to go from there."

What he was not saying was how he needed space away from her. Arkimedes wanted to keep her close enough so his soul wouldn't hurt, but far so his heart wouldn't get too attached. Nava wasn't sure who she had pissed off in a previous life, but she must have done a mighty good job at it.

Devon's voice broke the silence. "Are you thinking of us staying in the Society's safe house in town?"

Nava turned her head to the Crow, and her back crawled. She would rather stay in the forest than step foot inside a Society of Crows' house. She had grown more accepting in the last year, but not this much. "Absolutely *not.*"

"My father is bound by the treaty he signed not to enter that safe house. He can't destroy or harm the property either."

"Ask me if I care. I'm not stepping a foot inside that safe house."

Arkimedes pinched the bridge of his nose with two fingers. "Why not? Your mother was part of the Society."

"Yes, and I ran away from the two of you for a whole decade, just so I could keep my freedom from the Society. You seem to think you have control over me." She took a step closer and tapped her pointer finger over the hard planes of his chest, waves of anger burning in the pit of her stomach. "I'm not serving myself on a gold platter to them."

His hand captured hers in a gentle move, holding her as he studied her features with a puzzled expression. "There won't be any Crows there, other than Devon."

"My answer is still no."

"Nava. There is no other place I can think of where the king can't just pluck you from while in the city." His gaze turned wild and pleading. "I can't leave the city to burn."

She swallowed and pulled her hand away from his grasp, taking a healthy step back as her heart stuttered. "Wouldn't it send an alarm to the Society if nonmembers enter?"

"You will be invited by one of us."

"I'm not talking about me, Ark. Can either of you still walk in there? You deserted them over a decade ago, and Devon has been a prisoner for a year . . . which might have made them start their pursuit of another possible escapee. We all know how much they love those."

"What?" Arkimedes's face lost all color as he looked back at his brother. "What did you do?"

"She is such a charmer, isn't she?" Devon's voice dripped with venom. "Why don't you dig into the memories you are so desperately avoiding and see for yourself?"

With those words out, it wasn't about the Society's safe house or the fact that she believed Arkimedes wanted space. Time slowed down. She searched for answers in his expression, and the sudden tension in his shoulders gave it to her.

Did that mean Arkimedes had access to his memories of her and had been avoiding them?

"Nava . . ."

She hadn't meant to say her question out loud. "Are you avoiding your memories from the last decade? From us?"

"It's not the time nor place to talk about this."

In other words, yes. The ground beneath them shook as the pulse of her magic left her body in a thunderous wave.

He could work on recovering his memories, to love her again, to know all that had happened in the last ten years that had made him choose her over this. But he was making a different choice now.

She took a step back when he tried to come closer, presumably to calm her from unleashing an earthquake in this castle. The buzzing of her bees became stronger, and she battled her own need to disappear from this place and not come back.

Beyond her broken heart, the love she had for this man was strong enough that she knew being away meant their deaths—and she couldn't do that to him, nor to Cameron or Ari. Nava steeled her spine and called for strength she didn't know she had left. "If going to this safe house will buy us time, then I guess I will go there, but I won't play by these prisoner rules anymore. I will be going into that forest, with or without your consent." No matter what happened, after tonight she would be transferring to Ari every day.

Nava had lost Arkimedes, even though she had done all she could to prevent it. She had lost her identity as a potion maker and had lost her father. Memories she could never gain back, unlike him.

Her stomach churned and her skin turned warm, yet it wasn't anger alone, but despair. Hadn't he given up ten years for her, living like a hermit in a cabin in the woods, cursed to be a bird every night by her own mother? Unable to reach his soulmate or the destiny he had once believed was his.

Maybe it was her turn to suffer from a distance.

"So, let me get this straight. You want the both of us to go to the Society's house and pray we aren't caught by the guards on our way out?" Said Devon.

"No, *I* will take you tonight. We will leave after the sun goes down," Arkimedes said. "The guards are being dispatched to the forest tonight. The king is going as well. I'm to stay inside the city walls to keep the wards from collapsing in case we get more attacks than expected."

"So the king will find out you helped us escape and hurt you? No, thank you. We will all go or I won't be going anywhere."

"The only way he can hurt me is if he gets *you*." The way his expression shifted from worry to affection, then back to the former had her head spinning. "Tonight while he is out, I need to find the key to take the bracelets off you, which he keeps in his room. But I will come back and stay with the two of you in the safe house."

"So, you aren't staying in the castle?" she asked.

He shook his head, and there was a fair amount of hesitation flowing through their bond.

A horn echoed out in the gardens, along with the loud steps of metal on stone, as soldiers marched over gravel pathways to the forest. Their copper armor shone pink and brass under the golden shades of the setting sun. The three of them walked to the balcony and held onto the railing that was still warm from the day. Over a hundred Dark Ones headed to the outer walls of the castle, and in the very front, hidden by darkness, was the king himself.

CHAPTER THIRTY-TWO

ORION

It was hard not to make promises to Nava when she looked at him the way she did just now. Her lip quivered as her eyes dipped to the floor. Orion was ready to throw caution to the wind and do whatever she wanted from him.

It had to be a bond-induced drive that didn't line up with what he *needed* to do. Before she arrived at the castle, his strive to find answers had taken precedence. Why he'd been abandoned when he was just a toddler. What made his mother's spirit haunt him, repeatedly showing him a horrible nightmare of the night she died.

He had a bigger role in this kingdom, one he accepted before he ever met Nava, this time around . . . eleven years ago. Because of a soulmate, he'd abandoned this purpose—a whole kingdom—to the mercy of lost protection.

Still, he battled his primal need to say to hell with his role and the answers he always searched for.

Sensing her emotions through the pit of his stomach made his decision-making weak at best, and that alone was reason to break this irrational need to be what she needed him to be. He appreciated she wasn't asking for more than he was ready to give right now.

Orion brought his hand over his chest, massaging away the throbbing ache that built underneath. The guards marched toward the walls, and beyond them, a black smoke of fire already lifted in the air, clouding the forest behind.

"Do we leave now that the king is out of sight?" Nava swallowed. "We should be there too . . . Ari needs us."

Devon turned around to face them, his pale fingers tapping over the stone railing. "Who is this Ari person I keep hearing about?"

Orion ignored his brother's question. It was worth putting a pin in the way his stomach churned at the idea of revealing the Beekeeper to his brother. Then the flash came to him like a cold winter's breeze.

Devon held Nava by her neck, his face twisted with rage. Blue fire burned behind him in houses built on the sides of large trees. He made it to them fast. "Devon, let her go." The bitter taste of panic and dread coated his tongue.

Devon's grip tightened against her throat, and the smell of magic wafted around them. "And why would I do that?" Menace dripped off each word. "Keeping her will ensure you don't kill me, brother."

"If you don't let her go, I will kill you," he promised and meant every single word.

His breath tore out of his lungs as he shook off the memory and took a step back. He wished he could ignore that vision—the betrayal that churned in his gut. Orion stormed back inside the room.

His heartbeat drummed against his rib cage, and the air was too thick to get enough into his lungs. Were all the people he thought of as family meant to betray him?

"Are you all right?" Nava's heels clicked on the marble floor. Her voice was like a healing salve over a wound he had just reopened. She was by his side in a blink, grasping his forearm, blue and brown eyes studying him closely.

"I—" He cleared his throat, as the touch alone grounded him. "The king can take care of the demons tonight. It's better if you are away from him while he doesn't know you are my mate."

Why, if Devon had attacked her, was he here with her? Now her hostile predisposition toward his brother made sense. Why was she trusting him?

Everything fit into place. Devon was under some sort of bond. That much had been clear when they had talked about it, a life debt or a blood bond by the trust Nava had with him not hurting her.

Nava had said she almost died when the king took him from the Grey Island . . . and Devon had been in prison. Had the desperation of almost dying forced her hand to trust Devon, even after what he'd done to her?

They had traveled through a portal to get to this kingdom, and Nava had paid the price. She had lost memories that were too dear to her, which led her to a panic attack.

There was one person in this world who would do anything for him, and that wasn't his father or his brother, but this woman. Just like at one point in the last decade, he had dropped everything that made him the man he was for her. His identity as he knew it hung from a fine thread.

"I don't understand why we have to run and hide. If the rumors are correct, your father had a soulmate he loved. He should understand that he can't kill me and keep the heir he so desperately wants."

"My mother might have been his soulmate, Nava, but she ended up dead after she betrayed him. He won't look at this with a rational mind."

"Not to stir the pot further, but if he already took your memories once, he could do so again when he finds out you have let us go." Devon's voice was claws and poison gripping his gut, and the images of him hurting Nava were hard to ignore.

He closed his hands into fists and allowed his breath to even out. "I now know what he did to block my memories, which would lead me to a better defense against another attempt, but . . . it's always a possibility."

Orion was battling and losing a war against what he desired and what needed to be done. He needed to get the keys or else they would be tracked. Them being able to move around the city without trackers would give them freedom enough to live outside the castle while he figured out what needed to be done. With the kingdom, his past—and his future. Many questions were swimming in his mind, and he couldn't make a decision when lives depended on him.

Orion didn't want to keep Nava from being around nature even for her protection, especially when things like the Zorren were wreaking havoc.

With the new memory of what happened in the Grey Island with Devon, Orion couldn't leave Nava alone in that house with his brother while he was so far away in the castle. "We will go first to the king's room to get the keys and then head to the safe house."

"Why do we need the keys so badly?"

"I, for one, would like my magic back, especially if we are going to be hunted by the king and his dogs."

Nava's brows furrowed as she crossed her arms over her chest. "Who's to say you won't betray us when you get your magic back? Are you even still under the life debt?"

Ah, a life debt. "Who do you owe your debt to, Devon, Nava or me?"

Devon's lips pulled into a lazy smile. "Like I said, search your own damn memories."

"Enough with this. It's your life debt, Ark. You saved him last year from me." Nava cleared her throat, looking uncomfortable. "He had me and was hurting me—was hurting so many. I was angry, and I didn't know what I was doing with my magic."

His throat went dry, and he wished the images didn't flash through his mind the way they did.

Bees swarmed towards Devon from the sky, stinging him until he lay too still on the ground. He had asked Nava to stop.

Orion's heartbeats were too heavy. "I—remember it," he admitted. Nava's lips parted as she searched him for more. Hope glowed behind her dark lashes. "Did you call for the life debt?"

"I was running out of time, and I didn't know how else to get here."

Devon let out a heavy breath and walked to the sitting area, where he fell onto one of the chairs. "I have tried to leave multiple times, once during the solstice. The faes were too drunk and occupied to pay attention to me. I just had to slip past the gates, make it to the safe house, and wait for a member of the Society to come." He shrugged one shoulder and met Orion's gaze. "They have tools to get rid of jewelry like this bracelet—or the plan B was that I would bargain with the king after."

"Why are you telling us this?"

"I couldn't leave." He swung his head back with a dramatic sigh. "Not because of the debt, which is still active, but because . . . I had been searching for you for a decade, Arkimedes. Sometimes we do unimaginable things to try to get our family back. What I did doesn't make me different from the king, but I doubt anyone in this room has a clean conscience to condemn me for it."

Nava's mouth opened but shut soon after, and her guilt and shame flooded Orion's stomach like a tsunami.

"The reason we need to take the bracelets off is not because they cancel magic, Nava. It also allows the king to track you two."

"Oh."

"The location of the safe house is a secret only members of the Society know. Having a beacon leading him straight to it would mean you two would have to stay inside the house and not help with the Zorren situation."

"So we find the key and then head there?"

"This is the first time in the last four months the king has left the castle—it might be our chance to get the keys and avoid a confrontation."

"I can't believe I'm going to a Society's safe house of my own free will. Let it be known that I'm not happy about this."

Devon's forced laughter bounced over the walls of the room. "Cat, you haven't precisely made it a secret."

Finding the lost memories of what Devon had done last year didn't make Orion's choice any easier. Now there was a decade of secrets, of experiences, that had split them apart.

"I would like to get changed out of the dress that almost got me killed before we leave," Nava said, pulling at the fabric that wrapped around her narrow waist like a second skin. His eyes trailed up her body. He wished he could allow himself to help her out of the dress, if she would let him. But the reasons to keep his distance were present.

She had told him they'd met again a year ago, and that man she knew, it wasn't him. Not fully. And Orion wasn't ready to jump into those shoes. The thought of opening the weight of those memories, woven in a hazy web inside his brain, was haunting him, much like his mother.

Would he abandon it all again for her?

He swallowed and forced his eyes from her body to her face, and she raised a challenging brow at him, having caught him looking at her. His cheeks warmed. "Sorry."

CHAPTER THIRTY-THREE

NAVA

When they left Devon's room, the sky was turning black, away from the ominous gray and orange of the fires burning behind the walls of the castle.

The halls were deserted. The wind whistled through stone crevices, accompanied by the tapping of their quick steps over the marble floor. Her room wasn't far from Devon's, and as they paused outside, Nava noticed the door was ajar.

Had she and Fael left it open in their rush to make it to dinner on time? Maybe a maid had come to bring her dinner. She had not eaten anything since lunch, and her stomach growled at the reminder.

She walked forward, already anticipating the comfortable fit of her pants and well-worn boots over this tight gown. Nava hadn't taken three steps when Arkimedes's large hand grabbed her shoulder.

He stepped closer, and his lips touched the shell of her ear; the whisper of his breath sent goose bumps down the expanse of her skin. "Let's go to my room instead."

His aura was thick enough that it enveloped her body like a cool mist. She turned her head and met his intense gaze with a nod. Devon stood behind, observing everything around them. Both men moved like trained warriors, assessing for anything that could signal trouble, while she had just been coveting food and comfortable boots.

It hit her that the two of them had trained since boyhood to be like this.

While she baked cherry pies with Laurie or gardened with her mother, Ark and Devon had been forged into weapons.

Arkimedes opened the door to his room and entered after, leaving her outside in the hall with Devon. From where she stood, the room was dark; the light coming from the glass doors of the balcony cast rays of silver on the floor. It was too quiet around them, making her extra aware of the loud sound of her breaths.

"Clear."

At some point, she had stopped breathing. She turned to Devon to make sure he was following before entering the room.

It felt like ages since she had been here. Her eyes lingered over the bed as memories crashed through her of the night she and Arkimedes had shared here before he'd learned her secret and everything had gone wrong.

The room was cold enough that she took notice, but the flames in the fireplace rolled to life soon after the thought crossed her mind.

The scent of spices burned her nose and she focused on Arkimedes, who stood in the middle of the room, both hands extended in front of him, while dark mist spread out of his fingertips and leaked into the walls and floor.

The making of wards was a spell she had started to learn a month ago. There hadn't been much of a need for her to master it after Devon's soldiers had been placated. However, her mate had insisted she learn the basics just in case.

Just as she turned her palms up and called on her magic to ward this room for something she didn't know, Arkimedes opened his eyes and faced both Devon and her, frowning.

Her gut churned with an uneasiness that didn't belong to her. "Is everything all right?"

"I don't know. But we are closer now to the king's wing. We should head there as quickly as possible and then get out of here. You will need to bring your clothes to you. I'm afraid someone was in your room, and we should try to avoid a trap."

She swallowed; her scalp crawled with the sensation of being watched. This learned magic, wards and calling spells, was something she was very new and self-conscious about.

She wouldn't have been ashamed to have Ark watch and even instruct her on what to do, but this was not her normal soulmate, and now they were joined by none other than Devon Black.

"Calm down, cat, it's just a spell," Devon said, reading every single one of her insecurities that were no doubt painted on her face.

"Shut it."

His smirk grew wider, and Arkimedes stepped forward, his brows knitting together. "What's the problem?"

"I almost forget I might know more about your soulmate than you nowadays," Devon gloated, and that had both Nava's and Arkimedes's frown becoming more pronounced. "Celeste and the potion maker had Nava living in a non-magical town. The poor thing had barely any knowledge of magic when we met last year."

Arkimedes's eyes cut to her at the same time her cheeks burned.

"I know how to make a calling spell."

"Good, then you won't have to run in heels and that gown," Devon said.

Ark started, "I could go and—"

"You'd better not offer to get me my things from that room, Arkimedes, if you know what's good for you," she said, not even bothering to turn to face him, but by the cackling of Devon's laughter, she could imagine his face.

Nava swallowed the knot in her throat; she had learned earlier in the year that you could call on your things. Which was why Arkimedes couldn't manifest her clothing or the keys the king now held in his room.

It was why last year he could call the things that were in his cabin—though she'd never gotten him to explain how he could get fresh bread while they were traveling.

Nava walked to the bed and took a seat in the corner, opening her hands and closing her eyes. She pictured the armoire of the green bedroom, the musty scent inside, the now-black gowns, and the area where her clothes lay, neatly folded over.

Nava remembered the details of the white linen fabric of her shirt, the rough cotton of her pants. The worn leather of her boots, still caked with mud from her backyard. She wanted to bring anything she wore the day she'd left the Grey Island. Everything from those days was so far away now, but it represented a level of comfort she hadn't been able to reach.

Her skin turned warm as her magic became alive in her veins, right before the weight of her clothes appeared in her hands.

Devon's soft cackle turned into full-blown laughter, causing Nava to snap her eyes open and find to her horror that alongside her pants, shirt, and boots, her undergarments had appeared as well. Folded pieces of lace and thin fabric on top.

Bringing all her clothes to her chest to hide any evidence the Crow could see, she schooled her features and faced them both with what she hoped was a cool expression. "I know it has been a while since you have seen a woman's undergarments, but don't let it get you too worked up."

Devon choked, and she dared to look at Arkimedes, whose red face showed mirth, a smirk tilting his lips.

She stood from the bed and made her way into the washroom to get changed and put her embarrassment behind her.

By the time she got out of the room, wearing the clothes that fit her a bit too loose, she found Devon and Arkimedes talking in hushed tones, the latter removing cufflinks from the black shirt that peeked out of the sleeves of his jacket. "So what now?"

"Well, we—"

The knock on the door had Arkimedes stopping mid-sentence, his back straightening as he looked at the door with a deepening frown. No one spoke or moved a muscle.

"Your Highness, are you there?" Fael's familiar voice came from the other side of the door. "I haven't been able to find Miss Nava ever since dinner."

Arkimedes stood very still for a few heartbeats before he prowled to the door. Pausing in front of it, he looked back at Nava; the intensity in his gaze mirrored the turbulent feelings coming down the bond, making her nauseated.

He cracked the door and peeked through the hole, then without another word, he opened it fully. Fael stood in the doorframe, wearing his customary copper armor, holding his helmet in the crook of his arm.

Fael raised a bushy brow when his eyes met hers. "Well, now I know why I couldn't find her."

Arkimedes moved back into the room with no welcoming words. "Were you the one who opened her room?"

"Yes, I was worried something had happened, especially after what went on during dinner with the king."

"Sorry, Fael, I didn't mean to worry you," Nava said with a tilt of a smile, and the fae's golden eyes landed on Devon, then back on her, tracking down her body, catching the change of outfit.

"You are helping them escape?" Fael entered the room, his wings swaying with each step as his gaze traveled again over each of them, reaching Arkimedes last.

Nava paused and tightened her fingers around the fabric of her pants. Her shoulders tensed as the air crackled with tension.

Arkimedes shrugged off his black jacket and tossed it over the bed. "You recommended I do, a week ago if I remember correctly."

Nava's mouth fell open wide.

Fael crossed his arms over his chest with a wary expression. "Yet you were determined to keep them here. What has changed?"

Besides the king paralyzing her in front of everyone earlier?

Arkimedes's aura thickened enough that she was able to see it, the scent of magic spiking in the air. "What changed was I didn't know I was taken from a home I shared with her." His voice dropped lower. "I thought I had to save my brother from being under her spell. Turns out the one enchanted is me. You could have told me, yet you chose to leave me in the dark."

Fael's frown softened, his posture tensing at Arkimedes's tone. Devon, who sat on the edge of one of the chairs by the fireplace, stood and crossed the room with his iconic lazy steps, as if expecting a show at any moment. However, Nava could feel that Arkimedes's emotions didn't match his tone. He was calm enough; if anything, a tinge of panic started to burn in the middle of it.

He was acting angry, though he wasn't. Plans were forming inside that head of his, and that alone gave her pause.

"I swore I would follow you, my prince. But I can't defy a direct command from the king himself. His magic prevents me from doing so."

"Did he force you to swear your allegiance to me when I arrived to this kingdom? To make me feel like I had someone to trust?" Arkimedes's calculated moves were that of a predator. He opened his shirt with swift fingers, revealing light golden skin over muscle. Unlike the last time she had seen him, his ribs were bruised and his skin red. Had he been burned earlier in the forest but hadn't gotten around to seeing a healer?

She found herself taking a step toward him, her mind clawing at empty spots of memories where the potion for burns used to be. Arkimedes lifted his hand and a new, clean shirt flew out of the closet to his hand, making her gasp.

Show-off. No one else in the room cared about the flying garment or the lack of clothing.

"I swore to follow you 'till the end eleven years ago because I, like everyone in this kingdom, feared for our future. I wanted you to stay then—or to return to us of *your own free will.*" Fael's sincere tone shook at the end with pent-up emotion. "I was forced to come the day we took you, and I remembered her, which is why I offered to get them out of here."

Fael had told Nava earlier in the day that there was no future for her and Ark here, so she didn't expect the man to be trying to help her get out earlier.

The fae's chin pointed to Nava, who was already halfway toward Arkimedes. What the hell was she doing? She had no way of healing his wounds without a potion, even if she wanted to. Yet she *needed* to press her palms against his skin. To heal.

Maybe Fael had been right and she had been dropped on her head at some point.

"After what happened today with the dress—and what followed in the room with my father—I have to take them out of here to a safe place until the Zorren threat is removed and I'm able to talk with the king and not fear their safety."

"But he will follow the bracelets' trail," Fael protested. "Are you leaving us in the middle of this attack? What about the king's health? It ties to the health of this castle . . ."

Guilt churned in her gut like a festering disease. Had she been hoping Arkimedes would do that this whole time when these people were so desperate?

Arkimedes's eyes met hers. "I have to get the keys and then take them away. I'll be back after they are out of the city."

Out of the city? She'd thought he'd said the place they were going to was inside the city, but hidden. So he wasn't telling Fael about the Society's safe house. This gave her snippets of how far his trust went. Still, she was not understanding where all of this was going.

Devon brought his hand to his chin, scratching it as he followed the conversation with interest. Had he figured out what was happening? It would be extra annoying if he had, especially since she had a direct tap to Arkimedes's strongest feelings and all she was getting now was calm expectation, with a healthy dose of worry.

"I can get the keys for you, sir. Let me do this to mend what I have done. The king will believe it was me who let them go. I have been vocal about how wrong it was that we took you that way from the island. You won't have to answer for this or lose whatever memories you have just regained."

Wait. Arkimedes hadn't been trying to lead Fael to this point, right? He would never agree with letting an innocent man sacrifice his freedom and possible life for his own neck.

"I will go with you to the king's room, in case there are any spells that might delay it or harm you in any way."

"What about them?"

"They will wait for us here in the room." Arkimedes's gaze flashed to Devon, so quick she might have imagined it.

"Ark," she started, but Devon's fervent head shake distracted her long enough to miss stopping this madness from happening. Fael was already crossing the threshold and out of the room. Arkimedes walked behind the guard, buttoning his new shirt and avoiding her gaze. She grasped his arm, stopping him from going any farther. "You can't seriously consider letting

Fael throw himself to certain death when the king learns he betrayed him," she whispered.

His gaze was distant when it landed on her, but he couldn't fool her. His gut churned with building dread, tasting bitter in the back of her throat. He wasn't thrilled to do this. "It will buy us time to get you two out of here." His eyes bore into her before dropping to her lips, and his yearning exploded in her so strong her lips parted on a gasp. Then he stepped away, and the warm dizzying sensation was replaced by cool dread that pooled in her stomach.

"But you—you wouldn't let an innocent man get hurt like that," she pleaded, and that had him turning to her, his jaw clenching.

"The Arkimedes you remember wouldn't, but that's not me, Nava. It's about time you accept that." He paused, swallowing deeply, then whispered, "Become dust and leave."

She followed his retreating shape, her words getting caught on the knot forming in her throat, but he left the room without looking back. Then the door clicked shut right in front of her face, leaving Devon and her inside.

Nava gripped the door handle, which didn't move or budge, and she pounded on the wood as heat bubbled in her gut. "You asshole!" She was going to murder him, not only for locking her inside *again*, but for being such a dickhead. "I hate this new you!"

She turned in a whirlwind and ran to the balcony door. She had promised herself she wouldn't be a prisoner in one of these rooms again. The balcony door didn't move an inch, even though she shook it and pulled at it with all her strength. Bees crawled out of her skin as her magic awakened with her building panic.

Nava couldn't breathe. She didn't want to be responsible for Fael's death in the wake of his sacrifice. The king would kill him for it. Glancing at the glass of the door, she swallowed a second before she slammed her fist onto it. Pain extended past her knuckles and fingers, down her arm; however, the glass didn't crack, nor did it even shake.

"What . . . ?" Her clothes were too tight. She was going to combust with anger and desperation.

"This is very entertaining, but you should stop before you break your hand. I'm afraid neither of us can help you heal, and we will be running soon enough."

"I can't believe you are fine with this. Actually, never mind, of course you are. But Arkimedes . . . he is so ready to throw that man into certain death just to save our skin." Her throat thickened, and soon tears welled in her eyes.

"Calm down, cat. Even the Arkimedes I knew from a decade ago wouldn't do that—unless there was something else brewing beneath the surface."

She paused her movements at once, blinking as her heartbeat slowed down. He had been very calm, acting angry even though he hadn't felt it. "Do you think . . . he doesn't trust Fael?" she ventured.

Devon, who had been standing in the same spot as when Fael had been here, walked to where Arkimedes kept his armor hanging by the wall. So similar to how he had displayed his swords back in his cabin. The Crow picked the long sword, the moonlight shining over the blade's sharp edge.

Her bees flew around her with a warning—something was off. Ark's words before he parted rang in her head. They would make sense to no one but the two of them. Only Arkimedes knew she was a Beekeeper, capable of becoming dust. He had told her to leave.

"I think he realized he was being betrayed and tried to take the threat away from here."

"What are you doing?" Nava took a step back; her skin turned yellow as her power raised to her call. Was Devon going to attack her?

"He locked us here for protection, meaning he believes there is a chance we won't be alone for long. I can't open a portal and get us out of here. Do you have any better ideas?"

So he wasn't locking them in, but locking people out. "But we saw the king and the guards leave. Do you think it was a setup? It looked convincing. The fire . . ."

Oh, she hoped Aristaeus wasn't fighting this mess alone.

The pieces of the puzzle that Arkimedes had solved clicked for her all at once. He had been acting all along while Fael was here. Nava looked into Devon's eyes and knew she could leave him now, like Ark had told her to. Transfer out of this room under the crevices of that door and save herself.

He had been her enemy a year ago, but he wasn't that anymore. The realization hit her in the gut, along with acceptance. She couldn't leave Devon to fend off a group of Dark Ones when he was here because of her and couldn't use his magic.

"How long do you think we have?" Bees crawled over her body, and her stomach churned with anticipation.

Devon's eyes widened over her. "Believe it or not, cat, I'm not a soothsayer." She glared at the Crow and reconsidered her previous line of thought. "But probably not long. I'm guessing the king left guards behind just in case the prince decided to do this. If I were the mastermind behind this, I would have left enough of them to restrain him."

"You mean like you did with Mortimer when you had him stabbed?" she hissed, and her bees buzzed closer to Devon. Now real ones crawled down the crevices of the door, coming to her call.

"I asked him to *restrain* Arkimedes." Devon's face turned red, a vein popping on his forehead. "With magic, not with a physical injury that could have killed him."

Nava shook her head, refusing to go down that hole of memories that might sway her from staying and fighting alongside this man. "Back on the Grey Island, there were enough Dark Ones to restrain him and portal him back here." She exhaled. "They are going to kill us and take away his memories again."

"They will *try*. But they don't know they should fear you, cat. It will be their biggest mistake—take it from someone who has learned that lesson."

CHAPTER THIRTY-FOUR

ORION

Orion had been on this side of the castle twice—maybe trice since he'd found out he was part of the royal family. It seemed like such a long time ago but, at the same time, like it had just happened yesterday.

Large windows lined the walls, with metal black frames and intricate art that told stories of a millennia with bold colors that reflected onto the ground. This hall was so grand, it was hazy in the distance. Orion found it difficult to keep his steps calm but determined while walking next to Fael, a fae who had sworn his life to him but was betraying him in such a bold manner.

He was sure this was some sort of setup crafted by his father, but he didn't want to act irrationally and give away that he had sniffed the plan. His mind was somewhere back in his room, where he had left Nava. If his fears were confirmed, they would be in much more trouble than he.

Orion's gut churned with images of Nava getting hurt, and the fear racing through his veins felt like frozen water. Not a muscle of his face twitched under his well-crafted mask, and having put away his wings earlier in the night allowed him easier movements.

They turned a corner toward the king's room. Here in this wing, there was a clear lack of art, and they crossed many rooms that were often occupied by his women this late in the day. The couple of times Orion had been here, the halls had smelled of lavender and roses.

Right now, it smelled like smoke, ashes, and sweat.

The moan of the wind had the ends of his hair lifting on end, and just as the memory started to come to him, they walked across a marble sculpture of the queen holding a sun. A crown of thorns lay over her head, much like the one on top of his head. Orion's throat tightened as he focused on her face. Gentle doe eyes, small but sculpted lips that tilted into an innocent smile, and long, wavy hair that hit the top of her hips.

She couldn't have been older than seventeen when this had been made, which meant she'd been just a kid when she joined the messy, dark world of her father's magic. Orion's features weren't much like hers, as he had inherited all of the king's shapes, quirks, and malice.

That lovely figure had now haunted him through these very halls for the past four months, demanding some sort of justice he had been unable to fulfill.

They slowed when they reached the king's room; the door awaited ajar, which was the first indication this was too easy and he was about to walk into a trap.

He reached for the doorknob. The cool metal under his hand warmed with the ire raging beneath his calm mask. He pushed the door open to reveal a grand space. The fireplace came on, much like it did all over the castle, providing the dark quarters with the gentle orange light of the fire.

Orion's magic bubbled out of him, like waves of rage unleashing over the walls of his body, the cage the power was always suppressed in. "Tell me, Fael, what do you think is going to happen when we cross the threshold to get the keys?"

Fael stared wide-eyed at the power that billowed out of Orion like the fires outside of the castle walls. "Sir?"

Fragments of memories crashed into him then.

He ran barefoot down the wooden steps of a narrow staircase. The landing room led him to a short hallway and a small kitchen. He moved with the familiarity of someone who had used this space many times before. He rummaged through the contents of the cabinets, looking for a bottle of wine he had picked up earlier at the market. The flash of lightning illuminated the room briefly before thunder rolled in. The hairs on his neck stood on end as if called by static, and there he sensed it. The mild scent of spice hung in the air, masked by the familiar smells of his home.

A clear edge to cayenne that was more like his magic than Nava's earthy tones.

Arkimedes turned to the doors that led to their backyard. They appeared closed, but not quite. He walked to it, his heart picking speed as he inspected his surroundings. The living and dining areas were connected and, much like everything else around him, quaint. He was able to see everything.

Still, the sensation of being watched grew stronger. The wrongness of his surroundings closed in. Shadows in the room elongated, morphing into men with large wings. Fae from the Copper Kingdom. His family's kingdom.

How had they found him?

The wine bottle slipped from his grasp at the same time the grip of multiple spells crashed into him. They didn't know Nava was upstairs, and if they did, they were uninterested in her. He gasped for air and stumbled to the dining table; one of the chairs fell to the ground.

The fae stepped out of the shadows, his wings pale gray and spotted. Golden eyes shone behind a copper helmet. "We aren't here to hurt you, my prince."

Arkimedes's magic pushed against ten—twenty—spells that caged him in. It was hard to find a hole to sneak some counterattack when these spells wove around him like a skilled spiderweb. Too many materialized.

"Stop. Please," he gasped between labored breaths.

Fael's hand wrapped around his bicep, yanking him away from the table. He had used too much strength or Arkimedes was too weakened by their magic. His hand slipped from the wooden table, and with his loss of balance, he fell forward, but the fae caught him before he collapsed against the wood surface.

His forehead hit the edge, however, and pain erupted down his brow as a warm drip of blood trailed down the side of his face.

"Your father is tired of waiting," Fael said near his ear, and then many of them came around, grabbing his arms and pulling him out of the house.

"Ark?" Nava's voice echoed around the room, a tinge of fear spiking through the bond.

Stay. *He begged that Nava wouldn't come for him and be hurt by these people. He closed his eyes and threw all his strength into a paralyzing spell. He was too weak to hold her for long, but maybe it would buy time so she wouldn't get caught in the cross fire.*

The rain hit his body, and his bare feet dragged over muddied grass as the group of fae walked in silence to the edge of the property, outside of the wards he set to prevent portals to open inside his home.

It was naïve of him to think they wouldn't come.

Orion opened his eyes, dazed by the memories that tightened his gut. Nava's voice had been so familiar, and the panic of her being hurt was something he had felt even when he didn't remember who she was, back when she'd been attacked in the castle.

The guards shouldn't have been able to sneak up on him so easily, even with all their magical strength. He—*Arkimedes*—had been too distracted that night because of Nava to detect he was being ambushed.

Devon had been right; he had grown soft while living on that island. Even though right now Fael—who was working with his father—intended to repeat the ambush, Orion had all of his senses awakened. He was ready for this.

"Were you going to stab me in my back again when we walked inside this room or out here in the hall?" he asked, raising his brow as he turned to the fae next to him.

Fael's helmet fell to the ground as the spell Orion unleashed hit him full force. It wasn't different from what they had used that night when they kidnapped him away from his house. Strings of magic woven together to subdue and repress, closing like a cocoon over a man who had betrayed him not once but twice.

Fael gasped as he fell to the ground, both hands grasping at his throat as Orion's claiming magic pushed between the webs of the other lighter spell and took away fragments of his power. "Stop. Please."

"I asked that same thing when you took me away from my home." Orion's voice became colder, so similar to the one used by the king.

He didn't remember all that had happened in that old life on the Grey Island; a part of him was clawing at any chance to remember, wanting that warmth that represented safety and love—and her. But Orion had to remind himself that it was a weakness that had gotten him captured. A distraction to what he had wanted to do for so long.

To find the reason for his past, unravel the whys of his power. To find out what had happened with the queen.

"Who is waiting for me inside my father's room?"

Fael's arms shook as he was barely able to hold his body weight from the ground, and Orion lifted his hand to the man, fingers pulling strings off his essence, taking apart his power.

"Yes, let's show him what happens when we get played," a voice echoed in his mind. It had been a while since he'd lost control of his darkness enough for the spirits to come alive.

"Fool me once, shame on you. Fool me twice, shame on us," said another, and Orion's jaw hurt as he tasted blood from biting so hard.

"That's how I know you are my son." The king's voice, soft and mellow, echoed from the empty room ahead. The shadows trembled, and similar to how it had happened that night on the Grey Island, a Dark One walked out of the shadows.

Orion's throat tightened at the sight. What was his father doing here? He was sure he had seen him riding away to the forest. Had it been a decoy, or had he portaled his way back here while Orion had been talking to Nava and Devon in his room?

The king's steps were sure, and the sound of his silver armor didn't make a noise as he walked to the door. The shadows twitched, and soon the king's females walked out of every dark corner of the room, wearing the armor needed to fight the Zorren. Yet here they were, ready to fight *him* instead. He wasn't a fool to think he could defeat all of them. There was no chance of getting inside that room with so many Dark Ones and finding the keys to release Nava and Devon.

They were the closest guards to the king, always with him, ready to defend him in case of trouble. Had the king grown tired of his insubordination and was going to kill him as well? To hell with all of the reasons why he was supposed to care about his estranged son.

"I'm sure you don't want to take Fael's soul, Orion. His life is worth a lot more to our kingdom as a loyal guard. He just brought you back home."

"Against my will."

"Are we holding you against your will now?" The king opened his palms, stopping a mere foot away from him.

Orion hadn't considered leaving the castle until this moment, when he had been so clearly set up. For what? Was the king planning to kill him? Not if all he said about the kingdom needing him was true, and he knew that was the case.

Would he try to take Orion's memories away once again? He pulled his magic back a fraction, using some of his newly acquired energy to knit a shield around his memories. He wasn't as proficient in such spells, but he had been taught to fight mind attacks in the Society. The shields were similar to the spell he was under. Strings that layered together like strands of silver.

"I want the keys," he said instead.

"So you can release *my* prisoners?" The king's expression hardened. "I don't think so, son."

Orion's power thickened, mimicking the king's. If he were to get attacked now by all of his women *and* him, Orion wouldn't be able to hold his own for long. He layered the silver strings faster.

Orion's gaze flashed toward the women, who were approaching at a slow pace so as not to spook him, waiting for a sign. One of them—Fael's sister—shifted forward, catching some of the light from the hall. Her worried face was barely masked as her energy bounced off the room.

Her hand tightened around the hilt of her weapon, and Orion wondered if these women, who he had always sensed were bitter about his return, were looking forward to whatever might come out of this.

"Nava and Devon won't stay in this castle after tonight," Orion said, shifting back half a step, and Fael's still-warm body grazed his leg. Not dead . . . yet.

"Of that, we are in agreement."

Orion's stomach churned, his head prickling with worry. He hoped his wards would keep them safe for a while, but things weren't looking too positive here with so many Dark Ones waiting for him.

Nava should have left by now; even if she were tracked, her Beekeeper magic would keep her a step ahead. He doubted the king would kill him, but her . . . that was another story.

His jaw tightened hard enough that his temples throbbed. "I won't allow you to hurt them."

The king's smile didn't reach his eyes. "I would love to see how you intend on doing so." His voice wasn't mocking or happy. "I'm sure you have noticed I have the power of a kingdom behind me . . ." It wasn't quite the power of his whole army, though he guessed some had gone out to battle the demons.

"You promised."

"You like to bring up the promise I made to you. Yet you broke yours of returning to our kingdom ten years ago. Instead, you went to live with my enemy in that pitiful town you called your home." The king had abandoned all masks of politeness. His facial features twisted with anger, revealing aged skin and wrinkles that hadn't been present before.

"I wouldn't remember that I broke any promise since I have no memories of the last decade."

The king scowled. "You made peace with the man who helped your mother escape and took you away with her."

He had to be talking about Roman, the high commander of the Iron City's army. A soldier who once had been a high-ranking member of his father's guards. The only human he knew who'd been one.

From what he could remember, Orion hadn't seen the man since they had been in the Iron City, and they weren't close. Roman was busy with the armed guards for the kingdom and had little dealings with the Society of Crows. Orion's brows knitted, and he took another step back from his father.

This wasn't buying him any time; there was no way to get what he needed from that room and leave unharmed. The room's shadows moved as if listening to a mental command he was not privy to. Maybe he could call on the keys magically instead. If the castle already recognized him as the heir and prince, perhaps it would allow the keys to come to him.

It was something he hadn't even tried.

He pictured the aged brass skeleton key in his mind and called to it. His body warmed; the energy of his surroundings responded to him. The castle did recognize him—but the keys didn't come to his hand.

The king's smirk grew wider, but this time his eyes shone with a delight Orion didn't share. He lifted his hand, opening his palm wide. "Is this what you are calling for?"

Dammit.

"Our magic is interconnected, Orion. I can sense what you are trying to do. Whether it's to ward your room or call on *my* things."

Orion swallowed, and the weight of stones settled in his stomach. "I don't want to fight you."

"Of course you don't," the king said and took a step out of the room, his black aura increasing in size. Much like it happened with Orion's when he was ready for a fight, the shapes of people came out of the mist. Arms, faces—a trail of nightmares. "You will lose. But worry not, son, I will take away these memories, and tomorrow you will be free of them."

Them. Orion didn't think his father was referring to his memories, but having both Nava and Devon disappear. Orion's wings popped out with the increase of tension running through his body.

He gasped when a surge of energy hit his body, draining whatever it could take. The king's eyes shone brighter with unnatural cerulean light, while the storm of his inky power mixed with his.

His legs wavered, but he pushed back. The voices of the fragments of souls became louder once again. Probing in anger, demanding bloodshed. He took a step toward the king, flexing as their magic pushed against one another.

Then the extra waves of magic pushed onto him all at once as five—six—other fae attacked him with the same shadow magic. He struggled not to fall as the pressure extended down his muscles. An angry cry left his lips before he fell to the ground, pain extending from his knees to his hips.

"Coward." The word left his lips before he could think twice; the claws of magic fingers wrapped around his mind, and the memory of the night he'd arrived here flashed behind his closed lids. It had been too similar to this. Many powers used to subdue him while his mind was stripped open.

"I don't need to be just to save my kingdom."

The floor beneath his hand shook and he twitched forward, closing his eyes and focusing all his power to peel away the inky fingers that clutch his mind's shield. His head throbbed as pain extended through his temples.

"You learned to shield me," the king said with a strange waver in his voice that could be mistaken for pride, had he not been torturing him alongside his concubines. Orion's anger burned deeper in the pit of his stomach as flashes of what they had done to him before came back.

He pushed against their hold, stumbling up to his feet and leaping toward the king, who looked surprised for the first time. Orion's fist connected with his father's cheek, and the energy of his adrenaline drained with the contact.

They both stumbled into the room and to the commotion of winged women rushing in. Long nails dug into his arms and chest as the women pulled him away from his father. The king lifted to his elbows and cupped his wounded chin as a trail of blood dripped from the corner of his mouth.

"They trained you well," he said. His crown straightened on its own.

Orion guessed his father was referring to the Society of Crows, and right now he was thankful for their training as well. He moved against the hold of the women; words escaped his lips even though he didn't know what he was saying. His magic took from them, fed from all it could get. Some of them even dropped him, backing away from the pull of his power.

"Hands off my heir. His magic will feed on yours if you touch him." With the king's words, the women dropped him to the ground, but their magic kept pressing into him, paralyzing him.

The king stood from the ground, and Orion's arms shook as his father's power came harder now. It was too much—too many of them against him. The silver shield of his mind was struggling against his hold, the clawing of the king's power taking away strand after strand.

Maybe he should have stayed with Nava and Devon. Sure, he hadn't expected the king and his cohorts to be waiting for him, but facing all of this alone had been his choice.

With Devon being part of the Society, it was unlikely his father would kill the man. His memories might be altered much like his. But Nava . . . Orion's sudden decision of going at this alone weighed on his chest as fear gripped him. Adrenaline pumped through his system, dimming the ache that kept building inside his head.

His body turned cold, and he reached through the bond inside him, tugging at the cord that connected them. The warmth of it seeped through his bones with the soft drumming of a heart.

She was alive—but for how much longer?

CHAPTER THIRTY-FIVE

NAVA

The only sounds around them were the hissing of the sword as it cut through the air every time Devon swung it, the tapping of Nava's boot heels on stone, and the soft rolling of the flames in the fireplace.

How long had it been since Arkimedes left with Fael? Ten minutes? An hour? No, it couldn't have been that long, even though it felt like time was crawling by. Her gut flipped, raising up a wave of nausea that had her slowing her steps as the prick of anxiety grew larger.

"Would you stop it?" Nava snapped, turning to Devon, who put the sword down for a fraction of a moment before swinging it again and lifting a brow in defiance.

"I haven't used this weapon before. It will be good to get used to its weight before we have company."

A weapon, of course. She had been so paralyzed by all that had happened, she hadn't thought about her own defense against the possible attack.

Storming toward the wall where Arkimedes's armor still hung, she looked at the heavy copper plates and mesh. The scent of smoke still hung around it, and traces of soot stained its surface. The leather straps twisted at the ends, warped by the heat of the fires.

She stepped toward the weapons next. Much like in his cabin, another long sword rested upon wooden hooks on the wall. No special markings, just a plain sharp blade that would cut through people as if they were made of butter.

Nava had never been good with swords when she learned weaponry with her mother. Daggers, yes. Bow and arrow made her fingers hurt, but she had been decent with archery at some point.

Her eyes traveled down the wall of well-displayed weapons, and the knot in her throat thickened. Arkimedes had never asked to display anything like this in their home in the village, even though it was something he liked to do.

Had she been so into her own wants and needs that she had forgotten to pay attention to what he desired? Or had he always known the island was a momentary home for them? Maybe he had been waiting to tell her this truth, to find the right time to explain that he didn't want to stay there.

She swallowed, and the almost permanent ache in her heart bloomed larger.

Under the sword's wall mount, there were three knives. Not quite daggers, but closer than a sword was. She picked the two most similar to the daggers she'd learned to fight with, the ones she'd lost when she portaled into this kingdom.

The metal was balanced and heavy in her hands. The edge of the blade reflected her eyes back, and the leather that wrapped the handle was soft, stained a rich ebony color.

"It has been a while," she admitted. "They might not come. Maybe they will attack him instead—"

Devon put the sword down. "Let's hope they don't, and that he will come back with the keys so we can get the hell out of here."

Nava opened her mouth to answer him when the door handle dipped for the first time. The prickle of dread bloomed in her skull, and a heated silence descended. The door shook as someone outside tried to pry it open. Her heart raced as it happened a couple more times before a more forceful attempt was made.

Muffled, angry voices came from outside, then the first spell hit. The heavy door screeched under its pressing power. Once. Twice. The door shook but didn't open. Her skin went damp all over, her stomach swooping with anticipation.

Their heavy breathing became louder as another spell hit again. The room became unbearable with the scent of magic. Her eyes watered as the door trembled in distress.

A loud pop boomed, and a heavy crack extended from the ceiling, down the stone of the wall, across the doorframe, and through one of the doors.

Then someone hit it full force, and even though the door was still there, it moved a fraction, the broken pieces showing sections of exposed pulp. Nava hesitated before looking at Devon who, unlike her, had walked to the door and was standing on the side with the sword, ready to attack.

Where he stood, it would be easier to get anyone who entered through the hole. She walked to the other side, hoping to imitate someone who had been taught and had fought much more than her.

The crack extended farther as a heavy body hit it full force. The masculine voice coming from the outside was clearer when the wooden door began to collapse and the gap grew larger. Nava couldn't tell what the person was saying or the responses of the fae near him, but they were angry.

She trembled as her magic rose within, her skin glowed bright yellow. She had to do this again, fight for her life like she had last year. The building dread in her stomach wasn't just hers, which meant Arkimedes was in trouble, and he was alone.

She met Devon's gaze from the other end of the doorframe, and time halted right before the door blew off its hinges. Wood pieces flew across the room, and splinters went everywhere. She was protected from them by pushing closer to the wall. The bed screeched, hit by a large piece, and flew across the room as one of the posts broke in half.

She breathed out and steeled her nerves. Four winged men stormed into the room, weapons held high with their dark auras billowing around their bodies.

Devon attacked first, pure stealth and elegant use of the weapon, like an extension of his arms. The first guard who entered had not been waiting for the strike, and the blade went through the gap between the helmet and the bottom of the chain mail, slicing the head right off the body. Blood sprayed out of the severed neck, pooling on the floor.

Bile rose in her throat. She turned away from the body and focused on the guard closer to her, who didn't take long to spot her. He was taken aback by the clear vision of her magic aura blooming off her body. A scream left her lips as she attacked with her knives raised high.

Nava swiped across metal and hit one of the straps of his arm plate. The metal slid over his arms, and the second swipe of her blade hit the chain mail underneath. His magic wrapped around her, but she had practiced against this shadow magic before in all of her training sessions with Arkimedes.

Her body heated in reflex, and the mist evaporated with the touch, then she called her bees. In the past few days, everywhere she went, the insects had always followed. Crawling over walls, camouflaged by the warm tones of the castle stones. Devon or Arkimedes hadn't noticed or maybe hadn't mentioned it.

All at once, the bees flew off the walls and swarmed the other two guards, who were jumping on Devon with both magic and weapons. Maybe they thought he was the biggest threat—and the Crow had been right. They'd underestimated her. The guards, the king, even Arkimedes.

She was a Beekeeper, a sorceress, and she would show them how wrong they were.

"Bees everywhere!" one said with a hoarse scream. From her peripheral vision, she saw a large man jump back, avoiding Devon's blade. He swatted around his face as thousands of bees descended upon him.

His pink copper armor became a moving brown shade when her insects crawled over, searching for a crevice to get in. He ran closer to the bed, his panicked breathing one of the noises in the room. His aura turned black and heavy.

"I can't get them off!" he screamed, and the man who had attacked Nava turned toward him long enough for Nava to jump on him. Her skin was bright, and it illuminated this corner of the room, cutting through the darkness that surrounded him.

She slammed the blade of her knife in the gap where the chain mail met his helmet, and warm blood splattered her hand and the side of her cheek. Pulling back, she held her gag reflex as the man staggered to the wall, dropping down while holding his neck.

Devon was on the third man, his face shiny with sweat. The Dark One's aura surrounded him. However, the guard was overtaken by bees and was struggling to see anything beyond what was in front of him.

Her body temperature was high, and the stone beneath their feet swayed under their steps. The guard by the bed fell to the ground, screaming. The bees made it through the eyeholes of his mask and the crevices between his chest and arm plates.

Their screams echoed in the room, and she heard the sword cut the air once again and a pained cry a moment later. Looking at the last guard by the broken bed sent her a flashback of how her bees had attacked Devon last year and how Arkimedes had stopped her. The man's shaky arms held him on, and there was not a visible inch of his armor.

Nava swallowed and walked to the man, leaving Devon behind. Every step she took, the bees swarmed around in a protective circle.

"Help," she heard someone say. It might have been him or her subconscious yelling at her to hold off and exercise some humanity. He had come here to hurt her—maybe kill her—but Nava didn't need to be like these people.

She called off her insects, and all at once, they flew off his body, and his shaky arms gave way as he collapsed to the floor.

Silence descended upon them, and Nava found she could take a deep breath. She heard Devon's steps by the door. His eyes were wide as he looked at her, presumably remembering all that happened to him before.

"We need to get to Arkimedes," she said and wiped the blood off her hand onto her pants, trying to distract herself with anything else than whether or not she had killed the man or how much easier it had been this time.

"He would want us to go to the safe house."

"Too bad he isn't here to call the shots—and I'm going there, whether he wants me to or not."

Devon nodded, a smirk pulling his lips as they both exited the room. "I did say you seem like a fit mate for him."

Except Nava didn't like to think she would have stormed into a trap on her own. Ark—Orion—had done that. She was much more of a team player than a lone wolf. With the threat of the attack gone for now, she could fully sink into the changes of her mate.

How he had chosen to be alone, had decided he didn't want the memories of their life together. The ache in her chest grew as she stopped by the door. If he didn't want what they had, for whatever reason, she would have to be fine with it, even though it wrecked her.

Nava had been afraid of this very thing happening when she withheld the information about their bond. She wouldn't have abandoned him before and wouldn't now either.

CHAPTER THIRTY-SIX

NAVA

It was not the first time Nava had tracked Arkimedes after he had been taken. Back in the forest when Devon attacked the Northern Village, she had been new to their bond and magic as a whole. Now, as they ran down the wide hallways of this castle, she could sense his presence. It called to her like a beacon.

The halls were empty, dark, and quiet. As if everyone around them had gone to battle. Had the royal guard left to keep the demons at bay? Was Aristaeus on his own? Or had the king just kept a few guards here to take care of them?

Nava peered around the corner to check that it was empty. The area where Arkimedes's quarters were was beautiful, decorated, clean, and elegant. But this place was on another level. The runner that covered the ground was plush and muted their hurried steps. There were marble statues or urns placed on pedestals on each side of large windows. Nava could guess this was the king's wing.

Her lungs burned, and she gasped for air with the exertion of running nonstop. If she survived the night, she had to start exercising more often.

Out of nowhere, her heart faltered from a building pressure inside her, a constricting sensation that came through the bond, followed by a wave of searing pain. Nava stumbled, and one of her knives slipped out of her fingers as she gasped, bringing both hands over her stomach.

"Are you all right?" Devon took a step toward her, and Nava took long breaths to calm the ache.

"Arkimedes is in trouble." Her voice went cold, a whisper. "We aren't far."

"Then we shouldn't be running there and alerting them of the fact that we were able to fight the guards they sent," Devon whispered back, reaching for her but stopping short of touching her before pulling his hand back.

Her closeness to Arkimedes made the ache through the bond more real, and now that both she and Devon held still and quiet, voices traveled the distance.

Nava raised her eyes to the Crow. "I will transfer there. We aren't that far from where he is." She pointed in the direction, though she wasn't sure he would follow. "It will give me a better shot of a surprise."

"Transfer? What the hell are you talking about?"

Nava straightened, ignoring the throbbing pain deep in her gut. She didn't have time, nor did she want to explain to Devon what she could do and why she could do it. Nava closed her eyes and focused on Arkimedes. She had done it before, coming to him when he needed her that day in the library.

She could do it again now that she was able to control her skills. Peering around the corner again, she spotted a large statue nearby. If she transferred there, she would have a better vantage point to assess the surroundings and come up with another plan if needed. It wouldn't be smart if she accidentally appeared in a spot that would put her life in further danger.

Nava's body became light and transparent as it floated through the air. Devon's gasp was the last thing she heard before she moved across the hall toward the statue, but before she made it all the way there, Arkimedes's clear cry of pain came from inside the room with the open door.

Her speed increased as she crossed the threshold of the room. Inside, the image was clear. Arkimedes kneeled on the ground, with his wings spread out across the floor, his arms barely holding him up.

There were six women still dressed in armor nearby, and Nava didn't have to understand the Dark Ones' power to know they were all attacking her soulmate at the same time.

She had no body, but the emotion still swelled within her, bright and bitter anger. She swirled around the room like a cyclone, sending their long hair flying over their confused faces.

The king stood a foot or so away, his hand outstretched as his aura billowed. The cool air of his mist had the same cayenne notes she always sensed on Arkimedes, but there was something old in there too, like aged leather and parchment

Nava's body began to gain substance as her emotions became stronger, blurring the lines of her transferring phase with her corporeal one. She had promised weeks ago when these people took Arkimedes that they would pay.

For weeks she had been frozen from making the wrong move, for fear of the what-ifs.

It all happened fast. She became flesh and blood behind the king, still holding a long knife. Quicker than she could think, she grasped the king's shoulder with the other hand. With a swift, steady move, she brought her blade against her enemy's throat, and the whole room went quiet.

"Release him, or I will make sure this is the last thing you do," she said, ice in her words. There was no lie behind the meaning. Nava wasn't bluffing.

The king gasped, his back going rigid as he realized who was behind him. She couldn't see Arkimedes, not with the tall mass of the king's body in front of her.

Her soulmate groaned on the ground, and a sharp pain extended past their bond, indicating no one was listening to her—yet.

Nava lifted up on her tiptoes, holding the knife tighter against the king's porcelain skin. A drop of blood trailed down the silver blade that didn't shake or waver. "Call off your bitches from the prince. *Now.*"

"Do as she says." The king's words came out choppy as Nava brought her body closer to him, making sure she didn't lose her grip and not caring one bit if she cut him in the process.

Warmth swirled inside her gut. Relief mixed with a tinge of panic that was solely his. He regained his breath once all their spells lifted from him.

"If you hurt our king," one of the women started, her voice aiming to sound menacing but coming out panicked instead. The way Nava would have sounded if their roles were reversed.

"Be quiet," Nava snapped. "Now give Arkimedes the keys to the bracelets."

The king's jaw tightened, and his bright blue eyes met hers from the side. "This is impossible. You shouldn't be able to do magic. The bracelets are active. I can sense their magic. The only way they wouldn't is if . . ." His eyes widened, at a loss for words. He lifted the two keys hanging from a pale twine and threw it across the room to where Arkimedes was.

When Ark's eyes met hers across the king's shoulder, her body was inundated with a warm swirling sensation that took over. Something that felt a lot like awe and a touch of adoration made her stomach swoop.

He took a deep breath and reached for the keys with a shaky hand before struggling to get on his two feet, his black wings disappearing from view a moment later.

"What are you planning to do, Orion? Run away and forsake our whole kingdom again?" the king asked.

"We didn't forsake the kingdom, Father. *You did.*" Arkimedes's lips tightened into a thin line as he wiped his shiny forehead and took a step toward the door, his gaze never deviating from her. "You won't chase after us, and you will stop trying to kill Nava."

Devon appeared in the doorframe, holding his sword high. Arkimedes backed away in his direction and handed him the key, which he used to remove the bracelet from his pale wrist.

The jewel hadn't finished hitting the marble ground when the air crackled with static and a black portal started to form next to the Crow. Like a dot of spilled ink suspended in midair.

"Orion." The king's distressed voice broke the silence, and Nava held him tighter, the blade biting his skin deeper. "You can't leave us with the Zorren at our doorsteps."

The Zorren. She hadn't forgotten about those, even if the king had chosen to ambush his son instead of fighting them today.

"We will be in touch," Arkimedes said just as the portal became large enough for them to walk into it. Devon crossed it first, and the whole circle shook with energy, closing a fraction. Her soulmate stared at her, and she knew by the stubborn set of his jaw that he wouldn't leave with her still so close to the king.

Her body became lighter as her legs floated in the air, then her body and her arms, and just as her fingers started to become transparent, the king turned to her, his face pale.

"What are you?"

A Beekeeper, a sorceress—his son's soulmate.

Nava brought her face a bit closer to his ear, riding the wave of adrenaline still running through her. It was time he knew who he had been trying to kill. "If the queen's tree is anything to go by, I'm the future queen of this kingdom," she said before she disappeared, rushing toward the closing portal.

The whole room went dark, ink and mist exploding in the air as Arkimedes crossed the portal, but none of the king's concubines' powers hit her transferring body.

"Stop!" The king's voice echoed in the room, and she didn't know if it had been directed at her or his women. The portal narrowed to just the size of her hand, and the wind picked up speed, pushing her across the black hole before it snapped close.

The shadow land was empty and quiet, like all life and sound was sucked away from a never-ending room. Nava's shapelessness morphed back into her body, and soon it wasn't all quiet, but her fast breathing was almost as deafening as the pouncing of her heartbeat.

Floating with no gravity, she blinked, and the glow of her skin illuminated her surroundings. Moats of particles hung in the air, and a faint scent of smoke wrapped around her like a cold hug.

"Beekeeper." The voice was like the drop of melting ice on her skin. His voice held pent-up emotion. A mixture of mischief—or was it excitement? A long shape of a creature—no, it wasn't a monster or a demon, but a man—came closer. How could he walk in such a place where bodies weighed nothing?

His shifting expression was confusing. Her stomach churned with dread, and she knew she had to leave there as soon as possible. When she crossed this land before, there had been two entities, the one who'd claimed his prize, her memories . . . and this one. The one whose touch burned.

The closer he got to her, the clearer his face became with the glow of her skin. His features changed to the man she loved. It was the same wide nose, the shape of thick lips and bushy brows. His alabaster skin was jarring with the color—or lack thereof—and his moonlight hair hung down his back, swaying as he stepped closer, long like the king she had been fighting but a moment ago.

She flailed in her spot, trying to move away from this man, floating a few inches as he advanced to her. He looked like her soulmate, but he was her worst nightmare. Panic gripped her throat.

"Nava? Nava . . . ? Where the hell is she, Devon?"

She heard Arkimedes's voice from somewhere nearby. A small hole crackled in the distance and was closing. At first she hadn't seen it because, on the other side, it was still dark, except for the distant lights of a city.

Her skin broke out into a cold sweat as this other entity pursued her. She had forgotten she was supposed to be crossing, not staying here. The soft, earthy scent of her magic spiked as she moved with swimming strokes over the air, and the creature—man—began to run toward her.

He was fast, but she was so close. Her skin tingled the closer she got to Arkimedes, the real one. The city behind him became so clear and large, she could smell the faint scent of dew and food in the air.

"I don't think so, Beekeeper." A hand wrapped around her arm, thin long fingers coated in a charcoal layer. A scream escaped her lips as an agonizing, bone-melting ache ran through her arm

Her eyes watered as she focused on that lovely face she knew so well, but up close, his features were wrong, wrinkled and translucent like an old piece of wax paper. She focused on her trembling body, her racing heart, then took a sharp breath and brought her own hand on top of his.

She was fed up with these white-haired men trying to suffocate her. Her magic blazed through her veins, and he hissed, ripping his hand away from her. A flash of branches formed over his fingers, much too similar to the way the Zorren had become a tree that day she, Aristaeus, and Arkimedes was in the forest.

Nava took the chance, not wanting to overthink this for a second longer and get trapped inside this world. She moved across the last section toward the end of the portal, and her body fell out like she was being expelled from it.

The city noises were almost deafening. The warm summer night hugged her in a welcomed embrace, a clear contrast to the ice of winter she had been surrounded by in the shadow world. The cobblestone road dug into the soft curves of her body, and she looked around in a daze.

"Hey, hey—are you all right?" A warm hand rested on her shoulder.

Her vision sharpened on the man in front of her, and she flinched as her heart picked up speed.

"Nava?" Arkimedes dropped his hand. His brows knitted in the middle as he assessed her.

It was just Ark—her soulmate—her mind supplied as she studied his features. The healthy glow of a light gold skin tone and bright green eyes. Her body trembled, at odds with the dread and relief of being near him.

"I'm all right," she said, and even to her own ears, she sounded strained. Adrenaline still ran rampant through her body. She moved back farther before trying to get to her feet.

Arkimedes straightened from his crouched position as he assessed her with worry etched on his face.

Her arms hung over her legs, hunched over while she gathered her thoughts. The stones underneath her dug in, and her eyes drifted shut before she forced them open again. Devon, who had been standing nearby, came toward her, extending her a hand. Her limbs were heavy like a bag of rocks, the feeling all too familiar, and she knew that at any moment she would pass out.

She gripped the offered hand, and the Crow pulled her up with a swift move.

"Thank you," she whispered.

Devon dropped her hand and offered her the keys. The object was foreign now, like that problem had been years and not minutes ago. She didn't move a muscle to grab them, and soon the Crow snatched her wrist and took the bracelet off.

He disappeared from view after, presumably to dispose of the jewelry somewhere where the king couldn't trace it back to the safe house.

Arkimedes's eyes bore into hers before dropping down her body, stopping at her arms. "What happened?" he asked, taking a step toward her. She had to bite the inside of her mouth and urge her body not to back away in a panic.

It was just Arkimedes—*not* the shadow man. This was not an illusion. They were in the Copper City. He sounded and smelled like her soulmate.

She looked at her arm and gasped at the bright red burns in the shape of a hand, her skin already bubbling into angry blisters. "Oh."

"Did my father do this to you?"

She met Arkimedes's gaze and took a step back when he reached for her again, swallowing the bitter taste in her throat and the sudden need to leave. "It wasn't your father."

It was you.

THE SILVER KINGDOM

THE IRON KINGDOM

THE GOLD KINGDOM

THE CURSE OF THE FALLEN

BOOK 3

THE COPPER KINGDOM

1

ORION

Few could escape a Dark One when they were out for blood, and tonight, the fae were coming for him and his soulmate. Orion tightened his hand around Nava's and sped down the narrow alleyway, nearly stumbling over a pile of scraps that blocked their path.

At this speed, they would never make it to safety before sunrise, and that meant capture. Devon was likely halfway to the safe house by now. They had foolishly split up after the guards ambushed them hours ago.

Tall buildings on either side offered them sufficient cover from the flying fae above. Even though Orion's feet ached, adrenaline and fear propelled him forward.

He glanced at Nava. Her skin glowed yellow with power. She was beautiful—and a beacon for their enemies to find them in the dark.

"Can you dim your aura? The guards can see better than humans at night." The air burned his throat with every word he spoke. He hadn't realized how out of breath he was.

Every gentle feature of her face had long since morphed into panic and exhaustion. They had been running most of the night, and they both needed a break. Yet the guards were relentless, flying low over the rooftops of the city.

Orion didn't want his citizens forced into choosing who to betray: their prince or their king.

Nava breathed raggedly. "How could they catch up with us so easily? We left the tracking bracelets near the castle. Surely they won't find us without them." Her voice wavered on the last word. Because much like him, Nava had a deeper understanding of their current predicament. The guards would never stop hunting for him, not when the future of the kingdom depended on him staying.

The castle bells had been ringing ever since their escape, echoing down the streets of the Copper City, a command for its residents to stay inside their homes, for the Dark Ones were hunting. Any poor soul who didn't obey their call would be the first to be questioned.

Was there something more leading the guards straight to them? It didn't matter. No need to trouble Nava unnecessarily when he wasn't certain himself. "It's not a large city to track when you can fly."

"But what if they can still track one of us?" Her soft tone pulled at his insides, her words echoing his own fears, almost as if she could read his mind. That thought alone was sobering enough.

Orion's muscles quivered with strain. Time to slow down the grueling pace he had been maintaining.

Nava's aura flickered as her boot caught on an uneven cobblestone. She stumbled forward with a yelp, and he barely had enough time to wrap his arms around her body before she dropped to the ground, dragging him along with the force of her fall. His wings, which he had concealed while crossing the portal earlier that night, reflexively popped out of his back right before he hit the pavement. The weight of her body sucked the air out of his lungs. Hot pain shot through him as a sharp stone dug into his body.

"Are you hurt?" She scrambled off him. Her icy fingers touched his cheek.

"I'm fine." He sat and drew a deep breath. They didn't have time for this. As much as he longed for her touch, he could dwell on that later.

His gaze stuck to the injury that branded her forearm. Someone had attacked Nava when she'd crossed the portal, and in the hours since, she'd refused to tell him what had happened.

"There is a possibility my father put a secondary spell on me so I wouldn't escape my duties again. I don't remember if he did." He brought both hands to his temples, massaging away a burgeoning headache.

"That would explain how they found us back at the plaza." She craned her neck to take in the grimy alleyway. "Do you know where we are?"

Debatable. "Yes."

She narrowed her eyes at him. "There is a myth circulating in Caztian that fae can't lie. You prove them wrong. Constantly."

"You forget I'm half human. Besides, I didn't lie just now. This part of the city looks different from what I remember." He shouldn't feel amused by the crinkle on her forehead or the way she pouted ever so slightly. This was not the time to want to kiss her, not when his father's guards were hunting them down like animals. Not when he was supposed to be keeping her safe but failing miserably at doing so.

He rose, dusting his hands off on his coat and then offering one to Nava. "We should get going. I understand you're tired, and so am I, but it's imperative that we reach the safe house before sunrise."

She opened her mouth as if to speak—but jumped toward him, pressing her hands over her lips. Her skin glowed yellow, and bees buzzed around her.

Had she seen someone? Another Dark One? Orion moved swiftly, pulling her behind him, expecting the shadows to morph into the shape of a fae.

Instead, a fluffy gray shape skittered across the rubbish-strewn ground, its long, pink tail trailing after it.

Every muscle in his body instantly relaxed. "A rat, really?"

"It crawled over my foot," she defended herself, and he could not contain the smile that spread across his face. "What? They carry diseases."

Orion chuckled, already peering through the alleyway into the larger road that lay beyond. He recognized that wooden sign hanging from the storefront… He'd been to this part of town before. When Fael had found him roaming the streets months—no, years—ago.

The safe house was five blocks south. Yet he hesitated to leave what little cover this spot offered them. Out there in the open, they would become easy pickings for the flying guards.

After the torture he'd endured earlier when his father's concubines attacked him, he was too tired to fight anyone. Especially since they had already encountered three sentinels in the plaza. Nava was probably feeling much the same.

"We aren't far from the safe house, but using the street is risky right now."

Nava chewed her bottom lip, as she often did when she was feeling nervous. "Why don't we wait here until we're sure they're gone?" She sighed. "I wish we could just sneak out during the day. Blend in with people."

"You know that won't work. I stand out from everyone, including my own kind." He caught her beautiful, strange-colored eyes as they traveled down his body. Nava had told him once she couldn't see the dark shadows that always accompanied him. Some comfort, at least.

"You're easy to see during the day, and I'm easily spotted at night." She sounded as tired as he felt. "I can't continue to run this fast without using magic, Ark."

"I know." Orion placed his open palm against her lower back. Hope blossomed in his chest when she didn't flinch away from his touch. For the last few hours, she'd avoided being too close to him, so this was a minor victory.

It was clear that she was angry with him after everything that had happened at the castle. Admittedly, he shouldn't have locked her inside his chambers and left on his own to get the key to free her from the bracelets. Of course she needed time to forgive that. But why would she seem *scared* of him after crossing the portal? He didn't like it.

"We have to reach somewhere safe before daylight. There is a large population of humans in need who live in this area. Knowing my father, he will issue a reward to anyone who turns us in. Come on."

They walked in silence toward the main street, shielded by the balconies that jutted from the buildings on either side of them. Orion tightened his hand on Nava's waist, stopping her as they reached the end of the alley. Wind moved the wooden signs of the shops, carrying loose debris along the grimy, open road. It lay dark and empty before them, barely illuminated by gas lamps. All was quiet. Until…

Tap, tap, tap.

A rattle from the rooftops above. Like small pebbles trickling down the terracotta tiles.

The hairs on the back of Orion's neck stood on end. His skin grew cold and clammy. He pressed his hand over Nava's lips and pulled her into the shadows of the alleyway. She tensed under his touch but allowed him to move them swiftly beneath the ramshackle balconies.

A shadow drifted from above, and a silhouette appeared against the backdrop of the moon's silver light. A guard knelt down like a six-foot bird of prey, scanning the streets.

Nava's breath hitched as she spotted him, too. Orion called for a shielding spell, and his magic poured from him, fibers of power weaving around their bodies and making them invisible to everyone. A frustrating, draining spell, but it might buy them enough time for the Dark One to leave.

Thankfully, the guard leaned forward, his wings flapping. Then he leaped off the rooftop and took flight, vanishing off into the night.

Nava relaxed inside Orion's embrace, and he uncoiled his arms from her waist. He hadn't even noticed he held her so close.

A thick mist rolled down the street and wafted into the alleyway. Nava trailed her hand through the humid air, which was thick enough to blur the lanterns' yellow light.

"Mist is common near the canals." Orion crept toward the main road, careful not to draw further unwanted attention. "I think we need to hide inside one of these buildings."

He pointed at the shut-down shops in front of them. Many of them were boarded up. The sign he'd spotted a while back hung crookedly in front of what had once been a glass display, creaking in the night wind.

"I thought you said we should get to the safe house tonight?"

"I did. But that guard will return as soon as the mist clears."

Unfortunately, many of the shops they passed were still locked, with thick chains wound around their door handles. It would create too much noise if they tried to break into one of them.

His father hadn't mentioned how terrible a shape this part of town was in —the rats and the filth littering the streets. A decade ago, all these businesses had been flourishing.

"What if they're waiting for us down the road?" Nava took a deep breath, clearly struggling to keep up with his long strides.

"I doubt it. The guards are aware I can conceal my wings to blend in with the humans." Orion shrugged, still keeping an eye out for somewhere to hide. He needed to get Nava to some semblance of safety. A place to settle for the rest of the night. "They also know that fighting me can be deadly, as I possess the Curse of the Fallen."

Or, as his father liked to call it, the Gift of the Fallen.

It wasn't how Orion saw his particular type of magic.

"Don't tell me there's another curse on you I have to break?" Her voice rose to a frantic pitch. Too loud.

He turned to her and pressed a finger to his lips, signaling for her to remain quiet. Nava glared in response. It was almost enough to make him smile.

"I'm talking about my ability to remove fragments of people's souls. My power is my curse to bear, if not an actual curse. But you're already familiar with it. My father's guards know that engaging in a direct fight with me means that could happen to them. So they will hunt me down from above and then signal each other to ambush us instead."

Nava was quiet, but her gaze still burned with fury. "Is that why so many of them came when they kidnapped you from our home?"

They hadn't truly spoken about that night since she'd found him. His father had sealed his memories with a complicated spell, and before tonight, Orion hadn't even wanted to unravel it. Funny how, only a few days ago, he hadn't cared about his old life at all. He wouldn't have dreamed of abandoning this kingdom.

His father didn't know that the reason Orion had left the Copper Kingdom in the first place walked beside him now. If he'd understood that, Nava wouldn't have survived this long. The thought made his stomach clench in fear.

Whatever reason his old self may have had to avoid telling her the truth about his lineage—it wasn't good enough. A part of him was thankful those memories were gone. No need to remember the stupid decision he'd made. Or the glaring fact that it had put her in danger.

Nava tilted her chin up. "And was that why your father's consorts attacked you all at the same time tonight?"

Although his father's concubines were Dark Ones like Orion, they couldn't steal fragments of souls. They could, however, drain his energy instead.

"Yes," Orion said. They really shouldn't be speaking out here in the open, even if they were barely whispering. But his body throbbed from the concubines' attack, and the sting of his father's betrayal burned too hot to ignore his need to open up to Nava. Her pain and anger sang through their soulmate bond, churning in the pit of his stomach and gripping his heart.

All of a sudden, she froze mid-step, as if she'd seen a ghost.

Orion followed her line of sight. There. Something moved behind a slightly cracked door to their left. The mist was thick enough to make it hard to see farther than five feet ahead, let alone across the street into a filthy, locked-up shop.

A pale hand emerged from the shadows, and then Devon Black's familiar features rose like a wraith in the mist. His lips were moving soundlessly as he beckoned them in. But Orion didn't need to know the exact words his brother muttered to know they should follow.

2
NAVA

Inside, the shop reeked of mildew and body odor. Nava climbed over broken furniture, taking in the wide room. A wooden counter with shattered glass ran along the back wall. It must have held loaves of bread once upon a time, like Simone's shop in Willowbrook. If Nava closed her eyes and brought it to mind, she could still smell the scent of freshly baked goods. Her stomach immediately rumbled. Gods, she was hungry.

Tears pricked at her eyes as a wave of emotion surged through her. She couldn't deal with this now. Not when her life had turned into this hide-and-chase game that didn't seem to stop.

"Took you two long enough. I almost thought you'd let yourself get captured." Devon closed the door behind them.

"You shouldn't have left us behind to deal with those guards alone," Arkimedes complained. In the dark room, his magical eyes shone with green light.

Heavy footsteps echoed toward them from the hallway to their left. They drew close. And closer. "Watch what comes out of your mouth, brother," Devon said. "We aren't alone in this place."

Arkimedes fell still, his aura darkening as he turned toward the sound.

A young man who couldn't be older than eighteen stormed out of the corridor. He lifted the rusty sword he carried with shaking hands, scowling at Devon. "Fool! You brought a Dark One with you. Now we're all damned!"

"I discovered that this shop had prior occupants," Devon said, ignoring the young man's outburst as if he were a puppy waving a stick instead of a sharp weapon.

Admittedly, the sword's blade looked rather dull.

"Get out, or I'll—"

"You'll what?" Devon's cynical smile raised gooseflesh along Nava's arms. There he was, the old enemy she'd almost forgotten. "What do you plan to do to us?"

Hesitating briefly, the man glanced at where he had come from. Was there a room? Nava couldn't see much other than crumbling plaster walls. Without a warning, he lunged at Devon, sword raised over his head.

Devon effortlessly grasped the blade with one hand, his fingers turning white as ice quickly spread over the metal's edge. Then he pulled the sword from the young man's grasp and tossed it aside. His tall frame loomed over the stranger. "There is only one fool in this room, and it's not me."

The coldness of his tone instantly transported Nava to the day Devon had first set foot in her shop in Willowbrook. He hadn't used it with her for quite some time. Alarming, how fluidly he could transition to villainy.

The young man stepped back with wide eyes. His worn blouse slipped off his shoulder, revealing his bony torso as it nearly fell off him. With such a skeletal frame, he couldn't have been eating much during his time in hiding. Whoever he was protecting was clearly a loved one.

The stranger's wary eyes darted from Devon to Arkimedes. Nava felt sorry for him, even though they'd done nothing to deserve his outburst. Fear could make anyone do foolish things.

"Stop," Arkimedes growled and rested a hand over Devon's shoulder. He looked at the young man with a stern gaze. "We mean you no harm, but we *will* stay here tonight."

The young man heaved a shaky breath, even as he crossed his arms in a vain attempt to appear larger. "N-no, you won't."

This wouldn't end well. If the child persisted, he would get hurt. "We will be gone by morning," Nava said, hoping her calm tone would ease him. Unlike the other two brutes, she was used to dealing with teenagers. "Much like you, we need shelter tonight."

His arms loosened as his shoulders dropped, and for the first time, his eyes landed squarely on her, taking in her dirty features. His face softened somewhat. Perhaps the person he was protecting was a sister. Or a sick mother.

Devon made a move toward the hallway. The young man attempted to step in front of him, although the fight had clearly left him. "You're always the voice of reason, Cat," Devon said as he pushed past the boy.

"Are we going to follow Devon to the back?" Nava asked Arkimedes. Did she even want to? The stranger had claimed this shop as his home, right? It seemed rude to impose like that.

"I know it seems wrong." Arkimedes reached for her hand, pulling her down the narrow corridor, the floor creaking beneath their feet. "But it's better if we keep our eyes on our new friends while we rest. I'm uncertain who they are and what they are capable of."

The room turned out to be a kitchen. It was larger than the front room, with a clay oven in the corner and a large sofa in front of it. Tables that must have once been used for making pastries and bread were now propped up against the walls, broken and with chunks of them missing.

A family lived here. Used these tables as kindling for fire. Two heads of raven hair peeked out from behind the couch, hiding away from their inquisitive eyes. Children.

Devon prowled to the far end of the room, ignoring the young man's protests. He shrugged off his coat and draped it over a pottery rack.

"They are very young." Nava's horrified tone matched Arkimedes's expression as he too realized what they had stumbled upon. "Hardly anyone we should worry about."

Why was man, no older than eighteen, alone in this place, protecting them? Were they his siblings—or perhaps his offsprings?

Her brother, Cameron, instantly sprang to mind. He wasn't so little anymore. At fourteen years of age, he was a young man who would try to protect her if he needed to. Oh, how happy she was that he wasn't here with her and safe instead, traveling to Pearl Island with her friends Gavin and Violet.

Tears blurred her vision as she took in the little ones. How could she help them? She stomped toward Devon, rage burning through her.

"Why did you do that?" she accused. "You *knew* there were children in here!"

"Don't look so alarmed. I never claimed to be a good guy." Devon's smile deepened, although it didn't reach his eyes.

Nava faked a laugh, a strained sound that echoed through the large room. "You didn't have to be the monster I thought you would be."

"If only I cared about what you thought of me, Kitten."

Maybe Nava would have believed him a month ago, but not anymore. Working together to save Arkimedes from his evil father had revealed layers beneath Devon's cold exterior. Devon desired to appear as an all-powerful villain, but Nava was no longer buying it.

"I don't like deserters." He ran one of his hands through his hair and glanced over her head toward the family, who were huddled by the warmth of the oven. "A household who run away with their young usually cause more harm than good to the innocents. That man's cowardice and selfishness have left them starving in this dump."

"You have it all figured out, don't you?"

"Yes, I do. Unlike you, I haven't lived a sheltered life. I've seen suffering like this before. Every time the Society of Crows takes a child for the Crown, the families get paid a handsome sum they can use to feed the rest of them. The Crown values all magical children, so they're fed and clothed."

"How do you even know that's what they are?" Nava narrowed her eyes. And where was Arkimedes, so he could talk some sense into his brother? "Being poor doesn't automatically make someone a fugitive."

"Use your eyes, Nava."

Nava drew a deep breath. Although she'd never seen his face so serious, she didn't want to get into a nasty argument with him—even if he was baiting her like this.

"I've set some wards around the shop's front. It should give us time to escape through the back if we need to." Arkimedes rejoined them, seemingly unaware of the tension brewing in the room. Or perhaps he was choosing to ignore it.

Nava studied the family more closely. A smokeless blue fire burned gently underneath a pot in the clay oven. The only fire with that color was the magical kind. She had seen it a year ago when Devon's army burned the homes of the deserters on Grey Island.

Was that how he knew what they were? The fire?

She swallowed, blinking away more tears. She wanted to go over there and promise help she couldn't offer. What would she have done if that had been her and Cameron? Would she have allowed him to live in these conditions?

And underneath all these what-ifs, another question arose. Had the city fallen into ruin because of Arkimedes's absence? Had the businesses failed during that decade he'd spent waiting for her, far away from here? Was this all her fault?

They were safe from the guards for now. But what about the male Nava had encountered in the portal, back when she'd escaped from the castle? He'd looked just like Arkimedes.

Steam billowed from her lips as she sighed, and the chill air burned her wet cheeks. She wiped away silent tears with her hand and sniffled quietly. For now, Arkimedes had given her some time alone and left with Devon to check for other points of entry into the building.

She dropped her gaze to her arm and probed the tender skin of the burn her attacker had left behind. The raised blisters had popped open during their flight to this part of town, and now an oozing wound remained behind, at risk of getting infected.

Biting the inside of her cheek, she rolled up the sleeves of her blouse, trying to keep the dirty fabric off it. Her attacker hadn't called her by her name, but he'd known she was a Beekeeper.

Hours ago, when she fled through the portal and got stuck in the shadow world, her panic hadn't allowed her to truly think about who or what he was. And seeing Arkimedes waiting for her on the other side had been too much. The similarities between them were uncanny. But surely the gods wouldn't have made Arkimedes the Beekeepers' protector, let alone her soulmate, if he meant to hurt her. She had felt nothing for the man in the shadows who looked like her mate, other than that he was her worst nightmare. No stomach fluttering, no heart racing. None of the sensations she felt when Ark was around.

She let her head drop and allowed the weight of her body to relax against the wall.

The lingering scent of magic clung to the fibers of her clothes, an insistent reminder of her run-in with the guards at the castle.

If she closed her eyes for long enough, she could still picture the way her power had come to her aid when the shadow man attacked her. How wooden branches crawled over his arm, subduing his power and buying her just enough time to escape.

It had been a first for her to grow a tree vine over someone's body and a self-defense mechanism she hadn't known she possessed. One more thing she had to learn to control.

After all that time in the castle, she wouldn't stay locked inside the Society's safe house like a prisoner. Demons still wreaked havoc in the forest, burning trees and extinguishing life, hunting her fellow Beekeeper, Aristaeus, across the land. She should be out there with him.

With everything that had happened in her life, Nava couldn't brush off the connection between her and the shadow man, either. Why single her out when three of them had crossed the portal? It had to be part of a much bigger picture, right? She no longer believed in coincidence. That she was a Beekeeper seemed to be of importance to him.

Was it the Zorren?

"What are you thinking?"

Nava jumped, barely holding a scream. "You're going to frighten me to death."

"I've been sitting here for quite a while," Arkimedes said, sitting in the opposite corner, his long legs bent, his arms resting upon his knees. His green eyes dropped to her forearm, where the burn was clearly visible after she'd rolled up her sleeves. "Are you ready to tell me how *that* happened?"

"No." She swallowed the panic that rushed through her. It tasted sour on her tongue. "I don't want to talk about it."

"Nava..."

She needed time to sort through her feelings and thoughts before she told him. "It's been a long night."

Arkimedes was already teetering on the edge of self-loathing, of wanting to keep a distance—and secrets—from her. She didn't want to feed into that by telling him that his doppelgänger had attacked her.

"You're mad at me, I know that. I deserve it."

She tugged her sleeve down, covering her mottled skin. Thankfully, there weren't any tears left in her as she let out a shaky breath. "That's an understatement. You locked me inside a room with Devon, knowing the guards were coming to kill us. Then you told me to leave you both behind."

Arkimedes's gaze skittered away from her, toward the cracked tiles that had once made a beautiful design on the floor. "They wouldn't have killed Devon. A member of the Society of Crows cannot be killed by a kingdom's army unless they violate the rules of the treaty."

"Devon is a big boy. He can take care of himself," she agreed. Although him being roped into this situation was partially her fault, since she'd called upon the life debt he owed Arkimedes. "I'm upset because you made that decision for me. I get to choose whether I stay and fight for you, with you."

Arkimedes met her eyes. Even now, Nava wasn't sure he felt any regret. He looked completely unapologetic. "I knew you could leave that room using your power, and I hoped you would get as far away from my father as possible."

"And from you."

"I beg your pardon?"

"You wanted me as far away from you as humanly possible." If only the words didn't hurt so much. But her heart still ached inside her chest at his rejection, at the memory of the massive fight that had driven a wedge between them only days ago.

He didn't want her. He'd tried to get her away from him as soon as he'd learned what she was to him.

Arkimedes's forehead wrinkled, and he reached for her—then seemed to think better of it and pulled his hand away. "Nava, I was angry that you kept our bond a secret, but mostly, I needed time to figure out a way to reveal to my father who you are to me while you were out of his reach."

She swallowed the stone that had lodged in her throat. Gods, she was a mess.

His nervousness filtered through their soulmate bond, making her heart race. Was he afraid she wouldn't forgive him? That she would leave him? If he remembered their past, then he would know how impossible that was.

"When I locked you in the room, I couldn't think of anything else to prevent the guards from coming in and hurting you. I know it's not an excuse, and I shouldn't have done that. It will never happen again."

"You're damn right it won't," Nava said.

Arkimedes rubbed the back of his neck. The top button of his shirt came undone, revealing the angular lines of his clavicle, streaked with sweat, dirt, and—were those bruises? "Have patience with me, Bee."

Nava's skin tingled with the use of the nickname he'd given her a year ago, after she'd found out she was a Beekeeper. It warmed her from the inside out, bringing flutters to her stomach. She shifted on the cold, uneven floor. "Outside, you said this area of the city has changed since you were here last. Were the shops open ten years ago when you first came to the kingdom?"

"I bought bread in this bakery on my way to the Society's safe house," he whispered, glancing at the family who sat by the fire.

"Do you think it's because you were gone for so long?"

Nava wanted to believe that her mother hadn't known that cursing Arkimedes eleven years ago would condemn a whole kingdom. She'd been so focused on protecting Nava, who was only fifteen, that she hadn't asked any questions. And so she'd cursed him to become a crow every night until the moment Nava accepted him as her soulmate—of her own free will.

Arkimedes considered her words in silence, his face hard and lost in thought. He didn't need to answer for her to understand that he'd been asking himself the same question.

"I don't think I was the sole cause for this. I believe my father allowed the kingdom to harbor resentment toward humans, and so the wealth of these businesses flowed elsewhere. *Our* connection to the kingdom will allow nature's balance to continue. The crops will grow, and the animals will breed. This..." He pointed at the room, at the cobwebs accumulating in the corner above them, at the dusty surfaces everywhere. "Hate caused this."

Balance. That was how Aristaeus had described their role as Beekeepers. Their task was to create balance.

Small, shuffling steps drew their attention. A child not much older than her brother was approaching them with two steaming bowls. The girl wore a tattered dress and a wool sweater that was two sizes too big for her. "Would you care for a meal?"

"Oh! You don't have to give us your food."

The girl ignored Nava's protest and crouched forward, placing the small wooden bowls on the floor. The liquid inside them was still steaming.

"The broth will keep you warm at night. It gets cold in these old buildings." She stood and watched, as if she was waiting for either Nava or Arkimedes to accept her offering.

Nava reached for her bowl. It instantly warmed her stiff fingers. "Thank you."

"Kyle is just looking after us," the girl said, taking a long step away, her weary eyes bouncing from Arkimedes to Nava.

"You three are too young to be here on your own. Where are your parents?"

The girl flinched at the gravelly tones of Ark's voice. She moved back another few paces. "They are gone."

"How?"

"They came during the night, demanding that we surrender Caden, my youngest brother. My parents tried to fight since Caden is only seven. They said the Crown has no rights over us until we are twelve."

Arkimedes leaned forward, picking up the bowl near his feet. "Did the Crows come to take him?"

The old fear Nava had stopped feeling ever since she'd escaped Willowbrook flooded her in a flash. This was what Nava's mother had warned her would happen if the Crows ever discovered Cameron and her. The Crows and the Crown worked together in a way. First, the Crows tore young magic-wielders from their homes—usually between the ages of twelve and fifteen when they first presented their gift of magic. Then the kingdom's army took over the care and training of the children until they'd served the kings and queens for long enough to return home. But people died before that time ever came.

It was an abhorrent practice.

The girl nodded. "We heard they don't come to the Copper Kingdom, so we traveled here by ship, seeking refuge. But the Dark Ones are even worse. They hate humans."

"I'm half human," Arkimedes said with a curve to his lips. He took a small sip of his soup as he leaned against the wall. "Don't tell strangers about your story. It's true that Crows seldom come this way, but be wary."

The girl's shoulders dropped with a sigh, and a tentative smile lifted the corners of her chapped lips.

This. This was the Arkimedes she knew. How he'd been before his memories were taken. His good nature, forever masked by an indifferent frown and a scary aura, nevertheless shone through.

Her heart fluttered as she took him in: his long dark lashes and the straight profile of his nose. She loved him so much. Her earlier fears seemed idiotic now.

Nava glanced at the shop's door where Devon was taking the first watch. Then she looked at the children by the fire. Little did they know that a Crow stood right amongst them.

3

NAVA

"Is it true that you can speak to bees?" a small child's voice whispered through the webs of sleep.

Nava blinked, opening her eyes to a dark room and a stranger's face looming before her. The pungent smell of mold snapped her from a dreamless slumber, her body instinctively scrambling against the wall, trying to get away.

"What?" Blood rushed through her head, thundering inside her ears as she peered past the child's shoulder. Where was Arkimedes? Or even Devon?

"Are you looking for the large men?"

"Yes."

"They are in the front room." The boy moved closer. At this distance, he was close enough to count the freckles on her skin.

Nava eased him back by one of his bony shoulders and took a deep breath. Relax—she needed to relax. "You're supposed to be over there with your family. Are you Caden?"

"Did the bees tell you my name?"

Surely this was a dream. Right? How else could this child know that she could speak to bees? "No…" True panic settled in the pit of her stomach as the meaning of his words filtered through to her sleepy mind. "How did you know?"

"They tell you when danger is coming, right? Much like my dreams. Are they speaking to you now?" The child looked down at the ground, where three bees were crawling over her boots.

Caden possessed the very rare gift of the Sight. Was that the reason the Crows had murdered his family, even though he was so young?

"Why would they speak to me now? Are—are we in danger?"

As if they'd heard her, Arkimedes and Devon came rushing inside the kitchen, heading straight for her. Their eyes widened when they saw the boy still kneeling beside her. Perhaps, in her panic, she'd called Arkimedes through their bond.

The child's eyes glazed over as he looked at a spot on the crumbing wall above her head. Like he was lost somewhere all of a sudden. "The male lives in the shadows and lets the demons into our world. He is coming."

"What's happening here?"

Arkimedes's deep voice startled Caden out of his trance. He leaped away and scrambled swiftly around Devon, returning to his side of the room.

"Why was he here?" Devon asked. In the background, the family spoke in hectic, subdued voices.

The man lives in the shadows and lets the demons into our world.

Caden's words made her blood run cold. Did the child mean Arkimedes's doppelgänger? The man who had hurt her?

Was he letting the Zorren into this world? The shadow man had recognized her as a Beekeeper, the nemesis of those demons. Had he been working with them all along?

The first time Nava crossed the portal, the God of Shadows had ripped the memories of her father from her as payment and left her alone. She'd never even seen him. But he hadn't been alone that afternoon, had he?

Why was the other man—if that was even what he was—waiting for her in the portal crossings?

She stumbled to her feet, and a heavy piece of fabric tumbled to the floor as she rose. A black coat. She hadn't been wearing that, had she? The room spun around her as hundreds of bees suddenly circled her near the ground, expertly moving away from her clumsy feet.

Arkimedes tracked Nava's gaze, pausing as he spotted the insects, which were now crawling the walls and toward the ceiling. He picked up the coat from the ground and shrugged it on before reaching for her hand. "Let's go. The bells stopped ringing about half an hour ago, and the streets are full of people. We should leave now and take advantage the sun isn't out yet, and the morning mist is still thick."

Had the bees gathered around her because the man in the shadows was approaching, as Caden claimed? Or were they here because the guards were tracking Arkimedes across the city?

"Wouldn't they recognize you with your shadows—even if it's dark?"

"We are in the Kingdom of Dark Ones, and there are plenty other shadow-wielding-fae outside, I think the number of people outside will aid our cover."

Nava allowed Arkimedes to guide her toward the hall, feeling numb with cold and her rushing thoughts. But before they left, she turned and met the black gaze of the siblings by the fire. "Trouble is coming," she warned them. "Leave this place."

Arkimedes, Devon, and Nava walked for blocks in vigilant silence, filing past pedestrians who were setting up market stalls on the uneven cobble roads. The buildings' green copper rooftops contrasted with the terracotta color of their walls, made of bricks in varying shades of red, burnt orange, and ochre.

The people they encountered were obviously desperate for coin, selling a variety of knickknacks and dehydrated food.

Arkimedes tipped his head toward Nava, as if called by her turbulent thoughts. The endless questions running through her mind hadn't ceased since they'd left the shop. "We are close now," he said with a tentative smile.

He clearly meant to calm her down, but it achieved the opposite. Dread pooled in her stomach with each step that brought them closer to their temporary hideout. What if a group of Crows awaited them there? What if her enemy-turned-ally Devon Black betrayed them? After the way he'd acted in the bakery, she wasn't sure what to believe anymore.

Nava's legs burned as she attempted to match Ark's and Devon's pace. "If my mother were alive, she would die all over again if she learned I was marching into a Crow's safe house—willingly." She wiped off the sweat dripping down her temple. These giants had no sympathy for her much shorter legs.

Devon's smirk spread across his face as he turned the corner into a new, darker alley. "Do tell. What do you believe she would have said?"

"That I'm being reckless and foolish," she said, glancing at the sunrise peeking out from behind the roofs. It warmed her face despite the chilly morning air.

"Look at the positive side. We might find some of Celeste's old wanted posters in there. Perhaps you could take one back to your new castle as a keepsake."

"Hilarious..." Nava chewed at the inside of her mouth, trying to swallow the old grief that clutched at her heart as she remembered her mother's stern frown and the soft notes of her vanilla perfume. It wouldn't be so bad if she found something of hers in there, a little reminder to lend her strength. "What if we end up finding more trouble with the Crows instead?"

Arkimedes's dark gaze swept from Devon to her, his tall frame casting a wide shadow over them. "The Society hasn't sent the Corvus to the city in months. According to my father, none have come since my arrival."

What did he mean by the Corvus? It wasn't a term she'd heard before. She barely restrained a grunt of frustration. It was hard to make sense of what had happened when Arkimedes didn't remember the last decade of his life.

"So, has it been a decade since the Crows came here—or four months?" she asked. "Do you think the king lied to prevent you from coming here?"

"It's possible, although I keep hearing that the fae can't lie. So I assumed it's true..." Arkimedes's lips tilted into a wicked smile.

Nava smacked the side of his shoulder with an open palm. "Stop teasing me, Ark. I'm nervous. If you had asked me last year to walk willingly into a Crow's nest, I would have laughed and run away."

"I refuse to believe that," Devon said. "You crave danger. It's why you came to this kingdom to rescue Arkimedes with only me, your enemy, as your backup." He raised three fingers, counting out her recent questionable life choices. "Also, you're in love with a scary man who can rip people's souls away."

Nava's cheeks warmed. "That's not—"

Arkimedes's low chuckle cut through her words. "He's got a point."

"I don't crave danger!" Nava complained, though her tone lacked any heat. "I was *not* expecting you to be a prince without memories. Or that I would have to fight a mad king for your freedom." She cleared her throat, looking away from their irritating smirks. "In any case, what's our plan if the Crows do show up?"

"They won't. The safe house is the perfect place for us to regroup and plan our next move." The warmth of Ark's breath caressed her frozen knuckles, right before he dropped his soft lips to them.

Her stomach fluttered like dozens of butterflies had taken flight all at once. Arkimedes didn't blink or move, as if daring her to pull her hand back. Maybe she should, but she was having a hard time remembering why she was upset in the first place. Something about him locking her away somewhere.

Ah, there it was. The steady ember of her anger.

He smirked and let go of her hand. "Right now, the biggest threat to you is my father, not the Society."

Nava bit the inside of her cheek. Best not to blurt out her errant thoughts in the middle of an alleyway. Was the king truly her biggest threat? She was unsure who she should fear more, him or the Zorren. They were her mortal enemies.

If she were to believe Caden's words, the man in the shadows was coming for her and Aristaeus. She needed to return to the forest promptly.

Nava wanted no more secrets between her and Arkimedes. As soon as they escaped the streets, she had to inform him about the events in the shadow world—and about his doppelgänger.

Devon snatched a brown paper bag with roasted cashews from Arkimedes's hand. They'd bought them from a street vendor on their way. "Besides, the Society rarely sends the Corvus during the summer and winter solstice, for reasons the two of you are well acquainted with."

Arkimedes's cheeks burned red as he choked on the nuts he'd been chewing. Images of what had happened the night of the solstice flashed through Nava's mind, making her heart speed and blood pool straight into her core. The magically induced heat of the summer solstice had been sweet and hot, and the mere memory of it made her skin burn.

She stumbled, but before she could fall, Arkimedes had already grabbed her. He held her as if she weighed nothing.

"Watch your steps, Bee."

Their eyes met, and his pupils dilated. He must be remembering it, too. The way he'd ripped that ugly yellow dress off her body and made love to her after the masquerade ball. They'd discovered together that the queen's tree was, in fact, alive, signaling the arrival of a new queen. Nava.

If Arkimedes wasn't holding her so tightly against his chest, she would be dissolving into a puddle right where she stood. How could someone radiate so much heat in the chilly morning air?

Devon grunted in displeasure. The sound of his steps grew more distant as he left them behind.

Despite everything, this was where Nava wanted to be. Inside Arkimedes's arms. She pressed her open palms to his chest, knowing she had to tell him the truth about the man in the shadows. Trust that he wouldn't pull away from her, as he had done at the castle when he'd learned—rather abruptly—that she was his soulmate.

Admittedly, she couldn't truly blame him for being upset with her when he'd seen their soulmate mark on her chest after their passionate encounter during the solstice heat. She should've confessed their past long before, but her cowardice had prevailed.

Arkimedes released her and tilted his head to the side, studying her features. "Earlier this morning, you were afraid when the youngest child was speaking with you. Your fear called me. What did he say to you?"

Had he been waiting to ask until Devon gave them some privacy?

A renewed sense of dread clawed at her throat, and Nava scanned their surroundings, feeling it grow larger and larger the longer they stood there. "He had the soothsayer trait, and he knew about my connection with the bees—"

"What?"

"I'm afraid to tell you everything out here in the open." She pressed her lips together and eyed warily at the buildings surrounding them. They were alone in the street, but she wasn't foolish enough to think curious souls wouldn't listen in from the safety of their homes.

"All right. We can talk about it later. It'll be safer once we are out of here."

They resumed their walk, and soon they turned into a wide alley with uneven walls and deep puddles. It was eerily quiet. Not even the sounds of people buzzing about on the main road made it past the tall walls covered in ivy. There was only the heavy beat of Arkimedes's feet on the uneven ground. They followed a gentle curve in the alleyway, and the street behind them fell away altogether.

"There's something odd about these leaves," Nava said. She brought her finger up to the foliage, but right before she could touch it, Ark's hand closed around her wrist and pulled her away.

"Don't touch anything."

Nava met his gaze with growing curiosity. "Why not?" She could read the energy over the ivy. Pulsating waves of life gently enveloped each leaf, from the stems to the tips. A trail of pale blues and whites wrapped around each surface, the imprint of someone's spell. But unlike the flowers in the castle that spied on them, this energy was warm and vibrating with life.

"I don't know if it will consider you a friend or a foe. It's best to wait."

"Who…?"

"Not a who, but an it." He pulled her closer to where Devon was waiting for them. Arkimedes pointed to the barely visible sculpture of an old man's face amidst the greenery. A brass, deformed spout jutted out of his open mouth, and mold and algae hugged the porous texture of carved stone that formed a wide basin below. "We're here."

"Oh!" She studied the pipe once again. Contrary to initial appearances, the tube was actually a bird's head. A crow, to be exact, worn by age and decay. Its open beak served as a spout.

Devon leaned forward and placed his hand underneath it. A gust of wind descended around them. "I nearly didn't wait for you two. I'm tired and hungry." He glanced at Arkimedes, before his black eyes cut across to Nava and narrowed into slits. "The question is, will it allow you to pass?"

Water poured freely from the beak now, steaming hot into Devon's open hand. The sculpture of the man screeched, transforming into an arched door.

As Devon crossed the magical doorway, the scent of roses and gardenias bloomed around them. Then, just as fast as it opened, it closed again.

"It's our turn," Arkimedes said.

Nava shot him a worried look. "Why might it not let us through?"

He rolled his shoulders, as if readying himself—for what? "I'm going to place my hand underneath the spout. It won't let you in, Nava. But you can transfer inside with me when I cross."

"What happens if it deems you a foe?"

"It will burn my hand off and alert the Society of a break-in attempt."

"Wait, what?"

Arkimedes placed his hand underneath the open beak without answering her, and water burst out, gushing over his hand and filling the basin. The clear, steaming liquid thickened, and then it turned red like blood.

The Crow's fountain, illustration by Heather Souliere

Society of Crows

4
NAVA

Nava's stomach rolled at the sight of the thick liquid covering her soulmate's skin. Wasn't red a bad color? What did it mean?

Arkimedes's face scrunched in pain, and Nava dug her nails into his arm, attempting to pull him away. But he was as immovable as the statue. "We'll find another way. It's not worth it. Is it hurting you?"

He flinched at her words, and his face hardened further. "The spell's not hurting me badly. It doesn't know what to make of me..."

"You left the Society of Crows more than ten years ago. What were we thinking? This was foolish and—"

The blood-like water turned clear liquid, and the groove of the arched door reappeared before them. Arkimedes let out a sigh of relief, quickly withdrawing his hand from the liquid and wiping it on his leg.

"I'm fine," he said tightly. "Transfer with me. It may not allow me back in if I have to come and retrieve you."

Instantly, her body lost substance, and she became pollen, dust, and leaves. Wind moved through her, and in this state, her senses sharpened. She could hear the voices of her bees, warning her about the danger of crossing portals in this state, telling her to stay with her soulmate.

Telling her that a storm was coming...

Arkimedes crossed, and Nava embraced his body like a second skin, floating from the misty morning of the Copper City to the chill space of an unknown garden.

Gasping for air, she transformed back and strained to see the alley they had left behind. But it was pointless, as the gate had already closed, shutting them in.

Inside, the same ivy wall rose before them with an identical fountain sticking out from its other side, and yet everything else was different.

A worn stone pathway led them to a narrow house that stood on top of a hill, surrounded by massive trees. Dozens of colorful globes hung from their branches.

Nava narrowed her eyes at the strange spheres. They appeared to be fashioned from blown glass that caught the gray light and cast an array of colors over the garden. What were they? Sculptural decorations? Birdhouses?

An icy breeze seeped through layers of her clothes and pulled her focus to the house. She needed shelter and somewhere to rest her aching body.

With its gray stone and tapered rooftop, the safe house appeared to be hundreds of years old.

"Is this place in the Copper Kingdom?" Nava whispered, studying the climbing roses that grew over the arch of a pointed window with detailed ornamental stonework. Plants shouldn't bloom at such a temperature. Not when her breath billowed in front of her face, and the chill burned her cheeks.

"The fountain is a gateway to a secret location in Caztian. Even the Society members don't know where it really is."

They walked the rest of the way to the house in silence, not veering off the crumbling pathway. The place had a hauntingly beautiful atmosphere. Every plant, rock, and sculpture seemed to be spelled to survive unnatural conditions. Somehow, even the butterflies hovering over the flowers *felt* wrong.

Devon had left the front door wide open instead of waiting for them on the porch.

"Do all portals lead to the same safe house?" Nava asked as their steps led them across polished tiled floors and into a circular room with a winding staircase.

"There are twelve portals that lead to six safe houses. There is only one safe house in the Copper Kingdom."

Were there any safe houses on the islands? Cameron was traveling to Pearl Island with Gavin and Violet, and the thought of him being exposed to Crows made Nava's blood turn to ice.

She hadn't considered how the Society moved from kingdom to kingdom so quickly without having to pay the price to the God of Shadows each time they needed to use one of his portals. It made sense now. They had used their magic-wielders to create twelve portals to specific locations. No need to travel through the shadow world at all.

The house smelled...pleasant. Like lilacs and something warmer—vanilla, perhaps? Not like a place that hadn't been visited in years. Memories of Nava's youth came to her in flashes, of the manor she'd called her childhood home. Of tending to the front garden whenever her mother left.

Of course, Nava had been forbidden from setting foot outside during daylight hours, but she'd done it regardless, craving the feeling of dirt underneath her fingernails, wanting to be close to nature. That was, before Devon and Arkimedes had arrived on horseback one fateful afternoon and forced her and her family to leave the Iron City.

She wrinkled her nose, although a smile threatened to break free.

Arkimedes snaked a muscular arm around her waist, preventing her from heading deeper into what she assumed was the parlor.

"Stay here while I check if it's safe." His words drifted through her mind.

Nava blinked, surprised. They had communicated like this before. Sometimes accidentally. Sometimes when they were practicing how to use the mental bond they shared to its fullest extent. But only ever before he'd lost his memories.

Was he truly embracing their connection now?

Either way, she stayed behind until Ark crooked a finger at her from the doorway.

In the parlor, Devon sat in a large chair with green velvet upholstery. The warm colors of the fire burning in the hearth reflected off the blue jewel shades of the wallpaper.

Devon swirled the amber liquid inside the glass he held in one hand with lazy movements. "The house let you in. I can't decide if I'm pleasantly surprised or disappointed." He tilted his head back and swallowed his drink in a couple of gulps.

Nava propped up her hands on her hips, tapping her foot against the plush rug. "What would you have done if the house refused us entry and called upon the Crows?"

Devon shrugged. "I would thank the gods I won't get dragged into whatever suicidal mission you're about to embark on. It will surely get *me* killed. Then I'd send a get-well-soon letter to Arkimedes."

Nava frowned. "Why a get-well-soon letter?"

"Because his hand would have been severed by the fountain's water if the spell thought him a foe."

Nava shot a murderous glare at Arkimedes, who at least had the decency to look abashed. "I thought you were joking when you said that." She stalked toward Devon, her blood boiling. "And you *wanted* the Society to take us?"

Devon's lips tightened into a fine line.

Arkimedes reached for her shoulder and squeezed it lightly. "I wouldn't have risked it if I thought my loyalty was genuinely in question. Being heir to this kingdom has its benefits. The Society can't take me—nor you—and Devon knows that." Arkimedes's frown deepened, and even though his voice remained level, she could *feel* that he was, in fact, peeved.

"Right." Devon shook his head as if he couldn't believe it himself.

Arkimedes's jaw worked, and he took a deep breath to calm his temper. "And you don't have to follow us into our *suicidal mission*. If you don't want to, we can call our life debt even now."

Devon straightened in his seat, placing his empty glass on the side table. "Really?"

The magical string that still tied Devon to Nava flickered, the life debt slowly withering as Arkimedes continued to speak. "You hurt my soulmate last year. While I no longer possess all of my memories, I do recall that."

The room fell silent, except for the crackling of the fire. Nava's skull prickled with nervous tension. Would they be safe if the life debt was gone? Or would Devon betray them?

"Ark..."

He raised his hand, and she closed her mouth. This wasn't her choice, nor her life debt. Not really.

"You helped Nava escape my father last night. You deciphered the prophecy in the book I brought you, and you searched for me across the seas, although everyone else thought I was dead." Arkimedes took a step closer to his brother, his face torn between anger and something softer that she rarely got to witness. "I would save your life again, Devon, because you're the family I chose. I'm not forcing you to fight demons, nor die for me."

The string pulled tighter and tighter, leaving Nava's stomach roiling just before it snapped like a rubber band. She wheezed with the force of the recoil, bending forward as pain radiated through her chest. Then it was gone.

"Damn you!" Devon barely caught himself against his knees, visibly shaken. He buried his face in his palms. "It would be much easier to leave if you were a coward."

"Are you going to?" Arkimedes asked.

Nava wrapped her arms around her midriff, trying to catch her breath as they waited for Devon's response. Would he? Did she even care?

For so long, she had hated this man. Then circumstances had forced them into becoming allies. When had he turned into a friend?

"Not yet." Devon rose from his chair in one fluid motion. If the dissolution of the life debt was hurting him as much as it was hurting her, then he was a great actor. He strode to the doorway, pausing briefly on the threshold. "After all, someone from the Society needs to be here and make sure nothing gets damaged or stolen while Celeste's daughter is here." His expression lacked the unfriendliness of his words.

Devon was a master at playing a part. But in the end, he *had* gone to the end of the world to find Arkimedes. Even a decade after his disappearance.

Nava resisted the urge to smile. Emotionally constipated men were so frustrating, yet entertaining to watch. Hopefully, this wouldn't come back to haunt them later.

Devon ran a hand through his wavy, black hair. "I haven't checked if the pantry is stocked. Let's just hope there's something to eat in this place, or this little adventure was for nothing."

5

NAVA

An enormous limestone fireplace dominated one side of the kitchen. Thick stone columns held up its high, vaulted ceilings, and Nava shivered in the expansive cavern of a room. Devon busied himself by tending to the fire, and soon, the space warmed.

"Are you still cold?" Arkimedes asked a little while later, placing a steaming bowl of stew in front of her. "Do you want my coat?"

The remaining chill she felt had nothing to do with the room's temperature and everything to do with her surroundings. This safe house was a vipers' den. She'd never truly feel at ease here.

Devon pushed away his empty bowl of potato stew, his unnerving black eyes resting on her. "You've asked her five times already if she's all right. I'm sure her answer will stay the same."

Nava glared at him and smoothed the messy waves of her hair. "I'm fine," she said and met Arkimedes's eyes in an attempt to reassure him. But whatever he saw in her expression clearly didn't settle his doubts.

Never mind. She returned to studying her surroundings instead. A large chandelier hung low above the table, elegant swirls sculpted into its iron shape. Its candles burned with eternal magical flames that cast an orange light over the room.

Devon slid off his chair, strolling to the fireplace and feeding it a new log. "So, are you going to tell us or not? What happened when you crossed the portal?"

Nava glanced down at her arm and the wound, now covered by the sleeve of her blouse, but the words stuck in her throat.

"Stop," Arkimedes said, a warning in his tone. He inched toward her, as if he could protect her from the sudden darkening of her mood. Perhaps he knew she'd rather speak to him alone.

"We can fill the silence with useless chatter about the stew you just cooked with those lovely dehydrated potatoes or we could make a plan? We can't stay here forever."

"No, we can't." Arkimedes sighed, placing the glass of wine he'd been nursing on the table. He didn't have to say a word for Nava to know he desperately wanted some answers as well. His feelings were pushing loudly through their bond.

Nava sank deeper into her uncomfortable chair. "I know who is letting the Zorren into Caztian. The child in the bakery told me."

"The child?" Devon scoffed. "Just when I thought I'd heard it all…"

"Caden had the gift of the Sight. It's why the Crows killed his parents. He told me the man in the shadows was letting them in."

"The man in the shadows?" Devon scoffed. "Do you know how ridiculous that sounds? Now we have to base our plans on some tall tale a child told us?"

"Why would you think he made it up?"

"Because all deserters have a sad story, Cat. I already told you who I think is at fault for their living conditions."

"You can lie to yourself about your precious Society, but he wasn't lying. Caden knew things very few people know about me," Nava insisted. "And he knew about the demons."

"That means nothing. A lot of locals attended the king's dinner where Arkimedes publicly revealed that the Zorren are burning the forests. By now, the entire city is aware of them."

Arkimedes pressed his fingers to the bridge of his nose with a sigh. "Stop making this about the Crows and deserters, Devon."

"Why? We could call on the Society to help us fight the demons. You were their golden boy. They will bend over backward to assist you now that you are the heir to an entire kingdom. I, for one, think the Corvus could be of great help to subdue the Zorren. After all, we are the most powerful magic-wielders in Caztian."

"I'm no one's golden boy. They have used me for as long as I can remember."

"And yet here you are, using them…" Devon raised his hands above his head, narrowly missing the chandelier.

Arkimedes's frown deepened. Then he turned to her. "Who is the man in the shadows, Nava?"

"I don't know his true identity—" she began, but Devon's loud grunt cut her off. Nava glared at him and rolled up her sleeve, revealing the angry blisters. "He did this to me when I crossed."

Arkimedes stopped breathing. His chair scraped over the floor as he stood and bent forward to better inspect the wound she'd been hiding from him.

The imprint in the shape of a hand stood out sharply against her skin, and Nava's heart lurched in her chest as she spotted the black veins that now extended up her arm. They flared out from the new blisters that had formed during the day. "I didn't see the veins before. Is it infected?"

"Did you encounter a Dark One when you crossed the portal?" Arkimedes's anger flooded through the bond and blurred the edges of her panic. Was he upset with her for not telling him sooner?

"Yes."

"Why didn't you say anything before?"

Devon leaned across the table, his brows scrunching as he, too, inspected her wound.

"Because—he looked like you!" she blurted out over the thundering of her heart.

In the ensuing silence, one could have heard a pin drop.

"What do you mean, he looked like me?"

Nava cleared her throat and waited for the room to stop spinning around her. The gentle crackling of the fireplace in the background wasn't helping. It only reminded her of the fires brought by the Zorren. "I've crossed a portal twice in my life. When we came to this kingdom to rescue you. And then yesterday. Both times, a man approached me in the darkness. I had a hard time seeing him the first time, but that changed last night."

"Go on," Arkimedes urged, his face drained of color.

Her stomach churned, but there was nothing for it. She had to continue. She'd promised to tell him the truth, even if it would be easier in the short run to hold it in. "When I crossed the first time, one voice asked for a memory, which I expected, but there was someone else inside with me. Devon mentioned back in the castle that he heard no one else—"

"True," Devon confirmed. "You told me about it during our first dinner with the king."

Nava nodded. "He knew I was a Beekeeper, Ark. And he hurt me because of it."

"You're a *what?*" Devon exclaimed.

Arkimedes didn't pay him any attention. His eyes zeroed in on her wound instead, although he raised his gaze to search her face before he spoke. "He looked like me—but did you *feel* it was me?"

She understood what he was asking. Underneath all the fear and confusion, their unique soulmate bond allowed them to feel each other. Their love remained, despite the weakened bond.

The similarities had been jarring, but… "No. He had your face, the same nose and lips. His armor resembled the Zorren's." If only she could recall more details to fill in the missing pieces of this puzzle. "His hair was white like your father's."

"You know I would never hurt you, Nava."

"I know that." She cradled her arm against her chest. "It shocked me when it happened. But I've never doubted that I'm safe with you."

In the uncomfortable silence that took over the room, it was hard to ignore her soulmate's harsh breaths or Devon's intense gaze.

After an eternity, Devon spoke. *"The child of royal blood came to this world sick, poisoned by evil, and was taken into the world of shadows, away from the land and our people."* Nava shot him a questioning look, but he was clearly addressing Arkimedes. "Those were the words I translated from that burnt book you brought me back to the castle."

"What are you saying, Devon?" The urge to climb over the table and choke him for planting a seed of doubt in Arkimedes's mind was strong.

"I'm saying Arkimedes brought me a recorded prophecy and was worried that it referred to him," Devon said. "Perhaps the Dark One you discovered in the in-between world resembled him because it *was* him."

Nava shook her head. Devon could go and cram his negativity where the sun didn't shine. While she'd been caught by surprise the night before, the answer was clear as day right now.

There was no chance the shadow man and Arkimedes could be the same person.

"It might have been, but it wasn't." Arkimedes's tone was stern.

"How do you know?" Devon drummed his fingers against the tabletop. "You were worried weeks ago. We don't understand how time works in the shadow realm. Perhaps you could be in two places simultaneously."

Arkimedes shrugged off his royal coat and tossed it carelessly onto the table. "Because I'd rather die than hurt Nava, and because my power doesn't leave these marks."

And he pulled the shirt out of his pants, revealing his abdomen to both Devon and her. His golden skin wrapped over cords of muscle, but that wasn't what sucked the breath straight from her lungs. The black veins that snaked up his back and over his ribs were a terrible sight to behold. She rose so abruptly from her chair that it crashed to the ground. Then she ran her fingers over the lightning-shaped marks left behind by the Dark Ones.

"My father's concubines left these markings last night when they ambushed me. I will get better in a couple of days as my body recuperates." He wrapped one of his large hands over hers, pressing it into his skin. "A Dark One's power leaves blackened veins behind, but mine doesn't. If it had been me, I would have killed Nava, and a part of her soul would haunt me for the rest of my life."

And since they were soulmates, it would be a very short-lived life, since neither could survive for long without the other.

"I can't take just the essence of someone's magic, like most of my kind. My power rips a soul apart, steals bits of a person's essence. Only my father and I possess the ability to do that in this world."

Devon settled in his chair, evidently appeased by Arkimedes's explanation. "All right. Who was the Dark One, then? A lost twin brother or a shapeshifting demon?"

Nava's breath caught in her throat, and her blood ran cold at the very idea. There were other types of demons than the Zorren? "Do they exist?"

"They do." Devon poured himself more wine. "The scriptures say they borrow the likeness of the one you love the most. But they aren't from this world." He shrugged and downed his drink in one gulp. "Nasty little things. It's why I'm not recommending we open a portal and take this fight to whoever is doing this."

"Maybe that's what he wants. He seemed to move a lot faster than I could while in the shadow lands. I just floated, unable to do much."

Arkimedes scratched his chin. "The gods' realms are a mystery. Only those with the ability to open portals, like Devon, can access them. There's no way for a mortal to stay there. So we can't bring the fight there, either way."

No mortal...

Nava gasped, her eyes darting from Arkimedes to Devon and back again. "Could he be an immortal? A god?"

"Let's hope for all our sakes that he's not," Arkimedes said.

Could Aristaeus visit the shadow world and fight there alone? Perhaps that was why the demons singled out the Beekeepers. She made a mental note to ask Ari the next time she saw him, whether he was, in fact, an immortal.

"So, what's the plan, brother? We wait until the Zorren come to hunt Nava, our precious Beekeeper?"

For the first time since she had met Devon, he didn't sound cold or flippant. There was a touch of reverence in his tone. "I'm still the same woman you imprisoned on the island."

"If I had known you were a keeper of life, I wouldn't have done that."

"Why does it matter? You just thought I was a dirty deserter, like Caden in the bakery."

Devon lowered his gaze, staring at the table. "I don't see how that's the same."

"That boy you were so cruel to warn me about who was bringing the Zorren into this world. He gave us a vital clue we were missing." Was Devon following her? He was completely avoiding eye contact. "He deserves the family he lost because of that gift."

Arkimedes had once told her that Devon's family had abandoned him when he was not even ten and that the Society of Crows had taken him in. It was rare for the Society to take responsibility for children. Usually, they went to the armies.

What if the Society had killed Devon's family, exactly like Caden's? Both Ark and Devon were children of the Crows. Both had immense, unusual powers.

"What if the Crows were aware of your lineage all along?" she whispered and met her soulmate's gaze from under her lashes. "You said not all the Dark Ones possessed the Curse of the Fallen, except for the king—and *you*, his heir. Wouldn't the Society know that someone with your power was the lost royal of the Copper Kingdom?"

Arkimedes drew a ragged breath and leaned against the table. His brows scrunched together as if he were struggling to find a response that made sense. Perhaps he was attempting to revive lost memories. "I'd always thought it strange. Devon and I were the only children in the Society. All the others were taken to serve the royal guards."

"That's an imaginative idea." Devon's voice shook, and he cleared his throat before he spoke again. "But I don't think so."

Obviously, her imaginative idea had cut them both deeply. Nava only had to use her eyes to read them like an open book: their hunched postures, how they were struggling to speak. And beyond that, she could tap directly into Arkimedes's emotions through their bond.

"The gift of opening portals is rare, Devon," Arkimedes said. "In fact, I've only met three people who've had it in my lifetime, and they are all members of the Crows."

Nava closed her eyes and tried to sort through her jumbled thoughts. Some magical gifts, such as being a soothsayer or having Devon's power to control storms, were rare. But portal making—she'd never known that even existed.

Her sheltered upbringing had caused yet another gap in her knowledge.

"Let's stop talking nonsense." Devon's nostrils flared as he lifted his head and struggled to mask his emotions with false indifference. "The Society of Crows is unrelated to the Zorren."

"They might possess knowledge we lack, although I'm not implying that they're connected to the demons." Nava glanced around the room as if she might find the answers hiding in plain sight or in some dusty corner. If only it could be that simple.

"Each safe house has an archive," Arkimedes said. "We can try to find out what the Society knows about the royal prophecy, or how we can stop the...*shadow man*...from opening more portals."

"What is an archive?"

"They're libraries that only Society members can access. Every year, the librarians catalog prophecies, new spells, historic events, and so on."

"And there's one here?"

"A smaller version, yes." Arkimedes shifted on his feet.

"We should not step one foot inside that place unless you want the Crows to come here," Devon said, a warning infusing his tone. He slammed a hand on the table, and Nava's half-full glass of wine rattled in response. "You can't seriously think that's a good idea, Arkimedes."

"Do you have a better suggestion on how to move forward?"

"Sure. How about we *don't* go in there?"

"Why not?" Nava clutched her stomach with her wounded arm. She already knew she wouldn't like the answer to that question. "Is it not just a place for books?"

A stupid thing to ask, judging by Devon's clenched jaw and Arkimedes's tightened fists.

"Not quite," Devon said. "All archives have a scrying mirror. I haven't been to the one downstairs, but there must be one. The Society hides the mirrors in many shapes, and they communicate directly with its headquarters."

Now she definitely felt uneasy. She moved toward her chair, reaching for her discarded drink. Alcohol would do wonders to make her forget about her anxiety and bone-deep exhaustion.

"But the mirror can also find information," Arkimedes said. "The books will contain knowledge about the portals, and using the mirror can help us locate the right source quicker."

Devon rubbed his eyes. "The Vulcan will alert them, Arkimedes. She is Celeste's daughter. It's enough of a miracle that the house let you through. I'm not so certain the mirror will think you're one of us."

"Which is why I won't be the one handling it."

"You want me to do it?" A rough laugh escaped Devon's chapped lips, his chair scraping over the tile floor as he stood in a jagged motion. His jaw tightened before he spoke. "I'm too tired for this shit, and I'm not talking any more about this until I've had a wash and a good rest."

He picked up his empty bowl and dropped it in the sink on his way out of the kitchen. "I'm taking the first room to the left. Good luck finding a clean place to sleep. This house is not what it used to be."

SOCIETY OF CROWS

6
ORION

The halls on the second floor were long and narrow, with dark wooden panels that extended from floor to ceiling. Orion much preferred the murals downstairs. They reminded him of the forest.

Beside him, Nava's heavy steps dragged over the worn rug as she studied the paintings on the walls. All of them were group images depicting members of the Society of Crows, their faces a familiar anchor to a time that felt like an eternity ago.

"Are you in any of these?" She slowed to a stop and rose on tiptoes, studying the largest piece of art. Her brows were knitted tightly together with concentration.

"I'm sure they removed the one with me in it," he said.

"Why would they do that?" She moved on to the next image without waiting for his answer, her brown and blue eyes bouncing over neat brushstrokes. "Do you think my mother is here?"

Her tired voice lit up with a trace of hope. Of course. It made sense that she'd want to see Celeste's likeness immortalized in oil paint.

"No." The finality of his tone made her expression fall. He cleared his throat to unravel the heavy knot that had formed there. "They don't keep any paintings with members who have died or those featuring traitors."

"But these are group paintings. What about the other people who haven't died or betrayed the Society?"

"They commission a new artist, and the painting gets replaced. They don't want any of us to be reminded of our own mortality."

"Or that people can change allegiance?"

"Exactly."

Nava froze in front of the next painting, her eyes narrowing in on a dark shape that took over the bright picture. It wasn't hard to find him amongst the group of Crows. "You're still here…"

Orion moved closer to take in the old picture. That was him at twenty years of age. A month ago, before he'd discovered that he'd lost his memories, the image would have appeared recent to him.

But now…it seemed like so long ago, and he could tell the difference in his youthful face. He'd even forgotten what these people's voices sounded like, although some of them had been friends.

"This particular safe house we're standing in front of was in the Gold Kingdom." He remembered the rolling hills with tall grass, where it was less swelteringly hot in the summer.

Nava squinted at the picture. "Is she holding your arm?"

Orion blinked and inspected the picture again. Who did she mean? Ah, the woman beside him. He hadn't been paying such close attention to her before.

"I'd forgotten Faria used to do that…"

"She seems rather friendly with you." Nava's cheeks turned bright red. The pit of his stomach suddenly churned with feelings that weren't his but burned through his veins like wildfire.

"You know you've nothing to be jealous of, Nava," he whispered close to her ear, enjoying the way her skin pebbled beneath his breath. Then he grasped her elbow and turned her away from the painting to face him.

"I'm not…"

He touched her flushed cheeks and pulled her bottom lip free from beneath her teeth. She always did that when she was nervous or overwhelmed. "Tell me what you're thinking?"

Nava sighed, glancing at the offending portrait as if it might come alive at any moment. "When we met for the first time—you were about the same age, then. I see this picture, and I can't help but wonder if I ruined a relationship you had before me."

"That's not what happened."

"You don't remember what happened." She turned away, clearly not wanting him to read her as only he could. "Maybe if I hadn't been out gardening that afternoon when you came to speak to my mother, you would have stayed with Faria."

"I was never hers to begin with." Orion lowered his face enough that his lips were a mere hairsbreadth away from hers. Nava's breath stuttered, but yearning softened her features. "I've been yours from the moment I first laid eyes on you. Since before I understood who you were to me."

Nava crushed her lips to his in a kiss that caught fire as soon as he got a taste of her. It was right—perfect even—to chase her lips and marvel at the way she gasped for air as they broke apart.

"Stop saying things like that," she whispered. "I'm supposed to be mad at you."

Orion grinned. It was as if the weight of all their lies and problems had dropped off him, leaving him lighter. He felt drunk on a feeling he wasn't used to, on his love for this beautiful woman who belonged to him as much as he belonged to her.

Nava's hand traveled across his chest, pausing over the spot where the soulmate mark rested. Her touch was light, but even through his clothes, it sent a ripple of energy dancing over his skin.

Judging by her shivers and how her lips parted, she felt their connection, too. But then she stepped away from him, breaking the spell, and continued down the hallway until she stopped in front of the first door to the left. "Is this where Devon is staying?"

The double doors of the room were shut, hiding away the huge chambers inside. "Yes. It's the best room in the house, normally taken by high-ranking officers."

"I heard *you* were pretty high up in the ranks."

A smile curved his lips. "Was I?"

"Devon calls you the golden boy, and Roman used to say you called the shots. But you've never told me much about…any of this." She shrugged one shoulder, her eyes darting away again.

"It's hard to feel proud of being part of the Crows," Orion admitted. He didn't like to see that frown on her face, knowing the sadness it was hiding—or that his actions had put it there. "What do you want to know?"

"How many times did you come to this house before Fael found you?"

Fael—the guard who Orion had once thought of as a friend. Who'd betrayed him.

"I came here just once. The Society didn't allow me to visit this kingdom. They sent me to other places instead…" He broke off. Now that Nava had planted the seed of doubt in his mind, it was blooming.

What if the Society of Crows had known all along who he was?

"It looks like no one has been here in a long time," Nava said, lifting her chin to point at the spiderwebs that stretched from the corners of the ceiling. She was right. A thick layer of dust covered the pictures on the wall as well, dulling the gold tones of the frames.

"I was not supposed to come here when I did," he admitted, swallowing the nervousness that rose alongside the words. He hadn't told a soul. "They approved my leave and gave me permission to go to the Gold Kingdom to rest for two months."

Nava watched him, unblinking, as if waiting for him to open up further.

Orion dragged a hand over his greasy hair. He desperately needed a bath. "I knew the Copper Kingdom was the place where my kind lived, and I wanted to know if my family was still alive. I needed answers about the shadows that always follow me."

He pointed at his aura, although he already knew that Nava couldn't see it. She only ever saw him.

"And when you got here, you found more than you bargained for?"

A soft puff of air left his lips. "You could say that."

"Do you think no Crows have come here since you left the Society?"

Orion met her smart eyes, and for the first time, he yearned for those memories. He wanted to know what had happened when he headed to the Iron Kingdom eleven years ago after learning the truth about who he was.

He pressed his hands to his temple, massaging away an impending headache. If the Society of Crows had known who he was all along, then it stood to reason that they were now protecting their members from his father, the king. "I think they found out that I came here and learned who I was, and my disappearance suited them better than if I'd stayed to rule."

"Well, if we focus on the positives of this mess, at least we know they won't send any Crows while we're hiding here," she said.

"And that buys us time to go through the archives."

She hummed and pointed at the bee that was crawling across the wall underneath the picture. Its brown body blended almost seamlessly into the brown shades of the wooden panels. "Even if they don't come, we have little time. We have to go back to help Aristaeus in the forest. He can't battle the Zorren alone."

"I know, which is why I need to convince Devon to use the mirror to reveal the information we need."

"Do you think he's right? That it will call the Society if one of us uses it?"

"Probably. Do you remember how the fountain outside dripped blood over my hand until the very end?" She nodded at his words. "Well, on reflection, I believe that was because my allegiance to the Crows was already so weak. Now that I know they knew my true identity all along, whatever shred of it remained will be gone. And the mirror will see me as a traitor."

"You agree then? That they did know?"

The hollowness in Orion's chest deepened, and the voice of a spirit in his aura rose to his ears, as though the despair churning within him had brought it to life.

"I knew who you were, Arkimedes Valeron. Princeling of the Dark Ones. And now I am part of you."

Orion flinched at the sound, so twisted and hollow that it was impossible to distinguish its origin. A male voice. A fragment of one of his past victims. Panic snaked its icy fingers through his blood. If only he could tell who that voice belonged to. Perhaps if he could remember the person—their face—then he might finally gain some clarity. But with the number of souls he carried and the holes in his memories, it would be a challenge.

When he'd been a young Crow, Orion hadn't asked questions whenever the Society sent him to get rid of a problem. He'd believed everything served a greater purpose. They'd used him, molded him into a killer.

Had his mother not thought about what would become of him if she abandoned him in the Iron City, a place run by the Crows? She should have suspected it.

He swallowed the sour taste in his mouth and opened the next door after Devon's, waving Nava in. "This is your room."

The same dark wood panels as in the hallway wrapped around the walls, and on the opposite side of the door, a large, arched window with black trim let in the last rays of gray daylight. The floors creaked under Nava's tentative steps. "My room? Aren't you staying here with me?"

"I thought you might want space, after everything..." Orion hated how uncertain he sounded. The last thing he wanted was for Nava to think that he didn't want to be with her. He cleared his throat and moved toward her. "Do you want me to?"

A wave of her mixed feelings swirled in his gut: longing, desire...and hesitation.

"Yes," she whispered. "This place feels...wrong. Like there's something haunting the very fabric of what makes up this house. Is it cursed?"

Orion stilled as the image of the locked door in the basement flashed through his mind. He would have to tell her about the cellar tomorrow morning when they went to the archives. But there was no need to frighten her further by mentioning it right now.

"It's not cursed," he said and cleared his throat. "Are you sure you want me to stay? There's only one bed." He pointed at the piece of furniture in question. It was still shrouded by white dust covers.

"Are you embarrassed about sharing the bed with me?" Her words took on a teasing note, but the blush in her cheeks betrayed her nerves.

"No." A soft chuckle escaped his lips, and he grabbed the sheet, tugging it off the bed and tossing it into the corner in one movement. "I thought you were still upset with me."

Dust bloomed from the billowing fabric and itched his nose. He strolled to the other side of the room and closed the curtains, which were made of thick fabric, a blue so dark it was almost black.

The color reminded him of the dress Nava had worn to his father's dinner the previous afternoon. How the castle's magic had shown the king and the entire kingdom that she was royalty—for the sentient pile of stone and bricks allowed only the royal line to wear black inside its walls.

"It seems I can't stay mad at you for long," she mumbled, scrunching her freckled nose. "Even if this place gives me the creeps, you don't have to stay. I can handle it."

"I suspect there's nothing you *can't* handle." A warm wave of pride filled him. Pride and something more. Fuck, he'd been so lost without this woman in his life. He couldn't believe he'd tried to push her away.

Nava challenged him in every way. Made him want to be better. She'd come to this kingdom to save him and hadn't backed down, even when faced with a bastard as scary as his father.

Orion walked to her with long strides, stopping only when she was close enough that the warmth of her body seeped through his clothes. Her chin fit so easily between his fingers as he lifted her face to his.

"I was trying to be a gentleman and give you space. Don't mistake that for me not wanting to take all you give me, Nava. I'm a greedy creature." He touched her plush, parted lips and dropped his hand to her throat.

"Stay," she said and took hold of his hand with icy fingers. Her nervous breaths washed over his arm. "But only stay if you won't change your mind tomorrow. You asked me to marry you one night, and the next morning, you were planning on sending me away after you found out I was your soulmate."

"To protect you from my father," he said. "I'd just learned my whole life was a lie and that he took my memories of a past that scares me. I was upset about the truth you'd kept, but not about you being my soulmate."

"I'm sorry I didn't tell you." Her lips pressed into a flat line. "When I realized you had no memories of me, I was afraid you wouldn't choose me. But I realize I wasn't fair to you. All this time, I've been upset about the things you chose not to tell me. But when things got hard, I did the same to you."

He didn't even care about that nonsense anymore. Not when fear had nearly crippled him the night before when he almost lost her to his father and his guards. Even if they hadn't killed her, King Oberon would have made Nava disappear right along with his recent memories of her.

"Did you hear what I said in the hallway? I'm yours, and I will not change my mind. I love you, Nava. If you'll have me, I will stay."

Her lips trembled. "You love me?"

"I do. And I'm sorry I ever made you doubt it."

7
ORION

Devon sped past Orion on his black horse, loose pieces of gravel spraying around him as he went.

Then he pulled on the reins and slowed into a bouncy trot, turning around to meet Arkimedes's gaze from underneath the hood of his cloak. "Be prepared for Celeste to run as soon as she sees us. Better remember why we are here, brother."

As if he could ever forget. The branded letter in his pocket had five words written in red ink hidden behind the hard wax seal depicting the Society of Crows' emblem.

Deal with the traitor. Discreetly.

Arkimedes clenched his jaw as claws of dread buried themselves deep inside his chest. He dug his heels into his horse's flank, urging him to catch up with Devon. How he hated that he was the one to be sent to the outskirts of the Iron City to find Celeste.

The imposing, ornate iron gates hid the beautiful stone manor from the street, and tall twisting trees cast shadows upon the path that led to its entrance. The ground was littered with leaves in all shades of brown.

Arkimedes jumped from his saddle before his steed had even stopped moving, ignoring the ache in his thighs as he leaped up the steps, two at a time.

His dread grew, urging him to turn around and flee. He was not one to fear his fate when it came to handling most of his tasks. However, Celeste was a magnificent spell caster, and dangerous with a weapon in hand.

And he didn't want her soul to haunt him for the rest of his miserable existence.

Devon walked to the main door, and as Arkimedes followed him, movement to his right drew his attention. It was a girl, kneeling before a garden bed. She was lithe, with dark brown hair that flowed in messy waves over her round cheeks.

He took a step forward, attempting to get a better look, swallowing past the knot that stuck in his throat, past the fluttering of his erratic heartbeat.

Celeste? No. The girl was too young to be his old instructor. Still, the similarities were impossible to ignore.

Then her beautiful, strange eyes met his, and time stopped.

The air fled his lungs, and sudden pressure constricted his chest, burning him from the inside out. His hands dampened with sweat, yet he forced himself to step forward. Since when did he find it challenging to talk to a girl?

"Excuse me, do you know if anyone is home?" he said in an attempt to distract himself. He didn't want her to flee the moment she realized who they were.

Her brows shot up, and her throat worked as she swallowed. "N-no," she stuttered, dropping the shears she'd been using to cut the plants.

His body still blazed with this strange fire. So much so he struggled not to lower the hood that covered his face to get some air. Why was he feeling like this? He'd never been so unsettled by meeting anyone before. What was going on? "Do you live here?"

"No, I'm just...the gardener."

Her words pulled a distinct snort from Devon's lips. The girl was far too young to be a gardener. And she was the spitting image of Celeste.

She pulled a dead plant from the ground. Dirt spilled all over the aged stone floor that she knelt on.

His heart fluttered as her gaze met his once more. What the fuck was wrong with him?

"You have peculiar eyes," Devon said.

Arkimedes's shadows instantly surged out of control around him, the voices calling to him in hushed tones.

"He can't hurt her," *one soul fragment insisted, raising gooseflesh across his skin.*

"She is ours," *another hissed.*

"I get that a lot." The girl's trembling voice gave away her nerves. Surely, she didn't think she could fool them.

Arkimedes was about to ruin this girl's life. If the Society wanted him to kill Celeste, then they would recruit her daughter into the king's army without a second thought. That was, if she was fortunate enough not to suffer the same fate as her mother.

A new wave of dread crawled up his skull, chilling his body as the misty shapes around him grew ever angrier.

"You look too young to be a gardener," Devon drawled, and Arkimedes turned to meet his brother's perceptive gaze.

Devon had come to the same conclusion as he had: this girl was lying and was likely Celeste's daughter. Celeste's hidden child. If nobody knew of her, did that mean Arkimedes could help her vanish without facing consequences from the Society?

Either way, he doubted Celeste was here. She would never allow them to speak to her child freely. They needed to lie in wait for the traitor to return home. That would give him just enough time to convince his brother to let the girl go.

"Do you know when Miss Celeste will be back?" Devon asked.

The girl jumped, trembling like a rabbit under a predator's gaze. When she shook her head, her long, wavy hair stuck to her sweaty skin. "She's out at the market with my mother because we are the closest neighbors she has," she lied. "I can tell them—I mean, tell her you came around."

"Where did you say you lived?" Devon asked, moving forward. The look on his face only fed Arkimedes's rising panic.

What could he do? Push Devon away from her and give her a chance to run? Why was his chest burning like this, like a spell branding his skin?

"I didn't." The girl leveled them with a harsh look and placed her gardening tool inside the basket. Then she straightened her shoulders as if to make herself bigger. Brave and foolish, perhaps. It still warmed his dark heart either way.

Few dared to confront a Crow, let alone a Dark One like him.

"You aren't supposed to tell strangers where you live," she whispered. "I can tell Celeste you came by, or you can try to catch her at the market."

Arkimedes doubted Celeste would be near any market.

Devon moved toward the girl, but he froze when Arkimedes's shadows reached out for him, a silent warning to his brother to stay away from her. Devon glared at him from behind his hood.

"Not now," Arkimedes whispered to him.

His brother grunted his displeasure and turned around to head to the horses. It wasn't as easy for Arkimedes to leave, not with the way his heart suddenly ached. How could he even dream of leaving her here...

Arkimedes tightened his fists and shoved those unhinged feelings away. For crying out loud, the girl was too young to be anything other than a nuisance. And she would consider him a villain the moment he carried out the Society's orders. If he were a better man, he wouldn't return at all.

He turned away. Perhaps, in a few hours, this temporary madness would have passed. "Please tell her the Society of Crows came to see her."

Arkimedes descended the stairs, not looking back. That burning sensation seemed to be carving a hole in the center of his chest with each step he took.

Celeste had betrayed the Society. He had to remember that. She had brought this on herself.

"Why did you stop me?" Devon snarled at Arkimedes when he caught up with him past the imposing gate. "Since when do you have a vested interest in a random gardener?" Devon's last word dripped with sarcasm.

"I don't." If only he could explain it. The reaction of his aura had been purely

emotional, almost instinctive. He was clearly tired from his trip to the Copper Kingdom. And losing his damn mind.

Why had the girl not flinched when she'd seen him? As if not even the curse of his power intimidated her.

"If you don't care, then we should go back. Take the girl and wait for Celeste inside the house."

Arkimedes knew they should take care of the problem like the higher-ups had commanded. Devon was well aware of their orders. And this would be Arkimedes's last task before departing for the Copper Kingdom forever.

But he couldn't simply kill that girl's family and condemn her to serve the people who'd ordered the execution. It wasn't the first time the Society had requested an assassination of him. Still, this time, there was one simple difference.

Her.

If they saw this through, she would become a prisoner of the king's army. Or worse.

He could at least buy her the time to escape a fate he wouldn't wish on his worst enemy. Fuck the Society. He was leaving after this mission, regardless. They'd been happy enough to withhold the truth from him for so long. He could do the same.

"Let's check the market first," he said and rubbed the center of his chest. It still burned with remnants of whatever that girl had done to him. Perhaps she could already wield magic. If so, that was another problem he would have to deal with later. "We'll come at night when I'm harder to spot."

Devon narrowed his eyes and snapped his reins, signaling his beast to move down the road and farther away from the manor. "Don't tell me the visit to the Copper Kingdom has made you soft, brother."

Arkimedes's throat closed. All those truths he'd unearthed while he'd escaped to his birthplace for a few months... He'd promised his father, the king of the Copper Kingdom, that he would return as soon as he resigned from his duty.

A normal Crow might not have served enough time to retire, but as it turned out, Arkimedes was a prince, and that changed everything. Perhaps it was childish, how much he desired to see their faces fall when he told them he could leave.

He'd briefly considered not returning at all. Still, Devon deserved the truth, and this last mission together felt important somehow.

"Quite the contrary," Arkimedes whispered to himself. It had made him realize how petty the Society's actions were.

He followed his brother along the paved road that led them toward the center of town. With any luck, Celeste would be at the market. They would handle the problem, and he would never cross paths with that girl again.

Orion woke to the icy feeling of dread still crawling up his body. It invaded his head and transformed into a pounding migraine that rapidly grew in intensity.

He groaned, clutching his skull in agony as images from the dream continued to flood his mind. The scent of olive soap from the bath he'd taken last night lingered on his skin, and a steady warmth emanated from beside him.

His heart shrunk as he turned to Nava. She was still sleeping soundly, unaware of the state he was in. Even the tiniest detail of their first meeting rushed inside him, filling the gaps left behind by his father's spell.

He felt broken and unstable. A man caught between two minds...

He climbed out of bed, taking care not to wake her, and frowned as he took in the bees that were crawling all over the sheet and up his torso and arms.

Maybe a workout would ease the voices of his shadows. Maybe he'd even find Devon there—once upon a time, they used to train before sunrise on the regular. It was the perfect chance to convince his brother to help them with the mirror.

The solarium was situated toward the back of the house, on the ground floor. The rooms in every safe house had a similar appearance, regardless of where that safe house stood. It was a way for the Society to ensure its members always felt at home.

If his father had suspected the Crows knew who he was all along, then there was a possibility the king had watched Devon carefully during their stay at the castle. When they escaped a few nights ago, Orion had told Nava that the treaties between the Society and the royals would be enough to protect Devon. He'd been confident that his father wouldn't harm Devon when he'd locked them in that room and asked Nava to escape.

But Orion hadn't known all the facts then.

He stormed into the solarium, and its humidity wrapped around him. This was a place of life, with plants growing everywhere: an unseasonably warm spot of the house.

The faint scent of old magic welcomed him as he inspected the garden, full of lush greenery and blooms that wouldn't stand a chance in the cold outside. Here they thrived, aided by sorcery.

A crushed granite path led him to a wooden training deck, where Devon awaited.

His brother was swinging a longsword in an elegant arc with practiced ease. He froze in an attack pose as his black eyes fixed on Orion. "You are late."

"And you are shirtless."

"It's hot in here." Devon shrugged, then signaled for Orion to strike. "No magic. You know the drill."

Orion's magic tingled under his skin as it stirred, eager to be unleashed. "Why are you afraid? How long has it been since you've used your magic, Devon?" He smiled as he rolled up the sleeves of his shirt.

Devon glared. "A year, thanks to you and your wonderful soulmate." He tossed the sword onto the deck, and his aura bloomed around him, dark gray and sizzling with energy.

"You tortured her. Consider yourself lucky that it was only imprisonment..."

"So you remember?"

"Yes."

"All of it?" Devon's scaly tattoos moved down his arms like a real snake, slithering over his pale skin. They had both been marked as Crows on the same night. To assimilate into a fae-less kingdom, Orion had banished his wings with magic. He'd often longed for a symbol of them to remind himself he wasn't just human.

Devon's mark was a snake to represent his parents, who had given him away to the Society of Crows. After their discussion last night, seeing the tattoo sent chills down Orion's spine.

"I don't remember everything yet."

"Had I known she was a Beekeeper, I would have never harmed her."

Magical wind rushed through the leaves of plants around them, biting with unnatural coldness into their exposed skin. Devon's spell descended like a winter storm.

"You can help us and make it up to her," Orion said.

A laugh escaped Devon's pale lips. "Let me guess. You still want me to use the mirror?"

Orion dodged the ice spell, racing toward his brother. Frigid air burned down his throat. "You said it yourself. The house barely let me in. And we still need answers."

"You might not care about the allegiance we both swore to the Society, but I do." Devon's lips twisted into a snarl. "May I remind you that they protect the world from the very gods who sought to destroy us? Have you also forgotten that insignificant piece of history?"

Orion's back stiffened, his anger flaring. "We aren't talking about doing anything to harm your precious Society. We need to stop the demons from coming here and killing the Beekeepers. On our own, it will take us weeks to sift through the archives, and we don't have that time."

"Why not?" Devon raised his arms over his head. His alabaster skin glistened under the gray light. Frost or sweat? It didn't matter. "We're well hidden from your maniacal father here, and this place hasn't seen a Crow in ages."

"Because Aristaeus shouldn't have to deal with the Zorren on his own."

"Who the hell is this Aristes you two keep talking about?"

"Aristaeus," Orion corrected. "There are always two Beekeepers. You fill in the blank."

His brother's conflicted expression gave Orion hope. He stretched his arm across his chest, ready to get the training started. His stiff muscles really needed to unwind.

"What if it *was* you who hurt Nava when she crossed the portal? You were so worried at the castle about that prophecy referring to you..."

Orion stopped moving and met Devon's gaze across the darkness of his magic. "I would never purposely hurt my soulmate."

A cyclone of freezing air enveloped him not a second later, a wall of white blinding him as the moisture in the air transformed into snow that stuck to his clothes and body. He hissed and called on his shadows to shield him.

"Tsk. Getting sloppy in your old age, brother. No wonder your father's guards kidnapped you from the island. What was that thing you used to tell me? Rule one: do not allow your opponent to distract you. Not even if they're asking questions about your beautiful woman."

Heat surged within Orion's gut, and he raised both of his hands. His inky power exploded out of him in waves of faces and fierce voices that collided with Devon's stormy spell.

The glass above them shook with the wind now raging inside the solarium. Plants lifted from the ground and scattered dirt over the wooden floor beneath their feet.

Devon was right. He needed to get his head straight, or sooner or later, it would get him killed.

This round of training should at least help him release some of that pent-up tension and sharpen his priorities.

Protect Nava from his father. Find out what had happened to his mother, for her ghost still haunted him in this kingdom. And remove the Zorren from the land.

8
NAVA

Nava had been hovering on the threshold of their room for at least thirty minutes. Tapping the wooden doorframe with restless fingers, she studied the long hallway for any sign of either Arkimedes or Devon.

She'd woken up midmorning, aching from the fight with the guards two days prior, their evening of running, and the poor night's sleep on the bakery's floor. A yawn pushed its way past her lips, and she quickly pressed a hand over her mouth to mute any sound that might alert an enemy to her presence.

Gods, she was tired—and going mad with paranoia.

Rationally, she knew they were alone in this place. But the bees were her constant companions, a quiet warning that evil could be lurking behind every closed door. Since Nava was a child, her mother had instilled a deep fear of places like this in her, and she couldn't shake the undeniable sense of malevolence in the air.

A cold draft howled down the hall, making the hair on the back of her arms stand on end. She studied every inch of the space ahead of her. The bees were still with her, crawling over the walls and the clothes she'd borrowed from the set of drawers beside the bed.

She wrapped her injured arm around her grumbling stomach. Her burn had improved significantly compared to the night before, almost as if she'd used a healing potion.

Where was Arkimedes? Perhaps down in the kitchen having breakfast?

Her heart fluttered at the memories of what he'd told her last night. *"I will not change my mind. I love you, Nava. If you'll have me, I will stay."*

He loved her, even without the memories of their shared past. He was choosing to be with her, at least for now. They hadn't discussed their plans beyond defeating the demons and the man in the shadows.

Would he want to remain in the Copper Kingdom? Would she?

Her answer was simple. This wasn't her home, and she wasn't sure she ever wanted it to be. Why stay in a place that had only brought her pain?

She took a quick breath, shaking her head, and stepped out into the hall. She turned right and followed the path to the kitchen, tugging at the soulmate bond and letting it guide her toward Arkimedes.

The floor creaked and snapped beneath her feet. A sudden wind blew her hair into her face, just as the bees buzzed wildly around her.

Nava spun around, her heart in her throat. "Devon?" She hated how her voice sounded like that of a scared child.

The pads of her fingers prickled with nerves and magic. The hall remained empty, but one of the doors stood wide open, swaying slightly on its hinges. That had been shut before. Right?

"If you think this is funny, Devon, it's not. You're going to get stung," she called out, and her aura flashed bright yellow as bees of light joined their friends, wrapping her up in a cocoon.

There was no answer. Nava took a step toward the main stairs that would take her down to the ground floor. But…

Something called her to that room. And she couldn't resist its pull.

This was the kind of stupid behavior that caused a tragedy, and yet she couldn't force her feet forward. Even though she knew better. Even though she was hungry and wanted something to eat.

Her mother had loved to remind Nava that her childish curiosity would one day get her killed. And once upon a time, Nava had believed her. But now she was a powerful woman—not a frightened girl.

Sweat beaded on her temple as she crept to the mysterious door. If something or someone was there, they would regret trying to sneak up on her. And if danger awaited her, she could always transfer elsewhere and drag Arkimedes out of this hellhole while she was at it.

Her power surged through her veins, making her feet light. "Is there anyone here?"

An enormous window stretched across the far wall of the small room, flooding its wooden floors with gray morning light. Tattered curtains rustled in a breeze that whispered through shattered glass.

Nava's tense shoulders dropped as she breathed a sigh of relief. She had been ready to flee or fight for so long—the idea that a simple broken window might be the cause of this had never crossed her mind.

The room, similar to the one she'd slept in with Ark last night, held only a select few pieces of furniture: a small bed in one corner, a desk by the window, and a bookcase on the other side. Other than the mess of papers strewn all over the floor, it was empty. Chewing on her nail, Nava swallowed the remaining panic and edged closer to the table.

The scribbles on the yellowing parchment that lay on the desk were illegible. Nava skimmed the notes but couldn't comprehend them. Quickly losing interest, she moved on to a book with brown leather binding and uneven pages.

The gilded letters on it read: *The Book of the Dead. It's forbidden by the gods to kill a Crow.*

Its pages were thin and deceptively soft, the words inked with swirls of well-practiced calligraphy.

Gooseflesh raked over her skin. The Book of the Dead smelled like its name, and judging by the dust that pricked her nose, no one had opened it in a long time.

Delicate illustrations extended across each spread of pages, painted with burgundy ink that reminded her of dried blood. Roses framed the first image of a woman dressed in the Crows' black uniform.

She was beautiful, with light hair and youthful features.

Haerion C. Windsboe. Society of Crows member since the age of twenty-two. Killed by a deserter in the Iron Kingdom. Died aged thirty-four. No family survives her.

A heavy weight settled in her stomach as she turned the page, half expecting to see her mother's face next. Instead, she found one haunted-looking stranger after the other.

Page after page, portraits of dead Society members danced across her vision. The young and the old, each one remembered in detailed, etched drawings.

Nava closed the book with a thump when the scent of smoke rose to her nostrils. A cold draft slithered through the fabric of her wool trousers. She suddenly had the distinct feeling that she was being watched.

She turned slowly. In the corner of the room, a woman of nightmares floated above the bed.

Layers of a long petticoat moved in the air as if suspended in water. The figure was all black, with long bones for limbs that snapped about in jagged movements. She pointed at Nava with a gaping mouth and empty eyes.

Even though she wanted to scream, no sound left her lips.

She stumbled backward, hitting the table as the scent of burnt flesh and smoke clogged her nose. The spirit didn't move from her spot, but a bright string of magic shot through the room, straight from the center of her charred face and toward Nava.

The air crackled with energy, and the string cut through her shield of bees. Then it wrapped around Nava's skull, and images flashed through her mind, drowning her every thought beneath them.

Orange flames licked the bottom of the tree, red embers bursting into a flickering fire. She fought against the ropes around her body, trying to catch her breath between the sobs that tore through her throat.

"Please, don't do this. I love you," she called into the void, no longer able to see him behind the wall of smoke.

"Love? I wonder if you know the meaning of the word, Briar." His voice had once soothed her soul, but now it was cold and detached.

Briar closed her eyes and called on whatever strength remained inside her aching body. If this was her end, then she would die like the queen she was.

The smoke blurred her vision, and she choked on a breath. The flames licked at her skin, bursting it into blisters.

Her voice gave way, breaking with raw pain, and then there was darkness. For a moment, she floated above a dead tree in the forest, anger stealing her breath, but she couldn't even moan her lament.

The one she'd loved most of all had killed her.

Nava screamed until her throat was raw, her energy dwindling until everything went dark.

"Nava—Nava, look at me." Arkimedes's voice, smooth like honey, soothed her racing heart. She slowly opened her eyes and met a storm of green irises.

His muscular arms encircled her body, lifting her into the soft furnace of his embrace.

"Ark?"

"Yes, it's me." He cradled her tighter against his chest, and the quick thundering of his pulse calmed her. "What happened, Nava?"

His aura was so dark that she couldn't see anything else around her. Not even the spirit that had attacked her.

Her vision sharpened as she sat up straight, staring at the corner where the burnt woman had hovered a moment ago. "She was here," Nava said, twisting around in search of the spirit—only to find an empty room.

"She?" Arkimedes followed her line of sight, and his frown deepened. "Who was here?"

"There was a spirit in this room, but it wasn't a Neem. It was a burnt woman, and she attacked me with a strange spell."

Had it been an attack? It was hard to determine. Nava hugged herself tightly, trying to bring some warmth back to her body.

Ark's skin grew a few shades paler as he faced her. "What do you mean, a burnt woman?"

"Sh-she was wearing a long black dress and floated in that corner." Nava pointed to the spot where the spirit had been with a shaky finger.

Arkimedes's lips parted and then shut. He scrambled to his feet. "You saw her? Was she wearing a crown?"

A crown? In her panic, Nava hadn't noticed that detail. But…she had been a queen. That much had clearly filtered through to Nava while under her spell.

"How did you know about that? Is she the spirit that Devon claims haunts this house?"

"No." Arkimedes avoided her gaze and covered his face with his hand, rubbing it over his forehead again and again, as if he was trying to soothe himself. It left her concerned and curious in equal parts. "I didn't think she would follow me here."

"What do you mean?"

"That spirit was my mother. I'm not sure why she came to you. I'm the only one who has seen her so far. She doesn't reveal herself to my father."

"What do you mean, that was your *mother*?" The images of the woman dying still churned inside her. Nava leaned against the desk, lest she drop to the ground again.

A month ago, Arkimedes had shown her the spot in the forest where his mother had died. A centuries-old tree burned into lifelessness.

Had Arkimedes known how his mother died because she'd shown him, exactly like she'd shown Nava just now?

A long silence fell. Nava vaguely registered the sound of rain pattering against the broken glass of the window. As if this morning could get any gloomier.

Tears welled up in her eyes. "I saw her dying…"

Ark sucked in a sharp breath. "You saw the burning tree?"

"I did." Nava fought off a wave of nausea. "Has she been visiting you for long? How does it work?"

When Arkimedes told her how his mother had died that day in the woods, she'd never dreamed that he'd *seen* it. But if he'd witnessed the same visions the spirit had shared with her…no wonder he was fighting to find answers.

Arkimedes stopped pacing across the worn rug. "When I first visited the Copper Kingdom, Fael brought me to the castle to meet my father. I didn't know I was the lost prince. I thought I was in trouble somehow, and I put up a fight."

"Did you kill someone?"

"Initially, Fael and the other guards assumed I had abandoned my royal mandate." Arkimedes stared vacantly out of the window. "I already knew that using my power to kill would mean I'd hear their voices for the rest of my life, so I was trying not to use it. Still, the guard noticed that my magic was not like theirs."

"The Curse of the Fallen."

Arkimedes met Nava's eyes and nodded. "My father recognized me immediately."

Undoubtedly. Arkimedes was an exact copy of his father, down to the straight nose and full lips. And even though Ark was half fae, half human, he possessed that otherworldly beauty that only the fae could lay claim to.

Arkimedes walked toward the table, paging through the Book of the Dead, although Nava doubted he was actually paying attention to the obituaries. "I wasn't sure I was ready to stay, and when he saw me hesitate, the king offered me information about my past. He also promised to help me get a better handle on my curse."

"What do you mean by that?"

"That my shadows speak to me, and I thought I was going mad." He closed the book with a thump and frowned. "Now I only hear them when I'm overwhelmed, or if I lose my temper."

"So, the king promising to help you is what made you decide to stay?"

"No, it was the mystery surrounding my mother's death that tipped the scales. When I inquired about her, I was told the same lie they spin to everyone else." Arkimedes gripped the edges of the desk so tightly, his knuckles whitened with the pressure. "That she stole me away when I was a one-year-old boy and took me to a place where my father couldn't follow."

"The Iron Kingdom. Because the fae are allergic to iron." Arkimedes was half fae, so he could live there. "But why would she return? Surely, she would have expected to get in trouble?"

"I wondered about that, too," Arkimedes said, and something dark flickered over his expression. "My father told me she denied what she'd done, but he felt like she returned for something. They had no proof, and she claimed that someone else had stolen me."

Nava tucked a few errant strands of hair behind her ear. "But everyone at the castle claims that she took you. And back on the island, you told me she abandoned you at the orphanage."

"She did, Nava. The records say so, and so does everyone here. The castle workers, the citizens—everyone hated her. Her official postmortem report states that a few disgruntled citizens killed her in a fire in the castle's library and then killed themselves before the king could get to them." Arkimedes dragged a palm over his face and pushed away from the desk, reaching for her hand.

She took it, knowing deep inside he needed the physical touch. "But that's a lie."

"The night I learned about her supposed death, my mother's spirit visited for the first time. She showed me the day they burned her alive in the forest." His voice cracked with emotion, and that alone nearly broke Nava.

She pressed her lips tightly together as a heavy sorrow swarmed through her—an emotion that belonged to both of them. It wasn't the right time to bring out the stupid rumors about the fae she'd been teasing him with lately, but it was the first thing that crossed her mind.

"If the fae can't lie, how is any of this possible?"

Arkimedes blinked. Then his stern features softened. At least he continued to find this amusing. "Contrary to what you believe, full fae can lie—just not easily. They have to spin this kind of deceit carefully."

Nava hummed, not quite sure she believed him. "What happened after your mother revealed the truth to you?"

"I snuck into the forest. It took me three days to find the tree." Arkimedes was pulling her toward the door. Admittedly, Nava wanted to be as far away from this room as possible, too. Even now, it remained colder than the rest of the house, like the places in the forest that were haunted by the Neems. "Although she abandoned me in an orphanage, I can't help but think that she was protecting me from something worse."

"Yes, I think you're right."

This was why he was so keen to stay and explore the archive. While Nava understood that he wanted answers, the why hadn't registered as important before. He'd never known his mother, after all.

But after seeing the spirit—her charred skin and hollow eyes—she needed to discover the truth every bit as much as Arkimedes did. And she'd stay here for as long as that took.

"You left me in the midst of a duel, and there are feathers all the way up the steps. And you broke the chandelier. You know you can't fly in a house with low ceilings..." Devon burst into the room, in the middle of buttoning his shirt. His hair stuck to his face—from a recent bath or from sweat? Who knew.

Nava blinked. She hadn't even noticed that Arkimedes's wings were extended, crowding the small room with their impressive size.

"I was in a rush." Arkimedes shrugged and met her eyes, right as his wings disappeared behind his back.

Devon glanced around the room with a growing look of concern. "Who broke the window?"

9
NAVA

"Where are the dungeons in this place?" Nava's voice echoed through the massive room. The ceiling rose into a vault-like dome, decorated with intricate molding and painted in mauve gray. She stepped carefully down the wide staircase, her feet slipping against the polished stone.

Black feathers floated over the steps, carried by the air of their movements.

"Dungeons?" Arkimedes's serious expression broke as he glanced over his shoulder at her. He raised a dark, bushy eyebrow in response. "Why are you always asking about dungeons?"

Her cheeks burned. How long had it been since she'd challenged him to take her to his dungeon at the castle? Somehow, it felt like years ago. Not weeks.

With a shrug, she reached for the banister. "Where else would they keep their prisoners?"

He scoffed, shaking his head but continuing on his path.

"Seriously, though—where are the weapons the Crows used to murder all these innocents? This house seems rather normal."

Apart from the whole spirit thing, the reality of their environment was rather underwhelming.

"*We* are the weapons," Arkimedes tossed back and carried on down the rest of the steps. He sounded so much like his old self. Her heart squeezed tighter.

Hadn't he said those exact words to her the first time they'd trained together?

"Your modesty is astonishing." She ignored the fluttering in her stomach and the hope that blossomed somewhere so deep it blasted away the chill left behind by her ghostly encounter.

"Modesty is a waste of time," Devon called from behind.

A large iron chandelier lay shattered at the bottom of the stairs, fragments of wax candles peppered across the cracked floor. How hadn't she heard this break in the middle of her spirit-induced nightmare?

They cut through several rooms on the ground floor. She hadn't been here before, had she? They were taking her somewhere new. Although, admittedly, that covered most of the safe house.

"Are we going to the archives now?" Nava followed Arkimedes down an eerie corridor that led them to the back of the manor.

"Yes." He opened the first door into an empty ballroom. White sheets obscured every inch of furniture, except for the grand piano. "We should see if there's even a scrying mirror in there."

"I haven't agreed to do it," Devon warned. But he hadn't said no either. Clearly, he was only dragging out the inevitable.

They walked past a locked chamber with wards buzzing around it that would probably call the entire Society if they tried to break in. Then past the infirmary, a smallish room with a cot on one side as well as shelves packed full of old potions caked in dust and covered in spiderwebs.

It all gave her the creeps.

"After what just happened, I want us to get out of here as soon as possible," Arkimedes whispered so only she could hear. He hadn't told his brother about his mother's spirit, and Nava had kept her mouth shut.

Finally, they came to a set of narrow stairs that creaked under the weight of their steps and led them underground. Here, the wallpaper peeled from the corners of the wall: the same sage-green tones and dark wood paneling as inside the rest of the house.

Didn't the Society believe in the power of the arts? Of how color could change a person's mood and evoke emotions? Her skin crawled in anticipation of what the archive might look like—and of the truths it might hold.

It was too dark in here to see far. A lingering putrid smell she couldn't place mingled with the scent of dust and mold. Devon snapped his fingers, and gas lamps roared to life in quick succession, illuminating a circular room with an enormous door on one side and a hallway with no end in sight on the other.

The air around them was thick and humid, as if seawater had filled this entire floor before. Nava hummed and made for the door, studying it with growing dread. The Society had painted it cobalt blue. Gold rosettes embellished the surface. In its center, the crest of a Crow perched on top of a scale.

The emblem of the Society of Crows. Even now, it made her heart climb into her throat.

Nava wiped her sweaty palms against her trousers and forced her eyes away from the bird, called to the dark hallway to the far left of the room. The magic emanating from it left the back of her neck tingling.

Gray and white magic combined—something familiar that pulled at her and made her heartbeat run wild. Was her need to flee because of the blue door or due to the feeling emanating from that corridor?

"Since you're interested in the subject, the dungeons are over there. Home of the traitors." Devon's pink lips tilted up on one side as he pointed toward the hall.

Her stomach sank further. A bitter taste coated her tongue, making it hard to swallow. Even her bees were in disarray, crawling everywhere and sending mixed signals she found hard to decipher.

Whatever was down here, it wasn't good.

"Maybe we should leave," she croaked, shifting her weight from foot to foot. After the spirit upstairs, she'd had enough for the day.

"Stop tormenting Nava, Devon," Arkimedes growled. He pointed at a couple of bees that were circling in front of her, called by her burst of panic. "If you get stung, it'll be your own damn fault. I won't warn you again."

"But I'm not lying..."

Arkimedes's expression softened as he reached for her hand, squeezing it softly. "The cellar *is* cursed, Bee. It's meant to make you feel uneasy, so you won't enter it."

"The cellar? I thought—never mind." She narrowed her eyes at Devon and then at the hall. "Isn't that where normal people store their liquor? Why does it feel so wrong? Is the Society hiding something dangerous there?"

Arkimedes evaded her eyes, turning toward the blue door. "We don't want to release what's in there."

That must be where the actual spirit of this house was, the one Devon had hinted at the night before. Now that she knew, it made sense. Standing in this basement felt a lot like being in Neems territory. Damn, she didn't want to be here at all.

"Not such a boring house anymore, eh?" Devon ambled past her. Yes, she'd been naïve to make that comment earlier. This house was anything but normal.

Arkimedes inspected the emblem with a frown. "Let's just focus on one thing at a time. Our main goal is to discover what the Society knows about the prophecy and how the shadow man is letting the Zorren in."

His hand landed on her lower back in a comforting gesture. A spark of heat radiated from the point of contact, making her ache. His gaze was heavy as he traced the shape of her face, from her eyes to her lips. Despite her fear, their combined desire washed through her, leaving her legs weak.

Devon reached for the door handle, his lips peeling in a snarl, revealing straight white teeth. "If you want my help, then keep the—whatever you two do—behind closed doors."

The filigree Nava had initially thought a mere decoration moved across the painted panels. A mechanism that operated an intricate locking system. It rotated and clicked into shape. Metal scraped over metal as the spicy scent of magic wafted around them, mixing with the mustiness in the room. Then the blue door swung open.

Devon stepped through it without a glance back, leaving Ark and her alone outside. The dread in the pit of her stomach only grew. Her hands prickled with sweat. "Do you think he's going to help us?"

Arkimedes shook his head. "I don't know, but he understands what's at risk if he doesn't."

"What if one of us does it?" she asked, wetting her lips. "I know he said in the kitchen that the Vulcan will alert the Crows, but—"

"We can't. Like the fountain outside, they put a spell on the mirror to trigger a warning. If someone who isn't a Crow touches it, this place will be crawling with members of the Society before we know it. It will also poison whoever grabs it."

Her mouth went dry at his words. "Poison?"

Arkimedes nodded. "The Vulcan is a god's artifact. They say someone stole the first scrying mirror from the gods during the last war many centuries ago. The Crows split it into smaller fragments to use in the safe houses, but as with every artifact, you become poisoned if you hold it more than once—and if it considers you an enemy."

Nava almost turned around and headed the way they'd come, but Arkimedes cleared his throat and pushed her forward with the hand that was still pressed against her lower back. He'd read her emotions, her need to flee. And he was her anchor in a moment of weakness.

"When we enter, you'll find the Vulcan will call to you with what you want to hear. But it's not a call you want to answer, Nava."

"What will it say?"

There was something dark in his expression. "It's different for everyone. I don't know how this particular Vulcan looks, so please be alert and don't respond to anything that feels strange. Come on."

They walked into the archives, Nava's steps stiff, her neck aching from the tense set of her shoulders. Flickering candelabra on the walls illuminated the room with magical candlelight so dim that it was hard to make out any detail.

"Easy there." Arkimedes soothed her with a smile that didn't quite reach his eyes. His wide hands grasped her shoulders, and her quickened heartbeat eased to a pleasant drumming that made her skin tingle with awareness.

She took a deep breath to calm her heavy breathing. "I'm fine."

"You're glowing."

Nava looked at her arms. She was shining such a bright yellow she was easily the most intense source of light in this place. Her energy rolled like waves from the magical core beneath her skin, and she didn't even feel all that threatened now they were inside the room. The bees that had accompanied her from the castle still circled her body.

Something was wrong, and she couldn't ignore it any longer. Did it have anything to do with the mirror? Perhaps, perhaps not. She was just happy Cameron was as far away from her as possible.

The archive wasn't quite a library. Two of its walls held bookcases that extended to the tall ceiling. The other two were covered in large glass cases that contained old weapons and unfamiliar gadgets. In the center of the room, several circular wooden desks surrounded a mirror sphere that rested upon a limestone pedestal.

Any spot on the walls that wasn't hidden by books or artifacts was covered in beautiful landscape paintings and portraits.

Nava followed Arkimedes deeper into the room, glancing at Devon, who stood frozen before the scrying mirror.

A song flowed down from the ceiling, gentle like the buzzing of bees and leaves rustling in the open air. The globe in the center shone white and yellow, like her own aura. Ari's voice called for her to return. She only had to touch it, and she would be back in the forest with him.

The sphere's yellow glow flickered, and Ari's voice grew distant. He was asking for her help. He was hurting. The Zorren had returned.

She collided with a mass of muscle, and strong iron-clad arms wrapped around her body right before she could sprint toward the Vulcan. The warm air of Arkimedes's breath hit the side of her ear, and panic flooded Nava. She couldn't move.

Her body began to lose matter. She had to transfer... "I have to answer Ari's call!" she shouted, pushing against the wall that held her.

"Ignore its call," Arkimedes urged.

It took several long seconds for his words to filter past the fog in her mind.

This wasn't real—it was a trick from the artifact, designed to get her to touch it. Hadn't Arkimedes warned her?

She let out a shaky breath and sagged against his hold. "I don't know what happened to me…"

His hand caressed her arm in a soothing motion, before he intertwined his fingers with hers and pulled her in the opposite direction. "The Society trained us to handle the calling, but it's very hard to ignore the first time you experience it."

Nava's limbs felt heavy. She'd been tired ever since she'd woken up, but adrenaline had fooled her into believing she could push through. "Why is it called a Vulcan?"

"It's named after its creator, the god of truth and vision. He designed the mirrors to spy on our world."

Nava watched Devon as he threw his tunic onto the floor and rolled his shoulders. His forehead wrinkled as if he was sinking into a state of deep concentration.

"Is he preparing for a fight? Will the mirror hurt him?" Nava hated that she knew so little about all of this. It made her feel like a little girl asking silly questions.

"Devon has handled other Vulcans in the past. He will be fine," Arkimedes attempted to reassure her. However, the feeling coming through their bond didn't match his stoic face.

"I can sense you're nervous, Arkimedes. Why are you lying to me? And if he has handled a Vulcan before, wouldn't it poison him?"

A smirk tilted Arkimedes's full lips. "I didn't lie. Devon has handled the Vulcan before. The poison shouldn't be an issue because members of the Society use a potion that allows us to use it again—once enough time has passed. But I don't remember when he took the resetting potion, so…"

"You don't know if he'll be successful." She nodded, feeling dizzy.

"It'll be fine. Devon's not an idiot. And you know how much he values his life."

Nodding again, Nava stared at Devon as he reached for the orb. His hands glowed white as he clutched it. Energy buzzed through the room, making her hair stand on end with static.

Her skin itched; her stomach dropped. Ari's calls filled the air, much stronger now and so hard to resist.

Then Devon's deep rumble of a voice broke over Ari's screams. "Is Arkimedes B. Valeron the one opening the portals for the Zorren?"

Wait. That wasn't the question they needed answers to.

"No!" Nava screamed. The surge that blasted through the room in the next instant cut her words off, rattling the glass cases and blowing loose parchment from the tables.

Devon snarled, holding the glowing sphere aloft with both hands. His long black hair fluttered behind him, blown out of his face by the force of the magic from the artifact.

Arkimedes strode toward his brother. Was he readying himself to intervene if needed? The sphere's outer edges still glowed in a silver shade, but it was turning bright red at its center.

Nava didn't know how long they stood there, paralyzed by the intensity of its power. Of an old magic that smelled so similar to her own.

Then one of Devon's hands fell away from the glowing ball, dangling lifelessly at his side. His eyes glowed bright white. *"No mortal can stay in Dargan's world and speak the demon's tongue,"* Devon said in a distorted voice, and from a far shelf, a book flew out and landed with a bang on the floor.

Its pages flapped like a fan, moved by air that seemed to come from everywhere and nowhere at once.

Devon gasped, his body shaking.

Arkimedes's wings popped out of his back, and he flew forward just as Devon stumbled and placed Vulcan on its pedestal—and then dropped like a dead weight.

Time slowed as Arkimedes's immense wings closed in around his brother's body. He slid across the polished floor, barely getting underneath Devon before his head hit the hard ground.

For a long moment, the rustle of paper settling on the floor was the only sound in the room beyond the fast beat of Nava's heart. Then Arkimedes rose, carrying an unconscious Devon to a settee beside the blue door. He placed him against its cushions and turned to Nava. Shame twisted his features as he averted his eyes.

Anger bloomed hot in her stomach. How could Devon believe that Arkimedes had done it? They'd talked it through in the kitchen. This had *not* been the plan.

Undoubtedly, Arkimedes needed some space to lick his wounds and make peace with his brother's actions. Nava had to keep herself busy so she wouldn't swoop in and try to console him. To reassure him that she believed he was good...

She also needed to resist the urge to smother Devon with a pillow. So instead, she turned to the book that had fallen to the floor. This was the answer to a useless question the god's artifact had given them.

10
ORION

Orion didn't know how long he stood there, unmoving. He breathed deeply, trying to quiet the whispers from his shadows. To ignore the sting of betrayal.

A part of him wanted to give in to the anger simmering in the pit of his stomach, threatening to boil over. Why would Devon think he was capable of causing this disaster and hurting Nava or Aristaeus?

Orion always feared he was teetering on the edge of some wicked act. His nature demanded it. But he tried to rise above the darkness of his power. To not take life for granted, not for a moment.

And he loved, fervently. This world, and especially Nava.

He'd told Devon while they were training what they needed from the mirror: a way to shut the portals permanently. Devon shouldn't—couldn't—use the Vulcan again or it would poison him.

Even if they had access to the Society's potion, they wouldn't be able to ask another question for at least half a year. Fuck, they were in trouble. Orion dragged his eyes over his brother's unmoving body, and his heart ached. It shouldn't hurt this badly…but it did.

"Ark," Nava called from the other end of the room. She was kneeling by the book on the ground, her arms draped over her legs, not touching the pages.

He made it back to her in a few strides. Better to mask his disappointment with something that would bring her hope. "Is the book useful?" he asked, leaning forward to glance at the ancient book, its parchment thin and waxy.

She raised her head to meet his eyes. A crinkle appeared in between her brows. "It seems to be about the history of our world. Not sure how it can help?"

Orion grabbed the book, turning it around so he could read the elegant calligraphy.

The Creation of the Kingdoms:

The people of Caztian destroyed the land. They murdered and burned the land. The gods were angry and caused all that once was alive to perish.

The four leaders of the lands brought offerings to the deities to banish their ire.

The sorcerer brought mechanical inventions made of IRON. A gift of ingenuity.

The fae brought a creature of great intelligence and strength with a COPPER mane. A gift of creation.

The witch harvested SILVER and spun it like webs to link the magic of beings to the land. A gift of cunning resourcefulness.

Last, the creature of the night offered the gods their second-born. Her GOLD hair flowed like sand dunes. A gift of sacrifice.

The benevolent gods accepted the leaders' offerings, but they demanded one final gift of sacrifice from all rulers. In return, they would grant their bloodlines great power.

"What does that last part mean…about the gift of sacrifice?"

"Have you heard about the tithes?" he asked.

Nava pursed her lips and shook her head.

"It's said that the founders had to pay the tithes to the gods to save the world by forfeiting their second-born magical heir. Then, in their grief and to prevent the gods from waging another war we couldn't win, they mandated the creation of magical armies to fight the deities."

"Is that why families have to give away their magical children?"

Orion nodded, glancing at the pages that detailed a history he'd learned a long time ago. "At first, when the memories of the devastation brought by the gods were still raw, magic-wielders volunteered for the armies. And so did their sons and daughters, for a few generations. Then, slowly, they stopped, and the magic dwindled. First from families that held less power—out of four children, only two inherited the trait. After that, just one, and then an entire generation would go without magic."

Nava's frown deepened. "It sounds like the propaganda my mother used to tell me the Crows spread, so they could take the children away."

"The *kings and queens* set the tithe, Bee. The Crows uphold it. Every person born with magic needs to be trained to defend our world in case the gods come for us again."

Nava raised an eyebrow at that, silently challenging his words. "But how can we defeat a god? They can't die."

"They can, if you use the right weapons—or so the story goes." Not that talking about the gods would help them at all with their current predicament.

"So the founders created the Society of Crows to uphold the balance." Nava tapped her chin, but her voice turned high-pitched with irritation. "I don't like it."

Remnants of memories he still had to unveil tickled his mind, making the ghost of his headache resurface once again. He cleared his throat and rubbed his index finger over his temple. "Later generations forgot why the drafts happen in the first place, and it's the Society's job to keep records of those years of pestilence, war, famine, and death."

"Do all the kingdoms take tithes?"

"My father rarely does. He only demands that the Dark Ones join the royal guards. But there is no need to take them as children. Every Dark One born with enough power to wield it comes to serve the king willingly."

"I see how they serve him," Nava said tightly, shaking her head. "All the women ended up as his consorts."

Orion rested his elbows on his knees, meeting her unrelenting gaze. "They wanted to, Nava—they told me that much."

"I doubt they would say otherwise when the truth could get them in trouble."

He didn't want to get into this argument with her. Her hate for the king wouldn't allow her to see that some people regarded him as something close to a god. "I've heard the Gold Kingdom doesn't draft children either, but I'm unsure whether that's true or not. Their politics are complicated."

"How so?"

"For starters, they have two monarchies fighting for the same crown. The shifters who lost the last war and the vampires."

"Vampires?" She blinked rapidly. "Really?"

"It's not a place I would head to for a break, even though it's beautiful." Orion shrugged and continued paging through the book. Surely there was something in here that could help them?

"So the Society upholds the tithes, which keeps their armies strong with magic to fight the gods?"

"When I was a Crow, they taught us to be prepared for when the gods returned. They didn't teach us to harm people simply because they wanted the citizens of Caztian to suffer. Every family has given up something precious. The founders who became the royals paid the first tithe when they gave the gods their second-born child."

"But why does it have to be children?" Nava's lips flattened just as a wave of anger, mixed with sorrow, flared through their bond. "No matter how frightening the decline of magic is—or the supposed end of the world at the hands of the gods—a child should remain with their family."

"I agree." Orion nodded. "But if children stay with their non-magical parents, they can't be taught or trained properly. They might hurt themselves or others by accident. Some villages are so poor Nava, they lack education and sometimes they punish the innocent magical kids because of their powers, which they can't control." He'd prefer not to remember everything he had seen in his time. The innocents who'd suffered unspeakable torture. "It's hard to grow up when you're always the scary one. When people don't understand you."

Nava's expression softened, and she reached for his hand, pausing briefly before taking it. "You never told me about this..."

"It's not a good story to tell." Orion's chest felt tight all of a sudden. Why hadn't he shared any of this with her before? Regardless of the reason, he wanted her to know now. "Once, the Crows commanded me to check up on several families. The rumor was that they'd harmed their children because of their powers. When I found them locked in dark rooms, barely more than skin and bones, I nearly lost it."

"Gods..." Nava turned pale.

He ground his teeth. If only he could lose those memories, shake the echo of the rage that had consumed him, demanding he seek retribution. "And when I asked for the children to be released, the families demanded the price the Crown pays per head." Shame forced his eyes away from her compassionate gaze. "Of course, I also took some children who were loved because I thought I had to."

"And now you believe the drafts are wrong?"

"I believe the Crowns should invest in better education for their people. Also, I wish they wouldn't treat their armies like disposable human camps."

"I enjoy learning all this. It makes a bit more sense—I just don't understand why the Vulcan showed us this book."

Orion smirked, squeezing her shoulder. Nava was right. This was the legend behind the creation of the kingdoms. Not much use for closing the portals—nor for understanding who was sending the Zorren.

"Devon Black did this. Force him to hold the Vulcan again and get us the answers we need," one of his shadows spat, and its venom rushed through Orion's blood, awakening his power.

Orion took a breath to calm himself and clenched his jaw tight against the throbbing within his skull.

"I'm sorry about what happened," Nava said, as if she were reading him like the open book beneath his hand.

The crawling sensation under his skin intensified alongside the need to disappear into the shadows of the room. To hide and lick his wounds. "You've done nothing to be sorry for."

"Maybe I'm sorry for how you feel right now. Maybe it's time we show Devon who the wicked one in this relationship is."

Surprise pushed a laugh past Orion's lips. "You don't have a drop of blood in your body that's truly wicked, Bee."

"May I remind you that the life debt only existed because I almost killed him?" She let out a shaky breath. "Not that I'm proud of it. And I have grown to care for Devon—against my better judgment."

"I'm not angry about him wanting to make sure you are safe. He understands your role as a Beekeeper. You found a Dark One who looks like me and is letting the demons in."

"But we agreed it couldn't be you," she grumbled.

"Yes, and it hurts that he doubted me, but I would have done the same, and I will get over it. Devon needed to be sure he could trust me, and I understand that."

He was done talking about it, to be honest. He flicked back to the page the book had originally opened on and pointed to the line of text that mentioned the Silver Kingdom. "The witches tied the four rulers and their descendants to their new kingdoms. It's the very reason my father kidnapped me from our home on Grey Island."

She returned her focus to the book. "Because your magic feeds the land..."

"*Our* magic. You are the future queen, Nava." If only she didn't look so defeated. It tore him from the inside out. He reached for her again, as if one simple touch might revive him, but she turned her face away from him.

"I do understand that."

She hated it in the Copper Kingdom. How could she not? Everything she'd experienced here had been negative. The burning forests, the Zorren, the king—hell, even Orion had played a part in Nava facing trial after trial. The knowledge only made his stomach sink further.

"I understand why I chose not to come back of my own free will," he whispered, grasping her chin and lifting her face to meet his. The answer was simple. The Arkimedes from a year ago had known Nava wasn't ready for this. That she was too new to the world of magic—a world where her soulmate was a Dark One with a giant secret in the shape of a kingdom. "If you really don't want to be a queen, we will leave once all of this is over."

"Really?" Her lips parted, and she searched his face as if she was trying to find the lie there.

"Yes."

"What about the kingdom?"

"Perhaps we can live somewhere in our land but far away from the castle and the king." He paused, and the memory of a red-haired boy flashed through his mind. Cameron—Nava's little brother.

Another reminder of the family his father had stolen from him. He could keep the reality of him regaining his memories to himself, so it wouldn't detract from the bigger problems at hand. But he craved honesty between them. Her happiness was the most important thing.

"I bet Cameron will like it here. There are creatures neither of you have ever seen before."

Nava nodded and then froze. Her eyes widened as she seemed to realize what his words meant, but she didn't say a thing. Instead, she threw herself at him across the old book, barely giving him a chance to catch her.

She laced her fingers behind his neck and crushed her lips to his in a bruising kiss. He could taste the salt from the tears that were streaming down her cheeks on her tongue.

The kiss was too short. She withdrew and hiccuped before taking a deep breath. "How much do you remember?"

"Not everything. Just fragments. But they're coming back faster now that I'm away from the castle and my father."

She ran her hands over her face, wiping away all traces of her tears. Then she flashed him a blinding smile. Now they only had to defeat the man in the shadows before the Zorren destroyed the kingdom. It seemed easy enough, with her looking at him like that.

"When can Devon use the mirror again?" Nava settled on her knees, wincing as she spotted the wrinkled pages of the book wedged between them. She flattened her palms over them again and again, attempting to get rid of the creases, but all to no avail.

Orion sighed, glancing at Devon's pale form on the settee. His chest was rising and falling with slow, shallow breaths.

"We can't use the Vulcan again," he said, and the burning frustration returned like an old foe that had never left him. "It will kill Devon. Or hurt him very badly."

"So Devon ruined our chance to learn how to stop the man in the shadows and all we got out of it was a useless history lesson?"

Well, when she put it like that...perhaps hurting his brother wasn't such a bad idea. But maybe all wasn't lost. Devon had asked the wrong question, but the mirror had given them one useful answer. Even if it wasn't the one they'd been looking for.

"No mortal can stay in Dargan's world and speak the demon's tongue," he repeated.

It made little sense why this book had flown over to them when Devon had asked whether Arkimedes was the one opening the portals. Nevertheless, the Vulcan had answered clearly by speaking through Devon's lips.

It couldn't possibly be Orion because he was mortal.

Whoever Nava had encountered in Dargan's realm was immortal, able to stay in Dargan's realm and talk to demons.

"He is an emissary of the gods." The words left his lips before the thought had fully formed in his mind. He looked up to see Nava's blank expression and grabbed the book from the floor, carrying it to the nearest table.

She scrambled after him. "A what?"

"Emissaries are the messengers of the gods. They walk both this world and their realms and deliver the gods' messages to the royals."

Orion found the sentence he was looking for. He reread it, his heart lurching in his chest.

> *The benevolent gods accepted the leaders' offerings but demanded one last gift of sacrifice from all rulers. In return, they would grant their bloodlines great power.*

"A gift of sacrifice." He pointed at the swirls of ancient calligraphy. "The Society of Crows believes the emissaries are magic-wielders. That families across the world offer sacrifice to the gods to gain something holy."

"So...you think the shadow man is a sacrifice to the God of Shadows?" Nava's voice came out strained, but she nodded as if it made sense. "If that's the case, then he has to be your kin, not a shapeshifting demon."

They stared at each other in silence. Orion knew with a terrifying certainty what Nava was thinking.

What if the man in the shadows was Orion's twin brother?

Maybe that was the reason his mother had whisked him away? Perhaps she hadn't realized what would happen until it was too late, and in her terror at losing one child, she'd wanted Arkimedes as far away from his father's reach as possible.

"If he's an emissary of the God of Shadows, Nava, it would explain why he was there each time you crossed."

"How are we supposed to defeat him if we can't kill him?" Her face twisted with shame, and she swallowed hard. "I mean…I don't mean we *have* to kill your blood brother, but—"

"He's trying to kill you," Orion growled. "I will do anything—and I mean that—to protect you." The words burned in his mouth, and dread squeezed his throat tightly.

But how? Without the Vulcan, they wouldn't be able to get a straightforward answer to that question, and finding another mirror was nigh on impossible.

"If we can't take him down, we might have to return to the castle and speak with my father."

But that would be the very last thing they would do.

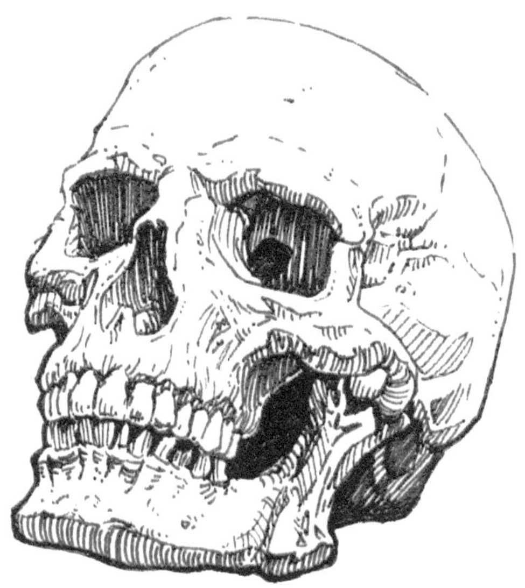

11
ORION

By the time Orion got Devon into his room, night had fallen. It was particularly cold tonight, the chill sneaking past the thin window-panes and creeping under the layers of his clothes. He threw a log into the chimney, and golden flames ate it up, roaring to life.

Devon lay on the bed, barely moving. He had said very little ever since he'd woken up.

Now he pressed his cheek against the pillow, his features drawn as he tracked Orion's movements with care. "If you're angry with me, Arkimedes, you can speak now or forever hold your peace."

"Peace?" Orion scoffed, straightening as he dusted wood fibers and ash off his hands. "We needed to know how to stop the Zorren, Devon. Not whether I was behind it all."

For someone so tall and strong, Devon looked frail now, weakened by the ancient magic of the mirror. "Just because you said you wouldn't do it, doesn't mean your blabber convinced me."

Could he storm out of this place like Nava had done mere minutes ago? Tempting. Still, deep down, Orion was glad Devon had tried to protect her from harm. Even if it felt a lot like betrayal.

"At least your question gave us something to work with." Orion headed over to the window and tugged at the curtain to shut it. This cold wouldn't do much to help Devon heal.

"Out with it."

"The one opening the portals is an immortal, and we have no idea how we will stop him."

Devon's lips parted in obvious shock.

"Unless you know how to defeat an immortal?" Orion crossed his arms.

"Of course I don't."

"That's the information we needed from the Vulcan. If we're to survive this mess, we have to work together, not against each other."

"She's a Beekeeper, Arkimedes." Devon slammed his open palm against the bed. Particles of dust rose, encircling him in a halo. "I want to protect her, and if you were destined to kill her in some strange twist of timelines, I wasn't going to make it easy on you."

"You knew as well as I did that we only had one shot at the Vulcan—"

Devon's harsh laughter cut him off. "Only weeks ago, you brought me a burnt book and asked me to translate it. When I told you the prophecy, you thought it referred to you."

Orion didn't need to hear his brother's justifications. In the logical part of his brain, he understood. But that didn't mean it hurt any less.

He turned his face away. "I'd hoped you'd believed me when I reassured you that I couldn't hurt Nava. Not in this lifetime, nor the next."

"You're in love now, but how many fall out of love?" Devon reasoned. "What if you stop loving her tomorrow morning and destroy the world by nightfall?"

Anger boiled over as he crossed to the bed with wide strides. Heat flooded his cheeks, and his shadows darkened, crawling over the bed. "That's not how soulmates work. I'd rather die than hurt her!" In fact, he would die, too, if Nava were to be killed.

"How would I know? I don't have a soulmate of my own for comparison. You have the girl and the father who wants you home. You have the kingdom, the power, and a life full of purpose."

"So what is it, Devon?" Orion narrowed his eyes. His shadows retreated, inch by inch, as his anger cooled, replaced by the bitterness of heartbreak. "Were you truly doubting my nature because you were concerned about Nava's well-being? Or were you secretly hoping I was going to be the villain all along because you're jealous?"

Devon's mouth opened, then snapped shut. His brows furrowed as he took in Orion's words. "You're twisting this..."

"Am I?" Orion backed away to the door. He just wanted to get out of here. To be alone. He swallowed a few times before speaking again to make sure his voice wouldn't crack. "Tell me it's not true, then. Swear it to me."

The silence was absolute.

Orion nodded and turned to leave, pausing by the door when Devon's breath hitched.

"I wanted nothing bad to happen to you, that I swear." His brother's voice was raw with emotion.

They both knew jealousy was a venom that could kill, even in relationships like theirs. "If you want to be the hero, I'd start by looking into what your precious Society is doing to innocents."

The creaking of the bedsprings made Orion pivot on his heel to meet his brother's haunted gaze. Devon was sitting up straight, his back like an iron rod against the headboard. "Don't bring them into our private affairs."

"I believe the Society knew who I was when they took me as a five-year-old boy. They kept me away from my kingdom."

"You don't know that for sure. Just because Nava whispers sweet nothings into your ear, doesn't mean she's right about everything."

Orion had neither time nor patience to get into this with Devon. He wrapped his hand around the handle and opened the door into the dark, cold hallway. "I believe they took your family from you, exactly like they did to the children in the bakery. I've been the villain to many, and I never truly questioned the Society. We were young and ignorant when we first met. But I don't have that excuse anymore, and neither do you. You don't get to blame me for the decisions you make when you continue to follow them blindly."

And without another look back, he left the room.

12
NAVA

Nava hated being alone, but especially so in this haunted place. With all that had happened three days ago with the Vulcan, tension had been running high between Arkimedes and Devon.

She hadn't left their room for fear of running into the spirit of Arkimedes's mother again—or, worse yet, meeting Devon in the hall and having to pretend not to be bothered by what he'd done.

She paced across the creaking floor, pausing by the window and peering outside. Mist enveloped the front garden, so thick she couldn't see beyond the rock wall that fenced off the manor from the wilderness outside. Her skin crawled with the need to be out of these four walls as soon as possible.

Where was Arkimedes? He'd said something earlier about catching some fresh air. She pressed her face to the glass, trying to spot him. Nava drew a fortifying breath. She had to leave this room eventually.

Venturing out into the haunted halls, she kept her eyes wide open and a shield of bees buzzing around her. The kitchen was empty, but there was hot coffee in the pot and porridge waiting for her on the stove. Wonderful.

She blew on the steam rising from her mug and closed her eyes as the bittersweet scent promised a boost of energy. If there was one thing she was grateful to the Crows for, it was the reserves of coffee beans they kept in this place. They could go to the shadow realm for everything else.

It didn't take her long to discover Arkimedes in the solarium. His bare, muscular chest came into view through its double doors, the glass distorting some of the detail. But what she couldn't make out, her mind filled in from memory.

Arkimedes stood in a wide stance, his charcoal pants slung low on his hips, showing off his well-defined abdominal muscles. He wiped his forehead. His skin glistened with sweat.

Nava swallowed against the sudden dryness in her mouth. Despite sharing a room, they'd been too exhausted for intimacy, except for the two kisses she had stolen from him.

She needed time to heal from the heartbreak of believing he'd chosen the kingdom over her. That wasn't the case, of course—but words only healed part of the wounds. Time and proof of his commitment would do the rest.

But it didn't hurt his case one bit that he looked the way he did. Heat rushed through her, coiling tight in her center. She rose up on tiptoes to catch a better view of her mate.

He bounced on his feet while rotating his shoulders. His power—rich and black—morphed into waves that swirled around him like a cyclone, shaking the wooden boards of the training deck. The shapes of his victims peered from the swirls. His aura was only visible to her when he was actively using magic, and perhaps it should have frightened her, but she loved that he was power incarnate. That he could choose to bring destruction but refrained from doing so.

He'd been coming here to train each morning at sunrise. Then he came to collect her for breakfast before they went to the archives to find the answers Devon had robbed them of. It was useless, as there were thousands of books to go through—and they didn't even know where to start.

"Are you going to stay out there or come inside?" Arkimedes's bright green eyes caught hers from across the solarium and past the dirty glass door. His gaze pinned her down like he was the predator and she was his prey.

"Hello." Nava scrambled forward, her heart beating wildly in her throat, and she lifted a hand in the most awkward wave any human could possibly give their soulmate.

He smiled, the sun catching the firm muscle of his abdomen, and the visual was so distracting that her foot caught on the step up to the training deck. She screeched as she fell forward, her coffee spilling everywhere.

His hands caught her before she could hit the ground. "Watch where you're going, Bee."

Nava met his knowing gaze, and her face heated. How could he still have the same effect on her after all this time? "You made me spill my coffee."

"What a catastrophe." His hands settled on her hips, the warmth of his touch seeping through the thin layer of her trousers. "You can always go back for more. I brewed you a big pot."

Desire rippled through her, making her shudder. "Apparently not enough if you're going to strut around the house shirtless," she whispered, her fingertips tingling as she pressed a hand to his chest. The touch alone sparked energy.

His laugh was breathy, music to her ears after he had spent the past few days sulking. "Are you here to train with me?"

"I don't know. You like to cheat."

"When have I ever cheated while training?" he challenged. His fingers dug into her flesh, and he pulled her forward with a sudden, possessive tug until their bodies touched.

"Please. Back on the island, you did all the time." Did he remember their training sessions again? Her heart was beating so fast, she could barely think straight. There was no greater gift than him regaining his memories.

"You're a sore loser..."

Nava pursed her lips. "I win if I reach the weapons rack first." Lifting her chin, she pointed in the general direction of the target. Her skin glowed yellow as a rush of magic came to her call, feeding the adrenaline already rushing through her veins.

"Since you're intent on tainting my name, I get to call the prize if I take you down." Arkimedes stepped away, depriving her of his nearness. He dusted off his pants and stalked around her like a predator inspecting his next meal. Oh, she wanted to be that. Badly. If only to forget about everything else.

"Do your worst." The challenge died on her lips when Arkimedes launched himself at her. She squeaked, darting out of the way of his shadows.

He'd always waited for her to attack first, and him making the first move unsettled her. But she transferred out of his grasp just in time. Her blood buzzed, warm with the delicious exhilaration of being chased across the wide expanse of this room, surrounded by tropical plants that lent their energy to her.

She laughed, half running, half transferring in a billow of dust and pollen toward the weaponry stack. Arkimedes's wings beat in sharp bursts as he swooped into the air and toward her like a bird of prey. She was almost there, but the reach of his magic was too great.

The air crackled with black particles that swarmed her. He was anticipating her moves, perhaps reading her emotions. Each time she appeared in a new place, he was almost there, ready to catch her.

The peppery scent of his magic brought tears to her eyes, blinding her and slowing her down. Through the gust of dark ink that wrapped around her like a secondary shield and refused to let go, Nava could see the shelves a mere four feet away. They beckoned her forward, calling for her triumph.

Suddenly, Arkimedes landed behind her with silent steps. Someone else might not have noticed, but Nava sensed the spike of excitement through the bond. Two could play the game of guessing where the other would go. She didn't need to see him or hear his steps to know he was running toward her.

He was close, too close.

She bolted in the opposite direction and reached for the shelves. Her fingers wrapped around the polished wooden handle of a dagger, just as his fingerlike mist grabbed her ankles and dragged her backward.

Nava kicked at the tendrils of magic and pulled the entire rack of training weapons from the wall to the floor. The ground shook, and Arkimedes tackled her from the side, emerging from the pitch-black wall of his power.

A scream escaped her as they tumbled to the ground, collapsing in a pile of sweaty limbs away from the weapons. Slowly, both their auras faded away to nothing.

"You're heavy," she groaned. Having the full weight of his body on top of her made her keenly aware of how perfectly it fit against every plane and curve of her body. Her blood sang with his nearness.

He lifted himself off her, although one of his hands lingered on her stomach, right over the spot where she could feel their bond the strongest, where his emotions blended with hers, intangible but real.

His need for her ran rampant, merging with her desire for him. She lifted the small wooden dagger she'd picked from the rack before Arkimedes had reached her.

"It seems you won. What's your prize, Bee?"

Nava dropped the practice weapon to the side and placed both hands over his sweaty skin. Gods, she loved the thundering of his heart under her palms. She trembled beneath him with the force of her craving. "I want you to touch me."

Arkimedes let out a low groan. His eyes darkened with something primal as he caressed the side of her face with one hand, before closing the gap that separated them with a kiss.

Their lips touched gently at first, but the kiss soon caught fire as he deepened it. His tongue traced her lips, then slipped inside her mouth, tangling with hers in an obscene dance that left Nava breathless. She shuddered, her entire body tingling with the need to feel him, to have him explore every inch of her.

She swallowed as his hand splayed over her stomach, traveling over her blouse, slowing down to trace her breasts, grasping the mounds and flicking a finger over her nipples.

"Devon could come at any moment." She dug her fingers into his scalp, pulling him closer.

"I don't want to hear my brother's name on your lips when I'm touching you like this." Arkimedes slipped his hand inside her trousers, and the breath caught in Nava's throat when his fingers met her aching center.

A gentle wind chime rang in the air, and his lips closed on her neck, sucking. His tongue lapped at her skin with the same intensity that his fingers danced over the point where she craved him most.

"Don't stop," she pleaded in a ragged tone, writhing beneath him as he slid a finger inside her, pumping harder.

Her hips moved of their own accord, rising and falling as she met each thrust of his hand until she was a tight coil ready to snap.

"Nava, I want to devour you whole."

Pleasure burst through her as her orgasm crashed down on her like waves, dragging another moan from her lips. He kissed her then, but unlike their previous kisses, this one was slow and languid, sweet.

Arkimedes pulled away and met her gaze. In his expression, she found love, desire—and fear. He pressed his lips to hers again, a gentle caress that made her heart stutter. She never wanted to be apart from him again.

The thought sparked the fire in her veins once more, and as it rushed through her, she reached for the strings of his trousers, eager to be rid of them. She needed to touch him…

The chime pierced the solarium again, followed by a loud ringing sound that echoed through the room.

"What's happening?" Nava blinked, dizzy as she tried to locate its source.

"Fuck," Arkimedes growled, and he was off her in a matter of seconds. His head snapped from side to side as he searched for the origin of the noise. "Something's triggered the alarm."

The fire raging through Nava's body died as if doused in water. He helped her up and hunted for his discarded shirt while she straightened her clothes.

"What does that mean?" Her mind raced as she looked around, half expecting to see a Crow bursting into the solarium at any moment. Had someone attempted to enter through the fountain? One of the king's guards, perhaps?

"It means the Society now knows we are here. We have to go."

13
ORION

The alarm rang louder inside the house. It morphed from a soft chime to a sound so high-pitched that it punctured Orion's ears and brought the remnants of the headache he had been fighting for days.

They ran to the entrance hall and the winding stairs that led to the second floor. "We need to get Devon before we—"

As if called by his words, his brother stumbled into the room from the other direction, clinging to the wall with trembling arms. His wide black eyes met Arkimedes's, bulging from their sockets as he gasped for air.

"Devon?" Orion rushed to him. His fingers went numb when he caught Devon's body just as he collapsed. He was cold as ice and soaked in a layer of perspiration that was seeping through his white shirt.

"I'm sorry, Arkimedes," Devon rasped. Whatever softness his cheeks had held before was gone now. His skin sagged over every bone of his skull.

Nava hurried to them, the glow of her body illuminating the dark room, bringing warmth to the greenish-gray shades of Devon's skin. "What's happening to him?"

Devon closed his eyes, his weight sinking more heavily into Orion's arms. "I wanted to get you the answers." He grimaced in pain as his body rattled with shivers.

Unease crawled over Orion's skin. "What did you do?" he demanded, fighting the need to shake his brother.

But he already knew the answer, even without an explanation. Devon had gone back to the archives and sought out the Vulcan once again. Orion pushed aside the anger that boiled within him and picked up his brother from the ground. Devon's weight was considerable. Even with the Vulcan's poison sucking the life out of him, he was still all thick bones and muscles.

Nava followed them into the parlor where Orion placed Devon onto the green velvet sofa. "What can we do to help him?"

The alarm bells were still ringing. They needed to leave. Orion turned to her and read the unspoken question in her eyes. *Is he going to die?*

Not today. Not if he had anything to say about it.

"We need to find a healing potion before we leave. It should keep him alive until we make it to the city." Orion rose, making for the small infirmary down the hall. The likelihood of discovering a non-expired potion was slim, but Orion had seen people perish under the poison's grip before. It was a fast and ugly death.

"I'll get it," Nava said, placing a trembling hand on his shoulder. "You stay with him. I know where the infirmary is."

Before he could argue, she was already transferring away, disappearing past the archway toward the long, dark hall. She could get there and back faster than he ever could. But it was too dangerous. He doubted the Crows would arrive so quickly, but she shouldn't be too far from him…

"I asked about the portal." Devon grabbed Orion's wrist, stopping him from dashing after Nava. His black hair stuck to the sharp angles of his pale face. "But I have been thinking about the children in the bakery a lot, and the thought sprang to mind."

Devon had triggered the alarm when his allegiance had changed while he was holding the Vulcan. Arkimedes squeezed his brother's shoulder.

The cold air enveloped Orion as he stepped out onto the porch after administering two healing potions. Nava awaited him in the front garden, both arms wrapped around her chest. She was wearing a Society ensemble today, with black pants tucked into tall leather boots—but the long dagger on her black belt was new.

Had he not allowed his nature cloud his mind while they were training, perhaps he could have stopped Devon from triggering the alarm and poisoning himself. He'd promised himself he wouldn't let things go too far with her, and he'd truly intended to kiss her senseless and nothing more—well, and maybe tease her a bit. But her beauty, how she'd glowed with happiness, had weakened his resolve.

He cleared his throat, descending the steps to stand beside her. He was still craving her warmth and her lips, but now they had to run and hide again. All he wanted was a warm meal and to take his woman to bed. To rest without having to worry about whether they'd have to fight for their lives and freedom. When would they get another reprieve like this one?

"How long does Devon have?" Nava asked, worry etched on her face.

"A couple of days. A week at most." Orion rubbed his tired eyes.

"We need to leave soon, don't we?"

"Yes. Soon. As soon as Devon is ready." Orion stared at the humming spheres that hung from the trees before them. Dozens of colorful globes spelled by the Society of Crows to act as alarm bells if someone broke in. The scent of magic swirled around them in a cloud of spice as they watched the chiming bells vibrate at a high speed.

"What if they get here before that?" Nava asked.

"They won't make it here so fast. We have at least a few hours," Orion reassured her, although he wasn't certain he believed it himself. "There are steps they need to follow before sending someone over. First, they have to find out which Society safe house was breached. This rarely takes long. Then they have to check what triggered the alarm in the first place. That way, they know who to send here. And then they need to travel, which will take some time..."

The movement of the spheres was far too rapid to be visible to the human eye. However, Arkimedes could trace its lingering echo, a faint blur that encapsulated each orb. The sound should have been one of breaking glass, but instead, it was the blaring song of wind chimes.

"How will they get here?"

"My father doesn't allow the Corvus to portal into the city anymore. They would have to come to the outskirts of the actual safe house." His ears ached from the noise that seemed to be building the longer they stood out here. "They have hidden passages all over Caztian." He sighed. "The truth is, I really don't know how long we have."

"You keep using that word. Corvus. Is it another way to refer to the Crows?" Her voice managed to both soothe his growing dread and set his nerve endings aflame.

"The Society doesn't consider all Crows to be part of the Corvus. Think of them as the elite. They send selected members with enhanced skills to eradicate problems quickly. The hope is that the Corvus deals with it before they have to send a larger group."

"Enhanced skills?" Nava swallowed, fear clear in her eyes. "You mean they are more powerful?"

Orion tilted his head with a shrug. He couldn't lie, but he also didn't want to add to her nervousness.

Of course, Nava read him with ease. Her face lost its beautiful flush from before. She reached for his hand with clammy fingers. "How many Corvus do they usually send?"

"They usually sent us in pairs, Bee."

Her eyes widened. "You and Devon were Corvus? Was that why they sent you to my house ten years ago?"

"We were." Devon's voice came from behind them. Orion turned around to see him stepping out of the manor, bracing himself against the doorframe. "Once upon a time, before everything turned to shit."

Was he referring to their current situation? Or how things had changed after they'd found Nava?

"You shouldn't be up." Orion clicked his tongue. But if he was...perhaps that meant he'd gathered enough strength already to leave. Orion craned his neck, searching for the portal disguised as a wall fountain. He could have sworn it had been in that wall over there, surrounded by the ivy. Perhaps it was too far away to make out...

"I created this mess, so I need to get us out of it," Devon said. Some color had returned to his face. The old potions were clearly doing the trick.

Nava stared at the nothingness of the misty grounds around them, her eyes glazed over, as if she was stuck in her thoughts. "When you came to my home, back in the Iron City, did my mother trigger an alarm like this?" If her trembling lips weren't already giving away her nerves, the painful tightening of her grip around his hand certainly did a fine job of it.

"Celeste set off all the alarms. Her, your father, and their little team burned establishments from people who were loyal to the Crows. She killed members and freed convicted criminals." Devon wheezed before a cough rattled his chest.

"You are lying..."

Did Devon understand the concept of self-preservation? Clearly not, not even after poisoning himself. The distant buzzing of bees circled him as Nava's grip tightened even further.

Orion hissed in pain, pulling his hand from her grasp. "You're going to break my hand."

"Sorry," she said sheepishly. "So where do we go from here?"

Where was the gate? Orion walked along the path, toward the fountain they'd used to enter. There. What was that? The bowl that had previously jutted from the wall lay in pieces all over the pathway, partially hidden by the tall grasses around them. Gooseflesh erupted all over his skin as dread flooded him, overwhelming his senses with cold shivers.

"The fountain is gone. They've trapped us here." He kicked at the debris on the ground, his power surging in a bright flare. The piece of concrete bounced off the ivy-covered stone wall and landed somewhere he couldn't see. The edges of the safe house grounds wavered with an invisible shield of power.

Orion brought his hand to his temple and tried to massage the blinding pain away. Meanwhile, Nava inched forward, likely sensing the panic that gripped him.

"Don't get too close, Nava. We don't know what spells are circling the perimeter of the property."

"So what, then? We wait here to be captured?"

"No one is taking you from me again." The things he would do if that happened, and so soon after the debacle with his father... It didn't bear thinking about.

Nava glared at Devon. "Look at the mess you got us into! Why didn't you come and talk to us before—"

"I know!" Devon's voice trembled. He was hunched over with the cough still shaking him at intervals, and his eyes shone with remorse.

The need to leave grew more urgent with each passing second. The sound of the bells culminated in an ear-piercing crack of shattering glass.

"Ark?" Her voice boomed past the fierce thunder of his migraine.

"We can't be here when the Corvus arrives. We have to go through the cellar."

"The room downstairs?"

Devon magically seemed to regain some energy as he straightened to his full height, his eyes sharpening with worry. "You can't be serious."

"There are only two ways left out of this place. Now that the fountain is gone, that's not an option. The second is through the hills, and since we don't know where this house is located, we can't commit to traveling for weeks—months, even—back to the Copper City. Not with the emissary letting the Zorren in."

"You know we can't open the cellar. It's flooded and cursed," Devon said.

Nava's lips parted, but no sound emerged, although her growing anxiety pushed through their bond. She leaned against the wall, her gaze shuttered. "Why would the Society curse their only exit out of this place if a problem were to arise?"

Her eyes jumped from Devon to Orion. It had been difficult for him to wrap his head around the truths of the curse that lay underneath all the safe houses when he was young. He half hoped Devon might offer the information, but his brother remained quiet.

"So?"

"The Society did not curse the cellar, but what they did to its previous owners meant the spirits stayed." Orion got the impression she already knew what sort of spirits he was referring to. Neems were always the haunted, angry souls of those murdered on magical grounds.

"And it's flooded?" she asked.

Orion placed his hands on her hips, guiding her toward the house. "There is a spell on the cellar that allows for safe passage by loyal members of the Society."

Devon watched them approach, his face pleading. "Which we're not. They will kill us before we can get out of here. I can't be much help with the way I feel now. We should head the other way."

Taking the steps two at a time, Orion barely spared his brother a side glance as he crossed the front porch. "You know they'll discover it was you who held the Vulcan, which means they'll expect us to go through the hills. The Corvus will travel in that direction, hoping to catch us along the way. You know that."

Nava followed closely after him, the soles of her boots squeaking against the polished marble tiles. "How many spirits are we talking about? Two? Four?"

"The records don't specify the number, but the rumor is ten."

She lost her step, barely catching her balance as she stumbled into the circular entrance hall. Somehow, the house felt icy cold, as if the ground itself could read their intent.

Devon grasped Orion's arm, hard enough to send a ripple of pain through him. "You two should go without me, Arkimedes. Nava can transfer out of here, and you can fly. This is my fault. You don't have to go through the spirits to leave."

Orion's jaw ached from clenching it so hard. He shrugged off Devon's hand. "I don't have time to discuss this ridiculous notion that I don't care about what happens to you. I won't abandon you here, even if you've made some questionable choices. If you want to help, then find some more of those potions because you're going to need them."

Devon's lips thinned, and he nodded before shuffling down the hall.

"What if Devon opens a portal?" Nava's voice broke the momentary silence. "We don't have to go through the cellar."

Time froze as the image of her burnt skin and all she had confessed to him rose in his mind's eye. "No. Not after last time. The Neems are dangerous but mindless."

"I know what to expect now, Ark. And I'll be fine."

"You know what to expect, and so does the emissary. We aren't taking any chances, Bee. If he's working with the Zorren, he wants you dead. We can't risk it."

14
ORION

"I can't believe we're doing this. It's suicide." Devon stood in front of the cellar door, a monstrosity of aged, rotting wood.

If only he would stop pacing, then Orion could focus on something other than the crunching of broken tiles beneath his brother's feet. "Are you going to tell us how to open it or just continue to complain endlessly?"

Out of the three of them, only Devon had studied the languages of the old world, which meant he was the only one who could break the lock. Orion was fast losing his patience with his brother's lack of cooperation.

Devon sent him a withering look and stepped closer to the script etched into the wood. The Crows had carved magical runes into the doorframe and woven them into a powerful ward that prevented the room from being opened from either side. Magic was probably the only thing that kept this door standing.

Beside him, Nava was rocking on her heels. Her skin remained pale as she kept a respectable distance from the door. "I rarely like to agree with Devon openly, but this is suicidal."

The spell's warning compelled everyone to run from the cellar. They had been standing there for an hour, attempting to figure out how to break in.

"I'm not sure if the Crows are truly more dangerous than a room full of angry spirits," Nava continued, tapping her index finger against her lips.

Orion sighed, nodding curtly. "I know this is far from ideal, but we have no idea how many Corvus the Society will send. What we do know is that they're aware of who triggered the alarm, which means they might send multiple teams. The Neems are predictable, at least."

A crinkle formed between Nava's brows as she studied their surroundings. "It makes me sick to my stomach to think about this place. Why would they trap people in there to die?"

"The Crows aren't known for acts of mercy, and Neems are an effective security measure to block off the secret entrance." He swallowed thickly as her lips parted in indignation. Whatever else he could say would only anger her further and get her to feel more empathy for the spirits they would soon face.

"Or from breaking in," Devon said.

"They are using dead people as watchdogs?" Nava's nostrils flared. "You stood behind this society, even after knowing they would do something like this?"

"They were all I knew..." What more could he say? Orion stilled, his heart racing as an ache spread all over his body like a sickness. "They committed this crime long before I joined them."

"You were a five-year-old boy when they took you." She blew away an errant strand of hair that had curled around her chin, and her expression softened. "I feel like they lost their best member they had the day you left them."

"Careful there." It was a challenge to hold her gaze. "You're feeding my ego. I might start to believe that I'm worthy of you."

"You're more than worthy."

"Not of you."

Her lips curved into a sad but genuine smile that reached her eyes. "I think you are..."

The more time he spent away from the castle and his father, the clearer it became how much of an idiot he'd been to push her away. He brought his hand to her face, his heart still beating too fast. He hated the dark rings under her eyes from the lack of sleep.

"How are you feeling about being away from Aristaeus?"

"Tired." She glanced warily at the door. "If you're worried about me fighting the Neems, you can stop. I can do this."

"I know you can handle yourself."

"Useless," Devon muttered, moving away from the door. His skin was shining with sweat as he brushed his ebony hair out of his face. "I can't get close enough to see all the symbols because of the spell, and my Tharent skills aren't good enough to make sense of it."

Tharent was the old language of the gods, not spoken widely for centuries.

Orion's father seemed to know it, and a lot of the old books in the castle's library were written in it.

"Is there nothing you can glean from it?"

Devon huffed and returned to his task. "Maybe. *We reclaimed our truth and stole your lies.*" Devon pointed a finger at another line of runes, not quite touching it but tracing their shapes. *"Your curious mind won't get you through. Only those seeking balance will escape unharmed, or else they will face the wrath of the dead."*

"Perhaps it's simple. It won't open it if you're just curious." Nava stepped closer to get a better look. "You're always talking about balance, Devon. Maybe it will open for you?"

"It would have opened for me before I touched the Vulcan the second time." Devon drew a labored breath and pulled a small vial from his pocket, emptying it into his mouth. The healing potion brought some color back to his face almost immediately.

"And that made you not care about your precious balance...?" She matched his flat tone.

"You've figured me out, Cat."

Orion suppressed a smile. At least their banter was somewhat entertaining in such a grim situation. "It's simple. The door prevents any trespasser from leaving who isn't loyal to the Crows, and that's not us."

What if they didn't need a counter-spell to open the cellar? The safe house *had* to be in the Copper Kingdom, didn't it?

A kingdom connected to Orion's magic.

He stepped forward. The closer he came to the cellar, the more the wards pushed him away. He called on his magic, gathering energy from every inch of the building. The walls shook and crackled, raining dust over them.

"Ark, what are you doing?" Nava's wide eyes darted toward the cracks that split the ceiling apart.

Orion took another step closer, so close that the spell burned his skin. He pressed his lips together and pushed harder, reaching for the iron handle of the door. His misty aura rose, the voices of his shadows loud as they growled, lending him pieces of their energy.

He felt like he was stepping into a shield of hot coals or the embers of a fire.

Nava rushed up behind him, and the considerable weight of her magic warmed his spine. He pushed into the ward, and the house groaned. The land knew what it needed to do for its prince, and the Crow's spell crumbled.

"You two are sickening," Devon grunted from behind them, but he joined them a moment later. The air crackled with the energy of his magic, further weakening the shielding spell.

The burning sensation against Orion's skin eased, and the spell cracked further, right before popping like a bubble. Dread crawled up the back of his skull, increasing tenfold now that the protection had vanished.

Multiple haunted moans seeped from the crevices of the door, raising the hairs on his arms. He quickly pushed Nava and Devon backward, and they retreated to the circular room in front of the archives.

With the spell gone, would the spirits pass through the walls?

Orion waited until the first white hand pushed the door ajar. Five long fingers wrapped around the edge of the frame, skin tight around bones.

He stepped in front of Nava, shielding her with his body. Another hand, attached to a decaying arm, crossed the threshold. Then another. Devon cursed loudly and broke into a fit of coughs.

"Get ready," Orion warned.

Nava lifted her hand, her skin shining, and the bees that crawled the walls took flight all at once. They surrounded them in a cocoon of buzzing bodies.

"We are too large for me to hide us completely, but if they don't see us, they won't attack," she said.

"Cover yourself, Nava. Don't waste your energy on us."

She scoffed and continued to hold the shield around them, her skin shimmering with a thin sheen of sweat.

The first spirit that burst from the door had once been a woman. Her long hair stuck to her white face, the rest of her continuously decomposing. She resembled a walking corpse more than a spirit. Devon's magic flowed from the tips of his fingers, sparking with energy—and she was gone.

Two more followed immediately. Dark blood dripped from their faces, their jaws clanking open and shut. Their ghastly dead cries froze the blood in Orion's veins.

They fought them down the funnel of the hall, dissipating them, only for three more to emerge hot on their heels. He took a deep breath to calm his erratic breathing and regretted it immediately when the pungent scent of rot mixed with the spice of magic.

A small ball of light floated next to Devon. Where had it come from? Orion opened his mouth to warn his brother just as a Neem materialized out of thin air. Nava gasped, and Orion's head jerked to the side as another spirit rose from the ground. Its teeth dug into his hand, cutting through layers of skin and flesh. Intense pain shot up his arm, and he fought to pull his hand away, the ripping sensation bringing tears to his eyes.

He hissed, and the shadows of his aura snapped at the spirit that still clung to his body, its nails scratching his neck as it tried to bite his face.

He needed to focus. With a blast of energy, he dissipated the spirits until none remained outside the cellar door.

Well. Almost none. Devon was screaming as a spirit dragged him down the corridor, its thin lips opening wide as a ball of energy glowed in its pitch-black, gaping mouth. Orion flew toward his brother, his wings tearing as they collided with the rock walls around him. He bit his tongue so hard blood coated it.

He barely managed to grab Devon's flailing hand before the spirit dragged him into the cave-like cellar. Digging his heels into the ground, Orion found purchase. His throbbing hand spilled blood down his wrist and onto Devon's pale skin.

A ray of black magic snapped from his aura, and the Neem puffed out of existence, leaving them both gasping for air.

"Ark!" Nava transferred to them. She, too, was breathless. "Are you all right?"

Her face was scratched and bloodied. Fuck, he hadn't even noticed that happening. He stepped closer and reached for her chin, lifting her face to his to better inspect it. He traced every freckle, the curve of her lips, the long line of her neck.

Nava forced a smile, but the gesture didn't fool anyone. Then she glanced down. "Your hand!"

"I'm fine," Orion said past gritted teeth and pulled his hand away before she could grab it. It hurt too much, and they couldn't linger here for much longer. They had already wasted too much time.

She cleared her throat, clearly not happy at this turn of events.

Devon stood, winded and bloodied, much like Orion. The number of spirits had far exceeded their expectations. "Someone failed with the records they kept about this place," his brother choked out and spat blood on the ground.

The family trapped in the cellar had been a large one. Perhaps even their servants had suffered the same fate alongside them.

It gave him pause. What if Nava's family had shared their destiny? Would the Society of Crows have converted Celeste's manor into a hidden safe house?

The thought of her loved ones being cursed to be Neems for eternity crushed his heart. He felt for these people—now they were liberated from their haunted forms.

"We need to go," he said. Gods, he hated how his voice broke. He let go of Nava. He wasn't good enough for her. Not in this life. Not in the next.

Carefully, they crept forward. Brown water pooled in front of the cracked door. No more spirits emerged, but the air still crackled with angry energy.

While the Neems appeared corporeal enough to push this door open, once dissipated, they vanished into nothingness. Their true bodies rested inside the cellar they were heading into.

It took Orion only a moment to rip off a strip from the bottom of his shirt, and with Nava's help, they wrapped it around his bleeding hand to stem the flow. Then he pushed the door open. The light from the candelabra outside trickled inside the dark cave, illuminating rotten wooden stairs and deep green water beneath. The back of his throat ached, and his tongue tasted bitter.

His legs felt heavy—both from exhaustion and from the horror of stepping into that water alongside the corpses of those poor people.

"Do you think there are any more Neems down there?" Nava's voice shook, as if she was contemplating the same thoughts.

Devon brushed the long strands of hair out of his face. "I'm going to guess not." His mouth was set in a hard line. "They would kill us. They have no need to hide, especially since we've disturbed their haunting grounds."

Well. Wasn't it their lucky day if they escaped with only a few bites and scratches?

Orion moved down the first creaking step. It bowed under his weight. The stone walls were slick with algae, and the smell of seawater and rot was overwhelming.

His aura swirled around his body in a protective shield, much like Nava's did. The whispers of his souls warned him to stay away. He tested the second step before committing to the next. On his third step, the wood underneath him creaked and snapped, and he stumbled forward with the weight of his body.

Orion fought to regain his balance as his heart lodged in his throat. Thankfully, he steadied himself before he could tumble all the way down. The remnants of the previous step fell into the dark water beneath him.

Nava stood by the doorframe, illuminating the room more than any magical candle could. "Are you all right?"

"Fine," he breathed, trying to calm his erratic breathing. He didn't want to step into the water and walk over bones, but he had little choice. "Don't come down yet. It's all rotten."

The stale, humid air stuck to the back of his throat, tasting like old magic. If only he could be far away from it.

Shuffling forward, Nava moved close behind him, although she didn't follow him into the cellar yet. Surprising, that she wouldn't challenge his request when she usually enjoyed it so much.

Still, Orion knew her well enough by now to comprehend that she was one word away from transferring inside this hell and fighting whoever might harm him, before he'd even had time to inspect the place.

"I could transfer there…" she offered.

Hah. "Not yet. It's not safe."

"Why is it that you are so keen to believe you're more disposable than me?"

He glanced at her over his shoulder. His wing shrouded most of her body. Dammit, they had no time to get into this discussion. Still…he'd been trying to mend the rupture between them. Best not to aggravate her further.

"If you aren't safe, my head's not in the right place, which could get me killed. I want to protect you more than anything."

She didn't say a word but narrowed her smart eyes at him.

Devon, who had been too quiet ever since the Neems had poured out of the cellar, poked his head through the doorframe. "Do you need one of these?" he asked, dipping one hand inside his pocket, pulling out a healing potion, and extending it to Orion.

Orion shook his head. The bite had gone numb a while ago. Perhaps it was the adrenaline, or maybe the Neem had torn a nerve. Either way, he wasn't feeling much.

They had discovered a large stack of potions in the infirmary, but worry prickled Orion's mind. His brother needed too many of them, too quickly. He was weakening too fast for them to keep up.

Devon shrugged and emptied the potion into his mouth without preamble. Then he stared down at the cellar, his brows dipping. "Can you see a way out of this hole? Or did we open this place for nothing? Because if the bells didn't call the Corvus, opening this cellar sure did."

Devon was right. If they continued to destroy the wards, the Corvus might choose to break all rules and portal here against the king's demands.

The dark water mirrored the cavernous ceiling. Orion steadied the weight of his body with one hand against the roof and crept down a few steps. His fae eyes could spot more than any regular human. He rarely needed light to see in the dark. And whatever he didn't see, the souls in his aura would pick up. But they were quiet now…too quiet. It left him uneasy.

"The safe house must be near the coast. This is seawater," he said, finding a steady drip from a corner of the room. The waterline appeared to be three feet high at most. Shallow enough to wade through.

The cellar was about the size of the bedroom he'd shared with Nava for the past few days. Shelves extended on either side of it. They must once have been thick wood but now lay rotten and broken in the murky depths of the water.

The spell the Crows had cast upon this place must have resembled a typhoon, tearing this room to pieces.

Nava had finally had enough and followed him down the stairs. "If there's a way out, is it going to be a portal like the fountain that will take us back into the Copper City?" The wood groaned beneath her feet, and Orion's heart jolted as he waited for the next step to break underneath her.

"Stay up there," he growled as she propped herself up against the poor excuse for a banister. At least it was still bolted to the wall. Barely.

"Calm down—it's not that big of a drop. Can you see a way out?"

Orion stepped into the frigid depths. His teeth chattered, the water sloshing as he inspected every single fallen shelf and anything else that might cover a hidden doorway.

His mind was yelling at him to get out of there. A sense of pressure seemed to emanate from everywhere, suffocating him the farther into the room he went. Nava followed him on light feet, with Devon trailing behind her.

Magic pushed against the power of Orion's aura. Heavy, ancient, and furious. A gust of wind howled through a crevice behind a tipped-over wine barrel right before him.

"I think I've found it," he said and rolled it away—only to reveal the angry Neem of a child.

It hurtled toward him with a biting gasp, and he barely got out of the way in time before its nails sliced his jacket and shirt. The eyes of what had once been a little girl glowed brilliant white.

She launched at him again, and he was too numb to move—too tired. Too sad. Devon's magic dissipated her right in front of Orion's eyes, leaving behind the black tunnel her family had likely tried to hide her in, right before the Crows had flooded this place and drowned them all in it.

15
NAVA

Cold water sloshed around Nava as they moved through a narrow, winding tunnel. If it weren't for the warm glow of her aura, they would be in absolute darkness. They had been walking for at least five miles in the smelly water, and her toes had long since gone numb inside her old boots.

After the last Neem had appeared, the crime the Crows had committed by trapping a child and leaving them to this kind of ending had overwhelmed them all. The three of them had been quiet ever since.

"We are here." Arkimedes's voice made her jump.

Nava watched his hand as he trailed his fingers across a muddy wall. They'd hit a dead end, and in her daze, she'd barely noticed. Everything was wet, and water clung to every surface, dripping off the jagged shapes of barnacles.

There was no door, no handle—no light leading them to believe this was the exit. Only the walls closing in on her.

"Is there a door?" She swallowed around the thick knot in her throat. Had that child tried to escape through here and found no way out?

Placing a hand across her chest, Nava gripped her neck. With her other hand, she reached past Arkimedes to shove at the wall. There was no nature here, only death and despair. She was itching to leave this place. "Can you see a way out?"

His glowing eyes flashed to her. "Are you feeling all right?"

"Seems I don't like tight spaces."

Arkimedes swallowed. Maybe her panic was filtering through to him. "I can feel what might be a stone door, but it's concealed in mud…" he dug out the grooves of a clear rectangular shape, but in the narrow space, only he could work on it while she was forced to stand behind him and watch.

He leaned against the wall with one shoulder, pushing against it with the force of his full weight. It creaked and gave way by a fraction, allowing a ray of light to peek through its rim.

Nava's heart fluttered with hope, just as Arkimedes slammed into the door. Mud splattered against his face on his third attempt, and finally, the slab of stone fell beneath the weight of his body and a spike of his magic.

He breathed raggedly as he wiped streaks of filth off his skin with the heel of his hand. Traces of blood mingled with the mud. They really needed better wraps and something to disinfect his wound.

"I'll go first. Let me inspect the area before you come out," he said and dragged his entire body out of the narrow door, which hovered several feet above the stagnant water.

The light streaming through the gap blinded her, and the air held a stale quality she couldn't place. Nava climbed up to the hole, not waiting for Arkimedes's signal. She wanted—no, *needed*—to be out of there.

She waited for the warmth of the sun to hit her skin. For nature to recharge her depleted energy. But something wasn't right with the light. It was strangely cool.

Arkimedes's arms coiled around her as she hoisted her body up and onto polished white marble floors. Her heart slammed against her ribcage as he helped her out, like she was made from paper. She collided with the planes of his chest, and his breath wafted over her cheek.

"I thought I asked you to wait there?" he whispered in a biting tone. His annoyance pulsed in waves through their bond.

"It's safe enough." She pushed against his chest, although she was too tired to put any force behind the movement. It was hard to even find the will to argue with him.

Everyone was on edge after fighting the Neems and then being forced to crawl through their remains to this—

"…is this a mausoleum?"

The room's imposing vaulted ceilings curved into a large white stone dome. Immense pillars and crossbeams created the visual effect of a ribcage holding up the roof. Sun spilled through the windows, though judging by the lingering scent, the building was sealed.

Five urns stood on top of marble pedestals. The withered flowers beside them had dropped their brown petals to the ground a long time ago.

The walls were covered in writing, and coffins dotted the room. Nava looked down at the slab of stone Arkimedes had pushed off for them to crawl out. It had aged into yellow and brown shades. Etched into it in black lettering were the words:

Here lies Rudolph Abercorn,
Beloved husband

What?

She blinked rapidly. Had the Society of Crows hidden the secret exit of the safe house behind a tomb in a mausoleum? How fitting.

Devon exited the tunnel, sliding over the ground, wet as a newborn fawn. "This has to be a joke..." he said with a dry laugh. His face distorted with fury as he attempted to clean off the mud that stuck to his black trousers.

Arkimedes spared Devon a glance, probably to make sure his brother wasn't actually dying. Then, cradling his wounded hand, he moved toward the locked metal gate at the front of the tomb. "They made this an iron gate, probably to keep the fae away. I'm sure it has allowed the Society's entrance to remain hidden for longer."

He squinted at the bars and reached across to the padlock hanging from a chain on the other side. His aura became so dark it was hard to see the shape of his body, and the metal groaned and snapped.

Nava tilted her head. How much did it hurt him to touch the metal? The Society of Crows had kept a lot of iron at the safe house, but Arkimedes hadn't complained.

"Being a hybrid means I can hold iron without being burned," he said, looking over his shoulder as if he was reading her mind.

Wait, had he read her mind? Their mental link wasn't as strong as it used to be, especially after he'd lost his memories.

The cemetery lay quiet and empty before them. Here, the open air was warmer, and the scent of decay from their clothes was less noticeable.

The castle was a hazy shape in the far distance, looming over a city of small homes and shops. From this hill, Nava could even see a turquoise canal of seawater cutting through the city.

It seemed so long ago since they had all visited town together, right before the solstice dance.

They walked down a cobblestone path with golden grasses growing on either side of it. Even this small amount of nature nearby helped to replenish some of her lost energy.

"Now what?" Devon asked, trailing a few steps behind them. "This is clearly the Copper City. I doubt the Crows will give up so easily, which means we'll have to deal with the royal guards and the Corvus coming after us."

Arkimedes grunted, scratching one of his brows. "Give me time to think."

A wet cough left Devon's lips. "Well, hurry. We're at the mercy of your father out here in the open." He reached for another potion with a shaking hand. "Don't you have any friends that can shelter us?"

"I'm afraid you ran them all away." Arkimedes stopped Devon's hand before he pulled the cork out of the small potion vial. "You've got to pace yourself with those, Devon. We don't have any more."

Even in broad daylight, Devon remained as pale as the Neems they'd encountered. Not even the continual potions were easing his symptoms.

If only Nava could remember how to brew the potions, then maybe they could keep him going until they found a healer willing to help them. The thought made her heart ache with longing. If only their friends were here. Gavin, who was such a wonderful healer and human being, would have fixed them up in no time.

She peered at her soulmate's wounded hand, and her stomach dropped. The temporary bandage he had wrapped around it back in the cellar had turned a brownish red.

Devon shook his head and opened the potion vial. "I used too much energy fighting the Neems. If you want me to walk anywhere, I have to take it."

"I'll get you a fresh potion later today," Arkimedes promised.

Nava turned away from the pair. Where could they go? To the bakery—or into any of these abandoned buildings? They would be right back where they'd started.

The memory of a fae with bright red hair flashed through her mind.

That was it! Leela, the maid who'd helped Nava during her stay at the castle, lived in this part of town. They had grown close, and Leela had even helped Nava alter her horrid yellow dress before the solstice ball.

"What about Leela?" Arkimedes's unyielding gaze met hers, making her want to squirm as butterflies fluttered in her stomach. Sometimes she was still surprised by how she reacted to him. Nava cleared her throat and reached for his bandaged hand. "I'm sure she would let us stay for one night to get our bearings. But I don't know exactly where she lives..."

Arkimedes's brows knitted together, his posture stiffening as she examined his injury. Her skin warmed, her magic humming to the surface as it called to him.

Arkimedes let her take apart the bindings. Although his wound was still fresh, it had stopped bleeding. Nava didn't want to further risk infection by keeping that filthy cloth pressed against it.

"I think I know where she lives, Bee. And it's not too far from here."

Unlike the cemetery, the streets were busy with fae going about their daily lives, bustling about. Some were cleaning their front steps while others fixed up the flower boxes underneath their small, uneven windows.

All seemed unaware that their prince was strolling along the streets, alongside two traitors of the Crown.

This area of the city differed from everywhere else Nava had visited in the Copper Kingdom. It reminded her a lot of home—of Willowbrook—when she was growing up. The homes were built close enough to one another that they appeared to be a single unit. The houses weren't extravagant, like the ones near the castle, nor dilapidated, like the ones near the bakery. Made of richly textured bricks and plaster and painted in a range of colors, they held the type of beauty that only came with age.

"At least nobody seems to be paying us much attention…" she mumbled as they crossed a bridge over the biggest water canal she'd seen. The rattle of carriage wheels and the cries of the seagulls drowned out the squelching noise of their hasty steps.

Somehow, the sounds of the city soothed her frazzled nerves. Finally, no alarms ringing in the distance—nor any guards flying above them.

"I think you need spectacles, Cat." Devon scoffed, shaking his head as he indicated a group of fae on the other side of the bridge who were pointing at them with wrinkled noses. "Look at them. If you read their lips, our appearance disgusts them."

Nava's cheeks warmed, and she glanced down at her scratched arms and filthy clothes. She could barely stand the scent emanating from them but doubted anyone that far away could smell them.

"Should we ask for directions?" Nava looked around the area, trying to find a place that would lead her to Leela and away from city folk. The longer they were out in the open, the greater the risk of someone recognizing them. Besides, they all needed a bath, proper healing, and a place to rest. "There!" Her heart skipped a beat when she spotted an old wooden sign bolted to the stone bricks of a building.

The name of Leela's partner stood out against the white background of the sign in green letters.

"Renna's Creations?" Arkimedes followed her pointed finger, his brow furrowing.

"Yes, I remember Leela saying her name. She's a seamstress."

They weren't far from the house, and the closer they got, the more

Nava's heart sped up. What would Leela do when she saw the prince outside her home? What if she shut the door in their faces and refused to help them?

"Let me be the one to knock—you're too intimidating." She dodged away from Ark's hand, ignoring his complaint.

Leela's door screeched open a second later, and she peered through the crack. "Miss Nava?" She gasped and stepped outside. "You can't be here!"

She reached for Nava's arm but froze when Arkimedes cleared his throat. "Leela."

"Your Highness!" she screeched and floundered into a low bow.

"There's no need for formalities out here. I don't want to call too much attention to us." Arkimedes's eyes darted about, worry etched onto his features. True to his words, several people on the other side of the street were glancing curiously at them.

"Please come in." Leela's freckles were prominent now that a blush covered her face. A deep crease appeared on her forehead as she looked up at the surrounding rooftops. "We don't know who might be watching."

Her friend hadn't been at the castle on the night the king had sent his guards to apprehend Nava and Devon. Did she know everything that had transpired?

She led them through the shop, past a small desk piled high with knick-knacks and pincushions. The back of the room was bathed in darkness, although Nava could spot large rolls of fabric lined up against the far wall.

Guilt churned deep within her. It was a good life the fae had here. And it might change forever if the king found out the palace's maid had helped them.

Why had Nava brought her into this mess?

Devon's harsh cough stopped her spinning thoughts. He needed more rest than what they could have found in a dusty abandoned shop on the other side of the city. This was by far the safest option for tonight.

Leela gathered her red tresses on top of her head in a messy bun. "I was not expecting your company. Although they came some days ago to ask me if Miss Nava came to visit me."

Oh no.

"Who came?" Arkimedes asked, striding across the cramped shop floor. A couple of wooden benches sat next to a large window, which was hidden behind thick velvet curtains. "My father's guards?"

"His ladies. Sir." Leela hastily added the last word and pressed her body against the desk, allowing them enough room to stand without touching each other.

Nava's heart was suddenly racing. In the absolute silence that fell, all she could hear was Devon's ragged breaths and the sound of crackling embers coming from the fireplace.

"Are they here now?" he whispered, low enough that only they could hear.

"They left that same night," Leela said, and her blue eyes dipped to take in Arkimedes's wounded hand and Nava's scratched skin. She frowned. "Nora said Miss Nava put a spell on you, sir."

"I knew this was a terrible idea," Devon said. "We should leave now."

Ark raised his hand to silence him and stepped closer to Leela, his voice gentle when he spoke. "Do you believe them? Do you think I'm under a spell now?"

Leela flinched, her eyes widening as she stared at what Nava presumed were Arkimedes's shadows. "I know Miss Nava was wearing the royal jewels when she was in the castle, and so was Mr. Black. There is no way she could've put a spell on you to betray us."

"This fae is lying, and we walked into a trap," Devon snarled, already shuffling toward the front door. Yet Arkimedes stayed right beside Leela, observing her quick breaths and studying her closely.

Was her friend lying? Nava didn't know what to believe anymore.

"Leela is not lying," Ark said. "Fae can't lie openly, Devon. You know that." His gaze flashed to Nava, whose mouth fell open at his words.

A flare of heat rose from the pit of her stomach all the way to her face. Fae can't lie... what ridiculous claptrap.

"If they can't lie, then how did they come here and *lie* to her about what happened?"

She hated to agree with Devon, and it pained her to think Leela would betray her—but she'd rather be safe somewhere else. This was a stupid idea. She shouldn't have brought them here.

Leela backed away behind the desk, paling further at Devon's sharp question and the wet cough that followed it.

"Nora *believes* Nava put me under a spell, which is why she attacked me in my father's room. It's also why my father's guards attacked me on the island and forced me back here." The tension in Arkimedes's face eased, and he nodded as if the pieces were falling into place. "They were convinced I was under a spell there."

Leela gasped, and the truth behind his words clicked for Nava as well. If the royal guards genuinely believed the heir and savior of the land was under the spell of an evil witch, then they would do anything to remove him from her reach.

Herous, the guard who'd hurt her the very day she'd arrived in the Copper Kingdom, had called her a witch. It made sense now.

"They all believe Nava has me under a spell." Arkimedes met her eyes, his expression heavy with meaning. "But Leela isn't lying because a full-blooded fae can blatantly not do so. They can bend the truth or avoid it."

Leela bowed her head, although her wary eyes flashed to Devon. Perhaps she was unsure what to believe.

Admittedly, there was some truth to it. Nava did have Arkimedes under a spell: fate had carved it into their skin and sealed it with a soulmate mark. They were magically bound and destined to fall for each other. No matter how much they pushed against it, that old, unbending magic always won.

"I would never hurt our prince. I know Miss Nava cares for him, and I don't think she's evil." Leela's lips thinned. "I don't believe she's forcing him to do anything."

Devon dropped his hand from the doorknob and pressed his forehead to the wooden surface. Then he reached for another potion with a shaky grip. This had to be the reason Arkimedes was choosing to stay as well.

"What else did my father's concubines say?" Arkimedes asked.

"They told me Miss Nava and Mr. Black wanted to kidnap you from our kingdom, which will make the land suffer."

The irony of those harpies blaming her for something they had done to him. They had kidnapped Arkimedes and taken him against his will.

Nava reached for her friend's hand. It was damp and cold inside. "Leela, we aren't leaving the kingdom. We need shelter in your home tonight, so we can figure out how to defeat what's causing the forest fires."

In the distance, thunder rolled, shaking the windows behind the velvet curtains. The gentle patter of raindrops followed it shortly.

Leela blinked. "The fires?"

"What Nava said is true." Arkimedes's expression sharpened with resolve. "We will have to go to the castle to speak with my father—eventually. But tonight, we need a meal, a place to wash off, and somewhere to sleep. We won't burden you for long."

Leela nodded and gestured toward the wooden stairs at the very end of the room. They were narrow and uneven, with metal spindles that swirled organically, like ferns.

Leela's home was a far cry from the opulent elegance of the Society manor or the castle itself. This was a working-class house, built with uneven materials. Imperfectly beautiful.

"My home is not fit for you, sir, but you may stay for as long as you need."

16
NAVA

They gathered around a small table on the second floor in front of a large, slender window with latticed metal running across its glass. Outside, a storm raged, blurring their view of the now-empty streets.

Their silverware scraped over ceramic plates, and the salty taste of buttery potatoes lingered in Nava's mouth as she chewed slowly. She was so tired. All of her itched to remove her stiff and filthy clothes.

"Leela, is there a potion maker nearby?" Arkimedes asked.

Yes, Nava wanted to say. *I'm here.* But the weight of the thought alone nearly brought tears to her eyes.

Leela took in Arkimedes's injured hand and Devon's general appearance. Then she shuddered and studied Nava's face. "There is no magic on the west side of the canals, sir. The potions available to us are only those of herbs and alchemy. If you require a true healing potion, then you must go to the center of town—or better yet, the castle's infirmary."

Devon's brows met in the middle, although he didn't lift his eyes. He'd been shifting his food from one side of his plate to the other, barely taking a bite. "You don't have to go anywhere because of me. I'll be fine."

Arkimedes dropped his cutlery on the table. "We both know what's coming for you."

Death by poisoning? A week, Arkimedes had told Nava as they escaped the safe house. Devon had a week at most if he didn't get proper help.

Nava cleared her throat, reaching for the blackberry wine to wash away the bitter taste that clung to her tongue. "Arkimedes also needs a potion and fresh bandages."

The silence grew thick. How much could Leela deduce from their conversation and appearance? Probably enough to grasp how dire their situation was.

Leela poured some orange and cardamom tea into a cup and pushed it across the rustic table at Devon, still quietly observing. "I—I could go to the center of town tomorrow and try to source you some potions. I'm afraid I'm unable to obtain one from the castle, as I'm no longer allowed inside the main walls. I would draw the attention of the guards if I tried to enter."

"Later today—" Arkimedes started with a smile, just as a flash of lightning cut through the sky, followed shortly thereafter by thunder. "Or tomorrow morning. I will be in your debt."

"I will, sir." Leela's face turned bright red, her eyes shining as she nodded. "Mr. Black, may I warm you up some stew? I know when I'm feeling unwell, it makes me feel better."

Devon leaned forward, interlacing his fingers in front of his face. Then he closed his eyes and sighed. "The food is not the problem, Leela. I'm not hungry. I'm quite spent and would like to retire for the night." He caught his breath as his cheeks turned a sickly green. "Can you show me where I'm staying?"

"I...I don't have a lot of space. Downstairs in the shop, there is a small room that we use mostly for storage. Mr. Black can use that one if he prefers. And there is a bed in there." She gestured to the dark hall on the other side of the living area, past the mismatched chairs and the narrow couch. "I suppose Miss Nava and I can sleep in the smaller room up here—unless she wants to share the downstairs with her fiancé?"

Fiancé?

"Why yes, where do you want to sleep, my love?" For someone as sick as him, Devon looked far too delighted. "Downstairs would be rather cozy for the both of us."

Heat pulsed through Nava's veins, flooding her cheeks as she stared at Devon open-mouthed. Fiancé? Gah! This was what everyone in the castle still believed them to be—the lie he'd told the king when they first arrived at the castle together.

"Stop, Devon," Arkimedes warned and flattened his palms against the table. "Since you are giving us shelter tonight, Leela, I will grant you some of my trust in return. Don't break it."

"Never, sir."

"Nava is not my brother's fiancée. She is mine."

"She is your—your fiancée, sir?" After a long, rather uncomfortable silence, she continued. "Is that why you escaped?"

It wasn't judgment that lurked behind her words, but an emotion Nava couldn't quite place tainted the inflection of her speech.

There was a vulnerability in Arkimedes's expression that he seldom displayed in front of others.

"Do you remember when I arrived at the castle and you kept saying the prince acted differently around me? You thought there was something happening between us," Nava said.

"Yes," Leela whispered. "He'd never invited anyone to stay in the green room next to his own…"

"Don't say it," Devon hissed at her, but Nava felt the rightness of what she was about to do in her gut.

Leela wholeheartedly believed in love and in Arkimedes's role in this kingdom. If she believed their story, she would guard their whereabouts. Maybe they could stay here for longer and find Devon some help.

"Well, that's because we are soulmates."

"Pardon?" Leela leaned forward, her eyes going wide as her gaze darted from Arkimedes to Nava and back again, as if she was trying to discover the hidden lie.

Arkimedes tensed at the revelation, his jaw tight. "Nava is telling you the truth. A few months ago, Fael and the other guards came into our home on the island where I was living with Nava and kidnapped me."

Leela reached for the steaming cup of tea she'd just poured and brought it to her lips with trembling hands. "But… you didn't know Miss Nava when she arrived at the castle a month ago."

"You don't need to know all the specifics. It's better that way. For your own safety." Arkimedes's displeasure rolled through the bond in intense waves.

Perhaps she shouldn't have revealed their secret without consulting him first. But Leela's loyalties seemed to be tethered to the king, and Nava needed her on their side if they were to rest safely in her home.

A drop of sweat trailed down Nava's neck, and she took another gulp of wine, hoping the alcohol would lend her some courage. "Do you know what happens to soulmates when they're apart from each other?"

Leela paled. "You… you die?"

"Nava…" Arkimedes warned in her mind. His voice was a growl that should have stopped her instantly—but she needed to drive her point home.

She avoided his burning gaze and the flare of anger that swept through their bond. "And yet the guards took him, and they left me behind."

"But that would have killed our prince! He is our only hope to breathe life back into our kingdom." Leela shook her head, placing her mug on the table. "The king wouldn't have done that."

"He didn't know I'd found her." Arkimedes rose from his rickety chair and slammed his hand on the table. "And that's the end of this conversation." He walked around to where Devon sat. His massive body filled so much of the space, it made the living area feel small. "Tonight, Nava and I will take the room downstairs. I want to trust you, Leela, but now you understand I would do *anything* to keep Nava safe."

"I wouldn't dream of betraying you or jeopardizing our future queen's safety, sir. You can trust me." Leela's lips trembled into a smile, and she bowed her head in their direction. "I knew Miss Nava was special from the very moment I saw her. I should have been a soothsayer." She scrambled to her feet. "I will get the rooms ready for you all and run the baths." She picked up the empty dishes from the table and hurried across to the small kitchen. Then she disappeared down the hall toward the bedroom.

Devon cracked an eye open, looking warily at the ceiling. "I can't believe you told her—"

"Leela and Fael were close, and I'm guessing she's also friendly with his sister, Nora," Arkimedes whispered.

"Exactly. So why did Nava think it was a good idea to tell her?" Devon got up on wobbly feet. "A year ago, I would have used that knowledge against you. In fact, when I suspected it, my original plan was to use the portal and take her to the Iron City to force your hand to follow me there."

A knot formed in Nava's throat. And he could easily have been successful if Nava's bees hadn't come to her aid.

"Because every citizen knows of the royals' connection to the land," Nava explained, rubbing her tired eyes. The weight of this truth being out in the open was frightening for both of them. "Which means that, as Ark's soulmate, I'm just as important to the kingdom's prosperity as he is."

"How can you both trust this girl after all the betrayals you've been through?"

"Girl? She's older than us." Arkimedes scoffed. "And I choose to trust, because the day I stop believing there is good in this world will be the day I become the monster you thought I was back at the safe house."

Devon clenched his teeth and faced the window. Outside, the storm still raged, with high winds slamming loose debris against the building. "I still think we should leave for one of those abandoned buildings—save ourselves the trouble."

Arkimedes shook his head, although he appeared to consider it for the briefest of moments. "You won't make it that far in this state. And even if Leela wants to tell my father where we are, she won't do it tonight."

"Is that the reason you're staying in the downstairs room?" Devon asked. "To block her way out?"

"We all need to rest, so let's take tonight to do that. How many potions do you have left?"

"Six." Devon coughed into a linen napkin. He quickly shoved it inside his pocket, but not fast enough for Nava not to notice the traces of blood on the ivory fabric. He reached for another potion, and as soon as the liquid hit his tongue, his skin regained some of the color he'd lost. "Call it five..."

Somewhere between their escape from Grey Island and Devon helping her rescue Arkimedes from his father, he'd become someone that she cared about. Nava hated seeing him this ill, even if it was his own fault for being so irritating.

Devon shuffled toward the door, following Leela's path, only to pause at the entrance to the hall. Darkness bathed half of his body, throwing the sallow angles of his face into sharp relief. "I respect that you can trust people after everything. I couldn't do that now. I will never forget what the Society did to my family—or the little girl in the cellar. I don't need to heal. What I need is revenge."

Leela hadn't been lying when she'd told them the room was tiny and disused. Nava's eyes prickled with the dust gathering on the sewing equipment and broken mannequins in the corner. Gauzy curtains did a half-decent job of covering the small window, which overlooked a dark alley.

The bed, which was considerably smaller than the one she had shared with Arkimedes at the safe house, had fresh linens and a patchwork quilt draped over the top.

Leela strolled out of the washroom, drying her damp hands on the skirt of her cotton dress. She jumped, barely suppressing a scream as she spotted Nava in the narrow, arched entryway. "Miss! You almost scared me to death!"

"Sorry." Quite the opposite of her intentions. She'd come downstairs so she could chat with her friend without the pressure of Arkimedes being in the same room. "I know it must be difficult to welcome us here, especially after Fael's sister visited you."

Leela walked over to a set of drawers, which leaned crookedly against the wall, and pulled out a nightgown. "My home is not fit for royalty, Miss Nava." She gestured at the surrounding mess. "Even less so this room."

"Ark—Orion and I have camped in a Neem-infested forest before, Leela. This is perfectly fine."

"Perhaps so, but I hate to make you both uncomfortable." The rain poured outside, and it was hard to hear her whispered words. "I—I can't believe you're the prince's soulmate. I mean, it makes so much sense now, why he looked at you the way he did. Why he defended you against our own, again and again, even though you'd only just met."

"What we told you today might put us in danger. Orion and I trusted you with our secret because helping us also puts your life at risk. But it's not something others should know."

It was still so strange to call him by his given name, but now that she'd been in this kingdom for a while, she was getting used to the idea of him being a royal and his connection to the land.

"Of course…" Leela shifted from foot to foot. "I'm afraid for you. What if the guards come while you're here? I'm—I'm not sure whether Nora has been watching over my house and waiting for you to come. She stays in the castle most of the day with His Majesty, so perhaps if we are lucky, nobody saw you come in…"

It was something that worried Nava as well—but surely if someone had been lying in wait and spotted them, they would know by now.

And even if the guards attacked them here, they would not hurt Arkimedes. After what she'd told the king before she'd left through the portal, he probably wouldn't hurt her either. Not if he knew the queen's tree was alive because of her.

The Crows were another problem entirely…

Leela laid the clean, lacy garment over the bed, before turning to Nava. "Mr. Black—is he cursed?"

Nava nodded and strolled toward the washroom. It was tiny, with lime-wash walls and a candle flickering on top of a rustic table. A barrel tub took up most of the space, and it was steaming with water full of salts and oils that made everything smell wonderful.

She almost moaned at the mere sight of it. Her aching muscles demanded she strip off her clothes and get in immediately.

"I used lavender oils to soothe your sore muscles. It seems like you need it." Leela hadn't commented on how battered they all appeared after their fight with the spirits, but they smelled and looked like death. "I also brought you my favorite soap from a local seller. I hope you enjoy it."

"This is perfect, Leela." Nava pulled the shirt she'd borrowed from the

Crows over her head. She was itching to get out of these clothes. "Do you have anything I could wear tomorrow?"

"I'm sure I can find something for all three of you in Renna's shop. I'm afraid my clothes won't quite fit you," Leela said.

It was true. She was lithe and tall, while Nava had wide round hips and narrow shoulders.

"Thank you, Leela." Nava tossed her filthy clothes aside, then groaned as she dipped her feet into the milky water. Leela quietly disappeared.

It was easy to push aside the burning from her scratched skin or the ache from the bruises marring her thighs and arms. They had escaped the Crows. They'd released those spirits from that awful place they'd been forced to haunt. Tears burned her eyes, and for the first time since they'd left the safe house, Nava allowed herself to cry.

"Nava?" Arkimedes's voice filtered across from the room next door. He sounded worried. "Are you here?"

"In the bath," she called, wiping her face. The water was still warm, and the oils were already doing wonders for her aching muscles. The only thing missing was a nice glass of wine.

She froze as Arkimedes stepped into sight, suddenly looming by the door-frame. His green glowing eyes cut through the room's darkness. A strong, gut-wrenching feeling took her by surprise. It was hard not to draw parallels with that night on Grey Island when he'd been taken from her.

"You disappeared on me." Arkimedes leaned against the door.

"I wanted to talk to Leela without you intimidating her." She hated that her voice wobbled, giving away her distress. Of course, it was silly of her to even worry about that. He could feel what she felt and was likely here because of that fact.

"What's happening? Your emotions are running wild." He pressed one of his fingers to his stomach, where she knew he could feel their connection. The floorboards creaked with each step he took toward her.

"Everything is overwhelming me," she said. "Then I remembered the night they took you from our home on the island. It was raining like tonight, and we were bathing." She glared at the soap that rested on the wooden stool next to her. "The scent of this damn soap is exactly like the one we used back at home." She almost tossed it across the room. But it wasn't Leela's fault.

Never again would she send Arkimedes away to bring her wine so they could relax in the bath. The experience had haunted her for almost two months and had forever changed the trajectory of her life.

"Ah. I regained that memory right before I showed Fael what happens when someone betrays me." Arkimedes rolled the cuffs of his shirt up over his toned arms and knelt behind her, dipping his fingers beneath the water's surface to caress the side of her arm.

She craned her neck to meet his eyes as he reached for the oil.

"We aren't on Grey Island now, but we are together. You came and saved me, Nava."

Tears welled up in her eyes as her throat constricted. "We are hiding in Leela's house from two different enemies. I can't claim to have saved you."

Arkimedes slid his hands over her shoulders, kneading her tense muscles. "I have regained most of my memories, and I'm closer to understanding what happened to my family, thanks to you."

He skimmed his fingers over her breasts, then along her ribcage. A light caress underneath her breasts soon dipped lower, bringing an intense flutter to her core.

Nava turned her neck to search for his lips. They were exploring the line of her jaw and traveling down her neck. "Are you going to stay there or come into the water already?"

"Where is your patience, Bee?" His laughter washed over her damp skin.

She twisted against the smooth surface of the tub, wrapped her arms around his neck, and pressed her lips to his. Their kiss grew to a languid dance of lips and tongues. Arkimedes leaned over the tub's edge, his free hand trailing down her spine and wrapping around her waist, pulling her closer.

"You know very well that I lack patience with everything, especially when it comes to wanting you," she said against his lips. She'd hoped to sound sexy, but her squeaky tone gave away her nerves.

Even after all this time, he still turned her into an awkward, fumbling mess.

"Good." He oozed the confidence she lacked. The bastard.

Nava moved her hands greedily down his torso, tracing the hard lines of his muscles beneath the wet fabric of his shirt. With his help, she pulled it free and wrestled it over his head. His pants soon followed, and then she lay back as he stepped into the tub.

Nava embraced him the moment he sat. She needed to feel his body. To silence everything sinister they'd experienced today.

Arkimedes's eyes darkened as his wet fingers crawled up her spine and wrapped around her skull. She settled her body weight on top of his, her knees falling on either side of his hips.

"Now I get to have you without secrets and without the *lies*," she whispered.

His eyes sparkled with mischief, and he tucked a strand of wet hair behind her ear. "I won't hide the truth from you again... I confess, I've been wicked." He trapped her face with one hand.

He had been. On Grey Island, when she'd first found out that he was her soulmate, Arkimedes had claimed that he never lied. But he could hide the truth. He could keep secrets and avoid questions by answering with other questions.

"All right, then no more of that fae wickedness. Not unless you're using it for its another purpose..." Her words brought those crinkles to the corners of his eyes he got whenever he smiled. Gods, how she loved them—how she loved him.

"And what, precisely, is that purpose? What sort of things do you want me to use my wickedness for?" He squeezed the round flesh of her ass, and his erection slid over her sensitive nub, again and again, pushing the air from her lungs.

Her insides fluttered with desire, and her skin grew warm at the huskiness of his voice. She rolled her hips over his, craving more friction against her aching center.

But Arkimedes held her tight, leaving her unable to move. Then he nipped at her neck and licked up the column of her throat until he was breathing against her ear. "Tell me."

"Ark," she whimpered. She needed more contact, but her words seemed to scramble each time she tried to find them. "I want you to touch me everywhere," she managed eventually.

"And?"

"I want you to make love to me..."

The moment she spoke the words, he slid inside her, kissing her hungrily.

Nava moved on top of him and found a steady pace while hanging onto his shoulders. She rocked against his body, until the water was splashing from the tub and his moans mixed with hers.

Her skin glowed as her magic soared through her veins. She was full to the brim, and pleasure ran through her body, making her toes curl. Goose bumps rushed over her skin as Arkimedes feathered his lips over her clavicle and up her neck and chin. The tension built, spiraling within her until she was about to burst, hovering right there on the edge.

She toppled over, her insides tightening around him as ecstasy pulsed through her. Arkimedes kissed her through it, lifting his hips from the tub's bottom and slamming into her with growing desperation. His movements grew erratic as he chased his own release, then he grunted, digging his fingers into her hips as he pushed himself deeper inside her.

For a long moment, they clung to one another, their ragged breaths easing slowly. Nava allowed herself to drift on the water until she could lay her head over his heart.

Now that they were separate beings once more, she felt empty—craving to be close and intimate again. But her mind was stuck between heated thoughts of repeating what had just happened and the weight of worry distracting her from her state of bliss.

The Crows were on their tail. The king was probably tracking them, and the Zorren were still wreaking havoc, assisted by an undying bastard. It seemed like the trifecta of trouble was intent on their ruin.

While they'd been at the safe house, for however short a period of time, at least they'd had a plan. Even if that plan was to find a solution. But now…

"What are we going to do, Ark?" Nava lifted her chin off his chest, studying the gentle flutter of his lashes as he closed his eyes.

He let his head fall against the edge of the tub, revealing the thick column of his neck as he swallowed. His hand drew lazy circles over the skin of her hip, and for a while, she thought he wouldn't answer.

"Be more specific," he said.

"Devon is poisoned and seems more ill with each passing hour. Then we have the issue with the emissary and the Zorren…"

"I don't want to talk about this right now." Arkimedes kept up his gentle caress.

Guilt swirled in her stomach, and she pressed her cheek against his chest, closing her eyes. If only she could push all her worries away. "Sorry. I just feel like we need to keep one step ahead of whatever is coming for us."

"We rarely get a moment of privacy where I can have you to myself, in peace." He sighed. "Right now, I want to trap you in this room where we don't have to worry about anything at all."

"Forget I brought anything up."

"Too late." He huffed a laugh and shifted, forcing her to sit up as well. The water had cooled down since she'd climbed into the tub, and unlike other washrooms, this one didn't have a stove to maintain the water temperature. "I've witnessed just one other person poisoned by the Vulcan, and the symptoms weren't as severe as Devon's."

"Why do you think it's different this time?"

"I don't know, Bee," he admitted and rubbed a hand over his face. "But whatever he asked hurt him badly. Or maybe he didn't let go of it in time."

"So tomorrow Leela will get us more healing potions. But do we need to find a healer?" She frowned. It didn't seem advisable if they wanted to remain hidden. "If only I could remember how to make a potion, I could sort this myself."

"You can relearn how to once things have settled."

She met his gaze, and hope blossomed. Perhaps she had given up on her old knowledge too fast. Why let the horrors of her circumstances defeat her? Why allow the God of Shadows to win when she could relearn what he'd taken from her? Sure, it wouldn't be her father's teachings, but she could regain that part of herself. In time.

Water dripped off Arkimedes's body as he stood and climbed from the tub, reaching for one of the fluffy towels Leela had set out for them on a wooden stool off to the side. Then he stilled, as if something had spooked him.

"Ark?"

"What if Aristaeus knows how to kill an immortal?" He turned to Nava, his eyes widening. "He's a creature of the gods. We lost access to the Vulcan and the archives, but we have a Beekeeper, and we can ask him things we don't know."

Her heart sped up as she thought it through. Unbelievable, that the answer might have been hiding in plain sight for so long. "Wouldn't he have told us about it the last time we fought the Zorren?"

"Not necessarily. Not if he hasn't seen the emissary." Arkimedes wrapped a towel around her body as soon as Nava emerged from the lukewarm water. "If the man in the shadows is opening the portals from inside the shadow world and allowing the Zorren into ours, then there is a possibility Aristaeus has never seen him."

He snaked both arms around her hips and lifted her with far too much ease, given her size. Then he walked her back to the bedroom, leaving a trail of wet tracks on the wooden floor.

"I guess that's possible. He has never mentioned who might be opening the portals." Nava steadied herself on his shoulders. Her heart was racing for an entirely different reason than the subject of their conversation.

Arkimedes's legs hit the side of the bed, and he lowered her until her nose was touching his. Her heart hammered in her throat as all her senses focused on her soulmate. What had they been talking about? Who even cared?

"Enough talking now," Arkimedes said and kissed her, before he dropped her into the bed.

17
ORION

Orion breathed a sigh of relief as the cool fall morning air hit his face the moment he cracked the window open. He studied the sky, still a deep shade of gray from the evening storm, and found nothing suspicious. No Crows appeared to be lurking on the streets, nor could he spot any Dark Ones flying above.

He shrugged off the long black coat Leela had brought him earlier and tossed it over a dining chair. Then he rolled up his sleeves while listening to Nava's gentle steps padding up the stairs to the second floor.

It was odd to sense someone without having to see them, but the more time they spent together, the stronger this bond they shared grew.

Nava walked into the living area, running her hands over the folds of an overly full, puffed-up skirt. "Leela's out of control with these clothes," she complained, frowning at the stairs. "Do something about it."

Orion grinned and headed over to her. "I thought you said I was *not* to scare your friend."

He reached for her waist and pulled her toward him to claim her lips. The gentle kiss lasted a few seconds at most—far too short for his liking.

"That was yesterday, before she turned me into her doll," Nava said and withdrew. She draped her arms over his shoulders. "I can't breathe in this." She pointed at her midsection, where a hidden corset cinched her waist behind the layers of silk and lace.

"I think she doesn't want her future queen to go out on the streets in anything but the best that she can offer." Orion fixed the suffocating collar of his stiff shirt. It was too warm in this place. "Even if it's ridiculous to wear it inside the house."

Nava pressed her lips together, clearly holding back whatever she was about to say. At a guess, it probably had to do with the notion of the royal title —and becoming his queen.

She changed the subject. "How is Devon this morning?"

"He was asleep when I checked on him earlier," Orion said. One day, they would get a reprieve from having to worry about their lives and Devon's. A moment to enjoy their togetherness without having to run.

But that day wasn't today. Not when the bees had been crawling over the ceiling of their bedroom this morning and were swarming all over Nava's dark dress right now. Had she even noticed? Or had she grown so used to them by now that it didn't seem odd anymore to be covered in insects?

"Has Leela left to get the potions?"

"Yes, when you were changing," he said.

He was just turning toward Devon's room when a sudden hissing sound called to him. It was an indistinct noise, so faint that Nava probably couldn't even hear it. Still, a chill instantly crawled under the layers of his clothes.

"You feel it too," Nava whispered.

Arkimedes nodded and crept along the corridor that led to Devon's room. The weight of a stone sat in his gut. There was no one else here—yet something was off.

"Devon?" Orion called. The hinges screeched as he pushed the door open, slowly revealing Devon's unmoving body on the rumpled bed. His chest was rising and falling with labored breaths, and his closed eyelids flickered as if he was stuck in a dream...or a nightmare.

Probably the latter.

"Is he...?"

"He's alive but not doing well." Orion knelt next to the bed and placed his palm over his brother's forehead. "He's burning up." He reached for the potions Devon had carefully lined up on the wooden nightstand. "We might need to take him to the healer in the center of town. I was being an overly optimistic fool last night."

Saving his brother was his priority. If he had to fight the guards to get him help, so be it. He brought the small vial to his eye. Were the potions spoiled? Too old, maybe? That would explain why they weren't working.

"I can fly him there, and you can wait for me here," he began.

"No." Devon grasped Arkimedes's arm with an impressive amount of strength for someone that ill. His eyes cracked open, and he stared unblinking at the ceiling. "It won't be my fault if you get caught..."

"You're dying, Devon." Orion pushed the words past the thick knot in his throat, resting a hand on his brother's burning skin. "The potions are doing very little. You need a healer."

"I don't. Want. It." Devon's chest rattled like a viper preparing to strike, and he shifted on the pillowy mattress. He looked so small for a six-foot man who was usually vibrating with life. "You've got to protect Nava. Not me."

"If only it were that simple to watch a person you care for die. Especially when you can do something about it."

"We must take him to the healer," one of his shadows insisted, becoming hard to ignore. *"We need his help to defeat the emissary."*

Devon's pale lips cracked and bled when he smiled, although the feeling didn't reach his eyes. Instead, he looked like a madman. "And what happens when the guards take you down? When the king wipes your memories again and you forget her and the emissary who is hunting the Beekeepers?"

Orion blinked away the images of that very thing happening. Perhaps his father wouldn't wipe his memories this time?

"I deserve this." Devon whispered. "I held the Crows in such esteem, yet they took everything from me."

Everything? Did he mean his family?

Orion remembered the day the Society brought Devon to its headquarters. Devon had been younger than him, and his body had been badly burned. He'd spent a month in the healer's quarters.

Devon shook his head, and blood pooled on the corner of his lips. "They told me my family dropped me on the Society's doorstep because they gambled their money away and couldn't pay for a proper healer to save me. I waited for months for them to return for me."

Nava covered her mouth with her hand and stepped forward from where she'd been hovering by the door. "They killed them?"

"I promise you, I asked the mirror about the emissary. But instead, it showed me what I *really* wanted to know. I didn't think it would take my wishes as a command, but it spoon-fed me my past like I was a starving man. I suppose in a way I always have been."

"Did they kill them because of your magic?" Orion asked. Devon's silence was answer enough.

"I'm sorry," Devon said to no one in particular, twisting to face Nava. "For the way I treated you in the past. For how I hunted you down like you were nothing but an animal. You were right all along."

Orion didn't know what he wanted more: to strangle his brother for reminding him of what he'd done, or to ask him to shut up and get him some help.

He handed Devon two new vials of the healing potion instead. Hopefully, Leela would be back soon with more.

Nava's lips trembled as she stopped beside the bed. "On the island, I healed Aristaeus and Arkimedes with an alchemist potion I brewed in Willowbrook. There was this warmth that came through me when I pressed my hand to your wound, Ark, and it helped you heal faster."

"You want to do the same with Devon?" he asked. Without warning, a tingling sensation clawed at his head. A sudden burst of images flashed through his mind, robbing him of his breath.

Orion leaned against the bed frame as the memories of the night Mortimer had betrayed him on Grey Island slotted into place, followed by a sense of foreboding. He relived it all in a strange time-lapse: Mort, one of the few friends he had—selling him to Devon by giving him spiked wine that made him pass out. How he'd stabbed Arkimedes in the side, so he couldn't escape.

Nava's face twisted with worry. "Is something wrong?"

He didn't want to worry her further. Trying to keep his face devoid of emotion, he handed Devon the potion with a forced smile. "No, I'm fine. It wouldn't hurt to use your magic…"

She leaned forward as the contents of the measly potion disappeared behind Devon's lips. Then she pressed her palms against Devon's chest and closed her eyes.

"This tastes like shit," Devon mumbled.

It didn't take long for Nava's palms to shine with white light—so different from the way her magic usually appeared. Perhaps some hope remained.

They stayed with Devon until his skin had gained some color, and his fever broke. When they returned to the living area, Leela had just arrived from her errand to the potion maker's shop and was fixing up some lunch on her small kitchen counter.

"Is Mr. Black all right?" she asked.

"He is doing a little better now," he said. "Did you encounter any issues while out?"

The fae's eyes crinkled with worry, and she glanced at the table. Orion turned just as Nava gasped, panic bursting through their bond.

"Ark…" She was holding a piece of parchment in one hand. The closer he came to his mate, the faster the dread pooled in his stomach.

It was a page of the *Russet Gazette*, the city's local newspaper. An illustration of a tree he knew by heart was etched onto the paper in forest-green ink. Above it, in printed letters, it read:

The queen has arrived in the Copper Kingdom.

"Leela, where did you get this?"

"The flyers were everywhere." Leela's face darkened. "They were on every lamppost, on all the shop windows. People were reading the *Gazette* and talking about it in the street..."

"Do you know if the king has announced anything?" Orion asked.

"No, sir." Leela shook her head and continued stirring her stew. "I asked the potion maker when the news came out, and he said they delivered it this morning before sunrise. I thought you might want to know, so I ripped the paper off a lamppost on my way home."

His palms dampened with perspiration, and he reached out for Nava. Did the king know the news had made its way past the castle grounds? Who could've leaked such information? Surely this wasn't his father's doing.

"Ark." Nava's small hand gripped his arm, but when he looked down, her lips shook as she pressed her palms to her dress, where her insects crawled all over.

So many more bees than this morning.

Orion frowned and stepped close enough that their bodies were almost touching. "Nava, what's happening to the bees?"

She lifted her hand, a pained expression on her face. A small bee was stinging her.

"I don't know," Nava whispered and then met his eyes with a wild expression. "It must be Ari. He needs us."

18
NAVA

It smelled faintly like a campfire out in the streets. On any other day, Nava would have thought it was the pleasant scent of firewood escaping through a chimney, but not today. Today it reminded her of destruction. Of death. The closer they got to the forest, the more nauseous she felt.

Of course, being this high up probably also contributed to the sick feeling in her stomach. They had left Leela's place a while ago, and now a mass of sepia tones blurred so far beneath them that she could barely distinguish a street from a building. If it weren't so dangerous for her to transfer to the forest on her own, she would have done it in a heartbeat. She'd prefer that over flying any day.

Her stomach was tied into knots as she snaked her arms around Arkimedes's shoulders, digging her fingers into the back of his neck to find purchase.

"You're going to choke me if you keep doing that." He glared at her, rolling his neck so she released him. "For the last time, Nava, I will not drop you."

"Sorry," she blurted, her cheeks warming as she moved her hands to his shoulders instead. "It's hard to hold on with the wings, and I don't want to rip any feathers and hurt you..."

He scoffed, tightening his grip around her and underneath her legs. "We're almost there."

They cut through the stormy gray sky. Thankfully, it wasn't raining as heavily anymore. Still, the icy drizzle remained, soaking her clothes and leaving her shivering. At least while it was so wet out here, the forest fire couldn't progress.

Arkimedes had taken the long way around the castle instead of flying over it to avoid any accidental encounters with the guards.

"It's been weeks since the demons came. I wonder if it takes the emissary this long to open a new portal or if there was something else holding him back?" If he needed time to regenerate his energy, that could be their saving grace.

"If a god owns his soul, then I'm sure he has other tasks that keep him from burning this world to the ground." Arkimedes's jaw tightened, and he brought Nava even closer to his body in a protective embrace. "Or from hunting you and Aristaeus."

Leela's home was a fair distance from the castle and even farther from the forest, so it took them a good hour to reach the trees. Arkimedes's aura helped him carry her all the way without stopping to rest.

Finally, he began his descent toward the immense block of greenery beneath them. The air whipped around them as gravity pulled them to the ground. The taste of smoke covered her tongue, although there wasn't a sign of flames to be seen.

"Fuck." Arkimedes opened his wings to glide over the treetops, his arms shaking with strain. "The air is changing. Hold on tight, Bee."

This time, he didn't complain when her arms wound around his neck like ropes. They were flying close enough to the canopy now that the leaves swatted at her dangling feet.

"The fires are over there." Nava pointed at the thick column of smoke that swirled angrily through the air, cutting the blue sky apart and casting a haze across the forest in the distance. "Ari has to be near the fire and the portal. That's where we need to go."

"I'm not flying you into the middle of a forest fire caused by your mortal enemies. We're landing in an unknown situation that could get us killed."

Nava thrived at solving problems as the situation arose, but perhaps this time she should put aside the need to find Ari immediately, for her soulmate's sake. Arkimedes was making sense, and if she expected him to listen to her, then she needed to do the same.

His wings beat steadily as he lowered them into the depths of the forest. Dry brush and leaves crunched under her feet as he set her down. Even this far away from the fires, smoke wafted over the ground.

The cries of nature resounded around her. The rumble beneath her feet as animals scurried through the darkness, invisible to their eyes but deafening to her senses.

"Let's find Aristaeus," Arkimedes said. Much like Nava, he didn't have a weapon to wield against the demons—and possibly the emissary.

All they had was their combined magic, and it had to be enough.

She closed her eyes and thought of Ari. His black eyes. The long trunks that formed his legs, permanently covered in moss and mushrooms. A gentle pull answered her, and Nava began walking—no, running—in its direction. Aristaeus was coming to her, and she needed to meet him.

She glanced at Arkimedes as her body shifted form. Her legs turned into swirling dust, her arms disappearing from view. "You can follow the pull of our bond. Find me there."

"Nava," Arkimedes called, wide-eyed, but he didn't stop her. "Be careful."

No mortal weapon could truly hurt an emissary of the gods. And with the demons he was letting in, the three of them might be the only thing that stood between this kingdom and certain destruction.

Nava flew through particles of ash, picking up speed as Aristaeus drew her to him like a magnet. She moved so fast her surroundings blurred into nothingness, until all that remained was the beacon calling to her. She could sense Ari, too: enveloped in a mixture of forest debris and blown across the place by a cyclone of ancient magic.

They collided in a cloud that momentarily pushed away the particles of ash raining down from above. And for a fraction of time, in the warmth of Aristaeus's embrace, Nava felt peace.

"Dearest one, you're back," he whispered inside her head. Oh, how she'd missed him. Then a burst of images flashed through her mind. A black portal opening in the middle of the forest. The Zorren passing through it, crossing the barriers between their land and this world.

Nava changed from air to flesh and bones, blinking away the daze left behind by the memories Ari had shared.

Ari popped into his own true form with the screeching noises of expanding wood. *"I feared the Dark Ones had imprisoned you, for I could sense you were alive, but I couldn't reach you anywhere."*

Guilt bubbled inside of her. Of course Ari wouldn't be able to locate her while she was in a strange safe house, guarded by spells and Neems. "I'm sorry. We had to escape the castle when my dress—" Oh, she didn't have time to go over the details. Not when a fire hissed so close to them, ravaging the forest. If only she could take her time to reconnect with him after this period of separation. "Are the demons nearby?"

Ari tilted his head toward the wall of smoke to her right. *"If you close your eyes and listen to the forest, it will tell you where they are."*

Nava clicked her tongue. Why couldn't Aristaeus give her a straight answer for once, instead of trying to teach her a lesson? They were already on borrowed time.

"I took care of the only Zorren who made it through the portal," he said, evidently sensing her frustration. *"Where is our protector? I sense him."*

"I came to find you first," she answered. The smoke burned her throat, and their bees flew around them in a shield of brown bodies, spilling from the hive on Aristaeus's head. The warning rang clear through their buzzing as a ragged line of flames pushed past the haze, crackling and reaching out toward them.

Behind the red glow of fire, black demons cast wide shadows over the area, watching, waiting—approaching with abrupt, broken movements across the land they hungered to destroy.

"Ari, I thought you said there weren't any demons," Nava gasped, jumping back with her heart suddenly in her throat. The imminent danger sharpened her senses.

"I closed the portal." Ari's voice lacked his usual calm. *"Another must have just opened."*

They looked at each other. They couldn't leave because this threat was coming for *them*.

"Listen to the forest, dearest, and follow its calling to the portal."

The changing wind blasted the fire through the underbrush. The dry bark on centuries-old trees caught on fire just as Aristaeus changed into his airy form and drifted away.

Nava closed her eyes, and the pained screams of the trees rang inside her ears. Tears sprang to her eyes at the sound of such devastation.

She needed to focus on her mission, on finding the portal. Like the air ruffling the leaves, she sifted through words in languages she shouldn't understand but did regardless. At long last, there was a clear call, beckoning her in. *There.*

She changed shape and followed their screams. Now that she was no longer in her human form, the smoke and flames didn't hurt her as she crossed the inferno toward the hum of the new portal.

Ari was already there, looming large like a magnificent tree. One of the four demons slipped straight through the fire. Its skull looked so similar to that of a human that Nava's hair stood on end. If it weren't for the small mandibles around the mouth that snapped in Ari's direction, she would have thought it was a monstrous human spirit.

Their shapes were all different. Some looked like a wasp and a human combined. Others had bones for horns, as if an elk had been stuck onto a human skull. They wore armor made of black metal—or dark stone, perhaps.

When they screeched, the entire forest fell silent. Nava swallowed the bile that rose in her throat, attempting to settle her nerves. The Zorren hadn't seen her yet, but they were attacking Aristaeus all at once.

Nava screamed and dashed toward them. Half of her body was still air, the other half human. She called on nature as she'd done many times before, and the earth beneath her rumbled, right before massive roots shot from the ground, slamming into a demon and preventing it from hurting Ari.

It battled with the ropes of tree roots as branches dropped from above and pinned it to the ground. But the wooden prison wouldn't hold the demon for long. She needed to use her power to subdue it, like she'd seen Ari do before.

She rushed to the fallen Zorren and jumped on top of it, ignoring the blisters that formed on her palms as she clawed at its neck. Her stubby human nails grew into magical claws. It hurt like hell, but she persevered, digging them into its head, avoiding its sharp teeth.

The screams of the forest grew louder inside her ears, feeding her anger and lending her strength.

She dug into the creature's slimy throat until she met the gristle of muscle and bone. Her magic burned hotter, and the scream of the Zorren drowned out the cries of the trees.

Her magic flowed through her fingers, swirling over the demon's body like wooden vines. They charred but didn't break when they wrapped around its burning skin.

It bucked under her, nearly throwing her off despite her iron grip. Her aura glowed yellow, and she ignored the intense pain shooting up her hands and arms. Instead, she tightened her magical claws around its throat until she heard bone break and the demon slumped within her grasp.

Nava transferred away just as the forest rumbled beneath her in a furious call. It demanded to be fed by its enemy, and the dirt underneath the demon cracked open into a giant hole that swallowed the Zorren's body whole.

Fire rained down on them as Nava moved across the battleground toward Ari. Everything hurt, even in her non-corporeal shape. But Ari couldn't fight the remaining demons on his own and close the portal. There would be time to lick her wounds later.

All of a sudden, a claw reached out from the shadows of the forest, hidden by the thick smoke, and sank into her. Nails that shouldn't be able to grab at her when she was just air dragged her down by her ribs, ripping through layers of clothing, skin, and muscle.

The wound burned deep, and her body flickered into its solid form as the demon threw her forward into a pile of brush. Sharp sticks, fallen branches, and small sharp rocks dug into Nava's crumpling body as she screamed in agony.

The Zorren's claws had been knife tips, curling under her ribs and tearing her flesh. The demon snapped its mandibles in her direction, walking to her with an unnatural gait that made her blood run cold.

So much pain flooded her body in waves that she could no longer move her limbs. Her body became a dead weight on the ground. It was too hot here. Too suffocating.

She gasped for air. Her fingers and legs had gone numb. All she could see was the trees around her, moving in unison and swinging their long branches at the demon that was coming for her.

A rough, guttural scream echoed through the burning woods. The Zorren growled and surged forward, its claws glowing with fire as it moved to strike her down. The leaves in the canopy shifted above her just before her vision blurred and darkness welcomed her in its soundless embrace.

19
ORION

Orion followed the pull of their bond toward the fire, gliding over the treetops and across the column of smoke that stung his eyes. He couldn't just land in there, not when he had so little visibility and it could cost him his life.

Instead, he flew a league away from the main source of the fire. Twigs snapped under his feet as he landed as gracefully as he could, folding his wings between enormous trees. Then he ran like hell through the deep wall of smoke that burned his lungs like acid.

He pulled out the handkerchief Leela had stuffed in his pocket that morning and tied it behind his head, covering his nose and mouth. It was woven from raw silk, the weave so fine it would help filter the air.

An icy wind blew around him despite the fire, raising the hairs on the nape of his neck. A crackling energy that felt and smelled familiar, like his magic coming to life. Perhaps it was the filthy stench from the demons or the weird scent that usually emanated from the portals.

It didn't matter. He didn't have time to linger. Through the bond, he could feel that Nava was nervous—she was probably getting closer to the fire as well.

"A Dark One is hiding nearby," a soul in his aura whispered, pulling him back to the present with a sharp spike of adrenaline. *"It thinks we can't see it—him."*

Fear stripped what little remained of Orion's sanity as he followed the pull of his shadows, trying to find whatever it was referring to.

A Dark One? Could it be one of the king's guards had found him? He was closer to the castle than he would have liked, and they might well still be on the lookout for him and Nava. The tree where his mother died wasn't too far away, either.

The smoke hovering near a tree shifted ever so slightly, as if a large body had vanished from the shadows of two knotted tree trunks, leaving a gaping hole in the middle.

Orion's throat went dry as he discovered a trail of ebony mist crawling across the forest floor like tiny claws. To an untrained eye, it was almost imperceptible in the surrounding haze. But Orion was familiar with this form of disguise, only used by his kind. His father's guards had kidnapped him by shielding themselves in the same manner on Grey Island.

Whoever this fool was, he wasn't even twelve feet away from Orion.

He propelled himself forward using the element of surprise and the power of his wings. The souls of his aura helped him, preventing him from nearly hitting a nearby tree. His energy left him drunk on power, and he stopped feeling the paralyzing fear, funneling his magic into anger instead.

Why would a guard try to attack him now? What if the fire had been a setup all along? Somehow, something was telling Orion that this was a dangerous opponent, intent on harming him.

He struck the perfectly hidden shadow hard. All of his magic collected into his fist as it connected with a gooey substance that burned his hand.

"Poison!" a soul shouted in his ear, so loud it mimicked his inner thoughts at the burning sensation spreading across his arm. He wanted to yank it back, but he had to weaken the Dark One further.

Inside the dark void of the tree trunk, he grasped at the slippery shape of a neck and heard a distinct gurgling noise. He closed his grip around it and threw the figure across the clearing before the venom could cause him true harm.

A shadow without a true shape collided against a tree that exploded into fragments of pulp, bark, and coal.

Orion heaved, nauseated by the use of his power and the poison of whatever had been in that hole, waiting to strike him. He'd thought it was a royal guard, but he wasn't so sure anymore.

A black figure rose from the dead ground, almost seven feet tall, with disheveled wings that lacked the splendor of full feathers. His face peered through a crack in his black helmet, revealing skin as pale as flawless alabaster and bright red eyes. Orion went numb as the realization hit.

This wasn't a normal Dark One. This was the emissary of the Shadow God. Fuck, the bastard did look exactly like Orion.

He was everything Orion had expected, yet different. Taller by at least five inches. Slimmer, too. With long, pointed ears that peeked from his silver hair.

A full fae—not a halfling like himself. This couldn't be his twin, even though their faces were nearly identical. No wonder Nava had been a trembling mess when she'd exited that portal.

The emissary swiped his purplish tongue over his bloodied lips and reached for the hilt of a sword that protruded from a belt around his waist. The handle was shaped from polished onyx, catching the pale gray light of the darkening sky.

"I wasn't expecting you..." he croaked as he took in Orion's fighting stance with wide eyes. The metal of his long sword hissed as it slid from a scabbard made of smoke. "But I'm glad you saved me the trouble of finding you later, *princeling*."

That last word was spat out with such hate it gave Orion pause. Why would this emissary be looking for him? So far, he'd only targeted the Beekeepers.

Did he know Orion was Nava's soulmate?

Vines were wrapped around one of the emissary's arms, contrasting with the ebony of his armor. The wood appeared to be slowing down his movements.

"Why are you trying to hurt the Beekeepers?" Sweat beaded on Orion's brow as he sidestepped the emissary. He needed the freedom to escape if necessary.

The ground trembled under his feet. A call from the Beekeepers, a trace of fear, surged through their bond. Was Nava hurt? Had she found Aristaeus before the Zorren? Were they fighting now?

The emissary advanced with the confidence of someone who couldn't die. His aura swirled around him, black like Orion's, although it lacked the spirits. Which meant he didn't possess the power to take souls.

"The Beekeepers have done nothing to me. I've naught against them—but I'll do anything to get my revenge on you."

What revenge? "I haven't done a thing to you."

"Your existence is a reminder of what he did." The emissary's eyes narrowed on Orion, shining with hate. "And you look just like him, which makes it easier to get rid of you."

"You're mad."

"You will be dead before the day is over, and your bloodline will be gone soon. Then, and only then, will I be free." He swung his sword at Orion, and it rippled through space, a force of nature that bent the air.

Orion's power pushed him back, although he barely dodged the deadly waves that disintegrated the tree beside him. The sword held a devastating kind of magic he'd never seen before, much less on a weapon.

"If you're trying to kill me because I look like my father, remember, I look like you, too." Orion took a shaky breath. His power was burning hot, demanding he take a soul, even though this immortal fool had none to be taken. "And if you kill the Beekeepers, you will forsake this land and all its inhabitants."

"The land is already barren. People are starving, sick, or both." The emissary laughed, a rough croaking sound. "Your bloodline will only wreak destruction upon this kingdom. I'm merely fixing the problem."

Orion didn't think his body could react any more viscerally to the emissary. But now his blood turned to ice—the emissary's words were far too close to the prophecy Devon had uncovered.

"So you'll kill the king and me to free yourself from your ties to the god, and then what? You'll take the throne?"

Surprise washed over the emissary's features. Perhaps he'd never expected that Orion would find out what he was. "I don't owe you an explanation, but a monkey could rule better than you."

The emissary gripped the hilt of his sword with white knuckles, and black power licked over his fingers. The swirls of his sorcery were mere wisps compared to the raw power the king possessed, or even compared to Orion's magic. But unlike them, the emissary was an immortal with a powerful weapon Orion didn't know how to avoid.

Without another word, the emissary unleashed himself upon Orion. His strikes were so fast that it was hard to see, let alone run or fly away from. Each time Orion managed to dodge it, he landed on the scalding hot ground that burned through the soles of his boots.

Ash rained down on them as the fire roared closer, strong winds pushing it in their direction.

"Behind you," a spirit warned, giving Orion just enough time to move out of the sword's path. Still, the dark tendrils of its attack sizzled through the hairs on his arm.

Another strike and the pointed blade nicked his white shirt. Orion stumbled back and fell to the ground, crushing his wings beneath his body.

The emissary kept a large enough distance between them to prevent Orion from using the full force of his powers. That damn weapon was too strong to approach.

Suddenly, panic and pain flooded the bond in a fierce rush. Orion clutched his stomach with a scream and stared past the dark shape of the undying fae, into the thicket of trees and to a point where he knew Nava must be... Injured.

He jumped to his feet, ignoring the sharp pain that shot from his wings down to his shoulder blades. The emissary couldn't die, and he might possess a weapon of incredible destruction—but he probably couldn't fly with those mangled wings.

The air cracked around Orion as he called for a shield of energy to protect him. Then he flew to the highest branch of the nearest tree.

The emissary's sword chopped it off before he could land somewhere that would hold his weight. Orion pivoted, aiming for an even larger branch instead.

With the distance between him and the magical weapon, it became easier to find the perfect moment to attack. The sword was clearly heavy, and each time the undying fae swung it at him, it seemed to tire him.

It was a marvelous weapon, likely forged by the gods for the gods. It demanded a price in exchange for its use, and his opponent's strength was fizzling out. The emissary's skin was shining with sweat. He had completely underestimated Orion's power and determination to not die.

The next time the fae swung the sword to strike, it took him longer. Orion jumped off the tree he was perching on, his aura calling for blood, and caught his opponent by surprise.

His fist connected with the emissary's jaw, whose shocked eyes rolled into the back of his head before he fell to the ground like a dead weight. But Orion didn't stop hitting him. Not even when his vision grayed out and all he felt was bone breaking beneath his knuckles.

The sound of a portal opening barely registered. A sudden force shoved him off the undying, and he skittered across the debris-covered forest floor.

The emissary sat up a heartbeat later, like a puppet pulled from the ground by invisible strings. The broken bones that deformed his face snapped into place. Then his eyes blinked open, and he looked around in a daze, before they widened in understanding.

Mad laughter escaped his bloodied lips, and his shattered teeth healed right in front of Orion's eyes. He tried to jump the fae again, but some kind of shield held him back.

The emissary hiccuped, a rattle in his breathing. He rose on shaking legs. A red cape slowly appeared on his shoulders, fluttering in the high winds behind him.

The portal grew and sucked the emissary into its black center like a magnet. He clicked his tongue, and for the first time, he abandoned the mask of madness he'd worn before. "Be glad the God of Shadows called me, Prince—for I'm done waiting for my freedom."

The whistling wind of the portal formed a shield of air that nearly burned Orion's lashes. Then darkness swallowed the emissary's body.

Nava. He needed to get to her. Now.

Orion jumped up to the sky, not wasting another second as he followed the pull of the bond through the thick layer of smoke, to where the warm rays of Aristaeus's magic beckoned him.

Three horned demons remained in the chaos below. But Orion had no trouble locating his soulmate, who lay on the ground, clearly injured. A demon hovered nearby, waiting to devour her.

Orion called her name and jumped on top of the demon. His aura burst around him, and the wisps of his power captured the creature of darkness before it could hurt her further. It screeched, its flames failing as he grabbed the Zorren by its slimy neck, ignoring the burn of its venom against his skin.

All the souls in him feasted on the demon—soulless but so full of power. The Zorren collapsed forward, its body shriveling like dry flowers as Orion drained it until there was nothing left, replenishing the energy he'd wasted while battling the emissary.

He was ready to destroy them all. To make them pay for even dreaming that they could hurt her.

20
NAVA

There was no time to waste. Arkimedes came for her, had saved her, but they weren't out of danger yet.

Nava rolled over onto her stomach, pushing her body off the ground with trembling arms. Blood dripped from her lesion, leaving warm, sticky trails over her hand as she tried to stem the flow.

How badly hurt was she? She had seconds—minutes at most—to do...something.

If she didn't die from her wound and stayed here much longer, the smoke would eventually kill her. She limped toward the portal that still hovered in the air.

It pulsed like a festering wound right in the middle of this forest. The scent of ammonia wafted from it in waves, growing stronger the closer she got to it.

Was this what the shadow world smelled like?

She shot a look at Aristaeus. He was still fighting a demon, unable to come and help her close the portal. But Ari always told her to trust herself—that her instincts were there to guide her to uncover her potential. And it was true. Whenever she'd done so, destiny had always surprised her.

Still, there was always that small voice of doubt that clutched her tight and refused to let go.

Nearly doubled over with pain and ignoring the black dots that danced across her vision, Nava raised her arms toward the magical gate.

Weeks ago, she had closed another portal, together with Ari and

Arkimedes. She hadn't spoken the language Ari chanted then, but had known what to say regardless. The spell had tapped into a piece of her soul that made her who she was. A Beekeeper.

Opening her fingers like Ari had done that afternoon, she closed her eyes and tuned out the screams of the forests and the growls of the remaining demons. Everything fell away.

Then the words came to her… first, quiet like a whisper, and then loud enough that she could chant them. They tasted strange on her tongue, but she chanted them, and the portal shrank right before her eyes. Yellow magic strings poured from her fingertips, beginning to seal the door to the shadow world shut.

Something landed at her side, but she didn't even blink, for she knew who it was.

Her heart soared as Arkimedes placed his hand on her shoulder, and his energy bled through her, intensifying the spell. The portal became smaller, condensing into a dot of ink—and popped.

"That was—" Pain cut her off. She doubled over, clutching her side with both hands, putting as much pressure as she could on the wound. But her body had turned cold, and she was trembling even though flames still burned all around them.

Arkimedes's arms wrapped under her legs and behind her back, and the air shifted as he took flight with Nava in his embrace, carrying her away from the inferno and, hopefully, somewhere safe.

They landed in a meadow. His limbs were shaking. He was probably exhausted. She was, too.

"Don't go to sleep, Bee," Ark pleaded as he set her down. The ground was so soft and pillowy. Covered in moss.

It was still drizzling icy water. She was so cold.

"Tired." She hissed when he lifted her arm to inspect the area the Zorren had dug its nails into. "Don't do that. Hurts."

"You're bleeding a lot." He shrugged off his coat and untied the green handkerchief he wore around his neck, folded it a few times, and pressed it against her stomach. "Hold it tight."

Then he pulled his shirt from his pants and tugged at the edges. The scent of spice filled the air, followed by the sound of fabric ripping.

The world spun around her, the treetops swirling above her. She tried to speak, but no words came to her lips, only senseless whimpers.

How bad was her wound? Did she even want to know? Ark looked paler than she'd ever seen him before. He wouldn't even meet her eyes.

"Sit still," he said in a clipped tone, and she obeyed. Who cared anyway? All she wanted was to go to sleep.

Arkimedes wrapped his shirt around her ribs tightly enough that it resembled a corset. When the white fabric turned pink and then red in a matter of minutes, he paled further.

"I need to get you to the city."

"Can't transfer anywhere." Nava's voice broke, her throat raw from inhaling so much smoke. She cleared it, wincing as she sank against the tree behind her. "And you're exhausted."

"I will take you to a healer even if it kills me."

She exhaled a shaky breath. No energy left to put up a fight...but she didn't want to move an inch either. "You'll kill us both. When you drop me."

"For the last time," Arkimedes growled, "I will not drop you."

A steady creaking sound alerted them to Aristaeus joining them in the meadow. His gentle voice was a whisper inside her mind. *"There are no demons around us now. I killed the last one, and you closed the portal. Well done, dearest."* His brows dipped slowly as he shifted, tilting his stiff neck forward to inspect her bloody shirt. *"Your body will heal faster if you remain here, close to nature. With your soulmate and me at your side."*

Would she heal? Or was Ari just trying to soothe her because he knew this was the end? If so, how long would that take? Surely blood loss would take her much faster than infection.

"What did he say?" Arkimedes asked.

"He said I'll heal f-faster if I stay in the forest by his side. And yours." She groaned in pain. Her skin felt so hot, but the heat didn't reach her.

"She needs a healer," Arkimedes argued, looking straight into Aristaeus's eyes.

"You are a Beekeeper with the gift of healing. When we met, the Zorren had hurt me, and you were the one to heal me. No human potion, healer, or fae could have saved me that day. Only you, dear one." Ari paused and glanced at Arkimedes. *"It's why you could heal your mate back on the island when he was a prisoner."*

"Ari says I'm able to heal." Could it be? That it had never been the alchemist potions her father had taught her, but always her magic? She'd denied it for so long.

"You're like Gavin?" Arkimedes blinked rapidly and pressed his hand to her wound, making the sharp stabs of pain worse.

She swatted his hand away. "I don't know."

Arkimedes's frown eased. He settled into a crouch and opened his hands, closing his eyes. His magic swirled, as she had seen thousands of times before, and a small wooden box materialized on his outstretched palms. What could it be? Her mind was too sluggish to ask.

He opened the lid, huffing as he removed a curved needle and rummaged through glass vials that clanked against each other. "If that's true, then we need to close the wound now, and then go there." He shot a cautious glance at the clearing over his shoulder.

"What's happening?" she asked, although she already knew. Before her, Arkimedes lit a dry branch with a fire spell and used it to sterilize the needle.

Then he dropped the contents of the potion—no, alcohol—on her wound without warning. Nava screamed, her heart hammering in her chest. She scrambled for his arm, stopping him before he could lower the sharp point to her injured skin.

"What the hell are you doing?" She swallowed, searching his panicked face.

Arkimedes caressed the side of her face. "You're losing a lot of blood, Nava. I've seen this kind of wound before. It will hurt just for a bit, but this way we can carry you to safety."

He peeked over his shoulder again when the wind rustled the leaves around them. The rain was falling harder now. Thunder rolled above.

"Why do you keep looking back there? Ari said there aren't any demons left?"

"It's not the demons I'm worried about..." He shook his head, and then without pausing, he pierced her skin and looped the first ring of black thread, pulling her skin tightly closed.

Nava barely suppressed another scream.

"The forest is not a safe place during the night." Ari knelt by her side. The absolute blackness of his eyes distracted her from the pain. He studied Nava like she did him, inspecting her for any other hurts the Zorren might have caused her.

Soot and mild charring darkened the bark of his body. The moss, once green and alive with mushrooms, had turned brown and now stuck to his side, shriveled and dry. *"I have a home of my own. It will keep us safe. "*

"You h-have a home?" Her breath stuttered as Arkimedes closed two more stitches.

Ari tilted his head, and while he lacked any human expressions, she could have sworn he raised one of his wooden brows at her. *"Where else would I rest and recover?"*

Damn. Of course. She'd always thought he slept in the trees.

Soon, her wound was closed and tightly wrapped. Aristaeus picked her up, and they set off for safe shelter.

This was an older part of the forest, untouched by civilization, and with trees so enormous that she couldn't see the tops. Not that she could make out anything clearly right now. Her vision was far too blurry. All she could focus on was the bandage around her ribs and how it kept slipping with each step Ari took farther into the forest. Nava pressed a hand to it to hold it in place.

Stray rays of sunlight filtered through the leaves, dancing like the sparkles on precious stones over the moss-covered ground. The trees looming over them rivaled even those on Grey Island.

Arkimedes trudged behind them in silence. He didn't need to say a word, for everything he felt howled at her through their bond. All his worry. All his love.

"I'm fine..." she slurred, cursing her stupid mouth and tongue. "Ark, I'm not even in pain."

The words wouldn't ease his concerns, and her rough voice did little to sell the lie.

"I met the emissary when I was trying to get to you," he said.

"What?" She raised her head from where it rested against Ari's chest. "You should have told me!"

"When, exactly? A demon nearly eviscerated you, Nava." He pointed at her bloody bandage, but his tone lacked any heat. He looked so tired and frightened. It broke her heart to see him like that.

"I'm fine," she whispered, and this time, she believed it. Although she was still in pain and weakened by the blood loss, she did feel more like herself.

Aristaeus was right. Being together—the three of them—helped her.

"I thought I was going to lose you." Arkimedes's voice cracked. He cleared his throat and continued. "It didn't matter that I found the emissary when your life was in danger."

All right. He had a point. If their roles had been reversed, she would have done the same. "What happened?"

"He was hiding in the shadows near the Zorren. I confronted him, and we fought. But then he got called away."

"What emissary is he speaking of?" Aristaeus asked, tilting his head to the side with a creak.

Of course Arkimedes couldn't hear him, so he continued. "I asked him why he was trying to hurt you two. From what he said, it's about earning his freedom. It made me wonder whether he's working with the demons as part of some kind of deal."

Nava covered her lips with a hand that smelled tangy and coppery, like blood. "He helps the Zorren come here to kill us, and then they help release him from his service to the god?"

"He wants to kill my father, too." Arkimedes hesitated. "And me. He wants revenge, although he didn't specify what for. But clearly, my father did something to annoy him."

She couldn't really blame the emissary. King Oberon knew how to make enemies.

"Ari, when I first found you—the day we met—there w-was another Beekeeper with you." She wished her voice didn't sound so weak. And that the throbbing pain would stop bringing tears to her eyes.

She swallowed heavily, trying to ease the knot in her throat as the memories caught up with her. The second Beekeeper had been dead and fading away into the ground. Smoke had lingered in the air that afternoon. Ari had told her that the Zorren had attacked them. But what if it hadn't been just the Zorren?

Arkimedes lengthened his strides to catch up to them. "What if the emissary killed the other Beekeeper?"

"His name was Illaris," Ari said and continued walking. *"I don't remember who or what struck him. But we were surprised by a large group of Zorren that day,"* he admitted in a sorrowful tone.

Could the demons come to this realm on their own? Or had the emissary been letting them in a year ago, too?

"They shouldn't be able to come to this land on their own. Every time we fight them, it's in the Beekeepers' realm."

Exactly as she'd feared. The Zorren, Ari, and Illaris—they'd all set her destiny in motion that day. Nothing was a coincidence.

"I don't know if the emissary can come into Caztian unless he's on a mission commanded by Dargan." Arkimedes shook his head, raking a hand through his hair. "Each time you've encountered him, Bee, has been in the shadow world."

That was true... Which would make defeating him that much more difficult because she couldn't move in his realm.

"I still must know about the emissary. This is confusing to me," Ari said.

Where to begin? It was such a long tale, and she was nearing the end of her reserves. Even with nature supporting her, the pain was becoming too much to bear.

"It would be much easier if I could share what happened with you—like you've done with me."

Ari inclined his head and reached for her with his empty hand. Without hesitation, she placed her much smaller hand inside his. *"Think of what you want to share. The clearer the image you gather, the better the picture I will receive in return."*

Nava brought her mind to their escape from the castle. To Devon opening the portal both times. To the Dark Fae approaching her. That he knew what she was and hurt her because of it.

She didn't want to remember that night or how afraid she'd been when she exited the portal.

Ari blinked those strange, beautiful eyes before glancing at Arkimedes. He could see the image of the man in shadows from her memories, and no doubt he was comparing his likeness to her soulmate. *"He looks like our protector—but is not."*

Undoubtedly, he could sense the fear that had gripped her then as well. It felt so long ago now. Such a silly thing to fear. "I know that."

"He wouldn't hurt you."

"What is he saying?" Arkimedes asked, peering at them with a frown.

"Open your mind. It will make communicating much easier." She repeated the words Ari had just whispered in her mind and pressed her cheek against the rough texture of his chest. "He saw my memories and what the emissary looks like."

"He isn't my twin brother, which is what I suspected him to be. But he was a full fae, unlike me," Arkimedes said. "The Vulcan showed us those scriptures from the earliest days of Caztian. About how the gods and the founders struck a deal of sacrifice. It could be that this emissary is my blood but from long ago. He certainly looked ancient."

"The Vulcan?" Ari brought his hand to Nava's arm, poking at the healed scar in the shape of a hand. *"Who used the god's artifact?"* Ari's alarm rang clear in his intonation, and the bees surrounding them buzzed into the air all at once. He studied Nava's body as if she might grow a second head at any moment. Then he did the same to Arkimedes.

"Devon did, and he isn't doing well," she said, wheezing a little. The air had turned so cold, like on a winter evening. "I healed him before we left. Perhaps he will be fine?"

Ari remained quiet. The wood covering his body creaked as he shook his head. Then his gaze swept to the tops of the trees above them, following the wind that moved them to and fro. *"No mortal magic can truly heal the poison that comes from a god's artifact. Yet I cannot understand why we ought to heal him. I thought he was our enemy?"*

She'd thought so too, and if Ari had asked her that same question half a year ago, her answer would have been very different. Now the man was not only Arkimedes's brother but also her friend. And after all that Ark had lost, it would break him to lose Devon as well.

"We shall go inside. It's not safe for you to be out here." Ari paused in front of

the largest tree Nava had seen in this kingdom. Mushrooms and ferns grew aplenty, sprouting from the crevices in its bark and from in between the rocks at its base.

The massive roots of the ancient tree moved aside like curtains, revealing an entrance to a deep cavern. Giant fireflies hovered before her face, at least as large as her palm. The gentle but uneven flutter of their wings matched her erratic heartbeats.

A cackle of laughter cut through her sluggish thoughts as the brightly lit shapes snatched her hair, pulling it gently and exposing her ears to the bite of the chill night.

Wait. Had she completely lost her mind? Nava blinked raindrops from her lashes and focused on one of the fireflies as it tugged at the bloody bandage around her ribs. It had long, black, human-like arms and even tinier hands. Its elongated face had large, slanted eyes that shone with eagerness.

"Be careful with the pixies." Arkimedes brushed away the one on her stomach, his voice deepening with his annoyance.

The pixie flew off, screeching in offense, then promptly tried to bat at Arkimedes's wings. It quickly changed its mind as the shapes of his aura appeared by his shoulder.

"Your soulmate is right. They are the worst nuisance. They eat the nectar in my hive and torment the bees." Ari sounded unlike himself as he swatted at a few pixies darting around them. Their golden glow left shimmering trails behind them when they flew to the ground after his wooden palm caught them.

They couldn't be that bad. Right? They were tiny. Nava wanted to laugh, but she couldn't seem to muster the energy. She hadn't been that cold until now. Perhaps Ari had been keeping her warm with magic, and their conversation had been keeping her awake.

Now her eyes were drooping, and it was a task to keep them open. Nava couldn't force another word to her lips. Sleep was pulling her under.

"Bee?" Arkimedes's palm pressed to her forehead, wet with sweat and rain.

"Mmm..." A clattering sound echoed around her. Wait. Were those her teeth?

"She needs to be out of this rain," Arkimedes muttered. "Now."

If Aristaeus answered, she didn't hear it. She floated in and out of a drowsy state as they moved swiftly into the cave. The roots shut behind them, leaving them in complete darkness.

Ari's aura illuminated the wide entrance. Huge crystals jutted from the ground and ceiling and began to glow with an orange light as he passed them.

It smelled of dirt and minerals down here, and fresh energy soared through her. Whatever this place was...the magic clinging to every speck of dirt around them helped dull her pain just enough.

She slept.

21
NAVA

Nava filtered in and out of a dreamless slumber for hours, perhaps even days. Who knew how to tell time inside a cave?

The first thing she noticed when she woke up was that her body was swinging in the air. Then pain ricocheted through her from the cut in her abdomen. She groaned.

Her agony meant she wasn't dead, and that was something to be grateful for.

"Ark?" Her mouth felt drier than ever before. Hadn't Arkimedes brought her water at some point? Or perhaps she had dreamed, after all.

When no answer came, Nava slowly sat up, swallowing the bile that rose in her throat as she shifted her body across the woven surface. Where was she? Ah. Inside a hammock of sorts, strung up in between two tall gem pillars—and far too high for someone like her to sleep in.

Gods, she hated heights.

"Ari?" she called into the nothingness but received no answer again. Worry prickled her mind as she struggled to the edge of the hammock. It was only five feet high at most, but the ground was spinning slightly, and she had to take a few deep breaths before she managed to climb down.

At least she'd regained enough strength to use some of her magic. Around her, magical crystals gently illuminated the cave. Their energy hummed like a heartbeat, gentle and soothing.

Ari's home was beautiful in a raw sort of way. Dozens of trees dotted the place, many still seedlings, judging by their size. It was like the forest above-ground but on a much smaller scale. How could a tree live here without daylight? She touched the bark, and it trembled under her fingertips.

She withdrew her hand with a gasp. Before her very eyes, the tree trunk grew a new branch in response to her touch, purple flowers and deep green leaves sprouting from it in an instant.

"The crystals mimic the sunlight and give life to the trees." Ari's voice in her mind made her jump, and a scream tore past her chapped lips, echoing off the vast ceiling.

She pressed her hand to her heart, taking deep gulps of air as she met his dark gaze. He was hunched over next to a crystal, his wood still charred from their fight with the Zorren. He tilted his head, probably puzzled by her human reactions.

Could she surprise him like that? Or would he feel her approaching?

"These are my sun stones." He pointed at the crystal by his side, choosing not to comment on her appearance or ask whether she felt better. He had never been one to waste time with small talk. *"All Beekeepers possess a different gift that gives life. Much like you can heal, I can create these."*

"Where do you sleep?" Nava turned around to inspect the place, noticing the hidden stones tucked in between trees, rocks, and even growing from the ceiling. This was not what she'd expected his cave to be like. The trees and the crystals divided it into discrete areas and made it feel like an actual home.

"I rest amongst the trees," he said, pointing up to the very top of the cavern, where a hammock was strung from one side to the other.

Nava limped toward him, her bare feet cushioned by moss. Where were her boots? "How long have I been out?"

"A couple of days," Ari said. *"Your mate is out hunting."*

"Isn't it dangerous for him to be out there alone?"

"It was dangerous for him to be here with me," Ari snarled, a rumbling sound rising from his chest. *"He kept pacing around my cave, worrying about you, even though you are healing. Then he worried about his human friend, who burned the forest back on the island. I had to send him out for both our sakes."*

She battled a smile. Ari was right, and he didn't need to forgive Devon for the damage he'd done to the people of the Northern Village or to the forest when he'd brought his army there.

Now that Aristaeus mentioned Devon, it left her wondering, though. Was he all right? Would the healing she'd bestowed upon him keep him well for long enough until they returned? She could only hope so.

Nava stretched slowly. Her body ached everywhere, even in places she didn't know existed. "Where did you find the hammocks?"

"I made them for myself and Illaris when we first discovered this place." His smile

displayed many sharp teeth that would make a more reasonable being run away.

But Nava had never claimed to be such a thing. Instead, all she could focus on was the sadness in the Beekeeper's gaze.

Ari picked at a charred layer of bark on his torso and ripped it away, revealing honey-like dew below.

"Ari!" Nava's scream bounced off the tall rock walls. But he remained unbothered, bending down to the nearest tree trunk and digging his iron claws deep into the pulp. Then he ripped off a long sheet of bark and stuck it to his newly opened wound, patching himself up like a patchwork quilt.

"I can't believe you just did that." Her stomach revolted at the images that kept repeating in her mind. Was that what Ari looked like in reality? A pale body covered in goop on which he stuck layers of bark, wax, moss, and everything else the forest offered?

"The layers protect me against the weather and fires, and it helps with camouflage," he said, reading her thoughts.

"You could have told me..."

"Why?" He blinked in confusion. *"I can't teach you how to do this on your frail body. You are one of us—and yet you are still human. A new creation I have never seen."* His body glowed in the same shade as the crystals, and his fresh layer of skin merged with the other parts, bit by bit, until it blended in seamlessly.

Well. He probably had a point. "You said these hammocks belonged to you and Illaris. Did you make this place together?"

"Yes, we built it decades ago. When the forests called us here for the first time. We suspected the Zorren would try to break into the land. We didn't find any demons then, but we found an underwater pool. It has magical properties that make it impossible for the demons to bridge in this area and a perfect home for the Beekeepers."

Nava straightened at the revelation. "You suspected the Zorren would come into this land decades ago?"

Ari tilted his head forward in acknowledgment, and Nava's heart raced while her tired mind grasped at the fickle details floating inside her head. Something was missing. "Could that have been thirty years ago? When Arkimedes was born?"

"Perhaps...perhaps not... Time works differently for me. I don't track it like you humans do."

Maybe she shouldn't ask all these questions. Not when it might bring back painful memories for Ari. If Illaris had been as important to Ari as he was to her, then she could understand how devastating it would have felt to lose him.

She glanced at the crystals, which were flickering like candlelight. "Can I have a small sun crystal? I would like to keep it with me when I return to town," she said, and he went still for a time, as if processing her words. Maybe he couldn't understand that she would like to maintain the connection to him and nature, even when they weren't together. "I'm sorry that you lost Illaris, Ari."

"There is no real life without death." Ari placed one hand on Nava's shoulder, squeezing gently. *"The immortals crave its finality—obsess over it. Even the trees die eventually, so a new one can thrive in its place."*

"Still..." Tears pricked at her eyes. Why was she about to cry when she hadn't even met the other Beekeeper? All she'd seen of him was his quickly decomposing body—and how pained Ari had been.

"Don't think it a coincidence. You crossed the edge of the Grey Forest and were called to me just as the Zorren took Illaris's life. I'm happy you are my companion. There is no need to be sad. The pain of abandoning these bodies we occupy is fleeting. I will meet Illaris again."

Was that true? Would she meet them once she died? Or was she different because she was human? If she went to the Beekeepers' realm, what happened to Ark's soul? Would they be separated?

The question brought such intense pain that it took her breath away.

"Arkimedes told me his magic came to him when he was five," she said. Hopefully, the change of subject would ease her panic. "I'm five years younger than him. Do you think the gods chose me to become a Beekeeper because I'm his soulmate? Or..."

"Yes?" Aristaeus narrowed his eyes as he tried to make sense of her questions.

"Was I always destined to become a Beekeeper and that's why Arkimedes is my soulmate?"

"The gods don't choose soulmates at random." Ari inspected Nava's changing emotions. *"Does the order matter?"*

Sometimes it was easy to forget that Ari's emotions worked differently than hers. "I—I guess I'd be disappointed if they chose me to be who I am because of who my mate is and not because of *me*." She leaned against a tree for support and lowered herself onto the ground.

His movements were slow as he took a seat next to her. *"I will not claim to understand the emotions you feel right now. The gods picked you to be his—just as much as they chose him to be yours. You're from the same soul, equal and perfect for this task."*

For a while, they sat in quiet companionship as his words settled inside her. He was right, of course. It didn't matter why or how, for she wouldn't change a thing. Even if, at first, she hadn't wanted a soulmate or a kingdom to rule. And definitely not the huge responsibility of defeating an immortal.

A year ago, all she'd longed for was to be free to choose her future. But that was precisely what she was doing now. She loved Arkimedes and fought for him. She could have stayed in a home in this kingdom, lived a quiet life alongside her brother, and allowed Ark to continue his royal life on his own without remembering her.

Having a soulmate wasn't what defined her choices—it only brought clarity to what she really wanted. Their love was a partnership. The gods had woven them together, but nobody was forcing them to remain committed to each other.

It was them clinging to each other that would shape the future of this kingdom. And she was ready to fight for the people who lived here, too.

"Wait, did you say there's an underground pool here?" she asked, perking up. She desperately needed to be out of these bloody clothes.

"Aristaeus told you about the pool?" Arkimedes's voice floated toward her, and he stepped around a crystal a mere moment later, carrying two dead rabbits over his shoulder. He set them aside and crouched beside them.

"Have you seen it?" He nodded, but Nava could have answered the question herself. He didn't look half as filthy as she did. Even his clothes lacked the gray tones of ash and soot. "I want a bath."

"How are you feeling?"

Like demons had tried to kill her and almost succeeded. "I've been better."

Arkimedes grabbed her hand and pulled her to her feet, guiding her away. Ari stayed, quietly watching them sidle past fruiting trees.

Nava's breath caught in her throat at the beauty that greeted her past the tall rock columns that held up the cavernous ceiling. The pool was bright turquoise and smelled strongly of minerals. Its shape extended like a winding serpent, far beyond what her eyes could see.

She'd never witnessed anything so magical before, and she'd visited many places.

A small island jutted from the center of the pool, made of white rock. On it, one lonely tree grew. Above it, a giant hole in the ceiling let in the morning sky.

Nava was undressing before she could think of a reason not to. "Do you think there are beasts under the water?"

"No." Arkimedes laughed, gaining a glare from her. "The only thing you have to worry about here is me. Now, let me see how your wound is healing."

22
NAVA

Nava hated worrying about everything and the powerlessness that took over her body whenever she did. It always began as a rolling ache in the middle of her chest that felt a lot like heartbreak.

Arkimedes handed her a piece of rabbit meat speared on a stick. The delicious smell called to her with a promise of warmth and savory goodness, but she struggled to find her appetite.

How was Devon doing back at Leela's house? Arkimedes had been fretting about it for days… Fine. She had been worried, too.

He refused to return to check on his brother if it meant leaving her there, although she doubted the emissary would come to hurt her so soon after the attack. But of course, she couldn't be certain.

Arkimedes had shared everything he'd learned from the emissary with them, and now, as they all sat around the fire in silence, the question circled her mind again and again.

How were they supposed to kill an immortal?

"There's no pattern we can use to predict when to expect the emissary next." Ark reached for a piece of dry kindling and fed it to the magical fire that raged hotter in return. "I'm concerned about both of you going out there to heal the forest. He was there recently."

The licks of the flames from their campfire were blue instead of orange, and yet they reminded her too much of the hell they'd just escaped. After what had happened in the forest, sitting by the fire should prove an impossibility. Yet here she was, soaking in its warmth on this chill autumn morning.

They had chosen a spot close to the pool to make the most of the natural light since Nava missed it so much.

"Why do you think so? Surely if he could come back that easily, he would have been here the entire time." Nava rubbed her tired eyes. Ari often said the crystals would help with her exhaustion, but healing this kind of wound took it out of her.

"We don't know that. You want to go out to the forest and bask in the sun" —Arkimedes paused his poking of the logs with his stick, sending her an all-knowing look—"but it's too dangerous."

"We can't hide here forever. You've been wanting to go to the city, and we should. If only to make sure Devon is alive."

Arkimedes opened his mouth but closed it again, clenching his jaw as he narrowed his eyes at her.

Sure, she'd played a little dirty by mentioning what he needed to hear, but there was no use in being afraid right now.

"If what I suspect is true," she continued, undeterred, "then the emissary can't come into this realm without the command of a god. He is probably on duty right now, and that's why he got called away."

"I believe you're right. Unless the emissary is on a mission for his god, he must not be allowed to come into our world. I hadn't seen him before."

Nava rubbed her chest, attempting to relieve the pressure that collected deep inside it, as if the forest was beckoning her to come and help. She'd taken so much of its energy, it was only fair to repay it, even if she was still healing. "Perhaps my need to leave the cave is because of the forest calling to me?"

She glanced at Ari, who inclined his head in confirmation. He looked so out of place in front of the campfire, with his massive tree-like legs bent at angles no human limbs could comfortably—healthily—achieve.

"The call is strong once you connect with your powers and the nature that surrounds you," he said.

Nava pulled at the bandages around her torso, which had gone brown with dried blood. No matter how much she'd washed it in the pool, the stain remained.

The gray morning light trickled over the water, bringing a gentle breeze that seeped through the thin layers of her clothes. Thank gods for Leela and the wool coat she'd insisted Nava wear. It was burnt in places, but it kept her warm.

Hopefully, her friend was all right. And she was still helping Devon heal.

"All right, let's assume the best. The forest is calling you because it needs you." Arkimedes tapped his fingers against his thighs, but his expression was strained. "Let's prepare for the worst, regardless. What are we going to do if we get there and the emissary attacks us?"

"What if we call upon Dargan?" She scratched her arm as the crawling sensation under her skin worsened. "Each time someone crosses a portal, they meet with him to pay the price. We can ask Devon to open a portal and tell the God of Shadows his emissary is attempting to break free. Perhaps he will want to get rid of the problem for us?"

"The gods have been fighting their own war for decades, dearest. They don't care enough about Caztian to intervene, not when they have bigger problems to attend to." Aristaeus looked somber.

"I heard that." Arkimedes straightened, his eyes growing wide as he stared at Ari.

"You heard Ari speak?" Nava asked. She would have smiled if the information being shared was about a happier subject.

Arkimedes nodded and placed his half-eaten meal aside, looking dazed and a little horrified. "I felt this pressure in my head and assumed more memories were coming. I haven't been pushing them away for a while now, so I let it through..."

"He let me in. At last." Ari's expression softened. *"I would assume Dargan is aware of what the emissary is doing. Even if he believes he is fooling the god."*

"How can we kill him?" Arkimedes asked.

"Only an immortal can."

"Isn't your soul immortal—couldn't *you* do it?" Nava asked.

"My soul, yes. But my body is as mortal as the tree standing in the middle of this lagoon." Ari pointed at the aforementioned tree. The morning mist covered its roots and part of the trunk. It lost its leaves long ago, although Nava could see the ribbons of life weaving around it, even at this distance.

Well, that brilliant plan lasted about two seconds.

"You could search for a god's artifact," Ari added, although they could all hear the doubt in his inflection. *"At the beginning of time, many Caztanians stole these items from the gods. They soon learned that most mortals can't wield godly weapons, so they perished, and the artifacts went missing. Some deities have sent their emissaries on a hunt to collect them. Yet some remain."*

"Why does everything have to be so difficult?" Nava groaned and stabbed the fire with the stick holding her food until its embers were dancing and sweat beaded on her temple. "Does the Society of Crows keep artifacts in the archives?" she asked, looking at Arkimedes. Because if so, she would gladly crawl back down that long tunnel of nightmares to retrieve one.

"Not in the Copper Kingdom. Perhaps in its main headquarters. But even if they do, Nava, we can't touch them without triggering an alarm. They will send the Corvus, and we can't win against the entire Society on our own."

The sunlight changed from silver to pink as morning fully embraced the forest. And they still had no clue how to move forward.

"It's rumored that the founders kept some artifacts hidden from the deities. Your father might have one inside your castle."

Arkimedes's breath caught. His eyes fixed on a spot in the distance, almost as if he could see it—feel it, even. "My father wouldn't give it to us even if he had it. He's mentioned nothing about the prophecy of our bloodline. He kidnapped me and lied about my mother's death."

"What are you saying?" Nava asked.

"I wonder why the emissary is letting demons into the kingdom to get revenge against my father?" Arkimedes's gravel voice trailed off as he reached toward the fire, opening his palm. The flames slowly suffocated, leaving behind a thin trail of smoke that dissipated into the open air.

Nava stood, dusting her pants off with more vigor than necessary. She needed to vent some of her frustrations. "You've said many times that the fires started right as you came to the kingdom. But what if they began before and that's the reason the king had you taken from our home?"

Arkimedes nodded. "When I went into his study to get the keys to free you from the bracelet, I saw a piece of art that depicted a king tossing a babe into a cloud. It looked ancient, like something that recorded history. I believe the emissary is my father's brother and that he wants to take the throne."

"And if there aren't any living members of the royal line, then the God of Shadows would release his emissary. It's a failsafe to protect the godly magic they gifted to the founders."

What Arkimedes was saying made sense. It would be a good enough reason for a mad fae to try to kill the prince as well. He needed everyone from his bloodline gone so he could be free from his ties to the god.

"Do you think they are twins?" she asked.

"Yes," he said with enough confidence that she believed it.

There was bad blood between the twins, and whatever had caused it, it had roped Aristaeus, Ark, and Nava into this mess.

"Why not ask the king himself?" Aristaeus reasoned, and his confusion was plain in the way he tilted his head to the side. *"If he possesses the artifact, then he can part with it for his own benefit."*

"I've been dreading having to go back to the castle and ask for help when he is far from an ally. He's all I have left of my family, but he wants to hurt Nava." Arkimedes shook his head and rose from the ground, shrugging on his coat, and offered Nava his hand. It was probably time to go and heal the forest. But then he carried on speaking, avoiding everyone's gazes. "I remember why I stayed away from here and why I didn't ask Nava to return with me. My father can't be trusted. I was gone for thirty years, and he didn't miss me. It seems odd that he is suddenly interested in being my father."

True.

"It's the nature of the fae to be cunning," Aristaeus agreed with a quiver in his voice that hadn't been there before. *"But your power has connected with the land. You are one with it, like the king. If I can sense the shift, so can he. I don't believe that putting you in danger benefits him."*

"Sure," Arkimedes agreed. He sounded stern. "A few days ago, I would have marched right in there and asked him if he has an artifact."

"So why the change of heart?" Nava asked.

"After finding out the emissary is after him, it gave me pause. What if he always wanted me to come back to deal with his brother? Just because he shouldn't hurt me doesn't mean he won't hurt you. He can keep you away from me and make me do things I don't want to—just to keep you safe."

Her mouth felt dry all of a sudden, and she fought the urge to wrap her arms around herself. He was right. They should try to defeat the emissary by themselves before attempting to forge an alliance with the king.

Ari shook his head, causing pieces of moss and bark to fly off him. *"If you're the heir, then she is the heiress. I'm not a human, nor a fae, but I know that much."*

"The king doesn't want a human queen, Ari, and neither do the citizens. Not since Ark's mother betrayed them."

Nava had tried not to think too hard about the spirit that had haunted her at the safe house, but now, the memories she'd shared that afternoon clicked into place, bringing with them a sudden burst of clarity.

The queen's final thought before her death had been that the one she'd loved the most of all had killed her. She'd told the man who'd tied her to a burning tree that she loved him, and yet he hadn't even flinched.

Nava had asked Arkimedes before, and he'd been adamant that his father hadn't been the culprit. "What if it was the emissary who killed her?"

Arkimedes froze and met her eyes. "My mother?"

"Yes. What if she was the first one to die in his quest for revenge?"

23

ORION

Orion followed Nava as she wove through the skeletal trees that remained after the fire. She glowed beneath the ash that streaked her skin, and the bees that always accompanied her seemed unfazed by the steady patter of rain. He'd grown used to the sight of them after they'd been in peril for so long, but that didn't ease his anxiety.

Mist billowed out of his lips as he exhaled. They were definitely heading into fall now, and with it came much shorter, colder days and the changing leaves of a new season.

"Stay near me," he said and turned to check on Aristaeus, who was too far away for his comfort. He had been using his Beekeeper magic to bring back some life to a large tree specimen. It had taken him an entire hour thus far, and he had still not moved away.

"It's cold out here." Nava blew some warm air into her hands and rubbed them together.

"Our coats have seen better days. It doesn't help." He poked at a hole in the fabric left behind by the fire and peered up at the husks of the trees. There was little left to shelter them from the weather, and lightning crawled across the dark, stormy sky, followed by loud thunder.

The weather was getting worse, and they were far from town.

Now that they'd left the sacred ground Aristaeus had built his home on, Orion couldn't wait to get back to Leela's house. He needed to make sure Devon wasn't dying. He'd barely slept during the past couple of nights, sick with worry.

Even though Aristaeus's home had offered them a semblance of safety away from his father's guards, the Crows, and the Zorren, they couldn't stay here another day.

"We must return to the city before nightfall and strategize about how to obtain the artifact. That's one thing we can't find in the forest."

Nava sniffed and shuffled close to him, seeking shelter under his wing. She cast a knowing look at him. "Do you know where we can start?" At least she didn't mention Devon again.

"No."

"Seriously, that's all you're going to say?" She pursed her lips. They had turned a light shade of mauve from the cold. Orion had to get her out of there, even if she needed to heal the trees. They'd endured hours of relentless rain with no end in sight, and he was done.

"While I was working for the Society, they used to hunt for smugglers around the ports. People frequently come here to poach rare animals and sell them to other kingdoms. Sometimes they trade in magical weapons." Orion wrapped an arm around Nava's slim shoulders and extended his wing to shelter her further.

"Like a god's artifact?"

"It's unlikely, but they might tell us where we can find one, for a price."

"So… our plan is to find a smuggler in the ports and hope that they'll give us the information we need?" She huffed a laugh.

"I know how it sounds." His face grew warm. "And no. They won't exactly give it to us willingly…"

That sobered her up. She blinked rapidly to banish the raindrops that had accumulated on her lashes. "It's just me and you, Ark. How are we going to fight anyone?"

"And Devon, too. If he is well." A heavy knot formed in his throat, and it took everything he had not to grab her and rush back to his brother. "We can offer them money, and if—when—that fails, then…" He didn't need to say the words.

Nava nodded, and her face set into a resolute expression that showed him how fucking brave she was.

Fighting pirates was less risky than going into the castle to take part in whatever game his father was playing. He couldn't take the chance. Not when Nava's and Aristaeus's safety was at stake.

He studied the surrounding area, his heart drumming in his throat. His fingertips prickled as his power awakened. What if the emissary heard them discuss their plan? Was there a shadow lurking nearby? A portal?

Nava's hand wrapped around his wrist, squeezing it gently. "We're safe. The forest and the bees would alert us otherwise."

He glanced down at her and the small smile that pulled at the corners of her pillowy lips. Then she pointedly glanced at her feet, where moss and grass were sprouting from beneath the ash.

The demons had taken life, and the Beekeepers had brought it back. This power was how Aristaeus had disposed of the Zorren weeks ago when he'd turned one of their bodies into a tree.

Orion had never noticed Nava doing anything like this on Grey Island when she'd called upon her power, but he had seen the signs of her magic crawling all over the emissary's arm.

She was sprouting life from death.

"I haven't been able to replicate this—this spell, or whatever you'd call this. I did it to him after he attacked me when I crossed the portal. While in the cave, I could only grow lichen over the rock." She stomped her feet over her newly made grass and smiled so wide he almost forgot all about the horrible destruction around them.

Meanwhile, Aristaeus seemed to have finally given up on the dead tree and was heading over to them. *"The life you give the forest will return to us when the Zorren strike again."* Aristaeus's eyes softened as he took in Nava's work, which continued to flourish a few feet away, returning color to the ashen tree trunks nearby. *"Mastering it is the quickest way to kill the demons. Practice using it even when you are away."*

Another peal of thunder rang through the air before the skies opened up and rain pelted them so hard it became difficult to see.

"I'm taking Nava to the city. We need to find the artifact. We'll be back when we have something." The rain rolled off Orion's feathers as he shielded Nava's shivering body from the worst of it. Still, flying in this tempest would be tricky.

"The emissary is on borrowed time for this world. We have time," Aristaeus said in their minds. The bees, which had been flying around them, rushed to hide in the hive on his head, disappearing under its protective cover. *"No demon can cross into my home. I shall wait there until I sense you've returned."*

Nava stepped out from under Orion's wing and wrapped Aristaeus in a hug that looked far from comfortable. Aristaeus seemed surprised but awkwardly patted her shoulder until she was ready to let go.

"I hope it doesn't take me so long to see you again," she said.

"Let us hope that when we meet, it's not because of another attack on this forest. Not even Beekeepers can bring back life once it's left for good."

Orion and Nava arrived at Leela's house at nightfall, chilled to the bone by the cold front that had descended onto the city. It was far too early in the year to be that freezing.

The silver lining on flying through a storm was that none of the guards or the Crows would bother to keep an eye out for them.

The wooden awning that covered Leela's front door sheltered them from the downpour as Orion knocked on the glass. As soon as he could, he shoved both his hands inside his wet pockets.

The hinges screeched as Leela's red hair popped out to greet them, and a sudden wind slammed the door against the wall. "Your Highness!" she gasped and reached for Nava's wrist, dragging her into the house. "You can't be outside in this storm!"

The inside was much warmer than the cave had been and smelled of sweet tea and pigments used to dye fabric. He turned toward the closed door and placed a hand over it, whispering a warding spell that locked into place.

When he turned, Nava was standing beside Leela, speaking in hushed tones as her friend fretted over her wet appearance.

"Is Devon upstairs?" Orion asked, already ascending the narrow staircase, two steps at a time.

"He's fine, sir, just warming up by the fire. We've had quite the storm today."

Orion needed to see him with his own eyes, to hear his voice... To make sure his brother was actually alive and doing well. They'd left in such a rush, and Nava's healing had only just set in—there had been no way to tell how long it would last.

They'd been gone for far too long.

"You're alive." Devon's voice broke over the sound of a hissing teapot by the fire. He uncrossed one long leg, clad in elegant, wine-colored pants, and stood from the chair. It seemed Leela had found him a new set of clothes.

"I should be the one saying that," Orion said, fighting a smile.

Behind him, the stairs creaked under Nava's feet. She entered the room moments later, wringing out her long hair, and a mixture of rain, ash, and dirt dripped onto the wooden floor. "Devon," she greeted. "I trust you're feeling better?"

"Perfect, as always. You two, however, look like drowned rats and are making a mess of this wonderful place." He stretched like a cat, extending both arms over his head. "I take it you encountered demons?"

"And the emissary." Orion helped Nava remove her coat. It was so heavy with rain it nearly swallowed her whole. He draped it over the balustrade and peeked over it to see where Leela had gone.

A distant rustle of fabric emerged from the seamstress's shop. She was probably looking for dry clothes.

Devon was right. Perhaps they should have cleaned up and changed downstairs to avoid getting the floor dirty. They had inconvenienced Leela enough.

As if called by his thoughts, she bustled up the stairs not long after, piles of clothing stuffed between her slim arms. She dropped the lot on one of the empty chairs.

"I know I shouldn't interrupt." Leela patted her forehead with her arm, drying a thin layer of perspiration that clung to her skin. "You three are always talking about such pressing matters… But it's so cold outside, and I don't want you—nor Miss Nava—to get ill. I brought everything I could find that might fit you, sir. My partner doesn't sew for males as often as she would like."

"These will be fine." Nava joined them and began rifling through the pile with a smile. "I'll be glad to be out of these clothes, even if I have to wear a potato sack."

"Who hurt you, miss?" Leela's fingers reached out to touch the scars left behind by the demon's claws. The wet, white shirt stuck to Nava's ribs, revealing the darker color of her skin and the makeshift bandage Orion had created beneath.

"The Zorren," Nava said in a soothing tone he remembered her using with her little brother. It didn't work with Leela, whose face twisted with fear. "I'm fine. I'm desperate to change and toss these clothes. They smell like smoke no matter how much I wash them."

Orion wanted to see the back of them as well. They only reminded him how close she'd been to dying—an inch more and she wouldn't be here. They'd almost lost, and all before they'd even given that bastard emissary a good fight.

Leela took a few steps away, her eyes still wide. "I will run you two a bath. I got some new oils from the market a couple of days ago that will help with healing."

She was out of their sight faster than Orion thought anyone could move with the layers of her dress. No matter how all this ended, Leela deserved some reward for helping them without asking hard questions he wouldn't be able to answer.

When he turned to Devon, his eyes were trailing the curves of Nava's body with far too much interest. Her breasts were now visible under the layers of her sheer, wet shirt.

Orion stepped in front of Devon's line of vision and glared down at him.

Nava covered her torso with the item of clothing she was holding, but it did little to help matters—it was the type of frilly thing he'd rather Devon *not* see in the context of wherever his mind had clearly just ventured.

"I'm going downstairs to get clean," Nava announced, picked up a few things from where Leela had dropped them, and followed her friend to their room below.

"I wasn't looking..." Devon said, and his face turned bright red as he glanced away toward the fireplace. He took a quick breath before reaching for the tea. "Not like *that*. I just realized why it took you so long to get back here."

Rubbish. But Orion wasn't about to get into this fight, even if his blood was rushing wildly within him. "The demons hurt her, so we stayed until she was out of danger and could fight if we encountered trouble in the city."

"And what happened to the second Beekeeper—Arisfaeus or whatever?"

"He is fine." Arkimedes rifled through the clothing, trying to find something large enough to fit him. The awkward silence extended. "I see you're feeling better."

Devon shrugged, his face still hollow. The shadows under his eyes were more pronounced in the flickering light of the fireplace. "Better, but not great. The potion and whatever Nava did helped. I improved within a day." He refilled his mug and sat down in the chair. "Leela went and bought more healing potions today since I ran out and my energy has been dwindling."

"It wasn't the potion that helped you, Devon, it was Nava's magic." Orion shrugged off his shirt and reached for a black one. It was at least a size too small, with ridiculous billowing sleeves.

Devon settled against the chair's backrest. "I thought I'd dreamed that. Her healing me."

"No. The other Beekeeper confirmed she has the gift of healing—which is why she's walking around right now instead of fighting an infection back in the forest." Orion sniffed at the clothes. A mild scent of mildew and dust lingered on the fabric, but it was dry, and that was an improvement.

To his surprise, Devon didn't comment at all about Nava's powers. Instead, he sat quietly for a while, observing the hissing pot hanging over the fire. "What happened with the emissary?"

Orion told Devon all that he could, leaving out only the details about Aristaeus's cave and the magical pool inside it. He hooked his fingers under the waistband of his trousers as he spoke but stopped when he thought better of it. While he had no qualms about undressing in front of his brother, he was not about to get caught in the nude by Leela.

"Let me get this straight. You want us to find some pirates and make a trade for an artifact? Have you lost your mind? They kill for those." Devon laughed, although the sound lacked emotion.

"I'm well aware. But it's either that or going to my father and asking him if he has an artifact we can use. We have better odds with pirates than with escaping my father a second time."

"I'm not insinuating we should go back to the castle."

Orion's shoes squeaked as he made his way toward the couch. "If it were up to me, we'd leave this place and never look back."

"Isn't it interesting how the mind works? Last month you were moping about it, and now here you are—making strides to become the old you. I bet Nava's happy."

Devon was right, much to his chagrin. Orion had groveled about the man he'd been without his memories. But as appalling as his actions had been before, things had changed. His father had attempted to hurt Nava, and nothing else mattered as much as she did.

"Let's not pretend you care how happy I make her and move on to what we need to do next." Orion pushed the words past stiff lips. Who could blame him for wanting to punch Devon's shit-eating grin off his face? Especially when he'd caught him gawking at his soulmate mere moments ago.

"It's been a while since we've tracked illegal trades in the ports." Devon stared past Orion's shoulder, out of the large window above the dining table. Perhaps he was remembering all the times the Society of Crows had sent them to fight pirates. "Are you expecting us to recognize some of the old crews from the Iron Kingdom? I'm confident they aren't running the black markets anymore."

"The life of those who live at sea is fleeting. We both know that." Orion sighed, rubbing the exhaustion from his eyes. Had he secretly been hoping for that? Finding a familiar face would save them time from sorting out the pirates from the regular sea merchants, but he wasn't that naïve. "I'm just grasping at straws, really."

"Even if we stumble over someone we know from the past, I doubt they'd be happy to see us, let alone work with us. They will never forget the Reaper."

Orion let his head fall back, suppressing a groan. "I know they'll remember me. Perhaps that'll give them an incentive to offer what we need, though."

"So, you want to go on the offense from the very beginning?"

"Do you have any better ideas, Devon? I'm all ears."

"Any suggestion is better than that. Nava just got hurt. I'm slowly dying, and you look like shit. No offense."

"Go on."

"What if we let *her* deal with them?"

Orion stiffened and frowned at his brother. "You want Nava to speak to the pirates? She's powerful, but I want her as far away from them as humanly possible."

"I know it sounds ridiculous, but hear me out. She has that newness about her that would allow her to get close enough to ask the questions we need to answer." Devon took a sip of his tea, placed the cup on the side table, and leaned against his chair. "We can count on them underestimating her. We've all made that mistake."

"So, your idea is, we go to the ports, track a ship, and send her in there to ask questions?"

No one parted with a god's artifact without bloodshed, and Orion sincerely doubted the bag of gold he carried inside his pocket would be enough to buy them one.

"We go to the bar they frequent at night. Nava heads in, disguised as a deserter, and lets it slip that she has something to trade for a ride out of this place."

"That sounds vaguely familiar..." They had done that same stint several times in the Iron Kingdom.

"And it always works. A pirate overhears that she has money, and it gets her a one-to-one meeting with the captain—or second-in-command."

"Fuck, I don't know if I can stand back and watch her go in there on her own."

"She won't be by herself. We'll be in the tavern, also in disguise. There will be blood eventually, and I doubt they'll even have what we're looking for, but that's our best option."

Orion hated to agree, but the odds of them getting closer were better if the pirates didn't see either of them. "Does Leela have anything stronger than tea in this place?"

"She offered me some sort of fae honey wine. I passed, of course. I wouldn't have benefited from being completely out of it for a day." He tapped his bottom lip with a long finger. "I always wondered, does the wine affect you like a human, or are you immune because you're also a fae?"

"You've asked me this at least a dozen times."

"I keep forgetting. So, what happens if you drink it, would you get all... loose and relaxed?"

He narrowed his eyes at Devon and stood, moving to the kitchen to search for that wine. "We will head to the port tomorrow and see if there are any merchants around."

"Merchants? What a boring way to describe them."

True. But Orion didn't want Leela to overhear any more than she probably already had. There was some movement downstairs, faint noises traveling to his ears. He opened a cupboard and discovered a large bottle full of amber liquid. Honey wine. If Nava knew what he was about to drink, it would horrify her. He poured himself a glass and downed half in one gulp before walking to the living area.

Leela greeted him with a nervous wave, peering at the glass in his hand. "I see you've found something with a bit more punch to it. It's the best in the kingdom."

"It's the best I've had," he agreed and returned her tentative smile.

"So, what's the answer to my previous question, brother? Is it just liquor, or are you drinking it to get heated with your soulmate?"

"Mr. Black!" Leela exclaimed.

Orion maintained his flat expression and raised his glass in Devon's general direction. "Be ready first thing in the morning or we will leave without you." And he made for the stairs, plucking a pair of pants from the pile on his way.

24
NAVA

Pirates, fae, and sorcery—those three words would never have crossed Nava's mind a year ago. Alas, this was what her life had become. She pulled the metal stamp from the black wax, revealing an uneven seal stuck to the parchment.

"Everything will be fine. I just have to play the part," she repeated to herself for the hundredth time. Maybe this time she would believe it.

Arkimedes's voice carried through the floorboards as he called to her from downstairs. He'd been on edge ever since they'd woken up before sunrise and gone over the details of their plan. A plan that sounded completely ridiculous, given how awkward she became when she was nervous.

Even Arkimedes hadn't seemed convinced it was a good idea, so why should she be? It wouldn't surprise her if he changed his mind and demanded that she stay behind while he took care of the rest with Devon.

Nava handed the letter to Leela, who'd been waiting by the bedroom door. "Are you sure it's not too much trouble to take this to the post?"

"Not at all. It's near the house, and I'm glad to help."

When they arrived the night before, the first thing on her mind had been Cameron. What would happen to him if things went awry and disaster struck? She could have lost her life in the fight with the Zorren and he would never have known.

Nava had no home to return to on Grey Island, even if they succeeded—because she'd freed their prisoner and that would never be forgiven.

So she poured the truth about everything that had happened onto pages.

When her parents died, she'd promised Cameron the truth. Her little brother deserved that much, and the situation was dangerous enough now that, if she died, she wanted him to know what had happened. In the end, Cameron would never forgive her if she'd kept it all from him.

Leela tightened the strings of her tunic around her neck. It was the same color as Nava's, a deep shade of green that brought out the blue hue of her friend's eyes.

Nava reached inside her coat pocket and grabbed the sun stone. Its warmth seeped through her cold, clammy fingers, lending her some strength to move forward. At least she had this small piece of Ari coming with her.

Devon and Arkimedes were waiting for her outside the shop. Both leaned against the wall, talking in hushed voices as they watched the fae pass up and down the busy street. Arkimedes's eyes settled on her as she exited the building, and Nava's heart jolted, butterflies flying in her stomach as she took in his handsome features. The chill of the morning did nothing to cool off the heat washing through her body.

"You've got everything you need?" he asked, and the intensity behind his eyes told her he was having the same reaction to her.

She nodded. The gentle hum of the sun stone inside her pocket comforted her, even in this dreary weather.

"You won't return?" Leela asked, locking the door of her shop behind her.

"Not tonight," Arkimedes answered. He offered Nava the crook of his elbow. "It's best if we don't stay with you for long stretches of time. We have imposed for long enough."

"It's not a problem, Your Highness. Please come back if you need a place to stay." Leela bowed, clearly missing Arkimedes's sharp exhale as he attempted to stop her but wasn't quite fast enough. "I will deliver the letter, miss. Good luck with what you're doing tonight."

"What letter?" he whispered to her as strolled down the wide street.

"I wrote to Cameron. To let him know about what's happening here…"

"Cameron?" Arkimedes's brow arched, and he brought his face closer to hers, so Devon couldn't catch what he said next. "You think it's safe for him to know you're here? What if he comes and we're in the middle of fighting the demons?"

"Well, I don't know," she mumbled and focused on their surroundings instead of Arkimedes. Of course, she didn't want her little brother to come to this kingdom when they were under attack. But what else could she do when she didn't know what would happen to her next?

If she didn't do this, what would become of him? While Violet and Gavin had taken him along on their journey, it was too much pressure to expect their friends to care for a teenager indefinitely.

Never mind that he was mature beyond his years—he was *her* family and responsibility.

"I hope he won't receive the letter too quickly, and we'll have some time to deal with this." She gestured around them. The town was alive with flower carts on the sidewalks, and large carriages pulled up and down the streets by orrus. She'd only ever seen these beasts in the Copper Kingdom, a strange blend between a buffalo and a horse.

Arkimedes nodded. "Even if the worst comes to pass, he won't be left penniless, Nava."

"Our old property in Willowbrook is still there, but I don't think he'll live there."

"When I stayed at the castle, I discovered that I inherited a large estate from my mother, and I also have some gold stowed away from my time with the Crows. It'll be tricky to access right now—but not impossible."

Nava nodded, tightening her fists as a rush of adrenaline surged through her. Overwhelm didn't begin to cover how she felt at the thought of leaving Cameron with all that, without him understanding why or how to manage it.

She cleared her throat and focused on the odd behavior the citizens were displaying instead. Why were they all dressed in white and yellow?

"I don't remember exactly where Cameron is and why he's there," Arkimedes admitted, scratching his forehead with his free hand.

Had he noticed the change yet? Or perhaps this wasn't a change at all, but a regular occurrence. Nava hadn't been in the city long enough to fully understand its customs.

"He's with Gavin and Violet on Pearl Island. Violet needed to go there to research something about how to prevent the drafts of children for the armies—I think." Her friend hadn't been exactly specific about her aims, and Nava hadn't asked too many questions. "Cameron wanted to go so badly and see the largest library in Caztian. We were in Willowbrook for so long. I didn't want to force him to stay behind with me—but I also couldn't just leave Aristaeus."

"He's always wanted to be a librarian," Arkimedes said, his eyes turning glassy, right before he brought his hand to his head with a grunt. Another headache, perhaps? "I don't know how long it will take for the letter to reach him, Nava. I understand why you want them to know, but it's risky. It could be intercepted."

She knew that, and still, she didn't regret sending it. "We can't go up against the Zorren and not tell Cameron he might lose the only family he has left. I also needed to tell Gavin and Violet that I released Devon, so they know not to return with my little brother, just in case Roman gets any ideas. Devon hurt all of us, and not everyone is ready to forgive."

"I heard that," Devon said from behind them.

"It's not untrue." Nava huffed. A part of her would forever be unhappy at having released him—not continuing to hate him like she should.

But she now also understood the other side of the story. How desperate Devon had been to locate Arkimedes at any cost. How angry and betrayed he'd felt when he discovered Ark alive and well, hiding in the forest.

She couldn't forgive him for what he'd done or how many people he'd hurt... but she *understood* him. And now she had to explain her reasons to Cameron and her friends, just in case the emissary won.

"I didn't know the kitten had a baby brother. What a revelation."

Arkimedes glanced over his shoulder and shot Devon a sharp look that would quieten almost everyone. "Don't say another word."

"You two need to lighten up and stop treating me like I'm the villain. I'm heading into a pirate lair with you because I want to help." Devon's face lacked any of his usual mischief. He was serious now. His black eyes met hers, and he placed his hand over his heart. "I would never betray your brother's existence to the Crows if that's what you're concerned about."

Strangely enough, Nava wasn't. Not now that he was aware of what the Society had done to his family. "Devon, to earn our trust, you've got to work for it. Not so long ago, you went against our request and asked the Vulcan the wrong question."

Devon's cheeks flushed as he averted his eyes and shoved both hands inside his wine-colored coat. It matched the striped pants he was wearing.

Leela had been fussing over all of their clothes for the better part of the morning. Little did she know they would have to change into less elegant attires soon enough.

Arkimedes placed a large gloved hand over hers. "Have you considered what might happen if Cameron, Gavin, and Violet come here before we defeat the emissary?"

Nava chewed her bottom lip. Her insecurities grabbed her in a chokehold. "Then we will ensure his safety."

If only she'd mastered her long-distance transfer before all of this. She could have simply visited Pearl Island and spoken to them there. But she'd just begun to hone her skills, and it was impossible for her to travel to the forest in one trip, let alone to an island far across the world.

"We'll work it out," Arkimedes said. "It would be nice to see them again."

"Even Violet?" she teased with a grin that widened as his expression sobered.

"No, just Cameron and Gavin. Violet can stay there for all I care."

They crossed a large bridge made of worn stone. Aged copper railings lined the sides, painted in green and white shades that matched the turquoise water in the canal below. A trading vessel was crossing beneath it right now, sporting impressive gray sails.

The seagulls squawked in the skies, circling the bridge and flying too close to their heads for comfort in their search for food. This part of the city differed from all the other areas Nava had visited. The road led them to an open plaza with the biggest fountain she'd ever seen, sparkling right in the center of the square.

Although breathtaking, it wasn't the beautiful sights that called to her. It was the flags hanging from every streetlamp and balcony above a shop. A black tree rose against the golden yellow background, framed by white trim. The fae walking about were all dressed in similar colors, and they were heading toward a stage right next to the fountain.

Was that the queen's tree? Were they wearing masks? Was this another celebration, like the solstice?

They approached cautiously, sneaking through a crowd surrounded by the loud chattering of people as they awaited the play.

"What's this celebration?" Nava asked Arkimedes, taking in every detail—from the street seller waving golden feather masks, to the small children in white, waving bouquets of equally white flowers.

"Not sure..." Arkimedes whispered, but his emotions were tumultuous. Which meant he was lying at least a little bit. Even if he still claimed that he couldn't.

Three-foot-long banners were draped over either side of the stage. In the center of its wooden deck, a table stood, covered with white linens. A fae sat on a throne, dressed in white and wearing a golden mask. He had huge black wings—evidently fake, as they hung crookedly over his shoulders and didn't move.

The fae's costume was eerily similar to what Arkimedes had worn on the night of the masquerade ball during the summer solstice. Nava remembered it vividly. Especially after she'd removed every item of clothing from his body during their mating heat.

Her throat went dry at the same time that Arkimedes stiffened beside her. This was a reenactment of that night. She knew it like she knew her own name.

A bell chimed once, twice, thrice, and the audience fell quiet as another fae actor entered the stage. He was wire thin, sporting pale wings with gold tips and a silver mask, the same color as his hair. He stayed near the side of the stage and bowed to the false prince sitting at the table and then to his audience.

"Gentle fae of our city, thank you for joining us in celebrations of *The Solstice Queen*." The host's voice projected widely across the plaza, carried by magic and echoing off the buildings behind them.

The audience clapped, and laughter rippled through the crowd. The actor's voice was deep and pleasant, but nothing could lift the sinking feeling in Nava's stomach.

Arkimedes's breath caught in his throat as a woman in a canary-yellow dress stepped out from behind the curtains. The crowd howled.

Fuck. They'd even gotten her dress right. It looked so close to the monstrosity they'd forced her to wear that night.

"It looks like you two got caught," Devon said with a chuckle. His black eyes twinkled when they landed on her. "This should be interesting."

The narrator cleared his throat and silence fell once more. "Many of you saw a bright beauty on the night of the solstice, and no one could ignore how she captivated our prince." The female fae prowled across the stage, flirting with several of the dancers before crooking her finger at the prince.

What? Nava had never done that. She hadn't flirted with *anyone*. And Arkimedes had come to her on his own.

"My prince, would you care to have some wine?" the woman purred and traced a finger over her large bosom with one dainty, gloved hand. The fake prince followed her moves with false interest.

Something hot and feral flared in Nava's stomach as she watched them. How dare they make a mockery out of that moment—out of her and Arkimedes.

"We should leave before someone finds us here." Arkimedes's breath hit the exposed skin of her neck and raised gooseflesh wherever it touched. "We don't need to see this."

"I disagree. This is quite entertaining," Devon said. "I don't remember Nava being that…sultry, but I might be remembering it wrong."

Arkimedes glared at Devon and reached for her hand. He lowered his face to hers, and when their eyes met, the crowd disappeared behind them. "We know what truly happened that night. This is just going to upset us."

"But what if they overheard our conversation?" she breathed in a panic, right before his lips met hers. The gentle kiss wasn't enough to douse the sudden heat that swept through her. It was almost as if they were back to that night, when her skin had burned and desire for her mate had become too much to ignore.

Her chest tingled as Ark traced his tongue over her bottom lip, and the sensation traveled down to her core, leaving her wanting more. But he pulled away from the kiss before it caught fire. His pupils swallowed his irises, leaving behind only a trace of green.

"I don't want to lose my temper and hurt them. It will be worse if I give away who we are in the middle of the city. We have to blend in tonight to get the artifact."

The artifact—right. Nava nodded and kept her eyes glued to him, allowing Arkimedes to be her anchor. It was wise to escape from here. There was no point in getting overwhelmed by her need for him in the middle of a crowd.

"Devon?" Arkimedes studiously avoided looking at the play, although his gaze had turned more serious. Even Nava could see a flick of his power emanating from his skin.

Devon shook his head and pointed at the stage. "I'm staying to *mingle* with the good fae of this town... Perhaps I'll take a stroll around the piers later."

Arkimedes frowned, and he reached for his brother, draping an arm over his shoulder. "You're feeling fine to do that on your own?"

"Indeed."

"What do you mean by mingle?" she asked.

"He's going to find the location we need for tonight. It's easier if only he looks for it," Arkimedes whispered into her ear. His voice was so soft she could barely hear him through the loud clapping around them.

Then he led her away from the crowd and toward a large building near the edge of the town square. *The Lost Chariot* read the sign above the inn's door.

Arkimedes had already informed her that they'd be staying here tonight. Close enough to the docks but far away from the unsavory *merchants*. Nava's natural curiosity had replaced the fear she'd felt for most of the morning. The more she kept hearing about the pirates, the more she wanted to see what all the fuss was about.

"At least now we know how they found out about me," she said. It also explained the pamphlet Leela had brought with her when she went to the potion store a week ago.

The waves of laughter called her attention to the stage. More and more spectators were gathering to witness a moment in their lives that was supposed to stay private. "Do you think your father knows?"

"Let's hope for the safety of these fools—and for the sake of our plan—that he hasn't learned of this play yet." His brows scrunched in the middle as he glanced to where his brother stood. "But the distraction will serve as a good cover for what Devon has to do."

25
NAVA

Nava stopped in front of a black door. The paint had peeled around its edges, and time had faded the gold numbers on the black plate in its center. 211.

The keys jingled inside her grasp as she unlocked the door, feeling Arkimedes's body pressed against her back as he leaned over her. Her grip trembled when he wrapped his fingers around her hand.

"Let me go in first. I want to make sure the room is safe."

She met his bright gaze over her shoulder. "How can it be dangerous inside? We just got here."

"Indulge me," he pleaded, his tone rough. His grin did little to calm the speed of her racing heart. She dropped her hand from the doorknob and stepped aside on wobbly legs.

That play had left her in a tangle of heated thoughts and immense want. With the reminders of the solstice dance swirling around her head, it was hard to stay focused on their reasons for being here.

Arkimedes soon waved her inside. Nava eyed every corner of the small space, from the cobwebs accumulating in one corner to the lantern hanging from the wall, which lit up as she wandered past it. The room was empty and musty, with a bed that would barely fit both of them.

"It will do for tonight," Arkimedes said and tossed the brass skeleton key onto the stiff mattress. Dust billowed as it bounced over the edge and clanked onto the wooden floor.

"I guess it's not too bad, since we won't be sleeping much tonight." Her cheeks warmed as her mind caught up with her words. "Because of the night we have planned. I meant nothing else by that—though I wouldn't oppose it either, I guess."

Arkimedes's grin widened as he grabbed her by the waist and pulled her close. "Are you nervous, Bee?"

"A little?" She craned her neck to meet his gaze and pressed her body to his.

"Devon and I will go to the tavern first to make sure it's safe. You can follow our bond to find me. Once we are settled, I'll let you know if we've found some pirates."

"How are you going to talk to me in there if we aren't supposed to know each other?"

"I'll find a way." He traced her cheeks with his rough fingertips. "We have our mind connection, too."

"I like that." Their mind link didn't work all the time, but it was an option. She nodded, and her eyelids drooped as his caress traveled to her neck, making her stomach flutter and her insides melt. "If you've already spotted our target, then I won't have to ask the bartender for a ship to take me out of the city. I'm not the best of liars."

"If they hear a new deserter is offering gold for a chance to leave this kingdom, it will get you noticed."

"And not all traders are pirates—I get it."

"And not all pirates deal in magical artifacts. Don't trust anyone in there. From the bartender to the old hag drinking ale by the bar."

"The old hag?" She chuckled, pleased that he was trying to ease her worries.

"There is always some crummy-looking woman using her fragility to steal from you. They are the worst of all." The air of his breath washed over her face, warm and inviting. And now her heart was beating fast, too—not from fear or nerves but with anticipation.

"Are you trying to distract me, Arkimedes?" She walked her fingers up the lapels of his coat and wrapped her arms around his neck.

"Is it working?" he asked and kissed her, stealing her answer. His demanding lips and expert tongue were fuel for her desire. Nava dug her fingers into his hair, giving in to the heat running through her veins. The little intimacy they might have for a while.

She trailed her tongue over his lips, rejoicing when he met it with his own in a slow, languid dance.

"You're going to kill me if you don't kiss me again," he whispered against her lips. He sounded drunk on the same desire that churned inside her, his body warm and hard against hers. Gods, she wanted to throw caution to the wind and allow herself to let go.

The background noise from the play seeped through the crevices in the walls. The glass was thin enough that it rattled with the wind, letting in the icy air. Outside, the crowd erupted with laughter, presumably about a particularly funny punchline she wouldn't have found funny at all.

"Bee." Arkimedes pulled away, tracing her face with his hand again. "Are you still with me?"

"Yes." Nava frowned. She hated the people of this town all over again—and herself for allowing them to get under her skin. "But I can hear everything happening out there. And Devon could come at any moment."

They had informed the innkeeper that someone else from their party would be joining them. They'd left no key behind, so Devon would have to knock on the door to be let in, but Nava really didn't want to get caught making love.

"We can't get carried away," Arkimedes agreed and shrugged off his coat, tossing it onto the bed. Even with him gone, she could still feel the ghost of his lips against her own. "But we need to change out of these fancy clothes."

"Let me help you." Her fingers untied the cravat around his neck, and she swallowed against the rock that lodged in her throat. The afternoon had come too fast, and he had to leave first, to make sure everything was *safe,* whatever that meant. There was no safety out there for either of them.

Arkimedes kissed her again as he loosened the ribbons of her complicated gown with needy fingers, giving away his lack of control. Whatever she'd been thinking before no longer mattered.

He cupped her left breast, then looped his other arm under her ass and lifted her in one fluid motion. Pressing her to the wall, Arkimedes devoured her neck, licking all the way down to her clavicle and up again.

The lamp trembled, its light flickering with the movement of her body colliding with the cool surface of the wall. Nava wrapped her legs around Ark's waist, momentarily struggling with the thick layers of her dress.

She squirmed, stuck in between him and the wall. A mewl escaped her lips when two of his fingers snaked their way over the thin layer of her drawers, pressing against her center, which throbbed with need.

"These won't do," Arkimedes breathed. The air rippled with his magic, and her skin felt cold and hot right before the distinct sound of ripping fabric filled the room. He exposed her to the cold air just as he bit and licked her neck.

"I don't think this wall can hold us—" Nava began, supporting her entire body weight on his shoulders as he roughly pulled down his pants. She couldn't see him, but she could feel the warmth emanating from the bare skin that touched her thigh.

"Not another word, Nava," he growled and resumed the path his hand had followed before: up her thighs and toward her aching center.

The strength of his kiss and the rough texture of his stubble bruised her lips. Her body coiled tight with want when he touched her where she needed him most.

"So wet," he purred. His fingers moved in maddening circles over her clit, and he trailed his other hand down her neck and chest, over the peak of her nipple.

The touch drove her wild, and she struggled to find purchase on his shoulders as her pleasure built. He kissed her again, hard. She would never tire of his taste.

Continuing, he moved two fingers inside her, pumping in and out. How he managed it with the little space left between their bodies was anyone's guess.

Her hips jerked, and her pleasure neared a crescendo. She trembled as a loud moan escaped her lips. Any second now. Gods, she felt as if she might break.

"Ark."

"Come for me, Bee."

Nava cried out as the tension built until it snapped, and the orgasm swept through her body in waves while she rode his hand.

"Good girl," he purred, removing his hand and taking a firm hold of her ass. She felt him line himself up against her entrance, and then he pushed into her in one fluid movement.

His groan of pleasure was all she could hear, and the lantern on the wall rattled before falling to the ground. The sound of breaking glass didn't stop them, not even as darkness bathed the room, except for the trickle of gray light that filtered through the thick velvet curtains.

Arkimedes's punishing rhythm extended her pleasure. Time slowed until only the two of them remained, until her skin went tight again and she shattered into a million pieces. He slammed into her one last time and followed with a grunt, letting his body weight rest against her.

The world slowly returned, blurred at the edges of her vision as Arkimedes withdrew and set her down on trembling legs. The long skirts of her dress fell around her as she dropped her head to the firm planes of his chest, waiting for her breathing to calm down.

Her heart was so full, and her body ached in the best possible way. "I love you."

"And I love you." He pressed his lips to her head and held her tight for a while until her blood stopped rushing inside her ears. This felt right. It was worth fighting for.

"It held up fine," he whispered at last, a hint of smugness in his tone.

"What?" she croaked, still in a daze.

Arkimedes stepped away and tucked himself back into his trousers, tidying up his black shirt and messing his hair. Now he looked properly rumpled in his fine clothes. Then he tapped the wall with one hand.

A cough from the neighboring room answered him.

Horror cooled Nava's heated flesh as she stared at the wall with wide eyes. "Do you think they could hear us?"

"I would assume so," Arkimedes said with a rakish smile.

"Why aren't you more disturbed by this?" she accused, horrified, and paced around the pile of broken glass left on the floor. At least now that the room was dark, she couldn't fixate on all the suspicious stains the cleaners had missed—if anyone had even attempted to clean this room, that was.

"Where are my undergarments?" she asked. She'd smelled magic and heard her clothes tear, but surely Ark hadn't destroyed them. Right?

Sticky wetness clung to the inside of her legs as she kept hunting for her clothes without success. She couldn't possibly head out to that tavern wearing nothing under the dress.

He looked away sheepishly. Oh dear gods. He had.

"Ark." She glared. "I don't want to take a bath in this place—much less go out there without underwear."

"Let it be. It will send a message."

She gaped at him. "Arkimedes! Did you ravage me in this dirty room just so you could leave a mark on me like some sort of animal?"

A smile tugged at the corners of his lips, and at his shrug, her face warmed. "I never claimed not to be. The fae in me demands things from me humans don't do. But make no mistake, you are mine, and I intend for anyone out there to know."

Nava crossed her arms, flaring her nostrils. "And you are *mine*."

"Yes, and now when I go to that awful place, I'll get to smell you."

Thankfully, a tiny washroom adjoined their chamber. Arkimedes left to gather some items for the night while she cleaned up a bit. By the time she was ready, he'd returned and was standing by the window. He'd opened the thick green curtains, allowing daylight to pour into the room.

"I got you a new dress," he said and pointed at the garment lying over the bed. He was wearing different clothes, too. Black and a hooded tunic that hugged his wide shoulders.

Nava joined him, glancing outside. The play had ended, and the crowds were dispersing, leaving rubbish strewn across the wide courtyard.

Who'd dared to spy on the prince of the Copper Kingdom that night? They clearly had been an eyewitness. The costumes were too accurate for anything else.

She dragged her fingers through the messy waves of her hair before braiding the sides tight to her scalp and tying it all behind her neck into a low bun.

"When do you think you'll leave?" she asked, hating how worried she sounded—and felt. Her nervousness wouldn't help with their task.

"When Devon gets here and tells us what he's found." His eyes moved up to the sky. It had darkened considerably. "If he isn't here by sunset, we will both leave together and make sure he hasn't got himself in trouble."

Nava rose on her tiptoes, trying to get a better view of the square below. "How can Devon mingle with the fae and gather information when they all seem to hate humans?"

"Not all do. Although I'm sure meeting Devon won't help their views on humankind." Arkimedes smirked. The playful expression made her stomach flutter, and the need that should be satiated began anew. He arched a brow, and his smile grew. "Are you all right? You seem flustered."

"Oh, hush."

He huffed a laugh with a shake of his head. "To answer your previous question, Devon is good at intimidating people, and he uses as many tactics as he needs to make them believe he is someone to fear."

True. Nava still remembered the afternoon Devon Black the Crow had walked into her potion shop in Willowbrook. He'd put the fear of the gods into her and sent her into a frenzy to escape the threat of imprisonment and protect Cameron. He'd set all of this into motion.

Damn him, but she loved him for it.

"I remember him doing that… He did it to me," she said. And to think it was all a mask Devon wore to get the job done. Much like the indifference Arkimedes hid behind. It was all to show the world that he didn't care about their judgment of him.

"Most fae out there possess little magic. Having someone like Devon ask them questions will force them to answer if he displays just a small fraction of his power."

"Do you think he's going to get in trouble?" And if so, with whom? The royal guards, the Society of Crows, or the pirates?

"If he isn't indulging in frivolities and is, in fact, scoping out information as he's supposed to, then no." His growing frown did little to calm Nava's dread.

"How often does he indulge?"

"Enough for me to be concerned."

Great.

Arkimedes cleared his throat. "In the meantime, I need to get some things to prepare for tonight. You should call upon your daggers."

"Which one? The one I left on Grey Island or the one your father's guards took from me?"

It had been a year since Nava had learned to use her magic and to accept it. She hadn't used the spell to portal the things she owned often enough. It took a lot of energy, especially if the items were far away.

"Not the dagger the guards took. While that one is closer, they might track it to the inn. You'll have some time to recover your energy this afternoon."

Arkimedes sat on the bed and opened his palms to the ceiling. He closed his eyes, and his shadow power deepened, extending like a halo of darkness around his body. Swirls of magic began to resolve into the shape of a longsword in his grasp until the substantial weight of his weapon filled his hands. The air vibrated in response to his power.

He'd done the same in the forest when he'd called upon his first aid kit, but that time, she'd been too out of sorts to really grasp what he was doing.

His sword from back home had made it all the way here. The sweat beading his temple and the fact that he remained seated told her all she needed to know about how much the spell would take from her.

Nava dragged her finger over the cool metal of his blade and shivered when she traced the etched shape of the naked queen's tree. Her tree. The first time she'd seen this sword, it had been hanging from Arkimedes's cabin wall. Now she understood the meaning behind the symbol.

Had he known the tree would bloom if she made it here? When she was snooping through his things that afternoon, Arkimedes had been well aware that she was his soulmate—and what the tree meant.

"Why do we need weapons if most people are without magic?" she asked.

"Because of where we are going. We might encounter the blinding spell."

"I don't like how that sounds."

"The Society of Crows crafted it to daze magic users for a short period. Just long enough to allow them to deal with a problematic magic-wielder." Arkimedes paused and shook his head, as if getting rid of a bad memory. "Years ago, someone leaked the spell, and now it's available on the black market."

"And of course, we are going to deal with pirates..."

"Many pirates are deserters, Nava. Former magic-wielders. But the ones that aren't usually carry crafted spells."

"Well, on the plus side, I miss my old dagger," she said with a weak smile and sat on the bed beside him. The light from her spell blinded her, and the familiar cool metal of her mother's dagger filled her palms a second later. It felt like forever since she'd seen this weapon—let alone held it.

A rapid knock on the door startled them, and Arkimedes was up on his feet, sword in hand, and across the room before her mind had caught up to the fact that someone was there.

"It's me," Devon said.

The room spun when she stood on shaking legs, her blood rushing in her ears—a clear sign of how much the spell had drained her.

Arkimedes cracked the door open, and a moment later, Devon strolled into the room.

"I'm not sleeping in here." He whistled and glanced at the broken glass on the floor and then up at the ceiling. "Seems you two have been busy…"

Nava's cheeks warmed, but she didn't dignify his comment with an answer. It was true either way, so she couldn't exactly deny it.

"Did you discover anything useful?" Arkimedes asked.

"Lots." Devon paused a few feet away from her and turned to face Arkimedes. He coughed, but the noise wasn't as terrible as it once had been. "It seems someone followed you two into the castle's garden the night of the solstice, but they didn't listen to anything important—or they are smart enough not to divulge it to the crowds."

"What about the ships?"

"There are a couple of promising leads docked nearby. When I inquired with the local fishermen, they said they'd been docked for a week already, which means we don't have long to get what we need."

"Did you see any familiar faces?"

"I'm afraid not." Devon took a deep breath and promptly choked. He pulled a handkerchief from his pocket. Then he coughed loudly into it.

"I thought you were feeling better?" Nava stepped toward him, studying his pale face. It wasn't odd for him to look like this. Nava had met no one as fair as Devon Black.

"It's dusty here." He met her gaze evenly, but worry was etched onto his features.

"Don't lie to her, Devon. It won't help you." Arkimedes dropped his sword on the bed before he brought over the sheath and a long, aged black belt.

She sniffed. It was true that the air was musty here. "I can try to heal you once more before you leave?"

"No, save your energy. You aren't mentally ready to deal with the shifters and the lowlifes we are going to encounter. But you should at least be prepared by keeping some energy."

"Suit yourself," Nava said with more bite than she'd intended. But she hated the feeling of not being prepared and knowing less than everyone else in the room. It was how she'd felt for months after first being thrust into this dizzying world of magic.

Ark eyed her knowingly and reached for her hand, squeezing it lightly. "You'll be fine."

Was he trying to reassure her or himself?

"We should go soon. The sun isn't too far away from setting, and Nava shouldn't be walking the docks on her own at night."

Arkimedes nodded and knelt in front of her. "Here, let me get this ready for you."

She stood still, watching his hand trace the shapes of her legs underneath the skirt of her dress. Up and up they traveled as he met her gaze with a defiance that made her heart skip.

Devon walked toward the door, muttering something under his breath.

Nava's heart nearly leaped out of her chest. "Stop that." She slapped his hand away, even as her stomach twisted in delight.

Arkimedes chuckled and finished strapping the dagger belt around her thigh. Then he whispered, "You smell delicious."

"Did you know there's a blade with your name on the bed?" She narrowed her eyes at him and stepped away. She was half ready to stomp on him for teasing her—or push him into the bed. To hell with their mission.

Devon popped his head back into the room from the dark hallway beyond. "The name of the tavern is the Flying Boar. Don't leave this place after sunset, Kitten, or you will be sorry."

26
ORION

"It's not looking promising. Where are the merchants in this place?" Devon took a sip from his second pint of ale.

They had been in the Flying Boar for at least a couple of hours, although it was hard to tell the time when the windows were closed with wooden shutters and the walls were a uniform shade of brown.

Everything was dark in this place, undoubtedly to hide the layers of filth caking the floor and every sticky surface. Orion couldn't see the sunlight from where they sat at the far end of the room, but he hadn't felt Nava approach yet.

She should have left the inn by now…right?

"You should pace yourself with the drinks," he said as Devon gulped down his drink almost without breathing. He wasn't sure if his brother was drinking this much to take the edge off or to dull the pain he was under because of the Vulcan.

"I'm fine," Devon assured him, although his eyes were starting to glaze over. "Maybe you've forgotten I can handle my liquor."

"Everything but fae wine, apparently," Orion said with a smirk, bringing his own drink to his lips. Gods, it was terrible. Bitter and way too yeasty.

The dip in temperatures and the constant rain seemed to be driving everyone into this establishment. Most were local fae. The few traveling merchants Orion had spotted when they'd arrived all looked unfamiliar.

He sighed, rubbing his brow and trying to swallow his discomfort. Most pirates were shifters, humans, or former magic-wielders. He couldn't blame them for not wanting to come to the Copper Kingdom when the fae held a grudge against their kind.

Nava was right. He should have known this trip would be in vain.

"There is no one here to trade with. It's why so many shops have shut down," he whispered, unsure if Devon could hear him through the roar of drunken laughter and singing from the stage at the other end of the room.

Devon reached for a buttery roll in the center of the table and pulled a sizable chunk from it before dunking it into his broth. "You got your work cut out for you, brother. Fixing this place once the ol' man croaks won't be easy."

That almost made him laugh, but Devon was right. Orion's father's complete disregard for the human population that lived in the kingdom had proved atrocious for the economy. Perhaps that had been the true reason behind the kingdom's decline instead of his absence.

Then again, if he'd stayed, perhaps he'd never have allowed things to become this bad.

Even though the king rarely enforced the tithes, he'd also done little to provide for and protect the humans in his kingdom who lived in poverty.

The hair of Orion's arms suddenly stood on end as strings of energy rose from the ground. It was the same power that had come to help him when they'd escaped the safe house, but it felt different, too. Like a warning.

He shifted on his chair and secured the hood over his head, making sure none of his features peeked out.

"I doubt any of the fools dining here are trading on the black market. Look at them, they're happy and drunk. Perhaps we should check the rooms upstairs?" Devon pointed behind Orion's shoulder, looking grim.

Orion glanced in the direction his brother indicated, up the narrow steps that led to an open second floor. Even in the darkness, Orion could spot doors up there. A woman exited a room, wearing nothing but a sheer slip, her tits bouncing for everyone to see. Someone nearby howled at the sight of her, but she didn't pay them any heed as she fanned her shiny face. She looked utterly fucked and rumpled.

Orion raised his brows and looked back to Devon. "Do you think the rooms are rented by the hour?"

"Indeed, and I think sailors traveling across the sea for months can get awfully lonely. I wouldn't put it past the worst kind of *merchant* to be up there. Which could explain why there's no one down here—" A cough tore past Devon's lips, interrupting his speech. He took a deep breath and reached for a new potion from his pocket, avoiding Orion's eyes when he took it. "Perhaps you and Nava can accidentally stumble inside one of those rooms? It might be a way to discover if a pirate is exercising up there."

"*Exercising*, really? What are you, twelve?" Orion scoffed. "Either way, we shouldn't be calling more attention to ourselves than we have to. Coming here is already a risky move."

"I guess you're right. Sometimes I forget you're important."

"It's not about being important, Devon. But we are on the run." And he was feeling so on edge already. Like the tavern was telling him someone watched him. But there weren't any Dark Ones here, and everyone else was too drunk, dirty, and definitively not paying attention to them.

"Isn't being on the run and being important the same thing? I'm just fed up with hiding away from everything," Devon said in a pensive tone. "It must be nice, being in this kingdom where you actually fit in." He turned and patted the wooden backrest of his chair. "I've noticed the chairs here are designed for people with wings. Even the coat Leela gave me has discreet slits all across the back. It would accommodate someone like you, so you don't have to hide your true nature."

"I do like that," Orion admitted. "Here, I'm not an outsider simply for being a fae."

He paused and studied their surroundings again. Nothing had changed, but the anxiety within him was ramping up. It wasn't Nava who needed him this time, but something else. The same old patrons he'd become familiar with over the last couple of hours sat around them. The same band played a merry tune.

Where was the source of danger?

Devon ate his meal without a worry in the world. Pottery shattered as a scuffle broke out to their left, the stranger's drunken yells muffled by the general noise of chatter.

Most people ignored what was happening, but Orion couldn't. Instead, he was inspecting the very shadows of the tavern, half expecting a royal guard to emerge from them to drag them away. Or perhaps it would be a Crow, blending into the busy night, much like the two of them were doing.

"You look tense. Talk to me," Devon said.

"Something is off." And there wasn't a point staying here waiting if Nava could arrive in a potentially dangerous situation at any moment. "We're being watched."

"Now?" Devon stilled. His dark eyes darted from side to side as he slowly placed his spoon on the table. The air shifted with the spice of magic, and his fingers whitened with shimmering ice. "I see nothing."

"I don't think it's anyone here, but I can't be sure." Orion stood, leaving his untouched meal on the table and closing his coat. "It's like the city is telling me something is coming. We should search the area."

Devon not even questioning how strange that sounded was perhaps even more unsettling than the fact that Orion was connected to the very land they stood upon.

"You check from the sky, and I will take the streets around the tavern. We'll meet in the side alley in an hour. If you don't come, I'll assume something happened to you."

"And if that's the case, make sure Nava stays safe."

"I swear it."

From the sky, the ports looked small and the streets eerie in the wet night. Nava should've been here well before dark, and it complicated matters that she hadn't arrived. Judging by the pull of the bond, though, she wasn't far.

There was movement down in the streets, the sounds of footsteps amplified by the puddles on the ground. Women in ornate gowns clutched their parasols close to their bodies, taking refuge from the early evening drizzle. Their silhouettes moved beneath the gaslight, casting long shadows over the wooden planks.

Orion didn't know how to explain the odd feeling he had. At least not without sounding like a madman, for it churned inside his blood, nearly suffocating him. But he'd learned that he needed to trust his gut, and if the land was speaking to him, then he would listen.

The cold bit at his cheeks as he circled the block around the tavern, inspecting the shadowy gable rooftops with care. It was unlikely that anyone would be able to stand on slick terracotta tiles. Not unless they were fae that hid in the shadows. Which could be the case...

He followed the instinctive pull that had led him here and landed in a crouch on one of the building's rooftops. His feet fit inside the terracotta tile grooves as he stabilized himself low to the surface. The clay was still warm from the afternoon's sun, and mist rose from it, warming his hands.

"Come out now. I know you're there, and I'd rather not have to hurt you," Orion said to the nothingness. He didn't want to harm a guard. Many of them had become friendly with him over the past five months he'd spent in this kingdom.

He focused on the chimney that jutted out of the building, where the shadows shifted with barely perceptible movements.

After the emissary's attack, the only thing consuming Orion's mind had been to find the artifact. His father and the guards had been the last thing on his mind today. How foolish of him, to walk around the place without a proper disguise.

Slowly, a winged figure appeared from the darkness, wearing copper armor from head to toe.

"Your Highness." The fae dipped his head as a sign of respect. His gravelly voice was one he recognized. The crashing waves rumbled in the distance, just as Cyrus's wings materialized on his back. They were as black as Orion's, not something common in their kind. Right now, it helped him blend further into his surroundings.

"Are there any more of you here?"

"No, sir. It's just me. I didn't mean to bother you."

Full fae couldn't lie outright, which made Orion inclined to believe him. The real question was, how much of the truth was he hiding? "Did you just find me this afternoon, and have you told my father?"

Cyrus tilted his head forward in acknowledgment. Something the fae usually did when they didn't want to answer straight away. Cyrus's armor screeched with the movement as raindrops dripped over the curves of the metal. "The king has sent two sentinels to watch over you ever since you escaped. We found you when you left the Crow's nest, sir."

Orion blinked rapidly as his mind caught up with Cyrus's words. "You have been following me all this time?" He couldn't believe it. How had he missed this?

But the guard nodded. "We have, Your Highness."

"Where is the second sentinel?"

"He's back at the inn, guarding your mate, sir."

Fuck. "If either of you hurt her…" Orion snarled. His wings fluttered up and down, sending debris flying off the roof as he readied himself to take off and return to Nava.

"The king commanded us not to harm the future queen, nor to be seen by either of you." Cyrus's voice held shame as he looked down. "Which I failed to do tonight."

Orion's chest tightened. After what had happened in the castle, his father had put it all together. He clearly understood Nava's importance in this entire story, so much so that he'd commanded a sentinel to stay with her.

Yet Leela had said that Nora, one of his father's concubines, had told her everyone believed Nava had put him under a spell.

Did his father believe a soulmate bond was a spell that clouded a person's judgment? A weakness? Wasn't Orion's mother rumored to have been the king's soulmate?

His throat went dry all at once as Orion focused on the bond he shared with Nava. Thankfully, she was fine, for her overriding feelings were nerves about their assignment—not fear or anger. And she was getting closer.

"My father commanded you to leave us alone?"

"That's correct, sir. We are here to secure your safety."

There was something not being said here, and Orion knew better than to fully believe all that the guard shared. "So long as we don't leave the kingdom?"

"If you remain in our land, sir, then we are supposed to stay in the shadows." The guard hesitated in silence, then pulled off his helmet, revealing bright blue eyes that shone in the night as they met Orion's from across the rooftop. "We lost track of you for a few days, and we feared you'd gone into the forest to fight the demons on your own."

Ah. So they'd known the Zorren were attacking but hadn't come to help? "Why didn't you come to my aid if you thought that was the case?"

"The king commanded us to report back if you left the city. I attempted to follow you while Eris went to the king. But with the storm, I lost your scent, and by the time I reached the fires, there were no demons, and you were gone."

Somehow Orion doubted his nervousness was the city warning him about the guards. Especially if this had been going on for so long. Was he feeling watched because something had changed with Cyrus, or was it a warning about something else entirely?

No matter what Cyrus had said, Orion had to ensure Nava was safe. "Don't follow me anymore," he commanded.

"Your wish shall become my command, Your Highness," Cyrus said after a long pause. He put his helmet on, beginning to fade back into the shadows. A well-considered choice of words. For in the future, Orion would come to overrule everyone else. But tonight, King Oberon still had the final say.

Cyrus was smart enough to know to give Orion space, and he wasn't ready to get into a fight and harm this guard because he was following orders. Not unless either of them hurt Nava.

Intent on following the soulmate bond and intercepting Nava as she approached the tavern, Orion leaped off the roof.

He found her fast. Her steps clicked against the wet stone, speeding up as she shouted over her shoulder at a nearby man. Her gown was puffier than what she usually wore, adorned by a corset that shimmered beneath the gaslight.

He could stop her. Tell her all he'd just learned. Then they could leave, still with no idea of how or where to get an artifact. Trouble seemed to pile higher with each passing day, but the threat to the world and the Beekeepers remained.

Now more than ever, they couldn't go to his father for help.

Orion landed on the cobblestone and rushed into the alleyway where Devon awaited. He'd allow his mate to go into the tavern on her own—for now.

"You come empty-handed. Does that mean I left my perfectly good meal inside that hole for nothing?" Devon asked in a flat tone, mist billowing from his lips.

Orion opened his mouth to tell him everything and promptly shut it again. The weird vibrations continued, coming at him in waves, rising from the ground.

"I take it you found nothing strange either?" Orion clicked his tongue and walked to the end of the alley, all the way up to the tavern's back door, where old produce crates were stacked against the wall.

"Of course I didn't. Have I mentioned that I hate walking in this muggy place when I can barely breathe?" A cough rattled past Devon's lips, as if to drive his point home.

His hair was sticking to the sides of his sharp cheekbones. He'd lost considerable weight ever since they'd escaped the safe house. Perhaps Arkimedes shouldn't have stopped him mid-dinner.

"It's probably a pirate who followed me when I returned from the piers. I haven't done this for so long now. I'm rusty."

It might be—or maybe not. "My father's guards have been trailing us ever since we left the safe house."

"What?" Devon looked up to the sky and the empty balconies that jutted from the surrounding buildings. "How do you know?"

"I just finished talking to Cyrus, a sentinel." Was Eris still with Nava?

"Well, that was it, no? You were right to feel watched. What are we supposed to do now?"

"I don't know if it was my father's guards triggering this feeling or someone else," he whispered. "Nava is in the tavern. We should head back in."

"So we continue with our existing plan?" Devon pushed off the wall, his brows dipping over his black eyes as he crept toward the back door.

They were soaked from the gentle but steady drizzle of rain by now, and the cold had snaked its way through all the layers of Orion's clothing. "I don't trust my father, even if for some strange reason he has known where we were and has done nothing about it," he admitted. He ran a hand over his hair.

"Do you think he commanded Leela to house us all this time?"

"It stands to reason he would," Orion said.

Devon cursed. "If I were the king, I wouldn't want either you or your soulmate harmed. Especially if it's true that the health of the kingdom depends on your bloodline." Devon's lips pressed into a fine line. "But I wouldn't trust him any further than that."

Exactly. Orion sighed. The air was thick with the rich scent of coal smoke and dampness. The distant rumble of a carriage in the distance drowned out the obnoxious laughter from the hansom cab drivers who were loitering outside the tavern, waiting for customers to drive home.

Orion opened the door that would lead them back into the warm hell-house they'd just left, but he paused and studied his brother for a moment. "How are you truly holding up?"

"Still dying," Devon said. "And fine to do whatever needs doing today."

27
NAVA

Nava dragged her sweaty hands over the bodice of her dress for the tenth time in a row. By this point, if any crease remained, it was meant to stay. It was a full moon tonight, not that anyone could tell with the stormy weather.

The ocean waves crashed against the barrier of stone beside her, sending droplets of salty water into the air.

It had been drizzling ever since she'd left the inn, and it was far too cold to get wet. Would her dress allow her to blend in with the other patrons at the tavern, even if she turned up looking like a drenched animal? She'd hoped at the very least she wouldn't stand out as the only human in a crowd of fae. All she had to do was play a role and gather information that might save the kingdom. No pressure.

Rolling an errant curl of hair around a finger, Nava prayed that, for one night, she'd manage to put on the best act of her life instead of ruining it all with awkward comments. She was a deserter on the run, and she needed to act like it. She'd fought far worse battles than this.

"My lady." A tall man shifted under a streetlamp, tipping his head in her direction with a feline smile. His hair was thick and plastered to his skull with grease. Light golden flecks lit his eyes, brought out by the warm tones of the lamp. "Do you need a ride tonight?" His tone alone raised gooseflesh across her body, an excellent incentive to quicken her steps.

Was he offering her a ride home—in a carriage or on a beast—or was this an offer of another type of ride?

"No, thank you," Nava said, while her stomach revolted at the stench that emanated from him. Alcohol and a general lack of hygiene.

The faster she was out of his sight, the safer she would feel.

His eyes brightened in that unnatural way that was neither human nor fae. A shifter. "Are you sure? I could keep you warm."

"I'm not interested," Nava said in between ragged breaths and felt for the pommel of the dagger Arkimedes had strapped around her thigh earlier. Hopefully, the shifter wouldn't chase after her.

The noise in the busy area in front of the tavern swallowed his distant growl. Devon had been right, as much as she hated to admit it. She was completely inexperienced in dealing with shifters. It had been silly of her to fall asleep earlier today when she should have left earlier.

People dressed in their work clothing were strolling along beneath the streetlights, but most of them looked too drunk to pay attention to her. The women wore bright-colored dresses, their skirts wide with wire petticoats underneath them, and tight corsets. Fashion from another kingdom, for the fae's fashion was much simpler. Yet the dress Nava wore was similar in many respects, except not as bright.

Were all of them shifters? They must be. They moved in a sinuous, smooth way, unlike any human she had ever seen.

She shivered and nearly ran the rest of the way. The ground changed from thick wooden planks to cobblestones, and she was now close enough to the building she could make out every detail.

Outside it, carriages with enormous horses and orrus were waiting. The few footmen lounging about in this weather sat on a bench, smoking and laughing at the poor soul whose task it was to clean up the beasts' droppings.

A wooden sign hung above the worn double doors, reading, in black letters, *The Flying Boar.*

There wasn't any reason to be this nervous. Not when she'd fought in magical wars, defeated demons, and escaped the king. She could do this.

Nava took a deep breath and went in.

Ale, roast pork, and odors she'd rather not identify greeted her as she entered the establishment. Circumstances stacked the odds against her favor, as she had rarely attended places like this, even before joining the world of magic.

She studied the wide space with dozens of small wooden tables, where customers gathered, eating, drinking, and playing games.

Across the room, a long counter stretched, tended by a woman with black clothing and thick rings of kohl around her eyes. Nava cleared her throat and forced her heavy feet to move forward. One step, two steps, and she rounded the first table.

"Look at this gorgeous creature that's just joined us," a male voice said, and a strong arm snaked around Nava's waist, gripping her so tightly she lost her balance. The man pulled her onto his lap a split second later.

His large group of friends howled loudly, banging their fists against the rickety table, almost like a song. Nava met his brown eyes, glazed by alcohol. Her stomach twisted, and she pushed off his chest and stumbled back onto her feet.

"Touch me again and you will lose your hand," she snarled and pulled out her dagger so quickly her mother would be proud.

"I meant no disrespect, magic-wielder." The man shrunk so far into his chair that it creaked under his considerable weight. The laughter around them died away. His eyes were wide, although he wasn't looking at the tip of her blade, which was so close to his throat. Instead, he stared at her glowing skin.

Nava could feel Arkimedes's anger brewing through their bond, blending with her own. He wasn't far and was likely watching and getting ready to intervene. Dammit all, she'd almost ruined this entire quest by not properly avoiding these drunken fools.

It was too dark and busy to find either Ark or Devon amongst the patrons. If she closed her eyes for long enough, she might be able to pinpoint exactly where Arkimedes was, but this wasn't the time to hold back and allow another of these men to touch her again if it risked blowing their cover. She straightened her clothes and headed toward the bar without another glance.

"Ya aren't from around here," the barkeeper observed. She was wiping a tall clay mug with a brown towel that had been clean once upon a time. Then she stacked it into the neat row of similar mugs behind the counter.

Liquor and ale jugs lined the wall all the way up to the high ceilings. Like most establishments in this city, they were evidently set up to accommodate the winged citizens.

The bartender turned to Nava with a steady gaze. "This not a place for a dame like yarself to come alone."

"I'll survive for one night." Nava sheathed her dagger in its strap. Good thing her dress had a side slit or she wouldn't be able to access her weapon so easily. "Can I have a glass of something other than fae wine, please?"

The woman raised a thin brow and tilted her head forward. Pointed ears peeked through the waves of her ebony hair. She had peculiar wings coming through the suede vest she wore, transparent and glass-like, like those of Nava's bees.

"Yar afraid of the fae wine?" She smiled knowingly and pushed a short cup over the smooth counter, filled to the brim with amber liquid.

"I'd rather keep my head on my shoulders tonight." Nava nodded and took a tentative sip of her drink. Smooth and bittersweet, with a smoky aftertaste. It burned down her throat and warmed her gut, right before it sent a cough rattling past her lips. The alcohol threatened to come back up.

"What on earth is this?" Nava pressed a hand to her lips, attempting to drown out her wheezing. This was not the way to blend in with a drunken crowd! She glanced around, hoping no one watched her almost spit up her drink.

"Not used to amber whiskey?" The fae continued drying mugs with the same towel, peering at the other patrons sitting at the bar. "It's two gold coins."

For one drink? Nava craved something to wash away the grit on her tongue, but this was not it. She studied her mostly full glass with a frown. Even though she was inexperienced with this general lifestyle, she knew this was very little liquid for such a price.

Still, her body had warmed significantly, and with one sip, she instantly felt less tense. This was no wine—nor any whiskey she'd had before. "Is this going to make me lose my mind like the fae wine?"

"Nah. It's what we serve the humans when they don't want ale."

Nava hummed and tapped her fingers against the surface of the bar. It had once been polished wood but now was stained with moisture rings and scrapes from the odd blade. "It's true I don't belong here, which is why I'm looking to leave."

"Leave the bar or the city?" The fae's tone filled with curiosity, although her bright eyes remained glued to her tasks. Then her expression changed to a conspiratorial look, and she rested her narrow hips against the edge of the countertop, finally looking up to meet Nava's gaze. "I saw yar doing magic back there. Ar ya a deserter?"

"I was not supposed to use magic out here. I don't want a Crow to find me," Nava whispered and glanced over her shoulder at the sea of faceless people. Coins were being slammed against surfaces and tossed to the floor. Nava straightened. Hopefully, if she voiced some of her real fears, her act would be believable enough.

"Haven't seen a Crow in years," the fae said and tapped her pouting lip with a long finger. "But the pricks usually use disguises."

The very thing Arkimedes and Devon were doing right now. Two ex-Society members who used the tactics they'd learned once upon a time when they were Crows.

Nava grabbed her drink with trembling hands and took a small sip. "I need a ship that can take me out of this kingdom. I heard I might find someone in this crowd? Perhaps you could point me in the right direction?"

The fae stood straight, her friendly expression dropping within an instant. She eyed Nava from beneath her long lashes. "Who told you to come here?"

"I heard it out in the streets. It was rather busy today, so I don't recall who said what, but the name of the bar stood out to me. Please. I really, *really* need to leave."

"Ya still got meat around your bones, which leads me to believe ya haven't been on the run for long." The bartender spoke with empathy. Nava hadn't expected that. "Have ya any clue how many deserters ask me that very question?"

Nava could not swallow past the thick lump that formed in her throat. Images of the family they'd found in the abandoned bakery weeks ago leaped to her mind's eye. Caden, the special boy who had the gift of the Sight, his brother the protector, and his sister who'd fed them broth. Children running away—unable to escape. Cameron and the way she'd had to leave him behind to protect his freedom when Devon came to her potion shop. "I'm well aware. But I'm not alone, and I have to leave."

"Another pint, Morgan!" someone yelled from the other side of the counter.

The bartender grunted a curse in another language and waved a dismissive hand toward the screamer. "For a price, I can pass yar information to the right *merchant.*" Her eyes said more than her words. A pirate, who was a lot more dangerous than a regular trading ship. "Like I do for most of those who come here asking the same."

"How much would that cost me?" A wave of annoyance rushed through Nava. Why would this fae prey upon the deserters when they had little to nothing left? When most, as she so gracefully pointed out, were only skin and bones?

"Twelve gold coins, and even if you pay, I can't guarantee that he will come to meet ya," Morgan said. The corners of her lips tilted down as she studied Nava's expression. She leaned forward, and her sour breath hit Nava straight in the face. "I know why yar looking at me like that, girl," she whispered. "But nothing in this world yar attempting to enter comes for free. This is not all for me. The merchants charge a hefty fee to even meet ya, and it won't be coming from me."

It wasn't worth getting into this argument. Nava would never understand what drove people to prey on the needy. But her main aim here was to find a magical artifact to save the kingdom from the Zorren. And the pirates were the only lead they had.

Nava reached inside her pocket and counted out fourteen round coins. Two for her overpriced drink and twelve for a meeting with a pirate. The uneven texture of the gold clanked loudly against the counter as Nava allowed it to drop from her hand. Greed was the downfall of all sentient species of this world.

28
NAVA

Nava rolled her shoulders to ease the ache that extended down her back from sitting too stiffly on that uncomfortable stool. How long had she been waiting for this supposed pirate to appear? A long time, if the lack of circulation in her legs was any measure at all.

Morgan had disappeared from behind the bar at least half an hour ago, and a younger server had taken her place. The new fae's shifty eyes kept flicking at Nava like she was trouble. And perhaps he was right.

Had she lost fourteen pieces of gold for nothing? Surely this was why Arkimedes had attempted to warn her about not trusting anyone in this place. Heat rushed to her face as she finished what remained of her drink and glanced discreetly toward the main area. Come to think of it, where was he?

His feelings were very much present and filtered through to her in waves, which could only mean he was in the room. He wasn't pleased, either, but hadn't approached her yet.

A sudden shadow fell over her before the largest man Nava had ever seen settled on the stool beside her. He smelled like the sea and the lingering scent of pure sunlight, but not entirely pleasant at the same time.

What a ridiculous thing to think—who smelled like sunlight? Clearly, that amber whiskey had some of the fae juju in it, and she was losing her mind, after all. Nava blinked rapidly and turned away from the man so she wouldn't catch his attention.

"Are you the mouse Morgan came yapping about?" He tipped his head toward the scrawny bartender, not sparing a look at her. The leathers of his clothes creaked as he leaned forward on the counter. "The magic-wielder looking to leave this fine piece of dirt?"

There was a healthy dose of sarcasm in his tone, and it bothered her. What did he have against her kingdom? No, not her kingdom. But even she could admit it had potential.

Nava looked at him and attempted to keep her features blank. He carried himself with the confidence of someone who had no troubles in the world. The complete opposite of how she felt because her nerves had returned with new vigor. This man wasn't human, although she couldn't quite place *what* he was.

He moved with the edge of someone dangerous enough that they weren't one bit concerned about her potential to harm them. "I don't have all night, mouse. Speak or this meeting is over."

Nava straightened, pushing down her bubbling temper. She couldn't afford to lose this lead. "I'm looking to leave…and have gold to buy me and my family passage." She kept her words simple and close to what she'd told Morgan.

The pirate faced her straight on, and the breath caught in Nava's throat as she noticed his missing eye. He studied her, not in a salacious way but with curiosity. A discolored scar ran from one end of his forehead, across his brow bone, and all the way down his cheek.

"The answer is no."

"No? That simple?" Her lips parted in shock. "You won't help me even if I pay you?"

He grimaced. "You have freaky eyes."

Nava fought the sudden urge to turn away and hide her face behind her hair, like she always did when people made negative remarks about her different-colored eyes.

"You're one to talk," she said heatedly and pointedly looked at his missing eye. She usually wasn't the petty kind, but she also wouldn't let this man walk all over her and insult her to her face. She had no time to waste. "I can't see what my eyes have to do with what I need."

The pirate grinned, revealing sharp, yellowing teeth. A shifter? What was he? "Neil! A pint of ale." He slammed his tattooed hand on the counter. There was a snake—or a dragon?—inked on his tan skin. It appeared to slither with the movement of his muscles. An optical illusion, perhaps?

The server, who'd been avoiding the area where Nava sat ever since Morgan had left, was with them in the blink of an eye. Up close, he was a mousy thing, shaking under his thin clothes. He picked up a clay mug and filled it with bubbling beer. "Here, Draken."

"Put it on the mouse's tab." He pointed at Nava but didn't turn to look at her.

"Excuse me?" Nava's lips parted in a silent gasp as she stood from her stool. "You don't get to decide whether I buy you a drink or not. Especially after you just denied me what I need."

"Sit. I'm not done with you," Draken ordered. "To answer your question, your eyes could easily be bad luck. In a world of magic, I'm not one to take risks." He took a long swig of his drink.

And what did that mean? Perhaps he'd had a premonition that warned him of someone with different-colored eyes?

Nava didn't sit. Instead, she gripped the pommel of her dagger, narrowing her eyes at him. "I'm not paying for your drink, but I have gold to pay for passage."

"No gold can get me to take you on my ship. It's not worth the risk. But I can give you information about who might—for a price."

All of these bastards were leeches. "If you can't take me, then I'm interested in a trade." She lowered her voice so the bartender and the surrounding patrons wouldn't hear her. "The Crows are trailing me and my family, and I need a weapon that will help me fight them."

"A weapon to defeat the Crows?" He laughed from his belly up, a genuine sound that even reached his shimmering eye. Perhaps he was curious about her. Or he wasn't used to anyone answering him so directly.

He was a scary-looking shifter, but Nava possessed more power than he gave her credit for, and she wasn't a damsel in distress. Besides, Arkimedes was somewhere in the room.

"How much gold are you talking about? It seems you already have a fine dagger strapped to your body."

He'd noticed. Had he watched her threaten the other man? He was so large, Nava couldn't imagine him blending too well into the shadows of the dining area. "I have enough to buy a god's artifact…with no one being the wiser."

Of course, that was a bald-faced lie. She had maybe ten coins left. He would never sell her an artifact for that little.

"A god's arti—" Drake sobered and looked around them, as if he expected someone to jump him from the shadows. Not that he was that far off with his fear. "I'm thinking you're a Crow. Hiding behind this act of a powerless mouse." His growl began in the very center of his chest, and his eyes sizzled orange and yellow, like the embers of fire. A dragon shifter. "Speak the truth or face the consequence of wasting my time."

Grit stuck in her throat, and she *felt* Arkimedes move toward her. His shadows floated around the tavern like cool mist that raised the hair on the back of her neck.

There were a few gasps in the distance, but Nava focused on Draken, unblinking.

She craved more of the bitter amber whiskey. They didn't need to add another foe to their growing list. Ari always spoke the truth, and it was what she longed for as well. She was tired of lies.

"I'm not a Crow, but I'm not a deserter either." She hesitated but didn't release the handle of her weapon. Her bees began to circle her body. Drake swatted at a few of them that flew too close to his hook nose. "I would like to purchase the item if you have one."

Dragon shifters were dangerous, according to legend, and Nava wanted nothing to do with them. The tavern darkened further. Undoubtedly, nobody was paying attention to her and the pirate because they were gawking at her soulmate.

The dragon eased onto his stool and regained the edge of curiosity he'd almost lost. "I commend you for being brave enough to tell me the truth, after all your lies. But even if I owned such an artifact, what makes you dream I would ever part with it? I kill for my treasure."

"We both know they possess great power—but also that they curse those who wield them." Nava pressed her lips together. That was an important detail they had avoided discussing while devising this plan.

Who was going to wield the weapon?

"I also know the emissaries of the gods have been tracking these artifacts across the world. So if you do have one, it's only a matter of time before you find yourself pitched against an immortal."

The dragon shifted his gaze toward the crowd in the back. The silence had finally caught his attention. He instantly paled. "A Dark One," he exclaimed and rose, his body growing hotter and the tattoo on his arm moving with light.

"He is with me. He won't hurt you if you don't hurt me..."

"You said you weren't a Crow. But I would recognize the Reaper anywhere. He's one of them." The dragon reached for Nava, his fingers turning to long claws covered in golden scales.

"Don't touch her," Arkimedes growled as he reached the bar, his hand on the hilt of his sword. He was almost a head shorter than the pirate but stood just as tall with the shapes of his shadows.

The tavern was so quiet Nava could hear her own ragged breaths as she racked her brain for something to say. "Let's go talk somewhere more private. I promise you we aren't part of the Crows."

"Fuck that. Like I'd believe shit you say." His distorted voice held nothing back, and the scales growing on his body had extended past his elbows. He smelled like smoke and fire, and the scent turned her stomach as she remembered the Zorren.

"Settle down, dragon. There are more of us than you right now, and we aren't looking for a fight," Devon said as he came up beside Arkimedes. Although they were all speaking in hushed whispers, everyone could probably hear them.

This was it, their one opportunity—and he was shifting to fight them. Nava's heart was in her throat, beating quickly as she dipped her hand into her pocket and held the sun stone, wanting Ari to give her strength. The sun stone beat inside her grasp, warm as a newborn chick. She had to get the artifact to protect Ari and Arkimedes and to avenge Illaris.

"I've got this." She withdrew the stone, light against her palm but hidden from view of the crowd by her lap. The dragon's eye snapped to the stone, and his scales retreated as he settled into his normal size.

"What's that?" His voice wasn't the same as before, but he suddenly seemed more interested in the treasure than even his fear of Arkimedes.

Nava pocketed the sun stone and raised her chin. "We want to talk, in private, about what I already told you. I wasn't lying then, nor am I now."

Drake glared at Devon and Arkimedes. "I don't like to be outnumbered. If you want a deal, mouse, then meet me at the night market. There, we can talk business." He reached for his clay mug and gulped down its contents, making sure he was taking his time—even though a minute ago, he'd been itching to leave.

Then he walked in between Ark and Devon, knocking the latter with his shoulder as he passed him.

Devon stumbled, barely catching himself against the counter. Ice traveled across the wooden surface, triggered by his temper. "That fucking bastard always pisses me off when he gets away. I told you, Arkimedes, one of them was bound to be up in the rooms fucking a whore."

Nava's lips parted, and she blinked rapidly as she caught up to what Devon said. "You've met him before?"

"Draken? Yes, he and his crew are always in trouble with the Corvus. His captain is vicious. That fucking snake is not who we should work with. He's dangerous." Devon coughed loudly.

He wasn't even a ship's captain? Given his size and how alpha he acted, Nava had assumed he was in charge and used to make demands.

She looked at Arkimedes, who was staring daggers at the door through which the dragon shifter had disappeared. Both of them were soaking wet, as if they'd been standing outside in the rain instead of waiting inside for her to arrive.

It didn't take long for the patrons to resume their chatter, although uneasy tension lingered in the room.

Nava patted her pockets to make sure she still had her sun stone and the leftover gold, and followed them to the front door. "You didn't see Draken before I arrived?"

"No," Arkimedes said. "Everyone here isn't anyone we recognize—but everyone knows him." Arkimedes opened the swinging door for her and Devon to exit.

The cold evening air enveloped her like a thick, unwanted hug. She wasn't wearing warm enough clothing for this kind of weather, and she cursed her own stupidity for leaving her coat at the inn.

The server caught up to them before Nava could fully step outside the establishment, gripping the billowing sleeve of her dress. "Miss! You may not leave until you pay for Drake's drink. We won't welcome you back if you don't."

The nerve of him.

Nava yanked her arm away. "I never ordered that drink, and I won't pay for it. Next time, ask the person to see if they agree instead of ignoring them the entire night."

They left the round-eyed fae and loud place behind. Nava doubted she would ever step foot in there.

"Is there such a thing as a night market?" she whispered to Arkimedes. Devon was leading the way, a mere silhouette in the dark street before them.

"The guards often spoke about it, but I haven't been to it myself." Worry was etched onto the lines of Arkimedes's face. Even though they were outside and had the information they'd come for, something was wrong. "Speaking of the guards, two of them have been following us ever since we left the safe house."

29
NAVA

The whereabouts of the night market cost them another five gold coins, given to a drunken shifter they encountered while walking down the old port road.

How could Nava focus on the magical market around her and the pirate they needed to find when the king's guards were lurking somewhere in the shadows?

Arkimedes had filled her in on everything that had happened while they'd been apart. Was this the reason the bees had been around her at all times, even after they'd escaped the castle?

Nava shook her head and wrapped her arms around her body. She'd been wearing Arkimedes's coat for the entire walk here, and it almost swallowed her whole. The bottom edge fell right below her knees. Besides keeping her warm, his scent eased some of her nervousness.

"Do you think Leela sent the letter to Cameron?" she asked.

"You know what I believe."

She did. He'd told her that he believed Leela had provided a roof over their heads while informing the guards of everything that had taken place inside the house.

"She didn't seem to know that we are...you know."

"If my father believes it's a spell, then he wouldn't use a word the entirety of Caztian reveres to describe our relationship."

That made sense. Soulmates were rare and coveted by so many, supposedly designed by a higher power. Many had stopped believing they even existed. At one point, Nava had been like the king. She'd hated that she had no choice but to love Arkimedes.

But the reality was so different from the pictures painted by folklore and fairytales. When they met, his beauty had overwhelmed her. But love had grown gradually, born from trust and friendship. And, of course, there was the intense chemistry neither of them could deny.

Devon glanced at her with pity in his eyes. Nava expected a scathing remark about Leela to hit at any moment. "I hate to advocate for her," he said instead, "especially if she betrayed us, but the guards would've killed her, had she not agreed to do their bidding. Just like they almost killed us on the night we escaped."

"I agree." Arkimedes nodded, and hot air billowed out of his lips with a sigh. Dark circles were smudged beneath his eyes, an exhaustion that ran deep—like hers. "If Leela has been working with my father, then she had no choice in the matter. She is a victim here. Let's not forget that and lose focus on what's truly important."

Nava sucked in a breath and held her words. Of course they were right. Their words were for her, not for them. But it was hard to keep on fighting when everything good in her life kept being torn away. Her family, her home, her friends, her potion-making skills, her father. It was selfish of her to burden Cameron with the truth of it all when he couldn't do anything to help her. But it mattered to her—that he would know she'd never meant to leave him behind.

The scent of spices and magic permeated the air, and the distant chatter of strangers distracted her from the suffocating feeling. "I've only been to one magical market before, on Grey Island, right before Devon attacked the village."

"You had to bring that up, didn't you?" Devon said, although his tone lacked his usual mockery. He dodged around a cart, which held massive gourds in rust and green colors, and adjusted the lapels of his coat so they hid his grimace.

It was far too easy to forgive him for the disaster he'd caused then, especially now that he'd stopped being nasty to her. It was a terrible disaster not to hate him. If only the remorse didn't taste so bitter as it churned in her stomach. Nava forced her eyes away and hoped Gavin and Violet would forgive her. Hopefully, they would be understanding at the very least. She didn't know if she could lose another person she trusted, not right now. Not when the list of foes by far exceeded their friends.

"This won't be the same," Arkimedes said. He kept glancing up at the metal balconies of the narrow townhouses around them with a growing frown.

Did he remember that day? He'd been regaining his memories, and it was unclear how much he'd truly lost in the spell. He felt a lot more like his old self than several weeks ago.

The market spilled onto the narrow street that had brought them here from the tavern. When they entered, it was as if they were transported into a new world entirely. Wooden carts rested under a canopy of draped silks, illuminated by the soft glow of enchanted lanterns that swayed gently in the sea's breeze. Fae and humans wandered about, carrying their loot in carts or burlap sacks.

Nava itched her nose as the exotic spices blended with the briny tang of the ocean. "How are we supposed to find Drake in this chaos?"

Just as the words left her lips, Arkimedes's arms wrapped around her torso, and he pulled her out of the path of a small running creature.

"Stop the thief!" a woman with strange clothing and wiry wings screamed, chasing the small shape out of the alley and into the street.

Nava's heart hammered as Arkimedes let her go. "Was that a child? Should we help him?" she asked in a high-pitched tone as the three of them watched in horror as the two figures disappeared around the corner of the building.

The vendors, who had quieted after the commotion, continued as if nothing had happened, traveling from stall to stall, carrying baskets with trinkets, strange-looking plants, or bugs bottled in small potion jars.

"I want to help him, Nava, but we can't do that and find the artifact. We have to keep moving," Arkimedes said. His jaw clenched tightly, as if the words burned his tongue. "What we have to do will save them all."

It was true, but it felt wrong all the same.

"You two go ahead. I'll make sure she doesn't hurt him. I'll find you back at the pirate's den," Devon said in a strained tone. Darkness flashed behind his gaze as his aura deepened around him, and the air around them seemed to grow colder. Then he dashed toward the exit of the market, following the woman's footsteps.

"I'm sorry, Ark. I'm just not cut out for this kind of job. My heart is too soft." She'd been so ready to drop everything to help that child, and to hell with their actual task. She turned her head away, her cheeks growing warm. "I don't think it's a good idea for us to split up."

"This is a tough job, and your soul is beautiful. It's good to know what's happening here, especially because of who we are." Arkimedes reached for her hand and dragged her through the narrow path in between stalls. His grip was firm and kept her grounded. "A pirate's den is the term we used in the Society of Crows to refer to the black market stalls the pirates set up in places like this."

"How can we find it?" Her eyes darted around the narrow, busy space. The cries of the sellers advertising their wares made it hard to hear, their shouts echoing off the labyrinthine alleys.

"Their contraband usually contains magic, much like the artifacts. Most humans, fae, or shifters can't detect it because they don't have magic like me and you."

"Does that mean we will sense it when we come close? That's how Devon can find us later?"

"Exactly."

They walked in silence after that, surrounded by displays of curiosities she'd never seen before. Pools of light spilled onto the slick, rain-soaked ground, coming from the lanterns strung above their heads. It didn't take long to sense it, the gentle poke to her subconscious that warned her of the presence of magic.

Nava's skin prickled. This was similar to how she felt near a place haunted by Neems, and yet different somehow. This time she didn't want to run away—she felt drawn toward the sensation.

She craned her neck to look at the passersby. A year ago, she could not see things like auras or wards, much less sense the old magic lying dormant in an object. Especially in a place like this, where a myriad of impressions overwhelmed her senses.

And yet there it was. Clear waves of magic radiating in shades of green from a tent made of thick canvas. Nava approached with tentative steps, driven by her burning curiosity.

"Is that the place?" she whispered and pressed her body against the wall of the building beside them, allowing people to flow through the riverlike alley with ease. Arkimedes didn't need to answer her, regardless. They were almost at the end of the market, and she could spot the street beyond the pitched ceiling of the tent.

"You can feel the artifact in there as much as I do. What remains to be seen is whether the gods crafted it or if it was made by a Caztanian." Arkimedes pointed at the street, empty this late at night. Or this early, really—the first glimmers of sunrise marked the bottom of the clouds with hints of orange. "This is a pirate's den. Usually, they set up their stalls in a place where they can escape easily."

"Should we wait for Devon?" Nava asked. They'd been walking through the market for at least an hour, and her legs ached just as much as her body demanded rest. Having Devon's help inside the pirate's den couldn't hurt.

"No, we shouldn't stay here for long. I haven't stopped feeling uneasy this entire evening, and I'm not sure if it's because of the guards that are following us." Arkimedes glanced to the rooftops, tracking the shapeless shadows.

Worry churned in her gut.

Nava nodded and moved toward the thick canvas flap that served as a door. But before she could enter, Arkimedes's hand grabbed hers, making her pause.

"Are you sure you want to part with the sun stone?" His words rose clear in her mind, much like they had back at the safe house. This connection gave them an immense advantage when the walls could listen.

"No, but we have nothing else to offer." Ari had given her the stone so she could maintain a connection with him. Even now, it gently thrummed inside her pocket, a reminder that he was out there, alive and well.

A wall of smoke greeted them as soon as they crossed the threshold. Nava's heart leaped, and the image of a Zorren floated from the depths of her mind, of nails made of iron digging into her skin. The phantom ache of her old wound became a sharp throb as she gripped the pommel of the dagger strapped to her leg.

"No weapons in our shop," a man close to the door said. He pointed at a wooden sign that hung crookedly from a rusty hook jutting out of the canvas wall.

Sweat beaded on her temple as she took in the enclosed space. Logically, Nava knew this wasn't the smoke of fire, but her mind continued to spin, and nausea racked her body, making her wheeze.

"Breathe, Bee." Arkimedes's voice was a gentle whisper and helped bring her back to reality.

She took a deep breath and tried to focus on something that could anchor her to the here and now.

There. The two narrow tables on either side of the shop, and the three men waiting for them inside. Drake was sitting on a stool, casually leaning on his knee as he smoked a long wooden pipe.

"I told you, captain, the magic-wielder is small like a mouse." He rose and pointed in her direction with his sharp jaw.

"And she walks with the Reaper." The second man—the captain—picked a random trinket off one of the tables with a gloved hand. He didn't turn to meet them. "You aren't welcome here, Crow. Not after Aliyah."

The town of Aliyah in the Iron Kingdom? Nava turned to Arkimedes with a raised brow.

"That was a long time ago, and I was doing my job," Arkimedes said. "You should have known better than to sell contraband in the city. The ports are always crawling with Crows."

"Yes, it was a long time ago, but a dragon never forgets..." Heavy tobacco use had roughened the captain's voice. He took a long draw from his pipe and blew the smoke in their direction.

"We didn't come here to fight. We came to trade," Nava said, hoping to derail the conversation from old vendettas.

The captain wore very few clothes for someone managing a shop, as if he were ready to change into his animal form at any given moment. He'd rolled up the legs of his trousers, revealing muscular calves and ankles marked with scars. A leather vest did little to cover his tattooed torso, where a silver necklace hung, contrasting with the deep shade of his skin.

"Drake said you know about the emissaries? How did you hear about them?" he asked.

Aristaeus had told her the emissaries were hunting for the artifacts, and he'd lived for a long time. He'd watched the world go around the sun more times than one could count and all that happened within it. Nature whispered to him, sharing the truths of what he couldn't see.

But of course, the pirates would know about emissaries. They had probably encountered them many times before and undoubtedly feared them. It had to be why Drake had agreed to even consider this exchange.

Arkimedes glared daggers at the captain. "We don't have time to discuss our sources, Emir. If you have the artifact, let us see it and be on our way."

Emir's eyes were more beast than man when they landed on Nava again. "You know I have an artifact, Reaper. It's how you magic-wielders find us, no? But I haven't seen the stone the mouse wants to trade us for it. Show it to me."

Nava exhaled slowly and pulled the stone from her pocket with a sweaty hand. It flickered with the same warm light it had in the cave, illuminating the dark interior of the tent. They all went quiet. She couldn't even hear their breaths as they took it in.

If the market had been warm, standing inside this tent, so close to three dragon shifters, was like being back in the burning forest.

"What's that?" the third dragon asked.

"A sun stone made by a Beekeeper." Nava closed her hand around the glowing stone, hiding it from view. All three dragons tracked her hand as she shoved it inside the pocket of Arkimedes's coat.

"I have never heard of a gem made by the keepers of life. How did you obtain it?" Emir's voice rumbled in his chest as he blinked away the daze of utter desire from his face.

Aristaeus was going to kill her for trading away his creation, but perhaps he would understand that this was the only way to protect him from the evil immortal trying to kill them. "Now you've seen mine. It's your turn to show us the artifact."

"How do I know this supposed stone is even real and not a spell you're trying to trick me with?" Emir's eyes flashed to Arkimedes, who stood beside Nava. Her soulmate's wariness continued to bleed through their bond.

"It's real, and I can prove it," Nava said.

No one here knew what she truly was, so they wouldn't understand the stone was irrelevant to what she was about to do. Nava raised her hand and called to the bees that had been crawling this place ever since she'd entered. She asked them to fly, and all at once, they listened.

Her insects circled the bright stone in a cloud of dozens, drawing surprised gasps from all three shifters.

The spectacle lasted for a few seconds until she lowered the stone and the bees settled down. "Is that proof enough? If you aren't interested, we will leave with our stone."

"Let's take that little trinket of hers. It's just two of them against three of us." The third dragon shifter, who seemed younger than the rest, took a step forward, and his features elongated as he slowly changed into something inhuman. Nava took a hasty step away from the captain, who stood unmoving in front of her.

"I would like to see you try," Arkimedes growled, and his aura all but exploded around him. "She is mine to protect, and you'll keep your distance, or I won't blink before killing you all."

Nava's skin prickled with gooseflesh at the menacing tone Arkimedes used. He was deadly serious, too. And she didn't want her soulmate to carry these souls with him for the rest of his life.

The younger dragon laughed as if Arkimedes's warning was the funniest thing he'd heard in a while. It was likely the young one had never seen how quickly Arkimedes could kill. The captain, on the other hand, paled and lifted a hand, which stopped the man's cackle. "Drake, bring the table so we may begin the assessment."

Out of the corner of her eye, she saw Drake lift one of the wooden displays as if it weighed nothing. He carried it toward them, the few items on it rattling across the surface as he placed it in between the captain, Arkimedes, and Nava.

"When my man came back from the tavern and told me about your Beekeeper's stone, I returned to my ship to retrieve this," the captain said and removed the necklace hanging around his neck.

Drake slid a polished, wooden box in front of Emir, who used the pointed corner of his necklace to open the ornate lock. He picked up a small vial that rested on a deep purple velvet cushion.

A potion, really? Nava glanced around the table, hoping to find something a bit more...impressive. She focused on the green liquid sloshing against the glass walls of the vial. It stuck to them like a thick substance—the same color as the magic that had called her here. The vial vibrated faintly, like the flutter of her bees' wings.

This wasn't regular magic woven into the fabric of this object, but something much stronger and older, like the Vulcan the Crows kept in the safe house.

Made by the gods for the gods.

"You don't strike me as someone who trades illegal contraband often," Emir said, bringing his hand to his lips and slicing the skin of one finger open with his canines. Drake placed a dirty brass cup in the center of the table. "This is a blood oath. It protects the two parties from fake claims."

She brought her hand to her chest in response to his words. So they wanted her to bleed in that cup and make some sort of oath she had no protection against? No, thank you.

"The Reaper will testify. This is the way we do it. After the oath, we will tell you the truth of what we know of our artifact. Then you'll place the stone on the table and do the same. We can inspect it, and you may do the same with ours."

"If we choose to enter this trade. So far we have shown you we are indeed telling the truth," Arkimedes said, pushing the words past gritted teeth. A split second later, his voice filtered through to her mind. *"He is right, Bee. The blood oath won't bind you to anything other than speaking the truth about what the stone is. That's all. We have nothing to hide."*

Nava met Emir's expectant gaze, and sweat beaded on her temple as she brought her dagger out and pricked her hand. She allowed a couple of drops of blood to drip into the cup.

The scent of rotten flowers sitting in stagnant water drifted through the tent, although she wasn't sure if it was the oath or something else. But when she placed the sun stone on the table, her skin crawled with an odd numbing sensation that gripped her by the throat.

"This is a sun stone, made by the Beekeeper. It makes light and produces warmth. I don't know what other powers it has, but it gives me energy," Nava said. Her eyes opened wide as the words slipped from her lips. What the hell was happening to her? She glanced at Arkimedes, horrified but glad she'd said nothing that might give her away.

"Where did you get it?" the young dragon said from the back, just as Emir reached for the sun stone.

"In the forest." Nava pressed her lips tight, willing herself not to speak another word.

"She doesn't have to tell you anything else. The artifact is what we claimed. Now it's your turn." Arkimedes extended a hand to Emir for his artifact, and his misty aura wrapped around the vial as soon as it hit his palm.

"We discovered ours at a temple in the Gold Kingdom two years ago. The scriptures claimed it used to be a spell of auspices—or whatever. We don't have an excellent translator in our crew." Emir scratched his bald head and sneered at the wooden box. "I don't like you two, but I feel I should warn you. All of my men who dared to open that vial are now gone."

Auspices? What did that even mean? "Did it kill them?" Nava asked.

"It drove them mad, and that's what killed them."

Arkimedes glanced at her, probably reading every single one of her thoughts. "What else can you tell us about it?"

"We know nothing other than that Alera, the Goddess of Life, crafted this spell."

The Goddess of Life…? That must be why the magic waves had called so strongly to Nava, why they reminded her of her winged insects. Was the goddess somehow related to the Beekeepers?

"So it's a spell?" Arkimedes's flat expression gave away how unimpressed he was with this discovery. "Do you have anything else, like a weapon?"

"What do you think happens when we are out there searching for these, Reaper?" Drake scoffed, but he didn't move an inch from where he stood. His eyes were those of someone who'd spent too long out on the ocean. "Why don't you open it, Dark One, and tell us? You're a magic-wielder, no? You ought to know more than us." Drake spat to the side.

Arkimedes's lips peeled in a feral expression she rarely saw. Whoever these people were, her mate didn't like them one bit.

A random spell they knew nothing about was useless and would likely cause more harm than good. What were they going to do with a potion that drove people insane? Force it down the emissary's throat? He was already mad.

"This is all we have got, and this auspice protects whoever is strong enough to use it. I bet it won't harm you as it did us," the captain said. He seemed to be realizing the trade wasn't going in their favor and was still holding on to her stone.

"We need a weapon, not this." Arkimedes offered the vial back, but the dragon did not reach for it.

"You used to be a Crow, Reaper. You should know there isn't a vast array of artifacts left undiscovered. One thing I can assure you of, we are the only traders currently docked in this city in possession of a god's artifact. I urge you to reconsider." The captain's voice had grown deeper, and now his nose extended into the shape of a scaled snout. "I very much desire this."

Arkimedes's entire body stiffened, and for a second, Nava thought he might fight the dragon. But then he spun toward the tent's door just as an explosion shook the ground.

Nava lost her footing, pushed back by an intense pressure that sent her flying against the wooden table.

"Nava!" Arkimedes shouted, running toward her. A cloud of dust and smoke blew the tent's door open, right as the screams began outside.

30

ORION

Orion's ears rang, and his vision blurred. Everything inside the tent rattled as the ground shook. He clutched the goddess artifact in his hand, while orange-tinted smoke poured in from the outside, smelling of sour tangerines. He would recognize the blinding spell anywhere. Now, it numbed his skin. Soon, his limbs would follow.

Disoriented, he knelt beside Nava, hoping she hadn't hurt herself in her fall and was still mobile. She looked dazed and coughed into her elbow, shielding her face from the bite of the magic surrounding them.

"Try not to inhale too deeply." He wheezed out the command and pulled his scarf over his nose with his free hand. But it was too late, even for him—he could feel his power dull beneath the effects of the spell.

The sound of ripping fabric drew his attention. The younger dragon was clawing at the wall of the tent, right before the three of them left through the back, shapeshifting into large, winged beasts.

The captain glanced at Orion, baring long teeth and still cradling the sun stone. He was escaping, taking the Beekeeper's stone with him and leaving this useless vial as a trade-in.

"W-what's happening?" Nava slurred. He would have gone after the shifter, but he couldn't abandon her. The effect of the stunning spell was twofold: it numbed the magic-wielder's power and their motor skills. Even the bees crawled aimlessly over the ground, unable to find Nava easily.

"It's the blinding spell I mentioned before. Someone must have crafted it into a bomb of sorts. We have to go through the back." He dragged her off the ground and past the mess of trinkets the dragons had left behind.

"It couldn't be the dragons who did it—right? Was it the guards?" Nava asked once they were out in the alleyway. If anything, it was worse there than inside. People were crawling on the ground in a vain attempt to escape what they all knew was coming.

A couple of shifters stumbled past them, clinging to each other as they dropped bags of contraband that would land them in prison for a long time. Orion reached for Nava, pulling her under his wings for protection. His memories might have been patchy, but he knew she'd never experienced the Society of Crows in true pursuit.

Smoke clouded almost everything except for the shadows that approached, unbothered by the spell they were using to punish everyone. They wore gas masks with rounded glass eyes and pointed beaks.

It had been foolish not to think of them anymore after they'd escaped the safe house. All night long, the city had warned him that someone followed him around the streets as they prepared for the attack.

"It's the Corvus. They finally tracked us down."

Nava's stiff movements slowed as she looked over her shoulder. "They are here?" Her wide eyes barely seemed to focus on anything, and her aura flickered on and off as her ragged, panicked breaths intensified.

Out in the main street, where the air was clearer, he could finally think straight. The sooner they were out by the sea, the better they would fare. He moved them farther away from the alley, toward the pier and the ships with their hollering crews. "Try to calm your breathing, Bee. Put the coat over your nose."

He would have given her the scarf, but at that point, it was best if he kept a handle on whatever was left of his magic, for she had already inhaled too much of the bomb to have full control of hers.

"I can't feel anything. How am I going to fight them?" Nava asked.

Orion doubted the Crows had spotted either of them yet. They'd been lost in the throng of people who had fled from the market and into the streets. If they got away fast enough, they wouldn't have to fight them at all.

"Most establishments in town have basic protective wards. It prevents stun weapons—like the bombs—from being detonated inside the shops. My guess is the Crows waited to attack us once we were no longer under the tavern's protection."

Nava exhaled. "How long is the effect going to last? I can't feel my magic..."

Orion peered over her head at what remained visible of the night market.

The Crows' silhouettes loomed clear against the bright light of the lanterns, stalking closer and closer to the main street.

They should keep moving. But something nagged at him. Some detail at the back of his mind that didn't allow him to continue.

The heavy beating of his heart nearly drowned the screams of the crowds. And then he spotted it: the Corvus were dragging someone behind them. A tall male figure tied with a rope, pulled like cattle into the open streets of the ports. The man stumbled with each step he took, his features hidden behind his messy hair.

Orion's heart jolted as panic gripped him. Even at this distance, there was no mistaking him. "They have Devon," he choked out.

This place had been vibrant with colors only ten minutes ago. A haven for illegal trade that was harmless in the grand scheme of things. But the Crows had burst in and released a bomb where a child had been running but a moment ago.

If they had Devon, what would they have done to the small thief?

Orion pulled Nava behind an empty flower stand and crouched down. Its wooden edge dug into his palm as he rested his weight on it.

"How many Crows can you see?" Nava asked.

"Six."

His wings were too large to hide behind a small cart, but putting them away would use too much of his magic, and he had little to spare.

"Do they normally send that many when someone breaks into a safe house?" Nava flashed a panicked look at him. Then she peered around the corner of their hiding place to where the Crows were gathering in the middle of the main road. "Or is this a routine task and we are in the wrong place at the wrong time?"

"They are here for you and me..." he said, fully focused on the hunched shape of his brother. Devon was clutching his throat, as if he was having a hard time breathing. Of course. He was far too sick to deal with the effects of the bomb.

"But how could they know it was us? We didn't hold the Vulcan. And this is a large city."

"They likely used the Vulcan to track whoever broke in," Orion said. "It might have shown them Devon, and when they found him..."

"They found us."

Tonight had been the first time the city had warned him that something was wrong. Aristaeus had been right—his connection to the land was strengthening more with each day he remained in the kingdom.

Nava's brows knitted together, and determination set in. "My mother taught me to fight without relying on my magic because she knew that when we left Willowbrook, I might run into one of these bombs."

"Yes." If only Celeste had allowed Nava to learn about the world of magic sooner in addition to that. She'd been a cunning creature and always kept her cards close to her chest. And just like that, his annoyance at Nava's mother flooded back, like an old foe that had never left him. He was still too angry at her for taking Nava away—for cursing him to become a crow for a decade of solitude.

Fuck, he hated her.

"They are going the other way," Nava said.

Devon's legs faltered, and he nearly stumbled to the ground as a Crow pulled him down the street, away from where they were hiding.

Nava let out a shaky breath. "We are going to have to fight them, aren't we? To free him."

The rest of the group remained close to the exit of the market, searching through the unconscious people who littered the street, prodding them with their booted feet to turn them around and get a better look at their faces.

"Yes."

There wasn't an argument he could come up with that would convince Nava to run and hide while he attempted to release his brother. What was more shocking was that he didn't want to do this alone.

Nava was powerful and adept in battle. Her ability to heal would likely make the blinding spell dissipate from her blood faster than normal. Together, they were more powerful than alone.

"The Crows use this tactic when they are breaking up a group. Often, it's magic-wielding families who are protecting their youths from the draft."

"What tactic is that?"

"Staying out here in the open to make sure that I see they have Devon. They will start torturing him next," Orion said and turned toward her. Shame weighed heavily on his heart. How could he have stood back and allowed them to do this before?

"Here, in the middle of the city?" she gasped. Her feelings were bitter as they poured into his gut from their bond. Panic and anger blended together, fueling his own dread.

"It sends a message to the rest of the city as well," he said. "Do you have enough energy left to transfer one more time?"

Nava nodded, although she was frowning. Perhaps she thought he was about to ask her to leave him behind. Which, to her credit, would have been his first choice if he dreamed she would do it.

"There's a possibility they don't know you're here with me, which could give us an edge."

"You want to be the bait?"

"I will distract them long enough for you to transfer to the guy holding Devon. He has walked far from the rest. They won't be able to get to you fast enough. Once you free him, there will be three of us, which gives us better odds."

"Three of us without the full use of our magic," she mumbled but shrugged. "I guess I don't have a better plan."

Orion grabbed her face with both hands and pressed his forehead to hers. Gods, he wished they had more time to heal what they had gone through before having to fight again. He wished he could love her without having to fear that this might be a goodbye.

The waves crashed hard against the rock wall that divided the street and the sea.

"I'd rather fight them alongside you, even with half of my magic, than without you with the full use of my powers," he said, caressing her chin.

Her lips trembled into a sad smile. "Me too."

Orion pressed his lips to hers, and then he stepped out of the cover of their hiding place, his wings shifting before settling on his back. He swept toward the Crows, who paused the moment they noticed him.

"Let him go," he demanded, advancing on the group while tightening his grip around the pommel of his sword.

"Reaper." The first cloaked figure laughed and inched forward. Waves of bright gray power swirled around his wrists as he readied himself for an attack.

The helmet he wore muffled his voice, and Orion didn't recognize the tone or way he moved. He sounded too young to be someone he knew from his days in the Society.

"I've heard so much about you, the *dead* Dark One who disappeared a decade ago. Imagine our shock when we found you alive and assisting our traitor. Which makes you the same." The Crow moved with the cockiness of a recent but powerful recruit. The rest of the group kept their distance from the reach of Orion's powers. Smart.

"I'm the heir to this kingdom, and if you attack me or mine, you'll be breaking the treaties between the Society and the Crown," Orion said. It was a long shot, admittedly. He sincerely doubted the Crows cared about the treaties.

And if they got him out of here and back to the Iron Kingdom, they might use the same memory spell his father had employed to continue to use him as a weapon.

Or they might just try to kill him and be done with the whole thing, with no one being the wiser. There was no chance they understood how the kingdom spoke to his kin.

"What treaties?" The Crow barked another laugh and pointed to what remained of the market. "We discovered you in an illegal trading post just now, which King Oberon allows to exist in his land. I see broken treaties everywhere I look."

His steps slowed down, but he was close enough for Orion's power to reach him. The rest of his group were allowing this poor fool forward to test if he had, in fact, lost his ability to do magic. The silent figures had most likely met him in person before.

Interestingly, there hadn't even been a trace of shock when he'd mentioned that he was a prince. How many of his old comrades had known who he was all along?

"Next time I ask, it won't be so pleasant for you," Orion promised. Not an empty threat and that was even worse. His body craved to be replenished after the bomb had taken everything from him.

"Can you believe this fool?" The Crow scoffed, his magic on full display now, pure energy buzzing in between his fingertips. "You have no power left in you and no one even knows you're alive..."

All the Corvus' eyes rested on him. They still seemed unaware of Nava moving in the shadows as she transferred close to Devon's location, using her last reserves.

"Let's feed upon his delicious soul and show him what happens when they challenge us," a voice in his aura called.

Orion's magic returned to him slowly in swirls of black ink. They wrapped around his body as he gripped the wisps of what power remained awake after being stunned.

The ground and the surrounding buildings had lent him the energy he needed, and he'd accomplished his goal of distracting them. He had enough magic left for a single blast—and now it was time to move.

"Sahir, stand back..." A whispered warning came from the group, even as the young Crow sent his first attack swirling toward Orion.

But it was too late for Sahir to change his mind. Orion barely dodged the spell, and it singed a few feathers on his wings. Anger bloomed hot inside him, and he lifted a hand in the Crow's direction and gripped his soul.

Sahir moaned and drifted forward on his tiptoes, tugged by the energy of

Orion's curse. A song of laments pierced his surroundings as all the fragmented pieces of old souls swirled around Orion, greeting this new one.

The fresh energy he drew brought back his dormant power. His skin tingled as he fed on and on, until the Crow crumpled forward. It only left him hungering for more.

The Crow who held Devon lifted a trembling knife to his brother's neck. "Stop, Reaper, or I'll kill Black."

A second later, Nava materialized right next to him and stabbed him with her dagger. His scream pierced the silent night.

The ground trembled beneath Orion's feet. Was that Nava's doing or his magic? It didn't matter. They moved in unison, connected by a string of shared energy. Her skin glowed as she danced away from a Crow's spell and leaned forward to cut through the ropes that tied Devon.

Orion dodged another attack cast by one of the remaining four Crows who approached him. They were keeping a big enough distance that he wouldn't be able to pull at their souls. Four separate spells shot at him at once, and with his wings, it was near impossible to outmaneuver them all.

He rose up into the sky and flew toward the first, slashing with his sword until it cut through armor, flesh, and the bone of a ribcage. Then he pulled at the energy that remained to allow his magic shield to strengthen as he flew a few meters higher.

"Ark, watch out for—" Nava's words were drowned out by a battle scream. An arrow sliced through the air, striking his shoulder, followed by another that punctured his right wing.

He lost control and spiraled down to the ground.

Lightning illuminated the sky and struck somewhere nearby. Someone screamed, and the potent stench of singed hair and burnt flesh wafted up to his nostrils. Thunder boomed a second later as Orion landed roughly on the rocky ground, and the glass vial in his pocket cracked open, its gooey liquid seeping through his pants and onto his skin.

The god's spell took hold of his movements. For a moment, the adrenaline pumping through his veins dulled the ache from his rough landing and the arrows still jutting out of him. But the searing pain returned just as quickly. He needed to keep an eye on what was happening around him, dammit, but he couldn't. He couldn't breathe. He couldn't think.

Two blurred, winged figures touched down on the ground, chased by trails of shadows. The Dark Ones descended upon the Crows. Were there really just two of them? They looked more like ten.

Then his vision blurred as darkness claimed him.

"Ark, the guards are here."

Orion blinked. Nava was kneeling beside him. A magical rain fell on him, hot against his icy skin. There was a sound that didn't make sense until he realized she was repeating the same words again and again. "You are fine. You'll be fine."

Was she telling him or talking to herself? Even with his thoughts scattering like birds, he could feel the touch of her healing magic caressing him in spluttering waves that didn't quite reach him. At least the rain continued to fall. That meant Devon was still alive. Right?

"I need to take these out," Nava said, grabbing at the shaft of the arrow that stuck out of his shoulder.

"Leave them," he wheezed, lifting his body with trembling arms, chasing the warmth of her skin. Sometimes, the Society dipped their arrows in poison that was meant to slow down their victims. But he didn't think his body could handle the pain he was experiencing and the artifact at the same time. At least not without losing consciousness again. Even the blood pouring from the wound felt scalding. "The vial broke. The liquid is on me," he stuttered.

He tried to look over her shoulder to make out what was happening in the road, but all the shapes were blurry, and he couldn't tell friend from foe. He met her gaze and pressed his palm to her cheek, but the edges of his vision were already narrowing in.

"You had the artifact?" A brief look of comprehension flashed over her features, quickly replaced by pure panic.

"I do—did." He winced as everything continued to swirl around him. Tilting forward, he pressed his forehead to her chest, just as a spell cracked in the background, illuminating the wet street.

"Hold on, stay with me, all right? I can—I can use my magic to heal you. Just give me a moment."

Her arms wrapped around him, shaking with the effort to keep him sitting upright, but Arkimedes no longer possessed any control over his tired, aching body. He closed his heavy lids, chasing an odd sensation that began to brew inside his gut. It seemed to come from somewhere deep inside him and vibrated with power.

It felt similar to the warning he'd been getting all night but different somehow. While before, he'd sensed an enemy was tracking him, now he sensed a reprieve. The cavalry was coming, headed by the king himself.

How could he possibly know that?

"Bee, he...he is coming," Orion whispered, trying to swallow despite his parched throat.

And then darkness swallowed him whole.

31
NAVA

Enemies surrounded Nava, from the guards who had flown in minutes ago to the Crows who were fighting them from down the road. At least, they weren't paying attention to her and Arkimedes, which gave her a chance to get away.

"Wake up," she pleaded, choking as she gripped him by the shoulders. Arkimedes's eyes flickered under his eyelids. "Can you hear me? We need to leave now, Ark—please."

Tears blurred her vision as she struggled to pull air back into her lungs. She was teetering on the edge of losing what little composure she had left.

He is coming, Arkimedes had said before collapsing. His words ran circles through her mind as the urgency inside her grew. Who was on his way here? The emissary? She couldn't think of anyone else it might be. The two guards who had been trailing them were already here, and they couldn't have gone all the way back to the castle and warned the king of the Crows' attack. Right?

Nava hooked both arms beneath his armpits and pulled with all her strength, but she barely managed to move him a couple of feet along the bumpy road. No matter what, she needed to get Arkimedes out of the middle of the street and hide them away from further danger.

If she could catch a brief break, her body might regain some of its strength. Then she could attempt to heal him.

She wanted to puke as her arms slipped over the slick texture of his wet shirt and grazed the sharp point of an arrow jutting out of his shoulder blade.

A moan escaped his lips, but he remained unconscious—and far too heavy for her to drag under cover.

He was too big, too badly injured for her to lift without the full use of her magic. She pulled harder, and the veins in her forehead throbbed with exertion. The scent of magic burned her nostrils, drifting across from the spells the remaining two Crows were shooting at the guards.

"What are you doing?" Devon's voice broke through her ragged breaths.

She jumped and nearly dropped Arkimedes to the ground. "Out of the rain," she answered. If she hadn't been so tired, she would have screamed with frustration. "And away from them."

"It's not raining anymore, Nava," Devon said. He looked far worse than when she'd last seen him. Too pale, with purple lips that matched the circles around his eyes.

She leaned forward and continued to drag Arkimedes away from the battleground.

"Where are you taking him, exactly?"

"Behind the flower cart." Dammit, why did he keep slipping?

"Going at that pace, you won't make it there before they finish killing each other and come to find us."

She glanced at the battle still raging in the street. The two guards were using their shadow magic against one of the Crows, all the while avoiding the arrows still raining down from a nearby building.

"Can you help me, then? Or are you just going to criticize my handiwork while you stand there like a statue?"

"I don't think there's any way you could call *that* handiwork. Move over, Cat. I'll carry him from behind, you hold his legs. We'll go faster that way."

Nava pressed her lips tightly together so she wouldn't tell him where to shove his commands. Then she let Arkimedes sink to the ground. His skin felt like it was burning through the wet layers of his clothes—and through hers. Yet his face was as pale as Devon's.

Together, they managed to carry him behind the flower cart, skirting the large puddles that had formed while it rained. Devon leaned Arkimedes against the weathered wall behind it.

"Can you heal him?" he asked, crouching beside Arkimedes and pushing his hair away from his forehead. Then he examined the arrows jutting out from his wing and shoulder. "The Crows sometimes dip their arrowheads in poison… That must be why he is out."

Nava had used every last ounce of her magic to transfer to Devon and defeat the Crow who had held him. Gods, she hadn't realized how much she relied on her power until the bomb had dulled it. Now a hole gaped inside her.

It wasn't the arrowheads or the blood loss. Arkimedes had told her the artifact had shattered right before he fainted, and in the midst of her panic, she hadn't even considered what that meant.

"It wasn't the Crows, or at least not just their arrows." She shoved her hand inside Arkimedes's pocket. Pain shot through her finger as the broken glass pricked her skin. She withdrew it and examined the thick drop of blood that beaded on the tip of her finger.

"What is that?"

Devon watched in silent horror as she carefully pulled bloodied shards of the small bottle from inside Arkimedes's pocket, taking better care this time so she wouldn't get cut by the larger fragments. None of the green substance that had previously filled the vial remained.

"I need to make sure that the artifact isn't harming him further…" How much of the spell had Arkimedes's skin absorbed? Maybe it had only soaked into his woolen pants? She debated pulling the garment off to examine further.

A cloud of pure magic assaulted her nose as the guards and Crows shouted curses at each other in ancient languages. The smell alone was foul and brought tears to her eyes.

"We were trading for the artifact when the Crows attacked." Nava tossed the pieces she'd fished out of Ark's pocket to the side, eager to fill in the silence. Best not to focus on the fight going on around them or that it was growing quieter by the minute.

"You found it—and it's all over him?"

Nava sucked in a breath and pressed both hands to Arkimedes's chest. His rapid heartbeat was palpable beneath her touch, too fast for an unconscious person. Sorrow sank its claws deep inside her. If she still had the sun stone, it would have amplified her energy, and perhaps she would have been able to help her soulmate. But now it was gone, lost to the grimy hands of those dragon shifters.

"The pirates called it a spell, though it was a potion and not the weapon we were hoping for. I didn't even know Arkimedes had taken it until right before he fainted."

A curse slipped past Devon's lips, and he slammed his open hand against the cart's side. "I shouldn't have gone after that kid. I wasn't able to help him either way, and it distracted me from the Crows approaching." He frowned at Arkimedes's unmoving body. "If I'd been there with the two of you, perhaps it wouldn't have gone this way."

It was far too quiet all of a sudden. Not a single sound traveled toward them from the street.

As if reading her thoughts, Devon peered around the edge of the cart, then pulled back quickly. "There are two Crows left, and they're checking their dead. We don't have long until they search for us."

Nava swallowed and tried to grasp at whatever sliver of magic lay dormant within her. But there was nothing left for her to heal Arkimedes, let alone fight with. "Are the guards dead?"

"I don't see them. They might have gone after the archer." Devon sighed, pressing his body to the building behind him. "What a team we make..."

"Even the best team wouldn't be able to hold out against such odds," Nava said, forcing the words through the knot in her throat.

Soon, steps echoed through the empty street. The Crows were drawing closer, their words still muted by the crashing of the waves.

"More useless deserters and pirates. I don't see Devon Black, the Reaper, or the girl."

Too close. Devon pressed his finger to his lips, and Nava held her breath, waiting.

"They couldn't have gone far. The archers got the Reaper."

Nava slid the dagger from its sheath and tightened her sticky hand around its pommel. They could still fight and make it out of here alive, right? Surely this wasn't the end. She was tired, but so were the Crows.

A bell rang from a nearby rooftop, echoing over the two-story buildings that lined the boardwalk, and a sudden rush of shadows dropped from the sky. Nava counted at least twenty guards. They landed on the road with a rustle of flapping wings.

Looked like the Crows' lives wouldn't last long.

She peered around the edge of the cart. They all wore shiny metal armor in warm copper tones with brass details. She'd seen that same armor many times when they'd stopped her in her tracks in the castle. The final Dark One who descended had the longest wings, black like the shadows that wrapped around him, shrouding him in darkness. Why had the king come all the way to the ports when he could send out his people?

There weren't that many Crows left, right? Not unless there were many more archers than she'd originally thought. Nava glanced down at Arkimedes and pressed her hand harder to his chest. He'd known and tried to warn her. Not that it would have made a difference.

"Line up all the Crows on the street and find me my son—and *the girl*." The king's voice deepened on his last two words. Goose bumps rose on Nava's skin as she drew closer to Arkimedes.

His hot breaths were fleeing his lips in ragged puffs, hitting her face like burning coals. What was worse—to face the Crows or the king?

Fear paralyzed her, gluing her to the spot. How were they going to escape when they couldn't defend themselves with magic?

The next time she dared to peek, the guards were dragging the two remaining Crows across the cobblestone and toward the stunned bodies of the passersby. They fought against the guards' hold, no longer wearing those weird, bird-like helmets that had protected them from their stunning spell.

The king moved like a shadow, silent, although his shimmery metal armor should surely have made some noise. His silver hair stood out in contrast to his immense black wings. Like Ark, his aura billowed out angrily as he stepped closer to his prisoners.

"To kill a Crow is forbidden by the gods," one of the prisoners muttered. The same words she'd read in that book at the safe house.

"Is that so?" King Oberon drawled, looking over his shoulder as laughter rippled through the ranks of the guards behind him. "Are they here to protect you now?"

"We haven't broken our treaties. You agreed that we may seize the black markets."

"I remember the treaties I signed better than you, and I cannot recall where I gave you permission to harm the heir of my kingdom—my only son?"

"I saw no prince here." The Crow peeled his lips back to reveal jagged teeth stained with blood.

"You dare lie to our king?" The guard who held the Crow shoved him to the ground, nearly forcing him to kiss the puddle he knelt in. "Need I show you what we do to those who harm our royals, prick?"

"We're terribly sorry and meant no disrespect," the second Crow said in a shaky tone. Clearly, he was much more afraid than the first, or at least showing it more. "It was an accident, Your Majesty—we didn't know the prince was here. We've been hunting deserters, not Dark Ones."

She pitied them both—and herself, for soon she would be kneeling alongside Devon on that ground, ready to be killed. Or worse. "Do you think we can escape now?" she whispered, briefly turning to Devon. But he shook his head almost imperceptibly. He didn't have to say a word, for his emotions were written all over his face.

"You believe you can fool me? That I don't know exactly what happened here? I have eyes all over my city." King Oberon's steps grew louder. Was he moving away from the Crows and closer toward them? Could he sense Arkimedes?

Nava peered into the street, just as Arkimedes's father raised his hand and called upon the Curse of the Fallen. Not a second later, the first Crow crumpled onto the ground. Dead. The king turned abruptly, and his cerulean eyes met hers, and then he took the second Crow's soul.

32
NAVA

Nava's ass hit the ground as she jumped back behind the cart. Hopefully, it was all in her head, and the king hadn't seen her.

Of course, she wasn't that lucky. Not a minute later, King Oberon was standing four feet away from them. His face, barely visible behind the swirls of his power, twisted with ire. "Is Orion alive?"

She nodded, at a loss for words.

Devon's sword caught the light of the moon as he stood up, stepping between Arkimedes, Nava, and the king.

"Before you strike, consider if you want to die right now or live to see another day," the king said to Devon. "I know my son cares about you, but I've lost my will to care."

"I'm already dying." Devon gripped his sword with frosted, white knuckles. "I'd rather die right here than watch you hurt them."

Did Devon think he had enough magic left in him to actually harm King Oberon of the Dark Ones? Or was he stalling?

The king's brows knitted together as his lips twisted into a deep grimace. "I don't care if Orion can't forgive me for killing you, Crow. I won't warn you again."

Even through Nava's panic, her mind sharpened at the king's words and his hesitancy to strike. It didn't add up. He claimed not to care, but Nava got the impression that he cared a lot more than he would ever admit out loud. Was that why she'd remained alive back at the castle, even though he'd clearly seen through their lies at the time?

If she'd stayed inside her gilded cage like a good little prisoner, King Oberon would have had to devise a better way to get rid of her. Perhaps that was why he'd made her go to that horrid seamstress before the masquerade ball. To taunt her, make her hate this kingdom, and in hopes that it would drive her to leave.

It had almost worked...

Now that she thought about it, perhaps the king had always hoped that she would try to escape so he could kill her without having to hurt Arkimedes further.

But then her dress had changed from the customary blue all the guests in the castle wore to black, the color of the royals, and the king had realized she was more than just a thorn in his side. She was the future queen in Arkimedes's mind.

Devon stayed rooted to the spot, though his face turned toward the nightmare of black shapes that morphed out of the shadows of the buildings. She'd been so worried about the king and his reasons she hadn't noticed the flying fae approaching them. They were closing in from every direction.

Nava shot to her feet, lifting her short dagger with a steady hand. Unlike Devon, she had no resources left; all her magic was depleted, and she needed the sun or plants around her to regain some of it. But she wouldn't make it easy on them either.

"I don't want to fight you," she said in a trembling voice. "But I will not let you take him so you can erase his memories again."

The fate of the world depended on their success in defeating the emissary. He was letting the Zorren in, and the demons wanted to kill the Beekeepers. Without them, there wouldn't be balance in Caztian for a long time. She was a human blessed with the strange gift of being a Beekeeper, but it was Aristaeus they needed to protect the most.

He'd once told her it was up to them to keep the world of plants thriving, for dark creatures—like demons—intended to burn it all to ash. Together, they could travel the world like pollen and dust, flit from forest to jungle to make sure new seedlings would sprout when a large natural disaster took it all away.

If Arkimedes lost all his knowledge about his connection with Ari and Nava again, they wouldn't be able to defeat the evil coming into this land. She hated to admit it, but this went far beyond their love for one another.

"I can offer a healer who will help him, and you staging this little...performance is harming him more than I ever would." The king gestured at Arkimedes's unmoving shape.

Her heart ached at his words. He was right. She couldn't help Ark right now...

King Oberon took another step forward, ignoring Devon completely. Nava believed her initial assessment about the king not wanting to hurt him, but she also believed his warning. Did Devon not care whether he lived or died?

Whatever his wishes were, his life wouldn't be on her hands.

"You can't take Orion's memories again, Your Majesty, or your kingdom will suffer. We are working against something much bigger than politics," she said in an unwavering tone that conveyed her conviction. "I am a healer, and I can make him better. I just need time."

The king tilted his head and paused. His face softened, and so did his shadows. "Humans lie constantly, yet I sense you're speaking the truth. I have allowed you three to run around my city, searching for things I can't claim to understand. But I also know you went into the forest when new fires rose up. To fight the demons, I presume."

"Yes."

"My men couldn't find a trace of the Zorren when they got there." The king spoke more quietly than before and glanced around the wide-open street. On one side, the dark waters of the Leona Sea crashed in wild waves against a rocky wall, and on the other, two-story-high buildings shielded the view of the castle in the distance. "I don't intend to harm you today, sorceress, but you will come with us, and I recommend you comply."

A part of her wanted to fight him, to tell the king to go to the shadow lands himself. But when she looked at Arkimedes, all the fight left her. If she didn't come willingly, she would get hurt—or worse yet, he might command his guards to kill her. It seemed unlikely, as he probably suspected they were soulmates by now. But that didn't mean he wouldn't use Devon as a bargaining chip. Besides, while Nava possessed the gift to heal, she had no idea how far or how fast it would work with his kind of injury.

On Grey Island, when Mortimer stabbed him, her healing powers had worked remarkably fast. In a day, Arkimedes had been fighting Devon's army.

Nava glared at the king and shot Devon a look while she lowered her weapon. To think that this man had been her enemy a year ago. And now she was here, ready to comply with her other enemy so he wouldn't get hurt. Her softness knew no bounds.

The king stepped to her side, crouched down, and picked up his son from the ground as if he weighed nothing.

"Do you have to be the one taking him?" Nava returned her dagger into its sheath, her hands clenched into fists. She wanted to scream in frustration. And to fight him.

"Inar, Liure, and Olli—take our wounded civilians to the nearest healer. Kane, send a message to the Society of Crows and tell them that if they set foot in my kingdom again, we will kill them all," the king said.

Of course he'd ignore her question completely.

"Wait," she said. What did he mean by that? Surely he wouldn't hurt Devon, right?

King Oberon's blue eyes met hers for a long, suspended moment. "Eris, take the future queen back to the castle. She only gets to speak to you until I give permission otherwise."

Nava's lips parted as the king's words registered in her mind. He'd called her the future queen. Her heart hammered inside her chest so fast that it hurt. Arkimedes lay unmoving inside the king's arms.

Her hair blew into her face as the king flew away without another word. Debris scattered around them as most of the guards took off after him.

Unlike the time she'd arrived in the kingdom months ago, when all the guards had treated her as if she was the scum of the world, this time the guard approaching her from the shadows took off his helmet and dipped his head. A sign of reverence. Nava blinked, confused.

She recognized him as one of the two who had been fighting the Crows before the rest arrived alongside the king. He brushed his wavy, blond hair away from his face, revealing the sharp angles of his cheekbones and smooth skin, now covered in a thin layer of dirt and sweat. Blood dripped from a deep gash on his chin.

"Are you the sentinel that's been trailing us?" she asked. What was she meant to do with this? Was it all an act, a trap, or was he truly showing her respect?

"I am Eris," he confirmed. "The land compels us to obey and protect our royals. King Oberon commanded us to keep you safe, and we did so, gladly." The fae placed his open hand over his armor, right in the spot where his heart would be, and dipped his head once again.

Nava could only gawk at him. Surely she had spilled some of Alera's spell on herself and gone mad.

"Horseshit," Devon said, stepping forward, closer to Nava. He lifted his sword with the smooth motion of a trained warrior. "You almost killed her back at the castle, multiple times. And you called her a witch."

Faster than Nava could register, the fae scooped her up in his arms and lifted her off the ground before she could protest. She screamed, tightening her hands around the guard's wide neck and shoulders as they rose into the sky. The street below became smaller and smaller.

"Nava!" Devon screamed, and his hands brightened with his magic as a spell shot from the ground, grazing the long feathers of Eris's right wing.

"You didn't have to leave like that. Devon is part of our group!" Nava complained. She'd better not move too much. She couldn't transfer away from his arms and into a safe spot if he were to drop her.

If she survived this disaster, she would have to have a proper conversation with Devon about his inappropriate use of magic. Shooting at the wings of a fae who was flying away with her in his arms was hardly going to help her.

"The king commanded that no one should speak with you, milady, until further notice." Eris looked away—but she didn't miss the pained expression flashing through his features. He held her tighter to his body, as if that alone would prevent him from dropping her.

"Except you, apparently." She pressed her lips together, trying to spot Devon in the small city below.

"I'm your royal guard, madam," Eris said. Then he focused on the castle that loomed in the distance. "After what happened with Fael, your last guard, the king didn't think he would be the correct guard to protect you—or the prince."

"I'm aware of who Fael is, Eris. He betrayed Arkimedes's trust. He hurt him back on Grey Island. Kidnapped him and lied—" Which apparently the fae couldn't do but kept doing repeatedly.

While Nava had never been someone to opt for aggression first, she would do anything to protect Arkimedes from those who had betrayed him. She didn't understand the fae or their politics, but what Fael had done was wrong. He had hidden behind the mask of a friend when he had been a foe all along.

At least Devon never lied. When he wasn't a friend, he made sure Nava knew it. Even the king had the decency to be truthful about his intentions.

"Are the guards going to hurt Devon?"

"The king commanded us not to harm the prince's fake brother."

Ha. What a funny—and untruthful—way to refer to an adopted sibling. Clearly, they had no clue how strong their bond was. Admittedly, she hadn't really grasped it either a few months ago.

"Are you going to hurt me?"

"I would never harm the future queen of the Copper Kingdom. And if I did so before, it was because I didn't know who you were."

"How about the king?"

Eris was quiet when his eyes, blue and vibrant with light, met hers. "Be careful with the king, madam."

So much, so vague.

They'd been stuck near the port for a couple of hours at most, but it felt like an eternity. Nava glanced at the ships sailing in the orange-speckled seas, one of them carrying her precious sun stone. Hopefully, whatever the artifact was that had seeped into her soulmate's skin, it wouldn't hurt him.

Even if right now it had gotten them captured.

33
NAVA

The staff in the castle welcomed Nava as if she hadn't left as a fugitive. Even the maids who awaited them outside in the gardens, wearing their long orange dresses, beamed at both Eris and her. None of them said a word, though. They simply bowed as they walked by.

Their welcome wasn't the oddest thing to greet her, however. What truly shocked her was the strange burst of energy that instantly filled her depleted reserves and the gentle probing sensation at the back of her mind. Not entirely unpleasant, just odd.

Not even the creepy white flowers in the garden felt like they were spying on her. They had once frightened her, but not today. Right now, they were only offering to help.

From all around her, long tendrils of yellow energy reached out, moving like wispy fingers over the stone path. Being near the castle felt almost like being inside Ari's cave. The power running through each marble brick and every blade of grass knew who she was.

It didn't take long for the bees to find Nava once they'd stepped inside the actual building. They flew and crawled over the castle walls, demanding an explanation for her prolonged silence in their small voices. But through her exhaustion, Nava could only think of Arkimedes's well-being.

"Where is Orion?" she asked, turning toward Eris, who walked a couple of steps behind her. He hadn't said a word about the strange behavior of the staff, nor about what was going to happen to her now. The king hadn't specified where she would go once she was here.

"He might be in the infirmary or his chambers."

Was that where he was taking her? Their surroundings looked familiar. She'd been through these halls before.

Nava's shoulders tensed when the green room she'd stayed in before came into view. She'd never wanted to see its huge double doors again.

Eris had brought her here through a different route, expertly avoiding crossing in front of Arkimedes's room, which lay beside it. Nava understood why he had done it. Could he sense that the castle was returning some of her magic to her? She had enough now to transfer away a few times, and damn the consequences. But perhaps it was best to allow him to think she was still under the king's mercy. She could transfer to Arkimedes's room later.

The king's plans for her weren't her biggest worry at the moment.

Eris pushed the green room's doors open for her. "This will be your room. I'll be waiting right outside the door. If you require anything, just ask."

Nava didn't move. A sudden dread held her hostage. She couldn't bring herself to step right back into the cage she'd been a prisoner in for weeks on end. "I don't want to go in there," she said, breathing harshly as her palms dampened. "Please take me to see Orion."

"I'm afraid I can't do that," Eris said, shifting from foot to foot. He was clearly uncomfortable with what he had to tell her. "He is being tended to by the best magical healer of our kingdom. You have nothing to worry about."

Nava tapped her worn boot against the polished floor, trying to mask the panic that twisted her stomach into tight knots. "He will heal faster if he has me by his side."

It was common knowledge that soulmates benefited from being near each other. Which was probably why they'd brought her here, instead of to the dungeons downstairs—that was, if the king intended to imprison her again. It seemed doubtful when he had called her the future queen in front of his guards and whoever else was observing the fight outside.

"Right now, you're tired and could use some rest." Eris pointed at her clothes.

Nava looked down and gasped as her heart leaped. She'd been expecting to find the filth of the wet streets marking her dress or Arkimedes's blood staining the fabric. What she hadn't envisaged was for her previously maroon dress to have shifted to black, the color of the royals.

There it was. The real reason Eris did not whisk her away into some unknown tower in the castle to never see Arkimedes again. The citizens, guards, and workers knew of her. She hadn't caught a lot of good luck lately, but this she would take with a smile.

"I know it's hard to stay here," he said, gesturing to the dark room beyond.

"But you mustn't be afraid. I was told by the king's women that you can shapeshift into something magical—" Eris's voice faded into a breath, but he didn't look afraid of her. His expression turned reverent. "And that you can move through space without us being able to stop you. So why not go in and wash off? Rest. Later, you can see the prince."

Was it true that a guard wouldn't be able to stop her? The Zorren had cut through her in the middle of her transferring. Nava wrapped her arm across her wounded rib, feeling the ghostly pain of the demon's claw digging into her. "So don't stop me. Take me to see him now. I will wash off in his bathing chambers."

"The king commanded you not to speak with anyone," Eris said, shaking his head. "It's not you who will get punished if you go there, madam. It will be the healer and the nurses. If you ask them questions, they will answer you. It will seal their fate."

And just like that, her good luck vanished. The king was always one step ahead. "What about you? Will he hurt you?"

"I accepted my destiny when I offered to be your guard."

She wouldn't trust his words, not like she had trusted Fael. Yet it was hard to ignore how he pulled at her heartstrings.

There was no lie hiding in his expression. Still, the fae were cruel manipulators. "Why would you and the rest of the staff in the castle heed my command if the king has told you to do something different?"

"Because of his sickness. It's why we came to get the prince back on your island. Our allegiance changes as his health worsens."

Ah. That was why the castle felt different. "Fine," Nava said. "But I won't stay here for long. I'll bathe and change, and then you can take me to him."

Eris opened his mouth and then shut it again, standing rigidly against the door as she crossed the threshold.

A bath wasn't a bad idea. It was one of the few luxuries she'd enjoyed while being a prisoner here last time. And she was filthy.

The flames in the fireplace burst into life as she strolled in, warming her chilled body. The fine tapestry that hung behind the four-poster bed was new and depicted a white horse with a horn growing from its head. A new rug lay beneath the bed, handwoven to perfection in beautiful patterns of turquoise shades that reminded her of the Leona Sea.

Nava turned to thank Eris—and caught a look of pity flashing over his face as their eyes met.

Then the king's words rang through her mind. *"She only gets to speak to you until I give permission otherwise."*

When Eris mentioned the healer and the nurse, he had withheld Orion's name from the list. But the king wouldn't allow her to speak with anyone but Eris. Not even with Arkimedes.

"Wait, Eris." Her heart jolted as she rushed toward the door, reaching for it as a spike of magic surged through her fingertips. Her body became air, but the weight of her aching limbs held her back.

Eris slammed the door shut with such force that the glass panes of the balcony doors trembled. Nava slammed her entire body against the wooden surface that prevented her escape, trying the handle. Of course, it was locked.

They had imprisoned her in this hole, even though Arkimedes was hurting.

The brass heated under her grip, but the doorknob didn't move. "Eris!" she shouted, banging against the door with all her strength, until pain radiated from her hand to her elbow. "Let me out this very instance."

At first, it didn't seem like the guard would answer, but she waited, breathing heavily. If only she could force the door to explode into a million splinters and let her out.

"Try to rest, madam," Eris said. "It's been a rough day. I'll bring you breakfast in a while."

"Fuck you!" she shouted, slamming her body into the door again, until the pain traveling from her arms to her shoulders brought tears to her eyes.

These pricks wouldn't keep her locked inside this room ever again, as if she were a doll to be toyed with. Nava was a keeper of life and a magic-wielder, mate to the prince of the Dark Ones. She wouldn't be caged again.

The heat of her fury made her skin tighten and then loosen, and Nava transferred quickly in the air, heading toward the sliver of air beneath the door.

She hit a hard wall that prevented her exit.

It was transparent to the naked eye—which was why she'd missed it when she first entered. It had to be a spell that was triggered by the door closing. Otherwise, she would have felt it.

Hard air formed an invisible bubble, sealing off every crevice of the room. Now that Nava had hit it, she could see the markings of finely woven magic, crafted with tight black threads. Like a spider egg.

She couldn't allow this.

For the next several hours, she attempted to leave through every nook and cranny that appeared big enough for air to weave past. But the king had hermetically sealed the room from the inside.

Tremors raced through her as she reached for her dagger's pommel, gripping it so tight she lost the feeling in her fingers. Not that it did her any good here. "If you don't let me out, Eris, and take me to Arkimedes right now, I will kill you."

There was promise in her voice. She wasn't bluffing.

A cry tore past her lips. How stupid was she not to have seen this coming the moment the king appeared somewhat friendly in the ports?

It all made sense now. He'd let Arkimedes, Devon, and her roam around his city while the sentinels made sure neither Arkimedes nor Nava left the kingdom. Meanwhile, he'd crafted the perfect spell to keep her trapped in here.

Silence descended upon the room as she allowed her body to collapse against the smooth surface of the wall and onto the cold floor. She pressed her head to her knees and let her tired mind drift.

"It's not personal, madam," Eris said in a cautious tone, as if he didn't want to be overheard. "If I let you go, the king would kill me, and I would be a disgrace to my family. So you understand my predicament..."

She wanted to tell him that he'd lied to her, but then again, if she recalled every word he'd used carefully, he'd only told her she would get to see Arkimedes *later*.

Not at a specific time. Later could mean an hour from now or two years.

"You can't keep me away from him," she said, her voice trembling. "I told you, we heal better when we are together. You're harming your kingdom by keeping us apart."

Perhaps she could talk some sense into this fae?

"He is next door, madam, so you're very close." If Eris meant to make her feel better, he failed miserably. "The healers are with him, and the prince will survive," he continued, undeterred by her silence.

Sniffling, Nava wiped her face with the filthy sleeve of her coat. There was no use in crying. Tears wouldn't help her or Ark.

No, she had to come up with a better plan.

She focused on the webs of the king's spell right outside the balcony. Beyond it, the brown bodies of her bees crawled over the outside of the door, trying to get to her.

Unlike the last time she'd been locked in here, Nava now knew what her role in this family was. She was the future queen, and the gardens belonged to her. The plants outside had welcomed her. The castle had even restored her power.

It was as if it had known she was about to become a prisoner and wanted her to understand that she wasn't out of options. Slowly, she rose, the numbness in her body dissipating as she approached the doors and peered at her insects outside. There were so many of them she couldn't count them all.

Nava pressed her hand to the cool glass, and the threads of magic that were woven onto the surface reached toward her. The sensation was unfamiliar but welcoming, the same low voice that had whispered to her when she first arrived.

When Nava arrived here, a maid had told her the castle provided what people needed, as though it was alive. And right now, a whispering voice welcomed her home. *Home?*

Nava shut her eyes and focused on the strings of power that surrounded her. They were similar to the magic webs she often saw draped over plants, and that was something she could work with. She tugged on the soulmate bond but met only silence. Arkimedes was alive but sleeping.

But her connection to him would hopefully help her. *I can't be a prisoner in my own home,* she thought. If the castle was indeed a sentient being connected to Arkimedes, then it should hear her.

The glass trembled under her touch, and the bees accumulated where her hand rested, although they remained outside. More and more swarmed, so many that they obscured the bright daylight outside.

If you're the castle and you're happy that I'm here, then let me know, she thought, encouraged by the answering vibrations. The walls could hear her.

Once, when Leela had been fixing her hair, she'd spoken ill of the old queen. The room had gone cold and dark that time. Leela had been afraid to speak of Arkimedes's mother, as if the king had forbidden it. But now Nava wondered… Had the reaction been the castle all along?

Or perhaps she'd gone mad. *Why are you allowing the king to lock me in? I'm the queen.*

It was a stretch, and she could sense the magic threads of the walls as they pulsed in defiance. Was it aggravated by her questioning the king? Or at her referring to herself as the queen when she wasn't quite yet? But the tree was alive, and that had to count for something.

This was her only way out of there and to Arkimedes. Every fiber of her body told her as much. The glass of the door vibrated faster, ringing as if a storm were shaking it.

At any moment now, it would shatter.

"Madam?" Eris called from outside. He'd probably heard the tremble of the doors and felt the walls vibrate. The doorknob rattled as he tried to enter. The door cracked open an inch, and Eris's mane of blond locks came into view.

"Don't let him in," Nava said. "I need to go to my soulmate, castle. Let me out."

The door slammed shut in front of Eris's face, and his panicked gasp filtered through the door, making her smile.

"Won't you leave us if it lets you out, queen?" A voice, sweet and strange, rang inside Nava's ears. *"Won't you leave us and take the prince with you if it lets you out?"*

Nava's throat constricted, and she took sharp breaths at the intrusion in her head.

This didn't feel like it did when Arkimedes or Aristaeus spoke with their thoughts. That felt natural, like breathing. This, however, felt like an intrusion in her mind. Like the castle shouldn't be speaking to her so directly yet.

"You aren't the queen yet," the castle said with a touch more menace in its tone, and Nava's ears rang painfully. Like she shouldn't listen to its words, even if its energy felt warm and inviting.

"Let me out of this room so I can heal my mate, your future king, before the emissary gets to us."

"Madam, let me in at once. I don't want to call the others," Eris called, trying the doorknob again, but the door remained shut.

"Then don't," she responded, closing her eyes to fend off the pain that filled her skull. Gods, it hurt. "Are you going to take me to Orion?"

Eris grunted in frustration. "I... I can't."

Wrong answer.

Nava looked at the door. Her bees pressed on the balcony door, and a hairline crack crawled up the glass. Inside it, a fragment broke loose. The hole was so small she could barely see it, but it was there.

"Will the future queen leave if it helps her?" the castle asked.

"I won't leave the kingdom," Nava promised. And for the first time, those words didn't feel like a betrayal of herself.

"Then...it's time. The princeling of darkness is alone."

This didn't feel like home yet, but the kingdom was something she could learn to love. She wanted to help the citizens who were barely scraping by. She wanted to prevent people like those children in the bakery from ever having to suffer like that again.

Arkimedes had been right. Together, they had the power to make changes. To address the issues that others ignored.

The weblike black spell retreated around the hole. It was tiny but big enough for Nava to escape.

She reached for her bond with Arkimedes, but it remained empty. Panic seared through her, her body tensing as she looked over her shoulder.

"I don't want any guards in his bedroom, only the healer and the nurse," she said out loud to the room. Her ears were still ringing with a continuous high pitch from listening to its words.

Hopefully, this time, it wouldn't talk back.

No one stopped her as Nava moved through the humid air of the early afternoon toward her soulmate's room. His door was unlocked, and like the castle had told her, the room was empty.

Here, she didn't hear Eris's frantic knocks on the door anymore, and that alone brought her a semblance of peace. As soon as she'd crept past the balcony doors and into the darkness of Arkimedes's chambers, the weight of a thousand stones dropped from her shoulders.

She ran toward him across the expanse of the room, grinding to a halt beside the bed.

Arkimedes was fast asleep, clean and out of his bloody clothes. His bandaged wings lay beneath him in an awkward position that didn't look comfortable. His eyes were closed, his long dark lashes kissing the top of his cheekbones.

Nava pressed her lips together and ran her fingers over the soft velvet covers of his bed. It was the first time she'd seen him looking this ill, and her worry for him only increased with each step that brought her closer to him.

The slick marble floors were cold beneath her bare feet. She had left her boots in her old cage. She inspected every dark corner for anything odd—a hidden fae waiting to ambush her, perhaps.

The castle said he was alone, but how could someone be truly alone in a place like this?

"Ark?" she whispered, perching on the bed and reaching for his hand.

A thick green salve covered the deep gashes on his knuckles from where he'd fallen after the Crows had shot him. He didn't move or answer, and if it weren't for his shallow breaths, she might have thought he was dead.

"I'm here now," she said. Was she reassuring him or herself? Could he even hear her?

Best not to focus on his pale skin or the dark circles lining his eyes. The parallels between Ark's and Devon's appearance were a coincidence, surely. He'd only used the potion once, unlike Devon, who'd held the Vulcan twice.

Arkimedes's lips twitched into a grimace. Even in his slumber, he seemed to be in pain.

Nava's body sank into the plush mattress as she crawled closer to him. Her touch was the only way she knew how to use her healing magic. Even if, right now, she felt so depleted physically and emotionally that she could barely hold herself up.

Her eyelids drooped as her adrenaline dwindled further. The intense night and busy day had finally caught up with her. Still, she couldn't allow herself to go to sleep. What would happen when Eris found out she'd left the room?

Would he call the other guards, and would they try to break into this room to remove her?

What if he called the king? Even if the castle didn't allow the guards in, surely it would let *him* in.

With each blink, it took her longer to open her eyes. The ache in her body throbbed deep, resonating through every inch of skin and bones.

"With the king and prince asleep, you are the one I heed," the castle rumbled, and Nava's ears rang at the sound. *"Only those who intend no harm may enter until he wakes. When you wear the crown, then I shall answer to you."*

The mild pain dissipated quickly after the castle quieted. Or perhaps it had never spoken at all. Was she the one who had gone mad?

It didn't matter. Sleep claimed her.

34
NAVA

A bang jolted her awake. Blinking sleep out of her eyes, Nava focused on the fae standing on the balcony outside Arkimedes's room.

Eris stared at her through the glass, his arms crossed, his blond hair whipped around his face by the wind. She turned to Arkimedes, who was still asleep, but at least he felt warm to the touch once again.

Good. Whatever the healer—or Nava—had done to help him must have worked a bit, although he was still unconscious.

She scooted across the bed and walked toward the door. It was clear Eris couldn't enter. Judging by the sun setting behind the castle walls, she'd slept for a few hours.

Once she stood in front of him, she mimicked his pose by squaring off her shoulders and lifting her chin in defiance, glaring at him. "What do you want?"

She'd not forgotten her promise when he hadn't let her out. But now that she was here with Arkimedes, her fury had dimmed, and she didn't see the need to kill him.

"How did you escape?" he asked.

The castle's magic thickened before her, floating over the door with strings of gleaming power. It was keeping its promise to her.

"The castle released me," she said, not seeing the point in lying.

Eris blinked, once, twice, thrice. His face lost all color as his lips parted. "The castle?"

"That's what I said." Nava took a step back. She was just about ready for that bath she desperately needed.

"Wait, madam. Don't go yet," Eris pleaded, pressing his hand to the door. A snap of energy popped him, and he quickly pulled his hand away, shaking it as he squinted at the wood. "You've got to let the healer in, madam. The prince needs him."

"If the castle is not allowing them in, then it must sense they are a danger to me," she said. "Is the king still sleeping?"

Eris's jaw dropped, the knot in this throat bobbed as he swallowed. "How did you know…?"

A hint of worry pricked at the back of her mind. How long did she have left until King Oberon woke up? How long until the guards barged in here and tried to take her away?

"You won't lock me anywhere ever again, Eris," she said instead, shaking her head as she retreated into the room. "I'll stay right here, besides Arkimedes, as I'm meant to. Any fae who is loyal to me may enter and help us until Arkimedes recovers."

"And that's not me?" he asked, frowning. "I swore to our king that I would protect you from any danger, no matter what."

"And yet the castle doesn't allow you in." She pointed at the door and turned around, walking away without another look back.

Nava lay down next to Arkimedes. She draped a leg over his body and her arms around his torso. Her magic wove around them with a gentle buzz as it worked to heal him.

It was their second day since returning to the castle. The few fae who had come in to help had just left. They had brought them food and potions. Most were maids, and there had been one nurse as well, who had seemed thrilled to meet her.

Nava didn't know how long she lay there with her eyes closed while thinking of nothing except healing his wounds. She couldn't sense the poison in Arkimedes today, and his skin was already looking less sickly than before.

She tightened her grasp on his naked shoulder and felt his breathing stutter where it washed over her forehead.

When she raised her head, his long lashes were rippling with faint movements. "Are you awake?"

Arkimedes's eyes cracked open, revealing his bright green irises. "Are we in my chambers?" he asked, his voice like gravel.

Her heart beat so fast she felt light-headed. "Yes, we've been here for a few days." A sudden thickness clogged her throat, and she swallowed deeply, trying to stop herself from crying. "How are you feeling?"

"Like a beast ran me down," he said gruffly, rubbing his face before attempting to sit up.

Nava pushed him down with one hand. "Don't you dare try to get up. We are in enemy territory, and I need you to be well so we can handle whatever the king throws our way."

Arkimedes lifted a brow. "What happened?"

And she told him everything. From him passing out by the docks to her being locked inside the green room and then escaping with the help of the castle.

He shifted about as she spoke, clearly uncomfortable with his wings scrunched underneath his body. But he also attempted to stay still, staring at the ceiling unblinkingly while he digested all the information. "I got the potion on me…"

"Yes. How are you feeling?"

"Strangely good," he said, "So, Eris said my father was indisposed, and then the castle told you he was asleep? Has Eris attempted to come back here?"

"Not since last time."

"How long have I been out?" he asked. "And have you heard about Devon?"

She shook her head, worrying her bottom lip with her teeth. "You've been out for a couple of days. I have no idea how Devon is doing or where he is."

"Fuck. I need to get out of here and figure out what's happening with him —and with my father." Arkimedes sat up, his face twisting with pain.

Nava opened her mouth to demand that he lie back down but shut it when he shot her a warning look. "Before he locked me away, Eris told me that the kingdom's allegiance has been shifting to you—and to me—because your father's health is worsening. He said that's why they kidnapped you on the island. I guess that's why the castle helped me break your father's spell as well. I've been feeling like I've been going mad, because surely a castle can't speak, right?"

"Neither can bees, and yet they speak to you." Arkimedes reached for her hand and squeezed it tightly. "Like I said before, we have magical ties to this place."

True. She knew this, even if a part of her still struggled to accept it. The notion just felt so strange.

"I—I've been feeling the shift," he admitted, ruffling his hair with one hand like he usually did when he was nervous. "It's been building slowly. I sense things happening in the kingdom I didn't before. Like the city telling me the Crows were going to attack and that they were watching us. Or when I somehow knew my father and the guards were coming to aid us."

Just as she was about to answer, gooseflesh erupted all over her skin. A warning.

Arkimedes sat up straight, staring at the door. "Someone's coming."

If he felt it too, it couldn't be the bees warning her. It had to be the castle.

As if answering her thoughts, the walls trembled as the door handle moved. *"They have the king's permission,"* the castle rumbled in her ears. It sounded unhappy.

Pain shot through her head, and Nava scrambled to her feet, reaching for her dagger on the nightstand.

"The king is awake," she told Arkimedes. The doors swung open, and Eris stepped inside, along with two other guards. They paused, their eyes widening as they found Arkimedes awake and sitting on the bed.

"Your Royal Highness, we didn't realize you'd be up," one of the guards said. She'd never seen him before. His long copper wings matched his polished helmet.

The wisps of their shadows hugged their bodies, a reminder of the power they all possessed.

"No, you didn't," Arkimedes said darkly, shifting in bed with calculated movements. His aura deepened around him to match his low growl. "Were you planning to hurt my mate while I was unconscious?"

Their lips parted, and they retreated by several paces. Then they all dipped into a deep bow.

"The king commanded she shouldn't speak to anyone but her royal guard," Eris said, his skin shimmering with sweat. He looked at her with arched brows, and something shifted in his expression. Realization that she'd healed her soulmate as she had said she would—because Arkimedes was fine, even without the royal healer.

"He can't order her to stay away from me," Arkimedes said. "The laws of the gods demand that soulmates be respected." And he slipped out of bed in all his naked glory.

The three guards lowered their gazes.

"She was next door, Your Highness," the third guard said. The same ridiculous excuse Eris had given her.

"Did she request to come here?" Arkimedes asked, stepping dangerously close to the guards. Nava's stomach churned. His ire was spreading through their bond like a festering wound. "When you kidnapped me from my home and left her behind, you didn't know who she was to me, and therefore, you didn't break the godly laws. Now you do, and you will respect us. Or we shall leave."

Oh, he was angry.

These three fae were one wrong answer away from becoming a part of Arkimedes's aura. A couple of days ago, when Eris had first locked her away, perhaps Nava would have looked the other way. But right now, she had her head on her shoulders. She didn't want any of them to die simply because they were following a direct command from the king.

If anything, the guards' allegiance shifting to them faster would only help them. They couldn't fight the entire royal guard, the Zorren, and the emissary on their own. They needed allies, not more enemies.

The two guards near the back exchanged worried glances before one stepped forward. He passed his polished copper helmet from one hand to the other, giving away his nerves. "We wouldn't have come, sir. Th-the king sent us to get your mate so she could meet with him for a conference."

"My father wants Nava to come alone?"

"Well," the guard stammered, "we didn't know you were awake, sir. His Majesty wants to know how she could escape her chambers and what happened in the market."

"Shut up, Elliah." The third guard narrowed his eyes at him. "We can't divulge this information unless the king commands it."

He had white wings and was clearly incapable of reading the room. Or perhaps the other guards were feeling compelled to speak to Arkimedes more than he was. After everything that had happened, Nava doubted Arkimedes had the patience to deal with a disgruntled guard.

Nor did she.

"Well, I can tell you she isn't going anywhere near my father without me."

"His Royal Highness should continue to rest," said the guard with the white wings. "We won't harm her."

"And are you going to stop me from coming?" Arkimedes asked, and his shadows sneaked closer to the guard, who tensed visibly. Silence descended until only the sound of their heavy breaths cut through the air. "Where does he want Nava to meet him?"

"In his private library, sir," Eris said. "His Majesty isn't feeling well enough to come here."

"I see. You can tell my father that we are coming as soon as I've eaten and freshened up."

"And when will that be, sir? Your father is not a patient man."

"Tell him I'll be there after dinner." Ark paused, his eyes narrowed on Eris. "Send someone to the city to find my brother."

The three guards bowed in response and backed away one by one, leaving them alone in the room once more.

Nava's blood rushed in her ears. Gods, she felt light-headed, her palms damp with sweat.

"You two woke up at the same time. It seems strange, no?" she mumbled.

The hardness in Arkimedes's features softened when he took her in. She could only commend him for remaining so unaffected by standing naked in front of everyone. He'd resembled a statue.

"It's odd," he agreed and walked to the bed. For a moment, he sat, breathing heavily and pressing his hand to his forehead. "I wonder if me being ill affected him somehow?"

So many mysteries. It felt equally odd to grow used to another overwhelming connection to something else besides her bees.

"Why are you naked?" she asked after a moment of silence.

Arkimedes met her gaze. "The guards just came to bring you to my father, there is a building talking in your head, and you are wondering why I'm naked?"

Nava shrugged, her cheeks growing warm as she traced every hard edge of his body with greedy eyes. "I'm just a simple girl."

He huffed a laugh. "I suppose I've been secretly wondering the same thing. My guess is that the healer noticed there was a cut on my leg. He must have felt a remnant of Alera's spell on my trousers and skin and decided to strip me so he could examine it properly."

Ah. Well, that made sense and was a lot less nefarious than she'd feared.

"I don't want to go and meet your father," she said.

"I know, but now that we're here and have no artifact to speak of, we should talk to him about the emissary. We still have no way to kill him, and while I don't trust my father, we can't fight him and the emissary at the same time."

"Ari said that he might own an artifact we could use?" Hope seeped into her tone, but it was short-lived. No, that was stupid. How ridiculous of her to even dream that any good could originate from the king.

Arkimedes shook his head and lay down, covering his eyes with his forearm. "I doubt we're that lucky, Bee."

And while she preferred to be positive, she couldn't help but agree with him.

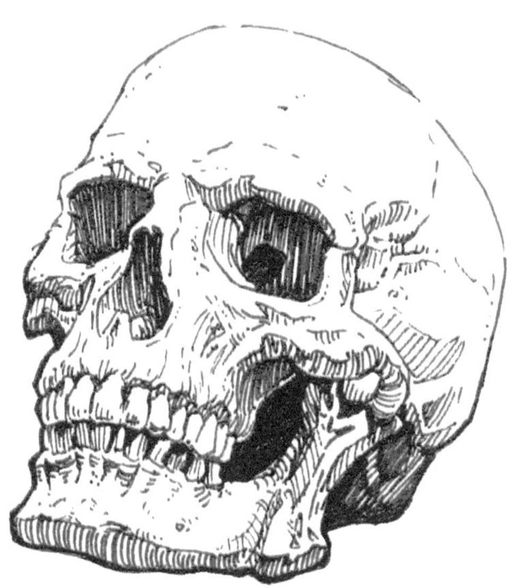

35
ORION

Seven guards came into Orion's chambers when the sun was setting. Perhaps the food they'd just eaten would be their last meal, although at least he had a strong feeling somewhere deep within that he didn't have to worry about most of these fae.

"You are well aware that I know how to get to my father's library," he said, by way of greeting. "Did he command all of you to come and get us? Seven against two? It seems unnecessary."

"No, sir," the guard nearest to him said. His glowing eyes shifted from side to side as he blinked rapidly. "All of us came just in case you needed our help. We thought a group of us could assist you with your journey. If His Royal Highness were to be in need of help."

"If it displeases you, sir, some of us can leave," Eris added from behind Nava.

Orion mulled it over. Other than the ache in his wings where the arrow wounds were still healing, he felt like himself. Sure, he was sore, but he had more energy than he'd had in weeks.

Nava's healing magic was working, though he wondered if, much like Devon, he would slowly deteriorate unless she helped him again. Poor Devon. Where was he right now? Had he left the kingdom? It weighed heavy on his heart to think of how he might be doing, as sick as he'd been when Orion had last seen him.

"No, it's fine. You may stay," Orion said, taking note of how carefully they examined him during his prolonged silence. Perhaps they expected him to collapse at any given moment, and that wasn't ideal. They had to believe he was at full use of his power so they wouldn't get any ideas about Nava.

Most of the group dipped their heads in a solemn bow, except for a couple near the front. The kingdom compelled them to obey the king, and yet Orion could sense some of their loyalties were slowly shifting. Like the castle and the city.

"Do you have any news about my brother?" He asked, as they began their trek to meet the King.

"No, sir," Cyrus said.

The tower holding his father's library was as grand as Orion remembered, but the closer they got to his room, the more trepidation Orion felt. His hands prickled with an unease that crawled over his skin, traveling up his arms and shoulders, all the way to his skull.

He spotted the ebony doors of his father's library at the far end of the hallway. The warm shades of the sunset spilled through the windows and caught the gilded patterns carved into the wood.

No fae waited outside to guard this place, so when they entered, it surprised him to see it wasn't empty.

Three wingback chairs stood in front of the marble fireplace. The king sat in one. Their eyes met, and Orion ground to a halt. This was the first time he'd seen his father ever since King Oberon had commanded his concubines to attack him.

The crawling sensation in his skull intensified as he forced himself to move forward, making sure his expression remained as blank as possible.

He'd been in this library many times before, but it had never felt as suffocating as it did now. Its tall, vaulted ceilings and stained glass windows closed in on him. He was stepping into a nightmare.

Orion tightened his hands into fists as his temper flared hot. Everything his father had done to him... Taking him away from his home with Nava. Almost killing her. Robbing him of his memories. Even if Orion could understand his father's reasons, it didn't make this easier. "You called?"

Two of his concubines stood unmoving by the bookcase, pretending to page through a book. Orion didn't think they were the sort to read. No, they liked to fight—to plot about how to remain in the influential position they held, whispering their thoughts into the king's ears.

Like the stories they had told Leela. They believed Nava had him under a spell, and perhaps that was what being a soulmate meant to them. If his mother had been his father's soulmate, as the whispers traveling around the castle suggested, then the mere mention of their rare bond could be upsetting to his women.

The king crossed one leg over the other and draped his hands on top of his knee. His white hair shrouded his face as he narrowed his eyes at Orion. "I don't recall asking *you* to come, son," he said in an icy tone. "But the guards informed me of your demands to join your mate. If you must be here, then sit down. I won't be looking up at you."

His father gestured at the two empty chairs, just as one of his ladies placed her book on the shelf and went to fetch wine from the cart. Orion glanced at Nava, who had been quiet since they'd left his room.

Where were the rest of the concubines? Hiding in the shadows, readying for an attack? Orion inspected every corner, expecting to see the dark, oily energy shifting in the air, but there was nothing there.

Much like him, Nava was perusing every shadow in the room. It was difficult to miss the insects that crawled around her.

"Can you blame me for wanting to come?" Orion pointed at the concubine Orna as she placed a carafe filled with burgundy liquid on the small table next to his father. "Last time I was here, they attacked me, and you commanded the guards to kill Nava, too. You knew we were together before you even kidnapped me."

"So you think you remember everything?" the king asked. "The real question you need to ask yourself is: are you going to put aside your own selfish desire to hate me for the good of our people?"

Manipulation didn't sit well with Orion, and realizing it was happening didn't make it any less difficult. Self-doubt crept in as he recalled his earlier promise to Nava: they would leave if she wanted to. He resisted the urge to fidget, unwilling to show vulnerability in front of his father. That would only give him what he wanted.

"That doesn't change what you did."

The king gave a dismissive wave. "I knew you'd recover from their punishment." He sounded far too lively for someone who looked as ill as he did. "It was the only way I could ensure that you wouldn't use your gift on one of them."

"You know full well I don't use the curse if I can help it." Orion pushed the words past gritted teeth. "And I don't forgive you for hurting Nava and me, not even if your reasoning was that you feared I would hurt them."

How could his father call something so wicked—stripping away the pieces of a soul—a gift?

The king reached for the wine and filled a crystal goblet before bringing it to his lips. The wine wasn't poison, but the alarming speed with which his father gulped it down made Orion wonder if he was using it to dull his pain.

"I didn't know who she was to us then. You never told me you had a soulmate. Had I known, things would have been…different."

"Perhaps I would have said something if I could remember a damn thing." Orion sank into the chair, and Nava followed his lead. "You don't look well. Why have you become this ill so quickly?"

"I didn't get an explanation from the gods, Orion. It may be because magic is dwindling in our world and the kingdom demands more of me." The king waved his hand again and placed his empty glass on the table. "I'll be better by morning. Going to the ports earlier took its toll on me."

That had been on Orion's mind ever since he'd woken up. Why *had* the king come all the way to the west side of the city when he could have simply sent the royal guards?

As if reading his thoughts, his father continued. "The treaties clearly specify the Crows can raid the night markets to search for deserters. However, they can't take one of mine. No fae, no guards—much less my son."

"So you came all the way because of the treaties?" Nava scratched her forehead. "I don't understand how that works."

"What is that you don't understand?" his father asked. The bite of his condescending tone made Orion's gut twist. Clearly, a civil conversation was *not* the king's aim.

"Why does the Society of Crows even exist?" She raised her arms above her head and stretched.

"I thought you magic-wielders received a special education on the subject from your prestigious schools. Aren't you all supposed to serve the Crown from youth? It's the first thing they teach you there."

"My parents did not send me to the army," Nava said. "And my mother shielded me from the Crows and the Crown. She was part of the Society, but she didn't agree with their methods."

The king tapped his chin, studiously watching Nava as she spoke. "The ignorance of humans never ceases to amaze me. It's unacceptable in a future queen."

"If you can't be nice, Nava and I will leave." Orion rose from his chair.

"Sit down, Orion. We have to talk about what happened in the market. To answer your question, *Nava,* when the gods nearly obliterated our world, it was because of the wars between humans and fae." The king continued to speak, undeterred by Orion's glower. "The destruction of the natural resources and the gods' favorite creations set them off. A few magic-wielding humans and fae managed to hold them at bay—for a time. But we were losing, so my family and those of the founders made a deal to pay the tithes in order to pacify them."

Orion hadn't heard this tale from his father before. Undoubtedly, the version that the Society of Crows taught their recruits wasn't quite the same. King Oberon was likely closer to the true source of this ancient knowledge, since his father's bloodline was directly connected to the fae founder.

"They also created the Society of Crows, who maintain balance in the world. Their primary purpose is to avoid us upsetting the gods again. But they have a secondary task, and that is to keep magic from disappearing, so if the gods were to strike us, we could fight back."

"But…?" Orion prompted.

"The Crows ceased to care about the fae and the balance held in the Copper Kingdom a long time ago. Everyone knows they favor the Iron Crown over the rest." His father's frown deepened. "To answer your previous question, I came to the ports because only the king can overrule a direct command coming from the higher-ups in the Society. No guard could have demanded that they release the three prisoners they found in the black market."

"Not even him?" Nava asked, pointing at Orion.

"You tell me, girl. The Society hid my only heir in a kingdom made of iron, knowing full well the fae can't visit a place like that. Now, I've answered your questions. It's your turn. Why were you at the night market?"

Nava and Orion exchanged a look. Could they trust the king? Did they even have a choice?

"We were looking for a god's artifact," Orion said.

The king reached for the carafe of wine again and refilled his glass. "The healer mentioned you had the markers of an artifact's poisoning. Why would you need one to defeat the Crows?"

"I don't care about the Crows—not right now, at least. We know who is letting the Zorren into the kingdom, and the only way to stop him is with an artifact. We were in the middle of striking a deal with the dragons when the Crows ambushed us." Orion let his weight sink into the chair with a heavy sigh. The ache in his wings became more prevalent the longer he sat. "But all the pirates could give us was a liquid spell. It cracked and soaked into my clothes and skin."

"Who is allowing the demons in?" the king asked, leaning forward slightly.

"An emissary of the gods. He has been opening portals to the forest and attacking the Beekeepers." As soon as the words left Orion's lips, Nava tensed all over. He would not tell his father what she was, but speaking of this at all with someone like him—it felt dirty.

Yet with the useless artifact broken, they didn't have a way to defeat the emissary.

"How could you possibly know that?" the second concubine asked. She'd been standing by the bookcase in complete silence. Orion had almost forgotten she was there.

Judging by his father's jolt, he must have, too.

"I know because he attacked me in the forest. He has a vendetta against our family."

"Did he look like me?" the king asked.

Orion sat unmoving in his chair, his lips parting as he looked from the king to Nava and back again. "Do you know him?"

"All of you. Leave the room. Now." His father pointed at the door. The guards hesitated but obeyed after making eye contact with Orion. The concubines hovered nearby, still watching their every move and overhearing every word. "That includes the two of you."

"Your Majesty can't be considering staying here alone with them..." Orna stepped forward, worry etched deep into her features. Out of all of his father's companions, she looked the oldest. Full fae seldom showed their true age, not until they were ancient. How long had she been serving the royals? She seemed the boldest of them all.

His father sighed, shooting her an exasperated look. "Do as you're told, Orna. I might be sick, but I'm not powerless. Now go."

The guards waited for the two concubines by the doors. The silence grew charged as they trailed from the room, an uncomfortable energy hanging in the air that was hard to tolerate.

As soon as the doors closed behind them, his father spoke again. "My twin brother has been a thorn stuck in my side for a long time. Ever since he went after my queen."

What?

Orion had been expecting them to be twins, but he'd assumed the fight must be about the right to the throne, not his mother. Shock rendered him speechless, and cold crawled up his body, numbing his mind. He suddenly struggled to think, unable to weave the disconnected strands of information into a cohesive whole. "W-what do you mean?"

"That before I realized what was happening, Leir had seduced Briar right under my nose."

Leir, his father's twin and the messenger of a god. Orion couldn't hear anything other than Nava's sharp intake of breath. He attempted to swallow, but even that seemed impossible.

"Why would an emissary care to seduce the queen—or bring destruction to your kin?" Nava asked.

"Jealousy drives those with weaker minds to madness. You can't reason with someone like that. No crime of passion warrants the destruction of an entire kingdom. But he is an emissary of the gods. It's not the first time they've attempted that."

What was his father trying to say? Jealousy, a crime of passion? Who'd committed it—him, her, or the emissary?

Nava's wide eyes and trembling lips told Orion that she was also putting together the horrible puzzle that he desperately longed to ignore. "Was he jealous because you and the queen were soulmates?"

Thunder cracked, rattling the stained glass windows. A storm was brewing.

The king's eyes skittered away from them, focusing on his drink instead. "She said we were soulmates at some point, but I never quite understood the bond she kept referring to. I have a connection with this castle—with my duty to its citizens." He paused and took a sip of the wine, which stained his lips deep red, like blood. "I loved her in my way, but she was always ill, and it was hard to connect."

They hadn't been soulmates, for there was no way to deny the pull that tied them together. But if his mother had believed them to be...had Leir been her true soulmate all along? Perhaps she had seen him in passing and assumed they were the same person?

Either way, Orion wouldn't like the answer. His mother's death looked more and more like an execution the longer he sat in this room.

Past the king's chair, a piece of wood hung from the wall. Orion had spotted it months ago when he'd visited here to obtain the key to unlock the magic-canceling bracelet Nava was wearing.

His father glanced over his shoulder, following Orion's line of sight. His face twisted as he realized what Orion was looking at. "You asked me once what that was..."

"And you said you like to collect art."

"I do, although I guess it was not the entire truth. The carvings were once part of the throne room's door, gifted to my father by a skilled soothsayer. They formed part of a prophecy that heralded he would have twins and lose one of them to the gods. I kept it here because I like to remind myself who is supposed to rule and claim the queen, and who is supposed to stay a servant."

The tithe. The royals of the Copper Kingdom parted with their second-born to Dargan as payment for his forgiveness. "When did you remove the panel? When you discovered they were having an affair or after she died?"

"I had it removed after Briar stole you from your crib and took you away from me."

"How did she die?" Orion pressed his body into the chair. His heart beat in his ears like a drum.

Thump, thump, thump.

"I don't like to repeat myself, Orion, and I've told you already. Your mother died in a fire, and as you know, the west side of the library was obliterated by one."

And there it was, the carefully concocted lie that hid behind half-truths. Months ago, when Orion first began to ask questions about his mother's fate, the king's answer had rung like a falsehood. But now the actual truth could only reveal how truly evil his own blood could be.

"You claim you want us to work together? Then stop lying to me!" Orion slapped his hand against his thigh. The stinging sensation grounded him in the present, pushing away the vivid memories the ghost of his mother had shared with him.

"Why are you so sure I am lying?" His father's sudden stillness was so absolute, so unnatural that it sent a shiver down Orion's spine.

Orion shot to his feet and strode around his chair and toward the fireplace. Nava continued to sit quietly, hands folded in her lap as she stared wide-eyed into space. The bond was a confusing cacophony of emotion, and he could no longer discern who was feeling what.

If Leir had been his mother's true soulmate, then he would never have hurt her. His motivations were becoming so crystal clear that Orion felt like throwing up.

"You never mentioned you had a twin who was an emissary, let alone that he was out for your blood. Instead, you sent me to the forest for weeks on end to track down the humans who were supposedly burning it down."

The king's pale skin was mottled with pink and red patches. He bared his teeth. "How was I supposed to know that bastard had anything to do with the fires? I haven't seen or heard of him in decades."

"If you care for the kingdom as much as you claim to, stop this deceit. I already know what truly happened."

"Full fae can't lie, and you know that. I don't have human blood like you." His father's eyes shone with a wickedness that would make most people cower. He wasn't technically lying—he was expertly avoiding and changing the subject.

"When I arrived at this castle, you insinuated that my mother died in that library. Gave me some clues and allowed me to fill in the blanks. I assume you gave the rest of the kingdom the same treatment. Yet I know it's not the truth." Orion's vision tunneled in on the king as he pushed away from the fireplace and strode back toward Nava. He needed to remain by her side, in case his father used his power to hurt her.

"How would you know where it happened? You were but a babe, and she abandoned you in another kingdom that hates our kind."

"I've seen her die," he growled. Those horrid dreams and how he longed to escape them. He'd never wanted to piece together the gruesome reality of what had happened to his mother. But now it all made sense. And he felt dizzy with it.

She'd taken Orion away because the king realized she had slept with his brother. Had she known they were two different people? How could she not? They were almost identical, but their eyes were different. While his father's were blue, Leir's had been blood red.

Then his father had burned her alive in that tree. Her final thought had been that the one she'd loved most had killed her. Even with her dying breath, his mother had believed he was her soulmate.

But that was impossible. Orion and Nava couldn't feel that strongly for anyone other than each other. She must have known.

"The queen thought you were going to hurt Orion, and that's why she took him away," Nava said, digging her fingers into the layers of her skirt, while her skin glowed bright yellow. "It had to be."

"Perhaps," the king said. "But I told her many times that I would never hurt my son. Even when I thought *Orion* was Leir's. I always intended for him to remain my heir."

Had the king become violent when he believed the baby was another's? Scared her enough to take him away to another kingdom—one he couldn't reach?

"Can immortals even have children with mortals?" Nava's voice held bitterness as she glared at the king. "Because I doubt they can."

"Orion didn't have pointed ears or the wings of our kind. Only a weaker fae could have produced such offspring. Not I, who possessed the Gift of the Fallen." The king stood on wobbly legs, leaning heavily against the chair.

Even now, the broken child inside Orion worried about this monster. But he would never refer to him as father ever again.

"The midwives told us that your lack of fae traits was an effect of mixed blood. That, since she was a magic-wielder, there was a possibility your fae traits would present along with the human magic."

Which was precisely what had happened when Orion turned five. The Crows had found him and whisked him away at a young age to become their weapon. "So you told everyone she had taken your heir, so no one would question how she died and know that you killed her."

King Oberon remained silent, still gripping the furniture hard enough for his knuckles to turn pale. He hadn't cared enough. Not about his queen, nor his son. To him, their union had been a transaction to obtain an heir and keep the kingdom alive.

"You never searched for me because you thought I was a bastard."

"What are you going to do, Orion? Kill me?" The king leaned forward. He didn't appear the slightest bit afraid to die. "Go on, I'm sure our people will believe you. After all, you didn't abandon them for more than a decade to chase after a woman."

The manipulative bastard...

"Then you also demanded to come here when I requested to speak with your soulmate, alone." The king circled the chair and dropped into it unceremoniously. Perhaps he'd thought Orion would do something rash, like actually kill him. "I have given you everything, even after you abandoned me. The knowledge to control your gift, power, gold..."

"Who would our people believe?" the spirits of Orion's shadows wailed in his ears, loud and clear, although the king had left the words unspoken.

"What if I don't care if they believe me? I don't need to be their king. I can live anywhere inside the kingdom to maintain whatever magical balance our ancestors bargained for. This castle can crumble into dust once you're gone for all I care."

The lie burned his tongue like acid rolling down the back of his throat, searing his vocal cords. Orion nearly choked, struggling to keep his arms stuck to his sides, to not grab at his throat and give the monster the satisfaction of watching him struggle.

It didn't matter, for the king's lips tilted up into a faint smile. "I always wondered if you were more human than fae and could lie, just like Briar did. It turns out you cannot."

Nava jumped out of her seat and rushed to Orion's side, her brows drawn together as she stroked his arm. The warmth of her magic soothed the pain.

"Ark?" Her voice came into his head, trembling with emotion. He couldn't tell where the anger that pulsed deep within him began and where the sorrow ended.

"If you're done trying to lie to me and yourself, we can both move past this setback—"

Setback? Was that all that burning his mother alive was to this bastard?

Orion flew forward, ignoring the pain that flared from his injured wings, and collided with the king in a pile of legs and arms. His fist met the king's jaw with a loud crack.

Then he punched him again and again. Blood splattered his knuckles from a deep cut in the king's lip. His wide blue eyes met Orion's right before the next blow rained down upon him.

Memories of his mother struggling against the burning tree flared inside him like wildfire. How much she'd suffered. How angry her spirit was. Darkness crept over the edges of Orion's vision, and the mist of his power crawled up his fingers slowly.

"Take him," a voice whispered in his ear.

"He deserves it," another goaded.

He pulled on the king's energy as he attempted to push him back and get Orion off him. But his efforts were a weak wisp of nothingness compared to Orion's rage.

"Ark, let him go. He doesn't deserve your humanity." Nava grasped Orion's hand and gently pulled him away. Her voice was a warm blanket in a sea of ice. He blinked away the haze of tears that clouded everything, and the room came into focus again.

Her hands framed his face, and as he focused on her features, illuminated by the flickering candlelight from the walls, his heartbeat slowed, making space for the true feeling—a sorrow so raw he nearly collapsed with it.

"You're pure evil," he heard Nava say. "I never understood Arkimedes's fears of what he would become if he let his darkness consume him, but I do now." She glared at the king, who lay groaning on the ground. "Even though you speak so righteously about sacrifice for your people, all you are is a monster."

The doors of the library swung open, and the seven guards and his father's women poured in, rushing to the king. Still, no one attempted to arrest him, not even the concubines.

"Thank you," he whispered to Nava through their mind bond, unable to gather the strength to say it out loud.

"I bet he wanted you to kill him. He would have died a martyr if you'd done so," she said.

Worse, still, a fragment of the king's soul would have stuck to him forever. Wouldn't the bastard have loved that—an easy way out but not a permanent end. To whisper in his son's ear and torment him for the rest of his life.

"I've not dismissed you, Orion. We must devise a plan to kill Leir!" the king slurred, hanging crookedly from the shoulder of one of his guards.

Orion paused by the door, resting his hand upon the gold handle. "My name is Arkimedes. After what I just learned, the name you gave me means nothing."

Nava had been right. In his attempt to hold on to the family he'd never had, he had pushed away the man he'd become on Grey Island. He regretted that he'd allowed this kingdom to suffer during his absence, but he wouldn't have changed it for the world now. Those precious years in seclusion had made him more human.

Months ago, when the king offered him the chance to take the name he'd been given at birth, to fill the role of prince, he'd been eager to impress. To be wanted by the father who he thought had abandoned him.

He'd wanted to forget all the crimes he had committed in the name of the Crows. Orion was a fresh start. A fit name for the ruler of a kingdom.

But his mother hadn't abandoned him. She had saved him and given him a chance to survive, to become a better man away from this. And for that, Arkimedes would be eternally grateful.

"He is bringing the demons in," the king urged. "We have to talk."

"Not tonight," Arkimedes said. He didn't look over his shoulder. What was there for him to see? Nothing. "We will meet tomorrow and discuss how to handle the villain you've brought to our doorstep."

He curled his fingers around Nava's hand and drew her out into the frigid hallway. The king had little time left, and Arkimedes would not be a part of his life any longer than necessary.

36
ARKIMEDES

Arkimedes needed to be as far away from the king as humanly possible, for the darkness within him still craved retribution. It was hard to silence the spirits of his aura when anger blinded him like it had back in that room.

He and Nava went down a set of long, wide steps until they reached a spacious hall. In the absence of daylight, its towering ceilings made him feel like the tiniest speck. The only illumination was wall sconces holding individual candles on either side and the promise of windows at the far end.

Nava's breaths came in short, quick puffs that gave away her exhaustion. She hadn't complained about his punishing pace so far, allowing him a moment of respite as they moved down the king's wing and toward—

Where were they?

He slowed down, taking in his surroundings, from the warm gray walls mottled with age to the tall columns and cobwebs that had accumulated in the corners.

"Do you know where we are?" Nava's voice had turned soft as her brows pinched together in the middle.

Arkimedes shook his head to clear his numb mind. "I don't think I've been here before," he admitted, dragging his hand over his face.

The space was unfamiliar and cold. Other than being built of the same stone as the rest of the castle, there were few similarities. It was desolate. There were sculptures but no wall tapestries or furnishings. Now that he thought about it, their steps had been echoing down the hall because of the lack of runners.

"Are these your ancestors?" Nava trailed a finger over a marble pedestal that supported an unfamiliar bust of a fae. This male wore a crown of thorns, molded perfectly to his thick, wavy hair with an impressive level of detail that depicted every last crevice of each sharp thorn. It looked very much like his own crown, so this must have been a prince from long ago.

Beside him, the statue of a female fae stood proudly. Both of them appeared young—perhaps in their twenties, although age showed differently in fae than humans.

"I suppose so," he said with a shrug, looking down the infinite hall. "It makes me wonder if all my family were as conniving as the king or my uncle. It seems to run in the family."

"Not you," she said.

Arkimedes nodded, feeling a weight lift off his heart. This time, he believed her. He was definitely not as wicked as them. Even in the Society, he'd never burned his wife alive, the woman who'd birthed his child. Much less threatened to kill an entire city for the sake of vengeance.

"I think you'll be a great king when the time comes for you to take your place here. We will show this kingdom what true soulmates can do when they work together instead of against each other."

Arkimedes sucked in a breath. After all that had happened with the pirates, the emissary, and the king, he had never expected that Nava would want to stay in this castle and assume their roles as monarchs. Of course, he had hoped she might, but even though this life called to him, he was ready to leave and never wear the crown again. So this meant a lot. "We are staying, then?"

"Why would I ever want to leave this cozy, lovely place that speaks to me?" She gestured at the creepy hallway with a quirk to her lips.

A laugh escaped him, and he shook his head. "Are you changing your mind because you know the castle is sentient now?"

"I admit, I'm curious." She shrugged, clearly doing her best to distract him from the awful truth that lay hidden within this place. It worked, somehow. "Does the castle speak to you?"

"Not like it does to you, apparently," he said. "But in this kingdom, the queen is the ruler of this place, which is why there is a tree that lives when a queen is here. It might have a stronger connection with you than with me—and even with the king."

Nava bit her nail, her eyes darting from dark corner to dark corner. "It's kind of overwhelming," she admitted. "Why do you think this area is so dirty?"

"I don't recall the last time I could roam the castle without a tail of guards behind me," he said, and they continued past the statues. If he really thought about it—had that ever happened? No. His fa—the king had tracked his every move from the moment he'd arrived in the kingdom. But now things had changed.

"There's nothing here." Nava's skin became a beacon of light in the darkness. Her nose wrinkled as she sniffled. "I don't think anyone has been here in a long, long time."

He reached out for her hand, and her warmth enveloped his cold skin. Tonight had been terrible, but being with Nava made it somewhat tolerable. Even when grief overwhelmed him, she anchored and guided him. He looked away, unable to find the right words to express himself. He would probably not make much sense if he tried.

His spirits were quiet now, eerily so. They moved to the end of the hall, where two stained glass windows let in long streaks of light, casting a myriad of colors onto the floor. His gaze fell on a single mahogany door within the wall. Painted black and decorated with gold accents, it seemed to shield a lonely room, surrounded by nothing.

A shiver ran down his spine, causing every hair on his body to stand on end. The castle didn't speak to him like it did to Nava, but had it guided him here, somehow?

His heartbeat sped as he inspected the familiar filigree adorning the entrance to the room, similarly designed to the ones in his father's room door. A cool breeze seeped under the layers of his clothes as he took in the marble statue standing on one side of the door.

He would recognize his mother anywhere. This bust was much like the ones of the fae they'd passed earlier. She wore the same crown of thorns, and her hair, long and billowy, covered her round ears.

The storm of his feelings matched the weather outside. He focused on the gentleness in her eyes and the smile that made her look so young. She was almost the mirror image of the full statue beside the king's room.

"I think this was my mother's room..." His voice shook with emotion. Moving away from Nava and the sculpture, he blinked as his vision blurred.

It was idiotic to feel this overwhelmed and sad for someone he'd never even known. Except that the ghost of her burnt body had chased him for so long, and it was impossible to ignore the devastating truth of what he'd just learned. He'd been looking for answers about what happened to her when Nava arrived at this castle. Now he knew the king had killed her.

"She was beautiful," Nava said gently and stepped toward the door, allowing him time to collect himself.

She could read him like an open book and could tell he wanted her nearby but needed space. He didn't like to be coddled, especially when he felt vulnerable. "My mother was so young when she became the queen. She wasn't ready to be married to the monster inside that room."

"Nor was she ready to be mated to the other monster," Nava whispered.

So she had come to the same conclusion: the emissary had been his mother's soulmate, not the king.

She took a shaky breath and met his eyes. "Although if Leir is immortal and can't die, then he has been stuck suffering for all these years. I think if that had happened to me, I would have gone insane, too."

Arkimedes nodded. "My father said she was always ill. Maybe she was sick because her soulmate was away for so long, much like what would happen to the both of us if we were separated."

"...you will be dead before the day is over, and your bloodline will be gone soon. Then, and only then, will I be free," the emissary had told him the afternoon they'd fought in the forest.

Arkimedes had thought it meant that Leir wanted the crown for himself, but it had never been about power. He had no interest in taking the throne. He only wanted to die so he wouldn't suffer anymore. This was about revenge and loss.

"Do you think she knew the king wasn't her soulmate and lied to him?" Nava asked.

The same question had been running through his mind ever since his father had told them the truth. "I don't know how she wouldn't know." He clasped his hands loosely and let his gaze drift over the edges of his mother's statue. "The first time I met you back at the manor, I didn't know you were my soulmate right away, not until I saw my mark later. I suppose it's possible that if she saw Leir first, got the mark, and then saw my father, she could have assumed they were the same person..."

But—that didn't add up, did it? They had different eye colors.

"I don't know. She wouldn't have found the soulmate mark on the king's body either... Not unless he never allowed her to see him naked."

He definitely didn't want to think about *that*.

"Leir's a blurred memory to me, but I remember his eyes were red." Her breath billowed from her lips, giving away the chill in the air just as thunder rolled over the castle, shaking the windows behind her. Her brows dipped low, and her expression turned serious. "We both know how lies can fester if they go on for too long, but someone is hiding the truth here."

"As I did back on Grey Island, when I didn't tell you we were soulmates."

"And then I did the same." She looked away, and her cheeks turned red.

Perhaps his mother hadn't been particularly bright and unable to tell the difference for that reason. A harsh thing to think, but how else could she not know?

Love made you blind to certain things, but even taking that into account, it didn't make sense. If she felt something special for Leir when he was toying with truths, then she might have looked the other way when she didn't feel the same for the king. Especially if she'd been as young as she appeared from the statue.

"Your mother showed me the moment before she died and what she said to the king."

"What did she say?"

"She told him she loved him."

Arkimedes had to prop himself up against the base of his mother's statue. It was as if the ground was dropping out from beneath him.

"I didn't remember everything she shared with me until your father was talking to us." Nava shook her head, anger ringing through her words. "But I thought his voice sounded familiar. I should have known earlier—"

"The memory she shares is a lot to take, Nava. Particularly the first time you experience it."

"What if the emissary actually *is* your father, Ark? Perhaps we can speak with him. Make him stop this madness before it's too late."

Arkimedes sympathized with Leir. He wouldn't survive with an intact mind either if someone tied Nava to a tree and sentenced her to die such a horrible death.

Still… He didn't think Leir was his father. Not that it mattered, because they were both evil. Even though the queen might have been his mate, she had also been with the king while he was away. Arkimedes had inherited the Curse of the Fallen, and only the king and Arkimedes possessed the power to strip souls from the people around them.

"Even if he is, there's no way we'll convince him to change his plans. He's out for blood because he can't die otherwise. He's willing to kill both you and Ari. He doesn't care about the thousands of innocents in this kingdom who will die if our bloodline disappears. He's neither a fatherly figure nor a lost soul."

"Which brings us to our initial problem," she said. "We have to stop him, and the only advantage we have is whatever godly magic you absorbed from Alera's potion. We don't even know what that is."

He'd be damned if he knew. Other than poisoning him at the docks, the spell had done nothing.

"I know." He rubbed his chin, studying the curve of his mother's round cheeks, made from polished marble, sculpted so exquisitely. "We can use her against him."

"How? Can you call on her spirit to come and beat some sense into him?"

"I would love to see that." He squashed a smile and cleared his throat. "We can't predict when or where she will show, but perhaps we can distract him if we find something of hers that she might have worn back in the day. Or a letter, a diary—a gown?"

Arkimedes opened the door, revealing a grand, yet bleak room shrouded in darkness. Someone had hastily draped blankets over its furnishings, and a fine layer of dust had accumulated on every surface. Spiderwebs covered the broad windows, the bedposts, and the end tables.

They tiptoed inside, taking in the abandoned chambers that had once belonged to his mother. Painted in light colors, they were the complete opposite of his father's. Blankets were piled up on the four-poster bed, and the drawers of the dresser by its side looked as if they had been closed in haste.

No one had bothered to come in here to make the bed. A wave of emotion rolled through him, starting in his gut and traveling up his body, taking hold of his throat and choking him. He drew an angry breath just as the fireplace sputtered to life, burning dust and sending fragments of old, ashy logs dancing into the room.

Nava jumped away from the fire with a scream. "That always scares me," she said, placing a hand over her chest as she took deep gulps of air. Then she glared at the ceiling, as if the castle had personally wronged her.

"At least it'll get warmer now." He wandered over to the dressing table and rubbed his fingers over the dusty surface, picking up a silver hairbrush with white bristles. "Leir is a skilled fighter, and his sword is unlike anything I've ever seen. He has been doing this for a long time, and he heals quickly."

Wait a minute. That was it. They had been going around in circles trying to find an artifact to defeat Leir—when he had been holding the perfect weapon the entire time.

"And there will probably be demons everywhere." Nava wrapped a protective arm around her stomach, gripping the fabric of her dress over the side of her ribs, where she'd been gored.

"We can steal his weapon," he whispered.

Her eyes widened as she met his gaze. "Of course. His sword is an artifact."

Arkimedes nodded slowly.

"So...we distract him with something that belonged to your mother and that way we can get close enough to steal his weapon?" Nava crept deeper into the room, pulling at the half-open drawers.

Every hair on Arkimedes's body stood on end all of a sudden. There it was again—the sensation of being watched. Frigid air seeped under his trousers, a touch of death in the little warmth they had gained. He dropped the hairbrush on the rug and glanced up at Nava, who was clutching the garments she'd plucked from the dresser to her chest.

Her mouth hung wide open before she screamed, and her skin had turned several shades paler. On the other side of the room, his mother's spirit floated, pointing at the settee by the fire.

Arkimedes jerked away, and pain shot through him from his healing wounds. He lost his balance and fell onto the carpeted floor. His heart thundered against his ribcage, and it took him a long moment to breathe past his panic.

The spirit was frightening but safe, and she was here to show him *something*. He checked to see where she was guiding him, then got to his feet and headed toward Nava first.

"She's not a Neem and won't hurt us." He touched her face, shrouding her vision of the ghost with his body and wings.

"How do you know? We're in her space, and she looks angry," Nava whispered. But she relaxed inside his arms. Her fear was almost too much as it poured through him from their bond, paralyzing him all over again.

"I know she is frightening, but ever since I arrived at the castle, she has been leading me to clues about what really happened." He stepped away from Nava and glanced over his shoulder. The ghost was still there. "When you'd just arrived at the castle, I was in the main library, trying to find some answers. She showed me a book, which I took to Devon to be translated, and we discovered an old prophecy."

"Was that the one Devon spoke about back at the Society's safe house?"

"Yes. *The child of royal blood came to this world sick, poisoned by evil, and was taken to the world of shadows, away from our land and our people,*" he recited. "I thought it referred to me, but it was always about Leir, and my mother must have known that."

"Even though the king killed her, she still wants us to stop her soulmate." Nava dropped the clothes she'd been clinging to for dear life and followed him across the room to the fireplace, skirting his mother.

Their steps left marks on the dusty ground, and for a good while, they searched behind the cushions of the sofa, only to come up empty-handed. Arkimedes flattened his lips and examined the mantlepiece, but other than the resident spiders, it was empty.

"There is something here that she wants us to see, but I can't seem to find it." He glanced at the ghost, who continued to point in their direction, unmoving. No matter how often he saw her, the image would never cease to upset him.

He frowned and glanced at Nava. She was kneeling on the floor, peering below the sofa. "Nothing— Wait… There might be something under here."

They pushed the settee aside. It didn't take them long to find the tile on the floor that had jagged edges, as if someone had repeatedly picked at the mortar. Arkimedes stepped on it, and it shifted under his feet. Nava sent him a charged look, and he opened his palm, his magic pouring from him in a burst of black ink. The tile moved aside, leaving behind a shallow hole carved into the stone beneath.

From a pile of rock debris and dust, he pulled out a rectangular wooden box that had lost its luster. Almost too large to fit in the hole, it had slumbered there, hidden for the past thirty years.

Settling on the ground, Arkimedes dusted off the top and found her name engraved in mother-of-pearl and gold. Briar. He looked for the ghost, but she had vanished. He swallowed and took a breath, hoping it would give him the strength to push forward. It was easier to keep going when anger drove his actions, and right now, he needed that focus to get her the revenge she deserved.

Inside the box was a small diary. Its leather binding had twisted with moisture and age, its parchment pages faded into a multitude of shades of browns. He withdrew it and placed it in Nava's expectant hands. Then he rummaged through the contents again, finding a small bundle of golden hair, wrapped in blue ribbon with a small tag with his name on it.

Orion, five months.

"I don't see how any of this will help us." He cleared his throat and placed the strands of his hair back into the box. He couldn't use it for anything other than to make himself spiral into sorrow at what the twins had stolen from him. Most of the remaining items weren't useful at first glance, except for the intricate ring made of silver. Symbols he didn't recognize were carved into it, and it was decorated with green emeralds.

"The ring—it says here that her soulmate gave it to her when they first met," Nava said, calling his attention to her. She was paging through the diary with a frown, her face an inch away from the pages. "It's very hard to understand her writing, but she drew a picture."

Arkimedes glanced over her shoulder as she continued to read.

"He told her that wearing it would ease the discomfort when they were apart, that it would call him back to her, except…"

"Except what?"

"She saw him again a few days later at the royal masquerade ball."

"And let me guess, he didn't remember who she was?"

"No." Nava's gaze cut to him, and he fell quiet, allowing her to continue uninterrupted. "He seemed to follow along with her story, though he didn't recognize the ring, so she didn't bring it up again. She wrote that the king told her he liked to change his eye color with magic."

They'd been right. His mother had met Leir, her soulmate, before she'd met the king. Probably when he was out on a mission for Dargan, and she was here traveling. Then he had been forced to leave, and she'd told his father about them being soulmates, sparking his curiosity.

Arkimedes brought the ring closer to his face, inspecting the designs carved into the band. If he closed his eyes and focused, he could sense the subtle vibrations of magic emanating from it. An artifact, although not one with a lot of power.

"Ark—your mother knew the king wasn't her soulmate." Her face shifted with an emotion that was hard to place. Disappointment—or anger? Her eyebrows pinched in the middle.

"What?"

"It's written here." She closed the diary and handed it to him. Her fingers were icy when he touched them.

Arkimedes put the ring aside, flicking to the page Nava had read last. His mother's writing was the finest calligraphy, elegant swirls written in deep green ink.

The twins believe I'm a naïve idiot if they think I haven't figured it out. And perhaps at first, I was for believing their lies. I suppose being seventeen will do that to a person, not that they would understand, with time holding such different meaning to fae.

I curse my heart for loving them, for having a soulmate who hasn't even shared his name with me. I shouldn't love Oberon, as he isn't even my mate. But here I am, a fool—lovesick and wondering when my king will decide to see me instead of one of his whores.

He insults me by bringing his female guards into his chambers while I rot in this room so far away from him. They are healthy—when I'm not. I hate him for even mentioning it, far more than I love him.

I never cared for a sacred love, even if at first it sounded like such a wonderful escape. What I long for is a family. My mate won't give me a child, for I know he isn't of this world. He's one of them—a messenger of the gods—at home somewhere I can't ever follow. So I must take matters into my own hands if I, too, want a home.

If fate is as cruel as binding me to a soulmate I can't ever be with, then I shall use my spare moments of health to carve out my own destiny. A child, a baby that will love me no matter how ill or how human I am.

His vision blurred. No matter how hard he tried, he couldn't seem to swallow the fresh surge of grief. He shut the diary and shoved it inside his coat pocket, unable to meet Nava's eyes. Of course, she could feel his emotions, regardless.

Arkimedes grabbed the ring from where he'd dropped it inside the box, and its magic buzzed in his hand. He cleared his throat, trying to steady his voice. "We can use this to call Leir to us. I believe what he told her was true. If my mother had worn this ring when she wanted to see him, he might have made it all the way here to save her."

"She loved you, and she saved you." Nava reached for his hand, and the warmth of her magic seeped through him. He fell into her sad eyes. "Leir had the upper hand all this time. He killed Illaris, tried to do the same to Ari and me. Now it's our turn, and when he comes, we will be ready."

37
NAVA

The king summoned Arkimedes and Nava to a meeting the following afternoon. They met in a room she hadn't visited before, which was decorated with dark murals. In its center, a bulky wooden table stood. It could easily seat forty people, although only four awaited them.

The sound of the heavy chairs scraping the floor welcomed them as three of the fae stood as soon as they entered.

"You're late, Orion," the king complained from his seat, the black of his wings and aura shrouding most of him. Yet the bright shades of his self-illuminating eyes cut through the haze as they burned into her. "The emissary might strike our kingdom at any moment, and you've been taking strolls around the city all morning."

Arkimedes pulled out a chair for Nava, his jaw tensing as he met her gaze with quiet fury. She sat in silence. The black velvet fabric of her seat was soft and warm.

"The guards conveniently left my brother back at the docks, and haven't located him. He's ill, and we were trying to find him," Arkimedes said. "But being out there this morning made us realize that there is a possibility the Zorren's next attack will spill over into our city, and I would like to open up the castle grounds to the citizens. The wards will keep them safe until we can defeat the demons."

"We can invite the high fae to seek refuge within our walls, Your Highness, but there isn't a way for everyone in the city to fit," a male sitting beside the king said. His skin was a rich brown, and his golden eyes were striking even from a distance.

"I don't care how, but you will find a way," Arkimedes said through gritted teeth. His dismissive tone held no room for argument.

The male opened his mouth as if to protest, but the king raised a hand. "That's enough, Finian."

"We can work on how to prevent the demons from getting to the city, but if we have to ruin the gardens to save our people, then we should," Arkimedes said.

"If our primary concern is the Copper City, we could send some of our people to our other major cities. In the meantime, of course," a female sitting to the king's right said. Her beautiful pale face grew pensive as her eyes traveled from Arkimedes to the king and then finally settled on Nava.

"Leir can open a portal anywhere in Caztian or the kingdom, but he'll likely target the city where King Oberon and Arkimedes are," Nava said. It wasn't the whole truth, given that Leir and the Zorren were targeting the Beekeepers.

The emissary had told Ark about it. Leir would help the demons kill Ari and Nava, and in return, the demons would help him burn the place down and kill the royals. It just so happened that, in this case, all of them were connected.

"While you were looking for your Crow, we've been discussing a way to stop Leir." The king gestured at the center of the table where a small jeweled dagger lay.

"Is that an artifact?" Nava pressed her hands to the polished table and leaned forward to study the hooked blade and the runes etched into the shiny black metal. Could it be? Although it looked ancient and clear traces of magic wafted over its surface, Nava was too new to this to sense the difference between a magic-wielder's power and something created by the gods.

"It's not," Ark said in an icy tone that matched his harsh expression, suffocating the hope bursting in her chest. She slumped into her seat.

"It's a *powerful* fae weapon and has belonged to our people for longer than I've been alive. It was crafted even before the gods waged war on our territory." The king's ire was plain. "Back in those days, our ancestors fought the gods with our own artifacts, and they even killed a few. My magic can and will defeat a god's *servant*."

Nava sucked in a breath and focused on the dagger and the magic flowing off it. Somehow, she knew with absolute certainty that this wouldn't be enough. This blade would never kill an emissary. They were back to square one, and their end was still nigh.

"You can't be serious and believe we can actually stop Leir with this knife. He won't let us get that close." Arkimedes reached for the weapon, touching the silk fabric wrapped around the hilt.

"Don't touch the artifact until you're ready to wield it, son. It may not look like much to you, but much like our power, it steals energy. It slows down our enemy's ability to heal and poisons their blood. But if there isn't a foe, it will drain your energy instead."

As if the king cared whether it hurt Arkimedes. Oberon poured himself some wine and leaned back like his fate didn't rest in the hands of his estranged son.

The nerve of him to assume Arkimedes would be the one to wield the knife. But then again, the king looked worse with each passing day. Right now, his face was an array of all possible shades of purple and red from the beating Arkimedes had given him the night before.

"I felt more magic coming from the useless potion the dragons gave us," Arkimedes challenged, allowing his hand to hover over the knife, his lips setting into a flat line.

"If you have a better way, I'm all ears."

Nava observed their interplay, much like everyone else in the room. How much of the advisors knew about Leir? Were they aware that the king had murdered the queen in a fit of jealousy and anger? If so, then they were keeping it quiet.

"When I fought Leir in the forest, I noticed he had a powerful sword. Nava and I have been talking about the possibility of stealing it."

"And how are you going to steal it if he is as strong as you make him sound?" The king's eyes glinted with curiosity.

"He won't know what's happening, and he won't see us coming." Arkimedes glanced down at the knife, pursing his lips.

"What did you find in your mother's chambers? I had it searched after she passed to discover where she took you, but there was nothing."

"How did you know…?" Blood rushed through Nava's head as she met the king's eyes from across the table. She had been extra vigilant of being followed, and her bees had been on high alert all night long.

"Don't be surprised, girl. The castle speaks to me. Soon enough, it will begin to communicate with you if you listen. It always prefers the queens."

Nava pressed her lips together. No need to reveal that the castle was already doing so.

"We found something Leir gifted my mother. It should call to him if one of us wears it. Our plan is to bring him to the tree my mother died on," Arkimedes said. "I do believe you know precisely where that is."

The king smirked, his eyes gleaming with something Nava couldn't decipher. But he didn't say a word.

Ark placed a hand over her shoulder as if the touch alone would soften the sorrow filtering in waves through their bond. It was hard not to empathize with the emissary's loss of his soulmate, not when they both knew how devastating that would be.

"Brilliant," the king declared. "And that's why you're my son."

"Indeed, Your Majesty," the male next to the king gushed, eyes bright with excitement. Instantly, the room darkened, and the scent of magic wafted through the air.

"These bastards know he killed her. I'm sure of it," Arkimedes growled through their mind bond, and his aura darkened further. The counselors sitting by his father shrunk back into their chairs with wide eyes, probably sensing they were one wrong word away from meeting Ark's power.

Her heart ached as she remembered the ghost of his mother and what she'd shown them. All her notes of how her life had spiraled due to her choices. How she'd tried not to fall for the king but had done so either way.

"What did you find in Briar's room, Orion?"

"A ring," Arkimedes said, steadying his temper. "You will wear it."

"Prince Orion, you can't be serious." The counselor laughed loud enough for the shrill sound to echo in the wide-open room, although his face showed nothing but panic. "His Majesty is ill. He can't fight an undying Dark One."

"Yes, he can. He is Leir's primary target. Leir will be too focused on his need for revenge to notice anything else, which will give us a chance to get close enough to steal his weapon."

"You won't need me as a distraction if you have a part of me within you," the king said. "Use that anger, take what's yours, and use my power to defeat him."

"You're mad," Arkimedes whispered, shaking his head in disbelief. Judging by his advisors' widened eyes, they felt the same. They had been right. All along, the king wanted to become a part of Arkimedes, to be absorbed so he could remain in this kingdom as a part of his shadows.

"The emissary's weapon will poison either of you if you were to hold it. A guard should do it instead," the female counselor said, calling their attention to her.

Nava felt numb. Why hadn't they even considered that?

"Miss Elina is right. The artifacts lose power the longer they remain in our mortal lands. Most artifacts will poison a person after they hold it only twice. I can only imagine what it would do to His Royal Highness if he were to steal it," Finian said.

"I agree as well. His Majesty should consider this." The last counselor indicated the guards standing by the door. "Neither of you two, nor the future queen, can be the ones to steal it. It has to be a guard."

Her life wasn't more important than those souls standing over there. This felt wrong, even if the gods had tied Arkimedes's life to the kingdom and Nava was a Beekeeper, tasked to maintain a balance in nature. They couldn't demand their lives, right?

Perhaps that was naïve, but she didn't care. The person who should get poisoned by that weapon was the king. He'd caused this entire debacle.

If she was reading Arkimedes's emotions right, he felt the same. "There is no need to sacrifice the guards."

"It's their duty to protect us, just as it's ours to protect their kingdom from collapsing," the king reasoned, glancing at the door where the guards stood, watching the hall. They hadn't moved an inch, although their shoulders had gone rigid as they'd listened in.

"His Majesty is right, as always," Finian said, dipping his head in reverence. "I'm proud to serve you and yours, and I shall protect you with my life, as my family has done for centuries as members of the royal guards. It's with great pride that I shall do my duty when we march to defeat the emissary."

Nava's throat tightened as her lips parted in shock. She studied all three counselors with renewed curiosity. At first, she had assumed they were merely fae who held influential positions alongside the king. She'd never seen a non-Dark fae wear a guard's armor.

And Finian wasn't a Dark One, even though his eyes glowed, making them appear like molten pools of gold. But his shoulders were wide, like those of a warrior.

"Finian, Elina, and Kaden have been the king's counselors for as long as he's held the throne. They served as royal guards when my grandfather was alive," Arkimedes's voice filtered into her mind.

"Well, they certainly don't look as old as your father," she grumbled in answer. While the king's features were breathtakingly similar to Arkimedes, his skin was cracking like dry mud. The other three fae looked young, much like Leela or even Fael.

Had the three of them helped King Oberon take the queen to the forest to burn her alive? Had they advised him to do so?

An additional guard entered from the hall, his breaths coming out in rapid puffs as he dodged the sentries guarding the door. He wore the polished copper armor most did and a long blue cape like the guards out front. He saluted rather stiffly before he spoke. "Pardon my interruption, but I come with an important message for Prince Orion."

He bowed, and his bright brown eyes traced every fae around the rectangular table, pausing for a moment on the king before settling on Arkimedes, who signaled him to approach. The guard tucked his chin into his chest and strode toward her mate, expertly ignoring everyone's disapproving gaze.

"Sir, a man is demanding an audience with you." The guard straightened and interlaced his fingers.

"Since when can random citizens request an audience with my son?" The king slammed his open palm against the table, making the poor guard nearly jump out of his skin. He opened his mouth as if to explain, then shut it as the king's frown deepened and his aura shrouded his sick appearance further. "You're already wasting our time. Speak now, for I also desire to hear what this is about."

"We tried to turn him away, but he kept talking about an emissary of the gods and insisted he had important information, for he believes the Zorren will attack soon. We thought it prudent to come and inform you before we got rid of him."

Arkimedes's eyes cut across to Nava. "Was his name Devon Black?"

"Yes, sir. I believe that sounds right." The guard stared at the floor, as if Arkimedes might hurt him if he dared to make eye contact. "He is quite ill, so we didn't want to bring him here."

"Take me to him." Arkimedes stood so fast, his chair fell to the ground.

"I'm not done agreeing with your plan. Surely finding the way to save your people is more important than seeing to the Crow," the king said.

"Devon is my family, and he is here saying he has information we need. I'm going."

"I don't trust the Crow, Orion. Eris told me that when the Corvus imprisoned him on that market, they didn't hurt him. It seems rather convenient that he wasn't with you when the time came for them to attack."

He was attempting to plant a seed of doubt. Two months ago, Nava would have fallen for it, but not now, not after everything that had happened at the safe house. Devon had been trying to save that child because he'd identified with it. The king didn't know that she'd saved Devon from the Corvus.

"And as I've stated before, I don't trust you. We can iron out the details once we know what Devon knows about the Zorren. Until then, I'm done with this conversation."

Nava rose to follow her mate, her back protesting from sitting for too long. In truth, she couldn't get away from the king fast enough.

"Did you find anything else in her room, Orion?" The king's face twisted with a strange sort of desperation. "Did she say anything about me—about him?"

Was he still jealous? Did he want to know about the emissary's gift to the queen because of their plan to defeat him or because of their love triangle?

He looked sick, but deep inside, Nava wondered. Had the king loved the queen? Had her betrayal driven him mad?

Could anyone have two soulmates? Perhaps Briar had two. It would explain why King Oberon was dying, when other fae older than him were still healthy. Perhaps his hate for her and love for himself kept him alive. It didn't matter. In the end, Ark's mother had died a horrible death, and he was still here.

38
NAVA

Devon had to be all right. It had only been a couple of days, and while his condition had advanced, he'd had a few more healing potions left the morning they'd been split up.

Nava took a deep breath, wiping a small bead of sweat from her temple. With Arkimedes's legs so much longer than hers, she had to use a spike of her power to keep up with him.

She glanced at the guard who was trailing after them with a serious expression. His vigilant eyes snapped to every open door they passed, as if he expected an ambush. "Are we worried that someone will attack us here in the castle?"

Eris tightened his hand around the rim of his helmet. "It's my duty to protect you at all costs. As I mentioned, our allegiance is shifting. His Majesty feels it, and so do the guards. To prevent unnecessary bloodshed among our ranks, the king commanded me to keep vigilant."

"Because I'm in danger?"

"Yes, my lady. There are rumors circling the castle about the prince being under a spell. One that will only be broken if you're gone."

Great. Nava pressed her lips together, and Leela's words echoed in her mind. She'd said Nora, Fael's sister, had claimed the same during her visit. Nava would have to be extra careful with the king's consorts.

Arkimedes's gravel tones floated into her mind. *"They will be dead before they can come close enough to hurt you."* It was a promise of blood—or, in his case, the fragment of a soul.

They walked past a group of maids who scattered as soon as they saw Arkimedes. Some smiled in their direction, bowing with an eagerness Nava hadn't seen from the staff other than the night before. The rest did so in a more restrained way, looking at them warily.

Arkimedes offered Nava the crook of his arm, gazing into the distance. "So the king thinks Nava might be attacked? Is that why none of his concubines were present during the meeting?"

Eris seemed to ponder his response. "It's for our future queen's benefit and for His Majesty's ladies. He fears for their safety from your mate—and from you."

"Fair enough," Arkimedes said.

A flare of anger rushed through Nava's body, and she swallowed the snarky response threatening to spill past her lips. She wouldn't hurt them unless she had to defend her life. This wasn't the time to make biting comments, though. Not when they were on the brink of a major attack and they had to work with the monster for just a little longer.

Two guards awaited them on either side of the gold room, the same place where Devon stayed when they were prisoners. Past its doors, a warm wash of air greeted them. A healer stood next to Devon, who lay on the bed looking paler than she'd ever seen him.

He coughed, and his black eyes met hers from across the room. "You're free," he breathed, and his expression softened with relief.

"How are you feeling, Devon?" Arkimedes asked, taking in his brother's condition with a growing frown. It was impossible not to notice the way his eyes had gone duller, how drab and thin his skin appeared.

"Your Highness." The healer bowed, stepping away from Devon and approaching them. The fae clasped his arms behind his back, not looking at his patient as he spoke. "Your…guest has a similar reaction to what I saw in you when you returned. I'm assuming it's the same poison. Except his runs deep within his body. I don't believe I have a spell that can heal him. I can only ease his pain and prolong the inevitable."

Devon's lips turned from a sickly shade of purple to lilac as he peeled them back to reveal his white teeth. "If you're going to tell my brother I'm dying, look at me while you do it. I'm very much still here."

How long had he been out there, exposed to the elements? Had he been walking the entire time while sick and hurting? Her heart ached for him.

Nava untangled her arm from Arkimedes and stepped forward, grasping the foot of the bed as she studied Devon's complexion. "Do you have any potions left?"

"No, but you can drop the concerned face, Kitten. I'm not dying just yet."

She cleared her throat and moved around the bed, doing her best to adopt a more neutral expression. Anything to set him at ease a bit. "How would you know? Have you been in this position before?"

"Have you seen someone who's dying look this good or have this cheerful a disposition?"

"I guess you've got a point." Nava smirked. She reached for his arm, knowing what she had to do. Her healing magic could help him as it had before, even though her body was still tired from using it so heavily.

Devon's face pinched as he inched away from her touch. "Don't waste your energy on me. You will need it soon."

Nava perched on the edge of the bed with a frown. It was soft and almost swallowed him whole. She heard the distinct steps of someone leaving the room, just as she sensed Arkimedes approaching slowly.

"What do you mean?" Ark asked. "The guard said you mentioned the emissary was coming. How would you know that?"

Devon took a deep breath and sat, reaching with a trembling hand for the carafe of water next to him. Nava stood up to help but paused when he glared at her. "As you two know, I'm able to change the weather—somewhat."

"Yes..."

"Well, after the guard took Nava, I was making my way here to ensure you were safe. I didn't know how I was going to get inside the castle, so I returned to the maid's home to ask for help. I overheard her neighbors say that the storms were unusual, much too cold for fall. It made me think, and it's true. They feel similar to the ones I'm able to conjure." He paused to cough.

Arkimedes's breaths quickened. "And you think it's a spell?"

Devon drained the glass of water as if he'd been thirsting for days. Then he refilled it and took another long drink before he spoke again. "It seems a strange coincidence that they happen every single time the Zorren attack. Before every fire over the past months, there has been some weather event. When you two left for the forest last time, it was coming down for days. I don't believe in coincidences."

Nava's breath caught in her throat. She looked down at the bees adorning her dress, their brown bodies standing out against the dark fabric. "You're right. After we arrived in the kingdom, I had a dream of Ari during the fires, but it had also been storming. It's odd that the fire demons should come when there is rain."

"Unless they don't have a choice but to come during a storm. As if it's a warning spell brought on by an emissary crossing a portal, perhaps." Devon drank the rest of his water and placed the glass on the table. "I believe the emissary is in the kingdom already. He's hiding away until he can bring the

Zorren without hurting his chances to destroy this place, as he promised you he would."

Nava stood, her skin prickling as she broke out in sweat, her skin suddenly cold and clammy. "He might hunt for Ari while he's alone in the forest." Her body began to shift into air and pollen, the bees taking flight, coalescing into a swarm.

Arkimedes's eyes widened, and he stumbled forward, trying to catch her. "You can't go without me!"

But she could, and she wouldn't wait here and do nothing while Leir killed her Beekeeper. Had she known deep down he was here all along? Was that why the bees had been following her the entire time?

"We have run out of time."

"Nava!" Arkimedes lunged for her, coiling his arms around her disappearing body. His magic bloomed black and enveloped her like a cocoon, shrouding everything around them. He was shaking. Or was it the ground beneath their feet as the very castle shifted in displeasure? "The only way to defeat him is by working together."

She breathed, her heart racing, although his muffled words made it through her fuzzy mind. "He doesn't know I'm coming."

"Remember when we went to the forest, when we thought Aristaeus was in danger, but then we got there and he was fine?" Arkimedes searched her gaze, and his resolve seeped through their bond. "Close your eyes and focus on your connection to Aristaeus, to the kingdom. To the forest."

Her eyes watered with the intensity of being contained while she was mid-transformation. The air tasted spicy, but Arkimedes's magic was relentless. He would not let her go. And would she, if their roles were reversed?

Her body collapsed back into her human form, cool inside Arkimedes's warm embrace. She closed her eyes and focused on the quick beating of his heart and then, beneath that, the fluttering of wings. Hundreds of thousands of bees were all whispering in small voices. All calling to her.

The headache was a gentle throb that built in her temples as she dug in deeper, following their whispers. It wasn't a human language; it had no words, only feelings.

Her body trembled, and in the darkness, she tugged on the trail of the gold ribbon that connected her to the castle and the gardens beyond the walls. To Aristaeus, beyond the trees, so far her body levitated from the ground.

"Nava..." Ark's tone was pure awe.

"Dearest one?" Ari's voice drifted into her head, and even Arkimedes tensed. Could he hear him? *"You're here, but far, too."*

There wasn't any panic or pain coming through Ari's bond. He was fine, likely inside his cavern, awaiting her return. So Nava returned and asked for the forest instead.

"Leir opened a portal last night." She repeated the strange thoughts of the trees, and her body shook harder as a sudden cold rippled all over her. Ark's hold tightened around her, and his nose pressed against her neck, his breaths burning fast and hot against her skin.

"Come back to me, Bee." His voice carried enough panic to pull at her. She retreated down the hills of the forest, over mossy ground, and past fallen branches.

She descended along the golden rope of magic that connected her to the kingdom. Her nose prickled as something wet dripped down to her lips. She blinked her eyes open into the bright, golden room, and although the fireplace was roaring, she shivered inside Arkimedes's arms.

"W-what happened?" Her teeth clattered together, but her mind was too full, fuzzy around the edges. What was she doing here? What was going on?

"I could hear Aristaeus through our connection. You reached him. How?"

"I don't know." She lifted her heavy eyelids and raised her face to meet his worried gaze. He swiped a finger under her nose, and it emerged covered in crimson. Blood.

Nava had bled while she'd been between planes, out there following magical ribbons that wrapped around things. Whatever power she'd tapped into was something new. Except—it wasn't. She'd always been able to see the strings. She'd just never attempted to follow them anywhere before.

"How do you feel?" Arkimedes whispered and tucked a strand of hair behind her ear.

Her mouth was dry, her body weak and still shaking with how much she'd drained herself, but she had her answer. "He's back."

Arkimedes already knew this. She was sure he'd heard her words through their connection. The sorrow, fear, and anger that filled her belonged to her and him in equal measure.

"Leir doesn't know *we* are coming. Let's set the trap."

"What trap?" Devon asked from his bed. He was leaning against the headboard, his eyebrows raised high as if he'd observed the entire spectacle in silence. "And who the fuck is Leir?"

39
ARKIMEDES

The armory wasn't as large as the golden room they'd left Devon in. Nor did it have sufficient ventilation, judging by the pungent smell of oil and the tang of metal that nearly suffocated Arkimedes as he strolled around the place.

He wiped his sweaty forehead with his handkerchief and watched closely as the armorer measured Nava's waist, the length of her torso, and the stretch of her arms, muttering subdued comments that not even Arkimedes's enhanced hearing could discern at this distance.

The armorer, Gallon, was an unassuming Dark Fae. He had a lithe build and smaller wings than the guards. His magic hadn't presented as strongly as most fae of his kind, yet his true gift lay in crafting protective spells for the armor he built.

"I don't have enough time to make the right chest plate for Miss Nava, Your Highness," Gallon said, shaking his head as the corners of his lips tilted down. His tone was harsher than most would dare to use with Arkimedes. But he'd visited this dungeon enough times to like the male, sharp edges and all.

"Do what you can, Gallon. The most important part will be to deflect the Zorren's claws and guard against the heat."

Nava's skin turned a few shades paler with every word he spoke. Sucking her lips in between her teeth, she traced her small hand over her ribs.

Gallon's eyes shifted from him to Nava, before he spoke with a softer tone.

"We haven't had a queen in thirty years, sir. I won't send her there with subpar armor. This is not the Iron Kingdom. We have standards here."

Arkimedes's lips twitched, and it took all his restraint to beat his smile back into submission. This was not the time to find something funny. In fact, they probably wouldn't return, but he wouldn't voice those thoughts for Nava to hear. Last time they'd met the emissary, only luck had saved them.

The armorer shuffled away in silence, taking with him all his parchment scraps of notes and scribbles. He selected a new chest plate from one of the floor-to-ceiling cases on his way out.

Now that they were alone, Nava's frustration and fear came through their bond with increasing intensity. He reached for her hand. "Is this the first time you're getting proper armor fitted?"

Nava grabbed his hand with clammy, stiff fingers. "Yes. I-I've worn armor before, usually when I trained with my mother, but it's been a while." She tried to smile, but the expression didn't reach her eyes. "Wouldn't metal make the heat of fire worse?"

"Gallon has a gift for casting spells onto metal. Earlier in the year, he created a special spell that helped us while investigating the fires." Arkimedes touched her cheek and caressed her soft skin until the pad of his finger met her bottom lip.

Her breaths stuttered just as she met his eyes, and the world around them fell away.

Arkimedes didn't need to read her thoughts to know she feared the same thing he did. They had no way of knowing how many demons Leir would bring through the portal this time around.

He swallowed against the suffocating pressure building in his chest and stepped closer to her. These were the last few minutes of peace they would have in a while, and the intensity of his need to be near her, to touch her, was as great as the fear that threatened to paralyze him.

"Don't look at me like that," she whispered and placed her hand over his heart. But the thick copper plate blocked the warmth of her touch.

"Like what?"

"Like we won't return."

If only he could lie to her. But the weapon they had to steal from Leir had disintegrated trees with each of his swings. None of the guards would be able to wield it long enough to kill the emissary. And if either of them managed to steal it instead, the poison would probably kill them within a few days. That was, if they even survived the fight that followed.

But going into battle without hope was a surefire way to seal their fate, and he wouldn't bring that upon his soulmate. No, he would fight for her with everything he had.

"What you did in the gold room was a marvel to witness, Bee. Your power goes far beyond what we imagined. I can't believe you could contact Aristaeus from the castle."

Nava narrowed her eyes, her lips tightening into a small pout. "You're changing the subject."

"I can't lie to you and claim we will be fine, but I can point out our strengths to give us hope," he said. A warm glow of pride spread in his chest, dulling the ache building there. "I believe you have untapped power. Let's see what it can do for us while we're in the forest."

Her lips parted with understanding. She was so beautiful inside and out. Powerful. Everything he shouldn't deserve.

One of his shadows billowed out on his side, the clear profile of a male flickering in and out of view. *"And she is ours to protect."*

"Fuck those who try to take her from us," another whispered, and for once, Arkimedes couldn't agree more.

Gallon came into the room an hour later with a stack of armor pieces inside his arms and glistening with sweat. "I have adapted one of the consorts' breastplates. I believe this shall work."

Arkimedes stepped away, giving Gallon enough space to fit her properly.

Nava lifted her arms, as she'd been doing for most of the afternoon, while Gallon tightened a thick leather corset around her torso. Then he draped lightweight chainmail over her head that the fae had developed during their last war with the gods. Finally, he affixed the copper breastplate.

Nava touched the hammered metal. It was usually shiny, but in this case, Gallon had beat it into shape during the little time they had left, lending it a dull patina.

"It's not as heavy as I thought it would be," she said.

"Of course it's not. Only humans create novice metalwork that weighs down their guardsmen." Gallon inspected his handwork so closely he didn't see Nava's yellow aura spike around her, nor the insects flying in waves, diving toward him. He swatted at a bee and hissed when he got stung.

"It seems you've forgotten I'm human, too," Nava said in an icy tone that cooled even the stifling humidity of this room.

The armorer hunched down to avoid another bee, and Arkimedes's lips curved into a smile. "I'd advise you not to upset my mate, Gallon."

Whether the fae understood that the warning was for his own protection against Nava's anger—not Arkimedes's—didn't matter in the end. Gallon voiced an apology that sounded sincere, and the bees ceased.

Eris entered the room not five minutes later, just as Gallon tightened the straps of the last gardebras. The guard's steps were every bit as loud as the screeching of his armor. He'd been waiting outside, keeping a watchful eye on the corridor. "Sir, madam, the king calls for you. He is out in the courtyard with the guards. It's time."

Nava tensed, then visibly willed herself to relax. She climbed off the pedestal she'd been standing on. "I guess I'm as ready as I will ever be."

They had gone over the plan multiple times. Even if Leir were to spot the guards heading into the forest, the ring should distract him enough to give them the upper hand.

By the time they made it out of the front entrance, the sun burned like fire as it set behind the castle and dipped past the horizon of tree tops.

The king walked ahead of the line of his guards, his armor made of a silver so light it appeared white in the distance. Only the chest plate was decorated with edges of copper and gold. "You're to remain out of sight until we can get close enough to the emissary to dispose of him."

Arkimedes tightened his hand around his mother's ring. He'd kept it hidden inside his pocket ever since they'd left her chambers last night. The metal was unnaturally cold, a clear sign that this jewelry wasn't of this world.

Nava strapped her long daggers to either side of her belt. "I don't think it's a good sign that it's stopped raining."

Arkimedes grunted in agreement and placed his crown-shaped helmet over his head. It was identical to the king's and a straightforward way for the guards to distinguish who was who.

Even with most of their features obscured, Arkimedes doubted anyone would confuse them, for the king stood taller than most, towering by a couple of inches over even his largest guard.

Nava reached for his crown. The pads of her fingers traced the edges of its pointed, thorny shapes. "The crown suits you."

"It was my father's before he became the king." Dammit, there he was, calling the monster his father again. He would destroy this piece of tin and never pass it down his family line if they were lucky enough to have children.

If they survived first.

"I will see you two in the forest. Good luck." Eris bowed to them, his features hidden by his helmet right before he, too, took off to the sky, following dozens of fae who were headed for the trees. Their wings and shadowy auras blended with the darkening sky.

The king remained, his braided hair billowing on the breeze. "Orion, if the time comes, you must take my power to defeat him. We can't let him destroy the kingdom. No matter if you hate me now, this is our duty." He nodded in their direction, his face strained before he took flight, not waiting for an answer.

There was no need to discuss where they would meet. Thinking about the tree his mother had died on clogged Arkimedes's throat and made him want to kill King Oberon all over again.

But tonight wasn't the night.

"Are you ready?" he asked.

"As ready as I will ever get." Nava held on to his shoulders as he wrapped one arm under her legs and the other around her back. He lifted her with ease, and her magic soared through him, warm and gentle. It dulled the ache flaring from the arrow wounds in his wings.

"Hold on tight, Bee," he said and rose into the rainy sky.

They flew in silence to a part of the forest he knew well. While he usually avoided it, he seemed to end up at the tree more often than not, as if destiny itself pulled him there.

Tonight, they would use the power of grief as a weapon to save thousands of innocent lives. To defeat an evil that festered in this kingdom, brought about by lies and jealousy.

The burnt tree stood in the clearing, commanding the same familiar dread. Charred and lacking life, its naked trunks twisted up onto spindly branches that allowed the stormy sky to peek through. A sense of unease sank underneath his skin and twisted his gut as he inspected the area.

"The trees are angry, but I don't sense the emissary is close." Nava drew a shaky breath. The silence was almost absolute. No creatures or insects dashed about in the undergrowth. Nothing lurked in the shadows of this cursed place.

"I've avoided returning here ever since my mother's spirit showed me the truth," he whispered, studying the blackened, gnarly branches. "I doubt Leir would come to the place where the king murdered my mother either."

"It's why this is a brilliant plan, Ark. We will get under his skin. You've outsmarted him."

"*We* did." Arkimedes gripped her chin and dropped a kiss on her forehead. He lingered for a moment, closing his eyes and enjoying her warm scent and the spice of her skin. She wrapped her arms around his neck, pulled him down to her face, and kissed him with a desperation that he matched.

This could be their last chance to do this.

He wrapped both arms around her waist and drew her close to him, tasting the sweetness of her lips. They had no time to lose—the guards could arrive at any moment. But he didn't want to let go, either.

This was the reminder of why they needed to fight, of what they might lose. He withdrew, brushing the hair out of her face. If only she hadn't been so stubborn and worn a damn helmet.

"Nava..." He clutched her hand, trying to inhale around the tightness squeezing his chest. "I'm glad I got to fall in love with you two times. You're the best thing that ever happened to me."

"We aren't saying goodbye, Arkimedes," she said.

"Do you have the knife?"

"Right here." She patted the satchel hanging across her chest.

However useless the artifact the king had provided was, it would probably be better than a regular iron sword. They had decided Nava would wield it, as she might be able to transfer close enough to use it.

"Good. Now hide and don't come out until you see Leir is distracted, even if I'm struggling."

"Don't ask me anything you wouldn't do yourself." Nava traced his jaw with a single finger before tapping his cheek. "So it's best if you don't get in too much trouble."

One moment she was solid, and the next she was gone, transferring away with the evening breeze that rustled the canopy of leaves above them.

40
ARKIMEDES

The first group of guards landed shortly after the king. They crept into the clearing with quiet steps, listening for anything that might be amiss. Only the crunch of debris under their boots and their heavy breathing broke the evening silence.

The king strolled toward Arkimedes as if he didn't have a care in the world. Was the kingdom lending him the energy he needed for this?

"I'm here as you demanded." The king frowned as his eyes cut to the tree, and his features morphed into an expression that was hard to read. Anger, disappointment—sadness?

No. Monsters didn't feel remorse.

"I did as you told me and used my connection to the forest," Nava's voice came through their bond. *"The trees told me the emissary is slightly north of here, close to Ari's home."*

She had tapped into the power she'd used back at the castle and found them a location.

Arkimedes withdrew the ring from his pocket, a feat with all the armor he wore, and placed it into his father's outstretched hand. Here, amidst the darkness, where there was almost no light, the green stone at the center of the ring glowed with magic.

"This should call Leir when you put it on. Nava said he is north of here, so you and the guards have enough time to hide."

The king's eyes flickered as he clenched the ring in his fist and stepped toward the tree, the nut in his throat bobbing as he swallowed. "I didn't want her to die, Orion."

"You didn't want her to die when you tied her to this tree and set it on fire?" Arkimedes asked and fell away toward the trees that would become his cover.

"Briar betrayed me long before I forsook her," the king continued. His shadows swirled around him as he stepped behind the tree. "She cheated on me for years. I didn't even know about Leir's existence. Then she took you away. She broke my heart first."

If only that were true. But Arkimedes had read the diary and all his mother had written about her feelings for the king and how insignificant he made her feel. She'd been lonely in that castle while he slept with his concubines.

"I don't care about your woes. You killed her, and that's all I need to know."

A gasp came from the edge of the clearing. Perhaps some of the guards hadn't known the truth, but it didn't matter if they discovered the king's true nature.

Arkimedes studied the guards. Some had raised their shields and pointed weapons in his direction. Shifting on their feet, they hid in between the trees. Their auras bloomed much like his, and their solid bodies became part of the shadows.

Arkimedes rolled his shoulders to ease the strain that had built in his injured wings. Closing his eyes, he focused on the way the ground trembled beneath his feet, a gentle murmur that responded to his power.

"The forest is uneasy. It remembers Leir brings the demons and fires. He is coming toward us now," Nava's voice rang in his mind.

Arkimedes dug his heels into the ground and rushed to a nearby tree, gripping its rough bark to keep his balance. He tucked his wings behind his back. He hadn't learned how to blend into the shadows like the others of his kind, but he'd mastered a spell that would hide him from view for a time.

A shield popped up in front of him, and he pressed his body against the rough texture of the tree behind him, just as slow steps resounded from somewhere nearby. The task should be straightforward. He had to strike fast.

Leaves ruffled in the distance as a large shadowy figure wandered into the clearing.

"Briar?" Leir's voice shook with hope as he stepped toward the burnt tree. His face was visible from Arkimedes's hiding place, but seeing that expression robbed him of his breath.

The emissary's confusion wouldn't last long. It would become clear soon enough that this was a trap. Arkimedes's heart constricted inside his chest as he watched his uncle walk toward the spot where his mother had died. An expression of pure pain took over his features.

None of this was fair.

Then understanding flashed through Leir's pale features as he twirled in his spot. He widened his blood-red eyes with a snarl. "You make a mockery of my pain." Leir swung his weapon like a pendulum, and waves of static bounced across the ground, cutting down limbs from the tree.

The king's aura exploded into a black sea of spilled ink, and he stepped out from behind the tree, the ring still on his finger. The stone hummed with green light, like a heartbeat.

Thump, thump, thump.

Time slowed as dead twigs crunched under the king's feet, and here, in the cursed clearing where the king had murdered the queen, the twins finally met face to face.

Leir straightened in a slow, calculated movement as he faced his brother. His arms fell to his sides. "I should've known it would be *you*."

They looked like mirror images of one another, standing so tall their shadows stretched up to the trees. The only difference other than the color of their glowing eyes were their wings, for Leir's were misshapen.

The king planted his feet wide, his neck corded with tension. "Last time we met, brother, you should have learned your lesson to stop messing with what belongs to me."

Their voices were so loud it was as if Arkimedes were kneeling right beside them. He swallowed. When had the king last met the emissary? Had they fought? Arkimedes wasn't surprised that the king had kept more secrets.

The ring continued to beat louder in the silence.

Thump. Thump. Thump.

The king pulled his sword from its sheath. "You would think losing your wings would be enough to teach you that lesson."

"This?" Leir reached over his shoulder with one hand, right before a laugh tore from his lips. The sound was wrong, like a banshee's cry. He advanced toward the king.

It was almost time. The moment the emissary attacked, Arkimedes and Nava had to strike.

Arkimedes's heart clenched. Part of him didn't want to. In his uncle, he saw everything that he could have become.

"You fool, my wings heal every day. I burn them to remind myself of the torture Briar went through." Leir's eyes took on a crazed look that turned

Arkimedes's blood to ice. Spit bubbled from his lips as they split to reveal pointed canines. "Now your kingdom will suffer the same fate as she did."

Leir was going to burn everyone who lived in the Copper Kingdom. His madness had reached a point of no return. The new information of how he mutilated his body only confirmed it.

Leir leaped toward the king, swinging his deadly artifact, which sucked the life out of the ground. Despite his illness, the king moved out of the way faster than anyone Arkimedes had seen. His aura enveloped the emissary in a cocoon of life-draining magic.

Leir stumbled back, his white skin recovering from the onslaught of the king's dark power, although blood trickled down from his tunic. The king hunched over with a pained expression, the façade of his strength vanishing quickly after commanding so much power to hold the emissary at bay.

Arkimedes abandoned his hiding place and ran toward the twins when his father's complexion turned even paler. With how sick he was, there wasn't a chance he would hold on for much longer.

Arkimedes lengthened his steps and beat his wings so he could cut through the space quickly. Thankfully, Leir hadn't spotted him yet. He was far too focused on the king.

"Allow me to bring the cavalry that will destroy your precious kingdom," Leir gloated. As he held his hand to the side, the first portal hummed with static magic. It looked like a small dot of petroleum suspended high up in the air, dark and shiny and thick in consistency. Its popping sounds became louder as it grew like a festering wound. Another one swiftly followed.

Arkimedes's steps faltered as he paused and stared at the portals. If the demons made it through, it would be impossible to steal the weapon. His aura burst around him, calling on the same magic Aristaeus had taught him, and the portal closest to him shrunk to nothingness before his eyes.

Then a dozen more appeared where the first had closed.

"Ark—" Nava's panicked voice invaded his head but quieted when the black dots appeared around the space, so many he couldn't count them all. They grew at a frantic pace, and the scent of sulfur thickened with each passing second.

The king barely ducked out of the path of Leir's sword, his eyes widening at the number of portals that had appeared. Amidst the commotion, a guard shouted something, but his words got lost.

Demons broke through the dark holes, wearing capes of fire. The temperature rose, and the drizzle of rain turned to steam, making the heat all the more suffocating. If it weren't for Gallon's armor, Arkimedes's skin would be blistering.

Leir glared at the armored guards who rushed out of the shadows and attacked the Zorren. Then he noticed Arkimedes.

Arkimedes dodged the emissary's attack that felled a tree ten feet behind him. Judging by the rage burning in Leir's features, he hadn't expected the guards, nor had he realized Arkimedes was also here.

A scream tore from the Emissary's lips when the king cut the side of his misshapen wing. The feathers melted away as soon as they touched the ground, like they hadn't been from this world to begin with.

"Now, Nava!"

She appeared right beside the emissary and swung the dagger into the cocoon of Leir's dark aura, slicing underneath one of his ribs. The knife should slow down even Leir's immortal healing, giving Arkimedes and the king a better chance to steal his weapon.

Inky waves wrapped around Nava's hand, and blotchy black veins rapidly extended up her arm. She pulled back with a pained scream. Her eyes cut to him before she disappeared.

Leir clutched his side with one hand while he swung his sword toward the king once more. A cloud of dry earth and ash billowed in the air, making it hard to see.

"Nava, where are you?" Panic rushed through Arkimedes, all-consuming like the fire. He couldn't focus on anything when she wasn't answering. *"Nava?"* he repeated, but only met silence.

He couldn't breathe. His eyes searched the clearing for a sign that she was all right. The air sizzled with such power it singed his lashes. He pulled at the bond in his gut, reaching further.

"Aristaeus, are you here?"

"Protector?"

The Beekeeper's voice shook him from his stupor. Now wasn't the time to get distracted, even if he wanted—no, needed—to make sure Nava was alright. If they didn't defeat Leir, no one in the entire kingdom would be fine. He needed to get a grip.

The air around the emissary seared Arkimedes's nostrils and burned down his throat as he approached. Blisters formed over the exposed skin of his body, and it took everything inside him not to take off in the other direction to find Nava.

He struck with his blade and cut Leir's hand off from his wrist. Leir's sword fell to the ground, much like it had done during their first fight.

The weapon steamed with black tendrils that wrapped around Arkimedes's fingers as he reached for it. He heaved as the sword scalded his skin. Bone-melting pain racked through him. Taking a sharp breath, he attempted to straighten, his ears ringing as Aristaeus materialized beside him.

A beastly snarl escaped the Beekeeper's jagged lips as he held a demon, shielding Arkimedes. *"Use our connection to nature to push through,"* Aristaeus commanded inside Arkimedes's throbbing skull.

Arkimedes breathed through the pain of holding the artifact, finding the strength to use it. *"Is Nava hurt?"* He hadn't sensed her in so long. *"Something is wrong."*

"Focus on the emissary and live." Aristaeus's voice was a growl, and then he disappeared.

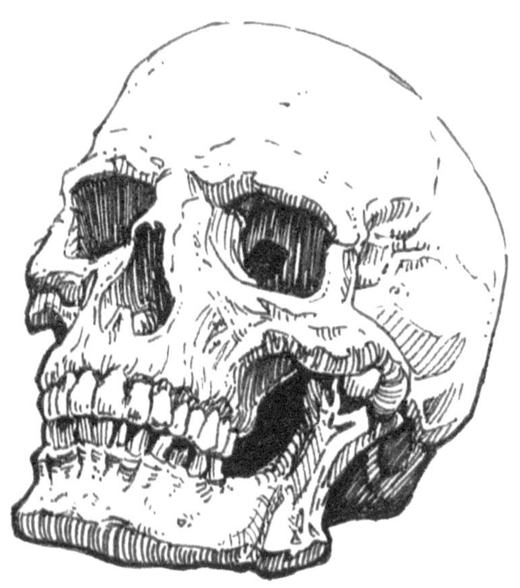

41
NAVA

Even as Nava transferred away, the burn from Leir's dark aura was immediate and it seared her flesh. Blood rushed in her ears, drowning out the demons' roars in the distance. Her body moved across the planes, barely evading a claw that reached up through the air and the sharp iron nails that scraped at her.

There were so many Zorren down in the clearing, Nava couldn't land anywhere as weak as she felt. She followed the call of the forest, and it led her to an area shrouded by tall bushes, untouched by fire.

Nausea bubbled up in her gut as she materialized behind one of the largest trees, not too far from Arkimedes. She could return to him once she'd neutralized the venom of the knife. She reached for the satchel hanging across her chest with shaking hands and pulled out one of the small vials Arkimedes had stuffed in there earlier.

The healing potion tasted of sweet lavender, and it immediately eased her pain. Blinking away her blurred vision, she inspected the cut in her hand. How had she managed to cut herself with the King's poisoned dagger during her attack? It hurt so damn much, and true to Oberon's words, the wound on her fingers oozed blood like it wasn't mending.

"Nava?" Arkimedes called to her through their bond. He was worried, and with reason. If the roles had been reversed, she would be looking for him everywhere. She shoved the knife into its sheath, cursing her clumsy fingers and her stupidity at getting injured by her own weapon.

"She's alone," a female hissed from the shadows, her voice eerily familiar.

Nava's head snapped to the side just as a Dark One emerged from behind a tree, moving so fast she was a blur of feathers and black mist.

The copper armor caught the glare of fire in the distance, right before the heavy mass of a bony fist collided with Nava's cheekbone. She staggered with a hiss, eyes wide as five females appeared around her.

They all wore the Copper Kingdom's armor, their faces streaked with soot from the ash raining from the forest canopy.

The king's consorts who had tortured Arkimedes in his father's chamber.

Nava held herself up against the tree, her bad arm dangling limply by her side and her head throbbing from the punch.

Using the last of her energy, Nava attempted to transfer away, but unlike normal transformations, she became a thick dust cloud that was too heavy to move away. Her exhaustion pulled her out of her transitory state, and her body became human again.

"Why?" Nava hated that her voice sounded so weak. But truly, she couldn't comprehend why they were attacking her now that they were fighting a common adversary.

There was no way she could bring down these warriors with only her bees. Five Dark Ones against her without the full use of her power—the odds were impossible.

Their sneers grew more pronounced in response to Nava's question.

They were going to kill her, and she couldn't transfer. Nor could she call on her magic or on her bonds to her mate and Aristaeus.

Another fist collided with the side of her head, and she crumpled to the ground.

The side of her face hit a fallen branch, and her teeth dug into her bottom lip. The tang of blood coated her tongue. She reached for Ark, for Aristaeus, but the five of them descended upon her, their gifts draining her energy like vampires drew blood.

"If you think you'll sit on our throne, witch, you are *wrong*." One of them hovered close to her ear, her spit splattering Nava's cheek as her spindly fingers tightened around Nava's neck. She squeezed hard, digging them into her skin. "You have them fooled, but not us."

"Nava?" Arkimedes's voice was a whisper through a fog of sleep. He was teetering on the edge of his own worry. His voice brought solace, strength.

"Hurry, Nora," another hissed, though Nava couldn't see her from where she lay. "We can't be gone for long or the guards will suspect us."

"Step aside and let me handle it," another Dark One said, her voice oddly pleasant for the words she spoke.

Nava met her eyes. A fair-haired fae—she had been in the king's study a day ago. Nava's anger brewed beneath the layers of pain and despair, just as the energy of the forest glowed like a heartbeat, strings of magic shivering over pebbles, fallen branches, and dried leaves.

It urged her to move, to use her power and show these harpies who she was. Its song was a gentle reminder that, even though the venom from the knife had dulled her connections to Arkimedes and Ari, she wasn't alone. She wasn't powerless.

A Zorren's screech pierced through the roar of fire. The clanking of metal swords colliding with matter brought her back to reality.

Even in the heat of battle, a chill crawled into her bones as a Dark One's power slid through her. The concubines drew more of Nava's essence with each passing second, and black spots danced across her vision.

A metallic taste spread across her tongue, and she dug her fingers into a dry layer of ash that covered the top of the forest ground. She pulled at the strings of energy nature offered up to her, just like she had done at the castle, and her power awoke with a gentle hum. The bond between Ark, Aristaeus, and Nava was a faint whisper beneath the layer of suffering.

Suddenly, Arkimedes's panic burst through their bond, so intense that it took over everything else. He was in danger, and she needed to help him. The guttural roar that left her lips startled the concubines. Nava twisted away from her assailant's claws, her power a shield of gold as she rolled over the debris, ignoring the rocks that dug into her body.

Her mother would've been proud of her strength, even if her form was sloppy at best. Nava withdrew the ancient dagger and stabbed Nora between her shoulders and neck. She brought down the blade again and again, ignoring the gurgling scream and the warm blood splattering her fingers.

"Nora!" a Dark One shouted, and Nora's body slumped to the ground as Nava pulled more energy from the earth and limped to her feet.

With adrenaline rushing through her, the pain had faded into the background, although she couldn't seem to move her right arm. The remaining four concubines jumped forward with enraged screams, out for blood. But they hadn't expected the swarm of bees that descended on them like a cyclone.

While the bees wouldn't be enough to defeat them, they bought her time. Nava climbed over a fallen tree, dropping the poisoned blade and pulling her longer dagger with her left arm.

The fair-haired fool with a sweet voice rushed over to Nava in the next instant. Every inch of her armor was crawling with insects. Red bumps were swelling her eyes shut and covered most of her creamy skin. Had she kept her helmet on, it would have protected her from the bees.

An ill-advised move, but it benefited Nava. She swiped at her legs, and the fae tumbled to the ground. Nava moved to finish her off, but the bees' warning made her dodge right instead. She barely missed a black swirling spell that singed her hair.

Her skin burned where the spell had touched her. She turned to meet her attacker's weapon with her dagger, and her arm shook as she tried to hold off the concubine's much larger sword with her weaker arm.

"You'll die here," the female snarled. Nava didn't recognize her voice. Not that it mattered who this was or why they hated her. All she cared about was to be done with this so she could find Arkimedes. Hopefully, her absence had at least given him enough time to focus on Leir.

"Not tonight."

She could protect herself.

And she called to the surrounding trees, and while their voices had turned into moans of pain, they still answered her. The wood screeched, and the branches swept toward them, swinging low as they took the fae by the head.

"What are you?" the fae with the sweet voice asked from the ground, her voice shaking and her pupils blown wide. She stared at Nava as if she were a demon, worse than the Zorren.

Nava's energy dwindled again as the surrounding trees caught fire, and the damned poison running through her veins kept fighting the healing potion—and even her own magic.

She reached for her bond, trying to locate Arkimedes, to sense how he was doing, but she couldn't feel a thing.

The final two fae lunged at her but ground to a halt when a massive tree-like creature appeared in between them and Nava. She shouldn't be surprised to see Aristaeus. He'd likely received her position during the split second she'd sensed him. The two Dark Ones screamed, but it was too late, for Aristaeus was furious.

The moss and bark on his body were burned. He'd probably been fighting the Zorren and trying to find her at the same time.

For the first time since Nava had learned she was a Beekeeper, she couldn't hear him speak in her mind. But he came to her either way, his claws and sharp teeth tearing at the fae with such ferocity that Nava had to look away.

It wasn't as if she cared for their lives when they had tried to kill her only minutes ago. Yet her heart ached that even while demons invaded their kingdom mere feet away, they had come for her instead of fighting for their people.

When Aristaeus approached Nava, his gaze searched her face and narrowed in on her limp arm.

"I can't hear you," she said, knowing he must be trying to speak. "The poison of the knife has dulled my connection to both you and Ark."

And if she were honest with herself, she wasn't even sure how she was still standing upright. She began to trudge to the clearing with a wobble to her steps. Arkimedes was just across the way.

"I need to get back to him," she said, knowing Ari would understand who she meant. And perhaps it was actually a blessing not to hear his sarcastic quip about how unfit to fight the Zorren she was in her current state. Although, since her mind filled in the blank void so easily, perhaps it wasn't.

After a second, he nodded. Then he walked to her and pointed to a spot right across the clearing, where the forest lay nearly untouched by the surrounding chaos.

The yellow lines of energy were thicker, more vibrant, showing her a path to where she could regain some of her power. The two of them moved, fluid like water, and the deeper they went into the forest, the more like herself she felt. A caress of their bond touched her mind.

"Turn to the right here, dearest." Aristaeus's voice startled her. He ran a few meters ahead, removing obstacles from her path. Her panic grew when she couldn't feel Arkimedes.

She'd transferred too far from him. It was idiotic to separate. Perhaps she should have let him try to save her. They might be in better shape now.

What if he was badly hurt? What if he was— No, she couldn't think of that. He was alive, and they were going to be fine.

The burnt tree the queen had died on became visible in between immense tree trunks. Behind it, a fire glowed. She couldn't make out how well the guards were holding up against the Zorren through the thick layer of smoke.

Aristaeus and her bees swarmed around them, right before a black shape jumped out in front of them. A demon with clanking mandibles swung one of its claws at her, and Nava barely got out of the way. Transferring a few meters away, she studied the dark shadow of the forest.

"Go to our protector. I've got this one," Aristaeus commanded.

42
ARKIMEDES

Aristaeus was gone, presumedly to find Nava somewhere in the clearing. But it was hard to focus on killing Leir with the stolen artifact, when demons popped out of portals all around him.

Panic, anger, and determination settled within Arkimedes as he turned toward the emissary once again. Leir was cradling his missing limb, a new one already growing from the stump of his arm, forming a new palm and fingers.

Arkimedes's aura bloomed thicker, although the pain from holding the artifact didn't subside, he tightened his grip around the sword's handle. He let everything around him fall silent and leaped forward, cutting through the two-feet gap between them, and speared Leir in between the ribs.

His blade met resistance, the emissary's body attempting to heal and push the magical weapon away. But it was no use. Its power was too great, and it sucked the life out of everything it touched. One of Leir's hands coiled around Arkimedes's throat, squeezing hard.

Past the slope of his shoulder and mangled wing, Arkimedes saw the horrid shape of his mother's ghost materialize, right in front of the tree where she'd met her end. The sockets of her eyes were wet with tears, and flames lapped the ripped edges of her dress as it flowed in the air.

Arkimedes's magic stuttered, drained by the artifact and Leir's hold. He pushed further, leaning his full body weight into the weapon, and the sharp point sank in a few more inches. A gurgling sound poured from his uncle's throat and their eyes met, frozen in time as warm liquid stained his fingers.

Leir's hand loosened just as an eerie moan escaped from his mother's lips. Then he crumpled to the ground, taking Arkimedes with him.

Arkimedes couldn't hear the warring demons and Dark Ones behind them. Nor did he know where the king had gone.

All he could see was the man underneath him.

"You're just like him. A back-stabbing monster that used my love for your own gain." Leir's blood dripped from his lips, trailing down his chin as he choked.

Tears stung Arkimedes's eyes. What could he say? This could so easily have been him if the same had happened to Nava. Losing her was the only thing he truly feared. "The king killed my mother, your soulmate, just as you tried to kill mine." Arkimedes tightened his burning fist around the handle of the weapon and held it steady.

Where was Nava? Her presence was stronger now. Was she coming to him?

Leir's eyes widened, his gaze drifting past Arkimedes's shoulder, up to the burning canopies of the forest. His lips parted and shut in a silent gasp for breath as comprehension flashed behind his uncle's red gaze. His expression softened. "The Beekeeper girl?"

"You shouldn't have come for her." And Arkimedes pushed the sword deeper. He didn't want Leir to suffer any more. The artifact clung to his fingers and wrist, seared into his skin.

Blood rushed through his head, numbing the sounds, the pain —everything.

"Arkimedes!" Nava's pounding feet brought her voice closer, her golden aura warm and beckoning him. But the tendrils of the magic emanating from the sword had taken over his body. He was cold. So cold and confused.

The land shook with tremors as more black shapes landed around the clearing. Zorren? Dark Ones? He couldn't tell anymore.

Nava scrambled past his shield and pushed him off the emissary's body. The chaos muffled her panicked screams as the demons continued to crawl out of the open portals. Was her face purple and bloodied?

"Stay with me," he read her lips, but his vision was already closing in.

He swallowed the bitterness in his mouth and tried to raise his hand to touch her skin. To reassure himself she was truly here. But his arm was too heavy to lift.

Her healing magic was a warm embrace chasing away the cold. *"Ark."*

Behind the blurry glow of Nava's and Aristaeus's combined power, darkness consumed his vision, and Arkimedes fell inside it.

43
NAVA

Nava reached for Arkimedes face—icy to the touch—and called on whatever power remained within her to funnel it into him.

She could feel Aristaeus's warmth coming from behind her before she heard his heavy feet settling on either side of her body. He loomed over them in a protective stance, looking out for attackers.

"Is Orion alive?"

She lifted her gaze and met the king's eyes. He lay on the ground a few meters away, supporting his body with trembling arms. His face was bloodied and burned, his hair a halo around his scalp.

Tears sprang to her eyes. She couldn't tell him that Arkimedes would make it. His skin remained too pale, and he wasn't responding to her touch. A sob tore past her cracked lips, and she sagged over his body, clinging to the metal chest plate.

He couldn't be dead. She would feel it in other ways, right?

"We need to take him to the cave," Aristaeus said, but he didn't sound as calm as he usually did. *"You're too ill to heal yourself, let alone properly help your mate."*

"But he is too weak to be moved."

Aristaeus shifted forward, the wood on his leg gracing her arm. *"There is something in his blood. An old magic that feels similar to the emissary's artifact."*

Old magic? Could it be Alera's potion?

Ari squinted at Ark's body, his face twisted with worry. *"He would be dead without it, but we need to go now. Can you transfer?"*

Nava nodded. Could she? She'd claw her way there if she had to. Aristaeus leaned forward and coiled his wooden arms under Arkimedes's body, lifting him up in the air. The branches above him blurred with her tears as Ari took one step and glanced at her over his shoulder.

"Meet me there, dearest, and don't longer here too long." And then he was gone, sprinting past the trees and away from her.

"Was that a Beekeeper?" The king stared at the spot where Ari had just stood. Nava looked at him, but there was no point in responding. She felt too numb to be angry.

She transferred away, back to Ari's cave and her soulmate.

"Our protector is lucky to be alive," Ari told her when they arrived at the cave. He placed Arkimedes in the same hammock they had slept in before. *"To hold a god's artifact charged with so much power would kill any mortal. He should be dead..."*

But he wasn't, and while they waited, Nava told Ari about everything that had happened since they'd parted ways. The pirates and their ill-fated trade that had turned into a terrible battle with the Crows—and what they'd initially thought was Alera's useless potion going to waste.

It had never been useless. It had saved Arkimedes's life.

In the cave's calm, Arkimedes's breathing steadied and grew gentle. While he rested in a magic-induced slumber, he was alive and well. He had even opened his eyes twice already.

Losing her sun stone seemed like a small price to pay, now that they'd defeated the emissary. It might have nearly cost Arkimedes his life, but they'd done it.

Nava never returned to the battleground that morning, even once Arkimedes was resting comfortably inside the relative safety of the cave. She was too badly injured to do much for him, and it took a while for the poison to leave her system.

Ari left the tree early in the morning and returned at night. He spent the day healing the forest and fighting the demons who'd escaped the king's army and were hunting for the Beekeepers. Thankfully, the Dark Ones had already taken care of most of them, and the portals eventually closed off.

"The portals only stay open if the spellcaster is alive," Ari explained when Nava worried about more Zorren sneaking up on him while he was alone in the forest.

Arkimedes woke up four days after the attack, although it felt more like two months had passed. Still, after the intensity of the battle, she welcomed the soft glow of the sun stones and the relative peace that came with the silence.

"So, are we going to stay in the Copper City, even though the king is still alive?" she asked, while they were eating breakfast. With a large part of the forest dead and the animals migrating north to higher grounds in search of food and untainted water, Ari had been eager to start the healing and for Nava to learn the ropes of her role.

"Or we could stay on the property I inherited down in the city of Milania," Arkimedes said with the rough voice of someone who hadn't spoken in days.

He took a bite of his rabbit meat and met her eyes. "It's a dukedom granted to my mother's family while the king was courting her. I was never interested in it, but I would prefer to stay there rather than anywhere near him..."

"You have a dukedom?" she asked, blinking rapidly. "When were you going to tell me about this?"

"I honestly didn't think I would ever need to go there."

"Would we need to return after he dies?"

"I don't know, Bee, but if you want to stay there even after that, then so be it." He coughed into the crook of his arm and leaned back against the rocky wall with a strained expression.

"I would like to know the kingdom before I'm to become its queen."

"Me too."

Who knew how long the king had left to live? Either way, it would be good to enjoy this place when they weren't fugitives or prisoners.

"The monster will undoubtedly want to have a ceremony for me to claim the official title of a duke, thus making you a duchess," he continued.

Nava didn't want any more titles. Although it didn't hurt to know she wouldn't have to worry about money again, or how to get Cameron clothes, pay for his education, or keep food on the table for him and Laurie. She had been worrying about that her entire life since her parents passed away. Not anymore.

Nor did she have to be concerned that the Society of Crows might stake a claim on Cameron, since he would become part of the Copper Kingdom's royal family. This was an opportunity. It gave them a chance to fight for something good. Hopefully, Gavin and Violet would decide to join them as well when they brought Cameron back here.

"We will have to wait for Cameron to return before we can get married." She took a small bite of one of those strange fruits Ari was growing. "He's already missed out on enough. Besides, I don't have a ring."

"A ring, huh?" Arkimedes's eyes crinkled as a rakish smile tugged at the corner of his lips.

Nava looked away, her cheeks growing warm. In the grand scheme of things, it seemed like such a stupid thing to consider. A ring—who cared when there were crowns and talking castles? "I'm just nervous."

"The dukedom is mine, and we can go there tomorrow if we wish. We are soulmates, and that overrides everything else."

What would Cameron think of all this? His life was about to change drastically—again.

If one day for her on Grey Island had been four months to Arkimedes, how much time had gone by for Cameron, now that she had been here for almost two months?

"Ark—since time works differently here to the rest of the world, what if Cameron takes a month to get here, but it's actually years for us?" Her chest constricted with a sudden surge of fear.

"They explained it to me. During summer, when the days are longer, gravity or magic—whatever you want to call it—has a different effect on the kingdom. Time passes quicker here. It evens out after the summer solstice, and we fall into line with the rest of Caztian. Then, during winter, the effect reverses. One day for us is four months for the rest of the world." Arkimedes searched through their bag of supplies for something else to snack on.

"So, toward the end of the year, the same time passes as in the other kingdoms?"

"It's why merchants travel during fall and spring."

That made sense. Was that why the pirates had been in the city on the night of the Crows' attack?

"I feel recovered enough to go back to the castle. We need to make sure Devon is alive and well at least," Arkimedes said. "And then we can leave this place and not return until the king dies."

44
NAVA

It had been a month since the big altercation with Leir in the forest, and life had settled into a peaceful routine. It turned out that the dukedom was in an uninhabitable state, so they couldn't leave as easily as they'd dreamed. Still, they refused to stay in the castle again. There were too many bad memories there, not least of which the consorts attempting to kill Nava.

Only one of them was still alive—the blonde with the sweet voice who had seen Aristaeus that night. She avoided both Nava and Arkimedes as if her life depended on it, which, given how angry her soulmate had been when he'd learned of her actions, it probably did.

For a time, they rented a place by the sea, waiting for Devon to return. On their arrival at the castle, they had spoken to him briefly while Nava healed him—only for him to vanish into thin air without leaving a word behind as to his whereabouts. After her initial panic, Arkimedes managed to reassure her that he would show up again in no time. But then a day turned into a week and then a month. And then another.

Now they were set to leave the Copper City for their new home, the city of Milania in the Dukedom of Elara, and Devon was still missing. Where was he? Was he well? And if he was, how would he ever find them in their new home?

"I left a message with the castle's staff yesterday. If Devon sends a letter there, they will forward it to Elara." Arkimedes's voice shook slightly when he mentioned his brother's name. His hand tightened around hers as they walked along the seawall toward the ports. The streets were busy with vendors, and the heavy scent of freshly caught fish and seawater hung in the air. A hint of hope bloomed through their bond, and Nava had to swallow past the thick knot in her throat at Arkimedes's emotions.

"Devon will find us, Ark," she said with a tentative smile. "Just like he was able to track you to Grey Island."

By the time they made it to port, the sun was setting behind the horizon. A gigantic ship, unlike anything she'd ever seen before, had docked an hour ago. It could easily transport a thousand people. However, instead of sails, a giant, elongated globe hovered above it.

"What's that?" Nava asked, standing on tiptoes.

"It's an Iron City ship. They call them blimps, and they've been circulating the world more as of late. They're hybrids, so people can travel by both sea and air." Arkimedes wrapped his arm around her waist and pulled her toward him.

She sighed, enjoying the way her stomach fluttered at his warmth. A feeling she could only describe as utter delight burst through her chest. "Does it fly with magic?" The giant ball appeared to be made from canvas, and aged brass beams ran along its sides like metal ribs. It matched the ship's circular windows.

"All I know is that magical crystals power them." Arkimedes's eyes crinkled at the corners. "Once, the Crows sent me to shut down a tinkerer's workshop. Since they are powered by magic, the Society thought it entitled them to the blimps. The king canceled my mission after it caused an uproar with the citizens. Thankfully."

"Of course they wanted first dibs." Nava indicated the ship with her open palm, shaking her head.

She had received Cameron's letter less than a week ago. Despite the difficult circumstances that had led to her contacting him, he had sounded excited to be reunited with her.

Would she spot him as he came down the ramp of the ship? Had his hair changed while they'd been apart? For her, four long months had passed.

"Are you nervous?" Arkimedes's deep voice called her attention back to him.

"Am I that obvious?"

"You haven't stopped fidgeting since we arrived here, so yes."

"I haven't seen him in so long," she admitted. "Last time we spoke in person, we had a new home and Devon was our enemy. Then I went ahead and released him." She drew a deep breath and rolled her shoulders to ease the tension building there. "I hope he can forgive me, that's all..."

"I don't think Cameron will have a hard time understanding why you did it."

"Nava!" Cameron's voice cut through the space. He stood at the very top of the ramp, energetically waving his arm over his head. His voice was deeper than she remembered it.

Raw emotion clogged her throat, and she moved toward him with a smile.

Cameron's hair was a long mess of bright red curls. Even at this distance, his happiness was already contagious. The people ahead of him turned and smiled as her brother bounced on his feet, taking in the port with curiosity.

Nava practically ran to meet him at the bottom of the ramp, and his hug was tight enough to squeeze the air from her lungs. He smelled like the sea, like cinnamon and home.

"You won't believe all the things I've seen!" His warm eyes studied her, a crinkle forming in between his brows. "Look at you, so elegant. It suits you."

"Thanks, Cam."

Her brother turned to Arkimedes, and they both hugged tightly. With how much Cameron had grown, the top of his head was almost at the same height as her mate's. Would he turn out to be even taller than him in the end?

"Look at those wings! I don't remember seeing them before."

Arkimedes's cheeks tinted red, uneasiness dripping through their bond as he shifted on his feet. "I don't need to hide them here."

"I love them." Cameron reached out a hand toward the black and blue feathers. "Can you move them independently?"

She blocked her brother's hand before he made Arkimedes more uncomfortable. "Cam, Arkimedes is still recovering his memories. Give him time to get used to you before you start grabbing at him. How would you feel if someone were to touch you without asking?"

Cameron paused, his eyes flashing to her before he shrugged. "I wouldn't care," he said and sneaked his other arm around her to touch the feathers of Arkimedes's wing.

Arkimedes laughed, and his weary gaze softened. "It's okay, Nava. I don't mind it."

"I'm not used to anyone touching my wings, but he is my family, too," he said through the bond, and her heart soared.

"You see? It's fine. You're always such a worrywart, Nava."

Cameron seemed so grown-up now, even though his attitude hadn't changed much.

"I never expected we would end up here, but I like it," Cameron said, glancing around the docks with interest.

"Where is Laurie?" Nava stretched her neck, trying to catch sight of their old caregiver, but she couldn't spot her anywhere. A heaviness settled in the pit of her stomach. "Is she all right?"

Cameron's face drained of its color. "About that..."

"What happened?"

"She became ill back on Pearl Island, and Gavin didn't think the trip here would suit her health. She needs to follow us when she feels better, using a regular ship. Not a blimp."

"So you left her there?" Nava tried to find Gavin in the crowd. "Who is taking care of her?"

"They didn't tell me, but I overheard them talking when we got the letter. We couldn't wait until she regained her strength. Gavin had some healer friends there who promised to help her and send her our way when the time was right."

While she hadn't seen Laurie for a while now, the worry ate a hole into Nava's chest. Time moved differently in this kingdom, which meant Laurie could only travel during fall or spring. It might be a long time before they were all together again once more.

Arkimedes stroked her back in a comforting gesture, helping to ease her anxiety.

"We wanted to come here and help you with the—well, with everything. We left as soon as we could, but it doesn't seem like you're in trouble now." Cameron's red brows scrunched as he studied them.

True. Leir was gone, and Nava counted her lucky stars that Cameron had never been in danger.

"It's for the best. I wouldn't want you anywhere near what we went through," she said.

"That's it, no? You never want me to be there for you, even though you need help sometimes, too." Cameron's face hardened. He looked so much like their mother when he was annoyed.

"You came at the perfect time," she said and reached for him again. She needed to be close and remind herself they were together again. Finally. "I'm no longer a wanted woman, and I have a feeling you will like our new home. There is a drawing room, like we had at the manor. You were so young then. I doubt you even remember it."

Laurie would have loved it, too. Perhaps she would get to see it soon.

"And a weapons room? Violet has been teaching me to fight."

"Yes." Nava nodded. It was the first thing she'd requested from Arkimedes when they'd planned the refurbishment of the ancient estate. It was far from the city, a day's trip past the forest and into the mountains, surrounded by nature and lush, sprawling gardens.

Gavin strolled down the ramp next, his brown coat gaping open to reveal a loosely tucked-in white shirt. He stopped when their eyes met across Cameron's shoulder. A lopsided smile spread over his face a moment later, and then he dipped into the lowest bow Nava had ever seen. "Your Majesties!"

Nava burst into laughter, just as Arkimedes said, "We aren't majesties yet, Gavin."

"It's good to see you again," Gavin said. "However, I must warn you we got two letters from Roman while we were on Pearl Island. He's not pleased with you."

Nava had been worried about that. Sure, Roman had been her friend of sorts, but he'd been spectacularly unhelpful when the Dark Ones kidnapped Arkimedes. Of course, protecting the village he ruled would be his priority, but he could have at least told her something about what to expect in the Copper Kingdom.

"Well, I'm not happy with him either." Nava crossed her arms. "He could have told me Arkimedes was a prince before I embarked on this mission and nearly got myself killed."

"You still released the Crow that killed so many of us," Violet said as she stepped out of the crowd. Nava steeled herself for the predictable tongue-lashing. Undoubtedly, it would follow soon.

Her friend had cropped her hair short. Much like Gavin, she was wearing traveling clothes: a long tunic and worn brown boots.

"I meant to bring him back," Nava said, and the words tasted of the guilt that still churned in her stomach. "It just didn't work out that way."

"She gets to pardon a prisoner, Violet. She's a queen now," Cameron said.

Nava brushed her sweaty hands over the skirt of her deep charcoal dress, and the gems embroidered on her long billowy sleeves caught the sunlight.

Violet shrugged and walked toward Gavin, handing him a heavy brown bag, presumably filled with their belongings. "I'm guessing the bastard ran?" Her eyes settled on Arkimedes. "Or maybe you let him go? Weren't you brothers before?"

"Violet…" Gavin warned.

"*I* let him go, Violet, not Arkimedes. But I believe he was remorseful for his actions in the end, unlike some others we have met recently." Nava looked at the ground. "He helped me come here and save Arkimedes—and this kingdom."

Silence followed, and Nava bit her tongue so she wouldn't fill it with nervous rambles. Still, Violet's face softened, and while she wasn't a hugger, her tentative smile spoke volumes. "For what it's worth, I'm sorry we weren't there to help you. We can talk about it all when we aren't out here in the open. But we tried to get to you as soon as we could."

Of course they had. Nava had no reason to doubt it.

"I'm loving the way this reunion is going." Gavin took a loud breath of air, patting Arkimedes on the shoulder. "What do you say—should we get something to eat? I'm ravenous, and clearly Violet is, too."

"So where are these magical creatures I keep hearing about that only live in this kingdom?" Cameron strolled ahead, as if this wasn't the first time he'd ever been here.

"Be more specific. There are many magical creatures in this kingdom." Arkimedes lengthened his steps to catch up to her brother.

"A fae on the ship said they looked like bulls—but bigger?"

"The orrus?"

"Yes! Those."

"You are in luck. We have some ready to take us home."

They walked across the dock's wide planks, bleached silver by the unforgiving salty air and the sun. Their carriage awaited them by the street, and its two guards and the driver promptly bowed as they approached.

"Do they always do that? Bow to you?" Cameron whispered into Nava's ear, his breathing loud and excited as they climbed inside.

No matter how many times Nava asked them not to, they always treated her like the queen they believed her to be. "Yes. I'm getting more used to it now."

"So where is home?" Gavin settled down on the squeaky leather seat, his long legs bent as Violet squeezed in next to him, while Cameron wriggled in between Ark and Nava. They'd stuffed the carriage to the brim with two large men, a muscular woman, a gangly teenager—and her.

"As far away from the castle and the king as possible," Arkimedes whispered, almost more to himself, although everyone heard him. No matter how much time had passed since they'd learned the horrible truth, it didn't make it any easier. Arkimedes battled daily with his darkness and the need to avenge his mother in a more ruthless way.

This wasn't something Nava wanted to talk about here, though.

"We are heading to the city of Milania. It's in a valley surrounded by beautiful mountains and nature," Nava said, hoping to lift the heaviness that had descended on the carriage. "We will tell you everything that happened once we are there. I promise."

45
NAVA

One year later

Nava pulled hard on the stem of a tomato plant, ignoring the small hairs that pricked the pads of her fingers. The cold temperatures last night had killed her crop, but it wasn't much of a surprise. Aristaeus had chastised her days ago when she'd mentioned she had been extending the plant's fruitful season.

"We don't go against nature's course," Ari had said, and she was rolling her eyes even now. What good did it do for her to have the power to grow things if she wasn't able to wield it in here?

She sighed at the wilting leaves and the young fruits that were too small to pick and glanced to the side, meeting the eyes of her fellow gardener. The fae waved at her and continued working.

Urlah wasn't talkative, but he kept his uniform impressively clean for someone who worked with dirt all day. He loved to teach Nava about native crops that grew in this part of the Copper Kingdom.

Tossing the tomato plant aside to the pile she had been working on the entire morning, she studied her very dead vegetable garden. She would have to wait until later in the spring to get her favorite crops blooming again.

The thundering hooves of a horse on the gravel road drew her attention. The ornate copper gates of their estate swung open as a gray stallion galloped toward the house. Its rider was a large male, wearing a black coat with a wide collar that matched his beast's shiny fur.

He jumped off the saddle before the horse stopped moving. His wings popped out from his back, casting a shadow over the stone steps that led to the entrance of the dwelling.

Nava dusted her palms off on her raw linen apron and rose to her feet. He came up the steps, two at a time. His clothing hugged his wide shoulders and a thick belt cinched in his narrow waist. Watching him approach made her heart soar.

Arkimedes's gaze dropped to her bare feet, then traveled upward as he studied her choice of clothing until their eyes met. "You must be the gardener," he said. "Do you know if anyone else is home?"

Nava's lips curled up into a smile, her stomach swirling with a mixture of nerves and anticipation. "I'm afraid they have all gone to the market. It's just me—and Urlah."

"I see." Arkimedes reached for her, but Nava swatted his hand away.

"Keep your hands off me, sir. While you're dashing, I'm a married woman."

Arkimedes peered at her from under his long, dark lashes, returning her smile. "I see no ring on your finger, milady…"

"He keeps me here with something much bigger than a ring."

Arkimedes choked on a laugh. "How big are we talking about?"

"I meant our soulmate bond!" Nava's cheeks warmed, and she fought the urge to fan her face. "You've a naughty mind."

"When it comes to you, I do." He reached for her again, so fast this time that Nava couldn't slip away. Then he pulled her close by her apron's front pocket, his face hovering a mere breath away from hers. "Perhaps you should wear the ring I gave you. It will ward off unwanted suitors."

"But it comes off while I'm gardening, and I don't want to lose it," she said, right before his lips descended onto hers. As if they hadn't seen each other in ages, when they had been a tangled mass of two bodies this very morning.

Arkimedes's kiss was soft but demanding, keeping a rhythm that made her blood sing. She wrapped her arms around his shoulders, pressing her body to his while tracing her tongue over his bottom lip before deepening the kiss. His hands traveled up her arms, across her shoulders, finally settling against her lower back.

Then he pulled away, his breath whispering over her well-kissed lips. "What do you say, should we get you out of these clothes?"

"Shh! Urlah is going to hear us…"

Again.

Nava should feel embarrassed that the poor staff kept stumbling over them in heated moments. However, with the rumors that they were soulmates, their insatiable desire for each other didn't appear to bother most of them.

"I think it's too late for that, Bee," he said, peering over her shoulder. She could hear the gardener's quick steps fade away as he made himself scarce. Arkimedes didn't wait. He dipped swiftly, wrapping one an arm underneath her bottom and the other behind her back, lifting her up with ease before he took off into the sky.

The crisp air bit her cheeks, and Nava smiled as she looked down on their home. The golden sunlight kissed its clay rooftop, and beyond the magnificent old edifice made of gray stone and climbing roses, the lake's water caught the light with a twinkle, like stars glimmering in the night sky.

"I hate that the meeting took me away from you this morning," Arkimedes said, and dipped his face into the crook of Nava's neck. A soft, approving noise left his lips. "Your scent is intoxicating, and it's driving me crazy."

Perhaps they were getting close to the winter solstice, and their primal nature was already taking over. Or perhaps this was how they always were.

His lips grazed the sensitive skin of her ear as he breathed her in, tightening his hold on her as they approached the house. Her core tingled with her awakened desire, and she dug her fingers into his scalp, kissing the side of his jaw and down to his lips. The longer they lived together, the more she was discovering Arkimedes's animalistic fae side, and she loved it.

They landed on the balcony. The stone beneath her bare feet was warm, and the view from here—she would never tire of it.

The beautiful, manicured gardens sprawled before her with their tall golden grasses, white winter honeysuckle bushes, and bright bursts of pansies. Each season brought a new delight. The entire estate took her breath away. Gods, she loved it here.

For the first time in a while, she felt at home. Sure, these walls didn't speak to her like the castle back in the Copper City had. But the flowers weren't spying on anyone either, and no spirits haunted the halls. Not unless one counted her nosy teenage brother amongst those.

Here they had a fountain with turquoise water and goldfish that glittered under the moon. No portals bled demons to allow them entrance, and no Neems guarded the doors. They were safe to grow old and love each other.

"How did the meeting go?" Nava asked, pulling away from Arkimedes to get a better look at his face.

One of his father's councilors came every three months to deliver important information about the kingdom as the king could no longer travel. Nava didn't want Oberon to spy on them here at home, so instead Arkimedes held the meeting in the city center.

It was always the same dark-skinned fae she'd met on the day of their battle with Leir. A little more than twelve months had passed, but it felt like a lifetime ago that Leir had let the Zorren in.

"We have a few months to continue enjoying our home here in Milania," Arkimedes said, but his face looked strained.

"But…?"

He took a deep breath and met her gaze. "But he is bedridden now, and he has summoned us to return for the coronation. He claims the citizens should see that we are still in the kingdom. That we should take up residence in the castle for a few months of the year."

"Months?" Nava pursed her lips while taking a hold of his hand. She pulled him back into their room, seeking the warmth of the house. "And the concubine?"

"She has been exiled. He set her up with a small residence on Rust Island, and she isn't allowed back in the Copper Kingdom." Arkimedes locked the balcony doors behind them.

Then he tugged off his coat and tossed it over a leather chair in the room's corner, leaving him wearing a fitted black shirt tucked into fitted trousers.

Her mouth watered just from looking at him. Who cared about the concubine or having to see King Oberon again when she had this in front of her now? The king's demands didn't matter. In the end, Arkimedes and Nava got to decide how to build their lives together. Sure, they had to bear their wider destinies in mind, but they were the ones who would choose where and when to go.

Still, it would be nice to make sure the situation with the deserters was improving. That had been their focus during the last year. They'd set up a funnel of funds to help the humans who were running away from the other kingdoms and offered them jobs to clean up the west side of the city.

They were also giving away grants to encourage businesses to return. But now it was her turn to visit that place where so much of her life had changed again. It was odd not to feel dread about the possibility of returning to the Copper City's streets, but to feel a prickle of excitement instead.

The manor sometimes felt too big for her. And still—never big enough to get the privacy they needed away from Cameron, Laurie, Gavin, or Violet.

"Hey." Arkimedes grasped her chin and tilted her face to him. His eyes shone with happiness and love. "Where did you go?"

Her heart squeezed tight as she shook her head, tracing her hands over his chest and over his soulmate mark. "I was just thinking about how much I like it here."

He grinned, and when he kissed her, the soft dance of their lips and tongues made her toes curl. When she'd arrived here in search of Arkimedes, she'd never expected that one day she would call this kingdom her home.

But time healed even the worst kind of wounds, and her anger toward everything that had happened had eased into acceptance, morphing into curiosity and love.

This place wasn't perfect. Far from it. It was occupied by creatures of raw power and an animal nature. But it reminded her of her mate. A place full of beauty and the dark magic that was only scary when misunderstood.

Nava had never expected this life, but here, in this beautiful place, beside the man she loved, she was grateful that destiny had brought them together. To call this manor her home until the day came when it was time for them to rule.

The End

EPILOGUE

DEVON

Nava and Arkimedes had left the room an hour ago, and Devon was feeling much better. They'd invited him to stay with them and travel to a city in the Copper Kingdom, but he already knew it was no place for him.

He'd stayed behind to help them fight the emissary. The guilt of everything he'd done on that useless island had demanded it. But now that they were off to live their happily ever after, Devon Black would not live and die in the shadow of their domestic bliss.

He scooted out of bed and picked out the best suit the damn magical wardrobe provided him. His hands ached as he popped the lapels of his coat, shielding his neck from the brisk air. Then he looked in the mirror and brushed his hair back, hating the sharp angles of his face and how fucking thin he'd become.

No matter how many potions he drank, every muscle in his body ached, and his energy dwindled far too quickly. He didn't have time to make sure he looked good. He needed to leave.

If he was going to die, he would do it on his own terms.

The tingling of his magic rose with his renewed energy, and a black portal popped into existence right in front of him, smelling of rancid acid and snapping at his skin with static.

Now that he'd learned the Crows had killed his family to get their hands on his rare magic-wielding abilities, he also knew he had something special to barter with.

A gift a god might be interested in. Especially since he'd just lost one of his emissaries.

He stepped forward and crossed into the portal. Blackness surrounded him. Here, Devon floated in air that felt thick and light at the same time. It was neither cold nor hot but the same temperature as his body, and the experience was—oddly comforting. Like he was floating in a dreamless sleep.

Devon had opened countless portals, ever since he'd learned to master the spell. It was second nature by now, almost like breathing. But never in his life had he actually seen the God of Shadows. He was always a deep voice in the darkness that demanded payment, but he never showed his face.

Today, it was different. Today, Devon heard the echo of distinct steps in the distance. When he turned, trying to locate the source, he found nothing.

He needed to keep his mind clear of any memories the Shadow God would grab and steal for payment. Instead, he thought only of his reason for being here.

To speak to Dargan himself and the deal he wanted to propose.

"You deny me my payment?" Dargan's voice was a velvet caress against Devon's skull, and an icy chill crawled up his back as the god finally came into view. "The deal is simple, human. You cross through my world and give me a memory, or I shall take something else. Your eyes, perhaps? Or your tongue?"

He was incredibly tall, with long, silky black hair that got lost in his fitted suit jacket. A glowing crown hovered above his head, casting yellow light over his sharp features and wide shoulders.

Fear clawed at Devon's throat. Nothing illuminated their surroundings, and Devon's body grew heavier, as if he was about to touch the ground.

But even with the fear growing like a sickness through him, he kept his mind blank. He'd been training his entire fucking existence not to let his mind wander. He could do it for a little longer to get what he truly wanted.

The god strolled around Devon, clasping his hands behind his back while he eyed Devon with growing curiosity. "You want to be immortal?"

"For a time..."

"For a time?" Dargan's dry laughter echoed in the cavernous emptiness. The darkness was beginning to clear, revealing an immense ceiling with stalactites hanging over them. Dargan's eyes shone brighter, and a cunning smile took over his features. "What makes you think I will release you once you're mine, pet?"

Devon recognized the look on Dargan's face. He was a god, but humans had descended from these beasts. He desired Devon's soul much more than a silly, insignificant memory.

"I don't owe you anything other than a memory, and my soul is mine to keep." Devon paused when the air caught in his throat. It was the same shortness of breath that had been winding him since he'd held the Vulcan that second time. But he couldn't dissolve into a fit of coughs right now, not when he was making a bargain with Dargan.

"Your soul is poisoned, and you have little time left to live," the God of Shadows said, and his magic moved in swirling shapes. It looked familiar. So much like Arkimedes's aura that it made Devon feel stupidly safe.

"I will manage. I have a friend who is a Beekeeper. She's fond of me and might keep me alive long enough for me to get my revenge..." Although Devon highly doubted that Nava and his brother were interested in following him to the Iron Kingdom to burn the Society of Crows to the ground.

Not when they'd just inherited an entire kingdom themselves.

"*Is* she fond of you, like you are of her?" Dargan questioned, inspecting his fingernails. They shone, black and long like claws. But it wasn't his inhuman hand that had Devon's heart racing.

Shame burned deep within his wretched heart as it ached with the feelings he'd been unable to shake for months.

"You look surprised that I know." Dargan stepped closer to Devon, and an intensity bled into his features that he couldn't place. "You think I don't know how much you *love* the Beekeeper?" Dargan chuckled. "Your brother's soulmate. You already know that those feelings are wasted, as she would never feel the same for you. Are you ashamed of your envy?"

He was. Devon had never wanted to fall for an untouchable woman. He hated being jealous of Arkimedes, who was his beloved brother. The bastard got it all, while Devon was stuck in here, making a deal with this devil.

He swallowed past the knot in his throat, digging his fingernails into the fleshy part of his palms. "You can read my feelings. Would you prefer that payment over my request? Because if you can take away my love for her, then be my guest."

Dargan tilted his head, looking more curious. "So why lend me your soul if you can live out there without my help?"

"Because I need immortality," Devon said. "Everyone has a reason to want something, and I'm not above bargaining what I have at my disposal to get what I desire. You're a god, and yet you want my soul, sick and all." A cough rattled past his lips, and he could taste copper on his tongue. But he wouldn't allow that to hold him back, not when he was so close he could taste it.

"You won't be immortal if our deal has a timeline," Dargan reasoned. "Why not give me your entire soul and then no mortal can touch you for an eternity?"

"Because I don't want to belong to anyone," Devon said. The truth brought a lightness to his chest. His breaths became shorter, the itching in his lungs increasing the longer he held off on coughing. He reached for his pocket but found his arm was too heavy to even grab at the potion he had stuffed in there.

"You can cough if you need to." Dargan stopped so close to Devon that his face hovered mere inches away. It was rather perfect, with a straight nose exactly the right size for his angular face, golden eyes and unblemished skin. "I'll take your soul for one hundred years of service, and when you're free, you will no longer be ill."

A century away from Caztian didn't sound half bad. The Society of Crows still wanted and remembered him. He could only visit in brief spurts of time, much like Leir had done whenever he'd let the Zorren in, before the shadow world had pulled him back.

But what if Arkimedes was gone by then? What if…?

"All those years away will make it easier to forget your love for the Beekeeper."

"Get out of my head," Devon growled, and his annoyance spiked further when Dargan's smile widened.

"You came into my land to bargain with a god, Devon Black. I'll do as I please."

Devon craned his head to make full eye contact with this giant. "Fifty years."

"One hundred years and not a day less." Dargan extended his hand to Devon, and what had once been black swirls like his brother's aura were now golden streaks dancing around him, like the light coming from his eyes.

"No," Devon said, and the portal somewhere behind him fizzled. He was running out of time, and he needed that potion. "Unless I get to return to Caztian and won't be brought here until you need me. I intend to use my immortal years to destroy the Crows."

"You will do as I command if we make a deal," Dargan said. His careful words wouldn't undo whatever spell of a treaty the gods had struck with the founders so many years ago. "What you do with your free time is not my problem. I don't meddle in the Caztanians' affairs, as long as they respect what I'm owed. One hundred years and that's my offer, pet."

"One hundred years," Devon agreed, and his knees touched hard ground. He couldn't see much around him, but the air grew crisp, full of a scent Devon couldn't place. "But I get to stay in Caztian if I choose to—until you call for me." Devon paused, and he slowly inched away toward his portal.

"Fine," Dargan said, and everything around Devon took on a solid shape.

The cavernous walls resolved into an enormous dome, as if he was standing inside a human-made throne room. Its interior was carved from dark onyx, and underneath him, a floor of polished, rounded stones spiraled into the center of the room where Dargan stood.

"Welcome home, Crow."

Acknowledgments

To my amazing friend Heather. Thank you for such an amazing illustration.

To my alpha and beta readers: Zar, Sarina and Rhian. You all rock!

To my editor Amber, who worked with my ever changing timelines and word count, and helped me polish this massive book.

To Ghbrookhorn, who helped me maintain my sanity as I wrote and re-wrote my blurb. PS. Writing a blurb is the absolute worst, but it's much better when a friend helps you <3.

To Carrie Sorens, your help meant the world to me.

To my PA, Margie.

To Jourdan, for being just an awesome human who worked with me to better promote my book.

And to my street and ARC team. I see you!

Thank you!

ALSO BY ABBEY FOX

Sign up to my newsletter to read The Curse of the Shadow God for free!

"If you enjoyed this book, please consider leaving a review!"

It *really* helps me out.

Goodreads

Amazon

Bookbub

ABOUT THE AUTHOR

Abbey Fox loves to write action packed Fantasy Romance stories, with powerful heroines, swoon-worthy heroes and a healthy dose of spice. When she is not crafting new worlds and putting her character's lives in peril, she enjoys tending to her indoor tropical jungle, changing her interior decor, and doing art.

facebook.com/abbeyfoxauthor
instagram.com/abbeyfoxauthor
tiktok.com/@abbeyfoxauthor
pinterest.com/Abbeyfoxauthor
amazon.com/Abbey-Fox

www.ingramcontent.com/pod-product-compliance
Lightning Source LLC
Chambersburg PA
CBHW020345310726
48979CB00015B/2507/J

* 9 7 8 1 9 6 0 2 7 9 0 2 6 *